LP
Fic
And

W9-CCS-625

CCAFGLP

34711203019932

FAMILY STORMS

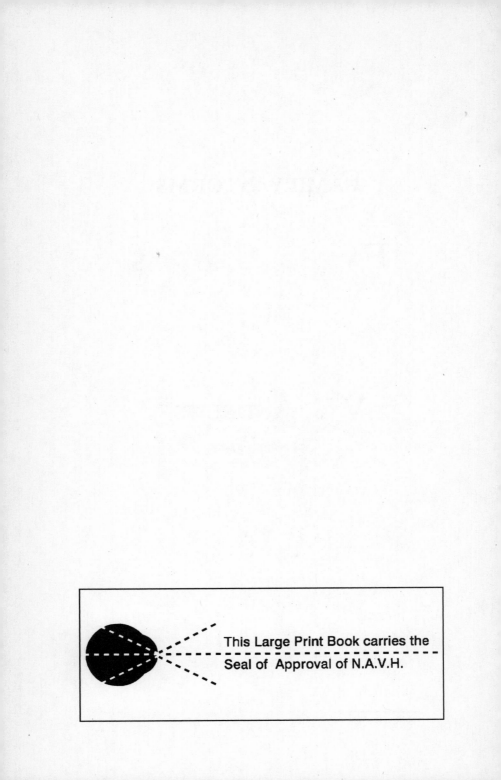

This Large Print Book carries the
Seal of Approval of N.A.V.H.

FAMILY STORMS

V.C. ANDREWS®

THORNDIKE PRESS

A part of Gale, Cengage Learning

Charlestown--Clark Co. Public Library
51 Clark Road
Charlestown, IN 47111

GALE
CENGAGE Learning™

Detroit • New York • San Francisco • New Haven, Conn • Waterville, Maine • London

Copyright © 2011 by the Vanda General Partnership.
V.C. ANDREWS® AND VIRGINIA ANDREWS® are registered trademarks of the Vanda General Partnership.
Thorndike Press, a part of Gale, Cengage Learning.

ALL RIGHTS RESERVED
Following the death of Virginia Andrews, the Andrews family worked with a carefully selected writer to organize and complete Virginia Andrews' stories and to create additional novels, of which this is one, inspired by her storytelling genius.
This book is a work of fiction. Names, characters, places, and incidents either are products of the author's imagination or are used fictitiously. Any resemblance to actual events or locales or persons, living or dead, is entirely coincidental.
Thorndike Press® Large Print Core.
The text of this Large Print edition is unabridged.
Other aspects of the book may vary from the original edition.
Set in 16 pt. Plantin.

LIBRARY OF CONGRESS CATALOGING-IN-PUBLICATION DATA

Andrews, V. C. (Virginia C.)
  Family storms / by V. C. Andrews.
    p. cm. — (Thorndike Press large print core)
  ISBN-13: 978-1-4104-3836-2 (hardcover)
  ISBN-10: 1-4104-3836-8 (hardcover)
  1. Teenage girls—Fiction. 2. Traffic accidents—Fiction. 3.
Deception—Fiction. 4. Adoption—Fiction. 5. Jealousy—Fiction.
6. Large type books. I. Title.
PS3551.N454F36 2011b
813'.54—dc22   2011012395

Published in 2011 by arrangement with Pocket Books, a division of Simon & Schuster, Inc.

Charlestown-Clark Co. Public Library
51 Clark Road
Charlestown, IN 47111

Printed in the United States of America
1 2 3 4 5 6 7 15 14 13 12 11

FAMILY STORMS

PROLOGUE

"We gotta move," Mama said.

I had just closed my eyes and curled up as tightly as a caterpillar in the heavy woolen blanket. Over the past few months, I had grown immune to the variety of unpleasant odors woven into it. Most nights, I think I held my breath as much as I breathed anyway. I was always anticipating something terrible would wake me, so I never slept much deeper than the very edge of unconsciousness. My ears were still open, my eyelids fluttering, and the dreams that came tiptoed in on cat's paws.

It had begun to rain harder, and the wind blowing in from the ocean made it impossible to stay dry under the cardboard roof that Mama had constructed from some choice cartons she had plucked out of a Dumpster behind the supermarket. In the beginning, I would tremble with embarrassment while she sorted through the garbage.

Now, I stood by quietly watching and waiting, as uninterested as someone who had lost all memory. I had learned how to shut out the world and not hear other people talking or see them gaping at us as they walked by. It was almost as if it were all happening to someone else anyway, someone who had borrowed my nearly fourteen-year-old body to suffer in and endure.

"Where will we go, Mama?" I asked.

"Home," she muttered.

"Home? Where's home?"

She didn't answer. Sometimes I thought she hoarded her words the way a squirrel hoarded acorns because she was afraid the day would soon come when she would have nothing left to say. Lately, she was saying less and less even to me. If I pressed her to talk, she would take on the look of terror that someone in the desert would have if she were asked to share her last cup of water. Consequently, I wouldn't talk very much to anyone, either. We both said only what was necessary. Anyone who watched us for a while would surely think we were actors in a silent movie.

I blocked my face from the drizzle and sat up. Mama was already stuffing her bedding into her suitcase, forcing it in as if it were screaming and fighting not to be locked away. She closed it and paused. The rain fell harder, but she stood there with her face fully exposed to it as if we were in bright sunlight, coating ourselves with suntan oil on the Santa Monica Beach the way we did years ago when Daddy was still with us. I knew she was looking at the ocean, expecting some boat to be rushing in to rescue us. A number of times over the past few days, she had told me she expected that to happen as we wandered up and down the beach searching for a good location to set up her Chinese calligraphy. Most people who bought any wanted their name in Chinese calligraphy and took Mama's word for it that she was doing just that. She could have been spelling out *toilet* for all they knew.

While she painted with expert strokes, I sat at her side and wove multicolored lanyard key chains that I sold for two dollars each. I usually began the day with a few dozen I had managed to do during the night. Between the two of us, we made enough to eat two, sometimes three, meals and occasionally have enough to buy some new article of clothing or old shoes from the thrift store. We had been doing this for nearly a year now, ever since we were evicted from our apartment and then from the hotel. Daddy had deserted us nearly two years before that.

Occasionally, someone would ask me why I wasn't in school. I would say I was on vacation or we were between locations and I'd be starting a new school soon. Most knew I was lying but didn't care, and when policemen looked our way, it seemed they either looked through us or didn't care, either. Sometimes I thought maybe we had become invisible and they could see right through us. Maybe it was painful to look at us. It was already past very painful to be us.

In the beginning, when Daddy first left, Mama had managed to keep us afloat, working first as a restaurant hostess and then as a waitress, but her depression led her to more and more drinking, and she had trouble holding on to any employment. Occasionally, she would sell one or two of her works of calligraphy to one of the arts-and-crafts stores. One of the better-known bars, the Gravediggers, had one prominently on a wall to the right of the bar. Mama told me it spelled *heaven.*

"The Gravediggers will take you to heaven," she joked.

Although I had never met her, my maternal grandmother was the one who taught Mama calligraphy. They had lived in Portland, Oregon. My grandparents had Mama late in life, and my grandfather, who was a fisherman, died in a fishing accident during a bad storm. Just like us, Mama and her mother were left to fend for themselves. Both of my maternal grandparents died before I was born, so I had never seen my grandfather in person, either. All I had were the few old photographs of her parents that Mama had brought with her. She told me they were taken when she was only ten, but her parents looked as if they could easily be her grandparents.

Mama said the struggle, which was what she called their lives after her father died, was responsible for aging and killing her mother. Her father hadn't made a lot of money and had had very little life insurance.

Despite our struggle, Mama would say that my daddy's desertion of us was no great loss. I knew she was just speaking out of anger. At least we ate and had a roof over our heads when he was with us. We never really expected to have much more. Daddy had barely graduated from high school and then enlisted in the army, where he learned some mechanical skills, and got a job as an appliance repairman when he was discharged. That was what he was doing when he met my mother at a bar in Venice Beach,

California.

Mama had left Portland with a girlfriend right after high school because her English teacher and drama-club coach lavished so much praise on her acting skills that she thought becoming a movie star was inevitable. She was in every one of her school drama productions since the eighth grade.

Of course, after endless rejection and only very minor acting opportunities, she blamed her teacher for ruining her life. "He got me full of myself until I couldn't see anything else, Sasha," she would say. According to her, he was right up there, just below Daddy, as the cause of all our troubles. "Beware of compliments," she told me. "Half the time people you know tell them to you so you'll like them more, not yourself."

She and her girlfriend were waitresses in the bar where she met Daddy. Her girlfriend was already going hot and heavy with someone she had met there, and according to my mother, "The writing was on the wall. I knew I'd be on my own very soon, and with what I was making, that was nearly impossible. The real possibility of my having to go home to Mama Pearl was looming. That's why I fell in love so quickly with a spineless, unambitious clod like your father."

She admitted, or rather used as an additional excuse, the fact that Daddy was very handsome, with his crystal-like cobalt-blue eyes, firm lips, and wavy light brown hair. I had his eyes but Mama's hair, which Mama said made me even more beautiful than she was.

"When I first met him," she said, "he looked like he could be a movie star himself. He had a sexy smile, the kind that could unlock anyone's chastity belt."

"What's a chastity belt?"

"Never mind that," she said. "He was built like a Greek god in those days, too, but I mistook his silence for strength. It took me a while to realize that most of the time, he was silent because he simply didn't know what to say. He never read anything, parroted whatever sound bite he had heard on television, and rarely went to a movie. At the time we first met, he had never been to the theater. Now that I think about it, Sasha, I must have been out of my mind."

She would eventually tell me that he had gotten her pregnant with me, and when he proposed, she thought maybe she should settle down and become a wife and a mother. She tried to make it sound as if I wasn't just a mistake. She said she was surely not going to be the famous movie star she had hoped to be, and she was just not tall enough to work as a model.

"Becoming a mother seemed to be the right thing for me to do. Besides, I needed you. I needed someone else. Your father wasn't much company."

There was no question, however, that she had once been very beautiful. Her half-Asian look was quite exotic, and she once had silky, long black hair down to her wing bones. Both men and women turned their heads to look at her when she sauntered down the street. I was proud to be walking beside her then. She walked like an angel, practically floating, her soft smile imprinting itself on the eyes of men who surely saw her often in their dreams. I wanted to be in that aura that rippled around her so I'd grow up to be just as special.

"If I would have had the sense to hang out where more well-to-do young men hung out, I'm sure I would have hooked a real catch instead of a mediocre clod. Almost as soon as we married, your father began cheating on me. He was never much help taking care of you. He hated having to stay home, so he would pretend he had to meet someone for a little while, maybe to get a better-paying job, and then not return until the wee hours and sometimes not until morning, bathed in the scent of another woman."

"Why didn't you go back to Portland?" I asked. "You said Mama Pearl's sister still lived there. Wouldn't she have helped you?"

"She had her own troubles and was fifteen years older than my mother. She was an old lady, and my mother's family wasn't happy she had married my father. His family wasn't happy he had married my mother. Everyone expects their children to make them happy," she added with a maddening laugh that always ended with her starting to cry, making me feel bad that I had asked anything.

By then, I was almost eleven. Daddy had just recently deserted us, but I was tired of hearing my mother complain about my father. It wasn't that I wanted to defend him. Even when I was only seven, I realized my father was not like the fathers of other girls at school. For one thing, he never came to a single parents' night and never seemed at all interested in my schoolwork. Sometimes I thought he wasn't interested in me, period. Once, when he and my mother were having an argument, which was most of the time, I heard him say, "Children are punish-

15

ment for sins committed earlier."

"That makes sense when it comes to your parents," she told him. He never talked about his parents or his sister, and none of his family ever called or showed interest in him — or any of us, for that matter.

Mama and Daddy's fights usually ended with Daddy pounding a table or a wall and sometimes breaking something and then running out of the house with curses trailing behind him like ugly car exhaust.

I'll never forget the day we were evicted from our apartment. I was twelve, nearly thirteen, and home from school because I had a bad cough. We had no medical insurance, so Mama would always try to cure me with some over-the-counter medicines. More often than not, she would just tell me to take a nap or sit in the sun. She was in and out so much in those days that she hardly noticed when I was sick, and she was not taking very good care of herself, either. I knew she was with different men frequently and drinking too much. I hated it when she came home late at night and began babbling and crying. She would stumble and bang into things. I would bury my face in my pillow and refuse to help her.

Eventually, her good looks began to fade like a week-old rose. Her hair lost its rich, soft look until it no longer flowed. The ends were always splitting, and she wasn't keeping it clean. She finally decided to cut it herself. When she was done, it looked as if someone had hacked it with a bread knife, but even if she hadn't done it while she was high on some cheap gin, she wouldn't have done a good job.

It wasn't only her hair and her complexion that grew worse. Her figure seemed to stretch and bulge like the walls of a water-filled balloon. She couldn't get into her jeans and had to wear baggy skirts. Because we didn't have a car and she couldn't afford taxis, she walked so much in old shoes that her feet were always aching or blotched with ugly blisters. She took to wearing oversized sneakers.

I remember once looking out the window and seeing a woman walking up the street, her eyes glassy, her gait uneven, and thinking, *How sad. Look at that bag lady.* When she drew close enough for me to realize it was my mother, I was stunned.

But I was frightened more than anything. The little there was of my own world was falling apart. I had long since stopped having friends over to visit, and no one was inviting me. My attention span in school was bad. I dozed off too much and took little or no pride in my work. My grades were tanking. My teachers said I had attention deficit disorder, which only made me feel more different from the others. Teachers were constantly asking me to bring my mother to school. We had no phone by then, so they didn't call, and letters were useless. She considered everything a bill and read nothing.

Now that I think back, I realize my mother was really the one who was stunned. She must have woken one morning and realized just how badly off we were and how helpless she was. Instead of the realization driving her to be more vigorous in search of solutions, it caused her to retreat to the gin and whiskey. It almost didn't matter what it was as long as it was alcoholic and could jumble up her thoughts and fears to the point where nothing seemed to bother her.

However, to this day, I don't think of her as having been an alcoholic. I believe she really could have stopped if she had wanted to stop. She didn't have the courage to stop. It was ironically easier to look into the mirror and see someone she didn't recognize. Otherwise, she would have committed suicide.

I suppose if we could have afforded psychoanalysis back then, she would have been diagnosed as a borderline schizophrenic. Something that had begun too subtly for me to realize right away had been happening in her head. At times, I thought she was talking to someone else. At first, I thought that occurred only when she was drunk, but I quickly realized it was happening even when she was stone sober. I think the person she was talking to was herself before I was born, and even before she had met Daddy. From what I heard and could understand, she was warning her younger self not to leave home, that if she did, this could be how she would be.

Of course, it made no sense to me, and if I asked her what she was doing or whom she was talking to, she would look at me angrily, as if I were intruding on a very private conversation.

"None of your business," she might say, or "It's not for your ears."

Whose ears is it for? I wanted to ask. *There's no one there.*

But I kept quiet. I was actually too frightened to push much further, anyway. Who knew what that might cause to happen, and enough had already happened.

She wasn't home when the police came to the apartment the day we were evicted. The landlord had followed all of the necessary legal steps, but Mama had ignored it all. I was home sick. I opened the door and looked up at two burly sheriff's deputies. One took off his hat and combed through his hair with his fingers as if he were searching for a lost thought. He looked sorrier than the other for what he was about to do.

"Your mother here?" he asked.

"No," I said.

"Where is she?" the other deputy asked.

"I don't know," I said, and coughed so hard and long that they both stepped back, fearing infection.

"Jesus," the first deputy muttered.

"Do you know when she'll be back, at least?" the second deputy asked me.

I shook my head.

"We'll wait in the car."

They turned and went to their vehicle parked right outside our first-floor apartment. At the time, I didn't know why they were there. I thought maybe they had found my father and needed to tell my mother.

After I closed the door, I went to the front window and waited, watching the street. Finally, I could see her coming. She didn't look drunk. She was walking fast, swinging her arms, with her purse wrapped around the front of her body like some shield. She had told me she did that to avoid having it grabbed. "Not that I ever have much in it," she'd added.

The deputies saw her heading our way and got out of their vehicle to approach her. She stood listening to them and then just nodded without comment and continued to the front door. When she entered, she saw me standing there and shook her head.

"You can thank your father someday for this," she said. "Pack only what you really need. We can't carry too much. I'm not spending money on a taxi."

"Why are we leaving?"

"We can't live here anymore. The landlord got the police on us."

"Where are we going?"

"To a hotel nearby," she said.

It sounded good, but when we arrived, I saw how small it was. The lobby was barely bigger than our living room had been, and we had one room with two double beds and a bathroom.

"What about a kitchen?" I asked.

"We'll eat out when we want hot food. This will have to do for now," she told me.

Her best hope was that "for now" was forever, only I didn't know that. I didn't know how serious the dying going on in her head was. Because we slept in the same room, I woke up often to hear her night-time chats with her invisible second self. Most of the time, it was done in whispers, but I often caught a word or two. None of it ever made much sense to me. *Maybe she's just dreaming aloud,* I thought, and went back to sleep.

She was doing it now as we trekked up the beach. The raindrops had become more like pellets. I kept my head down and lifted my eyes just enough to see her soaked old sneakers pasted with sand and mud plodding forward awkwardly.

"Where are we going?" I cried. I was tired and would have gladly just slept in the rain.

She didn't answer, but from the way she was moving her arms and hands, I knew she was talking to her imaginary self. I could see the top of a bottle of gin in her shabby coat pocket. There was no one else on the beach but us, so there was no one to appeal to for any help. I was feeling worse than ever. The only way I realized I was crying was by the shudder in my shoulders. My tears were mixed in with the rain.

Mama suddenly turned and started toward the sidewalk. I hurried to catch up. She carried her suitcase limply. It looked as if it was dragging. Even though I was exhausted myself, I wanted to help her, to take it from her, but she wouldn't let go of the handle.

"I'll carry it!" I cried.

"No, no. This is all I have. Let go," she said.

The way she looked at me sent a sharp pain through my heart. *She doesn't recognize me,* I thought. *My own mother doesn't know who I am. She thinks I'm some stranger trying to steal her things.*

"Mama, it's me, Sasha. Let go, and I'll help you."

"No!" she screamed, and tore it out of my grip.

We stared at each other for a moment in the rain. Maybe she realized her momentary amnesia and it frightened her as much as it had frightened me. Whatever, she turned and surged forward.

I sped to keep up with her. We were at a traffic light on Pacific Coast Highway, and it turned green for us. She stepped into the road, and I caught up with her to walk side-by-side. We were nearly to the other side when I heard car tires squealing and looked to my right.

The vehicle struck Mama first and literally lifted her over my head before it struck me hard in the right thigh. I saw Mama slap down on the pavement just before I fell and slid in her direction.

That was how my life began.

1
THE ACCIDENT

The pain was hot.

Although I was lying faceup in the road and the rain was sweeping over me in a downpour, I no longer felt the slightest chill. It was as if electric heaters had been placed all around me. I heard myself groan, but it seemed to come from someone else. My first thought was that I was dead and this was the way a soul left its body. Any moment, I expected to be looking down at myself lying there on the road, shocked, my eyes two balls of blue glass, my mouth opened in a silent scream. Souls don't cry, souls don't laugh, but they can be surprised when they realize they are no longer part of their bodies.

Cars began stopping, some nearly rear-ending the ones that had stopped already. Looking through what was to me a curtain of gauze, I could see some men directing traffic, shouting at drivers, waving off the curious. I started to move, but the pain shot so fast and sharply up the back of my leg, up my back, and into my neck that I immediately stopped and closed my eyes. I was vaguely aware of someone beside me, holding my hand. There was a man's voice and then a woman's. I realized the woman was trying to get me to talk. I heard more shouting. I tried to open my eyes, but they wouldn't open. The noise began to drift off, and then it came surfing back on the wave of sirens.

"Mama," I thought I finally managed to say. I wasn't sure I had spoken. I drifted away again and then opened my eyes when I felt my body being lifted. When they began to slide me into the ambulance, I had a funny thought. I envisioned a freshly made pizza being slid into the oven. Slices of pizza were our lunch more often than not and sometimes all we had for dinner.

I looked back and saw another ambulance. *They're getting Mama,* I thought, and that gave me some comfort. The paramedic beside me was saying soothing things and putting a blood-pressure cuff on me. There was so much conflicting noise, mumbling voices, cars, people still shouting, that I could make little sense of anything else the paramedic was saying. Finally, the doors were closed, and I heard the siren again as we began moving.

"Hot," I said, and lost consciousness.

I awoke in the hallway of the hospital emergency room. My clothing had been removed, and I was in a hospital gown. I saw what I knew to be an IV bottle and stand beside me. The tube was attached to my right arm. There was a blanket on me, but there was no doctor, nor was there a nurse tending to me. People were rushing around. No one spoke to me. Another pair of paramedics wheeled in another gurney, and I thought, *Maybe that's Mama,* but it turned out to be an elderly man with oxygen leads in his nostrils. His eyes were wide, as wide as those of someone who saw his own impending death. They pushed him past me without even looking at me, but it frightened me.

"Mama!" I cried. I waited, but either no one heard me or no one had time to answer. There was little I could do but lie there and wait. My arms, shoulders, legs, and neck were throbbing so much I felt I had turned into a drum. My ears were filled with the beat of my heart and the chugging of my blood through my veins.

When I saw a nurse hurrying up the corridor, I called to her as loudly as I could.

She paused, but before I could tell her anything or ask her anything, she said, "Someone will be with you soon. Be patient."

Don't you mean "be a patient"? I was the one who felt drunk now, not Mama.

I closed my eyes and tried to remember exactly what had happened. It had all happened so quickly. Mama was rushing through the rain as if she had an appointment. I ran behind her and kept calling to her. I was only a few inches away when I heard the sound of tires squealing. Right now, I could visualize the front of an automobile but little more.

Where was Mama now? Why had I been left in a hallway? Who had put me here? Who was looking after me? When I tried to lift my head, the whole corridor spun, and I was nauseated immediately. I kept my eyes closed and waited until the dizziness subsided, and then I opened my eyes slowly and took a deep breath. There was nothing I could do but wait.

Finally, I felt myself moving and looked down toward my feet to see a different nurse pushing the gurney. She looked younger than the first nurse and had a shock of brown hair drifting out from under her cap and down over her right eye. As she pushed my gurney, she blew the loose strands away from her eye.

"What's happening to me?" I asked.

"You're going to X-ray," she said. "Just relax."

"Where's my mother?"

"You're going to X-ray."

Didn't she understand my question?

"My mother," I said.

"Relax," she told me. "We're having a bad night here. We're doing our best to get to everyone as quickly as we possibly can. I've got to get you processed before I see about anyone or anything else."

Processed? What did that mean? With all that ached on me, it was hard to keep talking, keep asking questions, and she didn't seem to want to talk much, either.

I felt myself being navigated through the corridor to an elevator. When I was in it, I hoped she would tell me more now that we were away from all the bedlam, but there was another nurse in the elevator, and they started to have a conversation over me as if I weren't even there. I heard them complaining about some doctor who hadn't shown up and another nurse who was always late.

"Like any of us want to be here on time?" my nurse said.

When the elevator door opened, the other

nurse helped wheel me out and then went off in another direction. Outside radiology, there were two other gurneys lined up, one with a young man with a bloodstained face and a heavily bandaged arm and the other with an elderly African American woman. A younger African American woman stood beside her, holding her hand.

"Just try to relax," my nurse said again, and put a clipboard at my feet. "Someone will be out to get you soon."

"What about my mother?" I asked.

She walked off without replying. I began to wonder if anyone could hear me. Maybe I thought I was talking but I wasn't. The younger African American woman looked at me and smiled. The X-ray room door opened, and another patient was wheeled out in a wheelchair. He was an elderly man in a shirt and tie, wearing a blue cap with white letters that spelled "U.S.S. Enterprise." He looked perfectly healthy, even bored. A male nurse pulled the gurney with the young man into the radiology suite.

"Not much longer now," the younger woman told the older one.

"You hope," the older woman said. "You'll be on social security, too, by the time we get outta here."

The younger woman laughed. Then she

looked at me again. "What happened to you, honey?"

"We were hit by a car," I said. "My mother and me, but I don't know where my mother is."

"Downstairs waiting, for sure," she said. "Took us five hours to get this far."

I was relieved to see she heard me. "I don't know how long I've been here."

"Long," the older lady said. "You drip through this place like maple syrup."

The younger woman turned to me and smiled as she shook her head to tell me I shouldn't pay attention. "You'll be all right," she added, and turned to look firmly at the closed door as if she could will it to open.

I closed my eyes again. When I opened them, I realized I must have fallen asleep, because the two women were gone and there were two other gurneys lined up behind me. Finally, the doors opened again, the African American lady was wheeled out, and I was wheeled in. The young man bringing me to the X-ray machine was the nicest and warmest of anyone I had met so far. He assured me that he would do everything to make this easy and comfortable.

"Do you know where my mother is?" I asked him. Since he was being so nice, I thought he would give me an answer.

"Sorry," he said. "I'm just the X-ray technician. I'm sure someone will be getting your mother to visit you afterward."

"She was hit by the car, too," I said. "Was she here already?"

He paused, thought for a moment, and shook his head. "She's probably with the doctor somewhere else right now," he replied. "Let's get you going."

After my X-rays were taken, another nurse arrived to wheel me out and back into the elevator.

"Where am I going?" I asked.

"To wait for the doctor," she replied. "He'll look at your X-rays first. We have an examination room open for you, and I want to get you into it before someone else gets in there."

"What about my mother? She was in the accident, too."

"I don't know anything about her," she said. "I just came on duty."

She got me into the elevator and then out and into an examination room. I don't know how long I was in there before the doctor arrived, but I know I was in and out of sleep, and I was very thirsty. I called for someone to please get me some water, but everyone seemed too busy to hear me.

When my doctor finally arrived, I was

surprised at how young he looked. He had curly light brown hair and a round face with thin lips and a small nose, so small it looked as if half of it had still not emerged. In fact, it looked as if his facial features were sinking into his skull. His hazel eyes were that deeply set. His skin was as soft and clear as a little boy's skin. Maybe he hadn't begun to shave yet, I thought, which I knew was silly.

"Okay, now," he said, as if we had been having a conversation that had been interrupted. "I'm Dr. Decker, one of the ER doctors here. I've called for Dr. Milan to look at you. He's an orthopedic specialist. The reason," he said, "is that you have a serious fracture of the femur."

"I don't know what that is," I said.

"It means your thigh bone."

He held up the X-ray for me to see and pointed to my right leg bone.

"This is your thigh bone. There are four distinct parts to it, and your injury is at the head. See?" he asked as if he were teaching a class. "Look where the edge of my finger is."

I nodded, even though I had no idea what he was pointing to.

"The reason it's serious for someone your age is that it can and most likely will affect

33

the growth plate, the soft area of the bone located at the epiphysis near the head of the femur. As a result of all this, your right leg might end up a bit shorter than your left. So we want a specialist to handle the cast, okay? It might be a while."

"My head hurts, too, and so does my arm and my neck and shoulders."

"You've been banged up quite a bit. Luckily, nothing else is broken, but you do have a slight concussion. That's why you're nauseous and dizzy. In fact, I'm amazed you don't have a broken arm."

He lifted my right arm, and I saw the black-and-blue marks. They were ugly and frightening. I couldn't help but start to cry.

"Easy," he said. "I'll have the nurse give you something for the nausea. I don't want to give you anything else until Dr. Milan can get here. Okay?"

"What about my mother?"

"Your mother? What about her?"

"She was hit by the car first."

He nodded. "I'll check on it," he said. He patted my hand and left.

I expected the nurse to come in soon, but a long time went by before anyone came, and she wasn't a nurse. She wasn't wearing a uniform. She was an older lady with short gray hair that looked plastered around her head. She wore a pair of glasses with lenses so thick they looked more like the protective glasses mechanics wear. She approached me and lifted her clipboard.

"I'm Mrs. Muller. I work in admittance. You told the paramedic your name is Sasha Porter, is that correct?"

I couldn't remember telling anyone anything about myself. Maybe I had been talking in my sleep.

"My name is Sasha Fawne Porter, yes. Fawne is spelled with an *e* at the end. That was the way my grandmother spelled her Chinese name."

"You said you were thirteen years old?"

"I'll be fourteen in two months."

She lowered her head and looked at me over her glasses as if I had said something outrageous. "What is your present address? Where do you live?" she followed quickly, as though I needed a translation.

Maybe I shouldn't have let her know my grandmother was Chinese. She remained poised with her pen and didn't look at me until she realized I wasn't answering her question.

"Don't you know where you live? What's your address?"

"We don't have an address."

"What do you mean, you don't have an

address? I asked you where you were living." She had a thought. "Was it on a boat?"

"No. We live on the street, sleep on the
beach," I said.

She stared at me and pressed her thicker
lower lip over her upper one. It made the
brown spot at the bottom of her chin look
more like a teardrop. "How long has this
been going on?" she asked, as if it was my
fault.

"I don't know the exact number of days.
A year, I guess."

"Where do you go to school?"

"I don't right now," I said.

She smirked and shook her head.
"Where's your father?"

"I don't know. We don't know exactly. We
think he went to Hawaii."

"Hawaii? So your mother and father are
divorced?"

"No. He just left."

"Just left?" She nodded, as if she knew
him, and tapped the clipboard with her pen.
"Okay. What about other relatives here?"

"We don't have any here. My mother has
an aunt and cousins in Portland, Oregon.
My father's relatives are in Ohio, but we
don't talk to any. I don't even know their
names. His parents died a long time ago.
He has a sister, but she stopped talking to

him a long time ago, or he stopped talking to her." I nodded. Maybe these details were important. "Yes, Mama said he stopped talking to her."

"So you have no one to take responsibility for you?"

"Just my mother," I said.

"A lot of good that's going to do us," she muttered. She checked something on her clipboard and turned to leave.

"Where is my mother?" I called.

She paused and turned back to me. "Didn't anyone tell you?"

"No."

"Your mother is dead. She died instantly and was taken directly to the morgue."

2
ALONE

The nurse who finally came to give me the medicine Dr. Decker had promised started to check my pulse and take my blood pressure and then gave me a tablespoon of some syrup for my nausea, which she said was all she could do for me right then. She saw that I had been crying. I started to cry again, and she told me I should try to be a big girl.

"That lady said my mother died," I said through my tears.

"Yes. Very sad, but you have to be a big girl now. It will make everything go that much easier for you."

A big girl? How does a big girl react to the news of her mother's death? I wanted to ask. *Doesn't she cry?*

The nurse looked up when Dr. Decker came in quickly. "What's happening?" she asked him, sounding a little annoyed.

"Milan isn't coming. Once he heard she's

uninsured, he suddenly had another emergency."

"And?"

"I'll set the leg," he told her. "We've got to move her along. There's quite a backup out there."

"Tell me about it," the nurse said. "We should have a traffic cop."

"Okay, let's get to her." He finally looked at me. "We're going to get you on the way to getting better," he said.

He tried to explain everything he was doing every step of the way, but I had long since lost interest in myself and was only vaguely aware of the activity around and on me.

"This kid's practically in shock," the nurse said. "Besides the injuries, she just found out her mother died."

"The faster I get this done, the faster she'll get out of it," he said, obviously not wanting to stand around and have a conversation.

Get out of what, I wondered, *sorrow or pain?* I moaned, but because of my slight concussion, Dr. Decker said he didn't want to give me anything too strong for pain. He said he would prescribe some Tylenol, and he was sure it would help a little.

"Just hang in there," he said, and flashed

a smile as if it were on a spring in his face.

After my leg was set, they moved me to a ward. It was nearly morning now. Through the window across from my bed, I could see the sunlight creeping up on the horizon as if it were afraid night would slap it back. Everyone else in the ward, six others who looked like mostly elderly women, seemed to be still asleep. To me, the one nurse in charge, Mrs. Stanton, appeared to be as old and as sickly as the other patients. Her face was so pale and her eyes so watery I thought one of them might have gotten up and put on a nurse's uniform. She settled me in and told me to try to get some sleep.

"Do you need anything?" she asked.

What a question, I thought. *Yes, I need something. I need my mother not to be dead. I need a home. I need to be in school and have food and clothes. I need to remember how to laugh.* I saw from the look on her face that if I had said anything like that, she might have been the one to laugh, so I didn't say anything. I hadn't said anything to anyone since that woman had told me my mother was dead and in the morgue. All I had done was moan and cry. Mrs. Stanton went off to check on another patient, and I closed my eyes.

I slept on and off. The clatter of dishes

40

and trays woke me when breakfast was served. I looked at it but turned away and didn't eat or drink anything. The nurse who had replaced Mrs. Stanton shook me to tell me I should try to eat. "And you have to drink something. I don't want you to get dehydrated," she said, as if I worked for her. She stood there waiting to see me reach for the glass of juice and then handed it to me. I drank some, and she repeated that I should try to eat. "If you don't nourish your body, it won't heal," she warned. She said it as if it wouldn't be her fault or any doctor's. Whatever had happened and would now happen was my fault. It sounded as if she meant it was my fault that I had been born.

A different doctor stopped in to visit the patients in the ward. I heard the nurse complaining about me. He read the chart clipped to the bottom of the bed and then examined my bruises, checked my eyes, and listened to my heart and lungs through his stethoscope. His name tag read "Dr. Morton." He looked older than Dr. Decker, but something told me he wasn't. Later, I heard he was interning.

"You've had quite a shock to your body," he told me. He looked at my chart and added, "Sasha. You want to eat and drink so you get stronger, okay?"

He was talking to me in a tone of voice he might use with someone only about five years old. I didn't reply, and he turned to the nurse and said, "We might need the psychologist to stop by for this one."

"Is my mother really dead?" I asked when I saw that he was going to move off.

He looked at the nurse.

"Her mother was hit by the same car," the nurse told him. "She expired at the scene."

"Oh. Well, what about . . ." He nodded at me.

"There are no other relatives listed. I'm sure Social Services has been contacted. Homeless," she whispered, but not low enough for me to miss.

"Right. You hang in there, Sasha. We're going to look after you."

He smiled at me, patted my hand, and moved on to the next patient. The nurse trailed along like an obedient puppy as he went from bed to bed.

Look after me? How were they going to do that? I wondered. How was anyone? Despite how terrible our lives had become, I wished Mama and I were back on the boardwalk selling her calligraphy and I was selling my lanyards. I wished we were back in the struggle. At least we were together then, and I had someone. Besides, she might have gotten better. Maybe she would have stopped drinking and found a place to work again, and I would have been able to return to school, any school. I used to feel tears come into my eyes when I would see other girls my age in their school uniforms, laughing and talking as they walked to school. The furthest thing from their minds was wondering about where they would sleep and what they would eat. If only I could somehow turn back time and change everything.

I closed my eyes and dreamed about it. Mama was pretty again, and I had new clothes and friends. We had at least as good an apartment as we had had with Daddy. Because Mama worked, I would start dinner for us before she came home. She would be so proud of me, and we'd laugh and tell each other about all the things that happened to both of us during the day. I'd have very good grades to show her, and then I would go off and do my homework. She would still do calligraphy, but now only for her own enjoyment. Because she was happier when she was doing it, she would do more elaborate pictures, and before long, she would be selling them to art galleries, not arts-and-crafts stores or bars. We'd have more money than ever, and Mama would start talking about buying a car.

"We'll go on trips every weekend, see beautiful things, and stop at nice restaurants along the way," she would say. "I told you. We can get along without him, and we can keep the struggle from doing us any more harm, because we're together, partners, mother and daughter, more like sisters, good friends."

She would hug me and hold me, and I would inhale the sweet scent of her perfume and hair, which was long and soft again. Men would be very interested in her, of course, but this time, she would be far more careful and go out only with responsible ones. Someday someone like that would propose to her, and our lives would improve tenfold. We'd live in a house, not an apartment, and Mama would not have to work anymore. This wonderful, well-to-do man would love me and be a real father to me. He'd come to parents' nights and do homework with me and want to show me things and take me places, just as any other girl's father would want to do with his daughter.

It occurred to me that most other girls would think my dreams were too simple, too ordinary. They would be dreaming of being popular singers or movie and television stars. They'd want big houses and expensive cars, even boats. They'd dream of jewelry and fashionable dresses and shoes, love affairs, and romantic adventures.

"Even your dreams are poor, pathetic," they might say, and not want to be my friends.

I'd have to be very careful about telling anyone about my fantasies. I'd have to pretend I wanted exactly the same things they did. In fact, I'd have to keep many things secret, especially our struggle. What I would certainly have to do is come up with a story. In my dream, when I explained this to Mama, she nodded, understanding my problem, and said, "It's best you tell them that your father was killed in a car accident. That way, they'll feel sorry for you and not mock you."

Exactly, I thought. Daddy was dead to me, anyway. It was almost not a lie.

I dreamed so hard I began to believe it was real. For a while, I was happy, and I felt no pain or discomfort, and then someone in another bed screamed with her own pain, and I was ripped out of my fantasy and dropped right back into this gray ward, with other patients who I found out were also uninsured homeless or deserted people. One lady told another we were all in the "human Dumpster."

How long would they leave me in there? I

wondered. Would I have to be there until my leg healed? And then where would they send me? What was being done with Mama? Would I ever see her, or would she simply be taken away and buried somewhere without anyone present? She used to say she would end up in Potter's Field, a burying place for strangers, for people with no means.

"Where is Potter's Field?" I had asked her.

"There's one everywhere." She had looked at me, considering whether to tell me any more. I was thirteen by then and not attending school. Whenever she was sober enough, she always expressed regret about my not being in school and often tried to teach me things.

"It comes from the Bible," she'd continued. "My father was a Bible thumper. He would read aloud from it almost every night he was home. You know who Judas was, right?"

"Yes, he sold out Jesus for thirty pieces of silver."

"Good. Well, he regretted it afterward and went back to the high priests who had paid him. He threw the money on the floor. Afterward, he hung himself. The priests decided the money was tainted with blood and used it to create Potter's Field, where strangers and the poor were to be buried. They called it Potter's Field because it was located in a place where they mined clay for pots. As your father would stupidly say, that information and a dollar fifty will get you on the bus."

"But that's all it costs."

"Duh. That was your father's opinion of knowledge," she had told me.

It was almost impossible now to remember Mama from those early days, when she would have more sober hours than not. Before she began drinking for the day, her eyes were still clear; she was still standing straight and had a look of determination in her face. But that got to be less and less the rule and more the exception.

Sometimes I thought maybe an alien had gotten into her. The alien didn't have any of the self-pride and self-respect Mama used to have. Maybe Mama wasn't dead. Maybe just the alien in her had died on the highway, and she would wake up and come back to me. I was looking at the door of the ward just the way Mama used to look out at the ocean for that boat that would save us, hoping that she would suddenly just appear, smiling.

"It's going to be all right now," she would say. "We'll be fine, Sasha. I'm back."

I blinked when a tall woman dressed in a fashionable designer turquoise pantsuit with gold epaulets stepped into the doorway and caused my dream Mama to pop like a bubble.

This woman had thick light brown hair styled at shoulder length and carried a purse that matched her outfit. The nail polish on her long nails even matched her outfit. She gazed into the ward, looking carefully at each patient until her eyes came around to me. Once she saw me, she seemed to freeze, her eyes locked on me, her soft, puffy lips just slightly open. Whom was she trying to look like, Angelina Jolie?

I couldn't take my eyes off her. She had the look of a movie star, her makeup perfect, her complexion rich and peachy. But she looked somehow more important than a movie star. The regal way she held herself gave her an aura of authority, control, and power. The diamond ring on her left hand was so large that it seized on the ray of light spilling in from the nearest window and then seemed to brighten and become even more dazzling. She wore what looked like diamond teardrop earrings, too, and a necklace of small pearls.

A long moment passed before she stepped into the ward, and when she did, she stepped in as though she were trying to be careful, as careful as someone navigating a floor of mud. Maybe she thought the patients in the ward were contagious. She did look as if she was holding her breath. I waited when she paused at my bed.

"Are you Sasha Fawne Porter?" she asked.

She couldn't be someone from Social Services, I thought. Could she? Who else would be looking for me? Who else would know my full name?

"Yes," I said.

She nodded, opened her purse, and took out a very thin handkerchief to dab away something on her right eye. I saw nothing. Maybe she was wiping away imaginary germs. Why would there be a tear?

She focused on the area under the blanket where my cast was located.

"Are you in a lot of pain?" she asked, nodding at my legs.

"Only if I move too much," I said.

"I'm so sorry."

I looked at her and wondered why she was so sorry. "Are you with Social Services?" I asked, and she widened her eyes.

"Hardly," she said. She hesitated, and then she said, "I'm Jordan March. Mrs. Donald March."

The way she told me her name — announced it, I should say — caused me to scan my brain, searching for something in my memory that would tell me who she was. Had I seen her on a magazine cover? Was she really a movie star or on television, someone who visited patients in hospitals as an act of charity? Why would she think I would know who she was?

"It's your right leg that was broken?" she asked.

I pulled back the blanket to show her the cast. "My femur," I said, remembering Dr. Decker's description. "At the head."

"Yes, I know."

How did she know? Was she a special nurse? Or maybe she was a doctor. But she didn't call herself Dr. March. Would a doctor talk like that?

"You don't have any other broken bones, right?"

"No." If she were a doctor, she would have known that, I thought.

"But you're badly banged up," she concluded, her gaze fixed on my black-and-blue arms.

"I have a slight concussion, too. And my neck hurts, so it's hard to raise my head." I don't know why I wanted to tell her everything. Maybe it was because there was no one else really asking me.

"Oh, dear, you poor, poor child."

Poor is right, I thought.

I watched her look around the ward. Some of the others were looking our way and listening. She didn't smile at anyone. She pulled herself back a little and blew a small breath through her nearly closed lips.

"Well, this won't do," she said. It seemed to be something she was saying more to herself than to me. "It won't do at all." She turned and walked out quickly.

"That your mother?" the woman nearest to me asked.

"No way," I said. "My mother is prettier." *Was prettier,* I thought, and then argued with myself. This woman was beautiful, there was no denying that, but Mama had that exotic look, and she was natural. She wasn't just beautiful; she was different. In Los Angeles, women like the one who had just been to see me were not unusual. Mama used to say, "It's the only place where women don't care that beauty is only skin-deep. Few want to go any deeper."

Mrs. March didn't return for nearly half an hour, and when she did, the ward nurse and a male nurse's aide accompanied her. The aide pushed a gurney right up to my bed. Mrs. March stood back to watch.

"We're moving you," the nurse said.

"To where?"

"A room. A private room," she added, the corners of her lips dipping.

She and the aide guided me carefully onto the gurney.

"Does she have any possessions?" Mrs. March asked the nurse when they turned to roll me out.

"Possessions? No, nothing," the nurse said. "What would she have?"

Mrs. March smirked. "A watch, maybe? Any jewelry? These people carry everything they own on them."

"She had nothing I know of, and there's nothing listed anywhere."

"I hope not," Mrs. March said. "Anyone who would steal from this child should be shot."

I looked back at the other patients in the ward. A few watched with curiosity and amazement.

"Just relax," the nurse said, and I lowered my head and waited as I was rolled along.

We went to an elevator. Mrs. March followed us all the way and stood quietly in a corner of the elevator as it rose to a much higher floor. She kept her head high and looked forward, not looking at me at all now. She said nothing to the nurse or the aide.

The door opened on a quiet corridor with walls that looked freshly painted and a floor that glittered in the sunlight pouring through one of the windows. I saw the nurses' station, with at least a half dozen of them busy with their duties. The nurse on the far side sat watching monitors. I could see that she was doing some needlepoint. There was none of the frenzy here that I had seen in the emergency room.

I was rolled down to a doorway and then into the room, which was nicer than any bedroom I had ever had. There was a light maple armoire on the left, a closet on the right, small tables beside the bed, and a television on a metal shelf across from the bed. The room had two large windows that looked toward the Hollywood Hills. The bed was wider than the one down in the ward, and the blanket and pillows looked brand-new. The nurse and the aide gently transferred me. The aide started out with the gurney, and the nurse turned to Mrs. March.

"I'll get her paperwork to the desk," she said.

"Thank you," Mrs. March said.

The nurse left, and Mrs. March stepped up beside the bed and looked at me. "Now, this is better, isn't it?"

"Yes," I said.

"I have a private-duty nurse arriving within the hour. Her name is Jackie Knee." She leaned toward me to whisper. "She's younger than most of the nurses here, more tuned in to girls your age. She actually worked at a plastic surgeon's clinic in Brentwood but now freelances on private-duty assignments. I think she makes more money."

She straightened up and just stared at me for a few moments.

"I've arranged for a well-known orthopedist, Dr. Milan, to examine you."

"Dr. Milan?"

"You know who he is?" she asked with a slight smile.

"He was supposed to fix my leg last night but didn't come because I have no medical insurance, so Dr. Decker did it."

"Really? Is that what happened? Well, he's coming today," she said firmly. "You can be sure of that."

"Who's paying for all this?" I asked.

"I am. Well, I should say my husband and I are."

"Why?" I asked, expecting her to tell me they were in charge of some charity.

She looked as if she wasn't going to answer. She turned away, looked out the window a moment, and then turned back to me.

"It was my daughter, Kiera, who hit you and your mother," she said.

3
KIERA'S MISTAKE

I didn't know what to say when Mrs. March told me her daughter had hit Mama and me, so I just watched her as she began to pace back and forth, moving her hands as if she were speaking. I think she was trying to find the right words. Were there right words?

She turned, pressing her lips together. Then she took a deep breath and continued. "She was high on one of her recreational drugs. X they call it." She paused and turned to me. "Do you know what that is?"

I nodded.

"But you don't use that stuff, do you?"

"No," I said, but what difference would that possibly make to her?

"Good. Kiera has been more than a handful for us. She has everything any girl her age could possibly want. My husband, Donald, is one of the most successful builders in Southern California. Half the malls you see are malls he built, and he's busier than ever.

He gives everything he can to our daughter. Kiera has her own car. She's already been to Europe twice. She has a wardrobe that's even bigger than my own, not to mention expensive jewelry and watches that would choke an Arabian prince."

She shook her head. "You would think any girl would be grateful for the life Kiera has, but this is not the first time Kiera's been in big trouble. Each time, my husband has bailed her out, pulled strings, saved her. The result is that she never learns a lesson. I told him. I warned him something bigger like this would happen, but he didn't listen, and now he's already busy saving her again. I told him this time he should let her pay the piper, but he won't have it. He's hired a top attorney, but this is not the first time. You can't even begin to imagine the money we've had to spend on attorneys because of her."

She spoke quickly and excitedly, and her face turned crimson. Then she took a deep breath, looked out the window, and relaxed her shoulders. "Of course, I understand why he's like this," she said. "And it's hard to blame him."

She sat in the chair near the bed. For a few moments, she just sat there with her head lowered. Her words and actions had captured my full attention. I was holding my breath in anticipation of the next outburst, but she began in a low, soft tone.

"We lost our younger daughter, Alena, to acute leukemia three years ago. We took her to the best doctors and the best hospitals in the country, but we couldn't save her. You can have all the money in the world, Sasha, and still not be happy. Anyway, Donald doesn't want to lose Kiera, too. I don't, either, but I think that his always finding ways to excuse her misbehavior will lead to us losing her. It's like a slow disease, just getting worse and worse. You're probably too young to understand all of this," she added, and sighed. "Forgive me for throwing it all at you like this, especially at this time when you're soaked in your own horrible trouble."

I didn't say anything.

She looked at me again, her eyes narrowing. "Maybe you're *not* too young to understand what I'm saying. Children who live harder lives grow up faster. I'm sure you've seen more than your share of the dark side, and now look at what's happened to you. I'm sorry. I really am, and I'm going to do whatever I can to make things better."

"My mother's dead," I said. "They told me she died instantly."

Her whole face seemed to tremble. She understood that I meant there was no way to make my mother better, there was no nice room for her or expert doctors to fix her injuries. No one could promise her anything anymore, so Mrs. March couldn't make things much better for me. Mrs. March looked as if she would cry and did turn away to dab her eyes with her handkerchief.

I certainly didn't feel sorry for her. I didn't care how unhappy she was or what terrible things had happened to her. Maybe that was mean, but I didn't feel like feeling sorry for anyone else except Mama and myself at the moment. Did she expect me to say it wasn't her daughter's fault? Had she come here and done all this for me so I would forgive her daughter and help her feel better?

"It's terrible. I know," she said, still looking away. "That poor woman. On top of struggling just to exist." She sighed and turned back to me. "How did the two of you end up living on the street? I see so many people pushing carts and sleeping in tents or just under something. Some of them look so young. I can't help but look at them and wonder how in the world they ended up the way they are, especially in this great country. Are there many children out there like you all over?"

"I don't know. We've been only here. We never left after we were turned out on the street. Mama said it would be the same for us no matter where we went, and at least it wasn't cold here so much."

She blew through her lips and shook her head as she looked at me. "You should be in school, going to parties, not worrying about where your next meal is coming from or where you will sleep. What did you two do, just beg?"

"No, my mother wouldn't beg. She sold her calligraphy, and I sold lanyard key chains on the beach. I made them myself."

"Calligraphy?"

"It's Chinese writing."

"Oh, yes." She smiled.

We heard a knock on the door. A tall man in a black suit and blue tie stood there. He had thick gray hair and ebony eyes, a gray and black well-trimmed goatee, and a Hollywood tan. I thought he might be her husband. He looked just as wealthy.

"I received your message while I was still at the orthopedic convention at Shutters, Jordan. I came as soon as I could get away."

"Thank you, Michael. This," she said, turning back to me, "is the young girl I want you to treat, Sasha Porter."

He nodded and showed Mrs. March a clipboard in his right hand. "I picked up her file on the way."

"This is Dr. Milan, Sasha. Please, let him examine you."

He stepped into my room and, without saying hello or even smiling at me, took the blanket off my right leg and looked at the cast. He shook his head.

"What?" Mrs. March asked.

"It's not set high enough. I see this sort of sloppy work all the time. I'll have to redo this. I'm sorry," he told me.

"Did you see the X-rays, Michael?"

"Yes."

"How bad is the break?"

"It's pretty serious, in a bad place, Jordan. I'll do the best I can, but nine times out of ten, for someone her age, there is a residual effect when it's that high up."

"Do what you can, Michael. I mean it," she said firmly. "Think of her as you would my daughter," she told him.

I was surprised that she could speak to a doctor so sternly, but he didn't seem upset. He nodded.

"I have a private-duty nurse coming." She looked at her watch. "She should be here any minute. I'm sure she can assist you."

"I'll change my clothes and come back,"

he said. He hurried out.

I was quite impressed with how easily Mrs. March could order people to do things. I imagined she could get anything she wanted done.

"Do you know where my mother is?" I asked her.

"I'm sure she's in the hospital morgue, dear. I'm sorry."

"Will I see her again?"

"It's not pleasant to see someone who has passed away, especially a young person." She took a deep breath and nodded. "But a daughter should say good-bye to her mother. I'll look into it for you."

"She used to be very, very pretty," I said.

"Well, you're a very pretty young girl, so I know that's true. Now, don't you worry. Dr. Milan will get you up and about faster than any other doctor around here can."

I turned away to look out the window. It was another sunny California day. How could the world be so beautiful after my mother had died? I didn't mean to, but I started to cry.

"Oh, God," Mrs. March said. She stood and looked at me.

Just then, the nurse she had hired came into the room. Mrs. March didn't wait for her to introduce herself or anything. She practically lunged at her.

"Dr. Milan is going to reset that leg right now," she told her. "The cast wasn't done correctly. You make our little patient as comfortable as possible. She's been through the most horrible experience, especially for someone her age."

The nurse nodded. She was younger than any I had seen so far, younger but heavier, too. Mama would have said she had a body like a turnip. When she smiled at me, though, I saw she was warmer and friendlier than any other nurses I had met. Somewhere under those heavy cheeks slept a pretty face. That was something else Mama might have said.

"This is Jackie," Mrs. March said.

"Hi, Sasha," she said, coming over to me to take my hand.

She knew my name without looking at the clipboard. That was good, I thought. Whether she was doing it for Mrs. March's benefit or mine, I didn't know, but she started to rearrange my pillow and raise the back of the bed.

"You should be at this angle right now," she told me. Then she looked at my chart. "She has a mild concussion," Jackie read aloud, and then looked at Mrs. March.

"I know," she said.

"Are you nauseous, Sasha?"

"I was. I'm not so much now."

"I'll have a neurologist in to see her today," Mrs. March said. Jackie nodded. Mrs. March looked at her watch. "You'll be here until eight?"

"Yes, Mrs. March."

"I'm arranging for another nurse."

"She might not need round-the-clock, Mrs. March."

"I'm arranging for another nurse," she repeated, and looked at Jackie Knee as if she would have her shot if she said another word about it. She just nodded and looked at me, smiling again.

"Don't worry. We'll have a good time together," she told me.

In a surgical blue shirt and pants, Dr. Milan returned with another male aide pushing a gurney.

"I need to take her to another room," he told Mrs. March.

"Of course," she said. "I'll be back later," she told me. "You do your best to cooperate with Dr. Milan, okay, Sasha?"

I nodded. What else would I do? I wasn't about to get up and run out, although I wanted to more than anything.

"I'll look into your seeing your mother," she promised before she left.

Later, while Dr. Milan redid my cast, Jackie tried to distract me by telling me about the time she had broken her ankle.

"My little brother left one of his toy cars right outside my bedroom door. I was about your age, too. I think I flew ten feet. I was rushing out to meet some friends. Of course, everyone signed my cast and wrote silly things on it."

I didn't think Dr. Milan was paying any attention to Jackie's babbling, but he said, "She'll be able to write a novel on this cast."

Afterward, I was taken back to my private room and discovered that Mrs. March had sent flowers to dress it up. There were five different arrangements. Jackie raved about them. I knew she was trying her best to make everything seem better than it was. She made sure I ate most of my lunch. Soon after that, another doctor arrived, the neurologist. He was older and nicer than Dr. Milan. His name was Dr. Sander, and when he looked at me and talked to me, I felt he really saw me. Dr. Milan could have been working on a big doll.

"Well," Dr. Sander said after looking at my eyes, "no concussion is pleasant or should be ignored, but you'll be fine in a week or so. I'll stop in to check on you again soon. For now, you just take it easy. Your nurse has what you need if you get nauseous again." He turned to Jackie. "You know how to reach me if you need to," he said. Unlike Dr. Milan, he said good-bye before he left.

Everything was catching up with me. I tried to stay awake, but not long after Dr. Sander left, I fell asleep and didn't wake up until it was time for dinner. Jackie was getting it all set up for me. I saw a pile of magazines and books and a few boxes beside them on the table to my right.

"What's all that?" I asked.

"Oh, you're up. Good. Mrs. March sent up some magazines and books she thinks you'll like. There's a DVD player in the box with a dozen movies for someone your age. She knows it's no fun just lying around here waiting to get better. Let me fix your bed so you can have your dinner, and then you can look at everything, okay?"

She moved the tray over after she raised my bed for me.

"This looks good," she said, lifting the cover over the plate. "But if you don't like the food, Mrs. March left instructions for me to send out for something you do like. You have no dietary restrictions."

"It's all right," I said, trying to sound casual.

Dietary restrictions? We had dietary restrictions, such as some days only two meals. When Mama and I were on the street, meals like this would be like Christmas dinners. She'd be really angry if I didn't eat it.

Jackie had her dinner served, too, and pulled her chair up to my bed table. She smiled. "When I was your age, I'd hurry my meal just to get to the dessert. My mother always had something great. This chocolate cake looks delicious."

"Did you know Mrs. March before she asked you to be here?" I asked.

"Yes. She had work done by the plastic surgeon I used to work for. She liked the care I gave her. We had a special place for the patients to recuperate, and I was her private nurse four times for surgeries."

"Four times?"

She laughed. "I'm not supposed to talk out of school, but yes, she had a full face-lift, work on her rear end, breast implants, and a bit of a tummy tuck, not to mention her lips."

"All at once?"

"No," she said, laughing again. "But all of it over four years, I think. I don't want to tell you how much it all cost."

"You know why she's doing all this for me?" I asked.

"I know she does a great deal of work for different charities. I think that's very nice of her. There are lots of very rich people who don't do anything for anyone else." She smiled and started to eat again.

"I'm not a charity case," I said.

"Oh?"

For a moment, I wondered if I should say anything. Maybe it would make Mrs. March angry and she would stop doing nice things for me, but then I thought about Mama lying in a morgue and lost any hesitation.

"Her daughter killed my mother and did this to me," I said. "She said she was high on Ecstasy."

She stopped eating. And for a few moments, she looked as if she should be the one in the hospital bed, not me.

4
PEOPLE WITH INFLUENCE

I knew Jackie was thinking how much more horrible this was because I was a homeless child without anyone to care for me, and therefore I had to appreciate what Mrs. March was willing to give me and do for me. Another child who had a family would probably tell her to go to hell with her daughter.

"Well," she said after a few moments to gather her thoughts, "you just take whatever she gives you. You deserve it and more. Maybe her husband is afraid some alert attorney will come see you and get you to sue the Marches. A lot of money could be held in trust for you to have when you're eighteen. I bet that would bring your father back."

"Would it?"

"I imagine so. Of course, he might be returning just to get his hands on the money. How long has he been away?"

"Three years," I said.

"Three years? Has he called you often?"

"Never."

"Not even written or sent you things?"

"We don't even know where he really is."

"Well, don't you worry about it. Your first job is to get better."

"Maybe he'll come back when he hears what happened."

"He might not find out about it. I always read the newspaper from beginning to end, and I didn't see anything about this accident. I'm not surprised that the Marches were able to keep it out of the news, though," she added. "They are what you call 'people with influence.'"

She didn't have to convince me of that. Look at what Mrs. March had gotten done for me in so short a time.

After I finished eating, I began to look through the magazines and books. Most of it was what I would read when I could get my hands on it. I hadn't seen any of the movies she bought for me, and I had never had a DVD machine you could hold in your lap. Jackie checked my blood pressure and temperature and then sat and read some of my magazines, too.

We spent the next two days like this. Mrs. March didn't return during those days, but

I knew she called often to speak with Jackie. The nurse who came when Jackie left was older and less talkative, at least with me. She spent most of the night talking with other nurses. I guessed Jackie was right. I really didn't need the second nurse, because I slept through most of the night. I did look forward to seeing Jackie first thing in the morning.

Either because she really enjoyed talking about her family and her life or because she was just trying to keep me from thinking about things, Jackie told me all about her brothers and sisters, her parents, how she became a nurse, and her one disappointing love affair. She rattled on about her taste in music and things she loved to eat. It seemed there wasn't anything she didn't like. I enjoyed listening to her talk about her family. I imagined myself a part of it.

What was a family, anyway? Could just a mother and a daughter be considered a family, or did you have to have a father, too, not to mention at least one brother or sister? A house or an apartment didn't seem like much without a family living in it. When Jackie described her house, especially when all of her brothers and sisters had lived in it, I felt as though the house was alive, a warm place that embraced them and kept them happy and safe. How far that was from the cold apartment we had lived in and that small hotel room. How could I call either one a home?

Soon, though, instead of enjoying hearing Jackie describe her family and home life, I became sadder. Look at all I had been missing and would miss forever now. What sort of a woman could I become? I'd be like someone without any past. How could I ever do what Jackie was doing, describe my parents, where I lived? I'd be like so many of those homeless people I saw at the beach, panhandling or trying to sell something to survive. Their faces were caverns of despair, their eyes empty, a smile as hard to find as a decent meal or a place to stay the night. The sound of other people laughing was painful to them and to me. If one day we weren't there, no one would care; no one would look for us. Sometimes I wished the tide would come farther in and wash us all away. I was sure many people who saw us and shook their heads wished the same thing.

As I looked around my nice hospital room, I wondered where I would go from there. One day, the doctors would tell me I was recuperated enough to be discharged, but discharged to where? An orphanage?

Some foster home? When I thought about that, I almost wished Daddy would come rushing back to get me, even if it was just to get himself some money. At least I'd be with someone who was supposed to care about me.

Late on the third morning, Mrs. March appeared and told Jackie she had arranged for me to be brought down to the morgue.

Jackie's face lost color, and she turned sharply toward me. "Are you sure?"

"I know it's very, very unpleasant," Mrs. March said, "but she wants to say good-bye. Am I right, Sasha? We don't have to do this if you've changed your mind, and Jackie's right to be concerned for you. It's ugly."

"I don't care. I want to see her," I said. Mama could never be ugly to me, I thought.

"Then you will."

She stepped out and returned with an aide and a wheelchair. I was helped into it, and the four of us went to the elevator. No one spoke all the way down to the morgue. My heart was pounding, and my eyes were filling with tears so quickly I had trouble seeing as we went down the corridor and through a pair of doors. A man in a white lab coat was waiting for us just inside and had me wheeled sharply to the right to avoid seeing anything else.

We entered a cold room. I saw no bodies, just what looked like a giant file cabinet.

"You stay with her, Jackie," Mrs. March said. "We'll hang back here."

I looked at her and the aide. He didn't seem unhappy about that, and she looked as if she was trembling. It got me trembling. Jackie wheeled me deeper in and up to a cabinet. The man in the lab coat looked at me, and then he pulled on the handle and slid Mama out. She was under a sheet. He lifted it, and something inside me shattered like a windowpane.

It didn't look anything like Mama, and for a moment, I hoped it wasn't her. Maybe she was still alive somewhere in the hospital. Maybe there had been a terrible mix-up. I looked at Jackie, and she shook her head. It was no good to pretend, to lie to myself. I knew it was Mama.

Tears were trickling down my cheeks. "Mama," I whispered. "I love you. I'll always love you."

I reached out to touch her face and then recoiled when I felt how hard and cold it was. Suddenly, I was very nauseous and began to dry-heave. Jackie whisked me around and away. The aide stepped forward.

"Let's get her back upstairs," Mrs. March

said. "Quickly."

I kept my eyes closed and my head back until I was upstairs and in my bed. Then I slowly looked up at the ceiling.

Jackie rubbed my arm softly. "Don't think of her down there," she said. "That was no longer your mother. Think of her as being in a better place now, where she is always warm and happy and safe, okay?"

"Okay," I said in a voice so small I thought I had become three years old again. I closed my eyes and fell asleep.

Days passed. Mrs. March sent me more presents, more magazines and movies and boxes of candy. I could tell from the way other nurses looked when they gazed in at me that I was quite a curiosity. I had no visitors other than the doctors and my private nurses. I was sure that by now there were all sorts of stories about me. Despite Jackie and the gifts, I felt more and more as if I were in prison or in some cave in a human zoo.

Jackie tried to help me feel better about it. She got me into a wheelchair whenever she could and pushed me down to a small patio to get some air and sunshine. Except for a few visitors, only other hospital employees used the patio. Some ate their lunches out there. Jackie knew some people and introduced me. While I read or listened to music on the new iPod Mrs. March had sent, Jackie would move off and tell those people all about me. By the way they looked at me afterward, I could see that she had given them all the grisly details. I knew she didn't mean any harm, but soon, because of their looks of pity, I wasn't so eager to go down there anymore.

One afternoon, Mrs. March returned. I was sitting up in my bed and reading with my earphones on. They were plugged into the iPod, so I didn't see her or hear her, but out of the corner of my eye, I saw Jackie get up quickly and put her magazine down. I turned and saw Jordan March standing there. She looked as if she had just come from a fancy affair, and later she did say she had attended a charity luncheon. She wore a white wide-brim hat with a pink ribbon and a sleeveless V-neck dress, embellished with a pink scarf.

I took off my earphones.

"You can take a break now, Jackie," Mrs. March said.

Jackie nodded, smiled at me, and walked out. Mrs. March stepped up to my bed and smiled.

"I hear good things from your doctors," she began. "Your bruises are healing, the concussion has receded, and you do look a lot stronger. How are you feeling?"

"The cast itches," I said. "It's hard to get used to it."

"Yes, I imagine so. Dr. Milan says it's too early to know how the break will affect the growth of your leg, but it's important to remain hopeful. He's one of the best doctors in all of Southern California for this problem. Of course, when the cast is removed, you'll need therapy, and I'm arranging for all of that."

"Where will I have to go?"

"We'll see," she said, looking away for a few seconds. When she looked at me again, her face was full of sadness, the way it had been when we had first met and she told me about losing her younger daughter. I could see her eyes filling with tears. She took a breath. "I want you to know I've taken good care of your mother," she said.

Taken good care of my mother? She said it as if she meant that Mama hadn't died. Maybe that really wasn't Mama I had seen in the morgue. Maybe I wasn't lying to myself. I held my breath. I think she saw that I was misunderstanding her.

"What I mean is, I bought a plot in Greenlawn Cemetery for her. I wanted my husband to make my daughter come to the burial, but he wouldn't do that, so I went myself and made it as dignified as I could. I'll make sure you are taken to the grave as soon as you are able to go. I didn't have any stone put up yet. I thought you might want to have something besides her name and dates of birth and death. You might want something like 'Loving Mother,' whatever. You don't have to think about that right now."

At least Mama wasn't where she had feared she'd be, in that Potter's Field, I thought.

"I had one of our attorneys research your mother's family, and then I had any we could locate called, but no one wanted to attend the funeral. Your father was harder to find. He was in Honolulu for a while, and then he . . . well, he went off with someone to Australia. He hasn't responded to any calls or inquiries, I'm afraid. We have it from reliable sources that he has another daughter with this woman. I'm sorry to have to tell you all this, but I thought you should know. Any man who would desert a daughter like you isn't worth spending any time on, anyway," she added angrily.

"How old is his new daughter?"

"Not quite two."

Did he love her, I wondered, or did he

think of her the same way he thought of me, as a burden, a punishment for his past sins, as he had told Mama children were?

"He just left you two one day? He didn't tell you he was leaving?" Mrs. March asked.

I tried to recall the exact details. That day, Mama had made a meat loaf because she said if he didn't show for dinner, we could keep it for lunch the next day. When he didn't return home hours after we had eaten, she had gone into their bedroom and come out with a look of shock and anger on her face. I was doing my homework in the living room.

"That bastard," she had said. I looked up and waited for her to explain. "He took all the spare cash I thought I had hidden from him under my panties in the top drawer of my dresser. So I thought I had better check my mother's jewelry, the ring and necklace and that cameo my mother gave me. It was worth a few thousand, at least. Guess what? That's gone, too. He went and pawned it all, I'm sure."

I didn't know what to say. She wasn't sobbing, nor were her shoulders shaking, but tears were streaming down her cheeks.

"I went into the closet and saw that he's taken a lot of his clothes."

"Why?" I asked.

"Why? Why?" She sniffed, looked up at the ceiling and then at me. "He's gone, Sasha. That glob of flesh and bones who called himself my husband and your father is gone. I knew he was seeing this woman over in West L.A. My guess is, he's moved in with her. I'll find out, and I'll get the police on his back. You can be sure of that."

She returned to her bedroom and shut the door. I could barely breathe. Just remembering it took my breath away now. How could Jordan March expect me to relive it?

"No," I said. "He never told us he was leaving. My mother thought he had moved in with another woman, but when the police checked, both of them were gone. Later, she heard that someone thought he had gone to Hawaii. She tried to find him, but no one really helped us."

"How terrible for both of you. Your mother had stopped working, right?"

"Yes, but she went back to working at a restaurant the next week, and for a while, everything seemed okay. She was sad, though, and tired and . . ."

"Began to drink?"

I nodded.

"So she lost her job eventually?"

"Yes, but she got another and . . ."

"The same thing happened."

80

I nodded.

"So your bills began piling up. There are so many people, especially women who've been deserted, who are just like that out there. You lost the house, I imagine?"

"We didn't have a house. We had an apartment, and the police came one day and told us we had to leave right away."

"Evicted? Yes, of course, that would happen. Where did you go?"

"To a hotel, but Mama wasn't doing well. She didn't have a job anymore, so we couldn't pay the rent too long."

"And that's when you went out on the street?"

I nodded.

"You said she sold calligraphy she created?"

"And I sold lanyards."

"Yes, which you made. That's sweet, but how terribly difficult it had to be. Where did you sleep, exactly?"

"Sometimes just under the tree, sometimes in a big box Mama made. For a while, we slept in an old deserted car, but then someone came along and took it away."

"You stopped going to school?"

"It was too far and hard for me to go. I didn't have my old clothes."

"Of course, and anyway, where would you

do your schoolwork?" she said, nodding. "Didn't your mother try to get some help?"

How was I to explain what Mama had been like without making her sound terrible? I just shook my head.

"Your mother . . ." She hesitated and thought for a moment. I could see she was deciding whether or not to tell me something.

"What?"

"Your mother had quite a bit of alcohol in her at the time of the accident," she said. "I'm not saying that made it her fault or anything," she quickly added. "She was like that often, though? I mean, every day?"

I didn't say yes, but I didn't have to.

"I'm sure it made it all that much harder for you." She grew angry again. "That father of yours should be stood up and shot."

"Mama didn't want to drink whiskey," I said. "It made her feel better."

"Well, yes, I suppose . . ."

"She didn't have to think about us. She tried to change herself into another person so that she wouldn't have to think about all that had happened to her."

She stared at me. "That's very astute. You're a very bright young girl. I can see that, Sasha. It would be a waste to let you fall through the cracks. I'm sure you wanted to be in school."

"Uh-huh."

"I'm not usually someone who believes in fate. When Alena died, I knew there were some people who thought it was just something meant to be and that was why nothing we tried to do could stop it. It's like everything is designed, and we just follow the path we're given. Something like that. Donald believes that. I'd like to think that maybe some good could come out of Kiera being the one to have caused your accident, the injuries, and your mother's death."

I recoiled. *Good?*

"It brought me to you and you to me," she said. "I had a great loss when Alena died, and so did you when you lost your mother. We can help each other. Actually, you'll be helping me and Donald by giving us more to do with our lives, our family lives."

"How?" I asked.

She smiled. "I'd like you to think about something. I'd like you to come live with us, Sasha. First, we'll be your foster parents, and then, if you're happy, we will adopt you."

All I could do was stare at her. She wanted me to live with her? But I'd be living with her daughter Kiera, too?

"You'll only end up a ward of the state otherwise and be shipped off to some orphanage or multichild foster home," she quickly added. "You don't want that. Even your mother, in the condition she was in, that you were both in, avoided putting you there, and now that I have gotten to know you, it would make me very sad, too."

My continued silence unnerved her.

"Do you understand what I'm saying?" she asked.

I nodded, and she stood up.

"Okay. You just think about it. I'll be back tomorrow, and we'll talk again about it."

Jackie came to the door and hesitated, waiting to see if it was all right for her to return.

"You can come in," Mrs. March told her. "She's doing quite well, according to Dr. Milan."

"Yes, she is," Jackie said, smiling at me.

"We might only need you a few more days."

"Of course," Jackie said. She smiled at me. "In this case, I'll be glad to lose my job. She's been a delightful patient."

Mrs. March smiled and looked at me. "Yes, she's quite a wonderful young girl," she said. "Continue to take good care of her," she added, and left the room.

Jackie waited until she was sure she was gone and turned to me. "Well? What is she planning to buy you? What is she going to do for you now?"

"Have me take the place of her dead daughter," I said.

5

A NEW LIFE

"You mean she wants you to come live with her?"

"Yes. And if I like it, she and her husband would adopt me."

Jackie sat, a look of amazement flowing over her face. "I have never seen her house, but when I was working for the plastic surgeon, there was always a lot of gossiping about some of the patients. Some were famous movie stars, but I remember hearing that the Marches' house was bigger than any Hollywood movie star's or producer's and quite beautiful. In fact," she said, getting more excited, "I remember someone said it cost about one hundred million dollars. It's up in Pacific Palisades. Do you know where that is?"

"I think so."

"Wow. Well, what are you going to do? Did you say yes?"

"I didn't say anything," I said. "She wants

me to think about it."

"Don't you give it a second thought," Jackie advised angrily. "Don't you be bash-ful now. You take everything that woman is willing to give you. No matter what. You deserve more than they're willing to give you, in fact. Take it gladly."

I didn't say that I would, but somehow, because Jackie had heard that I might live in the Marches' house and even be adopted by them, she looked at me differently. I could feel the gap between us suddenly widen, and I didn't like it.

Then, as if Jordan March had been listen-ing in on our conversation, she sent more gifts. This time, it was clothes and shoes. Jackie unwrapped everything for me.

"This is all very expensive stuff. She wants to be sure you're dressed properly when you leave here and enter her world," she com-mented. Her voice didn't have the same tone of joy and wonder. I sensed the bitter-ness and wondered if I should be feeling it as well. "I bet this all costs more than I make in a week," Jackie added. "If this is any indication of what it's going to be like, you'll be fine."

"None of that replaces my mother," I said.

Instead of being upset, she smiled. "That's right. You keep that in mind. Take whatever you can get, but as I said, never let her and her husband forget that they can never give you enough. Sasha, don't ever feel like some charity case. Promise me that."

"I won't," I said, but I wasn't sure that I could keep such a promise. I wasn't even sure that I was going to say yes. I tried to imagine what Mama would have said before the struggle. Back then, she had so much self-pride. She wouldn't accept a nickel if she thought someone was giving it to her because he or she felt sorry for her. That's why she had worked so hard on her calligraphy.

"One of the worst things in the world," Mama had told me, "is being obligated to someone, especially someone who won't let you forget why. So the best thing you can do for yourself is always earn what you get or deserve it, Sasha. That's what it really means to be free."

Mrs. March, however, had made it sound as if I was doing her more of a favor than she was doing for me. She was the one who was obligated. I wondered if her husband felt the same way. Would I be treated like some kind of princess? Should I ever be satisfied and happy when I was with them?

I knew Jackie gossiped a little with the other nurses about me and Mrs. March, because when they stopped by, they, too, looked at me differently. I imagined I was no longer just someone's charity case. Was this how it would always be from now on? People would no longer look at me with disgust, disapproval, or disinterest? Should I be feeling good about it? Mama was dead and buried. Everything, all of the gifts, the clothes, the promise of a new life, was designed to make me forget what had happened. *I won't,* I vowed. *I never will.*

With the cast on my leg, I always had a hard time falling and staying asleep, but this particular night was the worst. I dreamed that Mama was in the room with me, sitting beside my bed and looking at me. She wasn't my mother before the struggle, either. She was just the way she was on the day of the accident.

She was staring at me and twisting her hands around each other. "I'm sorry," she said. "I'm sorry I did this to you."

"You didn't do it, Mama."

"I did. I did. I can't sleep in my grave, Sasha. You're alone in the street."

"No, I'm not. I won't be, Mama."

"You are. I did this. You are," she insisted, and then she began to shrink in the chair. I reached out to stop it, but I couldn't get to her. She kept dwindling.

"Mama!" I screamed, and woke up.

I apparently woke up my night nurse, too. She came quickly to the bed. "What's wrong? Are you in pain? What?"

I looked up at her. Her face seemed as white as her uniform in the dim light, and she didn't look sympathetic. She looked upset.

"No," I said. "Nothing." I lay back, closing my eyes.

"You'd think the ceiling had caved in," I heard her say.

"It has," I muttered. "For me."

The next morning, I saw how nervous Jackie was. She didn't say any more about Mrs. March's offer to take me into her home, but it was clearly on her mind. The more she flitted about, trying to make me more comfortable, keeping the sun out of my eyes and the room cool enough, making sure I ate well, the more nervous I became, too.

Finally, just before lunch, Jordan March arrived. She was dressed in a bright blue pantsuit and had her hair pulled back so that her opal teardrop earrings in a gold setting were quite prominent. As usual, it looked as if a professional had done her makeup and she was ready to step onto the cover of some fashion magazine.

"How's our patient doing today?" she asked Jackie.

"Fine, Mrs. March."

"Take a break," she told her.

Jackie nodded and left without glancing at me, keeping her head down.

"Well, now, Sasha, have you thought about our little discussion yesterday?"

"Yes," I said.

"How do you feel about it? Do you want to come live with Donald and me? I'll have the therapist come to our house, and when you're able to get around, we'll get you into school again. In the meantime, I'll also arrange for a tutor to come to the house and get you caught up. We don't want you entering class behind the others, do we?"

I shook my head.

"Of course, if you're terribly unhappy, we'll look for other arrangements for you. What do you say? Will you come?"

She was sitting where I had dreamed Mama sat. It was almost as if Mama's spirit was there, too.

"Yes," I said.

"Oh, that's wonderful, Sasha. It really is." She leaped to her feet. "I have lots to do, lots to arrange. You'll be out of here the day after tomorrow. Dr. Milan will discharge you, and then he'll follow up on your treatment. Now, tell me some important things. What are your favorite colors? I took a guess with some of the clothes I sent up. Do you like the baby pink, the metallic blues, and this green? I love this green," she said, holding up a blouse I had not yet put on.

"Yes. Everything is beautiful," I said. What else would I say? I hadn't had anything new for more than a year. Everything Mama and I had managed to buy during the struggle when we were on the street was used, from some thrift store. Colors were faded and dull, and the clothes were often long out of style and never quite fit.

"I'm glad. Those were Alena's favorite colors, too. Actually, she liked anything that was bright and happy. She was a bright and happy girl, never depressed. You'll be like that someday, too, Sasha, I just know you will. I can see that it's not in your nature to be unhappy. You did such a good job of helping your mother, and I'm sure you weren't crying and complaining all the time. You've got that same energy in you. We'll go shopping to get you more, of course. For the time being, you'll have plenty, however. You're just about the same age Alena was and about her size. That's how I figured out what to buy you, you know. I bet you were wondering how I knew."

"No," I said. "I thought you could just look at me and see."

"That's right, I could. Well, there's a ton more to do, a ton. I'm going right over to Donald's offices to tell him about your decision. I'll try to stop by later, but don't worry if I don't. You can be sure that you're all that's on my mind."

She moved toward me as if she were going to give me a kiss, but the look on my face slowed her down, and she paused and then smiled quickly, grabbed her purse, and left. For a moment, it was as if all the air had gone out of the room with her. I felt the blood rush to my face. Of course, I knew Mama was gone, but it still felt as if I were deserting her, leaving her to be alone on the street. My father had deserted her and now me. I couldn't help it. I started to cry softly.

"What happened?" Jackie demanded as she stepped into the room. "Did she say she changed her mind, or her husband said no, or what?"

I shook my head. "No. I'm going," I said.

"So why are you crying?"

"I'm not going home," I said.

She froze and then nodded and moved to hug me.

"That's where my mother said she was

taking us when we left the beach that night — home."

"You'll find a place to call home someday, Sasha. You'll make your own home when you're old enough. You'll marry someone wonderful and have your own children. You'll see."

I thanked her. Her words did give me hope. She was there the day I was discharged, and she followed Jordan March and me to the waiting limousine. I didn't know I'd be leaving in a limousine. I had never ridden in one. At first, I thought she had rented it, but I quickly learned that it belonged to the Marches. The driver was very tall, easily six foot four or five. He was slim but with such perfect military posture Mama would have called him a flagpole. He had a thick, well-trimmed black mustache, a nose that looked as if it had been pinched by the doctor who had delivered him, and coal-black eyes. Mrs. March called him Grover, which I would learn was his first name. His full name was Grover Morrison. He had been the Marches' limousine driver for nearly four years. I didn't know it yet, but the Marches owned five other vehicles, and Kiera had an additional one, the one she had been driving the night of the accident.

"You take care," Jackie told me after I had been transferred from the wheelchair into the limousine. She stood in the open doorway.

"I will," I said. "Thank you, Jackie."

She nodded and backed away as Grover closed the door. He opened the door on the other side for Mrs. March.

"Well, now," Mrs. March said. "Are you comfortable?"

"Yes."

"I could put a pillow under your leg."

"It's all right," I said.

"Don't worry," she said, patting my hand. "Everything's going to be fine."

I wasn't worried as much as I was afraid. Before Daddy had deserted us, I had slept over at a friend's house. That was really the only time I had ever been overnight at the home of strangers, and now I was going to live with some.

"You'll have to wear that cast for months yet, Sasha," she said, nodding at it, "but Dr. Milan's arranged for you to be up and about on a crutch soon. In the meantime, we have the wheelchair for you. I've already told Mrs. Caro that one of her duties now will be to wheel you out onto the patio in the afternoon. I want you to get some color and fresh air and not be shut up in a room like you were in the hospital."

"Who's Mrs. Caro?"

"Mrs. Caro is one of my housekeepers and also our cook. We have four housekeepers. The one in charge is Mrs. Duval. She's been with us the longest and was actually Kiera and Alena's nanny as well. Her husband, Alberto, is what Donald calls our house manager. He is in charge of the grounds people, house maintenance, that sort of thing."

"Four housekeepers? How many people work at the house?" I asked as we started away from the hospital.

"Fourteen full-time," she said. "There's a lot to do. You'll see."

Neither of us had mentioned her yet, but I didn't see how I could go much farther without bringing her up. "What about Kiera?"

"What about her?"

"Does she know about me?"

"She knows about you."

"But does she know I'm coming to live in her house?"

"It's not her house," Mrs. March said quickly and sharply. Then she smiled and added, "Don't worry about it."

"But she knows?" I asked.

"Not yet," Mrs. March said. "Right now,

I'm not concerned about what she thinks or how she feels about anything."

Her answer shocked me. How could such a thing be kept secret from her daughter? What sort of a family was this, anyway?

Maybe Mama and I, even during the struggle, had been more of a family after all.

It wouldn't be long before I knew.

6
CASTLE

Nothing I had seen in magazines, on television, or in a movie had prepared me for what I was about to see. I had thought castles were only in Europe and only kings and queens lived like this. We turned off a main road, went down a side road, and began to climb a hill. As we climbed, I realized there were no houses along the way.

Mrs. March sensed my curiosity. "All this land is ours," she said, "on both sides. That's why there are no other houses on the road."

Eventually, we reached what I could only describe as a hidden entrance to the road on which the Marches' house was located. There were no signs, mailboxes, or anything, just tall, full pine trees on both sides, so that when anyone drove in, he or she couldn't see the March house just yet.

"This isn't a public road," she said. "My husband built it, and we maintain it."

They own their own road? How can anyone own his own road? I wondered.

We came to a tall, solid, light orange wall at least ten or twelve feet high. Now, just over the wall, I could see the top of the house and what looked like a tower. Just looking at the wall ahead of us wouldn't tell anyone it opened, but when Grover pressed a button by the sun visor above him, the wall began to part. It revealed a beautiful cobblestone driveway that curved upward toward what I could only call a storybook house.

"Is it a castle?" I asked breathlessly.

Mrs. March laughed. "Donald thinks so. He was determined to build something different, so he built what's called a Richardsonian Romanesque house. It has the round-topped arches over the windows and entryway and masonry walls with a pattern of ruby and white. And yes," she said, laughing again, "that tower makes it look like a castle, but Donald will tell you a man's home is supposed to be his castle."

As we approached and we could see beyond the high bushes and trees, the house seemed to unfold to my right and to my left.

"It's so big."

"It might be the biggest house in Southern California, for all I know. I forget, but I think Donald said it's ninety thousand square feet. There are three floors if we count the rooms in the tower. We've been here nearly twenty years, but I'm still furnishing it. I suppose it will never be finished, but that's what makes it fun to go shopping here and in Europe. There's furniture from all over the world. Persian and Turkish rugs, French chandeliers, cabinets from England, settees and chairs from Spain, tapestries from both France and Spain. You can understand why we need so many employees."

She pointed to her left as we drew closer. "Over there, you'll find the swimming pool and the tennis courts. You can't tell, but part of the house is our multicar garage. The garage entrances are all around the side, so it makes the house look much bigger. Of course, there is an apartment over the garage. That's where Mrs. Duval and her husband, Alberto, live. There's another maid's apartment for Mrs. Caro at the rear of the house. Everyone else comes to work from his or her own home. We have another entrance for servants and deliveries at the west end of the property.

"There are security cameras everywhere. Donald loves his toys. He has a movie theater in the house, with the most up-to-date equipment. There's a full gym and a small indoor swimming pool, which will come in handy for your therapy, I bet. The house has an intercom system, of course. Just think of all the fun you'll have discovering new things in it when you're up and about."

As we drew closer, I looked out at the beautiful gardens and fountains, the statues and benches, the rolling lawns and trees. No wonder so many people had to work there, I thought. There was so much to take care of. How could anyone be so rich?

As soon as we pulled up to the front, a short, stout, dark-brown-haired woman came rushing out. She wore a dark blue one-piece dress with a skirt that flapped about her ankles as she hurried down the stairs. Her hair was clipped into a tight bun. Right behind her was a tall, gray-haired man with a dark brown mustache sprinkled with gray hairs. He wore a plaid shirt and jeans.

"That's Mrs. Duval and her husband, Alberto," Mrs. March told me.

Grover got out quickly and opened Mrs. March's door. He went around to get my wheelchair and my things, some of which he handed to Mrs. Duval. He and Alberto unfolded the wheelchair and brought it to my door.

"Careful with her," Mrs. March told them.

Grover looked for a graceful way to get me out and then simply decided to put his right arm under me and embrace me with his left. He lifted me out easily and gently lowered me to the wheelchair that Alberto held.

"This is Sasha," Mrs. March said.

"*Hola,* Sasha," Mrs. Duval said. "Hello and welcome."

"*Sí,* welcome," Alberto said.

He and Grover lifted me and the chair and carried me up the stone steps to the entrance. Mrs. Duval and Mrs. March followed us. At the grand door, they waited for her instructions.

"Take her in and to the elevator," Mrs. March told them. "We're bringing her right up to her suite."

Elevator? Suite? Had I heard right? This did sound more like a hotel than a house.

They hurried to do so.

The entryway had a floor of golden marble, and there were small statues of ivory-white angels in niches on both sides of the darker marble walls. Above us was a large chandelier shaped like an opened hand, and ahead of us was a curved stairway with steps that matched the marble in the entrance. The banister was made of marble, too. Everywhere I looked, I saw paintings and tapestries on the walls and pedestals with small statues.

Alberto wheeled me to the right, but before we went too far, a smaller, younger-looking lady with a pillbox chef's cap came hurrying down the long hallway. She didn't look much taller than five foot one or two, and her apron's hem was down to her ankles, making it look as if it was meant for a much taller person.

"This is Mrs. Caro," Mrs. March announced before she reached us. "Mrs. Caro, meet Sasha."

"Hello, dear," Mrs. Caro said in an accent I recognized as Irish only because Daddy had an Irish friend he had brought around from time to time. "My, what a pretty little girl," she told Mrs. March. "I'm fixing a nice lunch for you, dear."

"We'll let you know when she's settled in, Mrs. Caro. For today and perhaps tomorrow, we'll let her rest. Then we'll see about taking her out."

"Oh, of course, Mrs. March. I'll prepare some fresh lemonade," she said, and then asked, "You like lemonade?"

"Yes, thank you."

She smiled as if she rarely heard those words.

Mrs. March urged Alberto to continue, and he brought me to an elevator.

"We hardly use this," Mrs. March said when I was wheeled in. There wasn't room for Mrs. Duval, who had already gone up the stairway. "Donald thought it would be wise to have one, either to help us when we were too old or in the event of his wanting to sell, to have another attraction, an added advantage. If you ask me, it was just another toy for him, but now it does come in handy."

The elevator was slow. I saw that it could go up to the tower, too. When the door opened, Mrs. Duval was waiting for us. "I'll take her from here," she told her husband. Without comment, he turned and went to the stairway. Mrs. Duval wheeled me down another long corridor. More paintings and tapestries were spaced along its walls on both sides, with pedestals holding statues and busts here and there as well. We went almost to the end before she turned me into a room on the left. I nearly gasped.

Even in movies and magazines, I had never seen a bedroom this large. The walls were done in a baby pink, and the bed, which looked even larger than a king-size bed, had a cream frame with pink spirals, four posts, and a canopy. What surprised me, however, was the headboard. Embossed on it were two giraffes.

Before I could ask, *Why giraffes?* Mrs. March explained. "Giraffes were Alena's favorite animals. From the age of two or three, she was fascinated by them."

So, this was Alena's room, then. For someone who just weeks ago was sleeping in a carton on the beach, coming to such a house would have been overwhelming in and of itself. Even simply setting foot in it would have drowned me in amazement. The sight of it as we had approached it, the grounds, the landscaping, had taken my breath away and actually had numbed me. But now, realizing that I was stepping into the shoes and sleeping in the bed of Mrs. March's dead little girl did more than amaze and numb me. It actually frightened me. It was beautiful, the most beautiful room I had ever seen, but for a moment, it gave me the feeling that I was invading and violating another girl's sacred shrine. Prominent on one of the dressers was a picture of someone who was surely Alena. I avoided looking at it.

"Mrs. Duval and I have already gone through all of Alena's things and sorted out what we think would fit you properly," Mrs. March said as they brought me to the bed. "You don't have to put this on right now, but here's one of my favorite nightgowns." She lifted it off the bed where it had been neatly placed. She laughed. "As you can see . . . more giraffes. I'm afraid you're going to find them everywhere. She even had a toothbrush shaped like the neck of a giraffe with a giraffe's head. Donald went a little overboard with that stuff."

"Do you want her in bed right away?" Mrs. Duval asked Mrs. March. I looked up at her.

"I don't know. Are you tired, Sasha? You can explore the suite, if you like, or get into bed and rest. I imagine it's all been exhausting for you, considering you've been laid up so long and gone through so much. What would you like to do?"

Mrs. Duval pulled back the blanket in anticipation.

"I'll stay in the wheelchair a while longer," I said.

"Good. That way, you can have your lunch right over here," Mrs. March said, moving to her right to show me a separate sitting area. "This will become your private classroom, too, as soon as I have your tutor arranged. I was thinking we'd get that started as soon as we can, as long as you're up to it. You can work in here, don't you think?"

I wheeled myself toward it. There was a

small table, a desk with a computer, another television besides the one built into the wall directly across from the bed, and a very large dollhouse, large enough for a little girl to go into if she liked. Everywhere I looked, there were pictures of giraffes in different locales or just one or two close up. There was a beautiful painting of one as well.

The windows were low enough for me to look out, even sitting in the wheelchair. I wheeled to the one on the left and gazed down at the swimming pool, which looked huge, and the two tennis courts. Someone was cleaning the pool.

"That's an Olympic-size pool," Mrs. March said, standing over my shoulder. "Before she became very sick, Alena could do ten laps without stopping. I'm sure once you're fully recuperated, it will be great for your physical therapy. In no time at all, you'll be able to work up to ten laps, too, I'm sure. It's always heated, by the way."

There was a cabana with tables under a roof, a barbecue area, and what looked like a large hot tub, too. Around the pool were light yellow wood tables with yellow umbrellas. It looked more like the pool area in a hotel, not a home, but now that I was in it, I realized this house was bigger than many hotels. It would need everything to be larger and in bigger amounts than any normal house would. The hotel room Mama and I had slept in was probably no bigger than the wardrobe closet in this suite.

"Well, what do you think so far, Sasha?" Mrs. March asked. "Do you think you could be happy here?"

I looked up at her. Of course, there was a part of me that wanted to say, *Absolutely, this is like a dream,* but there was a part of me that still harbored anger and sadness. I was also reminded of the things Jackie had said to me. They could never do enough to compensate for what they had taken from me. Even all of this didn't come anywhere close.

"I don't know," I said, which obviously shocked Mrs. Duval and disappointed Mrs. March.

"It's understandable," she said, mostly for Mrs. Duval's sake, I thought. "You've been through so much so quickly. You need to catch your breath and get used to new things. I'd feel the same way," she added. "Well, don't hesitate to ask Mrs. Duval or Mrs. Caro or anyone, for that matter, for anything you want or need."

From the look on Mrs. Duval's face, I could see that she was thinking, *Need? What could she possibly want or need that she doesn't have already?*

I didn't know if I could blame her just yet for being insensitive. I had no idea how much she knew about me, about exactly what had happened or why I was there.

Another thought that was tying a knot in my brain was, where was Kiera? Where was her room? When would she and I meet? What would she say? What would I say? Did any of the people who worked there know what she had done?

"Okay, then, you look about, Sasha. Mrs. Duval will be bringing up your lunch soon. I have a few errands to run. All you have to do is pick up any of the phones in the suite if you need anything. Just picking one up rings Mrs. Duval's pager. That's another one of Donald's technical toys. I know sometimes Alena drove Mrs. Duval bonkers," she added.

"Only when she was sick," Mrs. Duval said sharply.

"Yes. She was a very thoughtful little girl, wasn't she?"

"The best. I can't imagine any little girl better," Mrs. Duval said, her eyes fixed on me.

"Well, let's not dilly-dally, as Mrs. Caro says. See you soon, Sasha." Mrs. March touched my shoulder and then turned and headed out.

Mrs. Duval hesitated. "Do you need to use the toilet?"

"No, not yet," I said.

"I'll go see about your lunch, then," she told me, and followed Mrs. March out. She closed the door behind her and left me in a silence so deep it made me feel as if I were asleep and dreaming.

It was truly like a medieval castle, with its walled-in grounds and security, its employees, some of whom I could see now cutting grass and trimming bushes. I was certain there was everything and anything that anyone like me could possibly want, if anyone like me could forget about love, especially a mother's love.

But to answer Mrs. March's question fully, no, I couldn't imagine ever calling this home. I was sure anyone else would think it strange, but as I sat there in my wheelchair and looked at all that was now at my disposal, I couldn't help wondering how and when I could escape.

7
ALENA'S ROOM

Mrs. Duval brought up my lunch on the same sort of cart I had seen at the hospital. I was stunned by how much food was on the tray. I thought maybe Mrs. March was going to eat with me, but she didn't follow Mrs. Duval into the suite, and I didn't hear her coming.

"Is this all for me?" I asked.

"Mrs. Caro made you one of her delicious chicken quesadillas, but in case you might not like it, she made a ham and cheese sandwich, and under here," she said, lifting a silver cover, "is a cheeseburger. There's a small salad for you and this piece of her homemade chocolate cake. This is the homemade lemonade she does. Do you think you want some ice cream, too?"

I sat with my mouth open. I would eat any one of the choices, but what would I do with the others? Maybe she'd take them back.

"I'll eat the chicken quesadilla," I said. I couldn't remember when I had eaten one last. "I don't need ice cream."

"Maybe you don't need it, but you can have it," Mrs. Duval said. "I'll bring some up later."

She turned to leave.

"But what about the rest? I can't eat everything."

"Just eat what you want and leave the rest," she said, shrugging. "That's what everyone does here."

After she left, I sat staring at the tray of food. There had been times when we were on the street when this much food would feed both Mama and me for a whole day. The thought of it being wasted and thrown out actually turned my stomach. Despite what I had said, I tried to eat more than I should have. I ate until I thought I would throw it all up and then stopped. Not long after, Mrs. Duval returned with a bowl of chocolate and vanilla ice cream.

"No," I said. "Please take it back. I can't eat any more."

She looked at me with indifference, put it on the tray, and rolled the food wagon out of the room. I closed my eyes and sat there trying to digest the food. Eating all of that food was stupid of me, I thought, but I couldn't change into a wasteful rich person overnight, could I? I dozed off in my chair and didn't wake until I heard voices outside. Fortunately, I no longer felt bloated and nauseous.

The voices grew louder, so I wheeled myself back to the window in the sitting room and looked out to see three teenage boys and four teenage girls getting ready to go into the pool. I had no idea what she looked like, but I knew one of them had to be Kiera March.

I concentrated on the four girls. One seemed too dark-haired and short to be Jordan March's daughter, but of course, I didn't know what Donald March looked like yet. I thought all four of the girls were pretty, but one did stand out more, because she looked slim and tall like a model and had Jordan March's light brown hair, which she had similarly styled. All of the girls wore two-piece bathing suits. One of the three boys was at least as tall as the tallest girl, but the other two were short and stocky. They all jumped in ahead of the girls and started to race across the pool. The girls cheered, but the shorter boys were far outclassed by the taller, more graceful boy and fell behind quickly.

Moments later, all four girls were in the

pool, too. Only one actually did any swimming. The other three bobbed and talked. I saw Mrs. Duval and Alberto arrive at the pool. Alberto carried what looked like a case of Cokes and began putting the bottles into a refrigerator in the roof-covered patio area. Mrs. Duval placed a tray of something on one of the poolside tables. No one seemed to pay any attention to them, but as soon as they left, the boys were out and at whatever was on the food tray.

Soon I heard some music start, and then the girls were out of the pool and dancing. One of the shorter boys went over to his bag and produced what looked like a bottle of some kind of whiskey. The tallest boy went to the refrigerator and filled glasses with Coke. He brought them to a table, and the shorter boy began adding from his bottle, and soon all seven of them were drinking, dancing, and occasionally embracing and kissing. No one seemed to be especially with anyone else. All of the girls kissed all of the boys.

I sat there mesmerized by the activity below me and wondered if anyone else in the house was watching from a window. None of the teenagers below seemed to worry or care. They began pushing one another into the pool, and then, to my shock, the boys, while they were in the pool, took off their bathing suits, swung them over their heads, and began swimming toward the girls, who screamed and rushed to the side of the pool. This went on until all of the girls were out and laughing.

The boys actually got out naked and put their bathing suits on in front of the girls, who, instead of being embarrassed, laughed. They all drank more, nibbled on the food, danced, and continued to tease and flirt. Finally, something drew their attention off to their right, and they quieted down. The boys went into the cabanas to change, and the girls followed. No one attempted to clean up anything. Tables were left with empty glasses and traces of what looked like half-eaten burgers, potato chips, and hot dogs. I leaned forward and struggled to see them walking off, but they were all soon out of sight.

I hadn't been in junior high school long enough and, of course, had never been in high school, but I had read about and seen enough of teenage romance to be curious about a group of girls and boys who didn't seem to favor anyone. None of them seemed to be boyfriend-and-girlfriend. Was this what was meant by an orgy? Nothing graphically sexual had occurred aside from the boys' nudity, but there was something different and strange about them. I couldn't help but be curious. Had the teenage world changed in ways I hadn't realized while Mama and I were living in the streets?

I heard a knock on the door and turned to see another maid, an African American woman quite a bit younger than Mrs. Caro or Mrs. Duval.

"You're Sasha, right?" she asked.

"Yes."

"I'm Rosie. Mrs. Duval sent me up to see if you needed any help going to the bathroom. I'm leaving for the day, so I gotta help you now."

"I don't need any help," I said. "I can do everything for myself."

"Okay." She started to turn and stopped. "Mind if I ask what happened to you? You got a disease or something?"

"I was hit by a car," I said.

"Oh, too bad," she said, and hurried off before I could add anything.

I was surprised she didn't know about me. If anyone else but the Marches knew what was going on, I thought, he or she certainly didn't gossip. Now that Rosie had mentioned the bathroom, I realized I did have to go. Because of the cast, it was hard to shift from my wheelchair to the toilet. I nearly fell twice but somehow managed to get it done and get back into the chair. At least I wouldn't have to depend on anyone for that, I thought happily, and went to watch television.

I tried to distract myself with a movie, but I kept my eyes and ears tuned to the door, anticipating Mrs. March and either her husband or Kiera. Hours later, Mrs. March did return, but she was alone. She burst in with an armful of packages.

"How are you doing, Sasha?" she asked, but before I could answer, she added, "I just had to buy these things for you."

She put everything on the table.

"Come, look. I was told that this is the newest iPod. Of course, I didn't know what songs you'd like on it, but I had them download everything that's popular now."

"But you already bought me one of these when I was in the hospital."

"Yes, but the salesman told me this one is the latest version, and you can do so many more things with it. I'll leave it up to you to read about it. You teenagers are so much more adept at figuring out all this technology. Donald says we were brought up with pages to read, and you guys are being brought up with megabytes or some such thing. Anyway, that's that."

She handed it to me. One of those would have probably paid for food for Mama and me for a month or so, I thought.

Mrs. March held up the first wrapped box. "I stopped at what used to be my favorite clothing store for Alena's things, and they just got in these darling outfits for the fall and winter."

She began to unwrap the box, and before I could really see what was in it, she had unwrapped the next and the next, pulling everything out quickly. There were skirt-and-blouse outfits with matching caps, jeans with sequins, and two leather jackets, one light pink and the other light green. They felt butter-soft.

"What do you think?" she asked when she was finished unwrapping and showing it all.

"It's all beautiful," I said. I wanted to sound grateful, but she was flooding me with so much I didn't have a chance to appreciate any of it.

"I thought so, too. Now, more news. I had the guidance counselor at the school Kiera attends contact the tutor he had recommended for us. Her name is Mrs. Kepler. She retired two years ago but is bored to death. Her husband does nothing but play golf. She'll be perfect, I'm sure. I've arranged for her to stop in tomorrow to meet you. Is that all right? We want you to be up to speed when the new school year begins."

"Where do I go to school?"

"You'll go to the private school Kiera attends, of course. It's just outside Pacific Palisades. Grover will take you and pick you up every day when that starts. I'm going to speak with Dr. Milan in a little while," she continued, barely taking a breath. "Do you have any complaints, pain, headaches, anything I need to report to him?"

"No."

"That's wonderful. It's so important not to linger in the hospital around all those other sick and injured people. It keeps it on your mind. There's plenty to distract you from that here."

She stood smiling down at me so long it made me feel a little uncomfortable. I deliberately turned away to look at the new iPod.

"Well," she said, "let's get your new clothes put away."

She gathered it all in her arms. I wheeled behind her to the walk-in closet. I had not yet looked into it, but now, when I did, I laughed to myself. I had imagined the hotel room that Mama and I had lived in not being much larger than a walk-in closet in this house. I was greatly underestimating. The closet was at least twice as large as that hotel room. It had a mirror and a vanity table in it and rows of clothing that probably rivaled the stock in most stores. How could any girl have been able to wear so much?

She paused as she hung up my new skirts and blouses and suddenly grew teary-eyed. She lifted one skirt, and I saw that it was hanging there with its label still attached. For a moment, it was as if she had forgotten I was there. Then she turned to me, still holding the skirt. After a deep breath, she nodded and said, "I'm being stupid again, I know."

"What do you mean?"

"When Alena was very sick, I went on a buying spree as I just did for you. Most of this," she said, pointing down the row of clothes, "she never had the chance to wear. I guess buying her new clothes, new shoes, anything, was my way of trying to deny what was happening to her. Here I am doing the same thing to you. I'm sorry. There is so much here that's still brand-new that will fit you. But I can't help it when I see something darling. When Alena was gone and I'd go into stores and see things she could wear and that would make her happy, I'd be tempted to buy them. In fact, I did buy some of this after she was gone. I know that sounds crazy to you, but . . . it helped me get by."

"I understand," I said. I really thought I did.

She looked at me and smiled. "I know you do. You're an exceptional young girl and will be an exceptional woman someday. I am determined to make you happy, healthy, and safe again," she said with such firm determination in her eyes that I couldn't help but believe her.

She hung up the rest, and we left the closet.

"Will I meet your husband tonight?" I asked.

"No. He's at a conference in Texas, something about new home-building materials. I'm not sure when he returns. I don't pay much attention to his work. It will just be you and me for dinner."

"But what about . . ."

"Kiera is at a friend's tonight," she said, almost before the words were out of my mouth. "I wasn't going to let her go, but I thought it would be nicer if you and I had your first night here alone. Okay?"

I nodded. Did she know that Kiera and her friends had spent the afternoon at the pool? Should I mention it? I felt funny about spying on them. What if she asked me what I had seen?

"Did you take a nap, at least?"

"I dozed off for a while. I don't feel tired."

"That's amazing. I know the excitement of going somewhere new can wear you out, but I forget how much energy you young girls have. I'll come up later and help you decide what you'd like to wear to dinner." She moved toward the door.

Why was it important what I would wear to dinner if it was going to be just the two of us?

"Enjoy your new iPod," she said, and left.

I simply sat there staring after her. My head was spinning. I looked at the closet, the sitting room, the magnificent bed, the television on the wall, everything I could have ever dreamed of having up until now was there. We hadn't had very much before my father deserted us, but it still had been sad to leave it. How much more difficult had it been for a little girl to lie here and know she was dying and would leave everything, especially parents who adored her?

I embraced myself as if I could feel the cold sorrow closing in around me, even in the wonderful suite full of color and warm things. Then I looked at the bed. Could I sleep in that bed, and when I did, would I hear Alena March's voice, maybe her sobs and cries? Would I dream her dreams?

I could feel what Jordan March was hoping for when she brought me there, and it intrigued me and yet at the same time made me feel sick and afraid. She wanted to look at me, blink her eyes, and see her daughter returned.

I wasn't all that different from her.

I'd want to look at her, blink my eyes, and see my mother returned.

Either we'd both be happy or, in the end, both of us would end up blind.

8
DINNER

I fell asleep again in my chair. I had wheeled myself to the window in the sitting room and sat gazing at the pool, the tennis courts, and the beautiful grounds. I opened the window slightly and could hear the drone of the lawn mowers. Because the house was so high up on the hill, I could see the ocean just behind the tops of the trees. At this time of the day, it looked like blue ice but gradually reddened with the sinking sun.

When I was eight, my father brought home a doll he had found on a job site. It was in a basement next to a washing machine he was repairing, and he just put it into his tool kit. Although it was old, faded, and dusty, I cherished it, because it was one of the only times I could remember that he thought of me while he was working and brought me something. Mama bawled him out for giving me something so dirty-looking and seized it to put into our washing machine. I never saw another doll like it.

The doll was a sailor girl. Daddy didn't know what it really was, but Mama did. She admitted it was something of a collector's item, because it was a doll depicting a member of the WAVES. She said she had a great-aunt on her father's side who had been a member of the Women Appointed for Voluntary Emergency Service, which was a U.S. Navy organization during World War II.

Once it was washed, the blue uniform had faded even more, but I thought it was the most beautiful doll in the world, and when I understood more about the WAVES, I began to fantasize about myself on boats and ships. Even during the struggle, when Mama and I were on the beach selling her calligraphy and my lanyards, I would look out at the sailboats and the bigger ships, and I would recall my fantasies.

Sailing off toward the horizon always seemed to be an escape from sadness and hardship. Nothing was as promising as the distant horizon. I envisioned myself standing at the bow and looking ahead toward a new life full of brightness and happiness. Mama was always on the boat with me, standing beside me or right behind me, with just as big a smile on her face, just as much hope in her eyes. We would never look back at the dark clouds.

I thought about my doll now as I looked out at the Pacific Ocean. I had played with it so much and kept it with me so much that the uniform thinned and the doll began to come apart. Mama tried sewing it a few times, but the threads would break. When I was older, I put it aside. Somewhere along the way, with our packing quickly, dragging our belongings along, it got lost. I told myself the doll had gone back to sea, back to that boat, to seek a better place than the places I could take her.

Now, I imagined her out there, sailing toward the horizon. I could vaguely make out a boat and watched it until I could see it no longer. *At least she's safe,* I thought. I smiled to myself and relived some of my childhood moments talking to my doll.

Mrs. March's return to help me decide what to wear for dinner broke the spell and ripped me out of the happier moments in my past and pulled me back to cold reality. It was as though I had lost my doll again.

"Let's look for something comfortable for you," she began, and headed back to that enormous closet. I wheeled myself to the doorway and watched her rake through the garments, pausing at some, shaking her head at others. What was she looking for? How could this be so important? I almost came right out and asked, but she plucked a blouse and a skirt off the rack as if she had found something she had tried and failed to locate many times. I saw the look of delight spread over her face.

"Yes," she said, talking more to herself than to me, "this was it."

When she turned and held it up to show me, I nearly fell out of my wheelchair. It was a sailor girl's outfit. I felt a hot flow move up from my chest and into my neck and face. The words crackled when I spoke. "Why that?"

"Alena was so excited when Donald bought our boat that I went right out and bought this outfit for her. When she tried it on, she didn't want to take it off. Donald and Kiera were away that evening, so it was just Alena and me for dinner. Even though we were alone, it was a very special night. I remember how talkative she was, how happy, and this was shortly after she had been diagnosed. Just like you, she refused to be depressed."

Just like me? What had I done to lead her to believe I wasn't depressed and unhappy? Did she think that just because I was overwhelmed with the house and the gifts, all of my sadness was dead and buried? Could she possibly believe that I had already forgotten what had happened to my mother?

I think she saw the look on my face and understood. Her smile flew off, and she grew serious as she approached me with the outfit.

"Oh, I know how unhappy and terrible you must feel," she began. "I don't want you to think for one moment that I don't know or don't care. I want you to remember and love your mother forever. I promised I would have whatever you wanted written on her tombstone, remember? As soon as you think of it, you tell me, and we'll have it done, and then you and I will go there to see it. But in the meantime, you've got to survive and grow and be healthy again. Don't blame me for trying to help you do that. I know you must hate me always talking about my Alena, but . . ."

"No, I don't hate you for that," I said quickly. I glanced at the framed photograph of her. "She was a very pretty girl, and I'm sure she was very nice."

"Thank you, dear. If you don't want to wear this," she added, holding up the skirt and blouse, "you don't have to. You can pick out something else."

"No, it's all right," I said. I almost told her about my doll but somehow felt that there were things so private that they still belonged only with Mama and me. Despite what Jackie called her charity, Mrs. March had not earned that trust. She was not my mother; she was not even a friend yet. She was simply someone who felt sorry for me and felt guilty because of what her daughter had done. It was I who was being the charitable one. I was letting her live with the guilt. That's what Jackie had told me, and it made sense to me now more than ever.

I reached for the outfit.

"Can I help you get dressed?" she asked.

I nodded, and she began by helping me take off the blouse I wore. She moaned at the sight of the fading black-and-blue marks and mumbled, "Poor child. What a horror you've gone through." She looked as if she was going to burst into tears, so I made sure to tell her that none of it hurt as much as it had.

After I was dressed in the sailor outfit, she wheeled me in front of the vanity table. I was amazed at how well it fit.

"Let's do something with your hair," she said, and began brushing it. "You do have beautiful hair, and thick, too. I bet your mother's hair was beautiful."

"Yes. She used to wear it down to her wing bones."

"I wish I could have long hair, but Donald says it makes me look older, and if there is one thing Donald hates, it's my looking older."

"What about him?"

"Men can always look older and call it distinguished, didn't you know?" she asked, smiling.

She opened a drawer in the vanity table and chose some hair clips. When I saw how she had shaped my hair, I looked at the framed photo of Alena and realized it was very similar.

"There now," she said, stepping back. "Don't you look very pretty?"

"I hope someday I'll be half as pretty as my mother was," I said.

She kept her smile, but it lost its excitement and warmth. She nodded and turned me away from the vanity table. "I do hope you like Irish stew. Mrs. Caro makes the best."

"I don't remember ever having it," I said as she pushed me to the doorway.

"Well, you eat just what you want. She's made a special dessert for us, a surprise, too. Here we go," she said, and turned me down the corridor toward the elevator.

I had seen only a small part of the house when I arrived. When the elevator door opened, she pushed me to the left and around a corner. The hallway seemed endless, but along the way, she pointed out the game room, the formal dining room, the den and library, the entertainment center, and then a hallway that branched off to the right. She said that was where the indoor pool was located.

Right off the kitchen was what she called their informal dining room. No room in this house was small to me, but she called it one of their smaller rooms. It had a beautiful dark hardwood table with twelve cushioned hardwood chairs. The walls were paneled in a lighter wood, and a large window looked toward the rear of the property.

"Is that a lake?" I asked, looking out.

"Donald's lake, yes. It's man-made. He says he's going to stock it with fish. What fun is that, right? It would be like shooting fish in a barrel, but once Donald sees something someone else has, he wants it, too. There are two rowboats. That's fun, at least."

She pulled a chair away next to the chair at the end of the table and fit me into that place. Two dinner settings, glasses, and silverware were already there. Almost as soon as Mrs. March took her seat, Mrs. Duval came through the door that led from the kitchen. She carried a bowl of rolls and a jug of water.

"Good evening, Mrs. Duval," Mrs. March said, sounding very formal all of a sudden.

"Good evening, Mrs. March."

"Doesn't our little girl look pretty tonight?"

Mrs. Duval paused after she poured Mrs. March's glass of water and looked at me as if I had just arrived. I caught the slight tic in her eyes, the little moment of surprise. She glanced at Mrs. March and then forced a smile and said, *"Sí, muy bonita."*

Mrs. March looked satisfied. She leaned toward me as Mrs. Duval returned to the kitchen. "That means 'very pretty' in Spanish," she whispered. "Do you know any Spanish?"

"Not really," I said. "I mean, I know some words."

"Alena spoke fluent Spanish, because Mrs. Duval had been her nanny since birth. I'm sure you'll learn quite a bit just being around her. It's the best way to learn a language, better than in a classroom. That's what Donald says."

"I know some Chinese words because of

my mother," I told her.

She didn't look that excited about it. "That's nice. Educating yourself as much as possible is important. I bet you are a good reader, too, right?"

Mrs. Duval brought in our salads and set them down without looking at me or speaking.

"I haven't read that much for a while," I said

"Of course. I understand. But you're going to see that Alena had a wonderful library in her sitting room. Unless you've already explored those shelves."

"No, I haven't yet."

"Getting Kiera to read anything is like trying to feed her cod-liver oil. She has barely passing grades. Donald's at his wit's end with that, and it isn't because we haven't paid for tutors. She never liked any, but I'm sure you're going to like Mrs. Kepler. Doesn't this salad look good? You like figs in your salad? We all like that. Alena loved it."

"I never had it before," I said, but I nodded. It did taste good.

That pleased her, and she became even more talkative, telling me about her own youth, her high school years, and her years at a private college she called "more of a charm school than a real educational institution. But I wasn't meant to have any sort of career," she added. "I was born to be who I am." She laughed. "That's what Donald says."

Everything was what Donald said, I thought. I couldn't help but wonder what he was really like and what he would think of me.

"Is he coming home tomorrow?" I asked.

"No. He'll be away the rest of the week, but that's all right. We'll have plenty of company, with your tutor coming tomorrow, your doctor checkup, lots to do. No worries," she said. I was waiting for her to add, "as Donald would say," but she didn't.

The Irish stew was delicious. I had eaten so much for lunch that I couldn't eat as much of it as I would have liked, especially with Mrs. March continually warning me to leave room for our special dessert. After the dishes were cleared off the table, I sat in anticipation. Moments later, Mrs. Duval returned, carrying a tray with something on fire. Mrs. Caro was right behind her, smiling. It remained in a flame until Mrs. Duval lowered it to the table.

"It looks beautiful," Mrs. March said.

"What is it?" I asked.

"Banana flambé," she said.

Mrs. Duval served us each a dish, and Mrs. Caro added scoops of vanilla ice cream. I couldn't remember anything so delicious.

"Wait until Kiera finds out we had this. She'll be sorry she wasn't here," Mrs. March said, and then clapped her mouth shut and lowered her eyes.

"It's wonderful," I said. It brightened her face.

"I'm so glad you enjoyed your first dinner here, dear. I hope there will be many, many more, and all happy and delicious."

After dinner, she gave me a more detailed tour of the rooms we had passed on our way to dinner. There was so much to see. I simply couldn't take it all in, and I was very tired by then. This did seem to be one of those days that Mama called longer than twenty-four hours. Mrs. March realized I was getting very tired and brought me quickly to the elevator. In fact, she fell into a kind of frenzy as she rushed to get me up and into bed.

"I know I shouldn't get you this tired," she said as we went up in the elevator. "I just forget. I'm sorry."

"It's all right. I'm fine," I told her, but she had the look on her face that people have when they realize they've done something terrible.

She hurried me down the corridor to my bedroom. "I'll help you get ready for bed," she said. "I know you're exhausted."

"It's all right," I insisted, but she was at me, getting me out of the sailor outfit. Then, after I had on the nightgown she had laid out earlier, she pushed me to the bathroom.

"There's a brand-new electric toothbrush here for you, and different kinds of toothpaste. Alena hated the peppermint-flavored ones. She said they burned her tongue. This one is sort of plain. She liked it the best," she told me. "You should have had a sponge bath. I'll send Mrs. Duval in first thing to help you have one in the morning."

"I can bathe myself," I said sharply.

"It's no disgrace to have help when you need it."

"I don't need it," I insisted.

"Okay. She'll be available if you do. Remember, if you need anything, you simply pick up the phone, okay?"

"Yes."

She stood watching me brush my teeth for a few moments. "Let me help you get into bed, at least," she said when I finished.

I didn't say no. I thought I might need her to do that. Despite someone's having come in to turn down the sheets while we were at dinner, the bed was a little high, and I was afraid of putting any pressure on my right leg. Mrs. March put her arms around me and guided me into the bed. Then she fixed the blanket and the pillow.

"Would you mind very much if I gave you a kiss good night?" she asked.

"I'd rather you not," I said, even more sharply than I intended.

Her face seemed to melt into a look of deep sadness. She forced a smile and wished me a good night's sleep.

How mean, I thought I heard my mother say.

"Mrs. March," I called. She turned abruptly at the door. "I'm sorry. You can kiss me good night."

She smiled and returned to kiss me on the cheek. "You're a brave little girl," she said. "Braver than I would be at your age. You must have grown very strong during your desperate time."

This is still my desperate time, I thought, but said nothing.

She turned and walked out slowly, shutting off the light and closing the door softly. There were so many lights on outside that the glow kept the room from being totally dark. I was glad of that, not that I was afraid of darkness. Mama and I had slept in too many dark and dingy places over the past year for me to have that sort of fear. Most of the time, the darkness had been more like a friend, keeping us from being seen by people who might prey upon us and take what little we had. Darkness became our cocoon.

But it wasn't like that now. There were probably not many safer places in the world to be than in this house, surrounded by its walls, lit brightly and protected by security cameras. Darkness made little difference. No, what frightened me the most was the utter loneliness I sensed, not only in Mrs. March's face and voice but also in the faces of her employees. When they looked at her, they, who had far less and were her servants, seemed to be pitying her.

I had come there to escape from loneliness, to escape from becoming no one in some orphanage or foster home. I wanted to hold on to my name and cherish my memories of Mama, but Alena March still haunted this house, this room. The thing was, she didn't haunt it because she wanted to haunt it.

She haunted it because her mother would not let her go.

Maybe she would never let me go, either.

Maybe I should be more afraid of that than of anything else.

9
MRS. KEPLER

Mrs. Duval was there first thing in the morning to wake me and ask me if I wanted her to help with my bathing. I was prepared to refuse any help, but I saw something different in her face. Yesterday she seemed not only quite indifferent to me but even a bit resentful. Perhaps she had been thinking, *Who is this poor nobody who has stolen her way into Alena's world?* Perhaps she thought I wanted to take Alena's place and was taking advantage of Mrs. March. Maybe, like that maid Rosie, she didn't know the whole story. Maybe now she had learned about it all. There was warmth in her eyes, a welcome in her smile.

"Yes," I said. "Thank you."

Dr. Milan had made sure that I left the hospital with plastic bags to put over the cast. Mrs. Duval took one out of the case and fastened it so that the cast would not get wet. She then helped me into the bathroom, and together we managed to get the rest of me washed and dried. She brought me one of my new outfits to wear and then called down and had Rosie bring up my breakfast, which she set out on the table in the sitting area. Even with Jackie in the hospital, I hadn't gotten that sort of treatment.

While I was having breakfast, Mrs. March came in to tell me that my tutor, Mrs. Kepler, would be arriving in about an hour.

"After I introduce her to you, I'll leave and let you two work, unless you want me to stay."

"I'll be all right, I think," I told her.

I couldn't imagine why she would want to stay, unless she wanted to see how smart or how stupid I was. If I didn't do well, perhaps she would change her mind and send me away. I hadn't been much of a student during the last year when I was in school. Mama took some interest in my work, but she was always overwhelmed with something herself, even when Daddy was still with us, or maybe because he was. The fighting took its toll on her, and I recalled many mornings when she was too tired or depressed to get out of bed before I left for school. Often, I made my own lunch to take. I never blamed her. I always blamed Daddy.

Despite my attempt to be indifferent about my tutoring, I couldn't help but be nervous. Even when we were living in the streets, I didn't like being thought of as stupid. No matter what the circumstances, most people who looked at the homeless thought their failures were their own fault. How could anyone not manage a roof over her head for herself and her child? How could she not find enough food and clothing?

Mrs. March expressed her pity and her sympathy for Mama and me, but what did she really think about Mama? Certainly, if her daughter had not been involved, she wouldn't have been there at the hospital to help me and wouldn't have seen to Mama's funeral arrangements. Perhaps she sent checks to charities or attended affairs as she told me, but did she really see the people the money was meant to help? More important for me right then was the question *Does she really see me?*

When Mrs. Kepler first appeared, I thought she was going to be as stern and as unsympathetic as the people who had walked past Mama and me on the street and either shook their heads in disgust or looked away quickly. Mrs. March had told her I had been out of school for some time, but she didn't say that her daughter had caused the accident. I could tell when we spoke afterward and I heard the way Mrs. Kepler made Mrs. March sound charitable.

"This is Sasha," Mrs. March said. "We want to get her up to speed so she can enter school on par with the other students who will be in her class. Sasha, Mrs. Kepler."

"Hello," I said.

Mrs. Kepler nodded, fixing her hazel eyes on me as intently as a doctor. She was a full-figured woman with dark-brown hair that showed gray roots. Nevertheless, she looked as if she had just come from a beauty salon. Her hair was nicely styled about her ears, with trimmed bangs. She stood about two inches shorter than Mrs. March but held herself stiffly erect. The weakness in her face was her far too thin lips, which looked in danger of disappearing entirely if she stretched them.

"What do you think of our little sitting area, Mrs. Kepler? It's quiet up here."

She studied the room for a moment as if it really mattered. It occurred to me that in her mind, she was being tested as much as I was and knew it. She was trying too hard to be a perfect schoolteacher.

"Yes, this will be fine," she said.

"I could have a blackboard brought up."

"No, that's not going to be necessary. There's just the two of us."

"I did try to make sure there were enough pens and pencils, paper, and such. Of course, the computer is there if you need it."

"I don't teach on a computer. Everything I need for now is right here," she said, patting her black leather briefcase. She walked into the sitting area to place it on the table. Then she looked around again and nodded. "Would it be all right if I opened these drapes to get more light?"

"Oh, of course. Let me help you," Mrs. March said, rushing to open the drapes.

"Why don't you come to the table, Sasha?" Mrs. Kepler said. She turned to Mrs. March. "I'll test her to see what levels she's at in math, science, reading, and history, and from there we'll know just how much we have to do to bring her up to speed."

"Yes, good idea. Would you like tea, coffee, a soft drink?"

"Not right now, thank you."

"Okay. Well, then, I'll have Mrs. Duval check back in an hour or so?"

"That would be fine," Mrs. Kepler said.

I noticed that after she said something, she pressed her lower lip tightly against her upper one, crinkling her chin. It was a small gesture, but one I thought she had used on her students in her classroom, because it made whatever she said sound like words chipped in cement. Arguing or challenging her was out of the question.

"All right. Good luck, Sasha," Mrs. March said, and left.

Mrs. Kepler opened her briefcase and began to take out some papers. "Come closer," she told me, and I wheeled myself right up to the table. "Are you comfortable?"

"Yes."

"All right. You were in what grade before you left school?"

"Seventh."

"So you've basically missed the entire eighth-grade year?"

"I guess so."

"Either you did or you didn't. Did you attend any school after you left the seventh grade?"

"No."

"Then you missed a whole year, which would have been your eighth-grade year. I like to start with reading skills," she said. "Everything we do requires a good foundation in reading."

"I still read a lot even though I wasn't in

school."

She looked at me long enough for me to feel she was finally seeing me. "What did you read?"

"Books other people on the street gave me from time to time. Sometimes we went into the library to get out of the rain, and I read there."

"What people gave you books?"

"Street people," I said, and she widened her eyes.

"I can just imagine what sort of things to read that was," she said.

"No, you can't," I replied sharply. She raised her eyebrows. "Unless you've been there," I added. "Not everyone was a bum. There were college graduates and people who had good jobs once. Someone gave me a copy of *Huckleberry Finn,* and someone else gave me a copy of *A Tale of Two Cities.*"

"Really?"

"Yes, really. I have no reason to lie about it. Not all street people are thieves and liars. Many try to keep themselves clean and have clean clothes, too."

I felt the heat in my face. I had never spoken to any of my teachers like that, but in my mind, any criticism of the street people was criticism of Mama, and I wouldn't permit it.

For a moment, I thought she was going to shove her paperwork back into her briefcase, shut it, and walk out, but she surprised me by finally smiling. "Well, you're not easily intimidated. Do you know what *intimidated* means?"

"Yes. Pushed around, made to give up or give in to someone or something," I recited.

"Okay, then. Maybe I'll be happily surprised. Let's get started."

She began explaining the tests she wanted me to take. We worked for hours. When Mrs. Duval stopped by to see if she wanted anything to drink, she had barely opened her mouth before Mrs. Kepler snapped, "Nothing, not now." She wouldn't tolerate the slightest interruption. I thought she would even make me work through lunch, but she agreed to stop so we could eat.

Mrs. Duval came up with the cart. Mrs. Caro had prepared chicken salad for us. I was afraid there would be a duplication of yesterday's mammoth lunch, but apparently the order had been put in earlier. We cleared the table, and Mrs. Duval served from the cart. It was when we began to eat our lunch that Mrs. Kepler stopped being the schoolteacher and spoke with warmth and concern. She wanted to know where I had lived and gone to school. I didn't know how much Mrs. March had told her about me and why I was there, but from the questions she asked and the way she spoke about Mrs. March, I was convinced that nothing had been said about Kiera.

"I'm sure this is all overwhelming for you," she said. Then she smiled and added, "It certainly is for me. I heard about this house, but until now, I had never set foot in it. I bet you feel a bit like Cinderella."

"Except there's no prince," I told her, and she laughed.

"No, I imagine not. There's not even a pumpkin."

Now we both laughed, and I finally relaxed. I hadn't thought I would, but I liked her. Even after lunch, she was different, warmer and more complimentary.

Mrs. March tiptoed into the room at about three o'clock. We were just finishing, and Mrs. Kepler was putting papers back into her briefcase.

"How is it going?" Mrs. March asked. Mrs. Kepler sat back and was silent for a long moment. I could see that Mrs. March was expecting bad news.

"I'm afraid I'm not going to earn very much money here, Mrs. March."

"Oh. Why not?"

"She's not as far behind as one would

expect. Her reading skills are better than those of most of the students going into the ninth grade, I'm sure. She certainly has a very good vocabulary, and she picked up very quickly on the math, too. There are some weak areas with history and science, but most of that she's going to strengthen with her own reading."

"That's wonderful," Mrs. March said.

Mrs. Kepler rose. "I'll prepare the work assignments to help her catch up quickly. I'll start her off tomorrow and then stop by every other day for a few hours at most. I hope she'll get out a bit, get some fresh air and sun."

"Oh, yes. For sure. Mrs. Caro will be taking her out after lunch in the afternoons. You certainly can work on one of our patios, if you like."

"We'd like," Mrs. Kepler said, winking at me. "I'll be by tomorrow, then, same time. I'll bring the books."

"Wonderful," Mrs. March said. "Are you happy, Sasha?"

"Yes," I said, even though I thought she meant about everything and not only Mrs. Kepler's tutoring.

"I'll see you out," she told Mrs. Kepler.

" 'Bye, then," Mrs. Kepler told me, and followed Mrs. March out of the suite. I heard Mrs. March's melodic laughter echo down the hallway.

Part of me didn't want her to feel better. Part of me wished she'd be suffering as much as I was, even though it wasn't literally she who had hit Mama and me. Just as Mama had once been responsible for everything I did, Mrs. March and her husband were responsible for everything Kiera did. Maybe her husband was more responsible, if I believed what she had told me, but still, it felt strange making anyone happy in that house. In that house, the cause of Mama's death resided.

From that house, Kiera March had emerged carefree and reckless, arrogant and self-centered. She had taken her drugs and, like some asteroid, come flying out of space to smash two people who had never done her any harm. Also like that asteroid, she was indifferent and unrepentant. *Look at how she was at the pool,* I thought. *She laughed and frolicked right beneath me.*

No, I hated the sound of laughter in that house. I even hated the sound of my own laughter. Eating well, trying to improve my education, wearing beautiful clothes, enjoying everything in that magnificent suite, suddenly felt more like a terrible betrayal. I almost wished I would never get better. I

150

had to suffer in order to honor Mama's memory.

Try as hard as she will, I thought, *Mrs. March will not take the pain away from me.* When and if she did, it would be like me burying Mama again and again. These thoughts overwhelmed me. I sat there sobbing and made no effort to stop the tears from dripping off my cheeks. It reminded me of that night when the rain came pouring down over us, pelting us so hard that it was as if the heavens were expressing their anger.

Or maybe it was meant to be a warning, to make us stay on that beach and not dare try to cross that highway, not dare try to go home.

10
FAMILY OF THE BLIND

Probably because Mrs. Kepler had made an issue of it, Mrs. March sent Mrs. Caro up immediately to wheel me down and onto the patio. She found me crying and rushed to me.

"What's wrong, dearie? Are you in pain?"

"No," I said, wiping my face quickly. *Not the kind of pain you mean,* I thought.

"Oh, I know," she said. "Being brought like this to a strange house ain't easy, I'm sure."

I didn't say anything, but *strange* seemed to be the perfect adjective.

"Well, let's get you out in the sunshine and fresh air. It's no good being indoors so much, anyway. People heal better and faster when they get into fresh air."

She turned my chair toward the doorway.

"I grew up in Cork, Ireland, and I can tell you it wasn't always easy getting into the fresh air. When I tell my family back home that I live in a place where the sun shines at least three hundred days a year without rain, they're amazed."

She pushed me onto the elevator.

"You always live in Southern California?" she asked.

"Yes. My mother was from Portland, though."

"Don't say? Weather there can be like weather in England, I hear. You have any of your people still there?"

Her question didn't surprise me. I was sure everyone who was working there wondered why I wasn't with family.

"I don't know," I said.

"Yes, it's a shame how fast we all lose track of each other in this world. I have a sister I haven't seen in nearly twenty years now. She married a man who lives in South Africa. You know how far away that is?"

"Yes. It's at the tip of Africa."

"I bet you've been a good student. How did your schoolin' work go today?"

"Good," I said.

"You'll be up and around in no time, I'm sure. Right now, it looks like forever to you. I can't think of a better place to recuperate from anything," she added.

I looked up at her. Was it really possible that no one in the house except the Marches knew what Kiera had done and why I was there rather than with some relatives or in an orphanage? Mrs. Caro looked sincere. I wondered if Mrs. March believed that I would never say anything, or was she so confident that even if I did, no one would risk repeating it or discussing it? From the way she described her husband and how he always excused and buried whatever wrong things Kiera did, I imagined that he had given Mrs. March strict orders to keep it all from their servants.

It didn't take me long to understand that it was a house built on secrets and whispers. There was more living in the shadows than in the light, despite the bright chandeliers and lamps. A family that lived more in the shadows was a family of the blind.

The patio Mrs. Caro wheeled me to faced the pool and the tennis courts. There were two tables with chairs, a settee with a small table, and what looked like a pile of stones in a circle with benches around it. I asked Mrs. Caro what it was, and she said it was a fire pit to keep people warm when they sat out there on cooler nights. Right then, the sun was still high in the blue, nearly cloudless sky. It was about the same time of day as when I had seen those teenagers there. Would they return? What would happen when they saw me, if they did return?

"I'll set you in this shady spot," Mrs. Caro said. "Not too warm for you?"

"No. I'm fine."

"Will you be all right here by yourself for a while? I have to check on some things in the kitchen for tonight's dinner," Mrs. Caro asked. "It could be twenty minutes."

"Yes, I'll be fine," I said.

"I'll bring some fresh lemonade when I return," she said, and left.

I sat staring out at the beautiful grounds. There was so much to see. It was still hard to believe that one family owned all of this. Just a short while ago, the only space Mama and I had had to ourselves was bordered by the cardboard walls of some box. It almost felt as though I had been taken to another planet.

The Marches' estate wasn't just big; it was busy. Judging by the short time I had been there, it seemed there was never a time of day when someone wasn't working on something. Right then, two men were repairing a pole lamp on the driveway to my right, and two others were working around the cabana. One was touching it up with some paint, and the other was adjusting a door.

Wheeling myself out a little farther, I could look to my left and see part of the long driveway that curved around the side of the grand house to where Mrs. March had said the garages were. When I heard the sound of a vehicle, I leaned as far as I could to see if it was the limousine that had brought me. If so, it was probably Mrs. March returning. Instead, I saw what I knew to be a gold-colored Rolls-Royce. I had seen a few of them in Santa Monica, and Daddy used to vow that he was going to have one. Mama always mocked that and made him angry.

"You're lucky you can afford the old truck you drive," she had told him. "If you're going to have a dream, at least have the sense to dream about something relatively possible."

As the Rolls approached, I could make out a good-looking, light-haired man driving. He didn't look my way and followed the driveway around the house. Was that Mr. March? I was sure Mrs. March had said he would be gone longer. I watched and listened but heard and saw no one. When Mrs. Caro returned with my lemonade, I asked her if Mr. March had returned.

"Yes," she said.

"Is Mrs. March here?"

"She is. I told her you had been out here about twenty minutes, and she told me to take you up in a little while so you could rest, maybe take a nap before dinner. I'll have to get started in the kitchen soon myself."

I drank the lemonade and nodded. I couldn't make myself ask about Kiera, and Mrs. Caro said nothing about her. She offered to wheel me around to see the garden before we went up to my suite. Gardening had been and still was a passion for her. She bragged about the way flowers grew in Ireland, and she said, "My duties here make it difficult to get my hands into Mother Earth." The garden was so big. It looked like something in a park. Mrs. Caro knew the names of every flower, when they bloomed, when they should be planted, even how they should be nurtured.

"Here I am going off at the mouth when I have to get you upstairs," she said, realizing the time. She pushed me back into the house.

When we entered, I anticipated either seeing or hearing Mr. March, but there was no one around. We went directly to the elevator. I expected that I might meet him when we reached the bedroom floor, but again, the hallway was quiet and empty. I was a little tired and let Mrs. Caro help me into bed. She wasn't gone two minutes before I did fall asleep. I didn't wake up again until I heard the cart in the hallway. When Mrs. Duval entered, pushing it with my dinner tray, I sat up quickly. Why wasn't I going down to the dining room?

"Let me help you get up and to the table," she said.

"How come I'm not going downstairs for dinner?"

"Dinner's being served later," she said. "The Marches don't normally have dinner until eight-thirty, and Mrs. March said that would be too late for you." She saw the look on my face and added, "That's what she told me." She said it the way someone who didn't believe it might say it.

I got into my wheelchair, and she pushed me to the table, where she had set out the dishes.

"This is Mrs. Caro's special chicken dish, and she prepared a pudding for you, too. Just leave everything when you're done. Rosie will come to clean up," she said. "I've got to get down to prepare for the Marches' dinner."

Mrs. Caro's food was delicious, but I didn't have as big an appetite as I had expected. I listened for sounds of footsteps in the hallway but heard none. I had no idea where the Marches' bedrooms were but imagined they couldn't be too far away. This had been Alena's bedroom. I was sure Mrs. March would have wanted to be close. Finally, I did hear a door open and close and some footsteps, but they weren't heading in my direction. Moments later, there were more footsteps, but again, they didn't bring anyone my way.

After I finished eating what I could, I watched television but kept listening for someone coming. Finally, someone did, but it was only Rosie to clear away my dinner dishes.

"You left a lot," she remarked. "Mrs. Caro will be upset." To my surprise, she began to eat some of my leftovers. "This is much better than what we get," she told me. "Didn't you like this pudding?"

"I ate what I could."

"Can't let it go to waste," she told me, and finished it. "There," she said. "Now Mrs. Caro won't be upset. Just don't tell anyone I finished your dinner."

She started to push the cart out and stopped.

"So, how did you get hit by a car?" she asked. "What, were you running where you shouldn't?"

"No. I didn't do anything wrong, and neither did my mother."

"Your mother? What happened to her?"

"She was killed," I said.

"Where's your daddy?"

"I don't know. He left us years ago."

She opened her mouth slowly and raised her head. "Oh. Well, now it makes sense," she said.

"What makes sense?"

"Mrs. March has been sponsoring little girl orphans, sending tons of money to these worldwide charities ever since her daughter died. She sits in her office and studies the pictures of those poor kids and compares them with the picture of her dead daughter. I've seen her doing it. She only sends money to those who look a little like her. You don't, but you're about her daughter's age and size, I guess."

She paused and looked at the doorway before turning back to me.

"Don't let her talk you into dyeing your hair."

"Dye my hair? Why would I do that?"

She shook her head. I watched her leave and then turned back to the television, but it was as if I could hear nothing, as if Rosie's words had put me into a daze. Hours passed. I prepared for bed and was just wheeling myself up to it when Mrs. March appeared.

"Oh, you're not asleep yet. Good. I'm so sorry I didn't get up here earlier, but Donald came home unexpectedly, and I had to spend all my time with him. He's always got a lot to tell me and new things for me to do."

I looked past her through the doorway but heard no one else. She saw where I was looking.

"Oh, Donald had some work to do in his office. He'll stop by some other time. Let me help you get into bed," she said, and moved quickly to my side. "Did you enjoy your dinner? Mrs. Caro said you ate almost everything."

"Yes."

"Good. Dr. Milan will be stopping by in the morning to check on you, so if there's anything to complain about, you make sure to tell him, okay?"

"Okay," I said.

She tucked me in, stood back, and smiled down at me. "Girls look so much smaller than they are when they're tucked into bed. No matter how old they are, they look like they could use a bedtime story. I used to read to Alena quite a bit. Would you like that?"

"Thank you, but I'm tired enough to fall asleep," I told her.

It didn't make her happy, but she kept her smile and then leaned down to kiss my cheek. "Sweet dreams," she said, then turned off the lights and closed my door as she left.

My second night there didn't feel any less strange than my first. I lay there with my eyes wide open and listened. There was a stronger breeze that night. I could hear it searching for nooks and crannies in the house, places, as Mama might have said, to scratch its back. The darkness seemed quite different from the darkness I had known when we lived in our apartment, stayed at the hotel, and then slept at the beach. There were no street sounds or sounds of the ocean. Oddly enough, I missed all that. Street sounds gave me the comfort of knowing we were not alone, completely lost and forgotten, and the ocean was reassuring.

The silence enhanced my sense of loneliness. There was not only too much emptiness in this family; there was too much emptiness in this big house, too many places unused, untouched, unnecessary. Cemeteries weren't only for dead people; there were cemeteries for the living, as well, and despite all that was there, I felt encased in a tomb. I wasn't shut in because of any lock. I was shut in because there was simply nowhere else to go.

What good would Lazarus's resurrection have been if he had had no family to embrace him?

Thinking of Lazarus reminded me of Mama quoting from the Bible, reminding me that her father was a Bible thumper, but I was tired of crying for myself and for Mama. Sleep was the only balm to soothe the pain in my heart. I closed my eyes and waited as eagerly as someone waiting for a train that would take her home. It came mercifully quickly, and I was deep in it when the sound of my door opening and footsteps woke me abruptly. The lamp by my bed was snapped on. I wiped my sleepy eyes and blinked to focus on the beautiful tall girl who stared down at me.

"What are you, Chinese, Japanese?" she asked. When I didn't respond quickly enough, she added, "Don't you speak English?"

"I speak English. I'm part Chinese, yes," I said.

"What part?" She laughed. "I can't believe this," she said, looking around. "She put you in my sister's room. If she was going to do this, she should have at least put you in one of the guest bedrooms. There are enough of them, for crissakes." She stared at me a moment and then reached down to feel the sleeve of my nightgown. "What, are you wearing one of my sister's nightgowns, too? Jesus."

I pulled out of her grasp. "I didn't ask to be put in here and be given your sister's clothing."

"I bet you didn't. I bet you didn't ask for anything." She paused and shrugged. "Actually, I'm not saying you did. I'm sure it's all been my mother's idea. This is all just one of my mother's new ways to punish me. She thinks this really bothers me, her taking you into the house, giving you Alena's things, and letting you sleep in her bed. Who cares? Half the time, I don't know who the hell is in this house, anyway."

She paused again and stared at me. I stared back at her. I was disappointed. When I first had heard Mrs. March say her daughter had caused the accident because she was on Ecstasy and was a selfish girl who had been in trouble often, I had expected the face and body of some spoiled rich girl, overweight and even ugly, with distorted features.

Instead, this girl was the one I had picked out yesterday, the one with the model's figure and, now that I saw her close up, a model's attractive facial features, too. She had soft, not cold, azure eyes, beautifully shaped full lips, and high cheekbones. When Mama and I would watch television together, she would always remark about the good-looking actors and actresses and say it was much more difficult for them to portray bad guys.

"We want our bad guys to look bad, have scars or ugly faces. It's not the way it really is, Sasha, not out there," she would say, and she would nod at the window.

Out there was always a desert, a jungle, a rocky cliff to climb. We were always safer inside, even inside a dingy hotel room.

Looking up at Kiera March, I especially didn't feel a bit safer in that castle of a house with its walls and security. She was beautiful, but she was bad.

She smirked and shook her head. "I bet you're really enjoying yourself immersed in all this," she said, lifting her hands. "This suite's actually a little bigger than mine. Where were you sleeping before the accident, in a carton?"

"Yes," I said. "We were. On the beach."

She dissolved her smirk, widened her eyes, and lost her arrogance for a moment. But it soon came rushing back into her face. "Well, I don't care. It was your and your mother's fault. No one crosses that highway there. That's why there's no crosswalk."

"The light was green for us," I said.

"So what? It was still stupid. It was raining too hard to see anything. Anyone would have hit you two. I was just the unfortunate one to be there at the wrong time."

"Weren't you on some drugs?"

"Who says? My mother? No one proved that." She smiled. "My attorney is confident. He'll make things right."

"He can't make things right."

"Oh, yeah, why not, smart-ass?"

"He can't bring back my mother," I said.

Her lips trembled. "You know what? Go to hell." She turned and marched out of the bedroom, slamming the door behind her.

"I'm already there!" I shouted. "That's how come you're here!"

I waited, but she didn't return.

That silence I was beginning to hate was the only thing that returned.

11
KIERA

Mrs. March came into my room before anyone else arrived in the morning. I wasn't even out of bed. She was visibly upset.

"Was Kiera in here last night?" she asked.

"Yes."

"I thought so. I heard her complaining to her father. Did she say terrible things to you? What did she say?"

"She said you were punishing her by having me live here."

Mrs. March nodded. "She's right about that. Not that I want you to feel bad," she added quickly. "But I don't want her to forget and ignore what a terrible thing she has done. Don't worry. She won't bother you or do you any harm. I'm so sorry. She snuck in here without my permission. I'm going to tell her father to speak with her."

"Maybe I shouldn't be here," I said. "Maybe it's only causing more trouble."

"Oh, no, no, no. Don't you ever, ever, ever

let that girl make you feel bad or think such a thing. Of course you should be here. If you left, you'd only be making her feel good about what she did. You're doing both Donald and me a favor by being here. Sometimes I think that girl has no conscience whatsoever. I look at her and wonder how I gave birth to her. Alena was so different. No, don't you think about leaving. Dr. Milan will be here in a few hours. Let's just think about that for now, okay?"

"Okay."

"Good. Do you want any help getting up and dressed?"

"I can do it."

"I'll go see about your breakfast and talk to Donald about Kiera before he leaves the house. I'm so sorry." She hurried out.

I rose and went to the closet to choose something to wear. I wondered how anyone could decide with all of these choices. How important had this been to Alena? I didn't want to keep thinking about being in her room, using her things, but at the same time, I couldn't help but be curious about her. Was she spoiled, too? Did she get along with Kiera? How could anyone? What did she think when she realized how sick she was, or did they keep the seriousness of her illness a secret from her until she was near the end of her life? Secrets were very comfortable living here. It seemed only natural for the Marches to lie to one another.

And yet, I thought, surely she must have felt very sick and knew because of all the things she couldn't do any longer that she was in danger of dying. Even a doctor like Dr. Milan couldn't keep the truth from peeking out of his eyes.

I realized, however, that death is not something someone so young thinks about very often and probably not until he or she hears about a relative or a friend dying. I didn't, not even when life was so difficult for Mama and me. Somehow I always thought we'd get through it. Something would happen to change things and make us healthy and whole again. Even when I saw her get hit just before me on the highway, I still believed it would be all right. The ambulances were there. Someone was helping Mama.

And when that woman told me she was dead, that she had been killed instantly, it didn't set right in. I kept hoping and thinking that there was a mistake. Alena must have been the same way when she was getting sicker and sicker. She must have thought the doctor would make her better. One morning, she'd wake up and it would be all over, just the way a cold ends. The younger you were, the more of a surprise death had to be, I thought.

After sifting through some of the clothes, I chose a light-blue skirt and the blouse that went with it. Everything fit well, but the more comfortable I was in Alena's things, the more frightened it made me feel. I almost took the blouse and skirt off and put on what I had worn the day before, but before I could do that, Mrs. Duval brought me my breakfast.

"What time does everyone else eat breakfast?" I asked her.

"Mr. March is the first down always. He eats very early and leaves for work before Kiera even gets up and dressed most of the time, especially during the summer months. Sometimes, like today, he takes a little longer, and Mrs. March joins him. On weekends, it's usually different. Everyone sleeps in. You look very nice this morning," she added. She smiled and left.

About an hour after I finished breakfast, Mrs. March returned with Dr. Milan. He examined me and said that one of the nurses at his office would stop by with a crutch for me to use.

"She'll show you how to use it so you can keep the pressure off that leg for a while."

"How long will I have to be in the cast?" I asked.

"We'll see. I'll get you over to my office for X-rays in three or four weeks. In the meantime," he said, looking around the suite, "you'll be fine. It doesn't look like you'll be lacking anything."

Nothing except love and a family, I thought. He and Mrs. March left together. I could hear them whispering in the hallway until they went down the stairs. Immediately afterward, Rosie came up to get my tray and dishes. She asked me how I was feeling and told me she thought Kiera was jealous.

"Jealous of what? Me?"

She laughed. "Well, she claims she's not feeling well and locked herself in her room. Mrs. Duval had to bring her breakfast, too, but it ain't the first time, and I'm sure it ain't the last."

After she left, I wheeled myself to the door and looked down the hallway. No one was there, so I continued a little until I heard music and laughter behind the door of the room next to mine. I imagined it was Kiera's and paused to see if I could hear anyone else. Perhaps one of her friends was already there. Whether she heard me or could see through some keyhole, I don't know, but suddenly, the door was thrust

171

open and she was standing there in her bathrobe. She was holding a portable phone in her right hand. It happened so quickly that I flinched and wheeled myself back a few feet.

"What are you doing, spying on me?" she asked.

"No. I didn't even know this was your room."

"Right. You don't know anything. Just keep out of my face," she said, and slammed the door. I heard her tell whoever was on the phone that one of the annoying maids had come to check on something.

Still trembling, I wheeled myself back to my room and closed the door. Just knowing that Kiera was so close made me nervous. She had already shown that she could burst in on me anytime, even when I was sleeping. I doubted that Mrs. March could stop her.

Moments later, I heard someone else coming, and I was happy to see that it was Mrs. Kepler. She could see I was upset.

"Are you feeling all right? I know the doctor was just here."

"I'm fine," I said, but I didn't say anything more. What good would it do to tell her about Kiera March?

"Would you rather we work outside?"

"No."

"You're probably right. There are too many distractions out there. Let's get to it," she said.

She went through the history and science workbooks with me and set out the books she wanted me to read. Finally, she paused and said, "You do look worried, Sasha. I hope I didn't lead you to believe that you must finish all of this in a week."

"I'm okay," I said.

She still looked suspicious but continued with her explanations and instructions. I tried to pay attention as well as I had done the day before, but I couldn't help anticipating Kiera March again. Perhaps she would come in to interrupt us and mock me. I could see that Mrs. Kepler wasn't pleased with my responses.

Mrs. March stopped by to see if Mrs. Kepler was going to stay for lunch. She told her she thought we had done enough for the day. From the looks they were giving each other, I knew Mrs. Kepler wanted to speak with her privately. She said she would return about the same time tomorrow and then left with Mrs. March. I hoped she wasn't going to tell her that it was too soon to have me do the schoolwork. I was happy to have it, to have something that would take my mind off everything. In fact, by the time Mrs. Duval stopped in with my lunch, I had already done everything Mrs. Kepler had assigned for the day. I knew that would both surprise and please Mrs. March.

When she returned, because of what Mrs. Kepler had obviously told her, she wanted to know if she was rushing me too fast. "With your recuperation and all that's happened, maybe we should wait on your schooling and . . ."

"Oh, no. I like it," I said. "I've done everything she left for me to do."

"Really? Well, that's wonderful, Sasha. She'll be pleased. If you're not too tired, I thought I'd replace Mrs. Caro today and take you out. I'll wheel you along and show you more of the property. Would you like that?"

"Yes."

"Good. I'll be back in about a half hour."

Almost as soon as her footsteps died away down the hall, Kiera came into my bedroom. I had my back to the door and was looking through the science workbook. I caught her reflection in the window and held my breath. She was still in her robe, but her image appeared so silently that she looked more like a ghost. I turned around slowly.

"So, Mother is going to show you the grounds. How sweet," she said, coming into the sitting room.

How did she know that? Did Mrs. March tell her, or could she hear what went on in my bedroom? Was she always going to be spying on me? She looked at my workbooks and the books on the table, tossing them aside as if they were someone's garbage.

"And you're getting private tutoring, too. I'm sure you need it." She stopped and put her hands on her hips. "So, what, do you expect to live here forever?"

"I don't expect anything."

"Yeah, right." She continued to inspect everything in the suite and saw my new iPod. She picked it up. "What's this? My mother bought you this? This is better than mine," she said, and dropped it. "Oh, sorry. I hope it didn't break." She didn't make an effort to see or to pick it up.

She continued to stroll through the suite.

"It's been some time since I've been in here for any length of time, actually. Mother kept it locked up, you know. She had it cleaned regularly but wasn't keen on anyone else but the maid being in here. I see nothing has been changed for you."

She wandered past the bed to open the closet.

"I heard she's been buying you some new clothes, too." She turned to look at me more carefully. "But that's not new. That's one of Alena's outfits you're wearing. Aren't you ashamed to wear a dead girl's clothes? No," she said before I could respond, "you were probably finding clothes in garbage heaps to wear."

"I'm not doing anything your mother told me not to do."

"I'll bet. You know, my father's not happy that you're here. They had a big fight about it. She tell you that?"

"No."

"I wouldn't count on being here much longer."

"I told you. I didn't ask to come here."

"You won't ask to leave, either, but you will."

I turned away from her. She returned to the sitting room and looked out the window.

"You know, I saw you watching us the other day. I didn't tell the others, because I didn't want anyone to know you were here. They'd have all sorts of stupid questions. It's embarrassing."

"Embarrassing? I think what you did was more than embarrassing."

"Aren't you smart. Anyway, did you get a good look at everything going on at the pool, a good look at all of my friends?"

I didn't answer.

"You'd better not be telling my mother about anything you saw out there. It's none of your business."

"I don't tell on people," I said. "I don't care what you do, anyway."

"You don't tell on people? You told her I came into the bedroom last night, didn't you?"

"She knew you had come in, but don't worry. I won't tell her about what you and your friends did at the pool."

"Probably jealous. You liked what you saw, though, didn't you? Ricky and Boyd and Tony? But I guess you've seen naked boys plenty of times in the streets, huh?"

"No."

"You still a little virgin?"

"Now, that's none of your business," I fired back.

She laughed. "I forgot you're a street kid," she said. She said it as if she admired it.

"I'm not a street kid. We didn't want to be living on the street."

"We all have to do things we don't want to do," she replied. I waited to see what she meant, but she stopped talking, looked out the window, then turned and walked out of the bedroom quickly.

I felt like shouting something nasty after her but wheeled myself back to the table, picked up the iPod she had deliberately dropped, and looked at my workbook again. But it was harder than ever to concentrate on anything. *What am I doing here?* I wondered. Maybe I'd be better off in some orphanage after all. Maybe I'd be happy to have her father kick me out.

"Ready?" I heard Mrs. March ask. She returned wearing a different outfit and a wide-brim hat. "Don't laugh at my hat," she said, seeing where my gaze went. "It's beautiful out there, but I've got to be careful in the sun. When you're my age, it only makes you look older, makes wrinkles come faster."

She stepped behind my wheelchair and started to turn me toward the door.

"When I was a young girl like you and like Kiera, I never thought about it. Now, when I think about all those days I spent on the beach without any protection, I shudder. How stupid we were. I tell Kiera that all the time, but does she listen? No."

In the elevator, I wondered if she was going to ask me if Kiera had come into my bedroom again. She didn't, and I didn't tell her.

She smiled at me and nodded. "You're doing a lot better, I can tell, and Dr. Milan thinks so, too. Where you are when you recuperate can make a great deal of difference."

Mrs. Caro had said something similar. Was everything anyone said to me planned?

The elevator opened, and she pushed me out and toward the French doors that opened to the patio Mrs. Caro had taken me to the day before.

"I used to wheel Alena out here when she was bedridden. Even though the poor thing had a hard time sitting up, she looked forward to it. Those were my last beautiful days with her, and I know she lived longer because of it. Look at what a beautiful afternoon we have for you, Sasha. There's even a breeze coming in off the ocean today. Feel it? I'll take you for a ride to the ocean soon, too. We'll go to lunch. I used to take Alena to lunch before she became too ill to travel."

"Did you take Kiera, too?"

"Kiera never liked to go with us. Kiera may act tough, but she wasn't able to deal with her sister's illness and death. None of us really was, but we did what we had to do and for Alena's sake tried not to show our sorrow. It was better not to include Kiera."

"Didn't Alena want her to come along

with you?"

"Oh, yes, but I found an excuse for Kiera not to be coming with us most of the time. Neither Alena nor I would have enjoyed ourselves. Now," she said, firmly changing the subject, "if we follow this path here, we can go around to the lake. I want you to see it close up. As I told you, Donald's very proud of our lake. He's always bringing someone in the construction industry here to see it, and it was featured in a prominent architecture magazine. When you are up and around, you can take one of the rowboats out. Did you ever row a boat?"

"No."

"Well, maybe I'll go with you the first time to be sure you're safe," she said. "After you start school, you'll probably make lots of friends and ask to bring them here. We'll ask that everyone wear a life vest, of course. The lake is seven feet deep and maybe deeper in some places."

Friends? I thought back to when I did have friends at school and when I would go to their homes or they would come to mine. It seemed so long ago that it was more like something I had dreamed. Would I have school friends again? All of them would surely be impressed if I brought them to the March house. The very idea of doing that set off all sorts of fantasies, but then I thought about Kiera and her threats and predictions. Maybe my days there were numbered. Maybe as soon as I was up on my feet again, I'd be sent away. Why even think about it?

We stopped at the dock, and I looked out at the lake. It was so still. Down on the left, the trees were reflected in the water, giving it a greenish tint. Toward the other side, I saw terns. They were visitors from the ocean. The two rowboats tied to the dock looked brand-new. Mrs. March stepped up beside me, folded her arms, and looked out as if she had never seen it until now.

"Isn't it beautiful?"

"Yes," I said. I hesitated but then asked, "Does Mr. March really want me here?"

She spun around and seemed about to say, *Of course.* Something she saw in my face made her pause. "Did Kiera say something terrible last night about her father?"

When you first meet someone, you can't help but wonder how much of the truth you should tell and how much you should hold back. It was something I had learned from the way Mama spoke to people, especially after Daddy had left us. Lying seemed to be an important way to protect yourself, and most people didn't seem to know or care that she was lying.

What should I do now? I wondered. *Get Kiera in more trouble?*

"I just wondered," I said.

"It's not for you to worry about," she replied quickly. "The reason I brought you here is to have your recuperation managed well so that you'll be up on your feet and get the opportunity to have a new, wonderful life. You let me worry about the rest of it, Sasha." She looked out at the water again for a moment before turning back to me. "I made a promise to your mother," she said.

"My mother? When?" Had my mother been alive for a while and no one had told me?

"At her burial, at the cemetery," she replied.

"Oh."

"I promised her that I would look after you, and I won't let anyone stop me from fulfilling the promise."

My daddy had made a lot of promises, I thought, and after we were thrown out on the street, Mama had made lots of promises, too. What was the real difference between a promise and a dream? Just like dreams, the day after, no one remembers them.

"Put your promises in writing," Mama would tell Daddy. "Not that it would mean

182

much more," she would mumble to me.

A promise was a wish made of smoke, I thought. You could see it, but you couldn't grasp it, and you couldn't take it anywhere. You had to wait for the wind to see where it would go or if it would just disappear.

I had no doubt that Mrs. March wanted to fulfill her promise to Mama, but even she, sitting on top of that beautiful, rich world, was helpless when it came to putting her fingers around the promise of happiness when it was for herself and her family.

What could she really do for me?

12
MR. MARCH

Two nights later, I finally met Donald March. Mrs. Duval came up to my room to tell me that dinner would be served earlier than usual, and that Mrs. March had requested that I be brought down to the dining room.

"She said you should choose anything you would like to wear except a tank top. Do you need help with anything?"

"No," I told her.

"Then I'll be back for you in twenty minutes," Mrs. Duval said.

I couldn't help being very nervous, so nervous I could feel myself trembling. Kiera told me that her father would send me away, and although Mrs. March told me not to be concerned about it, that it was her problem, I still felt I'd be more uncomfortable in Donald March's presence than I would be sleeping in a cardboard carton. Maybe because we had had so little that anyone would want, neither Mama nor I had been terribly afraid out there. Everyone living in the street appeared just as unconcerned. Perhaps we all thought nothing more could happen to us. Now I was in what had to be one of the most expensive homes in the whole country, if not the whole world, and I knew deep in my heart of hearts that much more could happen to me there.

I had a difficult time deciding what to wear. When I started to choose something, I stopped to wonder if it was too fancy or not fancy enough. I had no doubt that Kiera would laugh at me, even ridicule me, in front of her father if I made the wrong choice. He might look at Mrs. March and smirk as if to say, *How could you bring someone so common and stupid to our home? I don't care what your reasons were.*

Because of my cast, I could only wear skirts or dresses, and I wasn't sure which dresses of Alena's were formal. Mrs. March had made such a thing of what I would wear when it was only the two of us. Why wasn't she helping me choose tonight? Wasn't this a more important dinner? Perhaps she wanted me to prove that I could make the right choice without her.

A full ten minutes had gone by, and I still hadn't decided. Mama would surely laugh at my panic attack, especially over something to wear, I thought, and finally reached out and took a plain-looking dark blue skirt and its matching short-sleeved V-neck blouse. I was surprised at how well the blouse fit me. Earlier, I had brushed and pinned back my hair with one of Alena's clips. I hesitated to take any more of her things. There was a beautiful gold watch, bracelets and earrings and rings, but I touched none of it.

Mrs. Duval looked pleased with my choices when she returned. "Ready?"

"Yes," I said, and she wheeled me out to the elevator.

"Mrs. Caro has made an Irish dish that Mr. March favors. It's called Dublin Lawyer. It's made with lobster. Have you eaten lobster?"

"Once," I said.

"Once? Well, you're in for a delightful surprise."

The elevator doors opened. My heart felt as if it was shrinking in my chest as Mrs. Duval wheeled me toward the formal dining room. When we entered, I saw that they were all there and seated. Kiera wore a yellow keyhole-bust cap-sleeved top and a black skirt. I had seen other teenage girls wearing something like it lately and had wanted one for myself. She looked as if she had been born in hers; it fit her that well. As we drew closer to the long, dark wood table, I saw that her skirt was barely below her knees. She wore the most beautiful turquoise necklace I had ever seen and looked as glamorous as any young movie or television star.

How plain I look in comparison, I thought, but then again, I never imagined ever competing with her, especially for her father's attention. I couldn't help but wonder if Alena had felt the same way. Two daughters not all that many years apart must have been vying for their father's favor constantly. Once Alena became seriously ill, that competition had surely ended with Mr. March doting on Alena. I remembered reading a story about two sisters in which one did become ill and the other, jealous of the attention she received, pretended to be ill herself.

Being an only child, I often wondered what it would be like to have a sister or a brother and to share my mother's love. How could any mother have enough? It was clear to me that Mrs. March favored Alena, and Kiera perhaps still couldn't forgive her, even now, even with her sister dead and buried. Was that why she was afraid of my being there so much? I knew I wasn't any weight on her conscience, as Mrs. March had hoped I'd be. I wasn't sure she even had a conscience.

My gaze shifted to Mr. March, who sat at the head of the table with his elbows on the table, his hands clasped together, and I noticed his striking gold pinkie ring with a lapis, which I would find out later was his birthstone. He wore a dark blue velvet sports jacket and a black shirt opened at the collar. There was a gold chain around his neck with whatever was on it hidden under his shirt.

His light brown hair looked closer to blond. It was beautifully styled, with a slight wave in front. Against the color of his hair and his tanned face, his dark blue eyes were more prominent. They nearly matched his lapis ring. I could see that Kiera inherited most of her good looks from him, because the features of his face, his perfectly shaped nose and strong mouth, seemed as sculptured as hers were. He looked athletic, and later, when he stood, I'd see that he was a good four inches taller than Mrs. March.

He sat back when Mrs. March rose to take me from Mrs. Duval.

"Here she is," Mrs. March said. She put me to the right of Mr. March. Kiera sat across from him, and Mrs. March sat on his left. "Sasha, this is my husband, Donald."

"Hello," I said, or at least I thought I did. My voice seemed trapped inside my trembling body. I saw that Kiera had a look of disgust on her face.

Donald March sat back, still studying me. "How's your leg doing?" he asked as a greeting.

"It doesn't hurt anymore."

"Ugh," Kiera said. "Couldn't she put a shoe on that foot?"

Mrs. March pushed me closer to the table. My broken leg just slipped under it so she wouldn't have to look at my foot. She glared at Kiera and took her seat across from me.

"You're putting her in Alena's place, you know," Kiera said.

Mr. March raised his eyebrows as if he'd just realized that himself. The table could easily seat a dozen people. Why was Kiera sitting at the end? Shouldn't Mrs. March be sitting across from her husband?

"You could sit closer, Kiera."

"I'm fine where I am," she said. Then she smiled. "I can look at Daddy better."

I glanced at him. He obviously liked that and smiled back at her.

Mrs. Duval began to bring in our salads. Mr. March sat forward again and lifted his salad fork. Was that all he was going to say to me? I wondered as he began to eat.

"Sasha is off to a wonderful start with Mrs. Kepler, who says she has no doubt she'll have her up to speed before the end of the summer," Mrs. March said.

"Who's Mrs. Kepler again?" Mr. March asked.

"Her tutor, Donald, remember?"

"Oh, yes." He looked at me and nodded.

"I hate talking about the end of summer. I can't stand the idea of it ending," Kiera muttered. She pushed some of her salad off to the side. "Look at this! I keep telling her I don't like beets and artichokes. Why can't they remember?"

"Why can't you remember to hang up your clothes, especially those that we have dry-cleaned and pressed for you?" Mrs. March countered.

"I thought that was what servants are for," Kiera said.

"If you don't cherish the things we buy you, we shouldn't buy you so much."

"Whatever," Kiera said, shrugging. Then she smiled. "I'll buy my own things."

Mr. March seemed not to hear the exchange. He was too involved in his wine, bread, and salad. I began to eat my salad and thought it was wonderful. It had so many flavors and was crunchy, just the way I liked it. The hospital salad and the salads I had eaten at the March house before were not as good, I thought. Maybe special things were saved for dinners with Mr. March.

"We're going to have to do something with your fingernails," Mrs. March told me, smiling. "I'll take you to my manicurist."

I looked at my fingers. My nails were uneven, but the idea of trimming them and putting on nail polish was something I hadn't thought about for quite a while. Ages, it seemed. It was almost a foreign concept. Mama used to do them for me, but that was so long ago that it was like something I had seen in an old movie on television.

When Mr. March finished his salad, he sat back and turned to me again. "How long were you and your mother homeless?" he asked.

"Nearly a year."

"She lived in a carton, you know. Didn't you? You told me you did," Kiera added before I could admit to it or deny it.

"Yes, we did," I said.

"How did you bathe?" Kiera asked. "Or didn't you?"

"We bathed in the public restrooms. Mama always tried to keep us both clean."

"Yeah, right," Kiera muttered. "You need to take a bath as soon as you walk out of those places. I'd rather go in my pants."

"Kiera," Mrs. March snapped.

"Well, Kiera's not all wrong. It is quite difficult for people like that to take good care of their hygiene," Mr. March said. "It's lucky she didn't suffer from some disease."

"Who knows what she's brought into this house — or what Mother has brought into it, I should really say," Kiera said.

"I think, of all people, you should know what I brought into this house, Kiera, when I brought Sasha here," Mrs. March responded, her face reddening.

"No, Mother, I don't know. Do tell me."

"Please. Let's enjoy the dinner," Mr. March said sharply.

Rosie came in and began to clear away the salad dishes. Mrs. Duval followed with a tray holding the main dish, which she had called a Dublin Lawyer. She served it to Mr. March first and then to us.

"You're in for a special treat," Mrs. March told me.

"Just eating indoors is a special treat for her," Kiera said.

Mr. March poured himself some more white wine and then looked at Mrs. March.

"I'm fine," she said.

"Daddy, can I have some, please?" Kiera asked in a sweet, syrupy voice.

"I don't think . . ." Mrs. March began.

"White wine goes perfectly with this," he said. "It's harmless," he added, and looked to Mrs. Duval. She took the bottle and went around to pour a glass for Kiera.

"Thank you, Daddy."

He nodded. "This is as fantastic, as usual," he said after eating some Dublin Lawyer. "Give my compliments to Mrs. Caro, please, Mrs. Duval."

"I will, sir," she said. "Anyone need anything else?"

"My water glass is empty," Kiera said.

The bottled water was right in front of her. Mrs. Duval picked it up and put some in her glass. I waited to hear her say thank you, but she simply drank her water. Mrs. Duval looked at me and then went back to the kitchen. I started on my meal. It was delicious. I remembered the lobster Mama and I had had, but it was nothing like this.

"What did your mother do before things fell apart for you?" Mr. March asked me as he ate.

I looked at him. *Fell apart?* Did he mean before the accident or after Daddy left or before she met Daddy? I didn't know what to say.

"Before you were out on the street," he added, seeing my confusion.

"She was a waitress and she did her calligraphy."

"Really? Calligraphy?" He turned to Mrs. March. "You have something from our trip to China five years ago, don't you, Jordan?"

"It's in our bathroom," she replied.

"Right. So your mother did that sort of thing?"

"Yes. There's one hanging on the wall in the Gravediggers bar," I said proudly.

Kiera laughed. "Gravediggers. What is it, a bar in a cemetery?"

"I've heard of it," Mr. March said, and Kiera lost her smile.

"Well, what kind of a place is that for whatever she called it?"

"She called it 'heaven,' " I said.

"The bar?" Mr. March asked me.

"No, the word she had drawn and painted, the calligraphy. She would tell me that people go to the Gravediggers to see heaven."

He stared a moment and then burst out laughing. "That's really clever," he said.

I looked at Kiera. She pressed her lips together and dug into her food as if she hated it and wanted to kill it first. Mrs. March laughed, too. "It is clever," she said.

"Can you do calligraphy?"

"Yes," I told her. "I often did it with my mother, just as she had done with hers."

Mr. March's eyebrows rose.

"Well, we'll have to get you what you need so you can do some," Mrs. March said.

"I thought you said you sold lanyards on the beach," Kiera quipped.

"I did," I said. "My mother sold calligraphy."

What have you sold, I wanted to ask her, *besides unhappiness?*

But I didn't. I looked down at my food and continued to eat, thinking only of Mama and how pleased she would be to see me having such a wonderful dinner in so elegant a dining room with what was obviously expensive silverware and dishes.

She would have said, "You're in the pink, kiddo."

I was sure I heard it.

"What's so funny?" Kiera asked.

"What?"

"You're laughing. What are you laughing at?"

I shook my head. I hadn't realized I was smiling so widely.

"Well, there you are," Kiera said, nodding at me. "Smiling like an idiot. May I be excused, please? I have an important phone call to make."

"You haven't had dessert," Mrs. March said. "Mrs. Caro has made a very special cake in honor of Sasha."

"I don't need it. This was fattening enough," she said, pushing her plate away. There was at least half of her meal left. I had eaten every bit of mine. "Daddy?"

"Go ahead," he said. Mrs. March widened her eyes. "She'll only spoil our enjoyment pouting there, Jordan."

Mrs. March glanced at me. I could see that she wanted to respond but lowered her eyes instead.

"Thank you, Daddy," Kiera said. She rose and went over to give him a kiss. She looked at her mother and then brushed past me on her way out.

Both Mr. and Mrs. March were very quiet.

"You made a very nice choice of something to wear tonight, Sasha," Mrs. March told me.

Mr. March looked at me. I could see in the movement of his eyes and his mouth that he was just realizing that I was wearing one of Alena's outfits. I waited to see if he would say something, but he shifted his eyes down quickly and then turned to Mrs. March.

"I can't put off that trip to Hawaii any

longer," he told her. "It's too big an opportunity for us to lose. Are you or are you not coming along?"

"I can't just now, Donald," she said, nodding at me.

"You have doctors, tutors, servants looking after her, Jordan."

"I just can't," she said.

Mrs. Duval came in with the cake. It was chocolate with raspberry and looked scrumptious. Mrs. Caro had drawn my name with the raspberries. Now I was glad Kiera had left. She would probably have thrown it up later.

"How beautiful," Mrs. March said.

After we had dessert, Mr. March said he had to make some calls and rose. He looked down at me and said, "It was nice meeting you."

He had been quiet the whole time we were eating dessert. Before he reached the door, Mrs. March said, "I'll be right back," and followed him.

I wheeled myself away from the table and turned toward the door, too. I thought I might wheel myself outside to the patio. I stopped before I reached the door, because I could hear them arguing in the hallway.

"Can't you be nicer to her, Donald?" Mrs. March said.

"I don't know why you're making us do this."

"We can't escape our responsibility, Donald."

"Who says we should? We can simply set up a trust for her and have her live with some foster family, can't we? You can involve yourself in all that, if you like."

"That's what she's doing here now, Donald. We're her foster family, but you're right. We should set up a trust for her as well."

"I don't know, Jordan. You saw how Kiera's reacting to all this. I don't know."

"I do. It's good that she isn't permitted to forget, to ignore and minimize what a terrible thing she has done, Donald."

"How can she forget with you harping on it so much?" he said sharply. I heard him walking away.

I knew I would be embarrassed to be caught listening and started to turn. Mrs. Duval was standing right behind me. She had heard everything, too.

"People say things they don't really mean," she told me.

Mama did, I thought, *but she was half out of her mind with cheap gin.*

What's his excuse?

13
FAMILY

Why stay here now? I asked myself. *For the big room, the clothes, the food, my tutoring, and my doctor,* another part of me replied. *Remember Jackie's advice. No matter what, take everything they want to give you. You deserve more than what they give you. Take it.*

I really didn't know what I should do. Except for Mrs. March's obvious sense of guilt over what Kiera had done and the servants speaking some kind words to me, I felt not only unwanted but in some ways even more invisible than I was when Mama and I lived in the streets. How lucky other young girls my age were to have loving parents and caring friends to whom they could go for advice and sympathy. I had only the memory of Mama when she was healthy and strong, now speaking to me from the grave.

"Oh, did you want to go up to your

room?" Mrs. March asked when she returned to the dining room. She saw Mrs. Duval standing there, but Mrs. Duval went immediately to supervise the cleaning of the dining room. I saw that Mrs. March suspected that I had overheard the argument she had just had with her husband.

"I was going outside for a while first," I said.

"That's such a good idea. Let me take you." She got behind my wheelchair and started pushing me through the hallway, but this time she turned right. "We'll go to a different patio this time," she said. "This side of the house is better lit, and if we look east, we can see the lights of downtown Los Angeles."

She continued to talk, almost babbling, as we proceeded to another exit. The house did seem like a hotel to me. No wonder I couldn't think of it as someone's home. She pointed out some guest bedrooms and another, smaller living room.

"Donald had it designed just for the guests. He doesn't mind our having guests," she continued explaining, "but he likes us to have our private areas. Do you know who Citizen Kane was?"

"No," I said.

"It's a movie, actually, but in it, this man

Kane builds an enormous mansion, which is actually modeled on the Hearst Castle. Have you ever seen that?"

"No."

"I keep forgetting how limited your life was," she muttered, more like someone chastising herself or someone else living inside her. "Well, anyway, Donald always got a kick out of a line in the movie suggesting that there were guests still there, guests Kane and his wife had forgotten. Can you imagine a house so big that you'd forget your own guests were still there? It could almost happen here, I suppose. At least, some of Donald's friends tease him about it."

I could see myself very easily being forgotten here.

She turned us through the smaller living room, which was surely bigger than the living rooms in almost all of the other houses in America, and then to the French doors that opened onto the other patio. She was right about the lighting. The grounds were illuminated like some major league ball field. There were more beautiful gardens, pruned bushes, and an area that seemed to be under construction. I asked about it.

"Donald's building a hedge maze," she said. "Like the one in Hampton Court in

England." When I didn't say anything, she added, "Oh, but you probably don't know anything about that yet. You'll learn about such things in history when you return to school. There," she said, pushing me to the far left corner. "See downtown Los Angeles? Isn't it beautiful to be able to see it from here?"

"Were you always rich?" I asked.

"Rich?" She laughed. "Oh, well, yes, I suppose I was — or my family was, I should say. My father always says Donald interrupted my education. I was just graduating from Marlborough and on my way to attend Smith when I met Donald at a charity gala in Los Angeles. I had never met anyone like him. He was basically just starting out, but he was so sure of himself. You know how people often say there are no guarantees in life? Well, Donald behaved as if he had been given a guarantee of major success.

"But it wasn't only that. He was and is a very attractive man who believes your presentation is of paramount importance. My father believes the same thing. People usually, whether rightly or wrongly, judge you on first impressions, so it's essential to make the best first impression always. You'll never notice Donald looking sloppy or unkempt. He's never off duty, so to speak, whereas I'll let my hair down occasionally. Needless to say, my father loves Donald. In fact, he fell in love with him before I did."

She gave a trickle of a laugh. "I don't mean anything like gay love. He loved who Donald was and wanted to be. Can you imagine a father telling a girl just out of high school that this was the man for her? Oh, I know some people thought that was because my father believed I could never succeed at anything but being a wealthy man's wife." She laughed again. "Maybe that's true. So what?"

I don't know if she realized how much she had said so quickly or not, but she stopped talking and just stood there beside me looking out at the lights in the distance.

"What about your mother?" I asked, since she never had mentioned her.

"My mother was a rich man's wife," she replied, as though that answered everything. "Whatever my father said was gospel. She doted on my younger brother far more than me, anyway. He's a lawyer working for the Justice Department in Washington, a great success. They think he might become attorney general someday. I think every other sentence out of her mouth begins with his name, Gerald. Gerald Savoir Faire, his friends call him. You know what that means in French?"

"No."

"To know how to do . . . everything. Sophisticated," she said, but she didn't say it with pleasure and pride. "I'm just kidding," she quickly added. "He's terrific. His real name is Gerald Wilson. We're supposedly descendants of President Woodrow Wilson, you know. That's almost royalty in America."

"What about Mr. March's parents?"

"That's a different story. Donald's father was married to someone before he married Donald's mother, and he has children with his first wife. He and Donald's mother had only Donald, and his mother died two years ago while on holiday with Donald's father and two of his three other children and their families."

She sighed deeply. "Aren't families complicated sometimes?" she asked, but she didn't look at me. She looked out, as if she were asking someone else.

We were both quiet, and then, after a few moments, she turned sharply and said, "Don't let Kiera's behavior at dinner and Donald's tolerance of her discourage you. You belong here now. I'm determined about that. Give it time. Everything takes time. Otherwise," she continued with a smile, "babies wouldn't need nine months."

What was she thinking and saying? That I was going to be reborn in nine months?

"I'm so happy we had this little chat. We have to do it more and more so we get to know each other better. Soon Donald will open up more, as well, and before you know it, we'll be like a family, a family for you. Okay? Don't be discouraged, okay?"

I saw that she wasn't going to stop until she got me to agree. I nodded, and she smiled.

"Good. What was it Scarlett O'Hara said? 'Tomorrow is another day'? Well, tomorrow is another day, and every tomorrow thereafter. Would you like to watch television in the entertainment center? We have a screen as big as some small movie-theater screens. When was the last time you went to a movie?"

I thought about it and realized that it had been soon after Daddy had left us. Mama had taken me to a movie to cheer up both of us. That was years ago, because we never spent money on a movie after that, and my school friends had stopped asking me to go to movies with them.

"Years ago," I replied.

"Years?" She got behind my wheelchair. "Years, and you live in the movie capital of the world? We'll do something about that, although once you see a movie here, you might not care about going to a theater."

As she wheeled me along, she described some of their theater parties. She said that her husband knew an important movie executive at one of the studios, and he brought them first-run films to watch. The elaborate parties she described and the things they had done were as foreign to me as rituals in Africa or the Far East.

When we turned into the entertainment center, she stopped my wheelchair abruptly. Kiera was there with one of the girls I had seen at the pool, but what they were watching on the screen was more surprising. A naked man and woman were embracing as they lay on a beach. Mrs. March adjusted the lights so the room was blazing.

"What the hell!" Kiera cried, and turned around. She and her girlfriend were snacking on popcorn. They sat on two large red leather seats with a wide arm between them on which they had the bowl of delicious-smelling popcorn.

"What are you watching? Why didn't you tell me Deidre was coming here tonight?"

"Daddy said we could," Kiera said. "And for your information, this picture is going to be nominated for an Academy Award.

You're ruining it for us. Please turn off the lights."

"Hi, Mrs. March," Deidre said. She had auburn hair, smartly shaped, and was one of the prettiest girls I had seen.

"You can leave her here to watch if you want, Mother. I'm sure she's seen worse on the street."

Mrs. March seemed at a loss for words. She didn't move me or herself. The couple on the screen got up laughing and charged into the ocean, splashing each other.

"Deidre's mother would not like her watching this, I'm sure," she finally said.

"Are you kidding? She was jealous that she was getting to see it. Right, Deidre?"

"She was, Mrs. March."

Without further comment, Mrs. March turned me away and started out.

"Turn down the lights again, Mother!" Kiera screamed.

Mrs. March didn't. She continued to push me out and down the hallway.

"Thanks, Mother!" Kiera shouted after us.

"I'll take you up to your room. You can watch television in your own suite," Mrs. March said. I didn't look back at her, but from the way her voice trembled, I knew she was shaken.

As we went into the elevator, I realized that Kiera finally had told at least one of her friends about me, and surely once one found out, others would, as well. I wondered how she explained my presence in their home. Surely by now, her friends knew about the accident she had caused. One or two of them might have been with her in the car and probably high on drugs as well. They and their parents would have good reason not to let other people know what had happened.

After she had settled me in my suite, Mrs. March said that before going to bed herself, she would stop by again to be sure I was fine. She looked anxious to leave and hurried out, to speak with her husband I was sure. When she returned hours later, she didn't look much calmer. In fact, she looked as flushed as someone who had been in a nasty argument. I let her help me undress and get ready for bed, more out of sympathy for her than because of any need of my own. It seemed to help settle her down. After I was in bed, she tucked the blanket in around me, but she didn't leave. She pulled up a chair beside the bed and smiled.

"Did I tell you that when Alena was younger, she would often describe dreams she had? She loved telling stories, and to

208

her, the dreams she had were often her best. Even Donald, as busy as he seemed, enjoyed having her go on and on. Only Kiera would complain that Alena didn't leave much time to talk or hear about anything else. Did I tell you about all that?"

"No," I said. What made her think she had told me? We didn't speak that much about Alena.

"Anyway, to help her get to sleep the next night, I would sit here just as I am sitting now, and we would think of ways the dream story could continue or how it might lead to another dream. Sometimes Donald would stop in and participate. Who'd ever think that something so terrible would happen to such a lovely little girl?"

She continued after a little pause of sadness, "It seems I keep apologizing to you for what goes on here. It will get better. I promise." She patted my hand and started to get up, but then stopped and looked at me. "You didn't have any storylike dreams last night, did you?"

"No," I said.

"Well, if you ever feel like talking about a dream you've had, don't hesitate to tell me, okay? Good. Sweet dreams, then." She leaned over to kiss me on the forehead. She put the chair back, smiled at me, and put out the lights on her way out, closing the door softly behind her. The house was quiet, but when I adjusted myself to get a little more comfortable, I heard the music start in Kiera's room. It was so loud that I was sure Mr. and Mrs. March had to hear it, as well, but it continued.

She's doing that deliberately, I thought. Why couldn't she use earphones? Perhaps her friend Deidre was still there and in the room with her. Maybe she was showing off, showing her how she could annoy me. I imagined her bragging about how she would drive me out of there soon. Finally, the music was turned down or turned off, and the silence returned.

It was still difficult for me to fall asleep. I anticipated Kiera bursting in on me again to make more threats, but she didn't. I also thought about what Mrs. March had said about Alena's dreams. I wondered if her dreams would somehow become mine if I remained there. Maybe dreams lingered like cobwebs. They were floating about looking to settle in another young girl's mind.

I half wished they would. My interest in knowing more about Alena seemed to grow stronger with every minute I was in the suite. Whether it was wishful thinking or not, I half expected that someday, she would reach out to me to tell me that she would help me.

"Don't worry," she would whisper, "I'm here."

I so needed a friend.

Even one who had died.

14
UNCHAINED

Soon my days became more ordinary, or at least as ordinary as days living in such an enormous estate with servants could be. For the time being, Kiera seemed to lose interest in me and didn't come bursting into my room again. Often, she wasn't at dinner, and if she was, she acted as if I weren't even there. Perhaps she was convinced that my being sent away was only a matter of time and didn't require her interference or involvement. Mr. March was often gone on business or very involved in some project he was developing. I had seen little of him since our first dinner together. There was much to keep me busy, however.

Mrs. Kepler came to tutor me five days a week and always stayed the same amount of time. Dr. Milan came once more, and then I was taken to get the X-rays he wanted. He told Mrs. March and me that it was too soon to see if my right leg would continue to grow as normally as my left. I was instructed in how to use the crutch he promised, so the wheelchair was put away. The doctor wanted me to get more exercise and move about as much as possible, and I did feel myself getting stronger every day. As Mrs. Duval was fond of saying, there was light at the end of the tunnel.

Toward the end of the summer, Dr. Milan finally took off the cast, and I felt like a prisoner who had been unchained. But I was walking with a limp. The doctor said I would for a while, if not forever. Still, I was so happy not to have something attached to my body that I almost didn't care. Suddenly, the world seemed bright again, and hope dared show its face on my horizon. How I wished Mama would have lived to see my recuperation.

On the way back from Dr. Milan's office, I told Mrs. March that I had finally decided what to have written on my mother's tombstone. From the way she reacted, I had the feeling she thought I had completely forgotten about it.

"Oh, you have? Why, that's very nice, Sasha. What have you decided?"

"Under her name and the dates of her birth and death, I want to write 'who showed her daughter a little bit of heaven.'"

I could see she didn't fully understand. How could I want to write something like that after being on the streets for nearly a year before her death?

"I don't know if it can be done," I added, "but I'd like to see her calligraphy of the word *heaven* right under that."

"Oh. Oh, yes," she said, now realizing why I wanted that. "That work she has on that bar's wall. How clever. Well, we'll just find someone who can get it done for us. Do you think that calligraphy is still on the bar wall?"

"I don't know. I saw it only once when she took me there to see it."

"Of course. How stupid of me to ask. How would you know, after all? I'll make some calls when we get home," she said. "But right now, I thought I'd have Grover drive us to your new school so you can see it. It won't be long before you'll be attending. Mrs. Kepler says you're ready for day one right now."

I sat back, nervous and excited. I used to love school. Before Mama and I ended up on the streets, it was a wonderful escape from the dreariness of the life we were living. Even when my girlfriends stopped including me in things, I still enjoyed being in my classes. The girls I used to consider my closest friends had still talked to me. They just didn't suggest anything that would bring us together after school, and then, when they learned that Mama and I had lost our apartment and were living in a hotel room, they had even stopped talking to me unless I spoke to them, and even then, they would answer quickly and look to get away. It was as if they thought what was happening to me and Mama was as infectious as some terrible disease. In the end, I almost didn't mind not attending school.

When we made a turn and Mrs. March said, "Here we are," I thought she was mistaken. All I saw were beautiful green lawns, trees, and bushes, but then the building just at the top of a small incline appeared. Right at the bottom was the sign, "Pacifica Junior-Senior High School."

"Turn in, please, Grover," she told him, and we started up the driveway. It wasn't like any school building I had seen, and it looked very new. Everything around it sparkled. Our building at my old school had graffiti smeared on some of the walls, and almost as quickly as it was removed, it reappeared. The windows never looked as clear and as clean as the ones in this building. The frames here looked freshly painted.

The building had two floors, and as we drew closer, I realized it was in an L shape. Off to the right, I could see the ball fields. One had goals for field hockey or soccer, and the other was a baseball field. There was a parking lot on the left with only a half-dozen cars in it.

"The school has a very nice cafeteria and tables outside if you want to eat your lunch outdoors," Mrs. March began. "At the rear to the left is the gymnasium, and right next to that is the theater."

"Theater?"

"Well, it's a really small theater, but it's equipped with the most up-to-date sound system. I should tell you now that Donald's . . . our company . . . built this school."

"He builds schools, too?"

"Just this one," she said, laughing. "It was almost done as a favor. A group of well-to-do people, including two state senators, decided to establish it about twelve years ago and practically begged Donald to take charge of construction. So, if you hear Kiera tell people that it's her school, that's what she means. Actually," she added after a moment's thought, "I think she believes it really is her school."

"How many students go to it?"

"I think it's just less than three hundred

now. It's only for grades seven to twelve. There's a sort of sister elementary school that both Alena and Kiera attended. I'm sure you'll love it here. The classes aren't very big, so you'll get lots of personal attention."

Grover stopped, and I gazed out at it all.

"It looks better than any school I've ever seen," I said.

"The principal is a very nice woman named Dr. Steiner. She has a doctorate in education and has been the principal since the school was established. You're in Mr. Hoffman's homeroom class, and he's your math teacher, as well. I made sure you were in that homeroom. Your homeroom teacher is your personal adviser, too, and he's one of the best teachers in the school. So you can see, I'm getting everything set up perfectly for you. Doesn't it look wonderful?"

"Yes," I said.

"I thought you'd be impressed. Grover, you can take us home now," she said, and he started back down the driveway.

"Will Kiera go to school with me?" I asked.

"We'll see. That's something Donald has yet to decide. Seniors are permitted to drive to school. There's a parking lot for them."

After a long moment, she added, "Her court hearing has yet to happen. Donald's lawyer has successfully delayed it, which is a legal tactic, but as I tell him, you can postpone and postpone, but inevitably you have to face the music. But let's not talk about any of that, Sasha. It only brings back terrible memories and pain for you."

I sat back and was quiet. Her saying not to talk about it didn't do any good. It was like unringing a bell. It couldn't be done. I had been wondering for months what was going to happen to Kiera. How could what had happened be completely swept under the table? Were rich people that powerful?

Perhaps to cheer me up further, Mrs. March delivered on her promise to get me whatever I needed to do calligraphy. She even bought me a beautifully illustrated book about it, and I saw some of the words Mama had copied. I had told her exactly what I needed, and it was all set up in the sitting room. I began to work almost immediately. I wanted to do a copy of Mama's "heaven."

"Don't make me sorry I got you all this," Mrs. March told me two days after I began work. I had done little of anything else. "You can't shut yourself away all day, you know."

She was right, of course. Now that I was

free of my cast and did not have to depend on a crutch, Dr. Milan wanted me to take daily exercise. Mrs. March had a physical therapist come to the house to work with me every other day. "We've got to get your muscles strong again so you won't have any problem getting around in school," she said. The therapist, Sheila Toby, was very impressed with the Marches' indoor pool and, after some initial days of stretching exercises, decided we would do all of our work in the water.

One afternoon, Mr. March suddenly appeared to watch us. He was there for quite a while but said nothing. Later, when I was going up to my suite, he appeared in the hallway. I realized that this was the first time since I had come to his house that he and I were alone.

"You seem to be doing very well," he began. "I'm sure you feel stronger every day."

"Yes, I do."

I waited, expecting him to say, *Okay, since you're better and stronger, you don't have to live here anymore, and this idea of your going to Kiera's school is not really a good one,* but he didn't say that.

"I happened to glance in at the calligraphy you're doing," he continued, walking along with me toward my suite. "It's pretty impressive."

"Thank you."

"Tell me about it," he said.

"What do you want to know?"

"I'm not that familiar with it. Jordan bought something once, as I said, but I must admit, I didn't pay much attention to the explanation the salesman gave us at the gallery. I gather you told her exactly what you needed. What is needed?"

"I work with an ink brush, ink, a special type of paper, and an inkstone. Together, they are known as the Four Treasures of the Study."

"Really?" He smiled. "Go on. Tell me more."

We reached my doorway.

"The paper is weighed down with paperweights. Anything can be a paperweight, but my mother used to have wooden blocks that had pictorial designs on them, too. They had been her mother's."

"What happened to them?"

"I don't know. One day, they were gone and she used rocks we found on the beach instead. I think she might have sold them."

He nodded. "Go on in," he told me, and then he followed me in and went to my desk. "So, what is this inkstone?" he asked.

"You have to rub the ink stick on it with water to make the paint."

"Your mother did all this while you were homeless?"

"Yes. For her, it was more like . . . more like . . ."

"Therapy, relaxation?"

"No, I think something religious," I said, and his eyes widened and brightened.

"And for you?"

"The same," I said.

He smiled. He picked up the brush and studied it a moment.

"It has to be held a special way," I said.

"Show me."

I did.

"See, it's held vertically with the thumb and the middle finger. My mother told me you should be able to put an egg in your palm if you're holding it correctly."

He laughed and then tried it. I adjusted his fingers so that his ring finger and pinkie touched the bottom of the brush handle.

"This is hard," he said. "Must take a lot of practice."

"Yes. You start by practicing the Chinese character *yong* to master the eight basic strokes."

"And what does *yong* mean?"

"Forever," I said.

"Now, what does the one you're working on represent?"

"It means *mother,*" I said.

"I know you must really miss her."

"Yes."

He nodded, keeping his eyes on my calligraphy. "Well," he said, "your art teacher should be happily surprised once he learns what you can do. He'll probably have you teach the class."

"Oh, I couldn't do that," I said.

"Sure you could. Let me see this when it's finished," he told me, and started to turn to leave. He stopped, and I looked at the doorway.

Kiera was standing there. From the look on her face, I knew she must have been there for a while and heard what we had been saying.

"What's up?" he asked her.

"Nothing," she said sharply, and hurried away.

He hesitated, and then he walked out.

Not long before our accident, after Mama and I had spent most of our day on Venice Beach's boardwalk selling her calligraphy and my lanyards, she had paused while we were getting our things together and just sat there staring at people.

"What's wrong, Mama?" I had asked.

"Are you feeling sick again?"

"No, no," she had said. She'd smiled at me, and for a moment, I saw through her bloated face and tired eyes and saw the smile on her face years ago when she was beautiful and energetic. Nothing made me happier. I could go all the rest of the day without food and still feel content because I saw this smile.

"Then what, Mama?"

"I was just thinking how when they look at the calligraphy, they change."

"Who changes?"

"The people, the ones who pass by. It isn't until they're looking at the calligraphy that they suddenly see us as people. They look at both of us then, Sasha. Did you notice that?"

Now that she had said it, I realized it was true, and I nodded.

"Why is that, Mama?"

"The calligraphy, like anything beautiful, reminds us all about what we share as people. That's what your grandmother once told me," she had said. "But it wasn't until just now, today, that I realized what she meant."

She had smiled again and then continued gathering her things.

I looked down at my unfinished work and

nodded, thinking about Mr. March, his softer tone of voice, his curiosity, and his smile.

"Now I understand, too, Mama," I whispered.

It was truly as if she had reached from beyond the grave to speak to me through my own calligraphy. It filled my heart with warmth and gave me the strength even to face the jealous face of Kiera March.

Someday, I thought — no, vowed — I wouldn't hate her as much as I pitied her.

But I knew that the journey to that place would be a long one and over a road full of many traps and dangers. I just didn't know how soon it would all really begin.

15
JUDGMENT

A few days later, I learned that despite how powerful and influential Mr. March was and despite how good his attorney was, they couldn't put off Kiera's court hearing again. With only a week left before school began, she would have to go to court. No one discussed it in front of me, but I overheard enough to know the details, and by now, I understood that both Mrs. Caro and Mrs. Duval knew everything. In fact, Mrs. Duval apologized to me one day when I was sitting out on the patio that faced the pool, reading. Without my asking, she brought me a glass of Mrs. Caro's famous lemonade.

"Thank you very much, Mrs. Duval," I said, surprised. I started to drink, expecting her to leave, but she stood there looking out at the cabana. I could tell that she wanted to say something, and I waited.

"When you were first brought here," she began, "we all thought some organization had chosen you or singled you out for a special opportunity because of your accident and terrible loss and that Mrs. March had volunteered to take you in. She and Mr. March have done many wonderful charitable things. No one told us what or who caused the accident you and your mother suffered. We had some suspicions, but no one thought it was necessary for us to know the truth, so no one asked any questions."

I didn't say anything.

She shook her head. "If we had known the truth, we would have treated you better when you first arrived."

"You treated me just fine, Mrs. Duval. Everyone has."

"Not as fine as we would have if we had known how you lost your mother and who was responsible," she declared, and left.

I appreciated what she had told me, but I was worried that it would now cause even more friction between Kiera and me, especially now that her court hearing was scheduled. I felt the way Mama had always felt when she told me she was waiting for the second shoe to drop.

"What does that mean?" I had asked her.

"It means that when the second shoe drops, the whole ceiling comes down on you," she had told me. "The problem is, it doesn't happen right away, so you're always waiting for it, and that's nerve-wracking. That's the way my life has been with your miserable father. Every time the phone rings or someone comes to the door, I expect trouble."

Maybe that was why she had hated answering the phone and always made me look out the window to see who it was when someone came to the door before she would open it. I wished I had someone to do all that for me now, run interference. I had no doubt that the second shoe was about to drop.

Two days later, the Marches went to court. I practically locked myself away in my suite, reading, working on calligraphy, and watching television. The minutes went by like hours and the hours like days. Finally, a little before six o'clock, I heard footsteps in the hallway. I heard Kiera's door slam closed, and then I heard the recognizable *click-clack* of Mrs. March's stiletto heels on the tile floor as she headed in my direction.

"Well, that's over for now," Mrs. March said as she entered. I shut off the television. She came all the way into the sitting room and stood there looking at me. "The judge put her on probation, but only if she goes to serious therapy. If she doesn't go, she loses her driver's license indefinitely, so you know she'll go. What she'll get out of it is anyone's guess.

"I just don't want to think about it any-more," she continued. "Donald will handle the arrangements with the therapist. This is what we've come to in this country. A child will listen to a therapist but not her own parents. At least, that is what the judge believes. I can't say he's wrong."

I could see that she was waiting for me to say something, but I didn't know what I was supposed to say. *Good? That's all the punish-ment she gets? What?*

"I'm telling you all this so she doesn't tell you that the judge decided she was not at fault or something," Mrs. March continued. "She will probably tell her friends that, the ones who know the truth, but you should know different. I don't imagine any of this makes you feel any better, Sasha."

I realized that she thought I wanted to see Kiera get a far more severe punishment. It certainly wouldn't have bothered me if she had, but on the other hand, it wouldn't have brought back my mother. At this point, I really didn't care. I didn't like her, and I didn't expect that any therapist would, either. He or she would have to have a magic wand to turn Kiera into a different person, turn her into someone who wasn't selfish and spoiled.

"Let's just concentrate on happy new things, okay, Sasha?" Mrs. March said. She smiled, looked around the sitting room as if she was worried that something had been changed, and then left.

Kiera said nothing to me about the judge's orders. In fact, she made more effort to avoid me, often finding excuses not to be at the table for dinner and then getting herself away from the house as much as possible so that we wouldn't even cross each other's path. I did learn that Mr. March had forbidden her to have any friends over to party. However, I wasn't sure whether he did that as a punishment or out of concern for me. Ever since Kiera had given me her logic for defending herself, a logic that essentially blamed me and Mama for being there in the rain, I imagined that she used the same argument with her father and maybe even with the judge. At least I was sure the judge hadn't accepted her excuse.

Perhaps Mr. March had ordered Kiera to avoid me so as to avoid any more conflict. After all, not only was I still there, but I had been enrolled in her school. She could no longer barge in to tell me her father was going to throw me out. I was sure that she was upset about that, as well as what happened the day after I completed my calligraphy of *mother.*

I brought it down to dinner the following evening, an evening when I was sure that Mr. March was going to be there. Kiera was there, too, this time. She looked as if she was going to burst out laughing when I arrived carrying the framed calligraphy, but Mr. March's exclamation of "Wow!" stopped her dead in her tracks. He rose and came to me to take it and hold it up.

"Isn't this something?" he asked Mrs. March.

She smiled. "Amazing."

"You know," he said, still holding my calligraphy and looking at it, "this gives me an idea for something. I'm doing this co-development deal with some South Koreans. We should do a logo in calligraphy." He smiled at me. "Maybe we'll hire you to do it, Sasha."

I didn't know what to say. He laughed and handed the calligraphy back to me.

"No," I said, handing it back. "I brought this as a gift for you and Mrs. March."

"Oh, how sweet," Mrs. March said.

"It'll look good in the entertainment center," Mr. March said. "Thank you."

He took it back with him to his seat and set it aside.

"How can you hang that up in the house? I don't know what it's even supposed to be," Kiera said. "No one will."

"We've got a number of works of art that few can figure out in this house that your mother bought," Mr. March said, laughing. "But at least we do know what this means," he said, lifting the calligraphy.

"What?" Kiera demanded.

"Sasha?" Mr. March said, looking at me.

"It means *mother,*" I said. *"Love."*

Kiera looked as if she had swallowed an apple whole for a moment and then began to stab at her salad. I took my seat and, during most of our dinner, answered questions that Mr. and Mrs. March asked about calligraphy. It was actually the happiest and most pleasant dinner I had had at the March house. Afterward, Mr. March asked me to follow him to the entertainment center to help choose the wall space for my art. Kiera went directly up to her room.

The day before school was to begin was the last day that Sheila Toby, my physical therapist, came to the house. By now, I was doing twenty laps in the indoor pool. Toward the end of the session, Mrs. March came in to watch, and when I got out of the pool, she handed me my towel and said, "That was terrific, Sasha. I bet you can do ten laps in our outdoor Olympic-size pool now, just like Alena could do before she got sick."

Before I could say anything, she turned to Sheila Toby to compliment her on the job she had done with me.

"It wasn't hard working with a young girl who is so cooperative and determined," Sheila said.

"Exactly. She starts the ninth grade tomorrow," Mrs. March said. "Come, let me give you your check," she told Sheila, and they left together.

I dried myself and dressed and then went outside to walk over to the lake. I was still limping, but I had no pain and did feel much stronger. I probably could swim those ten laps Mrs. March wanted me to swim one day, I thought, but I felt conflicted about it. Almost everything she had done for me and wished for me were things she had done and wished for Alena.

I imagined that was only normal for a mother who had lost her daughter and had someone else wearing her things and staying in her room. There was no way for her to look at me and not think of Alena, but that also told me that as long as I lived there, I wouldn't be Sasha. I wouldn't be my mother's daughter. No matter what Mr. and Mrs. March did for me, I thought, the moment I could leave and be on my own, I would.

Did that make me ungrateful? Did it make me as self-centered as Kiera? Whenever I thought that, I had to remind myself of what my private nurse in the hospital, Jackie Knee, had told me. I could never be ungrateful, because they could never do enough for me.

I sat on the dock and dangled my feet over the water. The breeze drew ripples in the surface of the lake. I saw water bugs navigating through some floating leaves and blades of grass. The rowboats tied to the dock bobbed and swayed gently, and on the far end of the lake, those terns I had seen sailed what seemed to be inches above the water before lifting toward the tops of the trees.

Tomorrow, I would return to school. I'd be back in a classroom but sitting among boys and girls who came from wealthy families. When they looked at me, would they immediately see how poor and lost I had been, despite my living now in the March house? Not my tutor, my physical therapist, my clothes and shoes, my manicured fingernails and styled hair — none of it could disguise the pain of the past and the loss I had suffered. If anything, I'd be more of a curiosity than any other new student would be. *How did this one get here?* they would surely wonder. *She doesn't belong here. She belongs out there.*

Despite what Mrs. Kepler said, would I look inadequate? Would my voice falter and crack when I was called upon to answer questions aloud? Would I do so badly on tests that I would quickly become the class dunce? And when they all talked about their possessions, their family travels, their rich parents, and brothers and sisters who might be in expensive colleges, fashions and styles, famous people they had met and seen, shows they had gone to and were going to go to, what would I do? What would I say?

My silence would reveal everything. No matter how well Mrs. March dressed me, despite my being brought to the school in a limousine every day and living in a bigger house than any of them, they would recoil and whisper, "She's an imposter. She doesn't belong here. She's not really one of us."

If I thought I had been lonely during my final days at my last school, what did I think I'd be at this one? Lonely would probably be a choice I would take rather than what I would find now. Wouldn't it have been better, wiser, for Mrs. March to enroll me in an ordinary public school? The other students wouldn't seem so superior. I'd be more comfortable. Why hadn't she thought of that?

And then there was Kiera, waiting and watching, hoping for me to fail. If I did something wrong or did poorly in class, she would pounce on her mother. I could almost hear her claiming, "This is embarrassing, Mother. She's dragging me down with her. You're making us the laughingstock of the school. Put her in a public school, at least."

I certainly wouldn't argue about it. I half hoped that was exactly what would happen. Of course, I expected that when any of the other students went to Kiera to ask about me, she would tell them that I was her mother's charity case, a girl from the streets, homeless, carrying some contagious disease. I could see her whispering in ears, especially the ears of the other girls in my class. She would sabotage me anyway. What chance did I have to succeed? Why even bother to try?

When I heard her say my name, I thought I was thinking about her so hard that I had imagined it, but she said it again, and I turned around to see her standing there.

The sight of her startled me, and I got right to my feet.

"What do you want?" I asked her.

"What do I want? I want you to disappear," she said, and then smirked. "But that's not going to happen."

"So? What do you want?"

"Chill out," she said, and walked to the edge of the dock to look down at the rowboats. "I used to take my sister for rides," she said. "Especially when she first got sick."

Was she going to invite me to go for a ride? Maybe to drown me?

She turned to face me. "I've had two sessions with my therapist. Don't try to look surprised. I know Mother has told you everything."

"I'm not surprised that you're seeing a therapist, but I am surprised that you're telling me," I said.

"It wasn't my idea."

"Whose idea was it?" I asked, expecting her to say it was her mother's.

"My therapist's."

"The therapist's? Why?"

"It's part of my therapy, something I have to do."

"What is?"

"Talking to you. Not to get you to forgive me or anything like that," she added quickly.

"Why, then?"

"I told you. It's part of my therapy. I don't understand half of it myself, but if I don't do it . . ." She took a breath. "If I don't do it, he says the therapy won't work. Whatever that means. It could mean I would have to return to court, and then who knows?"

"What do you want from me?"

"Nothing. Just . . . I'll just talk to you," she said. She turned to walk away, then stopped and turned back. "Not that many people know about us, about what happened. I mean, what really happened. Just a couple of my very close girlfriends know. I'd like to keep it that way."

"What does that mean?"

"Don't you understand anything? I mean, keep your mouth shut in school. Just don't talk about it. No one has to know anything."

"They're going to want to know why I'm here, aren't they? They'll ask questions. They'll see that I come from a different world."

"They probably would. That's why I told Mother how hard this was going to be for me and that I wasn't going back to school unless she did something. Daddy agreed, and they made up a story about you."

"What story?"

"You're the daughter of one of my cousins

who was killed in a car accident. My mother, who is a walking soap opera, wanted to take you in, and so you're here. That way, no one will know you were homeless and sleeping in a carton."

"Why didn't your mother ever tell me this?"

"She waits until the last moment for anything. She'll tell you about it tonight. We agree that it will make things easier for both of us." She started to turn and stopped again. "But I'm not driving you to school, and don't expect me to hang out with you there."

"I don't think there's anything I expected less," I said.

"Ha ha. Aren't you hilarious," she said, and walked off.

I smiled.

It was as if she had really been listening to my thoughts and had heard my fears.

Maybe I would do well at this school.

I sat on the dock again to watch the bugs and the birds and the ripples and the trees and all the clouds that floated softly across the blue sky like great white birds migrating to another horizon.

Just like me.

16
ANOTHER HORIZON

Mr. March wasn't at dinner. He had a dinner meeting in San Francisco. Kiera obviously had not told her mother that she had revealed the story the Marches had created about me. When we were all seated, Mrs. March told Mrs. Duval to wait in the kitchen. She said she would let her know when to begin serving our dinner. Then she folded her hands on the table, looked down at them, and began.

"Both Mr. March and I have decided that it would be easier for both of you, but especially for you, Sasha," she said, raising her head to look at me, "if the other students in the school were not completely aware of your situation."

I looked at Kiera. She smiled and looked down.

"Situation?"

"What I mean to say is that it would be easier for you to assimilate if they all just assumed that you were part of our family. Which is something I am hoping you will actually become someday soon," she quickly added. "Anyway, for now, it would be better if you told your classmates that you were Kiera's cousin on Donald's side. That side is so mixed up no one would not believe it; not that many people know the details concerning his family."

"Don't forget the Chinese part, Mother," Kiera said.

"Please, Kiera, don't interrupt," Mrs. March said sharply. She turned back to me. "The story Kiera is referring to is simple. One of Donald's half brothers married a Chinese woman. You were born, and everything was fine until they were both killed in a car accident. That's when you came to live with us. Now, tell me, where have you visited outside California?"

"Nowhere," I said.

"Your story won't pass gas, Mother," Kiera sang.

"Kiera. You're not helping."

"All right, then," Mrs. March said. "Where have you been in California?"

"My father once took us to Santa Barbara, but I barely remember it."

"Wow, Santa Barbara," Kiera said.

Mrs. March glared at her. "That's fine.

That's perfect. You'll just say that's where you had lived. If anyone wants more detail, you just tell him or her that it's too sad for you to talk about it. That should work."

"But what about my teachers, the principal?" I asked. "Don't they know the truth?"

"Dr. Steiner, the principal, knows, but no one else does or will. I can assure you of that."

"Unless she tells them," Kiera muttered, nodding at me.

"Why should she do that?" Mrs. March smiled at me. "We just want you to succeed and be comfortable and happy at school, Sasha. Okay? You understand?"

"Yes," I said, and then suddenly thought, *I'm betraying Mama again, pretending she never existed.* "But I don't like lying," I added.

"Oh, please. Give us a break," Kiera said. "I can just imagine the things you told people when you were living on the street."

"That was different."

"Right. It's always different when you do it," she said. "I use the same excuse when I'm caught."

"I don't mean it to be an excuse. You just don't understand," I told her.

"That's the first thing you've said that makes any sense," she replied. "Who would

241

understand?"

"Stop. Let's not talk about this anymore," Mrs. March said. "She understands, and that's that." She called for Mrs. Duval.

At first, I was happy when Kiera told me the idea about what other students and my teachers would be told about me, but now that I heard it from Mrs. March, I was more nervous about it. I was entering my new school life on a raft of lies. I'd have to be very careful about what I said to anyone about my past, where I had been, what I had been doing. One slip, and I would fall out of the raft and into the sea of turmoil that raged around someone like me.

Mrs. March was eager to change the subject. During the remainder of our dinner, she went on and on about how wonderful it was going to be for me at this new school.

"Are you getting her out of PE, Mother? I don't expect she can play any sport with that limp."

"She certainly can swim better than you can," Mrs. March said. "She'll do fine. Her teacher will be understanding."

"Miz Raymond? The only thing she understands is a vibrator."

"Kiera!" Mrs. March screamed.

"I don't think she has innocent ears,

Mother. Look where she's been."

"I don't want that kind of talk at the dinner table. Your father is going to hear about this." She glared at her again and then turned to me and smiled. "Did you learn how to play an instrument when you were at your old school, Sasha?"

"Yeah, she played the lanyards, remember?"

"Kiera."

"No," I said. "We didn't have any instrumental music classes."

"Well you will here. You'll be in the senior high band. Alena played the clarinet."

"You're going to give her that, too?" Kiera asked.

"If she wants to play the clarinet, it would be foolish to let it just rot away, Kiera. No one stopped you from learning how to play an instrument."

"Yeah, right, the school band. There's nothing more appetizing than watching kids wipe their spit off mouthpieces."

"Don't listen to her. The band is highly regarded and goes on trips and is often asked to play at public events."

"Whoop-ti-doo," Kiera muttered. "You forgot to tell her she can wear the band uniform. There was nothing I hated more."

"I know you'll enjoy playing the clarinet,

Sasha," Mrs. March insisted. "It will be wonderful hearing that sound in this house again. And with your artistic talent, you might consider joining the theater group and working on sets, too."

"She'd be better as an actress," Kiera said.

"Is that how you got your training?" I asked her. She actually reddened, especially after Mrs. March laughed.

"Alena could give it back to you just like that, too," Mrs. March told her.

Kiera pressed her lips together hard. Her face puffed up and looked as if it might explode. She pushed her plate away from her and stood up. "I have things to do," she announced, and walked out.

"If your father was here, you'd remember to ask to be excused, Kiera," Mrs. March shouted after her. Kiera did not respond. "He'll hear about this, too," she added. I heard Kiera pounding the steps on her way up the stairway.

Mrs. March shook her head, and we continued eating. It took her a while to calm down, and then she talked more about the school and how sad it was that Alena never got to graduate.

"When you arrive at the school tomorrow, go directly to the principal's office," she told me after we finished dinner. She walked with me to the stairway. "Grover will be waiting for you right outside after breakfast, and he'll be at the school precisely at the end of the school day. I'll be waiting to hear all about your day."

I nodded and turned to go up the stairway, but she reached out to stop me.

"Don't let Kiera's silly remarks disturb you, and don't be nervous, Sasha. You're going to do fine." She released my arm and smiled. "I always loved the first day of school. There's such excitement, such expectation. Go to sleep early," she added. "I'll be there to make sure you get up early enough." She looked up the stairway. "Half the year, I'm banging on Kiera's door to get her up."

I started up the stairway again.

"Oh," she said. "I'll have a wonderful surprise for you. I'll have it with me in the morning."

"What?"

"Well, it wouldn't be a surprise if I told you, now, would it?" she said. She smiled and walked away.

What would it be? More clothes? Shoes? Jewelry? Gadgets? Or a special lunch on the beach to celebrate my finishing my first week at school? I never thought I'd see the day when I would be so disinterested in all of that. How different I was from Kiera. She never saw a day when she wasn't interested in all of that.

Her door was closed as I passed her room, but she must have been listening for me, because the moment I entered mine, she was right behind me. I turned as she closed my door.

"What do you want?" I asked.

"Rules," she said.

"Rules? What rules?"

"Rules for you regarding me," she replied with her right hand on her hip. "I told you that Mother was going to tell you the way my parents were explaining you to everyone at the school, but that didn't include my rules."

I folded my arms and squinted at her. "I didn't think you followed any rules," I said and she laughed.

"You really are a scrappy street kid."

"Stop saying that."

"Okay, rule one. Never tell any of your little ninth-grade friends anything about me. I don't mean just about the accident. I mean anything you see here or hear here, especially. I'm never to be a topic of discussion between you and the other infants."

"That's easy. You're the most uninteresting person I've ever met. I won't be talking about you. There's nothing much to say."

"Rule two," she said, ignoring me. "Don't dare come over to me in the cafeteria or if I'm outside eating to ask for anything. My friends already know what I think of my so-called cousin coming to live with us. As far as I'm concerned, you don't exist. You're not there."

"That works for me," I said.

"Rule three. Do not come home blabbing about anything you see me do, especially if I have someone in my car with me after school. My father has forbidden it for now, but he'll change his mind about it soon.

"Rule four," she added quickly, to prevent any comment I might have about that. "Don't dare ever mention to anyone that I'm in therapy."

"I imagine most people who know you probably expect that you are," I said.

She glared at me and then smiled like someone who had just discovered a big secret. "How do we know how old you really are?"

"What?"

"Maybe you're stunted or something, and you're really seventeen or eighteen."

"You mean because I seem to be as smart as you are? That's easy. You're not mentally seventeen."

"Keep it up, but remember this. Don't break any of my rules, or you'll be sorrier than you are."

She left, and I stood there for a few moments looking at the closed door. Alena couldn't have been happy to have her as an older sister, I thought. I went into my sitting room to watch television and get my mind off Kiera and the next day. I did go to bed early, but I didn't fall asleep for a long time. Would I be able to pull off the story Mr. and Mrs. March had created about me? That, plus wondering whether or not Mrs. Kepler was right about my readiness, was enough to keep me tossing and turning. Finally, I fell asleep, but I slept so deeply that if it weren't for Mrs. March shaking me in the morning, I wouldn't have gotten up in time. She looked more excited than I was.

"Although you're much older than Alena was when she first went to school, I feel as if it's the same sort of morning. She was such an independent little girl. She didn't want me to come along. 'I'll be just fine, Mother,' she told me. 'It isn't necessary for you to be there.' Can you imagine a five-year-old saying that? She never knew, but I was there watching her from a little distance to be sure she was all right.

"Well, don't worry," she continued, bringing my uniform in from the closet. "I won't be following you. I'm absolutely positive you'll be fine. Come right down to breakfast as soon as you're dressed. Now, I've got to see if Kiera is up. Just because her father has permitted her to drive, she'll wait until the last minute for everything. I'll be waiting for you in the breakfast dining area," she said, and left.

I washed and dressed and fixed my hair quickly and then hurried down to breakfast.

"Was Kiera up?" I asked, taking my seat and seeing that she wasn't there.

For a moment, I thought Mrs. March hadn't heard me, she was that deep in thought. But she had.

"Surprise of surprises. She wasn't only up and ready, but she was on her way out. Seems she and a few of her friends decided to have breakfast on the way to school."

Mrs. Duval came in with orange juice, Mrs. Caro's home-baked rolls, and a tray of jams.

"Mrs. Caro's preparing your scrambled eggs just the way you like them," she told me. I had mentioned once that I liked them with cheese, and she often made them for me that way. "Mrs. Caro says a good breakfast is the best way to start at a new school,"

Mrs. Duval added.

"I agree. I'm sure Kiera and her friends won't have half as good a breakfast as you will," Mrs. March said.

I started to drink my juice. "Is Mr. March back?"

"No," she said. "He had to stay over an extra day."

I thought she was angry about it, but then she smiled. "That's okay," she said. "I'm busy today with charity committee meetings, a lunch at the golf club, and then some quick shopping at Saks in Beverly Hills before I rush home to hear about your first day. Here," she said, reaching down to take something out of her purse. It was a cell phone. "This is yours. My number is right here already," she explained, showing me. "You simply press one, and it calls me. So, if you need anything, don't hesitate."

"Thank you," I said, taking it.

"That's a very sophisticated cell phone. It takes pictures, but I'm sure you know all about those things."

"No. We never had one," I said, looking at it.

"Oh. Here's the booklet for it," she said, and gave it to me. "But for now, all you need to know is how to call me if you need me."

"This is the surprise you promised?"

"No. That's waiting in the limousine," she said.

Now I was really curious.

Mrs. Duval brought in my scrambled eggs and stood back to watch me gobble them up. My nervousness made me hungry. Afterward, when I went out to get into the limousine, I saw that Mrs. Duval and Mrs. Caro had joined Mrs. March to watch me go. Grover opened the door for me, and I looked back at them.

"Good luck, dearie," Mrs. Caro called.

"Yes, good luck," Mrs. Duval said.

Mrs. March stood, smiling but looking like someone who was smiling through tears.

I got into the limousine. All alone in the big automobile, I felt even smaller and more helpless than ever. Grover got in, looked back at me, winked, and then drove us away.

Then I turned and saw the gift on the seat. Slowly, I unwrapped it.

Mrs. March had bought me a leather book bag, which she had filled with pens and pencils, pads, paper clips, almost anything any student would need. On the outside of the bag, embossed in gold, she had my name, but because of the fictional biography, it read "Sasha March."

She had managed to justify changing my

last name. Now I wondered if she would find a way to change my first name.

17
SCHOOL

No one seemed to pay any particular attention to me when I stepped out of the limousine, even with a uniformed driver holding my door. Perhaps to the students at that school, it was nothing out of the ordinary to see one of them dropped off in a limousine. From the looks on their faces as they hurried into the building, shouted to each other, embraced, shook hands, and even kissed, I could see that most of the students knew one another. Except for the ones coming into seventh grade from elementary school, I wondered how many new students like me there were.

Since they didn't take much notice of my limousine, I wondered if they would take much notice of my limp. Even though it had been a while, I was still quite conscious of it. I walked as if the bottom of my right foot was stepping on hot coals.

When I entered, I saw the sign on the

marble wall pointing to the principal's office. Everything looked immaculate, from the polished tile floors to the gleaming windows and the glittering desktops I could see through open classroom doors. It wasn't a very big school lobby, so the chatter reverberated all around me. A small blond boy, probably a seventh-grader, bumped into me and then turned to flash an excited smile, apologizing. Before I could respond, he was gone. I walked slowly to the principal's office.

The front desk was already crowded with other students who had questions and problems and two young women, dressed almost as stylishly as Mrs. March, were answering questions and passing out papers. I stepped up behind the last student in line.

The lady on the right saw me and whispered something to the other woman. Then she went around to the counter gate and beckoned. I wasn't sure she was beckoning to me, but she kept doing it until I pointed to myself and she nodded. All of the students waiting suddenly paused to look at me as I went up to the gate.

"You're Sasha March, right?"

"Yes." I imagined she had been told that I was someone with Asian features.

"I'm Mrs. Knox. Dr. Steiner wanted me

to bring you to her as soon as you arrived. Come through," she said, stepping back.

I followed her to the principal's office door. She smiled at me and knocked.

"Yes," we heard.

She opened it enough to peer in and told Dr. Steiner I was here.

"Send her right in, Louise," I heard her say. Mrs. Knox stepped back and held the door open for me.

Dr. Steiner was a stout woman with a heavy bosom. She wore a dark brown skirt suit with a frilly-collared blouse. She had curly, gray-stained dark brown hair and looked about five foot two at the most. Except for lipstick, she wore no makeup, not even to cover what looked like tiny freckles or age spots on the crests of her cheeks. She was standing behind her desk when I entered and for a few moments simply stared at me the way someone would study a stranger to see if he or she was what was expected.

"Welcome to Pacifica High School, Sasha," she said, and nodded at the chair in front of her desk. "I'm Dr. Steiner."

I sat. I didn't realize it, but I was clutching my new book bag against my stomach as if I was afraid someone would steal it. It reminded me of the way Mama had worn her purse in front to avoid it being stolen when she walked through the streets. Dr. Steiner looked at the way I was holding my book bag, smiled, and sat. I relaxed my grip.

"I imagine you're a little frightened about entering a new school, but I want you to know you needn't be. I have a wonderful, bright, and caring staff working here. You'll discover we're like one big family," she said.

When she spoke, she sounded a little nasal, like someone with a bad cold. Her grayish blue eyes widened at the ends of her sentences. She had her left hand palm down on the desk, but she held her right hand up with her index finger out and pumped it up and down to emphasize what she was saying. When I didn't say anything, she continued.

"I've spoken with your tutor, Mrs. Kepler, and she is confident that you are ready for the ninth-grade work ahead of you. I have a high regard for her opinion, so I'm sure she's correct. This is your class schedule," she said, lifting a card no bigger than a pack of cigarettes. "Your classes and your teachers' names are on it. On the back is our motto." She turned it over and read, "Pacifica High School, where everyone strives to be all he or she can be."

She leaned forward.

"Despite your recent history, Sasha, there is no reason for you not to be all you can be. I want you to know that I personally will do all that I can to help you achieve that, and I feel confident that your teachers here will do so, as well. They're a dedicated bunch.

"Now, then," she continued, sitting back. "I promised Mrs. March that I would personally see if you had any problems and personally escort you to your homeroom. There is a very nice young lady classmate of yours, Lisa Dirk, who has volunteered to be your big sister for today. She has the same schedule you have and will show you around, okay?"

I could see that it was bothering her that I hadn't spoken.

"Is there anything you'd like to ask me before we go to your homeroom and meet Mr. Hoffman?"

"No," I said.

"No? Well, I'm sure there will be things as you get started, and if you can't get the answers from your teachers or other students, you come knocking on my door, okay?"

I nodded.

"I have been told you are artistic. I know that Mr. Longo, our art teacher for the senior high, will be excited about that."

"I don't know if I'm artistic."

"Sasha," she said, leaning toward me and smiling, revealing tiny teeth. "You will quickly discover that at this school, modesty is a disadvantage. Take pride in what you can do. Of course," she added, "many of our students take pride even though they can't do. I don't know all that much about you, of course, but I'm willing to bet that self-confidence doesn't come easy to you right now. I hope that will change." Her eyes narrowed. She sounded and looked as if it had better change. "Okay, then, come along," she said, rising. "Let's get you started on a wonderful school year. I'll take you right to your locker first and give you the combination."

She reached out for me as she came around her desk and surprised me by putting her arm around my shoulders. When she opened the door, I saw that the students who had been in the outer office were gone. Mrs. Knox and her associate both turned and looked at us with a surprised smile. Dr. Steiner still had her arm around me.

"Mrs. Knox. Mrs. Frazer, this is Sasha March, our newest student. Please make her feel at home. We're going to her locker and then to Mr. Hoffman's homeroom," she told them. "Man the fort."

They both nodded and looked at me as if I, not Kiera March, were the rich man's daughter. Was Dr. Steiner giving me this special treatment because of Mrs. March or because of what Mrs. March had told her about me? Whichever reason it was, I didn't feel good about it. I hoped this would be the first and last time I'd be singled out for any privileged treatment. It wasn't that long ago since I was last in school, and I remembered all too well how students would resent others whom their teachers favored.

When we stepped into the lobby, it was empty and very quiet. So was the hallway we entered. Where had everyone gone so quickly? Dr. Steiner saw the confused look on my face.

"The bell for beginning of homeroom has rung, but the bells don't ring in my office," she said. "I have enough outside noise as it is. Loitering in the hallways after the bell rings will get you into detention as quickly as anything else."

I couldn't help but wonder if Kiera had made it to school on time. After Dr. Steiner showed me my locker and gave me the combination, we continued down the long corridor. We walked to the last room on that wing of the building. When we entered, the dozen or so students all turned to look. Mr. Hoffman, a man Mama would have called as slim as a butter knife, stopped what he was reading and looked at us.

"Mr. Hoffman, here is your new student, Sasha March. Miss Dirk is to be her big sister today."

A chubby, dark-haired, light-skinned African American girl stood. She looked to Mr. Hoffman, who nodded, and then she came around the end of her row to us. She wasn't much taller than I was, and if it were not for her full, round, bloated face, she could be very pretty, I thought. She had unique-colored eyes that were like a very dark blue. Everyone else continued to watch us as if we were about to begin some traditional ritual of greeting.

"Hi. I'm Lisa," she said, extending her hand. I took it and nodded. "You're sitting right behind me," she added loudly, and the boy who was sitting there stood up and moved to the back of the row.

Dr. Steiner watched it all unfold and smiled with satisfaction.

"You're in good hands now, Sasha. Everyone be sure to make Sasha feel at home," she said, her voice, though still with that nasal quality, sounding very authoritative. She nodded again at Mr. Hoffman, handed me my class-schedule card, and left.

I followed Lisa to my seat.

"Welcome, Sasha. I was just explaining that this homeroom period will be extended so we can go through some of the rule changes at the school," Mr. Hoffman told me, and then said, "Number three."

The only rule change that made the students around me groan was the prohibition against cell phones being on during classes. Texting during class would result in suspension.

The redheaded boy across from me leaned over to whisper. "That's because Jean Trombly was caught cheating. Someone was texting her the answers on the test."

I just widened my eyes. And then I realized that the phone Mrs. March had give me was on. I quickly dug into my book bag, took it out, and shut it off. The phone made a musical sound as it went off, and everyone looked at me, most smiling and laughing. Mr. Hoffman didn't crack a smile. I shoved the phone back into my book bag quickly.

"Number four," he said sharply, and they all turned back to look at him. He went through five more rule changes before finishing.

When the bell to end homeroom finally rang, Lisa spun around quickly.

"Let me see your class schedule," she said. I handed it to her. "Oh, good, you're in instrumental music next. I was afraid you weren't."

"Instrumental music?" I hadn't looked at the card. She handed it back to show me.

"Room fourteen," she said. "It's a bit of a walk. What instrument do you play?"

"I don't," I said.

She tilted her head and pressed her lips deeper into their corners. "Weren't you playing an instrument in the school you attended before you came here?"

"No. We didn't have a school band."

"We have an orchestra. Not a band," she corrected, and I followed her out. "We have three full minutes between classes, so being late is considered serious. Two times late for classes will result in one day's detention. And you don't want to be in detention here. Mr. McWaine runs it, and he doesn't let students do anything for the whole hour. No reading, no homework, nothing but sitting up straight with your hands clasped. Not that I've ever been in detention," she added. "Have you?"

"No."

"You might get away with it because of your limp."

"I don't want to get away with anything

because of my limp," I said sharply, but she didn't notice my annoyance, or if she did, she ignored it.

"That's the way to the cafeteria," she said, nodding to our left. "On Tuesdays and Wednesdays, they have pizza. It's thick and full of cheese, and you can ask for pepperoni to be put on it if you like. I love pepperoni. The juniors and seniors have their classes mostly down on this end," she continued. Then she leaned in to say, "Everyone's going to be asking me all sorts of questions about you. For starters, who was Chinese, your father or your mother?"

"My mother."

"Did you eat with chopsticks? I hate it. It takes too long to eat. My fingers are too fat and clumsy, anyway."

"We didn't eat with chopsticks at home," I said. "But always in an Asian restaurant. You shouldn't eat fast, anyway. It's not good for you."

"Oh, are you one of those health nuts?"

"No," I said. "I'm just nuts."

She looked at me and laughed. "You lived in Santa Barbara?"

I nodded.

"I've been there, of course. It's very nice. Do you miss it?"

"I miss a lot," I said sharply. I did, of

263

course, only it had mostly to do with Mama.

She saw the tears in my eyes. "Oh, let's hurry. We've only got another thirty seconds." She began to walk faster. Keeping up with her made me limp more dramatically, and for some reason, I felt pain in my hip.

Just before we turned into the music room, she paused and said, "The music teacher's name is Denacio. Everyone loves him, but they still call him Mussolini. You know who that was?"

"Yes."

"Then you know not to fool around in here," she said, and we entered.

Nothing could have made me more curious. Why was I assigned to instrumental music? Didn't I have a choice?

Room fourteen was a bigger classroom, but the class was half the size of my homeroom. Mr. Denacio was tall and lean, with coal-black hair and a coal-black thick mustache. He had piercing ebony eyes as well. He had his jacket off and the sleeves of his white shirt rolled up to his elbows.

"Let's not waste time," he said when the bell rang. "I want to see how many of you really practiced over the summer, and don't think any of you can fool me about that."

The students around me went to their

instruments. I stood there, feeling foolish.

"Okay," he said, nodding at me. "Sasha March?"

"Yes."

"I'm Mr. Denacio. I understand you're here to learn how to play the clarinet."

I stared dumbly. Before I could say anything, he reached back and picked up an instrument case.

"It's a pretty good piece," he said. "Just take your seat over there." He nodded at an empty desk on my right. "I'll get to you in a little while."

"I never played the clarinet," I said.

"No kidding. That's why you're here to learn, Miss March. Look around you. None of these geniuses knew anything much about the instruments they play now when they began here. This is why we call it an educational institution."

No one laughed, but everyone smiled. He handed me the instrument case, and I went over to my desk. Lisa was at the rear of the classroom, taking out a flute. I opened the case and saw the inscription on the inside cover.

Alena March.

Under that was her address, and at the very bottom was a tiny goldplated plaque that read, *We love you. Dad and Mom.*

I closed the case. Why hadn't Mrs. March told me she already had this for me? I had never said I wanted to play the clarinet. Would it be ungrateful of me to refuse?

I watched Mr. Denacio test every student. He complimented only two and told the others they had to make up for ignoring their instruments. Everyone was given something to do, and then he turned to me.

"Now, then," he began, "it just so happens I can use another clarinet in the senior orchestra. Hey, stop looking so worried. You're making me nervous." He finally smiled.

"I'm not nervous. I'm just surprised," I said.

"Surprised? Why?"

"I didn't know this was here waiting for me."

"Oh. Your aunt brought it in last week. She didn't tell you?"

I shook my head

"Well, I guess it is a surprise, then, but a nice surprise, right?"

I looked at the case and shrugged.

"Enthusiastic, I see. Okay, you're what I call a challenge, and why shouldn't I have one the first day of school? Why should anything come easier to me?"

He opened the case and began to show

me how to put the clarinet together, set up the reed, and hold the mouthpiece correctly. He told me to hold it between my teeth, pretend to say "doo," and blow.

"That's it," he said. "Blowing long tones will get your abdominal muscles used to the pressure."

I did it again and again, and he smiled.

"That's a pretty good sound. Something tells me I have my new clarinet player," he said. He said it as if he had been waiting for me for a long time.

It gave me chills, because sometimes that was just the way Mrs. March made me feel.

I looked back at Lisa, who lowered her flute and smiled. Maybe it was my imagination, but it looked as if everyone was looking at me and smiling.

It was as if everyone from Dr. Steiner down had been waiting for me, as if they had all known that what would happen some rainy night on the Santa Monica highway would deliver me to this very place.

18
FAST LEARNER

"You were a big hit with Mr. Denacio," Lisa said after the bell rang. I put the clarinet in the locker assigned to me. She put away her flute, and we were on our way to English class. "I could tell, because he always looks annoyed when he gets a student to start from scratch. He'd like everyone who enters his class to be concert-ready.

"So tell me the truth," she said almost in a whisper. "You really did play the clarinet at your previous school, right?"

"No. I didn't."

"Then why was an instrument left here for you?"

"It was meant to be a surprise."

She nodded as if she understood why I wasn't telling the truth. "Everybody tells little white lies here," she said.

"I don't."

She smiled coyly again and continued walking silently. I had little opportunity to speak with any of my other classmates until our lunch break. All the time I was with her in my classes and on the way to them, I could see that Lisa was using me to make herself look more important. When we entered the cafeteria, that was even clearer. Students who were eager to learn more about me looked up from their tables in expectation. She took her time deciding where and with whom we should sit and finally decided on a table with three other girls.

We set our books down first, and Lisa introduced me to Charlotte Harris, Jessica Taylor, and Sydney Woods. Charlotte and Jessica had light brown hair cut and styled almost identically. Sydney had auburn hair brushed shoulder-length. I didn't think any of them was particularly pretty, but after Lisa introduced them all to me and me to them, they acted and spoke as if they all had won teenage beauty contests.

Lisa began by telling them as much about me as she knew. I was a little more nervous, because all of them had been to Santa Barbara frequently, and I thought they would be asking me detailed questions about stores and places to go. I waited to hear what they liked about it and quickly agreed.

"Isn't there a place you liked more?" Sydney Woods asked me.

I pretended to think about it and then shook my head. "We didn't go out to eat that much, and my father hated the beach."

That was certainly true about Daddy, I thought. Mama practically had to drag him the few times he did come along, and all he did was complain about hot sand or the water being too cold.

"So, how did you get that limp? Born with it?" Jessica Taylor asked me.

"No, car accident," I said quickly.

While I was eating, I saw Lisa lean over to whisper in her ear. How long was it going to take for everyone in the school to hear the story the Marches had created for me?

"My parents know your aunt and uncle," Charlotte Harris said. "They say they are one of the richest families in Southern California. Is that true?"

"I don't know," I said. "I don't know the other rich families."

Everyone laughed, and when they saw that I didn't mean it to be funny, they looked at each other and laughed harder. Later, that was the information that flew around the school: "Sasha doesn't know the other rich families."

I told myself I didn't care, but who doesn't want to make new friends? Before the day ended, I saw Sydney Woods talking to some of the girls in PE and obviously imitating my limp as she recited my now-famous line: "I don't know the other rich families."

New girls are a threat, I thought — not that I saw myself as prettier or smarter or even simply nicer than the girls in my class. For a while, at least, I was a bit of a mystery to them and the boys. It was practically impossible for me to enter any room or even walk down the hallway to class without being watched and studied. I was even more self-conscious of my limping, and by the time the bell rang to indicate that the last class was over, I felt like a clam that had crawled completely into its shell.

Apparently, Lisa had decided that she would be better off not clinging so closely to me after that day.

"I guess you can get around yourself now, huh?" she asked as we headed toward the parking lot.

I had books in my new book bag and carried my clarinet in my other hand. Mr. Denacio had given me instructions on what to do. He said I had to practice every night for an hour at least and added that he would know if I hadn't.

"Yes, thank you for helping me today," I told Lisa.

She flashed a smile and then hurried to catch up with the other girls. They all laughed as they exited the school. Before I got to the door, Dr. Steiner called to me from the doorway of the principal's office.

"I hear you had a good first day," she said.

I thought, *Yes, I wasn't stoned to death.* I simply looked at her.

"That's what your teachers have been telling me. I didn't speak to Mr. Cohen yet, your history teacher, since you just finished the class, but all of the others think you'll do just fine, and Mr. Denacio is quite impressed. Did you enjoy the day? Was Lisa a good big sister?"

I tried to sound enthusiastic, but I could almost see her brain clicking.

"It's not easy for anyone to start somewhere new," she said, lowering her voice a bit, "but it has to be especially difficult for you, Sasha. I understand, and I'm confident you'll blend in well here. Concentrate on the schoolwork. Everything else will come in due time."

I thanked her and walked out. A few of the girls in my class had been watching us through the door. They rushed to catch up with Lisa and the others. Everyone turned to look my way. Did they think I had complained about them? They weren't laughing. They looked like a coven of witches mumbling curses in my direction. I watched them continue to their cars. Mothers waited in most of the cars, but I saw a few fathers. Grover stood by the limousine waiting for me, so I hurried toward him.

Before I reached him, Kiera caught up with me. Her girlfriend Deidre was with her, as well as one of the boys I had seen at the pool. Kiera deliberately bumped into me, and I turned.

"Oh, sorry, coz," she said. "So how did your day go? Feel like a little fool yet?" She walked off laughing. The boy smiled but turned to see my reaction. I lowered my head and continued to the limousine. Suddenly, it had become my cocoon, and I couldn't wait to be shut away inside.

Mrs. March was waiting for me when we drove up. She came toward us so fast that for a moment, I thought she was going to be the one to open my door and not Grover.

"I couldn't wait to hear how it went," she said when I got out. "I spoke with Dr. Steiner. I was so happy with the good reports about you. Did you like the school, your teachers? Isn't it wonderful?"

"Yes," I said. Anything else might have caused an earthquake. "But you didn't tell me you had brought this clarinet for me."

"Oh. Didn't I mention that? I thought I had. Apparently, Mr. Denacio thinks you could be a natural. I'm so happy for you. I bet you can't wait to go up to start your homework. Alena was like that. Kiera couldn't stand it. No matter what Kiera did or said, she couldn't get Alena to put off her work. She was such a responsible little girl, as I'm sure you are."

For a moment, I wanted to do something that would change her mind about me, even though she was right. I did want to get right to my homework. I was so happy to have it. After all, it had been a year since I had been asked to do anything for school.

"Did you make any nice friends?" she asked as we entered the house.

"Not yet," I said.

"Oh, I'm sure you will. Mr. March will be calling soon. He was anxious to hear about you, too."

"Was he?"

"Why, of course, Sasha. That school was his precious other child. He takes personal interest in it."

"Oh," I said. I thought he wasn't so interested in me, per se. He wanted to be sure the school lived up to its reputation for excellence. Mrs. March didn't realize the difference, I thought, and I went up to my room, where I did go right at my assignments.

I was so involved in it all that I didn't realize how much time passed. Mrs. March came in to tell me that we would be having dinner soon, but that wasn't the main reason she had come.

"Did you see Kiera at all today?" she asked.

"Yes, at the end of the day."

"Thank goodness for that," she muttered. "I was afraid she had cut school the first day. Last year, she and some friends did that, as if it were some sort of great accomplishment. Her father was furious."

Not furious enough to take away her driving privileges, I thought.

"Do you have any idea where she might have gone after school? Did she say anything to you? She doesn't answer her cell phone."

I shook my head.

She looked concerned but then shook it off to smile at me. "Well, let's concentrate on you for now. Come down to dinner in ten minutes, and tell me all about your homework. We're not holding up dinner for Kiera," she said, and left.

When I went down, Kiera was still not home, and Mr. March wasn't there, either. It was once again just Mrs. March and me.

She asked more questions about school and my teachers, but before I could really answer, she would go on again about Alena and her first days. I thought she was babbling to keep from showing how nervous she was about Kiera still not being home. Finally, just before we were going to have dessert, we heard her come in. Instantly, Mrs. March rose, intending to greet her before she went upstairs, but Kiera surprised her by coming quickly to the dining room.

"Sorry I'm late!" she cried.

"Where have you been? Why didn't you answer your cell phone?" Mrs. March demanded.

"I didn't see you had called until I was on my way home and thought you'd be at dinner, Mother. I was being considerate. See? When I am considerate, you complain."

For a moment, she threw Mrs. March off, but then Mrs. March got right back on track. "Where have you been? Why didn't you come right home after school? Both your father and I told you to do so. You didn't take anyone in your car, did you?"

"Oh, no, and that was such an inconvenience. I had to go with Clarissa in her car so no one would ask me why I couldn't take anyone."

"To where?" Mrs. March practically screamed.

"To Paula Dungan's house. I told you we had all decided to form a homework club."

"What?" Mrs. March looked at me to see if I knew. I said nothing, and she turned back to Kiera. "You never told me such a thing. A homework club?"

"We're seniors, and this is a very important first half of the year, Mother. Most of us will be sending out college applications soon."

For another long moment, Mrs. March just stared at Kiera.

"I'm hungry," Kiera said, and she went to the kitchen doorway to tell Mrs. Duval she was ready to eat. Then she went to her seat and poured herself some water. Mrs. March had still not returned to the table. She stared at her. "What?" Kiera asked.

"You never told me about a homework club."

"I did so. I told you that it was going to be difficult for me, because I have to go to that stupid therapy every Tuesday and Thursday after school. If I don't do well this first half, it's because of that."

Mrs. March returned to the table silently.

Kiera smiled at me. "I bet you haven't even started your homework," she said.

"I'm almost done," I told her.

"She went right to it after school, just like Alena," Mrs. March said, quickly coming to my defense.

Kiera shrugged. "They probably made it easier for her."

"Of course not," Mrs. March said.

Kiera shrugged again. "The kids will be coming here every other Wednesday until I get out of this therapy junk. Then I can have them here two or three days a week." She turned back to me. "I heard you made quite an impression on some of the girls in your class."

"Oh?" Mrs. March said.

"Yes," Kiera said. "She's got them all limping."

She laughed at her own joke just as Mrs. Duval brought in her dinner. Mrs. March sat back, looking as if all of the air had gone out of her lungs. I began to eat my dessert. Kiera was an expert when it came to throwing her mother off, I thought. First, she frustrated her with her responses, and then she went on to talk about things that she knew would interest her mother: what the other girls were wearing, what she had learned about where their parents went for the summer, and who had bought what for their homes.

I began to feel invisible again and asked to be excused.

"I want to finish my homework and practice the clarinet fundamentals," I said. They were like magic words for Mrs. March. I, too, knew how to manipulate her when I wanted to do that, but it didn't make me feel any better to compare myself with Kiera. She looked at me with a mixture of anger and awe. She realized then that I was more than a street girl. I could play on her field. I was a much faster learner than she had expected, and for the first time, I thought she might be afraid of me. I could almost hear her concerns.

For the first time in a long time, since Alena's death, actually, there was real competition in the house for her parents' attention. Soon it might be for their love, as well, and that was more than she could stand.

Maybe, Mama, I thought, *this is how we get our revenge, our justice.*

Why else would I be there?

19
NIGHTMARES

Because I really believed I had seen those things in Kiera's face that night, I began to settle more comfortably into school, as well as into the mansion. I made some acquaintances in my classes, but no one struck me as a possible best girlfriend. Maybe it was because of my limp. Maybe it was because of my looks. Or maybe it was because of the rumors that circulated about me, rumors Kiera probably had planted. Whatever the cause, I felt a gap between me and the other girls, a gap that seemed to be widening and not narrowing with every passing day.

As the first weeks and then months went by, I heard of parties some girls in my classes had, but no one ever invited me to any. I knew there were girls who got together on the weekends and went to movies or to hang out in malls, where they could flirt with boys, but no one had asked me to join them. Sometimes I felt that girls were friendly to me just in the hope that I would invite them to the March house. When they talked about it and I said nothing, they usually drifted away.

Mrs. March continually asked me about my days at school and how I was getting along with the other girls. I tried to sound as upbeat as I could, and she accepted it, either because she believed it or because she wanted to believe it. Reports about my initial work began to flow back to her and Mr. March. When he was home for dinner, he would compliment me about it, and Kiera would either sulk or try to ignore it. What really got to her, I thought, was how quickly I was picking up the skills to play the clarinet. Mr. March was even more impressed than Mrs. March and came to my suite a few times to listen to me practicing.

Kiera tried her best to make my accomplishments sound insignificant, especially after I played my first piece of music just before dinner one night in the living room. She didn't want to listen, but both Mr. and Mrs. March insisted. I tried not to look her way, because her sour expression was enough to make Mr. Denacio himself fumble the notes.

"I can't believe how quickly she learned

how to read music," Mr. March said when I finished.

"Maybe she already knew," Kiera suggested. "From her old school."

"We had no orchestra, no band," I said. "The school had major cutbacks in financing, and art and music were dropped."

"We know that to be true," Mr. March said.

"Well, her mother might have taught her stuff," Kiera insisted.

"I don't think so," Mrs. March said, her eyes fixed on me with such adoration I had to blush. "She had other things on her agenda." She turned to Kiera. "Like survival."

Frustrated, Kiera went into retreat. She didn't say anything more about me or my past. When our first report cards came out and I had all A's, she was practically a candidate for a straitjacket. She had nothing higher than a C and had two C-minuses. Mr. March looked disappointed, but it was Mrs. March who went after her at dinner that night.

"You told me you and your friends formed this homework club for after-school sessions because the first half of your senior year was so important, didn't you?"

"These teachers hate me," Kiera moaned.

"They resent us because we're so rich."

Her father looked up. "Why, did someone say something to you that would indicate that?"

"They don't come right out and say it, Daddy. They're too smart for that, but I can see it in their faces."

"That's ridiculous," Mrs. March said. "Every girl and boy in that school comes from a wealthy family. How else could they attend with the tuition being as high as it is? No one would single you out for that, Kiera. It's a pathetic excuse for your failure to care about your work."

"Your mother's right, Kiera," her father said. "If a girl like Sasha can do so well, considering her background, you can, too. I want to see more of an effort from you."

Her face deflated. Her eyes filled with tears. She looked at me and bit down on her upper lip. "It's the therapy!" she cried. "It's driving me nuts. I can't think."

"You could go to prison if you don't follow through on that," her mother said.

Kiera looked to her father, but he didn't disagree.

"Well, you'll just have to put up with me until I'm finished with it, then," she said in the exact manner and tone of a spoiled girl. She went back to her pouting and pecked at her food.

I didn't gloat, but inside I felt good about myself for the first time in a long time. It inspired me to work even harder. I was beginning to enjoy the clarinet, as well, and some nights I practiced for close to two hours. I overheard Kiera complain to her father about the noise, but he told her just to put on her earphones like she did most of the time. That brought a smile to my lips.

Kiera wasn't yet at the point where she would talk to me during the school day, but I did often notice her watching me when I was with other students in the cafeteria. A few times, I ate outside with some of my classmates, and I thought she was going to come over to say something, but she didn't. I thought she was looking at me differently, too. I didn't see the disdain or disrespect as much. It was more as if she was curious about me, which only made me feel even better about myself.

Usually, if she did say anything to me after school, it was sarcastic or biting, but one day, she followed me out and said, "You're hanging around with nerds and losers. If you stop, the other girls might invite you to something." She didn't wait for me to reply. She kept walking to catch up with her friends.

Did I hear right? I wondered. From her tone, it sounded as if she was trying to give me good advice, looking out for my interests. What was she up to now? Had Mr. and Mrs. March come down on her for not being friendlier to me? Had she been promised something if she was? I couldn't imagine ever trusting her or believing her, and yet there was a part of me that wanted to do just that.

All I should want to do is hate her, I thought. It was easier to hate her when she was so aggressive and arrogant and mean. I hated her for being rich and pretty and popular with her friends, too. However, somehow, no matter how I tried to fight it back, I was beginning to pity her. In her mind, she was losing her father and had already lost her mother. Maybe she was becoming more of an orphan like me.

With all that I was being given materially as well as emotionally now, it was sometimes hard to remember that I was an orphan. One afternoon, whether she had intended it or not, Mrs. March reminded me. As usual, Grover was there to take me home at the end of the school day, but when he opened the rear door for me, I saw Mrs. March sitting there smiling. I was so surprised that I didn't move.

"Get in, silly," she said.

I did, and Grover closed the door. Mrs. March had said nothing the night before or at breakfast to indicate that she would be with Grover. I first thought she was on her way back to the mansion and had timed it so she could detour with the limousine to the school, but that wasn't it.

"I'm taking you to see something," she said.

"Where?"

"You'll see very soon. How was your day?"

I showed her a math test I had taken. I had gotten a ninety-eight, and I had an A on my English essay. She looked at it all and widened her smile.

"Mr. March has gotten to where he's actually bragging about you. I heard him talking to Mrs. Duval yesterday. We're all very proud of your accomplishments in so short a time, Sasha."

"Thank you."

I saw that we were not going in the direction of the mansion.

"Where are we going?" I asked again.

"To see a promise fulfilled," she replied. "Is it true that you might actually be in the spring concert this year?"

"Mr. Denacio mentioned it, but he didn't say for sure," I replied.

She nodded but looked as if she knew something more. "It would be something for a first-year instrumental student to be included in the school's senior orchestra. I knew the clarinet would come naturally to you."

I had to admit that I didn't think I would enjoy playing it as much as I had.

"You deserve your moments of happiness," she told me. "That's what today is about."

She sat back, and we drove on. Soon it became obvious to me where we were heading, and the realization made me tremble in a way I hadn't for some time. Minutes later, we turned into the cemetery and drove as far as we could before Mrs. March and I had to get out and walk the rest of the way to Mama's grave. As we drew closer, I realized why she had brought me.

There on the tombstone was the inscription I had wanted. Under Mama's name and dates, it read, "who showed her daughter a little bit of heaven." And beneath that was the calligraphy for *heaven*. It looked just like Mama's work hanging in the Gravediggers.

Mrs. March stood back and smiled as I stepped up to the stone and touched the engraved words. The engraving certainly made the tombstone special, but as I stood looking at it, I simply couldn't imagine Mama lying below, shut up in the dark, cool earth. Most of the years we had been together, she had felt trapped, trapped by Daddy's betrayals and failure to provide for us as well as he should have, trapped after he had deserted us, and then trapped by our terrible fate. She had certainly trapped herself with her drinking, and now death had trapped her. How could I free her?

"Is it like you wanted it?" Mrs. March asked. Without turning, I nodded. "I'll wait for you in the car, Sasha," she said, and walked away.

I felt my legs weaken and sat on Mama's grave with my forehead just touching the cool headstone.

"Don't worry, Mama," I whispered. "I haven't forgotten you. I'll never forget you, no matter how much they give me or do for me, no matter where I go and what I become. You will always be with me."

I thought I was going to sit there and cry, but I didn't. Instead, I tightened up inside with a resolve that made me feel stronger, harder. I took some deep breaths, and then I kissed the tombstone, rose, and started back to the car.

When I got in, Mrs. March said, "I was

hoping this would please you and not make you sad, Sasha."

"Yes, I'm pleased. Thank you, Mrs. March."

She stared at me a moment, looking a bit hurt. What did she expect me to call her, "Mother"?

"Let's go home, Grover," she said, and we drove out of the cemetery.

Neither of us spoke for quite a while. I stared out my window. Just before we were home, she told me that for the first time since I had arrived, she had to go away that coming weekend with Mr. March.

"It's a traditional thing we do this time every year. We meet some of Donald's old friends in San Francisco and go to Carmel. I'll leave very specific instructions with Mrs. Duval, who is quite capable of looking after things, and after you, while I'm gone, and I'll call often."

"I'll be okay," I said.

"Of course you will. Why shouldn't you?"

I thought she might add that Alena had always been okay while she was gone, but she said nothing more. The night before they left, both Mr. and Mrs. March warned Kiera not to take advantage of their absence. Even Mr. March sounded firm and threatening. Kiera kept her head down and didn't come back with any smart remarks. The last few days, she had come home right after school and shut herself in her room, and when she returned from her therapy sessions, she not only shut herself in her room but also refused to come down to dinner.

At first, I thought all of this was her way of playing her parents again. She was hoping to punish them for forcing her to fulfill her obligations to the court and continue the therapy she hated, but she said nothing about it to them when she was at dinner. To my surprise, in fact, she showed them her math and science tests, on which she had received high-B grades.

Mr. March looked very pleased. "This is very good, Kiera," he said. He turned to Mrs. March. "Some people just take a little longer to wake up to what's important."

"Yes," she said, but she didn't look as convinced about any change as he did. "Do keep it up, Kiera."

Because of some change in her schedule, Kiera had a therapy session on the Friday the Marches left for their extended weekend holiday. As usual lately, when Kiera returned, she went directly into her room and asked that her dinner be brought up. I ate alone. Both Mrs. Duval and Mrs. Caro kept appearing to talk and keep me company.

They both seemed nervous for me.

"Don't worry," I told them. "I've eaten alone many times."

"I'm sure you have, dearie," Mrs. Caro said. She sighed deeply and returned to the kitchen.

Afterward, I watched some television and then practiced some music Mr. Denacio had given me. By nine-thirty, I was feeling tired enough to go to sleep and prepared for bed. After I put out the lights and slipped under my blanket, I listened to what I thought of as the grand house's sad silence, but suddenly I heard a different sound. I listened harder and then rose and pressed my ear to the wall between Kiera's suite and mine. I was sure of it now. She was crying. It wasn't someone on television. It was Kiera.

Full of curiosity, I put on my robe and stepped into the hallway and up to her door. I stood there for a moment, listening. Again and again, I heard the distinct sound of her sobbing. It was a sound that every part of me should enjoy, I thought, but I didn't feel the satisfaction I would have expected or hoped to feel. I even tried to ignore her sobbing and turn to go back to my suite, but it was as if my feet were glued to the floor. I had no idea what I expected, but I knocked softly. Her sobbing continued, so I knocked a bit harder, and then it stopped.

"Who is it?" I heard her ask.

"Sasha," I said, anticipating some nasty remark to send me back to my own suite. Instead, she opened the door.

She was in her nightgown. Her hair looked as if she had been standing in an open convertible going seventy miles an hour. She wiped tears away from her cheeks and turned to go back to her bed, surprising me again by leaving her door open. I stepped in and closed it behind me.

"Why are you crying?" I asked. She lay on her back, staring up at the ceiling.

"It's the therapy," she replied.

"Oh," I said, waiting for her to complain, but she surprised me again.

"It's been giving me nightmares."

"Nightmares?"

I stepped closer to her bed. I saw that she had taken off her clothing quickly, tossing it every which way, a blouse on the floor, her skirt on a chair, socks and shoes at another place on the floor, her panties beside them. In fact, the room looked as if someone had entered it in a rage and attacked it. Books and magazines were on the floor by a table, and items on her vanity table were turned over, uncovered, and scattered.

"What sort of nightmares?" I asked.

Still looking up, she spoke like someone in a trance. "Nightmares about that night. I can't get your mother's face out of my mind. I told my therapist, and he said that was good."

She finally looked at me.

"Can you imagine that? He said it was good, good that I see her almost every night now, good that I dream about that night. I don't sleep. I feel like I'm coming apart inside, and he nods and says, 'You're making progress, Kiera. That's good.'

"Every time I go to see him now, I begin to shake. He has this calm, soft voice, but it doesn't make it any less painful. And it makes it painful to look at you," she added in a louder, strained voice, her lips trembling. She turned away to illustrate her point.

I certainly didn't want to feel sorry for her, but I couldn't get myself to say anything nasty, either. I was waiting, probably hoping for her to do or say something that would drown any sympathy I could possibly have for her, but she sobbed and then wiped her eyes and sat up.

"What I hate about him, my therapist, is how low he makes me feel without saying anything. It's like he's become a mirror."

"Mirror?"

"Yes, a mirror in which I see myself differently. I see what I've become to the people I love, how much I've hurt my parents."

She took a deep breath and looked at me silently for a long moment.

"I hated you the first day my mother brought you here. I wanted to hate you forever, but my therapist pointed out that I was doing that to make myself feel better. If I could hate you, I could live with what I did much more easily, but hate doesn't ease the pain or stop the nightmares, and you've been . . . been far nicer to me than I would have ever been to you if the situation was reversed. In fact, I've tried hard to get you to hate me even more."

"That's true," I said.

She wiped away some more tears and smiled.

"When my mother put you in Alena's room and gave you Alena's things, I really hated you, but you've never taken advantage of it. I complained. Oh, I complained to both my mother and my father, but I saw it only brought more pain to them, so I stopped complaining. When I did that and when I talked about you with my therapist, I realized I was trying to hate you for being so much like Alena."

"Why would you hate me for that? Didn't you like your sister?"

"Of course I liked her. I loved her." She looked away and then turned back. "I wanted to be more like her, wanted to have my parents believe that and see that, but I couldn't, and then you came, and you could. My therapist made me realize all this."

"I'm not trying to be like anyone," I said.

"You don't have to try. You just are." She sighed, lifting and dropping her shoulders. "My mother doesn't know how close Alena and I really were. There were many, many nights when I went to her when she was sad and when she came to me. I hated that she got so sick. I hated everyone who was healthy. I even hated my parents for not giving her healthy genes, and I especially hated the world and God. Yes, I wasn't there as I should have been when she was dying. I couldn't face it. I wasn't strong enough.

"Maybe you can't believe this, but I was looking forward to being her older sister, to guiding her through the dangerous channels we all pass through as girls. I wanted to be there for her when she had her first boyfriend. I hated being left an only child. I hate it now. Everything I've done to displease my parents was done in anger.

"So," she concluded, "I have the night-mares."

"I'm sorry," I said. I really did feel sorry for her now. "But what can I do?"

"You can help me," she said quickly.

"Me? How could I help you?"

"You're just about Alena's age, what she would have been now. Maybe you'll let me be your older sister."

"Sister?"

"I'm not saying I won't still suffer. I can't ignore what I've done. Your limping about is clearly in my face every day, no matter what I do to forget, but as my therapist says, maybe it's better to confront what I've done and not try to ignore it."

"I'm not sure I know what to do," I said.

"You don't do anything, silly. I do it all. You're being kept like a prisoner here, and it's all my fault. You should enjoy being a teenager, too. I'll take you to places, to the malls, movies, parties."

"Parties?"

"I want all my friends to know you are part of my family now. I'll admit I have a selfish motive. I want to stop feeling terrible and having these nightmares, and I want people who think I'm so terrible to see me as a better person. If you're with me, they will. Well?" she asked when I said nothing.

Maybe I was very much like Alena. Maybe I was incapable of hate and being mean, and maybe my being with Kiera would change her. I tried to think of it as a selfish thing, too. I would enjoy living there more if we weren't at each other's throats.

"It's all right with me," I said.

She smiled and reached out for my hands. "Let's make a pact, then," she said. "Let's swear that we'll try to be like sisters."

"Okay," I said.

She squeezed my hands gently, and then she let them go and fell back to her pillow. "Do me a favor," she said.

"What?"

"Just return to your room and play the clarinet for a while. Will you?"

"Play my clarinet?"

"Yes."

"Okay."

"Thank you. It will put me to sleep, a good sleep," she said, and closed her eyes.

I stared at her a moment, and then I left, feeling as though I was the one who might begin to have nightmares.

20
NEW FRIENDS

Oddly, that night, I thought I played the clarinet better than I ever had. It was as if Alena possessed me for a while and had me do it well enough to help her older sister get through her own darkness. Afterward, I went to sleep feeling contented, too. I felt safer knowing that Kiera needed me.

For the first time, she was up before me in the morning. She knocked on my door, which was already different behavior for her. Usually, she would just burst in as if I didn't have any right to privacy, especially in her dead sister's suite. I thought it was Mrs. Duval and that I had overslept and was missing breakfast, but I saw it was early.

"Yes?"

Kiera peeked in first. "Hi," she said, and entered. She was already dressed in a pink and blue tennis outfit and wore a blue wristband. I had never seen her look as fresh and as buoyant this early. She practically bounced over to my bed.

"Get up, get up!" she cried. "We're having an early, simple breakfast, and then I'm going to teach you the fundamentals of tennis so that eventually we can play doubles. I've had all sorts of professional lessons, as you can imagine, so I'm qualified to give instruction. I'm not terrific, but I'm pretty good, better than most of the girls in my circle of friends, for sure. And it won't take you long to be as good as, if not better than, them, too."

"I've never played tennis."

"That's the point, silly. That's why I want you up and out there with me this morning." She smiled coyly. "I have a few friends coming over to play later, swim, and have lunch. I got my parents' permission," she added quickly.

"Really?" I said, feeling a little excitement but not rushing to get up.

"I know what's troubling you. Stop worrying about your limping. You get around pretty quickly when you want to, and you'll see that in doubles, you don't have to move that fast, anyway."

"But I can't expect to be too good at it, good enough to play with you and your friends."

"So? None of us is going to be in any

tournaments. It's just for fun. Stop arguing. If you're going to call yourself a March, you have to live up to the March reputation for self-confidence, if not downright arrogance. My father happens to be an excellent tennis player. My mother, however, is a professional sideliner."

"Sideliner? What's that?"

"Someone who sits on the sidelines, silly," she said. "She worries about breaking a fingernail even more than I do."

I couldn't help but laugh with her, even though it felt wrong to make fun of Mrs. March. Kiera was so lighthearted and happy, I didn't want to ruin her mood. I had gone to sleep wondering if everything she had said and claimed she wanted was just words that would drift away with all of the broken promises I had heard in my life, but this morning, that didn't seem to be happening.

I started to rise, and she went to the closet.

"Alena had a very cute tennis outfit that should fit you," she said, and began to look for it. While she did, I went to the bathroom and prepared to get dressed. She was waiting with the outfit when I came out, and she stood there watching me try it on.

"You have a pretty good figure for your age," she said. "With the right clothes and makeup, no one would say you were only fourteen. I didn't have boobs and a rear end like that until I was sixteen."

Her comments brought unexpected heat to my face. I caught my image in the closet wall mirror and saw that my cheeks were crimson. It wasn't that I never thought of myself as becoming a woman. I used to worry about it when Mama and I were living in the streets, in fact, because I had not gotten my first period. I expected that our poor diet would have an impact on my development, perhaps stunting me. When my first period came, I was excited and told Mama. She had looked at me and started to cry.

"I can't be happy for you," she had said. "Not now."

But I wanted to be happy for myself. *I'll be all right after all,* I thought. Mama had once had a beautiful figure, and when I looked at myself from time to time, I dared to think I might get to look just like her, like she was before this had all happened to us.

Kiera laughed at the way I blushed. "You're embarrassed, aren't you?"

"No," I said, but not very convincingly.

"Don't you ever think of yourself as being sexy?"

"Not really."

"I bet you never really had a boyfriend, did you?"

"Not the way you mean," I admitted.

She sat on my bed and looked at me. "The way I mean? What other way is there?" She smiled. "One of the first things I wondered about you was what happened to you living on the street. I mean, what happened to you sexually."

"Nothing," I said quickly. "My mother and I were rarely, if ever, separated, day or night."

She shrugged. "It wouldn't have been so terrible if you had some experiences, but on the street, you could pick up some diseases, I'm sure."

"I was only thirteen when we went on the street."

"I lost my virginity at fourteen," she replied casually, and then leaped to her feet. "We'll talk about all this later. Let's get to breakfast. There's a lot to do before they get here."

I followed her down to breakfast. Everyone was surprised to see Kiera up so early, but it was the look on Mrs. Duval's face that nearly made me laugh. Not only was it because both Kiera and I were wearing tennis outfits, but also because there was a new

302

tone of excitement and friendliness between us. Mrs. Duval's eyebrows rose, and she hurried back to the kitchen to say something to Mrs. Caro, who found little ways to observe us at breakfast, too.

Afterward, Kiera took me out to the tennis court, and with more patience and expertise than I ever imagined she would have, she began to teach me the fundamentals. We were out there for nearly two hours before we took a break to have something cold to drink. I didn't know if she was deliberately hitting the ball softly back to me the whole time or if that was as good as she was, but even with my limp, I found I could do decently for someone playing for the first time. She continually complimented me.

"I knew you could do this," she said. "In fact, you're doing a lot better than I did when I picked up a racket. My father was so frustrated, I thought he would give up on me. I guess he did. He hired professionals."

We sat at the pool cabana and sipped Mrs. Caro's famous homemade lemonade. Despite how well we were doing together, I remained on the lookout for some sign, some remark, something that would reveal that Kiera was just being nice to me to please her parents. Nothing like that occurred. In fact, she seemed even more interested in our being closer, and she was more willing to be honest with me than she had been the night before.

"I watched you all during these first months at school," she confessed. "I saw how badly your classmates were treating you, especially those snobby girls. In the beginning, as you know, I was hoping that would make you so unhappy that you'd want to leave no matter what my mother promised you." She laughed. "I was always complaining about you to my friends."

"How much did you tell them about me?"

"Not much. Only one of my friends knows the truth about what happened, and that's Deidre, who was in the car. The rest of my friends couldn't understand my attitude toward you. How could I hate my cousin so much? What was the big deal about her living in my house? A dozen more cousins could move in, and no one would notice in my house, they would say. I couldn't explain anything to them, so I didn't try. They're my friends, but they think I'm a bitch anyway. Half of them, if not all of them, are as well. You've heard of a coven of witches? Well, my girlfriends and I are a coven of bitches."

She laughed. Her being unconcerned about what other people, especially adults, thought of her intrigued me. Did she have that self-confidence only because her father was so rich? Not constantly worrying about the impression you were making or if people were looking at you with pity and disgust was very attractive to someone like me. No matter how Mama and I looked as if we were indifferent when we were on the streets, I know I was never anything but ashamed.

"What are you going to tell your friends about me and you now?"

"Simple. I had a change of heart. They know I'm capable of that always, and besides, I don't have to explain myself to them. They're lucky I let them be my friends."

She smiled and leaned toward me. "I can see that shocks you. You've got to develop an attitude, Sasha, especially with those snobs in your class. Tell yourself you're better than they are and you will be," she declared. She sat back. I supposed she thought she was acting like a big sister now, giving me worldly advice.

"Which of your friends are coming over?"

"Deidre, who you know was in the car with me that night, is coming over today. So is Margot. I'm the closest with Deidre. Her father's a business attorney and does lots of business with my father, so she and her family were always trusted. Margot is my next-best girlfriend, but I don't confide in her as much. And of course, none of the boys knows anything, so don't worry. Boyd Lewis and Ricky Burns are coming with Deidre and Margot. You've seen them here before," she said, and added, "completely."

She laughed, and I knew she was referring to their swimming nude.

"Is one of them your boyfriend?"

"Boyfriend? Not the way you're asking. We don't think of ourselves as with one or the other. In fact, last year, we all went to the prom as a group."

"You don't like one more than the others?"

"I like playing the field and so do they. Forget that *Romeo and Juliet* stuff, Sasha. It's only in the movies, and it gets boring. There's nothing as dull to me as going steady. Don't you know what we all are? We're friends with benefits. Ever hear of that?"

I shook my head, and she laughed.

"Friends with benefits have sex but don't have romantic relationships." Before I could ask anything else, she leaped to her feet and cried, "Here they come!"

A black Mercedes convertible with its top down was rushing up the drive. We could hear the girls screaming and laughing as the tires squealed.

"Boyd is such an idiot," Kiera said, but she said it as if being an idiot was great. She shouted and waved, and they got out and started in our direction. They were all carrying small bags and tennis rackets. The girls were in tennis outfits as cute as Kiera's, and the boys, whom I recognized as the taller two of the three who had been there that afternoon, were in short white shorts, tank tops, and white caps. Despite what I thought would happen and even what she seemed to have anticipated, none of them appeared surprised to see me there.

"Everybody knows Sasha, right?" Kiera said.

"Right. Hi, Sasha," Boyd said. He was as blond as a blond could be, I thought. He wore his hair long, but it was neatly styled. Like most of the boys in the school, he had a light tan, but even his tan couldn't hide the freckles that randomly ran over his forehead and down his temples.

"She's a tennis player?" Ricky asked. He had dark brown hair and soft brown eyes. A little taller with wider shoulders than Boyd,

Ricky looked more athletic, and I thought he was better-looking.

"What makes you think you are?" Boyd asked him before Kiera could respond. The girls laughed.

I had met Deidre before at the house when she had come to watch a movie with Kiera, and I had seen Margot with Kiera often at school. She was much shorter and overweight. From the way I saw her following Kiera around, she looked content to be in her shadow.

"Sasha is just learning," Kiera said. "Don't make a big thing of it," she added in a threatening tone.

"Who here isn't just learning?" Margot quipped. She smiled at the boys. "About everything." They all laughed, and she looked quickly to Kiera to be sure she had said something Kiera would appreciate.

"Whoever sits out takes Sasha on the other court and practices with her. Make sure she has the right form," Kiera said.

"She looks like her form's all right to me," Boyd said.

"Will you shut up and just do what I say? Didn't I tell you he was an idiot?" Kiera asked me as we headed for the tennis court. Everyone laughed. "Before we're finished, you can come in for me and get some experience."

"I can't be any good yet."

"Breaking news," Ricky said, turning back to me as we walked. "None of these girls is."

That started a playful argument and some challenges. Deidre was the one who sat out the first set, so she and I went to the second court. Before we did anything, she paused, looked at the others, and then leaned toward me.

"Hey," she said. She had her hair cut short, in almost a pageboy style. I hadn't noticed it before, but she had a dimple in her left cheek that flashed in and out when she spoke and smiled. "You're doing a very nice thing for Kiera. I think it's really big of you."

I had forgotten for the moment that she was the one who knew everything. From the way she spoke, I assumed that Kiera had told her about her therapy, too, and even what she would ask of me. I didn't know what to say, so I just nodded.

"Let's hit a few balls easy," she said. "Kiera showed you how to hold the racket and swing so you don't develop tennis elbow?"

"Yes."

"That's the most important thing. I'll keep an eye on it for you."

She went to the other side, and we began. Just like Kiera, she hit the ball softly right to me, which made me look better than I was, I'm sure. Before she changed with Margot, she showed me how to hit backhand and practiced it with me. Margot was just as considerate and nice. I couldn't help wondering if they were really this way or if they were afraid of Kiera, who kept an eye on us even while she played.

As she had promised, Kiera asked me to step in for her. "Just for a few minutes," she told me.

I was reluctant, but both of the boys insisted, too, and when I did take Kiera's place, I didn't do so badly. At least, that was what they all told me.

The whole time, I felt strange about how I was reacting to being with Kiera and her friends. I would never say I wasn't having a good time — a very good time, in fact — but the more fun it seemed, the more guilty I felt. They all continued to be very nice to me, and once, when Boyd made a slightly sarcastic remark about my being inoculated to live in the same house as Kiera lived in, she pounced on him so hard he seemed to wither under her words. I felt sorry for him and told him it was all right. I knew he was just joking.

Afterward, our lunch was brought out for us just as it had been when I saw them at the pool that first day. Rosie brought a tray of hamburgers, salads, and chips. I waited to see if one of the boys or even one of the girls would pour some whiskey into our drinks, but this time no one did. We sat at the tables, and I listened to them gossip about other kids in their classes. Even though I had nothing to say, I felt that they were including me. Every once in a while, one of them would ask if I knew this one or that one. Of course, I knew no one. Margot's comment each time was, "You're lucky. Isn't she, Kiera?"

"We're all lucky," Kiera said, and gave me a look to indicate that we shared some deep secret. I saw that Margot was actually jealous.

Afterward, we all did go swimming. Kiera, Margot, Deidre, and I went into the house so Kiera and I could get our suits. The boys changed in the cabana. I was nervous about it, of course, expecting a replay of what I had witnessed before, but everyone seemed different, a lot more restrained. I couldn't help but wonder if it was only for my sake. The boys fooled around, teased, and splashed, but no one did any nude swimming and when the music came on, they danced and invited me to join them. I refused, but Boyd insisted, and then he and Ricky pulled me onto the dance floor, and both danced with me, one turning me toward him after the other had danced with me a few minutes. I was very self-conscious about my movements, but no one seemed to notice or care. I couldn't even recall when I had danced last, but I was sure it had been in our apartment, when Mama and I had still been living in an apartment.

Later, when we were all pretty much exhausted, we sprawled on chaise longues and sipped lemonade. The afternoon sun was falling below a row of trees to the west, and the cool air was refreshing. I had to admit to myself that I hadn't felt this content since I had arrived there. Everyone was so quiet that I thought they had fallen asleep.

Then Boyd spoke up. "Hey, what are our plans for tonight? I think we should go to this new, fabulous pizza joint on Venice Beach that Julian was talking about yesterday," he added before anyone could reply. "Afterward, we could do the boardwalk and gape at the freaks. What do you say?"

Kiera turned to me sharply. "I'm not in the mood for Venice Beach," she said, still looking at me. "Let's do Westwood."

"Boring," Boyd sang.

"We'll buy you a yo-yo," Kiera said, and the girls laughed. "Besides, I thought we all wanted to see the new Belly Boys movie."

"You'll see that?" Boyd asked, excited.

"What do you say, Sasha?" she asked me. "Want to see the Belly Boys movie?"

"I don't know anything about it," I said.

"Perfect reason to go," Kiera said. "We'll meet you guys at the Big Burger. I want some shoestring french fries."

She rose, which the others took as the signal that the day at the March mansion had ended. Ricky screamed that he didn't want to leave. Boyd pulled him to his feet, and then everyone walked together to the front of the mansion, where Boyd had parked. Before they got into Boyd's car, they all kissed Kiera, and then, to my surprise, they kissed me, too. We watched them drive off.

"I have completely crazy friends," Kiera said. "But I wouldn't have it any other way. What do you think?"

I nodded. Who was I to challenge her, anyway? I could barely remember the names of any classmates I had once considered friends. As Mama might have said, beggars can't be choosers.

And I was still feeling like a beggar.

I had no way of knowing, but it wouldn't
be long before that feeling would change.

21
NIGHT OUT

Mrs. Duval looked nervous about my spending the day with Kiera. When Kiera told her we were going out for dinner and a movie, she wanted to know if Mrs. March was aware of it.

"I spoke to her this afternoon, and she didn't say anything about your taking Sasha anywhere," Mrs. Duval said.

Kiera groaned. "I'll call my mother and have her speak to you again, Mrs. Duval. Chill out."

To my surprise, Mrs. March did not call Mrs. Duval after Kiera spoke to her. She called me. "What's Kiera up to, Sasha?" she asked as soon as I went to the phone.

How could I even begin to explain what had occurred? I certainly felt funny doing it over the telephone in a quick conversation. Instead, I simply told her what we had been doing. "Kiera offered to show me how to play tennis, and then we had lunch by the pool with some of her friends and went swimming. Now everyone is going to dinner and a movie. Should I say no?"

She was quiet so long that I thought she might have lost the call on her cell phone. "What brought on this sudden generosity on her part?" she finally asked, but it sounded more like she was asking herself a question aloud.

"Her therapy," I said, looking for a short-cut.

"Is that what she said?"

"Yes."

I heard Mr. March in the background asking questions. She must have put her hand over her phone, because it all sounded muffled.

"All right, but I want you to be very careful, Sasha. I wish I was there to decide about all this, but I can't be."

"I'll be all right, Mrs. March," I said.

"Yes, you will, or someone is going to hear about it," she said. "I'll call you first thing in the morning."

Not long after I hung up, Kiera came to my suite. She had clothes in her arms. "My mother hasn't bought you anything worth wearing," she began, "and Alena's things are okay for just getting around, but there's nothing for going out. You'll look great in

316

this. I've outgrown them but hardly wore them."

She held up the skirt, which didn't look as if it would cover much. Before I could say anything, she pretended she was running a fashion show.

"I have one of our newest creations, Madam. This is a red and black buffalo plaid miniskirt with what they call flirty inverted pleats and a black scalloped lace hem."

She put it up against me.

"You must surely agree, Madam, that this will be perfect for you with this black top," she said. "Please, try it on, or our designer, Monsieur Daddier, will have a stroke and a half." She snapped her fingers and called for champagne.

I laughed at her antics.

"That's not too much of an exaggeration. I've been to these fancy-schmancy boutiques and fashion shows with my mother. It's enough to make you puke. Go on, try it all on already."

I did. The skirt was the shortest I had ever worn, and the top was so tight it felt like another layer of skin.

"Beautiful. Only you can't wear a bra with that. It looks stupid. It's no big deal anymore, Sasha," she added when I showed surprise. "Don't worry about your nipples. I'll show you a little trick, no shows," she said. She stepped back and looked at me hard for a moment. "You know, I think I remember Mother buying Alena some boots that would go with this. Let me look."

She went into the closet and was out so quickly that I suspected she had known exactly where they were. They were a pair of high black boots with black fur at the top.

"Try them on. You look like the same shoe size."

I had secretly tried on some of Alena's shoes, and they had fit, so I knew these probably would. After I put the boots on, Kiera smiled.

"Wow, you're really hot. I might get jealous," she said.

Of me? How could someone who looked like her ever be jealous of me? I looked at myself in the full-length mirror. The girl who looked back at me looked so different that, for a moment, I imagined I was looking through a window at someone else and not at a mirror. Did I dare wear this?

"Now that I see you, I've got to rethink what I'm wearing," Kiera said. "C'mon."

I followed her to her suite. This was the first time I had seen her walk-in closet. It was a little bigger than Alena's, and despite the way Mrs. March had been buying Alena clothes, Kiera's looked fuller. It didn't look as well organized, but Kiera seemed to know exactly where what she wanted was located. She told me to sit on the chair at her vanity table while she tried on one outfit after another — skirts, tight jeans, and dresses. She asked my opinion about each outfit, but they all looked great to me.

Finally, she decided on a pair of designer jeans with sequins up the sides and across the waist. She matched it with a blouse that wasn't as tight as mine but left a naked midriff. Then she went to her jewelry and found a pair of earrings for me, as well as a gold necklace. After I had everything on, she looked at me and shook her head.

"Makeup," she declared, and sat me down at her vanity table. I had never used lip gloss or mascara or eye shadow. As she applied it, she told me why I needed it. She used some blush and then decided we couldn't go out without my having my nails polished.

"We don't have time to do a real manicure, but let's get some color on those fingers," she said. "Didn't you ever do any of this?"

"Once my mother did my nails, but she didn't like me wearing lipstick yet. She didn't wear much makeup herself. She had such a beautiful complexion. Once," I added.

She nodded and averted her eyes. "I never really got the chance to do much of this with Alena," she said, as if she had to match my loss with her own. Then she smiled. "But now I have you."

She did my nails. She said she would have liked to do more with me but declared that we had to get moving. We hurried out. I couldn't help feeling very excited, but when we reached the bottom of the stairway, Mrs. Duval was there and nearly dropped her jaw to the floor at the sight of me.

"Mrs. March said you have to be back by eleven," she told Kiera, her eyes still fixed on me.

"That's very unlikely," Kiera said. "I won't drive fast, and the movie doesn't end until ten forty-five. It will be closer to midnight."

"I'm just telling you what your mother told me."

"Well, I'll explain it to her when she returns," Kiera said. She didn't sound condescending or nasty. She made it seem like nothing anyone should have the slightest concern about.

Mrs. Duval turned to me. "You be careful, Sasha," she said.

"She's with me, Mrs. Duval."

"That's why I said it," Mrs. Duval replied, and walked away.

"That woman has come to hate me," Kiera said. "She can't wait for me to go off to college or something. She used to love me." She sounded as if it saddened her, but then she smiled and added, "Oh, well, you can't get everyone to love you, can you? Let's go."

When I got into Kiera's car, the excitement of wearing those clothes, changing my image with the makeup, and going to socialize with older kids took a backseat to my realization that I was in the automobile that had struck Mama and me. A feeling of dark dread washed over me. It was truly as though I were committing a sin. I was surprised that Kiera hadn't thought of what this meant. Maybe she had but was just better at burying it. She seemed to be in an entirely different place, a place where she could remember only what she wanted to remember.

"Oh, this is really exciting," she said. "I feel like I'm taking my younger sister out for her first big night on the town."

She drove very slowly and carefully through the gate and turned down the road. Because of my silence, she asked if I was all right.

"Yes," I said, but my voice sounded small,

the voice of someone lost.

"Don't you be nervous about being with these guys," she told me, misreading my silence. "They may be a few years older, but they're not an inch better than us."

Us? Was she trying to make me feel better by including me, or did she really believe that? I knew little about psychotherapy, but now I wondered if it could really be this effective. She had been going to therapy for some time. Why would the court send her if the judge didn't believe it might change her, help her?

As if she could read my thoughts, she said, "I can't wait to tell Dr. Ralston about this. He'll surely be impressed, and maybe he'll see an end to my therapy. Therapists can keep you going for as long as they want and keep that cash register ringing along the way."

She looked at me. This time, I was sure she had read my mind.

"That's not why I'm doing this with you, Sasha. I don't really care if the therapy goes on for the rest of the year. My father can afford it, and it's no big deal. The fact is, Dr. Ralston is easy to talk to now. I don't resent him as much."

"Really?"

"Let's not talk about it anymore, especially

in front of these lamebrains, okay?"

"Why do you like them if they're lame-brains?"

"Simple. Because they're fun," she said, and laughed. "It's all about fun. You'll see," she told me, and drove on.

When we got to Westwood, Kiera parked, and we walked two streets over to meet her friends. The four of them were there already and also ready to complain about how late Kiera was, but when they saw me, they were speechless for a moment.

"Who's this?" Ricky asked, smiling. "This is not your little square cousin, is it?"

"You look terrific, Sasha," Boyd said. They both looked impressed. I didn't know what to say.

Kiera spoke up for me. "I made a few small improvements with her clothes and makeup. It's no big deal. Don't salivate in the street, Boyd. It's unbecoming."

"Oh, I'm becoming," he said, and everyone laughed.

We went into the restaurant. Maybe it was my imagination, but I thought the people already seated watched us from the moment we entered.

"There are UCLA college boys here," Deidre whispered, "and they're looking at you."

"Me?"

"Get used to it," Margot said. "As long as you hang out with your cousin."

I glanced at the college boys who were looking our way and smiling. Was she right? They were looking at me? It wasn't so long ago I had thought no boys would be looking at me with any interest, and not only because of my limp. Despite all I had now and all I had been given, the magnificent mansion in which I lived, the beautiful private school I attended, I couldn't help believing that the stigma of Mama's and my street life lingered. Somehow they would see through the expensive clothes and see the stains. Maybe they would still smell the odors of the street on me, no matter how much perfume I used.

Right from the first day I had entered Pacifica Junior-Senior High School, I had feared that someone might recognize me. So many people had walked past Mama and me while we were selling on the sidewalks or the boardwalk. Why wasn't it possible that one of these students, if not more, might look at me and think, *Isn't that the same girl who sold lanyards on the boardwalk?* Maybe one of these UCLA college boys was thinking that right now.

"Don't look back at them," Kiera whispered. "They'll get annoying if they think any of us is showing interest."

I looked down quickly, and she slipped me the menu.

"The burgers are out of this world here," Boyd told me.

"Since you're not from this planet, it makes sense that you'd know," Deidre told him.

"I've sent you out of this world from time to time," he retorted.

"Shut up," she said.

Everyone laughed, but I didn't. Why were they always trying to hurt each other if they were such good friends?

"You're wrong, anyway, Boyd," Ricky said. "I'm the one who sent her out of this world. You barely got her off the ground."

"Big shots," Margot told me, pointing her thumb at them. "Or should I say single shots?"

"Ha, ha," Boyd said. "It takes only one shot to hit your target."

Fortunately, the waitress came over, and they stopped their game of insults. It took so long to get served and to eat that we had to rush to make the movie. I held them all back with my limping, but no one seemed to care if they made the movie in time or not. It was just something to do. In the theater, I ended up sitting between Kiera and Ricky. He smiled at me and let his hand drop over the seat arm so that it was against my thigh. During the movie, his fingers played with my miniskirt. I didn't know what to do, but when he lifted it a little to touch my thigh, I jumped, and Kiera turned.

"What's going on?"

"Nothing much," Ricky said. "That's the problem."

"The problem is, you don't have any patience," she told him.

"That's Ricky," Boyd said. He was on Kiera's other side and leaned over her to talk to me. "PE Man," he said, jerking his thumb toward Ricky.

"Shut your mouth," Ricky told him.

Boyd laughed and sat back.

Ricky didn't bother me for the remainder of the movie, which had some very funny scenes but was basically pretty stupid, I thought. I didn't say so, because the others, including Kiera, seemed to think it was great. Later, after we parted to go home, I asked Kiera what Boyd meant when he called Ricky PE Man.

"He was just teasing him," she said.

"I know, but I don't know what that means."

"It means premature ejaculation. You know what that is?"

"I think so," I said. I wasn't really sure.

"It's when a boy, a man, gets excited too fast and the girl gets nothing out of it."

"Oh."

"Anyway, I can tell you for a fact that it isn't true, so don't worry about it."

I looked at her. She knew for a fact?

She smiled. "Hey," she said. "Don't look so shocked. Relax. This is your first day of real class in the real school. Here, I'm the best teacher. And," she added as we reached her car, "it's tuition-free."

She laughed, but something told me it wasn't tuition-free.

Something told me there was a price to pay.

22
THE PRICE

"Mrs. Duval will be happy," Kiera said as we drove through the opened gate just before eleven-fifteen.

"How will she know what time we arrived?" I asked.

"You'll see."

Sure enough, when we parked and went into the house, Mrs. Duval was there to greet us. Kiera glanced at me and smiled.

"As you can see, Mrs. Duval, you didn't have to worry. Both of us are still in one piece," Kiera said.

Mrs. Duval said nothing. She watched us go up the stairs, Kiera giggling.

"Did you have a good time today?" she asked when we reached her suite.

"Yes, thank you."

"No, thank *you,* Sasha," she said, and then she surprised me even more by hugging me. "Sweet dreams," she said, and went into her bedroom.

I hurried to mine. It was still difficult to think of it as mine. There was so much of Alena in it, not haunting it as much as continuing to possess it. I slept in what had been her bed with her choice of headboard. Most of the clothes I wore every day had been her clothes. Her pictures were still on the dressers, tables, and walls. I wished it was different, wished that her things were gone and it was really my bedroom suite, but I felt guilty wishing that. I now knew as well as anyone that those you loved died gradually after their funerals. The blood of their immortality consists of the memories you have of them. As they are gradually forgotten or thought of less and less, they drift farther away, closing the lid on that darkness. Mrs. March, as would any mother, refused to close the lid.

Perhaps by embracing me, if that was really what she was doing, Kiera was avoiding the pain of losing her sister. Would I be doing the same thing in relation to Mama if I accepted Mrs. March even as a surrogate mother? Could you really slip people in and out of your family the way you slipped your feet in and out of different shoes? It seemed so mean and horrible to me right now, but I knew that people did it all the time. Husbands and wives remarried and slipped new spouses into the spaces beside them on their beds, into the chairs across from them at their dinner tables, and into their arms when they danced.

Maybe loneliness was worse than grief after all. The guilty feeling that followed and grew as you began to accept someone else and bury your loved one deeper could be overcome. In the beginning, you did that by using anger. How dare the one you loved so much die? How dare he or she not fight off death, defy fate or destiny, or drive away some mysterious plan God supposedly had? There should have been some greater resistance so as not to leave you alone.

After that, you thought, if the person you loved was just as loving of you, he or she wouldn't want you to be lonely. When you found someone else, it was almost as if you were building a new relationship for your loved one who had passed away as much as for yourself. Why add grief to the soul already struggling in the afterlife?

Mama would want me to have someone fill the role of a mother — and a father, too. Mama would want me to have an older sister looking after me. Mama would want me to be happy and safe and healthy. After all, she drank whiskey and gin not only to escape who she had become but also to escape feeling guilty about not providing for me. I was like a can tied to the tail of a dog or a cat. No matter how fast she ran or what turn and twist she made, I was there, clanking behind her, reminding her of just how deep down she had fallen. Maybe that was why she refused my help carrying her suitcase and why she ran so blindly in the rain that night. Maybe she was only trying to escape.

Okay, I thought as I sat on the bed while I was still dressed in the clothing Kiera had chosen for me and still wore the makeup. *I'll put on Alena's clothes. I'll accept Mrs. March's affection. More important, I'll accept Kiera and let her be my big sister, at least for now, at least until I can stand as alone as anyone can stand. I'll try not to forget Mama, but I won't use her as a reason to reject any of this anymore.*

It was fun being with Kiera and her friends. It was exciting. I liked being a regular teenager, flirting, laughing, saying outrageous things. I wanted to have their dreams and possess that same invulnerability that made them reckless, carefree, and rebellious. Up to now, since Mama's death, I had been in some sort of cloudy, vague place. Because of the fiction that had been created about me, I no longer had my name. At least, with Mama, even on the street, I knew who I was. Whatever space we found in the parks, on the beach, even in that deserted automobile, became ours, whether it was for a short time or not. There was nothing I could call mine in my new place. It was funny to think about it, but I was living in one of the biggest homes in Southern California, and I was still homeless.

So, don't blame yourself for accepting Kiera's friendship, I told myself. *Don't go to sleep feeling guilty. If you need to justify it, justify it the way Jackie Knee, your nurse, proposed. Be selfish now. Take whatever you can get, even their affection. Embrace it. Turn something into yours.*

I gazed at myself one more time before taking off the clothes and washing off the makeup. As recently as just days ago, I would never have imagined myself looking and feeling like this. A new kind of energy had entered my body. I could see it in my eyes and could feel it everywhere, tingling right down to the small of my stomach. I loved the new feeling.

I looked back at the bed as if I expected to see my old self lying there, looking as lethargic and lost as ever but angry at me for leaving her behind.

Go away, I wanted to tell her. *Go your mousy way into the shadows, and drown yourself in self-pity. Dwell on your limp. Practice your "Yes, sir" and "No, sir," and remain a beggar hoping for some handout of love. Do that while I seize the tail of the wind.*

My old self disappeared like smoke. With a new bounce in my steps despite my limp, I prepared for bed, and when I went to sleep, I didn't think about Alena and my sleeping in her nightgown and in her bed with her favorites, the giraffes, above me. I thought about myself and about the way those UCLA college boys had been looking at me.

For the first time in a very long time, I couldn't wait for morning.

I was already dressed when Kiera came around. She was still in her robe and slippers. "Why did you get up so early?" she complained. "It's Sunday."

"I couldn't sleep anymore," I said. "I felt so awake and anxious to start the day." She saw and heard the change in me and smiled. "I'm hungry, too."

"Me, too. I know. We could have breakfast brought up to us. Let's have it in my suite. It's like room service in the best hotel, after all," she said, going to the phone.

I was sure that when she picked up the

receiver, Mrs. Duval thought I was calling.

"This is Kiera," she said. Although Mrs. Duval would certainly recognize her voice, Kiera obviously liked to announce herself as if she were a princess. "Sasha and I will be taking breakfast in my suite this morning, Mrs. Duval. I'll have my usual Sunday breakfast, and Sasha will have . . ." She listened and then shook her head. "I don't know if she wants that." She put her hand over the mouthpiece. "Do you want your usual cheese and egg omelet?" She grimaced and shook her head. "Or what I have?"

"I'll have what you have," I said. I knew that on Sundays, she had a cup of fruit sorbet with a dab of whipped cream, coffee, and glazed doughnuts. Mrs. March always complained about the way Kiera ate.

"She'll have exactly the same as me, Mrs. Duval. Thank you very much." After she hung up the phone, she laughed. "She didn't sound pleased, but they're here to please us, and not vice versa. I'm going to go take a quick shower. Oh," she added at the door, "I sorta agreed we'd go to Disneyland today. Ricky's getting his father's SUV. It will hold us all. They'll be here in about an hour."

"Disneyland?"

"Yes. Have you ever been there?"

"No, but . . . when will we return?"

"I don't know. What's the difference?"

"Homework left to do," I said.

"We'll get to it when we can. If we can," she added with a smile. She paused and tilted her head a little as she looked at me. "What are you wearing? I think Alena wore that to someone's baptism. Don't worry. When you come into my suite, I'll have something better for you."

"Okay," I said, and she left.

I looked at the clothes I had put on. Mrs. March sort of suggested things for me to wear by organizing the front of the walk-in closet so I could go from outfit to outfit. I hadn't thought much of it, but I certainly didn't want to go to Disneyland dressed the way I would dress if I were going to a baptism.

I had always wanted to go to Disneyland, but for Mama and me, it was too expensive after Daddy deserted us, and when he was still there, he never wanted to take me or spend the money. I imagined it would be more fun going with Kiera and her friends, anyway. I knew it was at least an hour away. It would certainly take up the whole day.

I gazed at the clarinet. Besides the homework I still had, I was also supposed to spend a good hour on the new music Mr.

Denacio had given me to practice on the weekend. He was so good at detecting when you didn't practice. Somehow, I thought, I'd get it all done.

Before I went to Kiera's suite to have breakfast, my phone rang. It was Mrs. March, and from the tone of her voice, I suspected that Mrs. Duval had called her as soon as she had hung up from Kiera's call.

"How are you this morning?" she asked.

"I'm fine, Mrs. March."

"Where did she take you last night?"

I told her about the restaurant and the movie and added that we had come right home after the movie. I also said that Kiera had driven carefully. Mrs. March was quiet a moment and then asked if any of Kiera's friends had tried to get me to smoke something or take something.

"No," I said. "Nothing like that happened. They were all very nice."

"Nice?" she said, as if I had said something good about Nazis. "Just be very, very careful with them and with Kiera," she reiterated. "Okay, we'll be flying into L.A. about five. I look forward to seeing you at dinner and hearing more about your day and night."

It was on the tip of my tongue to tell her we were going to Disneyland, but I hesitated, and she said good-bye. *Oh, well,* I thought. Surely Kiera knew we had to be back by dinner. She knew when her parents were returning. It would be all right.

She was still in her robe but drying her hair when I entered her suite.

"Ricky called," she said after she turned off the hair dryer. "He wanted to be sure you were coming along."

"Really?"

"He says there's something fresh about you."

"Fresh?"

"I explained that you were a virgin," she said, making it sound as if I had come from another country, maybe another planet.

"Oh. What did he say?"

"What do you think?" she asked. I waited. "He said too bad."

She laughed hard just as Mrs. Duval brought in our breakfast.

"Perfect. Thank you, Mrs. Duval," Kiera sang.

Mrs. Duval looked at me as she put the tray on the table. "Be sure to take your vitamin," she said. "Mrs. March was concerned."

"Oh, brother," Kiera muttered loudly. "You've already told my mother what we're eating for breakfast?"

Mrs. Duval turned to her. "You should be taking your vitamins, too, Kiera, especially the way you eat."

"I don't think I look so bad for it, Mrs. Duval."

"I'm not talking about the outside of you," she replied.

Kiera groaned.

Mrs. Duval shook her head, looked at me with a warning in her eyes, and left.

"I hope she didn't make the coffee as weak as she has been making it," Kiera said, coming to the table. "Oh, your clothes are laid out on my bed there. You can change after we enjoy our nutritionally worthless breakfast."

Now that I started to eat what she ate, I wondered why I had not asked for my special eggs. It was too much sugar, and just looking at it actually made me feel a little nauseated. She finished her sorbet almost before I had started.

She grimaced when she sipped her coffee. "It's more like tea. My mother tells her to make it like this for me."

"Your mother called me," I said as I nibbled at the doughnut.

"This morning?"

"Yes."

She stopped sipping her coffee and put

her doughnut down. "Probably after Mrs. Duval let her know what you were having for breakfast. What does my mother expect you to be, her little spy now?"

"No," I said.

"What did you tell her about our day together?"

"Nothing bad. I told her we had a very nice time."

She thought a moment and then shrugged. "Whatever," she said, and went at her doughnut.

After we ate, I put on the outfit she had chosen. It was a pair of slightly destroyed denim shorts with raw cuffs and a tank top that read "Fresh Air Turns Me On." I was surprised at how tightly the shorts fit. There was something uncomfortable in the rear, and I reached in and discovered a tag.

"You never wore these?" I asked.

"Oh," she said. "I probably never noticed." She grabbed some scissors and cut it off. "They look perfect on you."

"I think they're too tight."

"That's perfect, silly. You don't want to look like some old lady."

The top hung loose, however — too loose, I thought. My bra was half out. "I'm swimming in this."

"I'll give you a shell to wear instead of

your bra," she said. "It'll look great."

When she put on what she was going to wear, I thought she looked more conservative. Her jeans weren't tight, and she layered a shirt and a top but wore her bra.

"I'm not sure I look good," I said, gazing at myself in her full-length mirror.

"Trust me, you're dynamite. Now let's go find a reason to explode," she said. Her phone rang. "We'll be right down," she said, and hung up. "They're pulling in. Let's go."

We almost left the house without anyone knowing, but Mrs. Duval spotted us just as we reached the front door. "Where are you going?" she asked, hurrying toward us. "Your parents will definitely be home for dinner," she added.

"We're going to Disneyland with friends, Mrs. Duval. Didn't I mention it this morning?"

"No, you didn't."

"Didn't I? I'm sorry. We probably won't make it back in time for dinner. I'll call you if we can."

Before Mrs. Duval could respond, Kiera opened the door and shouted at Ricky and the others as they pulled up to the front of the mansion. She grabbed my hand to pull me out, and I looked back at Mrs. Duval. She gazed at me and shook her head as if I were about to step off the edge of a cliff.

It made me hesitate but only for a moment. The boys were howling as we stepped out.

"Who's that foxy girl with you, Kiera?" Ricky called.

The laughter and shouting replaced my worry with excitement. It hadn't been that long ago that I was desperate on a street. *Now look at yourself,* I thought.

You're a foxy girl.

23
HAPPIEST PLACE ON EARTH

Kiera decided that I should sit up front with Ricky since this was my first trip to Disneyland. On the way, everyone argued about the best rides and events. The boys liked Pirates of the Caribbean the most, and the girls favored Alice in Wonderland. I was surprised to hear that most of them had been there a dozen times at least. Because I didn't want to look and sound like some wide-eyed, dazzled child, I didn't want to say it, but I felt like Alice in Wonderland when we arrived and started down Main Street.

I was surprised at the attention I was receiving. Everyone wanted to show me something he or she liked. I was rushed along from one ride to another. Whether or not Kiera had coached the others about making me feel wanted, I did feel like part of their group and as if I had been for some time. Ricky was especially attentive and sat with me on every ride, especially Autopia. Boyd and Margot were right behind us in their car, deliberately bumping us every chance they had, but it was all great fun. I had never laughed and screamed so much.

After lunch, we went to Indiana Jones and then to Alice in Wonderland. Both Ricky and Boyd were ecstatic when I voted with them on best attraction and created a tie. The girls weren't upset. We joked about it and finished the day by going to the 3-D show of *Honey, I Shrunk the Kids.* I had not even looked at the time once and was shocked to see that it was nearly six-thirty. There was no question now that we would not be home for dinner. Kiera didn't seem at all nervous or upset about it. On the way home, we stopped at one of Deidre's favorite restaurants. By the time Ricky drove through the Marches' gate, it was nearly nine-fifteen.

No one worried about doing homework. In fact, nothing about school had been mentioned all day until Ricky said he'd see me the next day at school. Kiera and I got out and watched them drive off. I felt exhausted, but it was a happy sort of exhaustion that I would welcome again and again. I thanked Kiera. She had paid for everything for me, of course.

"Ricky seems to genuinely like you," she commented as we opened the door. "He's usually very critical of younger girls."

I basked in the compliment, but only for an instant, because Mrs. March came marching out of the living room with a look of anger I had not seen before.

"Earthquake coming," Kiera whispered.

"How dare you keep Sasha out all day and have her miss dinner?" she began. "Your father is too angry to come out of his office."

"She didn't miss dinner. We stopped on the way home."

"I don't mean that, and you know I don't mean that, Kiera. We worked out our travel schedule so we could have dinner together when we returned. And why didn't you answer your cell phone? Either of you?" she asked, looking at me.

"I didn't have mine with me," I said.

"Come to think of it, neither did I," Kiera said. "Everyone I wanted to talk to today was with us, anyway."

That brought blood into Mrs. March's face. For a moment, rage choked her throat, and she couldn't speak. Then she looked at me again. "What are you wearing? Where did you get those clothes?"

"They're mine," Kiera said.

344

"I never saw them before. Those shorts are inappropriate."

"Please, Mother, don't be a prude."

"And they're surely not warm enough."

"They were," Kiera said. "We weren't exactly on a hiking and camping outing. Can we go upstairs now? We both have homework."

"I'm very disappointed," Mrs. March said, stepping back. She was saying it mostly to me.

"You wouldn't have been if you had come along. Disneyland was great today. The lines weren't that long and . . ."

"Go to your room, Kiera. We'll discuss this tomorrow," Mrs. March said.

I lowered my head and followed Kiera to the stairway.

"My father's not as angry as she claims he is," she whispered as we went up. "Otherwise, he'd be out here, too."

I didn't say anything. The look of disappointment on Mrs. March's face was not only sobering, it was a little frightening. Maybe now all her of kindness and generosity would end. Perhaps she no longer saw me as being as good and as nice as her Alena. If anyone had told me months ago that I would fear being sent away, I would have practically laughed because it seemed such a ridiculous possibility. How could I ever get to care much about being with the girl who was driving the car that night or the family that protected her? All of the gifts, the money, the clothes, and the wonderful new school would not buy my forgiveness.

"Don't worry," Kiera said, seeing my silence and concern. "She won't be as angry tomorrow. That's the way she is."

"I'd better finish my homework," I said, and hurried to my bedroom.

When I entered it, I felt even worse. It was as if I had let down Alena as much as Mrs. March. *I thought you were going to be me for my mother,* her picture said to me. *I'd never have done that.*

Looking at myself in Kiera's clothes suddenly disgusted me. I took them off as quickly as I could and put on one of Alena's nightgowns before getting to my homework. It took me so long to finish that there was no time to practice the clarinet. I was so bleary-eyed by then anyway that I couldn't stay awake and, in fact, overslept.

Mrs. March came in to wake me. "You'll have to rush," she said, and then she just left without another word.

I got up quickly. I could hear her yelling in Kiera's bedroom, and a door slammed. I dressed as fast as I could and hurried down to breakfast. Mr. March apparently had left already. Mrs. March was at the table but had her head in her hands, her elbows on the table, and didn't look up when I entered.

"I want you to be sure to come directly home after school today," she said, still looking down at the table. "Do not permit Kiera to talk you into coming home with her and sending Grover back without you." She raised her head. "She wants you to go back and forth to school with her, but I refuse to permit it. In fact, I don't want you riding with her anywhere unless I specifically say. Understand, Sasha?"

"Yes."

"I don't know what went on here exactly while I was away, but I'm not pleased," she concluded.

"I'm sorry," I said.

Kiera sauntered in and poured herself a cup of coffee. "They're still making the coffee too weak," she told her mother after sipping some.

"I think you have more important things to think about than the strength of your coffee, Kiera."

"We just went to Disneyland, Mother. Don't make it into a federal case."

Mrs. March narrowed her eyes. "Rein

yourself in, Kiera. You're heading for another major disaster," she warned.

Kiera smirked and nibbled on a pastry. Then she just threw it down, got up, and left. Mrs. March didn't say anything, even to me.

I finished, got my things, and hurried out to the limousine. After being with Kiera and her friends, hearing their laughter and seeing their joy, it was even more depressing to be alone in the big vehicle. If anything, it made me feel as if I had shrunken again and was back to being the mousy little girl with a limp.

After homeroom, I dreaded walking into Mr. Denacio's class. The moment I took out the clarinet, his eyes shifted with suspicion. I hadn't played for more than thirty seconds before he stopped me.

"You didn't practice at all, did you?"

"No," I said.

He didn't say anything. He nodded and went to the next student, but that sort of quiet reaction of his was worse. I felt his disappointment and his conclusion that I was finally like most of the others and would not be anyone special after all. It was like almost getting to the top of a mountain and then sliding all the way back down. I wanted to cry. I tried to be enthusiastic for the remainder of the period but couldn't get my energy level up and was happy when the bell rang.

I wasn't as alert in any of my morning classes as I usually was and actually went into a daydream during math. I missed the entire explanation of a problem, and when called upon, I didn't know where we were in the lesson. There, too, my teacher didn't reprimand me. He just looked at me as if I had let him down and went on to another student. By the time lunch period came around, I felt as if I had stepped in quicksand and was nearly in it above my head. I certainly had no appetite.

But before I could settle into my funk and cry to myself, Ricky grabbed my arm. "We're eating outside," he said.

I looked at him with surprise. It was one thing to do things with Kiera and her friends on the weekend, but for them to want me with them at school, too, was quite another. My classmates and the girls with whom I usually sat looked up with as much surprise as I had when I filled my tray and followed Ricky out to their table.

He made a place for me, and I sat beside him.

"Why so sad a face?" Margot asked immediately.

"Not that it's any of your business, but my mother gave us a hard time for missing dinner with her and my father last night," Kiera said quickly. "I suppose that's still bothering her."

"Hey, don't mope, Sasha. It was worth it," Boyd said. "It was the best time I've had there."

That started us all reviewing the day at Disneyland. Before I knew it, I felt upbeat and happy again, especially with the way they were including me in everything they said. When the bell rang, Ricky helped me with my tray, and we walked out of the cafeteria together. Out of the corner of my eye, I saw the way Charlotte Harris, Jessica Taylor, and Sydney Woods were watching us. When Ricky and I parted in the hallway, they approached me quickly before I entered class.

"How come Ricky Burns is so interested in you?" Charlotte asked.

"Did you go out with him?" Sydney followed before I could answer.

I looked at the three of them. When I first came to the school and met them, I was of no interest. They mocked my limping and never thought to invite me to anything once I didn't invite them to the March mansion.

They rarely said a word or sent a smile my way.

"Who's Ricky Burns?" I asked, and went into the classroom, leaving them stone-faced behind me. I laughed to myself.

When I sat and looked back, they were in deep conversation among themselves and Lisa Dirk, my first-day big sister who had had nothing much to do with me thereafter. They all looked my way, and I smiled at them.

I did much better in my afternoon classes. Before my last class, Kiera tapped me on the shoulder and asked if I wanted to go with her after school. "We're heading to the Century City Mall."

I hadn't told her that her mother had forbidden me to ride with her without her specific permission and didn't want to do it now and start her on some tirade.

"I can't," I said. "I have too much to do."

"You're missing a great time," she sang. "If you change your mind, let me know as soon as the bell rings, and I'll send Grover back home without you."

I couldn't deny that I wanted to go, but I was too frightened this time. I deliberately took longer to leave my last class. Even so, Kiera loitered near the doorway.

"Change your mind?" she asked.

"No, I can't, but thanks," I said.

"Too bad," she said. "Tomorrow I have to go to therapy."

"I know. I'll see you at home."

"Home? Right," she said, and left me quickly. I saw her meeting the others in the parking lot. Ricky looked my way, shrugged, and then followed everyone else.

Did he really like me much? I wondered. I was fourteen, a girl who had never had a boyfriend or even a boy just interested in her, and a senior at my new school was looking at me romantically after spending only two days with me and his friends. He was one of the best-looking boys at the school, too. I hated seeming so young and innocent. I tried to talk and act more like Kiera when I was with her and her friends, but running home that afternoon probably made me look like a child again. Tomorrow they would have no interest in me, I thought, and my classmates would not be so friendly, either.

I sank back into a deep funk and remained there all the way back to the March mansion. When I entered the house, I headed for the stairway, waiting to get into my homework so I could have time to practice the clarinet. I paused when I heard some loud voices and realized that it was Mr. and

Mrs. March. When I heard my name mentioned, I turned toward the living room and listened.

"You're not making any sense, Jordan," Mr. March said. "You said you brought this girl here to save her from the streets and the orphanages or whatever. You wanted her to have a family, right?"

"Yes, but . . ."

"So why wouldn't having Kiera as an older sister make her more part of our family? And look what good this can do for Kiera. It's her way of achieving repentance, feeling remorse. Her therapy is going well, and now you want to stop her from being too close or influential with Sasha? It makes no sense to me. If you're that worried about Kiera being a bad influence, then maybe it would be better if we found another home for Sasha," he said.

Mrs. March was quiet. I held my breath. "It would be terrible to send her away now," she finally said.

"Well, then?"

"Okay, Donald, I'll try to keep an eye on both of them for now."

"If there's one thing we don't need, it's more tension in this house," he said.

They were both so quiet that I thought they'd be coming out and see that I was eavesdropping, so I turned away quickly and headed for the stairway. Once in my suite, I sat and pondered what I had heard. What was Mrs. March agreeing to let me do? I was as conflicted as she was at the moment.

On one hand, I wanted to be with Kiera and her friends, go out, go to their parties, go on their trips, everything, but on the other hand, I wanted to do well in school, too. Kiera and her friends didn't seem all that interested in school or concerned about their grades.

It would be like walking on a balance beam, I thought. Could I do it, do both?

If I fell this time, the fall might be too long and deep for me to make any sort of recovery, and then where would I be?

Probably following Mama's ghost on some backstreet and wondering how I had become so trapped in my recurring nightmare.

24
RULES

Mr. March was at dinner that night. This time, Kiera made sure she was there, as well. She didn't come to my room when she returned from the mall. I thought she was still upset about my deciding not to go with her and the others after school, but when she came down to dinner moments after I had arrived and taken my seat at the table, she smiled at me and apologized for not coming to my suite to fetch me.

"I wanted to be sure you got some of that homework done," she said. Then she looked at her father and added, "They give students in the ninth grade more work than they give us seniors. I remember." She turned to her mother. "You remember, Mother. I was complaining about it when I was in ninth grade, and they told you it was the transition grade from junior high to high school."

Mrs. March nodded but said nothing. Her eyes betrayed her deep suspicion of Kiera's sudden sweet talk. No one said anything while Mrs. Duval and Rosie began serving.

Then Mr. March clasped his hands and began what was obviously his and Mrs. March's compromise. "I'm pleased to see you including Sasha in some of your activities with your friends, Kiera, but you have to remember that for now, along with being younger than you, Sasha is a different sort of responsibility for us. We are acting as her foster parents, and therefore it doesn't begin and end with us.

"Naturally," he continued, looking at me, "we don't want her to feel strange or different. We want her to feel she's part of our family. However, we have to supervise her activities more closely. We need to maintain more control, follow more rules. So, before you decide to go anywhere with her, you must get either your mother's or my permission. We want her curfew maintained. For now, we don't think it's appropriate for her to be out later than eleven."

"Even on weekends?" Kiera cried.

"Even on weekends," her father said.

She shook her head, glanced at me, and looked down.

"The second we hear of any misbehavior, and you know by now what I mean by misbehavior, around her or including her, everything changes for both of you, understand?"

Kiera said nothing. She did glance at her mother, with what I thought was a look of such disgust and rage that it would surely have turned my heart into stone if I were Mrs. March.

"Now," he said, sounding softer, "if you're going straight to school in the morning and if you return straight home after school on the days you're not attending therapy, Sasha may ride with you. It would free up Grover and the limousine for your mother's use and mine at times."

Kiera started to smile.

"But if I hear of any bad driving, speeding, or anything of the like, I will take away your driving privileges, and of course, we'll forbid Sasha to go anywhere with you."

"We have to come right home all the time? Sometimes we like to get a snack or something, Daddy."

"If there is any change, call your mother and get her permission first," he said, relenting.

Kiera looked satisfied but wasn't. She was an expert when it came to manipulating her father.

"May I just say, Daddy, that it's very difficult for us to go to a movie or a house party or anything, for that matter, and have to be back by eleven on weekends. Half the time, the movie doesn't let out until nearly eleven, just like it did the other night. It's not good to have that sort of pressure on someone. I'll end up driving too fast just to make the curfew. Either I do that or not include Sasha in things."

"Eleven is late enough for a girl in the ninth grade," Mrs. March said.

"Not in today's world," Kiera countered.

"Let's leave it between eleven and twelve," her father said. "Call it the pumpkin factor."

"Pumpkin factor?" Kiera asked.

"Cinderella," I said.

Mr. March smiled. "That's right, Sasha. Remember? At twelve, her carriage turned into a pumpkin."

"Which one of us is Cinderella?" Kiera asked impishly.

I thought she was also looking for some clear expression of affection from her father, but before he could respond, her mother did. "I hardly think it's you, Kiera," she said. "You already live in a castle."

"You're right, Mother," Kiera said. She turned to me. "Then maybe Sasha will get her prince after all."

Her father laughed, but her mother didn't.

She heard something I heard, too. It sounded more like a threat than a promise of something nice. After that, the conversation changed to other topics, mostly between Mr. and Mrs. March. When we left to go up to our rooms, I wasn't sure who had won the argument I had overheard earlier, Mrs. March or Mr. March or Kiera. From the expression on Kiera's face, I was sure she believed she had.

"Don't worry," she told me, "we'll find ways to avoid coming right home on the days I can drive you."

"As long as I can get done what I have to get done," I said as a caution.

She didn't hear me or care to. Instead, she went into her room after she said, "Ricky really missed you after school today."

Her comment really distracted me. I had to concentrate harder to complete my homework and get to the clarinet. I was determined to impress Mr. Denacio in the morning, but a half hour into my practice, I had very bad cramps. I knew what it was; it was my time of the month, but it hadn't been this bad since I began to be regular again.

I don't know if it was because of our poor nutrition or simply the stress that came with living in the streets, but I had hardly begun to have periods before we were evicted from the apartment and then had to leave the hotel. In those early days, Mama was always there for me, but once we were on the street, I was on my own. I made sure I always had what I needed, but sometimes I would go weeks overdue, and once I went nearly two months. Since living with the Marches, I was clock-regular. I had merely forgotten that it was my time, but the severe cramps were more than a reminder; they were an alarm bell.

I prepared for my flow to begin and then curled up in bed, which was the way Kiera found me when she came to my room to tell me about something very secret. For a moment, she didn't realize what was happening to me. I had my eyes closed and my hands pressing on my tummy. She really didn't look at me. She entered and began to pace.

"I've been debating telling you about our secret club," she began. "There are the three of us, Deidre, Margot, and me, but we inducted Marcia Blumfield and Doris Norman recently, so now there are five of us, and . . ." She paused when she really looked at me. "What's your problem?"

"Monthlies," I said.

"Monthlies? What are monthlies? Is that

what you call it?"

"My mother did. I have very bad cramps this time."

"Isn't that something? I was just going to ask you about your period. Are you regular?"

"I am now," I said, "or have been since I've been here."

"Well, that's good. Don't worry. I have something for cramps. I'll go get it."

"You do?"

"Of course I do. Do you think I want to be all twisted up like you are right now? Besides, we have to stick together through pain and pleasure." She started out, then paused and turned. "Which, by the way, is the motto of our secret club."

"What secret club?"

"The one I was considering telling you about. Now," she added, "I definitely will."

She sauntered out, leaving me as confused as ever, but if she could help stop my cramps, I wouldn't care what silly thing she had to say next. She returned quickly and handed me a glass of water and a pill.

"What is it?"

"Something my doctor prescribed. It works fast. You'll see."

I took it and swallowed it down with water. "Thanks."

"No problem. I have more if you need it in the morning, but they usually work overnight."

Even though the cramps didn't lessen, I lay back and breathed easier. "What were you talking about before? I really wasn't listening."

"I know. It's not important right now. I'll tell you about it later. Hey," she said, starting out again. "You don't have to rush to get up. You're going to school with me tomorrow. I know a shortcut Grover doesn't know. Night." She left quickly, as if she had to talk to someone or do something.

Kiera's pill worked wonders. I felt a lot better in the morning and let her know at breakfast.

Mrs. March rose a little later than usual and entered just as we were talking about it. "What pill?" she asked immediately.

"My monthlies pill," Kiera said, teasing me.

"What?"

"You know what happens to us monthly, Mother."

"I repeat. What pill?"

"The one Dr. Baer gave me for cramps."

"Oh," she said. She looked at me. "I didn't know you were having any problems, Sasha."

"It's not a federal case, Mother. She came to me, and I helped her," Kiera said.

I practically spun around in my seat. *Came to her?*

"I'm getting tired of hearing that stupid expression, Kiera. I'm sorry your father taught it to you. No, it's not a federal case, but Sasha should know to come to me with her problems," Mrs. March said. She didn't sound angry as much as hurt.

Kiera shrugged. "I just happened to be around at the right time. It's not . . . it's no big deal."

Mrs. March stared at her a moment and then turned slowly back to me. "How are you now, Sasha?"

"I feel better, Mrs. March. Thank you."

"You know you can come to me with any problem, no matter how big or how small."

"I know. Thank you."

"We might stay after school tomorrow," Kiera said. "Mr. Bowman is casting for the school play."

"You would go out for the school play?"

"I might," Kiera said. "It's my last chance to do something like that, and I know Sasha will be interested, if not in being an actor, maybe in helping with the sets."

"That would be nice."

Again, I looked at Kiera. We had never

discussed anything like that, and besides, I didn't recall any casting for the school play being announced. Afterward, on our way to school, I brought that up.

"That's because he hasn't announced it yet," she said. "Don't worry. I'll just tell her I made a mistake. It's next week. I got the dates confused."

"You can't lie to your mother all the time, Kiera."

"Who's lying all the time?" She laughed. "Just when it's absolutely necessary, and tomorrow it's important that we don't go right home."

"Where are we going?"

"To a meeting."

"Meeting? What kind of meeting?"

"A meeting of the secret club I was trying to tell you about last night. It's at Deidre's house."

"What kind of club is this?"

"It's the VA."

"VA? Isn't that something to do with veterans?"

She laughed. "Absolutely. Everyone in the club is a veteran."

"Of what?"

"Sex, silly. VA stands for Virgins Anonymous," she said, laughing.

"I don't understand."

"You will," she said. "And it will be the most exciting club you've ever been in."

"I've never been in any."

"Perfect. You're a virgin when it comes to clubs, and tomorrow, we'll end that."

She sped up. I tried to ask more questions, but she said I should just be patient and promised I wouldn't be disappointed.

I wasn't disappointed at school. Once again, Ricky asked me to join him at lunch, which once again captured the attention of my classmates. I could almost feel the buzz about us growing with every word we spoke to each other and every step we took beside each other.

"I might be able to get my father's boat one of these weekends," Ricky told me on our way back to class. "It's at Marina Del Ray. If I can, we'll all go to Catalina Island. You ever been?"

"No," I said. I was sure I sounded like someone locked in a closet. No matter what place they all discussed or mentioned, I had not been there, and as far as I knew, all of them except Deidre thought I was Kiera's cousin. Either because Kiera would come down on them if they did or because they were just being kind, no one wondered aloud how I could not have done half of what they had done. I did hear Kiera whisper to Margot that my family was poorer relatives, but from what I could see of the Marches, ninety-eight or ninety-nine percent of the country was poorer than the Marches.

"Great. It's always fun to show someone places and things for the first time," Ricky said. It seemed, at least for now, that there was nothing I could do or say that would discourage his interest in me.

I was having a better day all around. Although Mr. Denacio wouldn't say anything nice about my playing that morning, I could see that he was cautiously optimistic about me again. I did better in all of my classes and got a ninety on a pop quiz in history. I could feel my confidence growing stronger all day and was quite convinced that I could walk that beam. I could do it all.

Grover was there waiting for me after school. I didn't see Kiera, but I knew she was off to her therapist. Grover rarely said anything to me, but this particular afternoon, he smiled and asked how my day had gone. I think he saw something new, healthier, and stronger in me and wasn't afraid that he might do or say something that would send a stampede of tears down my cheeks.

I even felt better about being in the limousine. I didn't feel shut up and alone. Maybe I was catching Kiera's arrogance, but I sat back and looked out the window at the other students emerging. I deliberately lowered my window so they could see me, too. Lisa Dirk stared at me a moment and then lifted her hand to wave. I flipped my hand like a queen I had once seen in a movie, and Grover drove us away.

Cinderella was in her carriage.

No pumpkins here, I thought.

25
CONSPIRATORS

"Even though Deidre and Margot know you a lot better now," Kiera began just before dinner, "they're still a little nervous, and the other two are very nervous, about my bringing you to a meeting of the VA club. It's a very private, secret club. You've practically got to take a blood oath that what you see and hear at Deidre's tomorrow after school will never leave your lips, even if you're not accepted. Can you promise to do that?"

I put down my math book. I had gone at my homework with a vengeance, partly because I was afraid that when she returned, she would take up all my time again, and I wouldn't have time to finish or practice the clarinet.

"Maybe I shouldn't go, then," I said.

"Oh, no. I've assured everyone that you're not the sort who betrays friends. In fact," she said, twirling a strand of her hair, "I told them you were very excited about it after I described it to you. I told them that in your heart, you were one of us and definitely no prude. However, for this first time, I wouldn't advise you to talk too much. Just listen, and look at me if anyone asks you anything you're not sure about or think you should answer."

"You didn't really describe it all to me, Kiera."

"We've got to leave something for a surprise," she protested. "Believe me, you're not going to be disappointed."

"What do they really know about me?"

"Just what we've told them. I added that your mother was controlling, and you were frustrated. That's why you never had a real boyfriend or even a friend with benefits. Except for Deidre, of course, they all bought everything I told them."

"Can't you at least tell me exactly what we do at this club?"

"We talk and advise and help each other."

"With sex?"

"You'll see. It's better if you see and hear it all yourself."

She stepped over to the dresser and looked at one of the pictures of Alena. There were about a dozen in the suite, but I noticed only one with both Alena and Kiera. Most of the others were of Alena with Mrs. March or both Mr. and Mrs. March. Either Kiera had been the one taking the pictures, or she simply hadn't been around when they took them.

She lifted the one on the dresser and studied it a moment before putting it down softly.

"How old was she in that picture?" I asked.

"Ten. This was a school photo taken when she was in the fifth grade."

"She would have been a very pretty woman."

"We have the exact same eyes and nose." She turned to me. "My therapist thinks it's healthy that I see you now as more like a younger sister. I told her how my mother was trying to come between us."

"Come between us?"

"She had a good explanation for it," Kiera went on, pacing now, like some teacher explaining a new idea. "She said my mother was jealous of our budding new relationship."

"She said that?"

She paused and looked at me with those narrowed eyes.

"She said my mother wants to dominate you, and the more she alienated you from me, the easier it would be for her to turn you into Alena. You don't want to be turned into someone else, do you? Or do you?"

"No, of course not," I said.

"Good." She stepped closer. "Just be alert. My mother will continue to warn you against me, if not call me the devil outright. That's why she was so angry when she saw you dressed in the clothes I gave you and wearing the makeup I put on you. That's why she wasn't for me taking you to school. She'd love to have you locked up in that limousine going and coming and then locked up in this room. She even has our servants working for her that way. They're all a bunch of spies, so be careful about what you say and do in front of any of them."

She smiled and relaxed her shoulders.

"But don't worry. My father sees through all that. He'll be on our side more and more."

I didn't say anything for a moment. She was making it sound as if there was a war going on in that great house, and now I was the prize, the spoils.

"Don't you love your mother?" I asked her.

She shrugged. "I love her the way a daughter is supposed to, I guess, but I've always gotten along better with my father, and after Alena was born, my mother didn't seem to care much about it, anyway. She doted on Alena. I could do nothing right, and Alena could do nothing wrong. It's back to that since you came," she said, but then she smiled again. "I don't mind. I'm fine. And so will you be, because I won't let her turn you into someone you're not. You've become . . . my cause célèbre. How's that? I learned something in French class," she added with a flair as if she were on a stage. "Oh, I heard Ricky's planning on getting his father's boat and taking you and the rest of us to Catalina one of these weekends."

"Yes, he said one of these weekends."

"His father makes him work every other weekend in one of their pharmacies."

"One? How many do they own?"

"About ten, I think. He expects Ricky will become a pharmacist, too, and take over someday. They have a beautiful boat. He hasn't invited many girls. I told you he likes you. I hope he can get it. His father lets him take it because he trusts him. My mother won't let my father give me use of the boat, even if I have someone like Ricky do the driving. Someday, though." She took a deep breath and smiled. "For the first time after a session of therapy, I've got an appetite. See you downstairs," she said, and left.

I rose and looked at the picture of Alena she had been looking at so intently. I didn't think they had the same eyes and nose, not at all. Alena's features were more doll-like, and her eyes looked warmer, friendlier. According to Kiera, Alena was only in fifth grade when the picture was taken, but she had an innocence that did remind me of myself, vulnerable, eager to trust and believe in someone and in the future. It wouldn't be all that difficult for Mrs. March to turn me into this girl. I was closer to her than I was to Kiera.

I returned to my homework and even got in twenty minutes of clarinet before I went down to dinner. Everyone was there. Kiera gave me a knowing smile, winking slightly as if we were conspirators now, both working her parents, manipulating them.

During dinner, Kiera reminded Mrs. March that we were staying after school to audition for the school play. Before her mother could say or question anything, her father went on and on about his own dramatic experiences when he was in high school.

"I was in a play called *Harvey,* the one about the invisible big rabbit."

I wasn't familiar with it, and apparently, neither was Kiera. He went on to tell us practically the whole story.

"Oh, Daddy!" Kiera cried when he described the ending. "That sounds like so much fun."

"It was. It is. In fact, your school should do it. At least, you guys should read it or maybe get the movie."

Mrs. March moved her dish to the side and said, "We have had that movie in our theater, Donald, and Kiera was bored and left."

He looked stunned for a moment, thought, and then nodded. "Yeah, I do remember that. Right."

"I was younger then," Kiera said quickly. "Besides, you never told me you were in the play when you were in high school, Daddy. I would have paid more attention and watched it to the end."

"He did tell you that, Kiera," Mrs. March said softly, "right before we began watching it."

"Well, I don't remember." She looked at me before firing back at her, "You're always finding something wrong with me."

"I'm just . . ."

"Just jumping on every opportunity you can to make me look bad in front of Sasha,"

Kiera added, and leaped to her feet. "I don't know why I'm still in therapy. I go there, make some progress, and then come home to have you ruin it," she moaned, and left the dining room.

The silence that followed was as deafening as that right after a bomb.

"Donald," Mrs. March finally said, "she can't . . ."

He put up his hand for silence. "Let's just finish our meal in peace," he said, and that was how we ate it, the three of us performing a show of simple gestures, passing dishes, salt and pepper and butter, as if we all were deaf.

When I went upstairs, I heard Kiera sobbing in her suite and knocked softly on her door.

"If that's you, Mother, go away."

"It's Sasha," I said.

She opened the door and then turned away quickly and returned to throw herself on her bed.

"You see? You see why my therapist is right? You were there!" she cried, and pounded the mattress. "No matter what I do or say, she's ready to destroy me." She turned to face me. "How can anyone be a better person in this house? Tell me that, will you? You were there. You saw it. You heard her."

She waited for my response. I didn't want to take sides, but I nodded.

"Well, we just have to stick together more," she said, sitting up. "Next time she's critical of me, something I do or say, you might come to my defense, say something."

"What could I say?"

"Say . . . 'Kiera's trying.' Just say that. My father will pick up on it. I can see he likes you. Maybe then my mother will get off both our backs."

I didn't think she was really on my back, but I didn't disagree.

Kiera smiled and reached for my hands. "Thanks for stopping by to see how I am, Sasha. That's very sweet of you. I don't deserve it, of course. I don't deserve even your being civil to me, but I plan on deserving it someday. Now, go practice the clarinet. I know it's important to you and you want to do well. Besides, I like hearing it through the wall."

I started toward the door.

"You can leave my door open a little," she said. "And yours, too. That way, I'll hear you better."

"Okay, but I'm not that good yet."

"You're better than me, not that that says much."

"Didn't you ever play an instrument?"

"The heart," she said.

"You mean the harp?"

"No. The heart," she said, and laughed.

For a moment, I thought she did look like Alena, innocent, young, and vulnerable.

Downstairs, you became deaf, a voice of warning inside me said. *Up here, you became blind.*

I practiced for more than an hour before getting ready for bed and reading ahead in my English textbook. I had forgotten that I had left my door open. Before she said anything, Mrs. March must have been standing in my doorway a while just looking in at me. I finally sensed someone and lowered my textbook.

She smiled. "Seeing you lying there like that, reading, reminded me so much of Alena. She was a voracious reader, unlike Kiera. She read all of those books you see on the shelves here, every single one. I know, because she would spend hours telling me the stories or talking about the characters. She always got so involved. She'd talk about her books with anyone who would listen."

She stepped in.

"It used to break my heart when she tried describing a story to Kiera, and Kiera would brush her off, tell her it was silly or a waste of time. I know Kiera can be a very exciting young woman, Sasha. She is beautiful, and boys trail after her like ants following honey, but she hasn't quite reached the level of maturity and responsibility she should, and I worry about her. Now I have to worry about you, as well. Please be careful," she said. "I know how easy it is to fall into traps when you're the age you are. Is there anything you want to tell me?"

"No. I'm fine, Mrs. March."

"I hope someday you'll be able to call me Mother. Not that I want to replace your mother," she quickly added. "I just want us to be closer."

"That's still difficult for me to do right now, Mrs. March," I said.

I saw how hard she took my answer. For a moment, she looked like she might burst into tears, but then she managed a smile. "Of course. Everything has its proper time and place."

She gazed around, smiled again, and said good night, closing the door softly behind her. Less than a minute later, the door opened again. I thought she had forgotten something, but it was Kiera.

"You left my door open a bit, remember?"

"Yes."

"I heard everything she said. I don't read. I wouldn't listen to Alena. I'm not mature and responsible. See what I was saying? That was a lie. I always listened to Alena. She would sit on the floor next to me and tell me her stories while I sat there filing my nails or doing my hair. Why, she'd even come in while I was soaking in the tub and sit on the bathroom floor and recite them."

Now she was the one who looked as if she might burst into tears.

"I hope you never call her Mother," she said. Then she turned and rushed out, closing the door sharply behind her.

It sounded so ridiculous, even outright funny to say it, but I muttered to myself, "Maybe I was better off in the streets."

26
THE VA CLUB

I was nervous from the moment I got into Kiera's car the next morning and never stopped being nervous all day. I did well enough in instrumental class to avoid any looks or words of dissatisfaction from Mr. Denacio, and I got an eighty-eight on a vocabulary test in English, but all through the day, I would have these moments when my heart would race and I would have a shortness of breath. I knew that this was because I was attending Kiera's secret VA club meeting and because of our lying to Mrs. March about a school play audition. If and when she found out, she would be very upset that I had gone along with it, but I felt that if I changed my mind, Kiera would return to the way she had been when I had first arrived.

I was good at keeping it all to myself. Ricky was the only one who sensed anything different about me. Kiera and her other friends were their usual buoyant selves, laughing, gossiping about other girls and boys in their classes and teachers as well. No one noticed that I was especially quiet. It wasn't until the very end of lunch period that anyone said anything about the VA club. Deidre came up beside me as we were all leaving for class and said, "We're all looking forward to you coming today."

Before I could say anything, she walked away and left me with Ricky, who now looked even more suspicious.

"What was she whispering about? What are you she-devils up to today?" he asked.

The first thing that came to my mind was that if I said anything that even suggested we were meeting after school, he would mention it, and Kiera and the other girls would think I had already betrayed them.

"Nothing very important," I said. "Girlie stuff."

"Well, that's no fun," he replied, and walked the rest of the way wearing an impish grin. Kiera never mentioned any boys knowing about or going to the VA club. Was that one of the surprises that awaited me?

When the final bell rang to end classes, my heart felt like a yo-yo. Kiera was at my classroom door before I got to it myself. She must have run all the way from her wing of the building the second the bell rang. She had told me that sometimes she faked a desperate need to go to the bathroom just to get a head start on leaving.

"C'mon," she said. "We can't stay at Deidre's longer than we would have stayed for a play audition, remember."

I followed her out as quickly as I could. I hated it when she or someone else made me move so quickly that my limp became more pronounced. I knew there were students, even in my own classes, who ridiculed me. I didn't see any of the other girls in Kiera's group of friends when we reached the parking lot. When I asked about them, she told me they had already left. Deidre had actually feigned an excuse to leave before the last period.

"They always get excited when we agree on a possible new candidate for the club," she said as we got into her car. "There are lots of girls who would love to join, but we're very particular. Usually, we don't ever consider a new student to the school, but since I vouched for you and all of them except Deidre believe you're my cousin, they agreed. Excited?"

"I don't know. I still don't know or understand what the club does."

"Oh, you will before today's meeting

ends." She stopped the car as we reached the driveway to the parking lot and turned to me, her face tightened into a look of seriousness and intensity I had not seen. "Nothing we can do together, nothing we say or promise each other, will ever bring us closer together than you being in the VA," she said. "I can assure you. We're closer than real sisters, and every girl in the club would rather tell her most secret thoughts and things to one of us than she would to her own real sister."

She drove out. I sat back, impressed. Never had I dreamed I'd be close friends with girls older than I was and in a new school, too. Now, according to Kiera, I would be even more special. I felt as if I had stepped onto a rocket ship, and it wasn't only because of Kiera's driving, either. Trips to Disneyland, parties, boat trips, all of it lay before me like some promised land filled with delight and pleasure. *Months from now,* I thought, *I won't even remember living on the streets.*

Deidre's house was in a gated community. The guard checked off Kiera and opened the gate for us. All of the houses were big and beautiful, but none was even half the size of the March mansion. That didn't mean Deidre's family's home wasn't a big, beautiful house in Pacific Palisades, too. As we approached, Kiera told me more about her. First, she explained that none of them talked about each other much with anyone who wasn't a member of the VA club.

"We hold each other's trust sacred," she said. "Any of us gossiping about any one of us would be considered worse than being a serial killer, but I can tell you more about Deidre now. Deidre, as you know, is an only child. I became friendlier with her than I was with the other girls because I frankly felt like an only child, especially after Alena came along. I think you're beginning to understand why.

"As I told you, Deidre's father is an important business attorney with beautiful offices in Century City. Her mother works with her father. She's his personal secretary. I think she became that because most men hire beautiful women to become their personal secretaries and then have affairs with them.

"Look, everyone's here already," she said, nodding at the three cars parked in the driveway. We pulled in behind the one on the right and got out.

Deidre's house was a sprawling Spanish-style hacienda with a large courtyard. It didn't have views of the ocean because of the tree line on the west side, but it was high enough to capture the sprawling vistas and the lights of sections of Los Angeles on the east side. Deidre opened the arched front door before we reached it.

"Everyone has to take off her shoes today," she said. "We just put in a new carpet in the living room, and my mother is anal about it."

Kiera kicked hers off, and I slipped out of mine. We put them next to the four other pairs there and followed Deidre over the tiled-floor entry, down a hallway, and into the living room, where the girls were sitting on settees. There were some soft drinks on the table and a bowl of popcorn with smaller bowls, but I was glad to see no whiskey. It looked as harmless as a gathering of teenage girls could look.

"Everyone knows who Sasha is," Deidre began. "Sasha, you know Marcia Blumfield and Doris Norman."

"Hi," Marcia said.

"Right," Doris said. She sipped her soda and shifted her gaze to Kiera.

"Sit anywhere you want," Deidre said. She flopped into the big armchair to the right of one of the settees. Kiera sat beside Margot, and they made a place for me. "If you want something besides soda, let me know," Deidre said. "Don't spill anything or drop anything on the floor, or I'll have my mother visit you late at night."

The girls laughed. I sat, and Kiera poured herself a Coke. She looked at me and offered some, but I shook my head.

"Who's first this time?" Margot asked. "I was first the day we inducted Doris."

"It might be instructive for Doris to lead off, then, don't you think?" Deidre said.

"You mean since the last meeting, no one's made lovey-dovey dangerously?" Marcia asked.

They all laughed again.

"Okay, I go first, then," Doris said. She looked at Kiera. "Unless I'm wrong."

"You're not wrong," Kiera said. "Go on."

"Well, you all know my father owns and operates a bowling alley in Manhattan Beach. On weekends, I often go in to waitress at the café. I've always had a crush on the bartender's son, Crawford."

"Crush. Give me a break," Margot said. I noticed how she looked at Kiera after practically everything she said to see if Kiera approved.

"Well, what would you call it?" Doris fired back.

"Hunger," she said, and everyone laughed, even Doris.

"Okay, hunger. No matter how I flirted with him whenever he was there, he didn't seem to notice or care. Last weekend," she said, smiling, "he did."

"Doesn't sound dangerous to me," Marcia said.

"I didn't get to it yet, genius."

I wanted to ask why it had to be dangerous but remembered Kiera's warning about asking questions. She must have sensed it, however, because she turned to me to explain.

"Sasha's probably wondering about this 'dangerous' thing, right, Sasha?"

I looked at the other girls. They were all focused on me. "Yes," I said.

"We came up with the idea to add some additional excitement," Kiera said.

"You mean you came up with it," Deidre told her.

Kiera smiled. "Whatever." She turned back to me. "You see, Sasha, some of the recent sexual episodes described here were quite mediocre."

"You say," Deidre told her. "I was quite satisfied the last time."

"It takes so little to satisfy Deidre," Kiera said, and everyone laughed again, including Deidre. "Anyway, a suggestion was made by *moi* to the effect of performing the ultimate sex act as close to in public or in the presence of a third party as possible, trying not to be discovered, of course. Therein lies the danger. Which brings us back to Doris. Go on, Doris," she said.

"Crawford hung around longer than usual this particular day. I could feel his eyes on me, and he was flashing that cute, sexy smile of his. To my surprise and delight, I might add, he waited until I was finished with my shift, and then he and I had something to eat and drink, mostly drink. He snuck me some of his vodka. His father asked him to get something for the bar in the storage room, and I went with him. When we got there, we began to kiss."

"Storage room?" Marcia moaned. "That's hardly dangerous."

"Will you wait!" Doris said, stamping her foot.

"She's right. Don't rush her. Don't ever rush it, girls," Kiera said. Everyone smiled. "Go on, Doris."

Doris sent some eye darts at Marcia and continued.

"He was trying to undo my skirt, and I said, 'No, not here.' I remembered our new VA pledge."

"Where did you go?" Margot asked, leaning toward her. All of the girls looked more interested now.

"I took him by the hand to an area right behind the pins. We made love to the sound of strikes and splits," she said proudly.

Marcia grimaced, shaking her head. "That's not much. I don't think it was possible for anyone to see you."

"You don't bowl at my father's bowling alley. Anyone looking past the pins might have seen us. That counts, doesn't it, Kiera?"

"It counts. It wasn't as dangerous as Margot's time with Perry Gordon just under her father's home-office window, however."

Doris looked disappointed. "Well, I thought it was clever," she said. "And it got Crawford very excited, just like you said it might. He couldn't believe I wanted to do it there."

"It was clever. That was very good, Doris. I don't mean to say it wasn't," Kiera told her, and her sour, disappointed expression flew off her face, to be replaced by a satisfied smile. She nodded at Marcia.

"From the look on her face, I don't think Sasha understands us or what we're talking about or what we believe," Margot said. Everyone turned to me.

"I thought I would let you guys talk a while to whet her appetite," Kiera said, and then turned to me. "You know what Alcoholics Anonymous is, right?"

For a moment, I lost my breath. She knew very well that I knew what Alcoholics Anonymous was. It was a place my mother should have been regularly, even before we were on the street. I glanced at Deidre and saw the way she was staring at me, poised to see my reaction. Every part of her face was perfectly still. She wasn't even blinking.

"Yes, I know what it is."

"Well, then, it's simple to understand," Kiera said. "Alcoholics go there to swear off alcohol. We meet here to swear off virginity."

As if they anticipated my reacting with shock or negativity, they each pounced with a defense.

"Why should boys be the only ones to be ashamed of being virgins?" Margot asked.

"Why should they be the only ones to enjoy having sex whenever they can or want?" Marcia added.

"Why should boys be the only ones who can brag about how good a lover they are?" Doris asked.

"Why do we have to be the ones who always say no?" Deidre asked.

"Most boys, the ones who really are good lovers, don't want to be with virgins, anyway," Kiera said. "When they are, they always act as though they're doing the girl a big favor."

"What we do here is support each other, advise each other, and protect each other," Deidre told me. "Any girl out there on her own is vulnerable and afraid. You're very lucky Kiera has brought you here. You may not realize it now, but you will soon enough."

"She thinks she doesn't have to worry because she's only fourteen," Kiera said, as if she were reading my mind.

"I was only fourteen the first time," Margot said.

"I wasn't quite fourteen," Marcia said.

"I confess. I was almost fifteen," Doris said.

"The way you look, you're not long for virginity, anyway," Deidre said. "When Kiera dresses you and gets you made up, you look at least eighteen, nineteen. That's why all those college boys were looking at you that night in Westwood."

"You don't have a mother or a father," Marcia said, "but every girl here will tell you it's easier for her to come to one of us than to go to her mother with questions. What mother would accept the VA club? Even though she probably lost her virginity when she was about our age, she'd make you feel terrible even thinking about it."

"Exactly," Doris said.

"Well, what do you think?" Kiera asked me. "Want to be with us, part of us, the sex sisters?"

They all smiled.

"Or do you want to be on your own out there?" she added.

I looked at each of them. They were all anxious to hear my answer. "I thought that once you lost your virginity, you couldn't get it back."

"No, not physically back," Deidre said, "but you can become a mental virgin, which is just as stupid."

"I'm still not sure about what I have to do," I said.

Doris laughed the hardest.

"First, you take the oath, and then you get the tattoo," Deidre said.

"What tattoo?"

"Girls?"

They all stood up. Doris and Marcia undid their jeans and lowered them as they turned to show me a tattoo of *VA* done in a fancy script just above the crack in their rears. Deidre and Margot lifted their skirts to reveal the same one in the same place, and then Kiera rose, lowered her jeans, and showed me hers.

"We'll take you to get yours on Friday after school," she said. "I think Sasha should have hers done in calligraphy. Her mother used to do calligraphy, and she's doing it in art class now. Anyone have any objections?"

No one spoke.

"Deidre, you schedule the tattoo, and tell him what we want him to do."

"First the oath," Deidre reminded her.

"Yes, the oath."

"And then?" I asked, my heart thumping.

"And then we help you break out of physical and mental virginity," Margot said.

"She began her period yesterday," Kiera told them.

"No rush," Doris said. "I trust her. She looks as innocent as I did."

"Hardly," Marcia said. "When you were born and your father asked what you were, a boy or a girl, the doctor said, 'Slut.' "

They all laughed. Doris threw a pillow at her. Marcia threatened to throw her drink at her.

"Watch the rug!" Deidre screamed.

"There's one major added benefit," Margot told me when things quieted down again. She looked to Kiera.

"She's right. When we say we'll help you break out, we'll make sure you break out with the right boy."

"No one knows the boys at school better than we do," Deidre said.

"The oath!" Doris cried.

"The oath," everyone else chanted.

Deidre reached under the chair and produced a diary. She brought it to me, and all of the girls stood up.

I looked at Kiera. "What is this?"

"This diary contains every member's description of her first sexual experience," Deidre said. "When you've had yours and you write it into the book, you can read the others. Place your right hand on the notebook."

Were they serious? Was this some sort of joke? There wasn't a smile on anyone's face, and no eyes betrayed any humor. No one was going to leap to cry "April fool" or anything. They couldn't have looked more serious in church.

I put my hand on the notebook.

"Repeat after me. I, Sasha Porter, do solemnly swear to share my most secret sexual thoughts with my sisters and with no one else."

I repeated it.

"I hereby renounce virginity, and I will never betray any sister's trust or speak of the VA club with anyone who is not a member."

After I repeated that, all of the girls placed their right hands over mine. They all closed their eyes as if in silent prayer. I closed mine.

Each one hugged me and returned to her seat.

"Now, then," Kiera said, smiling. "Let me tell you how I made love dangerously this week."

Like kindergarten students gathering around their teacher to hear a story, the girls leaned forward. Despite what Kiera was about to describe, I found myself lost in my own thoughts.

More a single question.

What had I just sworn to do and to be?

27
THE OATH

"I was really proud of you in there," Kiera said as we drove home. "A couple of the girls were worried you were too young. Of course, they don't know your history. Growing up in the streets, seeing the things you've seen, has made you more mature than they are, I'm sure."

"I didn't see much more than poor people struggling to eat, Kiera."

"You know what I mean."

I didn't, but I didn't disagree with her. If she wanted to believe those things about me, fine. Right now, it looked like something of an advantage to have her think that way about me.

"But you can't keep going to school dressed like a character in *Alice in Wonderland* or something," she continued. "I'm going to give you more of my things to wear. My mother has to realize you're not a ten-year-old, and boys won't take you seriously if you look like you just walked off *Sesame Street*."

"Ricky seems to like me," I said.

"He's one of us. Besides, he's only one boy. You don't want to become dependent upon one boy this early. That's the whole point of our club. Girls get into this frenzy to have a relationship. Heaven forbid they not be asked out on a date or not have a date to the prom or something. We're free of all that anxiety and pressure." She smiled. "And it drives the boys crazy because we act so indifferent. We're in more control of our own destinies. You see the point, right?"

"Yes," I said. I did see the point. What she was saying made me feel a little better about what I had just sworn to do and to be.

Luckily, Mrs. March wasn't home when we arrived. I didn't have to greet her with my face full of deception immediately. We went right up to our rooms, but Kiera wanted me to come into hers after I settled in so she could choose some clothes for me to wear to school. That was where Mrs. March found us. Kiera had at least five outfits laid out on her bed.

"What's all this?" she asked as soon as she entered Kiera's suite.

"Clothes I'm lending Sasha, Mother. She doesn't have anything really fashionable.

Alena's things are just not right for her now," Kiera said.

"Fashionable? I hardly think the clothes you wear to school are what I would call fashionable, Kiera."

"They are to me and to my friends, Mother," she said with what I thought for Kiera was remarkable control. She even smiled at her. "You just forget what it was like to be a teenager. I'm sure your mother complained about the things you wore."

Mrs. March stepped closer to examine what was on the bed. "I don't remember you wearing these things."

"Why am I not surprised?" Kiera said, rolling her eyes. "Sasha likes them," she added.

I hadn't really expressed any opinion yet, but Mrs. March looked at me as though she had caught me in a betrayal and then relaxed her shoulders like someone accepting defeat.

"How did the audition go?" she asked.

"Neither of us was thrilled with it," Kiera said. "We're rethinking it."

"Why?"

"Mother, will you ease up a little? Sasha has enough pressure adjusting to a new school, making new friends, learning the clarinet, and everything else."

Again, Mrs. March turned to me for a re-action. I was silent. *I'm already deep in a lie,* I thought, and felt trapped.

"Very well," she said. "I'm meeting your father at Palmeri for dinner. Don't give Mrs. Duval or Mrs. Caro any grief." She left.

I knew Mrs. March was very upset with us, but Kiera looked as if she couldn't care any less about it. She continued pulling clothing off hangers and tossing what she liked onto the bed with cries of "This will look great on you! This is perfect!"

She stood back from the clothes. "You need some jewelry, too, and I have a watch you could have. Here," she said, taking the watch off her wrist and handing it to me.

"But it's your watch."

"I have more than twenty, silly."

"Twenty?"

"Those are real diamonds in it, by the way."

I put it on my wrist.

"Looks nice on you."

She dumped a box of earrings, bracelets, and necklaces onto the bed beside the cloth-ing she had laid out and began putting the outfits together with the jewelry. She had so much I thought she could open her own jewelry store.

"Is any of this very expensive?" I asked.

"It's all very expensive. I don't buy junk, and I don't let my parents buy me junk, not that they would. You have nothing here that would make you ashamed to wear," she said.

"I don't mean that. I don't want to lose anything expensive. It makes me nervous."

She laughed. "First of all, Daddy has some kind of insurance policy on our jewelry, and second, I could replace anything anyway, even without insurance, so don't give it a second thought. I don't. There," she said, stepping back. "You have a different outfit for every day of the week with the right accompanying earrings, necklaces, bracelets, and rings. Start trying things on. Oh, wait a minute!" She examined my ears. "You don't have pierced ears. Didn't your mother ever want you to get your ears pierced?"

"No. She didn't think I was old enough."

"Damn. Most of these earrings are useless. We have to get your ears pierced. We'll do it this weekend."

I looked at the watch she had given me.

"Will you stop being such a worrywart about your homework? I'll leave you alone after dinner. Promise," she said, holding up her right hand.

I began trying her things on and was surprised at how well everything fit me. Everything looked and smelled new, too.

She raved about it all. All of the tops were skin-tight, shirred, with plunging necklines. The skirts were short and also tighter than I would normally wear. There was a fuchsia halter-top dress that left little to the imagination. In fact, I thought what she was giving me was even sexier than the clothes she wore.

"Are you sure I can wear all of these things to school?"

"Of course you can. You're not dressing much differently from most of the other girls. Besides, if you have it, flaunt it," she said. "That's my motto, and it should be yours, too. You have a great figure."

I was still reluctant. "Your mother was very upset about it."

"Of course she is. She has you in Alena's room, playing Alena's clarinet, and wearing Alena's things. We know why, and we know how we both feel about that, right?"

"Yes," I said.

"Good. I'm starving," she declared before I could say anything else. "Let's go eat dinner. Keep that on. I love the expression on Mrs. Duval's face when she sees you in something I would wear." She seized my hand and pulled me along.

She was right about Mrs. Duval. Her eyes widened, and she shook her head softly, mumbling to herself as she went back and forth from the dining room to the kitchen.

At dinner, Kiera reminded me about getting the club's tattoo on Friday.

"That's when we'll get your ears pierced, too," she said.

"What will be our reason for not coming right home after school?" I asked. Mrs. March probably would approve of pierced ears, but I couldn't imagine her approving of tattoos.

"I'll tell my mother I had to stop at the mall to pick up some makeup. That's one thing she understands and approves of, cosmetics. Besides, it is the start of the weekend. We don't have to rush home to do homework — not that I ever do, anyway."

"Does she know you have a tattoo?"

"I don't bathe in front of my mother anymore, Sasha, and certainly not in front of my father. Besides, they both know that if I wanted to do something like that, I'd do it with or without their permission."

I was still quite nervous about doing it, but I felt I couldn't back out now without turning all of the girls against me. Kiera didn't talk about it any more. She went on and on about different boys and other girls at school whom the club members were considering, and she told me more about each of the girls themselves, especially whom I should listen to more and trust more. It was truly as if I had been taken into her confidence now, and there was nothing she wouldn't tell me. She lived up to her word after dinner, however, and didn't disturb my homework and practicing of the clarinet.

Grover picked me up after school the following day, as Kiera had a therapy session. During the day, I did notice that more boys were looking at me because of the clothes I was wearing. Both Ricky and Boyd made a point of telling me I looked hot, and all of the girls in the VA club complimented me. I saw the envy in the faces of the girls in my classes, too.

"You'll need us more than ever," Deidre whispered. "Boys will be coming at you like flies to honey. Make no promises or commitments until you speak with one of us."

I thought I had felt as if I were floating when I had just entered such a school, but now I really was lightheaded and happy. I dared to think that maybe I was beautiful; maybe I was just as pretty as or even prettier than Kiera.

Grover was surprised and amused by how many boys accompanied me out to the parking lot, each trying to get me to pay him some special attention.

"I guess you're adapting pretty well," he said before driving off. He rarely said anything, so I was pleased and actually felt myself blushing. I waved when I saw Kiera driving away, but she didn't notice.

Either because we were friendlier now and she was assuming more of a big sister's role or because she had reached some important realizations about herself, Kiera complained less and less about her therapy and behaved much more nicely and kindly toward her mother. I still saw the suspicion flashing in Mrs. March's face, but even she began to relax more. On Thursday night, after dinner was over and we were heading up to our rooms, Kiera claiming that she was trying hard to do better in her schoolwork, Mr. March asked me to follow him to his office.

"I'd like to speak with you a moment, Sasha."

Kiera paused, too.

"You can go up, Kiera. I just need to talk to Sasha right now," he said.

Kiera looked at me with fear and warning in her face, but she didn't linger. Mrs. March followed Mr. March and me to his office. He smiled at me as soon as we entered.

"There's nothing wrong, Sasha," he said.

"You can wipe away your look of anxiety. On the contrary, there's something right."

He went to his desk and took a cigar out of a box. "Have a seat," he said, gesturing with his cigar toward the red bullet leather chairs. I sat, and he lit his cigar.

"You could wait until she leaves, Donald," Mrs. March said. "Not everyone loves the stench of cigar smoke."

"Oh. Sorry. Does this bother you, Sasha?"

"No, sir."

There had been a time not so long ago when the aroma of a lit cigar would have been more like perfume when compared with the odors surrounding me.

He leaned against the front of his desk.

"First," he began, "I want to thank you for giving Kiera a chance to redeem herself when it comes to you. You have every reason to hate every cell in her body. I know it looks like I'm totally aloof from all that goes on here, but I assure you, I'm not. Both Mrs. March and I have kept in close contact with Kiera's therapist, and we're very happy with her progress."

"We hope it's real," Mrs. March said.

"I think Dr. Ralston would be a better judge of that than we would, don't you, Jordan?"

"I'd hope so. I have a closet full of Kiera's

broken promises to us both."

He shook his head slightly at her, puffed on his cigar, and turned back to me. "In any case, you've been very generous in permitting her to rework herself into decent behavior. I'm also impressed with the influence you've had on her. Now, even more important perhaps, I wanted to tell you how pleased I am to hear about your own progress and achievements. I must admit I was wary when Jordan, Mrs. March, wanted to have this arrangement, but I'm very happy to be proven wrong. Is there anything you need? Anything I can do for you?"

I looked at Mrs. March. She was finally smiling warmly.

"No, sir. I have more than I ever dreamed I would have," I said, and he laughed.

"You and me both, Sasha. You and me both. Okay. I just wanted to have this little talk. Don't hesitate to come to me if I can do anything more or if anything bothers you, okay? I know you have Mrs. March to rely on, but I want you to know you have me as well."

"Thank you."

He smiled and went around to his desk chair. I rose, glanced at Mrs. March, and then hurried out and up the stairs. Kiera was waiting for me at her doorway.

"What did he want?" she asked. "Was he trying to get you to tell him something? My mother must have put him up to it. Well?"

"No, nothing like that," I said. "He wanted to tell me how pleased he was with how things were going between us and how both of us were doing now," I said. "He told me not to hesitate if I needed or wanted anything."

"My father said that?"

"Yes. He was very nice, nicer to me than ever."

She studied me a moment to see if I was telling the truth and then smiled. "That's my father. He can be a real charmer when he wants to be. This is great. Mother might ease up on us. Okay. Get to your homework," she said, and went into her room.

On Friday as planned, all of the girls in the VA club met us after school and followed as Kiera drove me to a tattoo parlor in West L.A. The man doing the tattoos looked as if he was tattooed on every possible area of his body. There was a snake up his right arm beginning at his wrist and what looked like a chain up his left arm. He even had a tattoo on his throat.

All of the girls followed us into a small area in the rear, and the tattooing began. It wasn't pleasant, and twice I was on the verge of screaming that I wanted him to stop, but Kiera stood right beside him, and the girls were right behind her. Afterward, I looked at it in a full-length mirror by holding another mirror to catch the reflection. It looked bigger than theirs, and he had done what they had asked, a form of calligraphy.

They insisted on celebrating. Kiera called Mrs. March and told her we had gone to the mall so that I could get my ears pierced. She asked her to let us hang out and go for pizza with some friends. Minutes after she hung up, my phone rang, and Mrs. March asked me if we were doing what Kiera had said we were doing. Kiera knew, of course, that it was her mother calling me, and she watched and listened. I had no choice but to lie.

"Let's get to the mall," Kiera said. "We really do need to get your ears pierced, remember?"

Instead of going someplace for pizza afterward, however, we all went to Marcia's house. She had a younger brother, but her parents had left for a weekend in San Diego and had taken him along. Kiera had told me that Marcia's father owned car dealerships up and down the coast. A girl whose parents were only middle-class would have a hard time being friends with members of the VA club, I thought. She would always be intimidated by their clothes, their jewelry, and their cars. That feeling was reinforced when I saw Marcia's family's home, a sprawling two-story in a place called Brentwood Park. She had a live-in maid, too, but her maid had the night off.

We did order in pizza, and then, to my surprise, boys began to arrive. Ricky and Boyd came first, and then three other boys followed — Tony Sussman, Jack Martin, and Ruben Weiner. They were all seniors as well. In fact, I was the only one there who wasn't. As before, no one seemed particularly involved with anyone else. When they danced, everyone was dancing with everyone. I saw the vodka being added to the soda and juice, but when Marcia offered me some, Kiera interfered.

"Sasha doesn't drink," she said. She said it so sharply that Marcia looked as if she had been slapped.

"Well, excuse me. I didn't know we had a Mormon in the club."

"She's not a Mormon. I promised my mother I wouldn't let her get into any drinking after what happened to her parents, remember? They were killed by a drunk driver."

"Oh. Sorry," Marcia said, turning to me

and looking as if she would burst into tears.

Kiera seemed to wink with her whole face. She leaned over to whisper, "She needs to drink to have fun. You and I don't."

Later, Ricky spent more time with me. We sat and talked and ate.

"I've got to work tomorrow," he said. "I have next weekend off, and I'm sure I'll get the boat."

"I've never been on a boat," I said.

"You will be next weekend." He looked at the others and then brought his lips to mine. It wasn't a quick peck, either. It was a soft, long kiss. I closed my eyes, and when I opened them, I expected that everyone would be looking at us, but no one was.

We kissed again and again before the party ended, but we didn't do much more. I wasn't disappointed, but I was anticipating it. When Kiera announced that we had to leave, Ricky followed us out. He kissed me again before I got into the car. I knew Kiera was watching.

"See you soon," he said, but he held on to my arm. Then he leaned in, bringing his lips to my ear. "I hear you were inducted into the VA club," he whispered. "I hope I'm the one."

He turned and walked back into the house before I could respond, not that I knew what to say. When I got into the car, Kiera asked me immediately what he had whispered. I told her. I was surprised that he knew about the club.

"He's okay. He has the Good Sexkeeping Seal of Approval," she said nonchalantly, and started the car. As we drove out, she slowed down and turned to me, "But as for him initiating you, that's not his decision — or yours, for that matter."

"What do you mean?"

"We'll bring it up at the next meeting, and the members will vote on it. There are four other boys who are approved for initiations, right now only four boys."

"You mean everyone votes on which boy each girl is with for the first time?"

"Of course. That way, no one makes a serious mistake. When I said I was going to be your protective older sister, I meant it," she said. "It's the least I can do for you, and I appreciate your letting me do it. We're all sisters now. The members of the club think clearly and carefully about each girl's sexual experiences. Everyone there has far more experience than you have. Why shouldn't you benefit from their experiences? Believe me, my mother wouldn't be any sort of adviser when it comes to sex. Sometimes I think she and my father stopped doing it.

"Despite what some people tell you, sex for the first time is the most important time. Our four boys know how to make love to a virgin. There have been no complaints," she added, smiling.

We drove on.

It was on the tip of my tongue to ask, but I didn't. *Whatever happened to love?*

28
DECISION

A strange thing happened at school during the days that followed. The more I hung out with the older students, whether at lunch or talking to them in the halls between classes and going with Kiera and the others to malls or restaurants, the more invisible I became to my classmates. Those who had once been impressed with my being so lovey-dovey with a senior boy were now indifferent to me. No one said hello or even nodded at me. They walked past me as though I weren't there.

I continued to do well in class and improve on the clarinet, but when Mr. Denacio announced that I would have a seat in the senior band and issued me a uniform, everyone else in the class took it as if it had been expected. It wasn't so much an achievement as simply another assumed step. *Big deal* was written across their faces. Ironically, Kiera and the club members were the only friends I had. No one my own age would give me the time of day.

One Wednesday, Kiera told me that we were having a meeting of the VA club at Deidre's house after school on Friday, and I was the main topic. She asked me how my period had been since she had given me her pill. I had gone through it far better than any time I had had it before and told her so.

"My doctor says we should take the pill afterward, too," she said. "It will prevent you from having those severe cramps next time. These are for you. Take one every day now."

I thanked her and took one every morning as her doctor had prescribed. As Friday drew closer, I was even more nervous for the VA club meeting than I had been the first time. After all, it was to be all about my first sexual experience.

The other girls were already there when we arrived, sitting in the same places. They all looked very serious. I saw the pictures of four boys on the coffee table: Ricky, Boyd, Ruben Weiner, and Tony Sussman. Deidre brought a chair for me and put it in the center so I'd face all of the girls.

"We didn't ask you last time," Margot began, "but how much experience do you have? How far have you gone with a boy?"

I looked at Kiera, but she was just as serious and stone-faced as they were.

"All I've ever done with a boy I did at Marcia's party with Ricky," I said.

"Just kiss?" Marcia said, squinting and crinkling her nose as though kissing were more disgusting. "What, did you grow up in Disneyland?"

"There's no reason to pick on her," Kiera said. "You weren't exactly Miss Sophisticated when we brought you into the club."

Marcia blushed and sat back.

"That still leaves Tony out. He moves too fast, assuming the girl has been on the verge," Deidre said. "Everyone agree?"

They all nodded, and she turned Tony's picture over.

"Can she go on a date? Will your mother permit it?" Doris asked.

"I doubt it," Kiera said. "My mother refuses to see her as anything but a ten-year-old, and she has this thing about added responsibility for her."

"She doesn't look ten now," Margot said. "I want to know where you got that fuchsia outfit you wore the other day."

I looked at Kiera. Hadn't she ever worn it?

"Like it will look as good on you," Doris

muttered.

"Can we get on with the business at hand?" Kiera said sharply.

"Ruben uses his love machine," Deidre says. "It's an SUV. All the seats go down, and he throws an air mattress in it. It feels like a waterbed."

"You should know," Doris said, smiling.

"Like you don't?"

Doris laughed.

"In any case, he'd be better if it was going to be a straight-out date, don't you think?" Deidre asked. Everyone nodded, and she turned his picture over.

"It's between Boyd and Ricky, and we know how you feel about Ricky already," Marcia said.

"Ricky's usually the most gentle," Doris added.

"I prefer Boyd," Margot said.

"It's not your initiation. It's hers," Doris told her.

"Boyd is more professional about it. He spends more time on foreplay," Margot insisted.

"I think this should be a secret ballot," Kiera announced. "There's a little too much personal business going on here."

"Whatever," Margot said.

Deidre produced a sticky pad and handed

each girl a sheet.

"I don't have a pen," Margot said.

"Use your lipstick," Doris told her.

"Then everyone will know it's my vote. That's not a secret ballot."

"I'm just kidding, stupid."

Deidre got up, walked out, and returned with pens for those who didn't have any.

"Just an *R* or a *B* is all that's necessary," Kiera said.

I watched as they spread out to vote. It wasn't until they all handed their folded papers to Kiera that the full realization of what they were deciding for me hit me. I had sworn their oath, and I had gotten the tattoo, but I wasn't confident that I could go through with the rest of it, especially if they had chosen Boyd. Kiera didn't announce the votes. She opened each slip and put it on the right. She put none on the left.

"It's settled," she said. "Unanimous. Ricky."

"When?" Margot asked immediately.

"As it happens, we're all going on Ricky's boat tomorrow," Kiera said. "I didn't say anything until I knew for sure and knew this would be the vote for sure. I mean, Boyd will be there, too, but Ricky's the one."

"And you can make it dangerous, too," Margot said, "if it happens on the boat."

"No, that wouldn't count as dangerous," Kiera said. "It's only us. Besides, you wanted real privacy the first time, as I recall. I heard Tony almost had to use a sheet with a hole."

"That's not true!" she cried.

Everyone laughed.

"Let's have some music," Deidre declared, "and order some Chinese."

Everyone rose to congratulate me as if I had done or would do something historic. Maybe I was naive about sex, but I knew that what they expected me to do, what I would do, was not all that much of an accomplishment, except, of course, that it would make me solid with these girls. I'd be part of their family, and for an orphan, that was some accomplishment.

"I bet you're really excited," Kiera said after we left Deidre's house.

"This is all supposed to happen tomorrow on Ricky's boat?"

"Sure. It has two staterooms. Don't look so worried. You'll do fine."

She made it sound like a performance or a test. When we arrived home, however, we were both almost grounded. Mrs. March had learned the truth. The drama teacher had not held auditions for the play yet. She intercepted us just before we were about to

418

go upstairs.

"In here," she commanded, standing in the living-room doorway.

Kiera and I looked at each other. On the way into the living room, she whispered, "Whatever it is, let me do all the talking."

Mrs. March was alone. She stood with her arms folded under her breasts and nodded toward one of the settees. We sat.

"What now, Mother?" Kiera asked.

"What now? Why did both of you lie to me about the auditions? There were no auditions that day. Well?"

"I was too embarrassed to tell you that I had made a mistake and misread the date on the bulletin-board announcement. We actually went to the auditorium and felt like idiots. At least, I did. It wasn't Sasha's fault, so don't blame her."

"But you continued the lie, giving me that story about changing your minds," Mrs. March said, looking from Kiera to me. I couldn't look directly at her.

"Yes."

"Why? Why wouldn't you just tell me the truth? You made a mistake?"

"I didn't think you'd believe me, and besides, we really did decide not to do it."

"Where did you go that day?"

"Nowhere. We just killed some time riding

around and then came home. It's not a federal case, Mother. It's not like we did some terrible thing instead."

"I don't believe you, Kiera."

"Don't believe me. Ask Sasha."

She looked at me. "Is what she's saying true? You just rode around?"

"Yes," I said softly, almost too softly for her to hear.

"I'm very disappointed in both of you. Why don't I see you working on your calligraphy anymore, Sasha?"

"I've done a little, but with my homework and clarinet practice . . ."

"And the time you're wasting riding around," she completed for me. "This is very discouraging. Alena never lied to me, ever."

"Oh, please, Mother. She had her little white lies, too."

"Never," she insisted. "Your bad habits never rubbed off on her. She was too good, an angel. That's why God took her back."

Kiera looked away, and when she turned back, her eyes were filled with tears.

"You just love making me out to be the bad one all the time. You did it when she was alive, and you still do it now. You hate me!" She leaped to her feet and ran out of the living room.

"Kiera!"

I sat there, frozen.

Slowly, Mrs. March turned back to me. "I don't hate her," she said. "She's my daughter. Of course I love her. I wouldn't put up with all her antics if I didn't care for her and love her, but I'm not one of those mothers who are so blind they will not see. I know her faults. Pretending, ignoring, excusing will not help her to change and improve. And you won't do her any good by supporting her when she lies or disobeys."

She took a deep breath and sat on the settee opposite me. After a moment, she looked up at me. "Sasha, I think, as Donald does, that it's wonderful you've found a way to get along with Kiera and perhaps help each other, but you must be wary. She has too many years of successfully manipulating both her father and me. She's an expert at it. Will you be careful?"

"Yes, Mrs. March."

"I don't mind your being a normal teenager, but please, be careful. I take my responsibility for you very seriously. Remember, I made that pledge to your mother the day she was buried."

I nodded, now nearly in tears myself.

"Donald is so happy at how things are going or seem to be going. I won't say anything to him about this, but no more lying, okay?"

"Okay, Mrs. March."

"Oh, I hate that 'Mrs. March.' At least call me Jordan," she said. She smiled. "So, you got your ears pierced?"

"Yes."

"Kiera has plenty of earrings to lend you. That's for sure. Alena always wanted her ears pierced, but we never got around to it." She was quiet a moment and then smiled again. "Donald is planning to take us all on a little trip, perhaps to San Francisco. Won't that be nice?"

"Yes, Mrs. . . . Jordan."

"Good. Okay, I won't keep you."

I rose and started out. She held her smile and then turned away. I paused once after I walked out of the living room and looked back at her. She suddenly looked like the saddest person in the world, alone, bedecked in expensive jewelry and her designer outfit, her hair recently cut and styled. But instead of looking wonderful, she looked like someone trapped and chained by her wealth, lost and alone with nothing but her expensive possessions to keep her warm.

Kiera's door was open. She wasn't crying, but she was facedown on her bed. She heard me enter her suite and turned.

"Why didn't you run out with me?"

"You jumped up and ran so fast I didn't know what to do," I said. It was the truth.

"What did she say? Did she tell you how terrible I am again?"

"No. She said she loves you, but she was worried. She liked that I got my ears pierced."

"That figures. Oh, well," she said, shaking off her rage and smiling. "At least I got us out of that one, even if she tells my father."

"She said she wouldn't."

"Did she? Great. I was afraid she would get him to lay down some new restrictions and ruin tomorrow. Perfect. We'll tell them both about it at dinner. Be sure you look and sound very excited about it." She studied me a moment. "You are, aren't you? You're not going to back out now?"

"No," I said, although I could hear a chorus of voices inside me saying *yes*.

"I'm going to take a bubble bath. Come in to talk if you want," she said, and headed for her bathroom.

I went to my suite and just sat for a while looking out the window. It was odd, I thought, but it wasn't until now that I realized I didn't even have a single picture of my mother. Everything we owned had disappeared in the road that night. Maybe it had all been tossed aside as junk. The sacks and the suitcases had been battered and stained. There had been some pictures in Mama's suitcase, but we had had nothing else of any real value. I couldn't recall anything that would have had our names. We had no address. If it had all been left on the side of the road, some other homeless person or persons might easily have come upon it and taken what they could use.

Of course, my thoughts went to the next day. *I like Ricky,* I thought. He was certainly very good-looking and so far very nice to me. It was exciting being with him. But to do what I was about to do, for the reasons I was about to do it, was troubling to me, and not because I was afraid. I wasn't old enough to have spent much time thinking about losing my virginity, but whenever I had thought about it, it was in terms of romance and love. Just doing it to get it over with diminished it, made it seem like such a common exercise. Was it just me? Why didn't these other girls feel and see that too?

Maybe they didn't really believe in love. From what I could see and what I heard them say, none of them had a particularly strong feeling for any one boy. If one of them had such a feeling, she surely kept it secret from the others. I had always dreamed of having a boyfriend who took me to school dances, movies, and restaurants. Maybe we would be too young to be really in love, but we would like each other so much that it would seem that way, and when we eventually broke up to go our separate ways, maybe for college, we would be brokenhearted, at least for a while. Years later, married to other people, we would meet and smile, almost laugh, at how intense we had once been. Yet in our heart of hearts, we would wonder what it would have been like if we had gone on together. The wondering would last only a second, but at least we would have had that.

None of the girls in the VA club would have anything remotely close to that. What would their memories of high school be like? How long could they continue to mock and belittle other girls who had had long and deep affections for boys in the past? Would they wake up one day years from now and realize what they had missed and lost and, most important, what they had given up when they treated their first sexual experience as just something they had to get over with?

I was tempted to go into Kiera's bathroom and sit beside her while she was in her bath and talk about all this, but I was afraid that the moment I brought it up, she would carry on with how I was not only betraying her but making her look bad to her friends. She might even find a way to blame it all on her mother, and things would return to the way they had been, a house full of thunder and lightning which would only bring us all to some new great tragedy. Whether Kiera would blame it on me or not, I would think I had caused it when all I had to do was make love with a boy I admittedly thought of as handsome and exciting.

How I wished I had a real mother to talk to now, even a mother who was in and out of sanity the way Mama was when we lived on the streets. I'd know when I could talk to her, when her mind was clear enough to hear me and care.

But I didn't even have that.

It was at times like this when I knew just how lost and alone I really was and that no amount of money, no house, no special school, nothing, would fill the great and deep hole in my heart.

29
INITIATION

Kiera was really very clever when it came to manipulating her father. I watched and listened to an expert at dinner that night. The excitement and sweetness in her voice was so well crafted, as were her smiles, her looks at me, and her way of bringing me in at the right times to support what she said. She had a way of tilting her head just slightly to the left while rolling her eyes to the right to look cute and innocent. She tossed back her hair with a flick of two fingers and pursed her lips as if she was sending her father a kiss across the table.

I looked at Mr. March as Kiera described what our outing on Ricky's boat was going to be. Mrs. March's face was more like a mask, nothing moving, her eyelids barely blinking as she listened. Although Kiera never came right out and said it, she implied that Ricky's father was going to keep close tabs on us. She reminded her parents that she had been on Ricky's father's boat before and how well it had gone. The weather was going to be perfect for boating, too. Most of all, this would be the most exciting thing I had ever done. She made it sound as if all the others, Ricky, even his father, were going along with this outing for my benefit. How could her parents reject it?

"Well, it sounds like you two are in for a great time," Mr. March said. "I'd take you myself, but I'm having so many problems with this project in Oregon that I've got to work all weekend. I don't know why I took on doing anything with Rick Stanton," he said to Mrs. March. "His preparation is always so sloppy."

"I couldn't agree more," Mrs. March said curtly, "but not because of Rick Stanton. You're taking on too much, Donald. We need you to spend more time with us."

The way she said "we" made it clear, at least to me, that she meant herself. He nodded and promised that he was going to cut back. He said he had already rejected two major projects. Kiera glanced at me as he spoke, a look of victory and satisfaction in her face. There was no other discussion about our going on Ricky's boat. She was happy they had gone on to other topics. Secretly, I had been hoping that they wouldn't let us go and my crisis would be postponed for a while, but I should have realized that there was little or nothing Kiera didn't get the way she wanted.

"I've picked out some things for you to wear tomorrow," she told me after dinner. "Boyd's picking us up at nine."

The outfit she had chosen looked more like a tennis outfit to me. When I put it on, I thought the skirt was too short, but she insisted that it was perfect. She gave me another watch to wear, with a band that matched the colors of my outfit, and different earrings, too. This watch, like the other, had diamonds.

"Now, don't worry about becoming seasick or anything," she said. "That pill I gave you actually helps prevent that, too. Don't ask me how or why. It just does. Tomorrow's your day, and we won't permit anything to ruin it."

I felt as if I were on the high seas already when I went to bed. I tossed and turned, struggling to fall asleep. The conflicting arguments going on inside me were fierce. I was caught in an echo chamber. A strong part of me was screaming how wrong it all was. I was doing it for the wrong reasons, and I would regret it for the rest of my life. The other part of me kept reminding me of what I had now and what I would have afterward. For a girl who had had few, if any, friends most of her life and none during the entire past year, the idea of being part of a group like the VA club brimmed with great promise. I'd be included in everything. I'd have trusted friends in school and out of school. Boys would like me even more. And besides, I had already gone too far. I had the tattoo. I had lost any chance of having friends my own age. They all thought I was too snobby because I was hanging around with the seniors. If I didn't do this, I'd be all alone again.

Sometime just before morning, I fell asleep and slept so late that Kiera came rushing with panic into my suite.

"You're still in bed?" she cried. I groaned and turned over to look up at her. She was already dressed in her boating outfit. "It's after eight! Get up. Get dressed. Get ready. I'll be back in fifteen minutes. You know my mother will make a big deal of us having a decent breakfast. C'mon. And don't forget to take your pill," she said, ripping the blanket off me.

I ground the sleep out of my eyes, sat up, and then, still half asleep, jumped into the shower to shock myself awake with cold water. I was just putting on my boat shoes when Kiera returned.

"Let's go," she said. "My mother is already wondering if you're sick or something. If you don't look good and full of energy, she'll find a reason to stop us. C'mon," she urged.

I hurried out after her.

Mrs. March was in the dining room waiting for us. "Are you all right?" she asked me immediately.

"Yes."

"She just stayed up too late doing her homework. You know how she is about her homework, even on weekends," Kiera said.

Mrs. March looked at me suspiciously but said nothing. I had to eat more than I wanted so she wouldn't think something was wrong with my appetite. At least, Kiera did most of the talking for us both, describing the day that lay ahead in Catalina and reminding her mother how much fun they'd had there when her father had taken them. She made the point of reminding her that Alena was alive then and loved the day.

"Never mind all that. You'd better make sure both you and Sasha are wearing your life jackets on that boat," her mother warned.

"Oh, of course. Ricky follows all the regulations to a T. What are you doing today,

431

Mother?" she asked to throw her off.

"I'm meeting Deidre's mother for lunch at the Ivy," she said. "It's a lunch meeting we've both been looking forward to for a while now." She made it sound as though they were meeting to discuss her and Deidre.

"That's nice," Kiera said without missing a beat.

"I want to hear from both of you periodically," Mrs. March said. "You both have cell phones, and this time they're not to be forgotten or turned off. Is that clear?"

"Of course, Mother. It's when we go on excursions like this that they come in most handy. We need to be excused now so we can both do last-minute things. Boyd will be here in ten minutes."

"Don't make any more mistakes, Kiera," Mrs. March warned. "There's no room for any more mistakes."

"That's all in the past, Mother. I'll let someone else make mistakes."

"Don't belittle what I say, Kiera."

"I never do, Mother. Sasha?"

I stood up and looked at Mrs. March. If she would or could ever see the hesitation in my face, she would see it now, I thought, and maybe she would forbid my going, but her mind was somewhere else. She nodded and looked down. Kiera tugged me, and we headed back up to our rooms. I was still brushing my teeth when she cried from my doorway that Boyd was there.

"Hurry up," she said, "before my mother finds some reason to stop us. Believe me," she continued as we went down the hallway, "she wishes she could."

"Why wouldn't she want us to have fun?"

"It's a long story, but it's because she had such a boring childhood. She's just jealous."

I shook my head as she descended in front of me. How could a daughter think her mother was jealous of her? Mothers wanted their daughters to have better lives than they had, didn't they? She certainly wanted a better life for me, even if it was just to ease her conscience. Besides, I couldn't believe Mrs. March had a boring childhood. Kiera just had a definition of "boring" that was different from most people's.

Deidre was waiting for us in the car with Boyd.

"The others are meeting us at the dock," she said. "Hurry up." When we drove off, she turned and leaned over to whisper, "Ready for VA day?"

Kiera pushed her to turn around. "Don't spook her," she said. "She's nervous enough."

"Nervous about what?" Boyd asked.

"Being on the same boat with you," Kiera said.

"Yeah, right. You have nothing to worry about as long as I'm there, Sasha," he said.

Ricky's boat was impressive. He had told me it was a seventy-five-foot Hatteras motor yacht. While everyone else waited, he took me on a tour to show me the galley, the salon, the master stateroom, and the guest stateroom. After that, he brought me up to the pilothouse, where I was to remain with him as he got us under way. Despite the conflicts going on inside me, I was very excited. When he started the boat and we were bouncing over the water, I couldn't help but squeal with delight. He let me steer for a while, too. Boyd started whining about not being permitted to do half the driving, as Ricky had promised, so he let him come up with Marcia, and he and I went down to join the others in the salon.

Kiera looked pretty cozy with Ruben Weiner, and Deidre was practically on Tony Sussman's lap. Margot was sprawled on a sofa with Jack Martin. The way everyone was smiling at us gave me the jitters. Did all of the boys also know what was supposed to happen on the boat?

"Looks crowded in here," Ricky said.

"Come on. We'll go to the front of the boat, and you can feel the wind and sea spray."

He took my hand and led me out. It was more exciting at the front of the boat. He pointed out Catalina and some of the other boats traveling to and fro. Because it was so bumpy, he held me around the waist, and we stood like that for a while. Afterward, we returned to the salon. I saw that Margot and Jack Martin were gone.

"Margot and Jack are in the guest stateroom," Kiera whispered. "You have the master, of course."

I glanced at Ricky.

"He already knows he's been chosen," she said.

Whether it was the prospect of really going forward with this or because this was my first time on a boat at sea, I don't know, but I felt the blood drain from my face and a wooziness come over me. I faltered for a moment as my legs turned into jelly beneath me.

Ricky saw it coming and had his arm around my waist again. "Whoa," he said, and scooped me up to carry me to the sofa.

"No," Kiera said, seizing his arm. "She needs to be in the bed."

He nodded and carried me to the master stateroom.

"I'll get Boyd to slow down. That will help," he said after he lowered me to the bed.

I closed my eyes. My stomach was doing flip-flops.

After he left, Kiera came in.

"Perfect," she said, as if I had planned it all out and was pretending. "We'll wait until the boat is docked."

"I'm not fooling," I said. "I feel sick."

"You'll get over it," she insisted. "Rest a little."

"But you said the pill would prevent this from happening."

"Everyone's different, Sasha. Don't be silly. I was hoping it would work for you, but I guess it doesn't. Next time, we'll get you to wear one of those patches to prevent seasickness. Relax. The best is yet to come."

"I don't want to," I said. "I don't feel good."

"What are you talking about? We go through all this effort to make it easy for you, and you want to back out now? Relax. You'll feel lots better after we dock, and that will be the best time for your initiation. Besides, you don't want to disappoint the girls after they voted to include you, and you especially don't want to disappoint Ricky," she added. "I'll be back in a few."

"I think I'm going to throw up."

She stood glaring at me for a moment and then sighed and shook her head. "Okay. If you have to throw up, go into the bathroom. I'll see if Ricky has anything onboard that will help," she said, and left.

I closed my eyes and kept my hands on my stomach while I fought back the urge to vomit. No one else was this seasick. I was embarrassed. The feeling didn't pass. I was about to get up when Ricky and Kiera returned. Kiera was holding a glass of something with a blue tint.

"We called Ricky's father, and he told us where this was in the galley," Kiera said. "You drink it all down as fast as you can."

She came to the bed. Ricky helped me sit up, and I took the glass. It didn't look like anything anyone would want to drink.

"Drink it fast," Kiera emphasized, "and you won't mind the taste."

I looked at Ricky. His face was so serious, his eyes intense. Was he that way because he thought that somehow this was his fault and he felt sorry for me?

"If she has a bad time, I'll never stop hearing about it from my mother," Kiera told him.

I looked at the glass again, took a deep breath, and gulped the contents. Kiera took the glass back immediately, and Ricky lowered me to the pillow again.

"Just rest. We're almost at the dock," he said.

Kiera was looking down at me in the strangest way. After a moment, they both left. I closed my eyes again and listened to the hum of the engines. I felt the boat slowing down, but I never felt it being docked. I fell asleep, I think, or maybe it would be better described as passing out.

The first thing I realized when I opened my eyes was that I was naked, and everyone was standing around the bed looking down at me, but their faces were going in and out of focus. Was I dreaming?

Then I saw the top of Ricky's head. He was moving between my legs and lifting them at the same time. Faces continued to go in and out and then diminished, as if I were looking at them through the wrong end of a telescope. When I felt him pushing into me, I was sure I heard a soft chanting that sounded like "VA, VA, VA." I know I cried out. My whole body was shaking. *It's really happening,* I thought. *This isn't a dream.*

I don't know how long it lasted. Minutes seemed to float into each other. I wasn't even sure how many times Ricky was there.

At one point, as if they were all suddenly bored, they filed out, and I was alone with him for a while. Then he left, too.

When I woke up again, I was dressed. I could feel the boat moving. I sat up. The stateroom spun and then settled. My stomach was still woozy but not as bad as it had been. I called for Kiera. I could hear them all laughing. There was music, too. I struggled to get to my feet and opened the door. Everyone but Ricky was in the salon. They were drinking vodka. I saw the bottle on the table. Deidre noticed me first and called out. They all stopped talking and laughing and looked at me.

"I hope you're feeling better, Sasha," Kiera said. "I can't bring you home seasick. My mother called, and I told her you were on the island. She tried your phone next and then called me back, and I told her you left it on the boat. Remember to say that," she added, and sipped her drink.

Everyone continued to stare at me.

"I want to talk to you," I said.

"So talk. We don't keep secrets from each other, remember?"

Everyone laughed.

I started to cry. "I want to talk to you," I insisted.

She groaned, finished her drink, and

stood. "Will you all excuse me? Babysitting duties call," she said, and came to the stateroom.

I closed the door.

"What?"

"What did you give me to drink?"

"I don't know. Something Ricky's father had on the boat."

"I don't know what happened to me. I think . . . was I raped?"

"Raped? You were initiated, Sasha. Don't think of it as being raped."

"But I think everyone was there."

She smiled. "No one was there but Ricky."

"I . . . it was like a rape."

"I told you. Don't think of it as a rape."

"What should I think of it as?"

She thought a moment and smiled. "Think of it the way you would think of a toothache. Now it's over," she said, and walked out.

30
LIES

I kept to myself for the remainder of the trip. No one tried to get me into any conversations, anyway. It made me feel like yesterday's news. Even Ricky was aloof and indifferent. He never asked me how I felt. When we docked in Marina Del Ray, Kiera called to me to hurry along. She was anticipating another call from her mother any minute.

"I'll call her first and let her know we're on the way home once we're started," she said. That seemed to be the only thing that mattered to her now.

As I stepped off the boat, I saw the way the others were looking at me. None of the girls said good-bye or "See you later." They all simply stared at me. When I looked back at them, they were huddled and whispering.

"Is everyone angry at me?" I asked Kiera after we got into a taxi she had waiting.

"Don't ask, don't tell," she replied, and laughed.

"What does that mean?"

"It means what happens in Vegas stays in Vegas, Sasha. Don't go blabbing about our trip. I'll describe some of the things on Catalina that you missed," she added. "Just in case my mother gives you the third degree or something."

She then narrated her version of our story, even elaborating on what we all had for lunch.

"Did you really do all that?" I asked.

"Of course," she said. "Why would I lie to you?"

"It's not that. I can't believe I slept through it all."

"Don't mention being seasick. You can say you were a little woozy but you got over it," she instructed. Then she put her earphones in and turned on her iPod and sang along. I couldn't remember when she had looked and acted so happy.

After the taxi dropped us off, I turned to her and said, "So now I'm a full-fledged member of the VA club, huh?"

She paused at the front door and looked at me with the most curious expression on her face. "Pardon me?"

"The club," I said.

"I don't know what you're talking about, Sasha," she said, and opened the door.

I hurried in after her to pursue and under-stand, but before I could say anything else, both Mr. and Mrs. March came strolling out of the entertainment center, laughing. They paused when they saw us.

"Hey," Mr. March called. "How was your day, girls?"

"Miserable," Kiera said, and charged up the stairway.

I stood looking after her with just as shocked a face as they had. She didn't look back. She pounded her way up as if she were trying to stamp out bugs on the steps.

"What happened?" Mrs. March asked me as she approached. "When I called, she said you were all at a restaurant and were having a great time."

I shook my head. What was I supposed to be saying? Had Kiera forgotten to prepare me?

"Did something bad happen on the boat?" Mr. March asked, stepping up beside Mrs. March. "No accidents, I hope."

"No," I said.

"Well, then, what is it?" he asked.

"I don't know," I said. "I'll go talk to her."

"What the hell . . ." He looked at Mrs. March, who just shook her head.

I moved quickly to get away from them, fearful that I would say the wrong thing. Kiera had her door closed, so I knocked. She didn't open it or respond.

"Kiera? What's going on? Your parents are confused, and so am I." I looked back to be sure they hadn't followed me up. "What am I supposed to say?"

She opened the door partway and looked out at me with a face so full of anger it took my breath away. I stepped back.

"Tell them whatever lies you want," she said. "I'm tired of covering up for you."

"What?"

She slammed the door. I stood there dumbfounded. When I looked toward the stairway, I saw that Mrs. March had come up and was standing there gaping at me. I hurried to my suite and went in quickly. My head was spinning. I was still woozy and a little confused from what had happened on the boat, but this added so much weight to it I felt as if my head had turned to stone. I sat on my bed, dazed, my heart thumping. I hadn't closed my door, so I heard Mrs. March knock on Kiera's door. Instead of the usual unfriendly "What do you want?" I heard the door being opened, muffled voices, what sounded like Kiera crying, and then the door being closed.

I sat absolutely still, trying to hear something more, but I heard nothing for the longest time. Then I thought I heard heavy footsteps in the hallway and got up to listen at my doorway. I heard Mr. March ask, "What's this all about?" Then he, too, went into Kiera's room, and the door closed again. I closed my door softly and retreated to my bathroom. From the moment I had stepped off the boat, I could think of nothing else but a hot shower. I felt so dirty inside and out. I decided to wash my hair as well. Afterward, I wrapped a bath towel around myself and went to my vanity table to blow-dry my hair and brush it out.

The shower had refreshed me, but I could feel the deep fatigue in every muscle in my body, even in my bones. My eyes wanted to close and did for a moment. When I opened them, I saw both Mr. and Mrs. March captured in the mirror. They were standing behind me, looking very upset. I spun around.

"Sasha," Mrs. March began. "Do you have a tattoo very low down on your back?"

For a moment, I couldn't speak. My throat tightened so hard I couldn't breathe. Why would Kiera have told them about that? There was no other way, no other reason, they would be asking about it.

"Yes," I finally said.

"I'd like to see it," Mr. March said, more

to Mrs. March than to me. "Now," he emphasized so sternly that I winced.

"Please turn around again, Sasha, and undo the bath towel so we can see the tattoo," Mrs. March asked. She looked as if she was going to burst into tears any second. "Please," she added.

I fumbled with the towel so I could open it and cover the front of my body while lifting the towel enough to expose the tattoo.

Mr. March stepped closer and looked at it. "Where's Alena's digital camera?" he asked Mrs. March.

"Donald, please."

"Where is it?" he practically shouted at her.

She looked flustered for a moment but then went to a drawer in the desk and took out a camera. She brought it to him. He turned it on and took a picture of my tattoo.

"You ask about the rest," he said. "I'm going to my office to send this to have it checked."

He left the suite, and I wrapped the towel around myself again. I had no idea what I was supposed to do or say. Had someone informed Kiera's parents about the VA club? Were we all in trouble? Mrs. March, her body looking as if it was slipping off her

446

bones, slinked over to a chair and sat.

"Kiera is upset," she began. "She says you stole her boyfriend today, Ricky Burns. She says you were intimate with him on the boat and didn't care that everyone knew it. She says you seduced Ricky."

It felt as if a sheet of ice was sliding from the back of my head down my back, over my stomach, and down my legs to my feet.

"That's not true," I said.

"She was so upset that she broke down and confessed about other things. She told us she took you to buy those clothes because you wanted them, and she thought we'd want her to make you happy."

"What?"

"I knew they weren't her clothes. They looked new, and they fit you."

"That's not true, either. She's lying. I don't know why, but she is."

"She said it was your idea to lie about the play audition."

"No."

"Otherwise, why would you go along with it? She says you have a reputation as a big flirt in school, and all the boys were after you, and she was frankly embarrassed about it since we had described you as her cousin. She claims she tried to get you to calm down, but today was the end. You could have had any boy on the boat, but you chose Ricky just because he was her boyfriend. She says that you were plotting and conniving to get your revenge in subtle ways, this being one."

How could she say these things? I thought. I wasn't going to let her get away with it.

"No, no, Mrs. March, I didn't choose Ricky. They did."

"Who's 'they,' Sasha?"

"The other girls . . . the VA club," I said.

She stared for a moment, looked away, and then turned back to me. "Now, what is this supposed to be, the VA club?"

"Virgins Anonymous. That's what this tattoo is about. It's calligraphy of the *V* and the *A*. All of the girls have a tattoo there."

"What's Virgins Anonymous? I don't understand."

"All of the girls in the club have given up their virginity to be members, and everyone has sex regularly with any boy. Kiera brought me to be a member, and they approved of me. I swore a vow on a notebook that contains the description of each girl's first time. We meet regularly at Deidre's house, because her mother works with her father and she has the house free after school. No one was supposed to talk about it, but Kiera's lying to you about me. I

448

didn't ask for new clothes, I didn't ask for the tattoo, and I didn't steal her boyfriend. What happened was that I got seasick very quickly on the boat, and Ricky put me in the master stateroom. I wasn't supposed to get seasick. Kiera said those pills she had given me would prevent it."

"What pills?"

"The pills to make my periods less severe. Here," I said, rising quickly and going to the drawer beside my bed. "I'll show you."

I opened the drawer and stared down in disbelief. The pills were gone. I looked carefully through the drawer.

"She must have taken them back," I said under my breath.

"Sasha, Mr. March is very, very upset."

"It's not true. None of what she's saying is true!"

"Get dressed," she said, rising. "We're all going to have a talk downstairs in Mr. March's office. I'm sick to my stomach."

I started to cry. She looked at me but not with the same compassion and sympathy I used to see in her face.

"Just get dressed. I'm calling Deidre's mother right now," she said, and left.

I couldn't stop sobbing, but I put on some clothes, making sure not to wear anything Kiera had given me. I wanted to confront her first, but she was already downstairs sitting in her father's office. She had her hands clasped on her lap and looked straight ahead, as though she was the one being accused of everything, as though she was the one so damaged and hurt.

Mr. March sat at his desk. Mrs. March was sitting across from Kiera.

"Just sit anywhere, Sasha," Mr. March said.

I looked at Kiera, but she wouldn't look at me. Nevertheless, I sat on the settee, too.

"Do you belong to or did you join a club?" Mr. March asked immediately.

Good, I thought. *They found out the truth. It serves her right.*

"Yes."

He held up a printout of the digital picture he had taken of my tattoo. "Is this the club's logo?"

"Yes, it is," I said.

"Hell Girl?" he asked.

"What?"

"That's what this calligraphy represents. I had it confirmed."

"No," I said, shaking my head. "It spells 'VA.' That's the club Kiera had me join, the VA club."

Kiera blew air through her lips. She smiled at her father. "Did you ever? VA club?"

"The girls took me to get the tattoo," I said quickly. "All of them."

"Do you know where this supposedly occurred?" Mr. March asked.

"Somewhere in L.A. I don't remember the address. If I saw it, I'd remember."

"First," Kiera began, "you know, Daddy, that someone under eighteen can't get a tattoo in California legally. Why would anyone risk his business to give her that ridiculous tattoo?"

"She's right. Sasha?"

"I don't know why he did it. Maybe they gave him more money," I said now, feeling real panic. "She has one. They all have one."

Kiera turned slowly. "Did you see it? Is that what you're telling my parents now?"

"Yes," I said, nodding at Mr. and Mrs. March. "I saw it on all of them in the same place."

Kiera stood up, undid her jeans, and lowered them. She turned to her father and mother and lowered her panties. Then she turned to me, and I gasped. It was gone.

"This is beginning to sound like *Psycho*," Kiera said as she pulled her jeans up. "I don't really care what my parents decide to do about you," she told me. "What you did with Ricky was mean. I'm not going to lie for you anymore, though. I can tell you that."

She turned to her parents.

"Haven't I tried to be a good older sister to her? I've lost friends because of her and some of the crude things she says. Now she goes and seduces Ricky after I talk him into taking us to Catalina on his father's boat. Don't just take my word for it. Ask my girlfriends. Go on and ask her if she's still a virgin or ever was when she first came here. Go on. You can have her examined if you don't believe me."

I couldn't keep the tears from streaming down my face. The looks on Mr. and Mrs. March's faces felt like knives in my heart. They both looked drained of any warmth and hope. I felt as if I were looking at them when they had first heard their younger daughter was terminally ill. I felt terminally ill. Kiera, always alert to an opportunity, had her finish perfected and perfectly timed.

"I told you, Mother. I warned you," Kiera said with a voice soft and sorrowful. "She's not Alena. She took advantage of you. She probably did know how to play the clarinet but pretended she didn't."

Mrs. March started to cry.

Kiera turned to me. "You're not my sister. You never could be," she said, and walked out of the office.

I took deep breaths to stop myself from crying. My chest ached. Mr. March rose and paced a bit behind his desk. Mrs. March stopped crying, wiped her face with her handkerchief, and, after a deep breath herself, turned to me.

"I spoke with Deidre. She confirmed Kiera's story about what happened on the boat," she began. "She doesn't know anything about any VA club, and her mother confirmed that she has no tattoo on her lower back."

"Deidre's lying for her," I muttered weakly.

"I called some of the other mothers, and they checked their daughters, too. No tattoos, Sasha."

"Theirs weren't permanent, then. They showed them to me to fool me," I said. "I'm not lying. I didn't seduce Ricky Burns on his boat. They gave me something to drink that was supposed to help my seasickness, only it made me feel weird. They were all in the room. I was raped!" I cried.

Mr. March stopped pacing and looked at Mrs. March. "This is no good, Jordan. We're talking about a first-class scandal here."

"I know," she said in a voice of defeat.

He pointed at me. "You don't go making

such an accusation, Sasha. Tom Burns is an influential businessman. His chain of pharmacies is one of the most successful in the state. He'd destroy us in such a fight. I don't want to hear that you've told this story to anyone at school. Is that understood? Is it?"

"Yes, but it's true."

"Don't dare speak it," he said, punching each word. He turned to Mrs. March. "I want you to move her out of Alena's room for now. Put her in one of the guest rooms away from Kiera. I don't know what's wrong with you, Sasha," he said, turning back to me. "Maybe your life on the streets made you sly and clever in your battle to survive. Maybe you saw an opportunity in Mrs. March. She's taken the loss of our daughter very hard. Maybe I need to send both you and Kiera to therapists. Whatever. But for now, I want no more talk about any of this. I'll look into seeing what the best alternatives for you are. For the time being, go to the school we have had you going to. Do your work, and stay out of trouble. Come directly home after your school activities, and do not go out and about on weekends. Am I clear?"

"Yes."

"You did impress me when you first came here. I have to believe that indicates you have good qualities. My advice is for you to nurture them and nothing else. You want to add anything, Jordan?"

"No," she said.

"Tell Mrs. Duval to move her things immediately, then."

She nodded and looked at me. "Go up and put together what you want to take to the guest room, Sasha. I'm sorry, but Mr. March is right. We want you away from Kiera."

"And out of Alena's room," he emphasized.

"Someday you'll know that I wasn't lying, and you'll be sorry," I said. "And I'll feel sorrier for you than I do for myself."

I walked out and up the stairs, but I felt like a sleep-walker. When I reached Kiera's room, she opened the door. She must have been waiting right there, listening for my footsteps. She stepped out and smiled at me.

"I feel I should tell you something," she began. "The second set of pills I gave you . . ."

"Where are they? What about them?"

"They were fertility pills. Ricky's father owns a drugstore chain, remember? He can get anything. Maybe you'll have twins."

The heat that came into my face made

me feel that I would go up in flames.

"Why did you do all this to me?" I asked.

She smiled. "My parents started to love you more than they loved me. That was the way it was when Alena was alive, and I wasn't going to let it happen again. Aren't my friends loyal? They're so wonderful.

"Besides," she said, losing her smile of satisfaction to the hard, cold face I had first known, "I told you. It was your mother's fault. She shouldn't have crossed the highway there." She closed the door softly.

I felt like someone in a coffin who wasn't really dead watching the lid being shut.

31
DARKNESS

Although the guest room wasn't as large as Alena's suite and didn't have a sitting area where I could set up my schoolwork, it was luxurious, with a king-size bed and a thick-carpeted floor. It had a very nice bathroom, too, but the room was in a wing of the house that was darker and lonelier, not that I wanted to be anywhere near Kiera ever again. She claimed the same about me and wouldn't eat dinner if I was at the table at the same time. Her father accommodated her wishes and ordered Mrs. March to have me served my dinner an hour earlier than when they ate. Every night of the following week, I ate dinner alone in the kitchen nook. By now, all of the servants working for the Marches knew that something was seriously wrong, but no one asked me any questions about why I was being isolated, nor did anyone speak much more to me than was absolutely necessary, even though I could see sympathy in both Mrs. Duval's and Mrs. Caro's faces. I imagined they were all worried about losing their jobs. Grover was driving me to school again but was back to his silent, formal ways.

I didn't know what to expect when I returned to school on Monday. At first, no one noticed anything really different until lunch hour, when I ended up sitting by myself. That was when the buzz began. The stories about me couldn't have been passed around quicker even in a general announcement over loudspeakers.

I had no idea exactly what the girls were saying about me yet, but Lisa Dirk couldn't wait to be a messenger. She came sauntering over and slid into the seat across from me.

"How come you're sitting all by yourself?" she asked. It was obvious that she knew the answer. My senior girlfriends didn't want me, and I didn't want them.

I didn't reply. I just ate with my gaze focused on nothing, least of all her.

"Is it true what we hear?" she asked. "About you and Ricky Burns?"

I put my sandwich down and leaned toward her. The expression on my face frightened her, and she pulled back.

"I don't know what you heard, and I really

don't care."

"We heard that you threw yourself at him on his boat. You called him from a stateroom, and you were naked," she blurted.

"They're spreading lies about me," I said, even though I knew it would be useless and a waste of time to defend myself. It was like holding back a waterfall with your bare hands. They were a chorus of gossipers, and I was a lone, lost voice.

"I'd never guess you were like that," Lisa said, ignoring my denial. "To go after a senior boy so desperately is sad."

"Sad?"

I was holding back a flood of truth with a dam made of paper. It was charging down my tongue. I was moments away from telling it all. *I'm not Kiera's cousin. While she was high on some drug, Kiera ran my mother and me over and killed my mother. Her mother took me in, enrolled me in this school, and made up that story.*

For a moment, I thought I had actually shouted it all, broken through the dam, but I quickly realized that what kept the dam secure was my fear that telling the truth about myself would only alienate me even more from my classmates. Who would want to be friends with a homeless girl? No one in that school would want to be seen talking to me. That was for sure.

I couldn't skip all of that and defend myself by telling Lisa I had been raped, either. Mr. March had forbidden me to say it. I could only swallow it all back and ignore everyone, but that was hard to do. By the end of the day, I felt covered in cobwebs of lies and distortions. There wasn't an eye not looking my way or a tongue not wagging about me. I might just as well have been walking around naked. My limping was nothing when it came to drawing attention compared with the globs of mud thrown at me. In fact, they almost didn't notice my limp, because they were too busy elaborating on the lies about my sexual exploits and sly ways. They saw only this promiscuous new student who probably had a bad reputation at her old school. In their minds, that was why I was so mysterious when it came to my past.

I did the best I could in my favorite class, art, but when I tried to start a new calligraphy project, I could only think of the horrible tattoo on my back and sat there for the longest time staring at blank paper. Mr. Longo kept coming over and encouraging me, but by the time the bell rang, I had hardly begun anything. I was the same earlier in music. I played my clarinet me-

chanically and so poorly that Mr. Denacio
threw one of his famous fits.

"If I don't see an improvement in you
soon," he threatened, "I will have to recon-
sider appointing you to a position in the
school band."

I didn't protest. I had no enthusiasm for
anything and plodded my way through the
corridors from class to class. Occasionally, I
caught sight of Kiera looking at me from
across a hallway. At one point, I thought
she looked amazed at how well her plan had
succeeded. She seemed in awe of herself.

Ricky never gave me a second glance. A
few times, I was tempted to walk up to him
to ask him how he could be so cruel, but he
and Boyd were always laughing, and I was
sure that if I did speak to either of them,
they would make me feel foolish and even
more embarrassed than I already was.

Except for band practice on Tuesday and
Thursday, I returned home immediately
after school and went up to the guest room.
I didn't start right in on my homework as I
used to do. I sat for quite a while just looking out the window, wondering what I could
possibly do now and where I would eventually end up. I was terribly worried about
becoming pregnant. I had no idea what I
would do if my period didn't come. I

wanted to visit Mama's grave, hoping that somehow she would talk to me and tell me what I should do, but I was afraid to ask Mrs. March for anything.

Mrs. March didn't say much to me all week. When we confronted each other, she looked as sad and as lost as I did. I was numb by now, but she still appeared to be on the verge of new tears. She did tell me that Mr. March was still researching what was best for me under the new circumstances. I understood that this didn't include my staying with them even like this. Sometimes, when I thought about all that Kiera had managed and how they had accepted everything she and her friends said as being true, I became more angry than sad for myself. I recalled the advice from Jackie, the nurse, and was tempted to threaten them with a lawsuit. I'd find my father, and he'd come back to do it.

Oddly, though, no matter how poorly I was being treated now, I couldn't harden my heart against Mrs. March, and I actually felt sorrier for Mr. March. Kiera had him so tightly wrapped around her finger that he couldn't see. Eventually, he would suffer some great tragedy. I went from wishing for it to chastising myself for wishing such evil things on someone.

In the midst of my misery, my loneliness in the dark side of the March mansion where my own footsteps echoed, I would find myself recalling some happier, sunnier moments with Mama, even on the streets after we had sold more than we had expected. She would splurge, and we'd have ice cream sundaes or get foot-long submarine sandwiches and sit out on the beach as if we were back to being as we once were. She didn't buy any alcohol with the extra money, so she was more like my mother again. She would tell me stories about her own youthful days in Portland, her boyfriends in high school, the plays she had been in, and the parties afterward.

I had heard many of the stories before, but for me, they were like the fairy tales other parents read to their children. Kids never heard them enough. You could recite them and know exactly what was coming next, but there was something special about having your mother or father read them repeatedly to you. It made you feel safe, wrapped securely in their love and in the magic they could conjure with their voices. The hard, cold world was kept outside. Nothing bad could happen, and you could slip softly into a comfortable sleep, unafraid of the darkness it necessarily had to bring along with it. There was always the promise of tomorrow.

Now there was no promise of tomorrow, and the cold, hard world had found its way to come back at me. There was no escape, no safety, and the darkness that came with sleep now was terrifying, not because it brought old ghosts and nightmares but because it made me blind and afraid to take another step forward, to have another thought, to dare to make another wish.

On Friday, Kiera broke her vow of silence when it came to me and approached me in the cafeteria, but it wasn't to express any regret or remorse. She didn't sit at my table. She stood across from me, keeping her distance as if she were afraid I might attack her.

"I see you're still having trouble making new friends," she began, nodding at the empty chairs.

"I'm not looking for new friends yet, but when I do, I'll be more careful about choosing them," I replied.

"You don't have to be careful about it or worry about it. I doubt you'll be here that much longer, anyway."

"Wherever I go can't be worse," I said, and she laughed.

"Ricky's having a party tonight at his

house. His parents are beginning a short Mexican Riviera vacation. We'd invite you just for entertainment, but everyone's afraid you might steal away another boyfriend."

I was silent. I felt my insides trembling, but I wasn't going to cry or even look sad and frightened. Instead, I said, "I feel sorry for you."

"You feel sorry for me? That's a laugh. When you end up in some foster home, sleeping in a two-by-four bedroom and going to some inferior public school, think of me. I'm going to think of you tonight. You can call it a celebration of sorts."

"You're good at what you do, Kiera, I won't deny it, but with all your money and your things, your cars and trips, you really don't have much more than I do. You're lonelier than I am, in fact."

"You're crazy," she said, but my firmness threw her. I could see her losing some of her confidence and arrogance.

"You had me believing that you really did have a good relationship with your sister, but I know now you couldn't possibly have had that. I imagine there were times when you wished bad things would happen to her, and when they did, you hated yourself. You know what?" I added, scooping up some fruit with my fork. "I think you still do."

For the first time, I saw blood rush into her cheeks and her eyes blaze. She was also speechless. There was so much anger in her eyes. I looked away, and she walked off, but I caught her looking at me every once in a while. There was no question in my mind that she was wishing she could do more harm to me. I had cut deeply past her hard steel surface and touched that place where all of her fears and regrets slept, waiting for something or someone to nudge them awake. Maybe now she would have bad dreams and fear the darkness, too, I thought.

Ironically, it didn't make me feel better to be able to hurt her, even after all she had done. I knew that for most people, that would be a weakness. How could I survive in a world where people were so cruel to one another if I didn't enjoy revenge?

I think the trouble was that I had grown too close to Alena. Dead and gone, she still had a presence in that suite, not only for Mrs. March but, after a while, also for me, wearing her clothes, using her things, and seeing her pictures, her face constantly in mine. I couldn't help but lie awake nights and think of her there, wondering what her thoughts were like when she realized how sick she was. Did she cry? Was she angry?

Was she simply afraid all the time? From the way Mr. and Mrs. March had described her, none of that seemed to be true. I knew that all parents saw their children as angels when they were so young and innocent, but maybe Alena really was angelic. Maybe she had been helping me find my way. Maybe, even now, she felt sorry for her sister and wished that somehow, some way, I could have changed her the way she had pretended to change.

Forgive me, Alena, both for failing and for wishing harm to Kiera, I thought, and I continued to the end of my school day.

Neither Mr. nor Mrs. March was home when I returned. I went directly up to my room. The hallway looked darker than ever, and the room was cold and lonely. I felt like one of those children we read about in class, the ones locked in the Tower of London. Like them, I was left to wither and die. For the first time since I had been brought to the March mansion, even in the beginning, when Kiera was so mean to me, I considered running away. I had survived in the streets before, so why not now? It was more than a passing thought. I considered what I would take with me and what I had that I could pawn to raise money. I still had the two watches Kiera had given me so nonchalantly. If she wasn't lying about those being real diamonds in them, I might have enough to get along for a while.

But then the reality of a girl my age trying to get by sank in. What hotel would rent me a room, even some of the fleabag ones I knew were out there? What would I do when the money ran out? Who would hire me to work, and what could I sell on the boardwalks now? The chances that the police would leave me alone without an adult were far lower, too. Running away was no answer.

Depressed, I lay down and soon fell asleep. I woke when I heard knocking on my door and saw Mrs. March standing there.

"Are you ill?" she asked.

"No, just a little tired."

"Mr. March called to tell me he's arranged a meeting for you with Social Services next week. I believe it's on Monday. They'll find a suitable new home for you," she said, and then pressed her lips together as if to hold back sobs. "I'm sorry, Sasha. I wish it would have worked out for you here. I truly do."

"Thank you," I said.

"Mrs. Duval has your dinner ready," she added, and left. I heard her footsteps dying away in the corridor, disappearing like my advantageous and hopeful future.

I rose, washed, and went down to dinner. Since the new arrangements had begun, I felt as if everyone around me was mute or deaf. The long silence hung in the air. Faces were averted from mine. Everything was done mechanically and as quickly as possible. It occurred to me, of course, that they had all been told Kiera's story and believed everything bad about me, too. The only friend I had left in the house was the imaginary friend I had in Alena. It seemed appropriate that I would be close only to the dead now.

I didn't linger downstairs after dinner. I went up the grand stairway slowly, walking like someone going to her execution, and went to my room. Doing my homework seemed pointless, as was practicing the clarinet. I wouldn't be finishing school there after all, it seemed. Nevertheless, out of either sadness or a need to keep up my connection with Alena, I did play the clarinet.

After that, I watched some television. I wanted to keep myself awake as long as possible so I would fall asleep faster and not toss and turn, worrying, reliving the pain and misery. It was close to midnight when I finally turned the television off. I was about to get ready for bed when I heard what sounded like quite a commotion, so I went out to the hallway to listen closer. It was coming from the wing of the house where Kiera's and the Marches' bedrooms were. Mrs. March was screaming something. I walked toward the noise slowly and then walked faster, almost running. She was heading toward the stairway when I saw her. She was buttoning her jacket. She stopped when she saw me.

"What's happening?" I asked.

"It's Kiera," she said. "She's being rushed to the hospital from her party. Something about . . . a drug overdose. She's in a coma," she muttered. "My husband . . ."

"What?"

"He's not been notified yet. He can't be reached. He's flying back from a meeting in San Francisco. I have to get to the hospital." She turned again to descend the stairway. She looked so small and frightened.

"Can I come with you?" I asked, rushing to the stairs. "I won't be in your way. I'll be there just to be with you." I wanted to add, *If Alena were here, you'd surely take her.* Perhaps she heard my thoughts, or perhaps Alena spoke to her.

"Yes," she said. "Thank you. Come."

I hurried down to join her, and without another word spoken between us, we got into her car.

"I knew this day would come," she said in a voice barely above a whisper. "I felt it inside me, the way people can feel the rain. The dark clouds were always on Kiera's horizon just waiting to be invited in. I try to blame it all on Donald, on his permissiveness, his blindness, his indifference, but I'm just as guilty."

I didn't tell her, but as we drove on through the night, I felt guilty, too.

I had wished hard for something like this. I had wanted it so much that I had almost tasted it. Was I going along with her now to gloat or to give her comfort?

Was I Alena, or was I Sasha Porter?

It wouldn't be long before I knew.

32
HOSPITAL

They were all there in the emergency room. Every one of them looked frightened, but when they saw me with Mrs. March, their looks of fear changed to surprise. Ricky looked up last. He was sitting, holding his head in his hands. Mrs. March didn't ask any of them anything, nor did she say anything to any of them. She went directly to the nurses' station and introduced herself. At almost the same moment, a doctor was at her side. He said something to her and then led her down a corridor.

Deidre was the first to speak to me. She approached me slowly. The shock of seeing me was replaced by confusion. "Why are you here?" she asked, loudly enough for the others to hear.

"Mrs. March needed someone with her," I said. After I said it, I realized I should have said "my aunt." "My uncle is on his way back from San Francisco and is on an airplane."

She lost her look of confusion, but then, in the tone of a confession, she said, "He's not your uncle. Everyone here knows the truth now. Kiera lost control of her tongue before anything else."

I looked at the others, all sitting there, their gazes now fixed on me.

To my surprise, Deidre added, "It was still very nice of you to come along with her. You can sit and wait with us," she said, indicating a chair next to her.

"Thanks. I'll sit here," I said, and sat.

She didn't look upset. She nodded, understanding, and returned to her seat. I looked at them all. I really hated them for what they had done to me, but they looked pathetic, more like terrified little children now, especially Ricky. In fact, he looked as if he had been crying. He turned away to avoid my gaze.

Two uniformed policemen arrived and went to the nurses' desk. She spoke to them for a while, and while she did, Kiera's friends were all like stone. The policemen turned and looked at them, and then the nurse nodded in the direction of the corridor and they walked down it.

Deidre stared at me thoughtfully. Finally,

she got up again and walked over to Ricky. She spoke to him, and they both looked at me. He nodded and got up. I felt my body tighten as he walked toward me.

"Can I talk to you?" he asked.

"What do you want?"

"Let's just go outside for a minute. Please," he added when I didn't move. The others all stared at us.

I got up and walked out to the parking area. He followed, and then I stopped and turned abruptly to him.

"What?" I said.

"I don't expect you to accept any apologies. I just wanted to tell you something about the pills Kiera gave you. She asked me to get them."

"So?"

"She wanted fertility pills. You know, pills for women who have trouble getting pregnant."

"I know what fertility pills are, Ricky."

"I got her pills and told her they were fertility pills, but they were only what we call placebos. There was nothing in them to make it easier for you to get pregnant."

"But thanks to you, I can still get pregnant, right?"

"I hope not. I don't expect it," he said.

"Why not?"

"Right afterward, without Kiera knowing, I had you drink some water and take another pill. It's called the morning-after pill. I wasn't going to be the father of anyone's baby at my age. Anyway," he said, looking back again and then at me, "whatever happens here, it's a wake-up call, at least for me. I'm probably going to be in a great deal of trouble."

"What happened to her?"

"She took something called G. I got it through someone I know. It's like the flavor of the week these days, you know? Everyone's always looking for a new kick. Kiera keeps up with this stuff more than anyone else. I didn't know what dosage people should take. This guy told me you take a shot like whiskey, but she took three. I warned her to go slowly, but it was pretty clear she had gone too far when she collapsed. She fell into a coma. We couldn't revive her, so we had to call for an ambulance. I had to tell them what it was. The police will be out here soon looking for me."

"How could you give her something like that? I guess I shouldn't ask. Look what you gave me."

"You're right. It was a terrible thing to do."

"You didn't seem sorry when I saw you

this week."

"I was, but I was afraid to show it."

"Your friends mean too much to you," I said.

He almost smiled. "You're pretty smart, Sasha. I wasn't with you just to do what Kiera wanted."

"It doesn't matter now," I said. "How seriously ill is she?"

"I don't know. Bad, I guess. They said she was having trouble breathing."

"Why was she so reckless?"

"She was just intent on having the best time ever. Actually, I thought she was doing the drugs to try to break out of a depression, not to have a great time. She was acting weird to start with, so I was nervous, and then this happened. Luckily, no one else went for any of the G before she had her reaction, but they would have, I'm sure. We all could be in there," he said, looking down and shaking his head. "Damn."

He looked up at me. "I didn't know the truth about you until tonight. No one except Deidre did, I guess. When Kiera told us about your mother and the accident . . . well, I think what she did bothers her more than she'd ever admit, which is another reason I think she went so heavily for the G. Of course, the others, like me, were surprised to hear the details about you. It made me feel pretty lousy. All this time, I thought you were just another spoiled relative of Kiera's. It's a poor excuse, I know, but I just wanted to say it. If the police ask you anything, you can tell them whatever you want. I won't deny it. Sorry," he said again, and walked back into the emergency waiting room.

I remained outside for a while, just pacing. When I looked through the glass doors, I saw the two policemen talking to Kiera's friends. Ricky stood up and walked out with them. He glanced my way as they led him to the patrol car. After he got into the rear, they drove off. When I turned back to the emergency room, I saw the rest of them at the door. They had been watching, too. They parted to make way for me when I entered, which was just when Mrs. March came out, too.

"Donald's here," she told me. "He came in through the main entrance and was brought to Kiera. He's with her now. We're going to wait for a specialist in a different lounge. If you want to go home, I'll get a taxi."

"No, I'd rather wait with you, if that's all right."

She looked at Kiera's friends, and they all

turned away. "I've very disappointed in you, Deidre. In all of you," she added.

Deidre started to cry.

"I'm getting this in bits and pieces," she said, turning back to me, "but I have a feeling you've been misjudged. Come along."

I looked back at the others. They were like people in a desert craving some water. No one was going to talk to them to tell them anything about Kiera. I went over to Deidre.

"Mr. March is here. They're expecting a specialist to examine Kiera."

"Thank you," she said. "We were told to stay here. Two other patrol cars are coming to get us, and our parents are being informed. I'm sorry about what we did to you," she added.

I didn't say thank you. I didn't say she should be. I simply nodded and hurried after Mrs. March. Someone from the hospital brought us to a private room outside the hospital administrator's office. He offered us something to drink and went off to get it.

"Donald and I make big contributions to this hospital," Mrs. March told me as a way of explaining our VIP treatment. "We'll soon see what good that does us." The man returned with some coffee for her and a soft drink for me. "Please let my husband know we're up here," she said, and he left.

As I looked at her now, I thought back to when I had first seen her in the hospital ward. She was so elegant, impressive, and powerful. I'd had no idea who she was and why she was there, but I had sensed that she had the power to get things done. Now, sipping her coffee and curling herself in the corner of the sofa, she looked so much smaller and as pathetic as some of the homeless women Mama and I had known as regulars on the streets. When I had gotten to know some of them, I often felt sorrier for them than I did for us. Many had children who had disowned them, or they had lost children, husbands, and all their friends. We were all hobos looking for a handout of love.

Just as I felt Mrs. March was now. It struck me that neither she nor Mr. March ever talked much about relatives. Their money and their power had lifted them into another realm, and if I did hear Mr. March talk about cousins and uncles, it was always in reference to some fear that they would be asking for money. I had never fully realized until now how lonely the three of them really were. They barely had each other, and now it was possible that after losing their younger daughter, they would lose their older one, too. As miserable as Kiera could be, she still filled some of the empty places in their lives. Their home was too kind to tragic memories. It welcomed them. They would never go away. They could live forever in the dark, empty hallways and rooms. Every shadow would protect a ghost, and there were already too many there.

"She'll be all right," I said.

Mrs. March nodded softly. "Why does she have to go to drugs for a good time? Why could she never see how dangerous it is?"

I didn't know what to say to her. We both sat sipping our drinks and waiting. At one point, she looked as if she had fallen asleep. I was very tired, too, but I wouldn't close my eyes.

I lost track of time, but finally, Mr. March, looking exhausted and defeated, that tall, self-confident posture gone, came into the lounge. His face was ashen. She looked up quickly.

"Mat Kindle is examining her," he said. Then he noticed me. "I got Deidre aside before the police returned for her and the others," he said. "What more can you tell us about this?"

"She wasn't there, Donald."

"I know, but she might know something,"

he said. "Something more. Well?"

I told him all that Ricky had told me about the party. I used his words to describe why Kiera had wanted the drug. I made a special effort not to sound happy or satisfied.

He nodded. "That's more or less how Deidre described it. She told me the rest, too," he added.

"What rest?" Mrs. March asked.

"It appears Sasha was telling us the truth about it all. They did a very cruel, sick thing to her at Kiera's bidding, I'm afraid." He turned to me. "I'll look into how we can get that tattoo off you."

I saw the mixed feelings in Mrs. March's face. She was happy for me but devastated about Kiera.

"We've got changes to make after this is over," Mr. March said. "Everything got out of hand. It's my fault. You were always right, Jordan. I'm sorry."

She started to cry. He went to her and held her. The two of them looked destroyed. Every part of me wanted to feel good, to feel vindicated and happy about their misery, but I couldn't stop myself from crying, too. Alena was there in me, I thought. I moved over on the sofa and found Mrs. March's hand. Mr. March looked at me, and then the two of them embraced me.

It was the way the doctor found us.

The three of us looked up at him.

"She took a severe dosage of this crap," he began. He was a short, stocky man with a dark brown mustache but a nearly bald head. I thought he looked more like one of those professional wrestlers on television, even in his suit and tie.

"What is it, exactly?" Mr. March asked.

"Technically, gamma-hydroxybutyric acid, known on the street as GHB or just G. It looks like plain water, but if you tasted it, you'd immediately know it wasn't. So there's no chance it was a mistake unless someone snuck it into a drink. That happens, but I don't think so this time."

"No, it didn't. You're right, Mat," Mr. March said.

"Why do they take it?" Mrs. March asked.

Dr. Kindle laughed. "You have a few days to hear the sociological and psychological explanations for the drug culture? Kids are taking it because it makes them feel energetic, sensual, intoxicated. They grow talkative, high. They even call it Liquid Ecstasy. People who take it often pass out. That's not unusual with this junk. In street talk, that's 'carpeting out' or 'scooping out.' It has a dramatic effect on respiration. If they hadn't gotten Kiera here quickly, she would most surely have died."

"How is she now?" Mrs. March asked in a soft, frightened voice.

"We have her breathing stabilized. I can't tell you exactly how much longer she'll remain in this coma, but it's usually not for days or weeks. In most cases, it's hours. We're moving her to a private room, and I have a private nurse there already, Donald. We'll need to do a full evaluation of her, of course, and see if there has been any other organ damage. This is one of those drugs there are not enough statistics on, because it leaves the body after twelve hours. More people have probably died from it than has been reported. Young people," he added.

"Thanks, Mat," Mr. March said, rising. "What room is she in?"

"Three-forty. I'll be up in a little while, too," he said.

Mrs. March stood up and took her husband's hand. Then she turned to me and held out her other hand for me. I rose quickly, took it, and walked with them to the elevator.

Our lives really do move in circles, I thought as we went up to Kiera's room. My life with the Marches had begun with my being in a hospital, and there I was again in a hospital with not much more time before my life with them would end.

Although they had both already seen Kiera, the sight of her in the hospital bed with her body connected to the monitors froze them. When I looked at her, I thought she had begun to fade away. Her rich complexion was washed out. Her skin looked grayer. Her hair was still beautiful, but the loose strands on the pillow reflected the havoc that surely had preceded all of this in the ambulance and the emergency room. Caught in the frenzy to save her life, she had been poked and prodded, tossed and turned, and attached to machinery. She seemed more like a doll that had been violently shaken until parts of it were beginning to detach themselves.

I still wanted to harden my heart against her, but Alena was pushing me forward. I could almost hear her pleading, *Help her. Help her.*

I went to the side of her bed. Her nurse stood back, and the Marches stood at the foot of the bed. I pulled a chair to the bed and sat, and then I reached for her hand.

"I know the truth about you, Kiera," I said. "I know you are in more pain than anger, and all you did to me and now have done to yourself was your way of covering up that pain. Don't be afraid of it anymore. It's there to clean away your guilt so you can live. Live for your parents. Live for the people who are waiting to love you. And live for Alena."

I let go of her hand, stood up, and put the chair back.

"I'll wait for you downstairs, Mrs. March," I said. I was sure they wanted to be alone with their daughter.

Neither of them said anything to me. They watched me leave. I fell asleep for a while in the waiting room. Mrs. March woke me, and for a few moments, I really didn't know where I was.

"She's coming out of it," she said, smiling through happy tears. "She has to be fully evaluated yet, but Dr. Kindle thinks the worst might be over."

"Good," I said, and got up.

"Donald's waiting for us in the parking lot. He's leaving his car here. He wants us to go home together."

I saw him standing by the car. He got in when he saw us and started the engine. I got into the rear quickly, and Mrs. March got in beside him. No one spoke for the longest time. I nearly fell asleep again, but when we reached the gate and it opened, Mr. March did not drive in. Instead, he turned to look at me.

"Thank you for what you said to Kiera in there, Sasha. You are a remarkable young lady after all. I apologize for the things I said to you."

I didn't know what to say. He was still staring at me, and we weren't moving. The gate remained wide open, and the March mansion loomed ahead, many lights on. I imagined that Mrs. Duval and Mrs. Caro and the others were all waiting for news.

"Maybe Mrs. March was right," he continued. "Maybe you are the daughter we lost. Maybe in an ironic and terribly painful way for us all, Kiera brought you here. I know this," he said as he turned around to drive in. "You're not leaving until you're old enough to say good-bye and be on your own."

Smiling, Mrs. March reached back for my hand. I took hers, and the three of us drove up the grand driveway to the waiting mansion.

And for the first time since I had arrived there, I felt that I was really coming home.

EPILOGUE

I had no idea what Kiera would be like when she came home from the hospital. Mrs. March said that when her husband told Kiera I was going to remain with them, she wasn't upset.

"I wouldn't tell you she was overjoyed with the news," Mrs. March told me, "but she looked relieved. Right now, that might simply be because she's not being blamed for something more. I don't know. I always had trouble understanding Kiera and expect I will continue to have trouble. I'll need your help."

"We'll have to help each other with that," I said, and she laughed.

I was moved back into Alena's suite. For me, it was like renewing an old friendship. I hadn't realized how much the suite and everything in it had become part of me. I shared it with the memory of Alena, but I felt it was more mine now, too.

My schoolwork improved considerably over the next week. Mr. Denacio even took time out in instrumental class to have me demonstrate what real practice could do. What I enjoyed most was the expressions on the faces of my classmates. Why, they surely wondered, was I so buoyant and energetic, as well as happy, after all that had happened? They knew how much trouble Ricky and Kiera's other friends were in because of what had happened to her. Perhaps they were friendlier to me because they were hungry for more details. Once I had felt as if I had celebrity status because I was friends with seniors and did things with seniors. Now I had it because I was simply an exciting person to get to know.

Of course, I gave them little information, but that just made them more determined to talk to me, be with me, and invite me to their homes. It all made me feel much better about myself. Why, Lisa Dirk even told me I looked as if I was limping less and less.

On Friday, they brought Kiera home. She was still confined to bed rest. All of her meals were brought to her, which was nothing new to her, I guessed. When I arrived home, Mrs. March told me she was upstairs and getting better. She knew that because Kiera was complaining.

"However, I think she's still a bit stunned," she said. "Dr. Kindle said psychological problems often follow such an event, so I wouldn't be upset about anything she might say or do right now."

I knew she was trying to prepare me for anything Kiera might say or do to me, but I had a new sense of power and strength. I was no longer afraid of Kiera. Her friends had practically crawled underground. They were meek mice in school now. Ricky's disposition remained unknown. If his parents hadn't had money and influence, he wouldn't even have been attending Pacifica. The few times I saw him, he said nothing to me, and I said nothing to him.

It was impossible to avoid seeing Kiera, so I thought it would be best if I simply went directly up to her suite. The door was open, and she was propped up on big pillows in her bed.

"How are you?" I asked.

She stared at me as if we had never met. "Terrible," she finally replied. "They want me to stay in bed another three days or so. I haven't been able to wash my hair, put on any makeup, or anything. Look at what I look like."

"Look at what you almost did," I told her.

"Another goody two-shoes." She looked

away and then back at me. "Deidre called me in the hospital and told me what was going on with Ricky. I heard he told you things."

"He did."

"Are you happy now?"

"More than I was last week, yes," I said.

She smirked. "It looks like I'm going to have to live with you."

"Looks like it."

"Why would you want to stay here after all you went through? They'd probably give you lots of money and place you in a comfortable new home."

"Probably."

"So?"

"I'm staying for Alena. I'm not *becoming* Alena," I quickly added, "but I'm staying because of her. Besides, someone has to look after you."

"Very funny." She paused, her eyes narrowing a little. *Here it comes,* I thought. "I'm not going to say I'm sorry, if that's what you're waiting to hear."

"That's all right. I can wait. Someday you will."

"How did you get so arrogant?"

"I had a good teacher," I said.

I saw her fighting a smile. "I don't want to like you," she said defiantly.

"You will, eventually."

"And I suppose you'll like me, is that it?"

"Maybe. Eventually."

"Eventually, eventually. Everything's 'eventually.' "

"Everything is. When my mother and I were living in the streets, I used to wonder if we'd ever get off them, get back into a home, into a life. If I asked her, she'd always say 'soon.' *Soon*'s a great word. It's full of promise and hope."

"Is it?"

"Sure. Soon you'll get out of this bed, and soon you'll go to school. Soon you'll graduate and go to college, and soon you'll meet someone you can love, who can love you, and soon you'll get married and have a daughter maybe just like you, too."

"Please. You sound like my mother now."

"We all get to sound like our mothers."

"She's not yours."

"No, but she knows where to stand, when to smile, when to laugh and comfort me."

"You're giving me a headache."

"Okay." I turned and started out.

"Hey."

"What?"

"I don't like you yet, but I don't hate you anymore. Don't ask me why not. And don't say I hate myself more or anything stupid

491

like that."

"Okay."

"They moved you back next door?"

"Yes."

"Come back later, maybe eat in here. If you can stand it."

"I think I can. I lived in the streets once, remember?"

Now she laughed.

I would eat with her, but before I did anything else, I asked Mrs. March for a favor, and she called Grover to bring the car around.

He drove me out to the cemetery where Mama was buried. It was one of those wonderful California late afternoons when the shadows from some scattered clouds were refreshing and the air cleaned out by the sea wind was sharp and fresh. When I entered the cemetery, the aroma of freshly cut grass surrounded me. It was a scent that spoke of life and renewal, even in a cemetery.

All week, I had felt guilty about being happy again. It was the old fear that by accepting the Marches' generosity and affection, I was betraying Mama. I was at the cemetery to ask for her forgiveness again, but I thought I would do it a different sort of way. When I reached her grave, I set down the case and took out the clarinet. Then I sat close to her tombstone and began to play.

And before I was finished, I was certain in my heart that wherever she was, she was smiling.

ABOUT THE AUTHOR

One of the most popular authors of all time, **V.C. Andrews** has been a bestselling phenomenon since the publication of her spellbinding classic *Flowers in the Attic.* That blockbuster novel began her renowned Dollanganger family saga, which includes *Petals on the Wind, If There Be Thorns, Seeds of Yesterday,* and *Garden of Shadows.* Since then, readers have been captivated by more than sixty novels in V.C. Andrews's bestselling series. With *Family Storms,* she begins a thrilling, all-new series. V.C. Andrews's novels have sold more than one hundred and five million copies and have been translated into twenty-two foreign languages.

The employees of Thorndike Press hope you have enjoyed this Large Print book. All our Thorndike, Wheeler, and Kennebec Large Print titles are designed for easy reading, and all our books are made to last. Other Thorndike Press Large Print books are available at your library, through selected bookstores, or directly from us.

For information about titles, please call:
(800) 223-1244

or visit our Web site at:
http://gale.cengage.com/thorndike

To share your comments, please write:
Publisher
Thorndike Press
10 Water St., Suite 310
Waterville, ME 04901

All the characters in this book have no existence outside the imagination of the author, and have no relation whatsoever to anyone bearing the same name or names. They are not even distantly inspired by any individual known or unknown to the author, and all the incidents are pure invention.

All Rights Reserved including the right of reproduction in whole or in part in any form. This edition is published by arrangement with Harlequin Enterprises II BV/S.à.r.l. The text of this publication or any part thereof may not be reproduced or transmitted in any form or by any means, electronic or mechanical, including photocopying, recording, storage in an information retrieval system, or otherwise, without the written permission of the publisher.

® and ™ are trademarks owned and used by the trademark owner and/or its licensee. Trademarks marked with ® are registered with the United Kingdom Patent Office and/or the Office for Harmonisation in the Internal Market and in other countries.

First published in Great Britain 2012
by Mills & Boon, an imprint of Harlequin (UK) Limited.
Large Print edition 2012
Harlequin (UK) Limited, Eton House,
18-24 Paradise Road, Richmond, Surrey TW9 1SR

© Lynne Graham 2012

ISBN: 978 0 263 22622 5

Harlequin (UK) policy is to use papers that are natural, renewable and recyclable products and made from wood grown in sustainable forests. The logging and manufacturing process conform to the legal environmental regulations of the country of origin.

Printed and bound in Great Britain
by CPI Antony Rowe, Chippenham, Wiltshire

THE SECRETS
SHE CARRIED

BY
LYNNE GRAHAM

WITHDRAWN

MILLS & BOON™

W9-BKZ-827

Merry Christmas

To Dad

with love

from Paul

1978

EX LIBRIS
TSM

Books by Isaac Bashevis Singer

NOVELS
THE MANOR

I. THE MANOR   II. THE ESTATE

THE FAMILY MOSKAT   THE MAGICIAN OF LUBLIN

SATAN IN GORAY   THE SLAVE

ENEMIES, A LOVE STORY

SHOSHA

STORIES
A FRIEND OF KAFKA   GIMPEL THE FOOL   SHORT FRIDAY

THE SÉANCE   THE SPINOZA OF MARKET STREET

A CROWN OF FEATHERS   PASSIONS

MEMOIRS
IN MY FATHER'S COURT

FOR CHILDREN
A DAY OF PLEASURE   THE FOOLS OF CHELM

MAZEL AND SHLIMAZEL OR THE MILK OF A LIONESS

WHEN SHLEMIEL WENT TO WARSAW   A TALE OF THREE WISHES

ELIJAH THE SLAVE   JOSEPH AND KOZA OR THE SACRIFICE TO THE VISTULA

ALONE IN THE WILD FOREST   THE WICKED CITY

NAFTALI THE STORYTELLER AND HIS HORSE, SUS

WHY NOAH CHOSE THE DOVE

COLLECTION
AN ISAAC BASHEVIS SINGER READER

Shosha

Isaac Bashevis Singer

SHOSHA

FARRAR, STRAUS AND GIROUX · New York

Copyright © 1978 by Isaac Bashevis Singer
All rights reserved
Second printing, 1978
Printed in the United States of America
Published simultaneously in Canada by
McGraw-Hill Ryerson Ltd., Toronto
Library of Congress Cataloging in Publication Data
Singer, Isaac Bashevis.
Shosha.
I. Title.

PZ3.S61657Sj   [PJ5129.S49]   839′.09′33   78-6921

AUTHOR'S NOTE

THIS novel does not represent the Jews of Poland in the pre-Hitler years by any means. It is a story of a few unique characters in unique circumstances. It appeared in the *Jewish Daily Forward* in 1974 under the title *Soul Expeditions*. A great part of it was translated into English by my nephew Joseph Singer. A number of chapters I dictated to my wife, Alma, and to my secretary, Dvorah Menashe. The entire work was edited by Rachel MacKenzie and Robert Giroux. My gratitude and love to all of them.

I.B.S.

· PART ONE ·

· CHAPTER ONE ·

1

I WAS brought up on three dead languages—Hebrew, Aramaic, and Yiddish (some consider the last not a language at all)—and in a culture that developed in Babylon: the Talmud. The cheder where I studied was a room in which the teacher ate and slept, and his wife cooked. There I studied not arithmetic, geography, physics, chemistry, or history, but the laws governing an egg laid on a holiday and sacrifices in a temple destroyed two thousand years ago. Although my ancestors had settled in Poland some six or seven hundred years before I was born, I knew only a few words of the Polish language. We lived in Warsaw on Krochmalna Street, which might well have been called a ghetto. Actually the Jews of Russian-occupied Poland were free to live wherever they chose. I was an anachronism in every way, but I didn't know it, just as I didn't know that my friendship with Shosha, the daughter of our neighbor Bashele and her husband, Zelig, had anything to do with love. Love affairs took place between worldly young men who shaved their beards and smoked cigarettes on the Sabbath and girls who wore blouses with short sleeves and dresses with a décolleté. Such follies did not touch a cheder boy of seven or eight from a Hasidic house.

Still, I was drawn to Shosha and I passed through the dark

hall that led from our apartment to Bashele's as often as I could. Shosha was about my age, but while I was considered a prodigy, knew several pages of the Gemara and chapters of the Mishnah by heart, could write in Yiddish as well as in Hebrew, and had already begun to ponder God, providence, time, space, and infinity, Shosha was considered a little fool in our building, No. 10. At nine, she spoke like a child of six. She was left behind two years in a class in the public school to which her parents sent her. Shosha had blond hair that fell to her shoulders when she undid her braids. Her eyes were blue, her nose straight, her neck long. She took after her mother, who had been known as a beauty in her youth. Her sister Yppe, two years younger than Shosha, was dark, like her father. She wore a brace on her left leg and limped. Teibele, the youngest, was still a baby when I began to visit at Bashele's. She had just been weaned and slept in a cradle.

One day Shosha came home from school crying—the teacher had dismissed her, with a letter saying there was no place there for her. She brought home two books—one in Russian, one in Polish—as well as some exercise books and a box with pens and pencils. She had not learned any Russian but could read Polish slowly. The Polish schoolbook had pictures of a hut in a village, a cow, a rooster, a cat, a dog, a hare, and a mother stork feeding her newly hatched offspring in their nest. Shosha knew some of the poems in the book by heart.

Her father, Zelig, worked in a leather store. He left home early in the morning and returned late in the evening. His black beard was always short and round, and the Hasidim in our building said that he had it trimmed—a violation of Hasidic practice. He wore a short gaberdine, a stiff collar, a tie, and kid shoes with rubber tops. Saturday he went to a synagogue frequented by tradesmen and workers.

Though Bashele wore a wig, she did not shave her head as did my mother, the wife of Rabbi Menahem Mendl Greidinger. Mother often told me it was wrong for a rabbi's son, a student of the Gemara, to be the companion of a girl, and one from a common home at that. She warned me never to taste anything there, since Bashele might feed me meat that was not strictly kosher. The Greidingers came from generations of rabbis, authors of sacred books, while Bashele's father was a furrier and Zelig had served in the Russian Army before they married. The children in our house mimicked Shosha's speech. Shosha made silly mistakes in her Yiddish; she began a sentence and rarely finished it. When she was sent to the grocery store to buy food, she lost the money. Bashele's neighbors told her she ought to take Shosha to a doctor because her brain didn't seem to be developing, but Bashele had neither time nor money for doctors. And how could they help? Bashele herself was as naïve as a child. Michael the shoemaker said about her that you could make her believe she was pregnant with a kitten and that a cow flew over the roof and laid brass eggs.

How different Bashele's apartment was from ours! We had almost no furniture. The walls were lined with books from floor to ceiling. My brother, Moishe, and I did not have toys. We played with my father's volumes, with a broken pen, an empty ink bottle, or pieces of paper. Our living room had no sofa, no upholstered chairs, no chest of drawers—only an ark for scrolls, a long table, and benches. People prayed there on the Sabbath. My father stood at a lectern all day long and looked into large books that lay open in a great pile. He wrote commentaries, trying to answer the contradictions that one commentator found in the works of another. He was short, had a red beard and blue eyes, and he smoked a long pipe. From the time I can first remember, I heard him repeat the phrase "It is forbidden." Everything I wanted to do was a transgression. I was not allowed to draw or paint a person—that violated the Second Commandment. I couldn't say a word against another boy—that was slander. I couldn't laugh at anyone—that was mockery. I couldn't make up a story—that represented a lie.

On Sabbaths we weren't allowed to touch a candlestick, a coin, any of the things we amused ourselves with. Father reminded us constantly that this world was a corridor in which one had to study the Torah and perform virtuous deeds, so that when one made one's way to the palace that was the next world, rewards would be waiting to be collected. He used to say, "How long does one live, anyhow? Before you turn around it's all over. When a person sins, his sins turn into devils, demons, hobgoblins. After death they chase the corpse and drag it through forsaken forests and deserts where people do not go or cattle tread."

Mother occasionally got angry at Father for talking so depressingly to us, but she was a moralizer herself. She was lean, with sunken cheeks, a pointed chin, and large gray eyes that expressed both sharpness and melancholy. My parents had lost three children before I was born.

At Bashele's, before I even opened the door, I could smell her stews, roasts, and desserts. Her kitchen contained rows of copper and brass pots and pans, painted and gold-rimmed plates, a mortar and pestle, a coffee mill, all kinds of pictures and knick-knacks. The children had a crate filled with dolls, balls, colored pencils, paints. The beds were covered with pretty bedspreads. Embroidered cushions lay across the sofa.

Yppe and Teibele were too young for me, but Shosha was just right. Neither of us went down to play in the courtyard, which was controlled by rough boys with sticks. They bullied any child younger or weaker than they. Their talk was mean. They singled me out in particular because I was the rabbi's son and wore a long gaberdine and a velvet cap. They taunted me with names like "Fancypants," "Little Rabbi," "Mollycoddle." If they heard me speak to Shosha, they jeered and called me "Sissy." I was teased for having red hair, blue eyes, and unusually white skin. Sometimes they flung a rock at me, a chip of wood, or a blob of mud. Sometimes they tripped me so that I fell into the gutter. Or they might sic the house watchman's dog on me because they knew I was afraid of it.

But inside Bashele's I received neither teasing nor roughness. The moment I arrived Bashele offered me a plate of groats, a glass of borscht, a cookie. Shosha took down her toy box with her dolls, doll-sized dishes and cooking things, her collection of human and animal figurines, shiny buttons, gaudy ribbons. We played jacks, knucklebones, hide-and-seek, husband and wife. I made believe I went to the synagogue and when I returned Shosha prepared a meal for me. Once I played the role of a blind man and Shosha let me touch her forehead, cheeks, mouth. She kissed the palm of my hand and said, "Don't tell Mama."

I repeated to Shosha stories I had read or heard from my mother and father, embellishing them freely. I told her of the wild forests of Siberia, of Mexican bandits, and of cannibals who ate their own children. Sometimes Bashele would sit with us and listen to my chatter. I boasted to them that I was familiar with the cabala and knew expressions so sacred they could draw wine from the wall, create live pigeons, and let me fly to Madagascar. One such name I knew contained seventy-two letters, and when it was uttered the sky would turn red, the moon topple, and the world be destroyed.

Shosha's eyes filled with alarm. "Arele, don't ever say the word!"

"No, Shoshele, don't be afraid. I will make it so that you'll live forever."

2

NOT only could I play with Shosha, but I could also tell her things I dared not speak of to anyone else. I could describe all my fantasies and daydreams. I confided that I was writing a book. I often saw this book in my dreams. It was written by me and also by some ancient scribe in Rashi script on parchment. I imagined that I had done it in a former life. My father had forbidden me to look into the cabala. He admonished me that anyone who indulges in the cabala before the age of thirty is in danger of falling into heresy or insanity. But I believed that I was a heretic and half mad anyhow. There stood on our shelves volumes of the Zohar, *The Tree of Life, The Book of Creation, The Orchard of Pomegranates,* and other cabalistic works. I found a calendar where many facts about kings, statesmen, millionaires, and scholars were set down. My mother often read *The Book of the Covenant,* which was an anthology packed with scientific information. There I could read about Archimedes, Copernicus, Newton, and about the philosophers Aristotle, Descartes, Leibnitz. The author, Reb Elijah from Wilna, engaged in long polemics with those who denied the existence of God, and so I learned their opinions. Though the book was forbidden to me, I used every opportunity to read it. Once my father mentioned the philosopher Spinoza—his name should be blotted out—and his theory that God is the world and the world is God. These words created turmoil in my mind. If the world is God, I, the boy Aaron, my gaberdine, my velvet cap, my red hair, my shoes were part of the Godhead. So were Bashele, Shosha—even my thoughts.

That day, I lectured to Shosha about Spinoza's philosophy as if I had studied all his works. Shosha listened while she laid out her collection of gilded buttons. I was sure that she didn't grasp a single word, but then she asked, "Is Leibele Bontz also God?"

Leibele Bontz was known in our courtyard as a hoodlum and a thief. When he played cards with the boys, he cheated. He had all kinds of tricks and excuses to beat up a weaker boy. He would approach a little boy and say, "Someone told me that my elbow stinks. Do me a favor and smell it." When the little boy obliged, Leibele Bontz punched him in the nose. The idea that he could be part of God destroyed my enthusiasm for Spinoza's philosophy and I immediately developed a theory that there were two Gods —a good one and a bad one—and Leibele Bontz belonged with the bad one. Shosha accepted my new version of Spinoza willingly.

Every day there used to come to the Radzymin studyhouse, where my father prayed, a man called Joshua the herring merchant. He also had a nickname—Joshua the philosopher. He was short, slight, with a beard that had all colors: yellow, gray, brown. He sold marinated herring and smoked herring, and his wife and daughters pickled cucumbers. He prayed late and with great speed after the other worshippers had left. One minute he put on his prayer shawl and phylacteries; a minute later—or so it seemed to me—he took them off. I had stopped going to cheder because my father could not afford the tuition; besides, I was now able to read a page of the Gemara by myself. I often went to the Radzymin studyhouse to converse with this man. He dabbled in logic and told me about the paradoxes of the Greek philosopher Zeno. He also told me that even though the atom was supposed to be the smallest particle of matter, from a mathematical point of view it could be divided infinitely. He explained the meaning of the words "microcosm" and "macrocosm."

The next day I spoke about all this to Shosha. I told her that each atom is a world in itself, with myriads of tiny human beings, animals, and birds. There are Gentiles there and Jews. The men build houses, towers, towns, bridges, without realizing how infinitely small they are. They speak many languages. "In one drop of water there may be myriads of such worlds."

"Don't they get drowned?" Shosha asked.

In order not to make things too complicated, I said, "They all know how to swim."

A day did not pass without my coming to Shosha with new stories. I had discovered a potion that, if you drank it, made you as strong as Samson. I had drunk it already and I was so strong I could drive the Turks from the Holy Land and become King of the Jews; I had found a cap that, if you put it on your head, made you invisible. I was about to grow as wise as King Solomon, who could speak the language of birds. I told Shosha about the Queen of Sheba, who came to learn wisdom from King Solomon and brought with her many slaves, as well as camels and donkeys

bearing gifts for the ruler of Israel. Before she came King Solomon ordered that the palace floor be replaced with glass. When
the Queen of Sheba entered, she mistook the glass for water and
lifted up her skirt. King Solomon sat on his golden throne, and
when he saw the queen's legs, he said, "You are famous for your
great beauty, but you have hair on your legs like a man."

"Was this true?" Shosha asked.

"Yes, true."

Shosha lifted up her skirt to look at her own legs, and I said,
"Shosha, you are more beautiful than the Queen of Sheba." I
promised her that when I was anointed and sat on Solomon's
throne, I would take her for a wife. She would be the queen and
wear on her head a crown of diamonds, emeralds, rubies, and
sapphires. The other wives and concubines would bow before her
with their faces to the earth.

"How many wives will you have?" Shosha asked.

"Together with you, a thousand."

"Why so many?"

"King Solomon had a thousand wives. It is written so in the
Song of Songs."

"Is this allowed?"

"A king may do anything."

"If you have a thousand wives, you will have no time for me."

"Shoshele, for you I will always have time. You will sit near
me on the throne and rest your feet on a footstool of topaz.
When the Messiah comes, all Jews will mount a cloud and fly to
the Holy Land. The Gentiles will become slaves to the Jews. The
daughter of a general will wash your feet."

"Oh, it will tickle." Shosha began to laugh, showing her white
teeth.

The day that Zelig and Bashele moved from No. 10 to No. 7
Krochmalna Street was like Tisha Bov for me. It happened suddenly. One day I stole a groschen from my mother's purse and
bought a piece of chocolate for Shosha in Esther's candy store; a
day later movers opened the door of Bashele's apartment and

carried out the wardrobes, the sofa, the beds, the Passover dishes, the all-year-round dishes. I didn't even have a chance to say goodbye to the family. Actually, I had become too old to have a girl for a friend. I was studying not only Gemara now but also Tosaphot. The morning they moved, I was reading with my father *Rabbi Chanina, the Assistant of Priests.* From time to time I glanced out the window. Bashele's possessions were loaded on a platform harnessed to two Belgian horses. Bashele carried Teibele. Shosha and Yppe walked behind the wagon. The distance from No. 10 to No. 7 was only two blocks, but I knew that this meant the end. It was one thing to sneak out of the apartment, pass quickly through a dark hall, and knock on Shosha's door, and quite another thing to pay a visit in a strange building. The members of the community that paid my father his weekly remuneration were watchful, always ready to find some sign of misconduct in his children.

It was summer 1914. A month later, a Serbian assassin shot the Austrian Crown Prince and his wife. Soon the Czar mobilized all the armed forces. I saw men who worshipped in our living room on the Sabbath pass by our house with round shiny buttons on their lapels as a sign that they had been called up and would have to fight against the Germans, the Austrians, and the Italians. Policemen entered Elozar's tavern at No. 17 and poured all his vodka into the gutter—in time of war, citizens should be sober. The storekeepers refused to sell merchandise for paper money; they demanded silver coins or gold pieces. The doors of the stores were kept half closed, and only customers with such coins were allowed in.

At home we soon began to go hungry. In the time between the assassination in Sarajevo and the outbreak of the war, many wealthy housewives had stocked their larders with flour, rice, beans, and groats, but my mother had been busy reading morality books. Besides, we had no money. The Jews on our street stopped paying my father. There were no more weddings, divorces, or lawsuits in his courtroom. Long lines formed at the bakeries for a loaf of bread. The price of meat soared. In Yanash's Bazaar the slaughterers stood with knives in their hands, looking out for a woman with a chicken, a duck, or a goose. The price of fowl went up from day to day. Herring could not be bought at all. Many housewives began to use cocoa butter instead of butter. There was a lack of kerosene. After the Succoth holiday the rains, the snow, the frosts began, but we couldn't afford coal for heating the oven. My brother Moishe stopped going to cheder because his shoes were torn. Father became his teacher. Weeks passed by and we never tasted meat, not even on the Sabbath. We drank watery tea without sugar. We learned from the newspapers that the Germans and Austrians had invaded many towns and villages in Poland, among them those where our relatives lived. The Czar's great-uncle Nikolai Nikolaievitch, the chief commander, decreed that all Jews be driven from the regions behind the front; they were considered German spies. The Jewish streets in Warsaw teemed with thousands of refugees. They slept in the studyhouses, even in synagogues. It wasn't long before we began to hear the shooting of heavy guns. The Germans attacked at the river Bzura, and the Russians launched a counterattack. In our apartment the windowpanes rattled day and night.

3

OUR family left Warsaw in the summer of 1917. My parents moved to a village occupied by the Austrians. Food was cheaper there. Mother had relatives in that part of the country. The city seemed on the verge of destruction. The war had already lasted three years. The Russians had evacuated Warsaw and in their retreat they had blown up the Praga Bridge. The Germans who ruled Poland were losing on the western front and they let the population starve. We never had enough to eat. Before we left, Moishe fell ill and was taken to the Hospital for Epidemic Diseases on Pokorna Street. Mother and I were taken to the disinfecting station on Szczesliwa Street near the Jewish cemetery. There they shaved off my earlocks and fed me soup flavored with pork. For me—the son of a rabbi—these were spiritual calamities. A Gentile nurse ordered me to strip naked and gave me a bath. When she lathered me, her fingers tickled and I felt like both laughing and crying. It must be that I had fallen into the hands of the demonic Lilith dispatched by her husband, Asmodeus, to corrupt yeshiva students and drag them down into the abyss of defilement. Later when I saw myself in a mirror and caught a glimpse of my image minus earlocks and ritual garment, and wearing some kind of bathrobe I had never seen on a Jewish lad and slippers with wooden soles, I didn't recognize myself. I was no longer formed in the image of God.

I told myself that what had happened to me this day was no mere consequence of the war and German decrees but rather a punishment for my sins—for doubting my faith. I had already read on the sly the works of Mendele Mocher Sforim, Sholem Aleichem, and Peretz, as well as Yiddish or Hebrew translations of Tolstoy, Dostoevsky, Strindberg, Knut Hamsun. I had glanced into Dr. Shlomo Rubin's Hebrew translation of Spinoza's *Ethics* and had gone through a popular history of philosophy. I had taught myself to read German—so similar to Yiddish—and had read in the original the Brothers Grimm, Heine, and whatever I could lay my hands on. I had kept secrets from my parents.

Simultaneously with the German soldiers, Enlightenment had invaded Krochmalna Street. I had heard of Darwin and was no longer sure that the miracles described in *The Assembly of Saints* had really occurred. Ever since war had broken out on the Ninth Day of Ab, the Yiddish newspaper was brought daily into our house and I read there about Zionism, socialism, and, following the Russian evacuation of Poland when the Russian censorship ceased, a series of articles about Rasputin.

Now revolution had taken over Russia, and the Czar had been

deposed. The news was full of the fights and disputes among the Social Revolutionaries, the Mensheviks, the Bolsheviks, the Anarchists—new names and concepts had emerged. I absorbed all this with an eagerness that couldn't be sated. In the years between 1914 and 1917, I didn't see Shosha and I never once met her in the street, not her or Bashele or the other children. I had grown up and had studied one semester in the Sochaczów yeshiva and another semester in Radzymin. Father became the rabbi of a hamlet in Galicia and I had to start to earn my own livelihood.

But I never forgot Shosha. I dreamed of her at night. In my dreams she was both dead and alive. I played with her in a garden which was also a cemetery. Dead girls joined us there, wearing garments that were ornate shrouds. They danced in circles and sang songs. They swung, skated, occasionally hovered in the air. I strolled with Shosha in a forest of gigantic trees that reached the sky. The birds there were different from any I knew. They were as big as eagles, as colorful as parrots. They spoke Yiddish. From the thickets surrounding the garden, beasts with human faces showed themselves. Shosha was at home in this garden, and instead of my pointing out and explaining to her as I had done in the past, she revealed to me things I hadn't known and whispered secrets in my ear. Her hair had grown long enough to reach her loins, and her flesh glowed like mother-of-pearl. I always awoke from this dream with a sweet taste in my mouth and the impression that Shosha was no longer living.

During the years I wandered through the villages of Poland trying to support myself by teaching Hebrew, I seldom thought of Shosha when I was awake. I had fallen in love with a girl whose parents wouldn't permit me to go near her. I began to write in Hebrew and later switched to Yiddish, and the editors rejected everything I submitted to them. I couldn't seem to find a style that might create a literary domain for myself. Discouraged, I gave up literature and concentrated on philosophy, but what I was seeking I did not find there. I knew I must return to Warsaw, but again and again the forces that direct the fate of man hurled me back to the muddy villages. I often considered suicide. When finally I managed to get to the city to find work as a proofreader and a translator, and to be invited to the Writers' Club, first as a guest, then as a member, I felt like one recovered from a state of coma.

Years had gone by, and I didn't know where. Writers my age had achieved fame and immortality, but here I was, still a beginner. My father had died. His manuscripts, like mine, had been scattered and lost, though he had managed to publish one small book.

In Warsaw, I began an affair with Dora Stolnitz, a girl whose goal was to settle in Soviet Russia, the land of socialism. I learned later that she was a functionary of the Communist Party. She had been arrested several times and had spent months in Pawiak and other prisons. I was anti-Communist—anti all "isms"—but I lived in constant fear of being arrested and imprisoned because of my connection with this girl, whom I later began to dislike for her hollow slogans and bombastic clichés about the "happy future," the "bright tomorrow."

The Jewish streets in which I now wandered were close to Krochmalna, but I never went near it. I told myself that I simply had no occasion to go into that section of the city, but there had to be other reasons. I had heard that half the residents of the street had died in the typhus epidemics, of influenza, of starvation. Boys with whom I attended cheder had served in the Polish Army and been killed in the 1920 Polish-Bolshevik War. Later, Krochmalna Street had become a hotbed of Communism. There were always Communist demonstrations in the neighborhood. Young Communists draped red flags over telephone and streetcar wires—even on the windows of the police station. On the Place, an area between No. 9 and No. 13, and in the den where the thieves, pimps, and whores hung out, they now planned the dictatorship of Comrade Stalin. The police were forever conducting raids. This was no longer my street. No one would remember me or my family. When I thought of it, I had the strange feeling that my experience there constituted something removed from the world. I was in my twenties, but it seemed as if I were already an old man. Krochmalna Street was like a deep stratum of an archaeological dig which I would never uncover. At the same time, I recalled every house, courtyard, cheder, Hasidic studyhouse, store; every girl, street loafer, housewife—their voices, gestures, manners of speaking, their peculiarities.

I believed that the aim of literature was to prevent time from vanishing, but my own time I had thrown away. The twenties had passed and the thirties had come. Hitler was fast becoming the ruler of Germany. In Russia, the purges had commenced. In Poland, Pilsudski had created a military dictatorship. Years earlier, America had established an immigration quota. The consulates of nearly all nations refused to issue visas to Jews. I was stranded in a country squeezed between two mighty foes, stuck with a language and culture no one recognized outside of a small circle of Yiddishists and radicals. Thank God, I found friends among members of the Writers' Club and its periphery. The greatest of them all was Dr. Morris Feitelzohn, who was considered by many to be a genius.

· CHAPTER TWO ·

1

D R. MORRIS FEITELZOHN wasn't widely known. His philosophical works, some written in German and some in Hebrew
and Yiddish, were not translated into English or French. To
this day I haven't found his name in any philosophical lexicon.
His book *Spiritual Hormones* got bad reviews in Germany and in
Switzerland. Dr. Feitelzohn was my friend, even though he was
some twenty-five years older than I. He could have become
famous if he hadn't squandered his energies. His erudition was
monumental. For a time he was a lecturer at the University of
Berne. He literally invented the Hebrew terminology for modern
philosophy. If Feitelzohn was the dilettante one reviewer labeled
him, his dilettantism was of the highest order. As a person, he
was a brilliant conversationalist and he enjoyed fantastic success
with women.

But this same Dr. Morris Feitelzohn often borrowed five zlotys
from me at the Writers' Club. Nor did he have any luck with the
Yiddish press in Warsaw, where articles that had been accepted
were delayed for weeks while the editors changed and corrupted
his style. They kept on finding defects in his work. There was
much gossip about him. He was the son of a rabbi, but he had
fled the house and became an agnostic. He divorced three wives

and constantly changed lovers. Someone told me that Feitelzohn
sold a sweetheart to a rich American tourist for five hundred
dollars. The bearer of this tale called him a charlatan. But the
one who slandered Feitelzohn most was Feitelzohn himself. He
boasted of his adventures. I once observed that if one combined
Arthur Schopenhauer, Oscar Wilde, and Solomon Maimon, one
might end up with Morris Feitelzohn. I should have included the
Kotzk rabbi, because in his own fashion Feitelzohn was a mystic
and a Hasid.

Morris Feitelzohn was of medium height, broad-shouldered,
with a square face, thick eyebrows that met over the bridge of
his wide nose, and full lips from between which a cigar always
jutted. In the Writers' Club they joked that he slept with the
cigar in his mouth. His eyes were almost black, but occasionally
I saw green glints in them. His dark hair had already begun to
recede. Poor as he was, he wore English suits and expensive ties.
In his conversation, he had praise for no one and derided world-
famous figures. Yet severe critic that he was, he had detected
talent in me, and when he told me this, it evoked in me a sense
of friendship that bordered on idolization. It didn't prevent me
from seeing his faults. At times, I dared to chide him, but he
only said, "It won't do you any good. I'll die an adventurer."

Like all skirt-chasers, he had to report his successes. One time
when I came to his furnished room, he pointed to the sofa and
said, "If you only knew who lay here just yesterday, you'd faint."

"I soon will know," I said.

"How?"

"You will tell me."

"Ah, you're even more cynical than I am." And he told me.

Strangely, Morris Feitelzohn could speak with ardor about the
wisdom found in *The Duty of the Hearts, The Path of the Righ-
teous,* and in some of the Hasidic books. He had written a work
about the cabala. In his own fashion, he loved the pious Jew and
admired his faith and power to resist temptation. He once said
to me, "I love the Jews even though I cannot stand them. No

evolution could have created them. For me they are the only proof of God's existence."

One of Feitelzohn's admirers was Celia Chentshiner. Celia's husband, Haiml, was descended from the famous Reb Shmuel Zbitkower, the millionaire who during the Kosciusko uprising gave away a fortune to save the Jews of Praga from the Czar's Cossacks. Haiml's father, Reb Gabriel, owned houses in Warsaw and Lodz. Haiml was his only son. In his youth, Haiml had spent half of each day with a Talmud teacher at the Sochaczów study-house, and the other half trying to learn languages—Russian until 1915, German after the Germans occupied Warsaw, and Polish after 1919, when Poland was liberated. But he knew only one language—Yiddish. He liked to discuss Darwin, Marx, and Einstein with Feitelzohn. Haiml read about them all in Yiddish.

Haiml had never had to concern himself with a livelihood. He was a runt of a man and frail. I sometimes thought there wasn't a trade or business for which he would have been suited. Even drinking tea didn't come easy to him. He lacked the dexterity to cut a slice of lemon and Celia had to do this for him. Haiml was capable only of a childlike love for his father and for his wife. His mother was no longer living. Reb Gabriel had a second wife, whose name I didn't dare mention before Haiml. I asked him only once about his stepmother. He turned pale, put his little hand over my mouth, and exclaimed, "Don't talk! Don't talk! Don't talk! My mother is alive!"

Celia was short too, but taller than Haiml. She was related to him on his mother's side. An orphan, she had been raised in Reb Gabriel's house. Haiml fell in love with her while he was still in cheder. When Haiml didn't want to eat, Celia fed him. When he was studying Russian, German, and Polish, Celia studied with him, and while he learned none of these languages, she did. Their marriage took place when Haiml's mother lay on her deathbed.

By the time I met this couple, they were in their late thirties. Haiml looked like a cheder boy who had been dressed in a man's

suit, stiff collar, and tie. He spoke in a piping voice, made childish gestures, laughed with a shriek, and when things didn't go his
way he burst out crying. He had dark eyes, a small nose, and a
wide mouth full of brackish teeth. The black ruff around his bald
head hung down in tufts. He was afraid of barbers and Celia cut
his hair. She also trimmed his nails. Celia considered herself an
atheist, but traces of her Hasidic upbringing lingered. She chose
dresses with long sleeves and high collars. She wore her long dark
hair in an unfashionable bun. She was pale, with brown eyes, a
straight nose, thin lips, and she moved with the lightness of a girl.
Haiml used to call her "my empress." Celia had borne Haiml a
daughter, who died at the age of two, and Feitelzohn once told
her that the child's death contained a measure of divine logic,
since Celia already had a child—Haiml. To Celia and Haiml,
Feitelzohn represented the big world and European culture. Feitelzohn did not need to suffer want. They were always proposing
that he move in with them in their big apartment on Zlota Street,
but Feitelzohn refused.

   He told me, "All my foibles and aberrations stem from my urge
to be absolutely free. This alleged freedom has transformed me
into a slave."

2

BECAUSE Feitelzohn praised me, the Chentshiners often invited
me to dinner, lunch, or for a glass of tea. When Feitelzohn was
present, no one else could speak. We were all content to listen.
He had traveled throughout the world. He knew practically
every important Jewish personality, as well as many non-Jewish
scholars, writers, and humanists. Haiml used to say that he was
a living encyclopedia. From time to time, Feitelzohn gave lectures in the Writers' Club in Warsaw and in the provinces, and

also on short trips he made abroad. On those occasions, Haiml, Celia, and I had a chance to talk among ourselves. Haiml liked opera and was interested in art. He attended exhibitions and bought paintings. Cubism and expressionism had been in fashion many years, but Haiml liked pastoral landscapes of woods, meadows, streams, and huts half hidden behind trees, where, as he put it, one could hide from Hitler, who was threatening to invade Poland. I myself had fantasies about a house in the woods or on an island where I would be safe from Nazis.

Celia's passion was literature. She bought and read nearly every new book that came out in Polish and Yiddish, as well as translations from other languages, and she possessed a sharp critical taste. I often wondered how this woman who had had no formal education could so accurately appraise not only belles lettres but also scientific works. I paid attention to her opinions regarding my writing; invariably they were correct, tactful, and clever.

One time Celia invited me to the apartment on an evening when Haiml was away at a conference of the Poale Zion. We talked so long she revealed a secret to me: she was having an affair with Morris Feitelzohn. That evening I realized that Celia had the same need to confess as everyone else. She was quite frank about the fact that when it came to love, Haiml was as inexpert as a child. He needed a mother, not a wife, while she was hot-blooded. She said, "I like gentleness, but not in bed."

This remark coming from a woman who dressed and behaved so conservatively and who watched her every word astounded me more than the fact that she was unfaithful to Haiml. Our conversation became nakedly intimate. The essence of what she said was that literature, theater, music, even accounts in the newspapers roused her erotically, yet at the same time her nature was such that she could give herself only to someone to whom she looked up. For a man to utter some foolishness or demonstrate weakness was enough to repel her.

She said, "I could be happy with Feitelzohn, but he's the worst liar I've ever met. He has hoodwinked me so many times that I've lost all respect for myself for still believing him once in a while. He possesses hypnotic powers. He could be the Mesmer or Svengali of our time. If you're convinced that you know him, you're only deluding yourself. Each time I tell myself that the man can no longer surprise me, I get a new shock. Do you know that Morris is superstitious to the point of absurdity? He is terrified of black cats. When he is on his way to a lecture and meets someone holding an empty vessel, he runs back. He carries around all kinds of amulets. When he sneezes he pulls his ear. There are certain words you can't use in his presence. Did you ever try to discuss death with him? He has more idiosyncrasies than a pomegranate has seeds. He considers all women witches. He goes to fortune-tellers who for a zloty tell him he will take a long trip and meet a dark woman. And his contradictions! He breaks every law of the Shulchan Aruch, yet at the same time he preaches Jewishness. He has a wife whom he's never divorced and a daughter he hasn't seen in years. When his mother died he didn't go to her funeral."

I remember that evening and the things Celia said to me, because this was the beginning of our intimacy. I suspected that she had decided to revenge herself upon Feitelzohn through me for his affairs with other women. There was a minute when I was ready to embrace her and whisper those smooth lies that come to the lips on such occasions. But I was sure that Feitelzohn possessed clairvoyant powers. Often when I was about to say something, he plucked the words right out of my mouth. I switched the conversation with Celia to a different topic and her eyes seemed to ask, "You're scared, eh? Yes, I understand."

A while later the doorbell rang. It was Haiml. The conference had been canceled because a quorum wasn't present. Winter had set in and Haiml wore a fur coat, fur boots, and a fur hat resembling a rabbinical *shtreimel*. He looked so funny I barely kept from laughing.

Celia said, "Haiml, our young friend here is as bashful as if he had left the yeshiva only yesterday. I tried to seduce him but he wouldn't cooperate."

"What is there to be bashful about?" Haiml said. "We're all created from the same protoplasm, we all feel the same urges. Don't you find Celia attractive?"

"Both attractive and intelligent."

"So what's the problem? You may kiss her."

"Come here, yeshiva boy!" Celia said, and she gave me a mighty kiss. She said, "He writes like a grown-up but he's still a child. Truly a mystery." After a while she added, "I have a name for him—Tsutsik. That's what I'll call him from now on."

3

DR. MORRIS FEITELZOHN had spent the years between 1920 and 1926 in America, where he had been on the staff of a Yiddish newspaper in New York and had given courses at some local college. I never found out exactly why he left the Golden Land. Each time I questioned him about it, he gave me a different answer. He said that he couldn't stand the New York climate because he suffered there from hay fever, rose fever, and other allergies. Or he said that he couldn't bear American materialism and reverence for the dollar. He hinted at romantic entanglements. I had heard that the writers at the newspaper conspired against him and got him fired. Also, he had problems at the college where he lectured. In his conversations with me, he often referred to the Yiddish theater in New York, to the Café Royal where the Yiddish intellectuals of the city gathered, and to such Zionist leaders there as Stephen Wise, Louis Lipsky, and Shemaryahu Levin.

In spite of his frequently expressed antipathy toward America and Americans, Morris Feitelzohn never severed his connections with them. He was a friend of the director of HIAS in Warsaw and was known at the American consulate. From time to time, tourists who had either known Feitelzohn in New York or to

whom one of his American friends had recommended him came
to Poland and Feitelzohn brought them up to the Writers' Club
and played the role of guide. He assured me he never took any
money from these Americans, but I knew that he went with them
to first-class restaurants, to the theater, to museums, and to con-
certs, and they often left him ties and other gifts. He confided
to me that one of the higher officials at the Warsaw American
consulate could be bribed to help obtain visas for alleged rabbis,
professors, and bogus relatives beyond the quota. The way of
transmitting the bribe was to play poker and allow the official to
win a large amount. The intermediary was a foreign correspon-
dent in Warsaw who took a percentage for himself. The fact that
despite all these contacts Feitelzohn remained a pauper who had
to borrow a few zlotys from a poor slob like me seemed proof that
he himself was basically honest.

For me that winter in the 1930's was one of the hardest I had
known since I left my parents' house. The literary magazine
where I read proof two days a week was on the verge of folding.
The publisher who printed my translations was facing bank-
ruptcy. I had sublet a room from a family who now wanted to
be rid of me. More than once when people telephoned me they
were told that I was out, even though I was right there in my
room. In order to go to the bathroom I had to walk through the
living room, and the door to this room was often locked at night.
I had been planning to move for weeks but hadn't found a room
for the little rent I could pay. I was still involved with Dora Stolnitz—I didn't want to marry her, yet wasn't willing to let go.

When I met Dora she had said that she considered marriage a
vestige of religious fanaticism. How could you sign a contract for
lifelong love? Only capitalists and clerics were dedicated to per-
petuating such a hypocritical institution. Although I had never
been a leftist, in this I concurred with her. Everything I saw and
read bore witness to the fact that modern man didn't take family
responsibility seriously. Dora's father, a widower, had gone bankrupt in Warsaw and, to avoid imprisonment, had fled to France

with a married woman. Dora had a sister who lived with a journalist, a married man who used to frequent the Writers' Club. Through him I came to know Dora. But in the very first months of our affair she began to insist that we marry. She said she wanted this for the sake of some aunt, a sister of her deceased mother, who was a pious woman.

On that winter day I looked for a room from ten in the morning until nightfall. The rooms I liked cost too much. Others were too small or stank of insecticide and bedbugs. The truth was that the way my affairs were going I couldn't afford even a cheap room. Around five o'clock, I headed for the Writers' Club. It was warm there and I could have a meal on credit. Going to the club gave me a feeling of shame. What kind of writer was I? I hadn't published a single book. It was a cold, wet day. Around evening, snow began to fall. I walked along Leszno Street, shivering under my thin coat, and imagined I had written a work that would startle the world. But what could startle the world? No crime, no misery, no sexual perversion, no madness. Twenty million people had perished in the Great War, and here the world was preparing for another conflagration. What could I write about that wasn't already known? A new style? Every experiment with words turned quickly into a collection of mannerisms.

I opened the door to the club and saw Morris Feitelzohn with an American couple. The man was short and stout, with a wide, ruddy face, a headful of hair white as foam, and a bulging belly. He wore a light-colored coat—a shade of yellow not seen in Poland. The woman was no taller, but young, slim, and dressed in a short fur coat I guessed to be sable. She wore a black velvet beret over her red hair. I wasn't in a mood to meet the Americans and tried to avoid them, but Feitelzohn had already seen me and called out, "Tsutsik, where are you going?"

He had never called me Tsutsik before—obviously he had talked with Celia. I stopped, my eyes bleary from the cold. I tried to dry my palms on the soaked tails of my overcoat.

Feitelzohn said, "Where are you running? I want you to meet

my American friends. This is Mr. Sam Dreiman and this is Betty Slonim, an actress. This young man is a writer."

Sam Dreiman's face seemed to have been pasted together from clay. He had a broad nose, thick lips, high cheekbones, and small, boring eyes beneath thick white brows. His tie was yellow, red, and gold, pierced with a diamond stickpin. He held a cigar between two fingers and spoke in a loud, grating voice. "Tsutsik?" he bellowed. "What kind of name is that? A pet name, what?"

Betty Slonim might have had the figure of a schoolgirl, but behind the makeup her face revealed maturity. She had hollow cheeks, a narrow chin, and eyes that by the dim glow of the overhead lamps seemed to be yellowish. She reminded me of trapeze artists in the circus. Her voice was that of a boy.

Sam Dreiman shouted at me as if I were deaf. "You write for the papers, eh?"

"For magazines, from time to time."

"What's the difference? In this world we need everything. On the ship I met a man and we played a little pinochle—that's a kind of card game. We got to talking and I asked him, 'What do you do?' and he told me he was going to Africa to capture lions and other wild animals for the zoos in the States. He had a group of hunters with him, and cages, nets, and the devil knows what. This lady, Betty Slonim, is a great actress who has come to Poland to appear in the Yiddish theater. If you have a play, we can do business immediately—"

"Sam, don't talk nonsense," Betty Slonim interrupted him.

"A young man like this could have just the play you're looking for. But before we get down to business, let's first go somewhere for a bite. Come along, young man. What's your real name?"

"Aaron Greidinger."

"Aaron what? That's a hard name. In America we don't go for long European names. There, time is money. A Russian came into our office and his name was Sergei Ivanovich Metropolitansky. You could get asthma just from trying to pronounce a name like that. We called him Met, and that's how it stuck. He's a plumber, a specialist. He puts an ear to a pipe in the basement and he knows what's going on on the top floor. I didn't have any lunch today, and I'm hungry as a dog."

"You can get a bite here," Feitelzohn said, pointing to the lunch counter.

"I'll tell you something. I never trust a writers' restaurant. I ordered dinner at the Café Royal and they gave me a steak as tough as leather. I noticed two restaurants down the street and they both looked pretty good to me. Come, young man, come along with us. May I call you Tsutsik?"

"Yes, of course. But I'm not hungry. I ate not long ago," I lied.

"What did you eat? You don't look like somebody who's overeaten. We'll have a drink of whiskey, too—maybe even champagne."

"Really, I'm not—"

"Don't be so stubborn," Feitelzohn interjected. "Come with us. I think you told me you'd written a play?" he went on, changing his tone.

"I only have the first act and it's just a first draft."

"What kind of play is it?" Betty Slonim asked.

I had stopped blushing when a woman addressed me, but now I felt the blood rush to my face. "Oh, it's not for the theater."

"Not for the theater?" Sam Dreiman shouted. "For who is it then—King Tut?"

"It wouldn't draw an audience."

"What's the subject?" Feitelzohn asked.

"The Maiden from Ludmir. She was a girl who wanted to live like a man. She studied the Torah, wore ritual fringes, a prayer shawl, and even put on phylacteries. She became a rabbi and held court for Hasidim. She covered her face with a veil and preached the Torah."

"If it's well written, it's exactly what I'm looking for," Betty Slonim said. "Can I see the first act?"

"Something will come of this meeting," Feitelzohn observed as if to himself. "Come along; we'll eat, drink, and talk business, as they say in America."

"Yes, come, young man!" Sam Dreiman shouted. "Keep your wits about you and you'll be swimming in gravy."

4

WE SAT in Gertner's Restaurant and Sam Dreiman spoke of his and Betty Slonim's plans. He had lost over a million dollars in the Wall Street crash, he said, but only on paper. Sooner or later the stocks would rise again. The economy in Uncle Sam's land was healthy. A good many of the stocks still paid dividends. Besides, he owned houses and was a partner in a factory. The manager was his brother's grandson, Bill, a lawyer. He himself was far from being a young man, so what need was there to worry? God had blessed him with a great love in his late years—he indicated Betty —and what he wanted was to enjoy himself and to provide her with enjoyment. She was a marvelous actress, but the hams on Second Avenue were jealous of her talent. They wouldn't even accept her in the Hebrew Actors Union, but the few times she managed to perform in spite of them, her reviews were sensational—not only from the Yiddish but from the English press as well. She could have appeared on Broadway, but she preferred to act in Yiddish. That was the language that really brought out her talent. Money was no problem. He would rent a theater for her here in Warsaw. The main thing was to find a play that suited her. Betty required dramatic roles. Her first choice was tragedy. She was no comedienne and despised the "dance, song, and strut" of the Yiddish theater in America.

He turned to me. "If you come up with the right goods, young man, I'll give you a five-hundred-dollar advance. If the play goes well, you'll get royalties. If it becomes a hit in Warsaw, I'll take it over to America. The first act is ready, you say? Have you started the second? Betty, you talk to him. You know better what to ask."

Betty was about to speak but Feitelzohn beat her to it: "Aaron, you'll be a millionaire. You'll become my patron and my publisher. Don't forget that I was the broker who brought it all about."

"If it comes to anything, you'll get your broker's fee from *me!*" Sam Dreiman bellowed. Each time he spoke he spread his hands, and I noticed a big diamond ring on his finger. He also wore a gold-banded wristwatch and jeweled studs.

Now that Betty had taken off her fur coat and sat there in a sleeveless black dress, I could see how thin she was. She had an Adam's apple like a boy's; her arms were like sticks. Warsaw was already talking about how healthy and fashionable it was to be thin, but this Betty seemed to me emaciated. It had become the style for Warsaw women to let their nails grow and cover them with red polish, but Betty's fingernails were uncolored and it was obvious that she bit them. Hair cut *à la garçon* was passé, but Betty still wore hers short. She barely tasted the food before her, and between bites she puffed on a cigarette. She wore a huge diamond bracelet on her left wrist and around her throat a necklace with smaller diamonds.

She leaned toward me and asked, "When did this girl live? In what century?"

"In the nineteenth. She died only a short while ago in Jerusalem. She may have been a hundred years old."

"I never heard of her. Was she that pious?"

"Yes, very pious. Many Hasidim felt that she had been possessed by the dybbuk of an ancient rabbi who uttered the Torah through her lips."

"What else did she do? Is there any action in this play?"

"Very little."

"A drama has to have action. The heroine can't just spout Torah through three or four acts. Something has to happen. Did she have a husband?"

"If I'm not mistaken, she married later on, but it seems she divorced her husband."

"Why don't you write in an affair for her? If a woman like that fell in love, it could create a strong conflict."

"Yes, that's an idea worth considering."

"Have her fall in love with a non-Jew, a Christian."

"A Christian? That couldn't be."

"Why not? Love knows no restrictions. Suppose she were to get sick and go to a Christian doctor. A love might very well develop between them."

"Why couldn't she fall in love with one of her own kind?" Feitelzohn asked. "I'm sure that the Hasidim who sat around her table and swallowed her leavings and listened to her Torah were all mad about her."

"Absolutely!" Sam Dreiman roared. "If I was one of those Hasidim and didn't have my Betty—may she outlive me—I would be mad about her myself! I admit to being an ignoramus, but I love educated women! Betty studied at the Gymnasium. She reads books by the hundreds. She performed in Stanislavsky's theater. Tell them, Betty, who you played with. Let them know who you are!"

Betty shook her head. "There's nothing to tell. I did perform in Russia in Yiddish and in Russian too, but it's just my luck that even before I got going, a whole network of intrigue formed around me. I'll never know why. I don't want power, I'm not rich, I've never tried to steal anyone's husband or lover. The men were attentive to me at first, but when I kept them at a distance, they became my enemies overnight. The women were all ready to drown me in a spoonful of warm water, as the saying goes. That's how it was in Russia and that's how it was in America, and it will be the same here, too—unless there's no competition to conspire against me."

"If anyone dares say a word against my Betty, I'll poke his eyes out!" Sam Dreiman shouted. "Here, they'll kiss your feet!"

"I don't want anyone to kiss my feet. All I want is to be left alone so that I can play with peace of mind."

"You'll play, Betty darling, and the whole world will learn

how great you are. They kept all the great ones down. You think Sarah Bernhardt's path was strewn with roses? Well, and what about the others? That one from Italy—whatever her name was. And Isadora Duncan, you think she didn't have trouble? Even Pavlova had it. When people sense the presence of a talent they turn into wolves. I once read in the paper—I forget the writer's name—about Rachel and how the anti-Semites in Paris tried to push her out of—"

"Sam, I want to talk about the play with the young man."

"Talk, darling. I like this play even before I've read it. I feel it was made for you. I bet a dybbuk sits inside you too, Betty darling." He turned to me. "At times when she begins to yell at me, she acts possessed herself—"

"Will you stop or not? Stop it."

"I'll stop. I'll only say one thing more to this young man. I'll give you a few hundred dollars so you can work without worrying where your next meal is coming from. Just make the play so that things happen. Let her fall in love with a doctor or a Hasid or a dogcatcher, you name it. The main thing is, the audience should be curious to know what's going to happen next. I'm no writer, but I would have her get pregnant and—"

"Sam, if you don't stop talking like a clown, I'm leaving."

"So be it. You won't hear another peep from me till we go home."

"I wanted to say something, but he's mixed me up to the point that I hardly know where I am," Betty complained. "Oh, yes— there has to be action. But you're the writer, not I."

"Really, I'm no playwright. I started to write the thing for my-self. I wanted to show the tragedy of the intellectual woman, particularly among Jews who—"

"I don't consider myself an intellectual but that is *my* tragedy. Why do you think they conspired against me? Because I had no patience with their gossip, intrigues, and stupidity. Ever since childhood I've been like a foreign element around women. My own sisters didn't understand me. My mother looked at me like a hen that had sat on a duck's egg and hatched a creature drawn to the water. My father was a scholar—a Hasid, a follower of the Husiatiner rabbi—and the Bolsheviks shot him. Why? He was rich once, but the war had ruined him. People fabricated stories and made false accusations against him. My whole family stayed on in Russia, but I couldn't remain among the murderers of my father. The truth is that the whole world is full of evildoers."

"Bettyle, stop talking like that. If I had a million for every good person, Rockefeller would be heating my stove."

"You're the first pessimistic woman I've ever met," Feitelzohn observed. "Pessimism is usually a male trait. I can envision a woman with masculine characteristics and gifts—a female Mozart, say, or even an Edison. But a female Schopenhauer is beyond the stretch of imagination. Blind optimism is essential to the concept of woman. All of a sudden, to hear such words from a female!"

"Maybe I'm not a woman?"

"That's for me to decide!" Sam shouted. "You are one hundred percent a woman—no, not one hundred percent, but a thousand! I've had many women in my life, but what she is—"

"Sam!"

"Well, I'll shut up. Start on the play first thing tomorrow, young man, and don't worry about the money. Betty sweetheart, stop smoking so much. You're on your third pack today."

"Sam, mind your own business."

5

BY THE time Feitelzohn and I said goodbye to Sam Dreiman and Betty, it was midnight. While shaking hands, Betty squeezed my palm once and then again. She tilted her face toward mine and I caught a whiff of liquor and tobacco. Betty had eaten little, but she had finished several glasses of cognac. She and Sam were

staying at the Hotel Bristol and they took a taxi there. Feitelzohn
had a room on Dluga Street, but he walked me to Nowolipki
Street, where Dora Stolnitz lived. He knew about my affairs. He
seldom went to bed before two.

He took my arm and said, "My boy, you caught Betty's eye for
sure—hoo hah! If that play of yours has anything to it, you're a
made man. Sam Dreiman is loaded and he's crazy about Betty.
Get out your manuscript and pack it with all the love and sex it
can take."

"I don't want to turn it into a piece of trash."

"Don't be an ass. Theater is trash by definition. There's no
such thing as a sustaining literary play. Literature must consist
of words, just as music must consist of sounds. Once you perform
the words on stage or even recite them, they're already secondhand goods."

"The audiences won't come."

"They'll come, they'll come. A guy like Sam Dreiman would
think nothing of bribing critics. He may even bribe audiences.
The main thing is, don't spare the schmaltz. Today's Jews like
three things—sex, Torah, and revolution, all mixed together.
Give them those and they'll raise you to the skies. Maybe you
have a zloty?"

"Two."

"Well, you're already acting like a millionaire. What do you
think about Betty?"

"She seems to be suffering from a persecution complex."

"Probably a lousy actress, too. But I'm having strange fantasies lately. We spoke of dybbuks today—I've been possessed by
a dybbuk. He tells me to found an institute of pure hedonism."

"Isn't life itself such an institute?"

"Yes and no. All people are hedonists, yes. From cradle to grave,
man thinks only of pleasure. What do the pious want? Pleasure
in the other world. And what do ascetics want? Spiritual pleasure
or whatever. I go even further. For me, pleasure takes in not only
life but the whole universe. Spinoza says that God has two attrib-

utes known to us—thought and extension. I say that God is pleasure. If pleasure is an attribute, then it must consist of infinite modes. This would mean that there are myriads of unknown pleasures still to be discovered. Of course, if God happens to have an attribute of evil, woe to us. Maybe He isn't so almighty after all and needs our cooperation. My dybbuk tells me that since we are all parts of Him and since men are the greatest egotists among all creatures—Spinoza says that man's love of himself is God's love for man—the pursuit of pleasure is man's only goal. If he fails here, he must fail in everything else."

"Doesn't your dybbuk know that man has already failed? Isn't the Great War proof enough?"

"It may be proof to me, but not to my dybbuk. He tells me that God suffers from a kind of divine amnesia that made Him lose the purpose of His creation. My dybbuk suspects that God tried to do too much in too short an eternity. He has lost both criterion and control and is badly in need of help."

"Really, you are joking."

"Of course I'm joking, but in some foolish way I am also serious. I see Him as a very sick God, so bewildered by His galaxies and the multitude of laws He established that He doesn't know what He aimed for to start with. Sometimes I look into my own scribblings and discover that I began one kind of work and it turned out to be the opposite of what I intended. Since we are supposed to have been formed in His image, why couldn't such a thing have happened to Him?"

"So you are going to refresh His memory. Is this the topic of your next article?"

"It could be, but these idiotic editors will not take anything from me. Lately they send everything back. They don't even bother to read it. By the way, your memory must also be refreshed. You promised me two zlotys."

"You're right. Here they are. I'm sorry."

"Thank you. Please don't laugh at me. First of all, this crazy Sam gave me too much to drink. Second, after midnight I let go of what is left of my mind. I am not responsible for anything I babble or even think. Since I cannot sleep I must dream with open eyes. Perhaps like me He suffers from insomnia. As a matter of fact, the Good Book tells us He doesn't doze or sleep but watches over the children of Israel. What a watchman! Good night."

"Good night. It was a great pleasure. Thank you."

"Try to write this lousy play. I have lost respect for everything, but I absolutely worship money. If we ever return to idolatry, my temple will be a bank. Here you are."

At Nowolipki Street, Feitelzohn held out a warm hand to me and headed home. I rang and the janitor let me in. All the windows in the courtyard were dark but for one on the third floor. For me, spending the night at Dora's was both a danger (they might raid the apartment and find illegal literature) and a humiliation (we had broken up). She was about to smuggle herself into Russia to take a course in propaganda. Although she denied it heatedly, almost every Communist who crossed the border from Poland was arrested by the Soviets—they were accused of espionage, sabotage, and Trotskyism. More than once I warned her that such a trip was sure suicide, but she said, "Those who have been arrested deserved it richly. Fascists, social Fascists, and all the other capitalist lackeys should be liquidated, the quicker the better."

"Was Hertzke Goldshlag a Fascist? Was Berel Guttman a Fascist? Was your friend Irka a Fascist?" I demanded.

"Innocent people aren't jailed in the Soviet Union! That's done in Warsaw, in Rome, and in New York."

No facts or arguments would convince her. She had hypnotized others and was herself under the spell. In my mind I could see her cross the border at Nieświez, fall to the ground to kiss the soil of the land of socialism, and promptly be dragged off to jail by the Red guards. There she would sit among dozens like her— hungry and thirsty beside a bucket of slops—and keep on asking herself, "Is this possible? What was my crime? I who gave my best years to the socialist ideal."

I walked slowly. I had vowed solemnly not to come here again,

but I needed her body. I knew that we would be parting forever.
Perhaps she was perplexed by doubts herself. Even the most pious
experience occasional heretical thoughts. I stopped for a moment
on the dark stairs and indulged in a brief introspection. What if
I should be arrested with her this night? What kind of justifica-
tion could I offer myself? Why, as the saying goes, did I crawl
with a healthy head to a sickbed? Well, and should I try to re-
fashion my play to suit Betty Slonim's whims? And what was it
Feitelzohn actually wanted? How strange, but during the last few
months I heard time and again at the Writers' Club that someone
was arranging an orgy. There was a table at the club that young
writers had dubbed the "Table of the Impotent." Each night
after the theater and movies, the older writers—the classicists,
newspaper editors, old journalists, and their ladies—gathered
there to discuss politics, Jewish topics, and the eroticism that had
come into fashion with Freud and the sexual upheavals in Russia,
Germany, and the whole Western world. A famous actor, Fritz
Bander, had come to Poland from Germany. The Nazi and conservative newspapers had for a time waged a campaign against
Bander for corrupting the German language ("Moischeling,"
they called it), for making insulting remarks about Ludendorff,
and for seducing a German aristocratic young lady and driving
her to suicide. Bander, a Galician Jew, fell into such a rage from
these attacks, as well as from the poor reviews he had been receiving, that he abandoned Berlin for Warsaw. He wanted to do
penance and return to the Yiddish theater. He had brought along
his Christian sweetheart, Gretel, the wife of a German film
director. Her husband had challenged Bander to a duel and
threatened him with a gun. Bander now sat every night with his
sweetheart at the Table of the Impotent and told jokes in Gali-
cian-accented Yiddish. He had been notorious in Berlin for his
sexual prowess. In the Romanisches Café on Grenadierstrasse
queer tales were told of his adventures. It was the joke at the
Warsaw Writers' Club that Bander's boastings had sparked the
ambitions of the old, sick writer, Roshbaum, to become another
Casanova.

Before knocking on Dora's door, I stopped to listen. Maybe a meeting of the District Committee was going on inside? Maybe the police were conducting a raid? In this compromised apartment, anything was possible. But no, all was quiet. I knocked three times—a signal between Dora and me—and waited. Soon I heard her footsteps. I never learned why there was no telephone in the apartment, but guessed it was so that the police couldn't tap the wire.

Dora was small, broad in the hips and with a huge bosom. She had a crooked nose. Her big, fluttering eyes were her only attractive feature. They reflected a blend of cunning and the solemnity of one who has assumed the mission of saving mankind. She stood at the door now in her nightgown, with a cigarette stuck between her lips. "I thought you'd left Warsaw," she said.

"Where to? Without saying goodbye?"

"I wouldn't put anything past you."

6

ALTHOUGH a Communist is forbidden to reveal Party secrets to a member of the enemy class, Dora told me that everything was ready for her departure. It was a matter of a few days. She had already sold pieces of her furniture to neighbors. A Party functionary was scheduled to take over the apartment. I had stored a bundle of manuscripts with her and she reminded me that I must take them away when I left in the morning. Although I had eaten a heavy dinner, Dora insisted I join her for rolls with marinated herring and tea.

"You brought this situation about yourself," she said accusingly. "If we had lived together like a normal couple, I wouldn't be going away. The Party doesn't compel a husband and wife to part, especially when there is a child. We could have had a couple of children by now."

"And who would support them? Comrade Stalin? I've been left without work. I owe two months' rent."

"Our children wouldn't have starved. Well, it's foolish and too late for such talk. You'll have your children with someone else."

"I don't want children with anyone," I said.

"The typical degenerate psychology of capitalist stooges. It's the collapse of the West, the end of civilization. There's nothing left but to lament the catastrophe. However, Mussolini and Hitler will bring order. Mother Rachel will rise from her grave and lead her children back to Zion. Mahatma Gandhi and his goat will triumph over English imperialism."

"Dora—enough!"

"Come to bed. This may well be the last time for us."

The wire springs of the bed had a depression in the middle and we couldn't lie apart even if we wanted to. We rolled toward each other and listened in on our own desire. Her flesh was plump, smooth, warm. Her enormous breasts amazed me each time we were together—how could she carry around such a load? She pressed her plump knees against mine and complained that I was hurting her. Our souls (or whatever they may be called) were battered and at odds, but our bodies had remained friendly. I had learned to curb my lust. We indulged in some foreplay, some during-play, and sometimes even some afterplay.

Dora put a hand on my loin. "Do you have my replacement standing by yet?"

"Well, and what about you?"

"There'll be so much to do there, I won't have time to think of such things. It's a hard course. It's not so easy to adjust to new circumstances. To me love is no game. I have to respect the person first, believe in him, have faith in his thoughts and character."

"A Russky with all these qualities is awaiting you there."

"Look who's talking! You were always ready to trade me for the first available yenta."

We kissed and bickered. I listed all her former lovers while she counted off all those with whom I might have betrayed her. "You don't even know the meaning of the word faithful!" she said. She kissed and bit me. We went to sleep sated and I woke up with lust renewed.

Dora spoke in a crooning chant, "I'll never forget you, never! My last thoughts on my deathbed will be of you, you reprobate!"

"Dora, I'm worried about you."

"What are you worried about, you lousy egotist?"

"Your Comrade Stalin is a madman."

"You're not even worthy to mention his name. Put your arms around me! It's better to die in a free land than to live among Fascist dogs."

"Will you write me?"

"You don't deserve it, but my first letter will be to you."

I dozed off again, and I was in Warsaw and in Moscow at the same time. I came to a square filled with graves. I knocked on a door and a huge Russian answered. He was mother-naked and uncircumcised. I asked for Dora and he replied, "Rotting in Siberia." A wild party was going on inside. Men played accordions, guitars, balalaikas; nude women danced. A yellow dog came out from the crowd and I recognized her—Jolka, who belonged to the Soltys of Miedzeszyn. But Jolka had died. What was she doing in Moscow? Oh, these trivial dreams, they have no meaning whatsoever, I said in my dream.

I opened my eyes and beyond the window a murky dawn seemed to be pondering its eternal return. Dora was banging pots in the kitchen. She drew water from the tap and mumbled a song about Charlie Chaplin. I lay still, dazed by the world and its absurdities. She appeared in the doorway. "I'm making your breakfast."

"How is it outside?"

"Snowing."

I washed at the kitchen sink. The water was icy.

Dora said, "A pair of your drawers was knocking around here. I washed them."

"Well, thank you."

"Put them on. And don't forget to take your Fascist manuscripts."

She brought me the drawers and from under the bed pulled a bundle of manuscripts tied with a string.

While I ate, Dora preached: "It's never too late to accept the truth. Spit on all this slime and come with me. Stop writing about those rabbis and spirits and see what the real world looks like. Everything here is corrupt. Over there life is beginning."

"It's corrupt all over."

"Is that your world concept? This could be our last breakfast together. Would you happen to have three zlotys?"

I counted out three zlotys and gave them to her. It left me with three zlotys and change. The magazine and the publisher owed me some money, but it was impossible to get so much as a groschen out of them. My only hope was an advance from Sam Dreiman. I said goodbye to Dora and promised to come back that evening. I took the bundle of manuscripts and went out into the cold courtyard. A dry snow was falling. On the top of the garbage bin a cat stood poised. She fixed her gooseberry-green eyes on me and meowed. Was she hungry? Forgive me, pussy, I have nothing for you. Dun the malefactor who created you. I went out the gate. There was an infirmary in the building, where the sick came to buy chits to see doctors. Some elderly women wrapped in shawls entered the gate. I imagined that they smelled of toothache and iodine. They spoke at the same time, each about her own sickness. The clouds hovered low. An icy wind blew. I headed for the street and my furnished room. It was just big enough to hold the bed and a single chair and almost as cold as outside. I opened the bundle of manuscripts and to my amazement saw the beginning of a second act of my play. Had Providence ordained this? Somewhere causality and purpose were firmly bonded. I began to read. The Ludmir Maiden bewailed the fact that God had granted all the favors to men and only the leavings to women—the laws connected with childbirth, ablutions in the mikvah, the lighting of the Sabbath candles. She

accused Moses of being antifeminist and blamed the evils of the
world upon the fact that God was a male. Should I add love and
sex to this play? Whom should she love—a doctor, a Cossack?
She could be a lesbian, but the Warsaw Jews weren't ready for
this theme. Suddenly I had an idea: she would fall in love with
the dybbuk who possessed her. The dybbuk was a man—I'd make
him a musician, a cynic, a lecher, an atheist. She would talk in
his voice as well as her own. There was a chance that Betty
Slonim could play this. She would portray a split personality.
She would supposedly wed the dybbuk inside her; he would mis-
treat her, disappoint her, and she would demand a divorce.

I felt an urge to tell Betty Slonim my idea that very moment.
I knew she was staying at the Hotel Bristol, but I couldn't bring
myself to drop in on a lady at a hotel unexpectedly. I lacked even
the courage to telephone her. I decided to go to the Writers'
Club. Feitelzohn might be there and I could describe my plot to
him. Although I was tired, a spark of interest in Betty Slonim
kindled in me. I had already indulged in a fantasy in which we
enjoyed fame together—she as an actress, and I as a playwright.
But Feitelzohn wasn't at the club. In the first room two unem-
ployed journalists played chess and I stopped for a while to look
on. The one who was winning—Pinie Machtei, a little man who
had only one leg—swayed over the chess board, pulled at his
goatee, and sang a Russian song:

> *"Happy or not happy*
> *As long as there is vodka and wine*
> *Let us not whine."*

He said to me, "You may look, but don't kibitz."

He had put his knight in such a situation that his opponent,
Zorach Leibkes, had to give up his queen for a castle. If not, he
would have been checkmated in two moves. Zorach Leibkes was
a temporary replacement in the Yiddish press when the proof-
readers were on vacation. He was small and round like a barrel.

He too swayed, and he was saying, "Machtei, stop singing. Your castle is nothing but an idiot. I'm afraid of him as much as I'm afraid of last year's frost. You have been a botcher and a botcher you'll remain until the tenth generation."

"Where does the queen go?" Machtei asked.

"She will go. She will go. Don't worry your silly head over it. Once she goes she will shatter your pieces to smithereens."

I went into the main room. There were only three writers there. At a small table sat Shloimele, a folk-poet who signed his poems only with his first name. He was writing a poem in a ledger like those used in grocery stores. He was known to write in almost microscopic letters that only he could decipher. While he wrote, he chirped a monotonous tune. At another table sat Daniel Liptzin, nicknamed the "Messiah." In 1905 he had taken part in the revolution against the Czar and was sent to Siberia. But there he became religious and began to write mystic stories. Nahum Zelikowitz—tall, thin, black like a gypsy, a pipe in his mouth—was pacing back and forth. He belonged to a minority in the Writers' Club that believed Hitler was bluffing and there would be no war. He had published twenty novels and all on the same subject: his love for the actress Fania Ephros, who betrayed him and married a union leader. Fania Ephros had been dead for ten years, but he continued to brood about her many treacheries. Zelikowitz had a continuing war with the Warsaw critics, who all put him down. He had slapped one of them across the face. I greeted him, but he didn't answer me. He was angry with young writers and considered them intruders.

I went back to the first room. Perhaps the Maiden should be possessed by *two* dybbuks, I thought, one a slut, the other a whoremonger? I had written a story of a girl possessed by both a whore and a blind musician. I was seized with boldness. From a phone booth I called information for the number of the Hotel Bristol, and when the hotel answered, I asked to be connected with Miss Betty Slonim. The telephone rang once and I heard her voice: "Hello?"

I was momentarily speechless. Then I said, "I'm the young man who had the honor of being with you at Gertner's Restaurant last night."

"Tsutsik?"

"Yes."

"I've been sitting here thinking about you. What's new with the play?"

"I have an idea I would like to talk over with you and Mr. Dreiman."

"Sam has gone to the American consulate, but come over, and you and I can discuss it."

"I won't be disturbing you?"

"Come right over!" She gave me her room number. I thanked her and hung up. I was tingling with delight over my own courage. Forces stronger than I propelled me. I wanted to take a cab but three zlotys might be too little to pay for it. Suddenly I remembered that I hadn't shaved, and fingered my stubble. I would have to visit a barber. I couldn't call on an American lady unshaven.

7

A DOORMAN in livery guarded the entrance of the Hotel Bristol, and going inside felt almost like entering a police station or a courtroom. But everything went off without a hitch. Although there was an elevator, I climbed the stairs to the fourth floor. The steps were made of marble and along the middle ran a carpet. Betty answered my knock at once. Her room had a huge window and was brighter than any room I had ever seen. The snow had stopped and the sun shone in. I seemed to have been transported to a different climate.

Betty wore a long houserobe and slippers with pompons. Having red hair and having been tormented by nicknames through my childhood—red dog, red cheater, red carrot—I had an aversion to redheads, but Betty's hair didn't repel me. In the sun it seemed a blend of fire and gold. Only now did I observe how white her skin was—as white as my own. Her eyebrows were brown.

A moment after I came in, the telephone rang and she conversed for a few minutes in English. How grand and worldly this language sounded! Betty was shorter than I but she carried herself with pride. She hung up and invited me to take off my coat and make myself comfortable. Even her Yiddish smacked of sophistication. She took my coat and hung it on a wooden hanger. This struck me as novel—so much respect for an old rag that was missing a button. When I was with Dora I felt like a mature man, but here I reverted to a youth. Betty waved me to a sofa and sat down in an easy chair facing me. Her robe parted, and for a fraction of a second I saw her dazzling legs. She offered me a cigarette. I didn't smoke but I wouldn't think of refusing her. She brought me a lighter. I took one puff and became intoxicated by the aroma.

She said, "Now tell me more about the play."

I began to talk and she listened. The expression in her eyes kept changing from anticipation to amazement. "This means I'll have to conduct a love affair with myself?"

"Yes, but in a sense we all do."

"True. I could easily play a man and a woman. Why didn't you bring the script along?"

"Everything is too rough to show."

"Couldn't you recall a few lines for me? I'd like to try it out right now. I'll give you paper and pen and you can write a few lines—some words for the musician and some for the harlot. Wait!" She stood up and from her purse that lay on the dresser took out a lady's fountain pen and a notebook.

I began to write as if automatically:

MUSICIAN

Come, girl, be mine. You're a corpse and I'm a corpse, and when two corpses dance the bedbugs prance. I'll make you a present of a pouch of earth from the Land of Israel and the shards that covered my eyelids. With the myrtle between my fingers I'll dig you a pit reaching from Tishevitz to the Mount of Olives. On the way, we'll do like Zimri the son of Solu, and Cozby the daughter of Zur.

HARLOT

Hold your tongue, foul whelp of a musician! I left the world a pure virgin while you wallowed with every whore from Lublin to Leipzig. A band of angels awaits me, while myriads of demons lie in ambush for you.

I handed Betty the pen and notebook and she began to read slowly. Her thin eyebrows lifted and remained raised. Her lips formed an inquisitive smile. She read through to the end, then asked, "Is this taken from your play?"

"Not really."

"You composed it right here and now?"

"More or less."

"Well, you're a strange young man. You have an exceptional imagination."

"That's about all I do have."

"What else do you need? Wait, I'll try to play this."

She began to mumble into the notebook, halting here and there over some word. Suddenly she began acting out the parts in two voices. I clenched my teeth to stop them from chattering. The powers that ruled the world had brought me together with a superb actress. It was hard to conceive that talent like this spent night after night in bed with Sam Dreiman. My cigarette had gone out. Betty walked up and down the room, repeating the dialogue over and over. It struck me that she was better as the musician than as the girl. The girl's voice sounded half masculine. Each time Betty concluded, she glanced at me and I nodded.

Finally she came up and said, "This is good to recite, but a play must have a plot. One of the Hasidim, a rich one, must be in love with me."

"I'll write it in."

"He should have a wife and children."

"Definitely."

"Let him offer to divorce his wife and marry the girl."

"Surely."

"But she won't be able to decide between the dead musician and the live Hasid."

"Right."

"What then?" she asked.

"She'll marry the Hasid."

"Aha."

"But on her wedding night the musician won't let her be with her husband."

"Yes."

"And she'll go off with the musician."

"Where to?"

"To be with him in the grave."

"How long will it take you to write the play? Mr. Dreiman is ready to rent a theater. You could become a famous playwright overnight."

"As it is fated, so shall it be," I said.

"You believe in fate?"

"Absolutely."

"So do I. I'm not religious—you see how I live—but I do believe in God. Before I go to sleep I say a prayer. On board ship I prayed to God each night to send me the right play. All of a sudden, along comes a young fellow, a Tsutsik, with a play that can express my soul. Isn't that miraculous?"

"Let's hope so."

"Don't you have faith in yourself?"

"How can one have faith in anything?"

"You must believe in yourself. That's my tragedy—I never have had that belief. As soon as something good begins to happen, I foresee nothing but difficulties and mishaps and I spoil whatever there is. That's how it's been in love and that's how it's been in my career. Do you have a director to suggest?"

"There's no point looking for a director until the play is finished."

"You're still doubtful, eh? This time I won't allow doubt. The play has to turn out well. Stick to the outline we put together just now. Sam Dreiman will give you a five-hundred-dollar advance and that's a lot of money here in Poland. Are you married?"

"No."

"You live alone?"

"I had a girl, but we've broken up."

"May I ask why?"

"She's a Communist and is going away to Stalin's land."

"Why didn't you marry?"

"I don't believe two people can make a contract to love each other forever."

"Do you have a comfortable apartment?"

"I have to move. I'm being dispossessed."

"Rent a nice room. Put aside any other work you're doing and concentrate on our play. What do you intend to call it?"

"The Ludmir Maiden and Her Two Dybbuks."

"Too long. Leave it to me to decide on the title. How much time will the rewriting take?"

"If it goes well, three weeks—a week for each act."

"How do you see the three acts?"

"In the first act, the Ludmir Maiden will become what she is and the rich Hasid will fall in love with her. In the second act, the dead musician must emerge and establish the conflict."

"In my opinion, the dead musician should appear in the very first act," Betty said after some hesitation.

"You're absolutely correct."

"Don't agree with me so quickly. Think it over first. A playwright shouldn't be so compliant."

"I'm no playwright."

"If you write a play, then you're a playwright. If you don't take yourself seriously, no one else will either. Forgive me for speaking to you this way, but I'm a few years older. Actually, everything I tell you I should tell myself as well. Sam Dreiman believes in me. He believes too much. He is perhaps the only person who believes in me and in my talent. That's why—"

"I believe in you, too."

"You do? Eh? Well, thank you. What did I do to deserve that? Apparently someone up there doesn't want my end just yet. Some sort of providence directed you to me."

· *CHAPTER THREE* ·

1

S<small>AM</small> D<small>REIMAN</small> offered me the five-hundred-dollar advance he had spoken of, but I refused to accept such a big sum. We agreed I would take two hundred dollars for now, and I traded them at a currency exchange for over eighteen hundred zlotys. This was a real windfall. I found a new place on Leszno Street that cost eighty zlotys a month. I put down three months' rent and got a wallpapered room with central heating, solid furniture, and an Oriental carpet. My landlord, Isidore Katzenberg, a former manufacturer, told me he had been ruined by exorbitant taxes. The apartment house lay close to Iron Street and was relatively new and modern. One floor was a Gymnasium, and there was an elevator at the front entrance, for which I was given a key.

Everything happened quickly. One evening Sam Dreiman handed me the money and the next day I moved into my new place. I had only to pack my possessions in two valises and carry them over. The maid, Tekla, a young country girl with brown hair and ruddy cheeks, had polished the floor until it gleamed. There was a bed in my room, a sofa, upholstered chairs, and in the long, wide corridor a telephone I was permitted to use at eight groschen a call. God in heaven, I had been thrown into the lap of luxury! I went to a tailor to be fitted for a suit. I lent

Feitelzohn fifty zlotys. He demurred, but I forced them on him. I invited him to dinner at a café on Bielanska Street. I had told him the theme of the play and he offered suggestions. Feitelzohn was going to earn money from this venture as well—Sam had asked him to do the "publicity." I had never heard this word, and it had to be explained to me.

Feitelzohn sipped his tea, puffed his cigar, and said, "What kind of publicity man will I make, anyway? If I don't like the play, I won't praise it. But Sam Dreiman is apparently a multimillionaire. He is seventy or more, he has a nasty wife and estranged children who are rich in their own right—what else does he have to do with the money? He wants to spend it as long as he can. This Betty must have brought back his potency. I didn't know either of them in America, but I heard about him. It seems I even met him once at the Café Royal. He is a carpenter by trade. He went to America in the 1880's and became a builder in Detroit. When Ford built his automobile factories there and began to pay his workers five dollars a day, men came flocking from all over America—from the whole world, in fact. Sam Dreiman built houses and he built factories. In America when the money starts flowing toward someone, there is no limit to it. In 1929 he lost a fortune but enough remained. You should have taken the whole five hundred. To him that's a trifle. He'll think you're a shlemiel."

"I can't accept money for goods that don't exist yet."

"Well then, write a good play. The American believes in paying. You can give him mud, but if he pays a lot for it, in his mind it becomes gold."

I was anxious to go home and get to work, but Feitelzohn had begun to expound on a "soul expedition" he was preparing to launch. Psychoanalysis wasn't the answer, he said. The patient comes to the analyst to be cured—that is, to become like everyone else. He wants to be rid of his complexes, and the analyst is supposed to help him in this effort. But where is it written that the cure is better than the disease? Those who would take part in his soul expedition wouldn't be bound by any restrictions. We would assemble in a room on an evening, with the lights off, and give our souls free rein. Man has to be granted the courage to reveal to himself and others what it is he truly desires. The real tyrants weren't those who repressed the body (which is confined anyhow) but those who enslaved the spirit. Alleged liberators, they have all been subjugators of the soul! Feitelzohn said, "Moses and Jesus, the author of the Bhagavad-Gita, and Spinoza, Karl Marx, and Freud. The spirit is a game uncontrolled by rules and laws. If Schopenhauer is right—if blind will is really the thing-in-itself, the essence of all—why not let the wanter want?"

"What's the purpose of only wanting?" I asked.

"Where is it written that there must be a purpose? Maybe chaos *is* the purpose. You've glanced into the cabala, and you know that before Ain Sof created the world He first dimmed His light and formed a void. It was only in this void that the Emanation commenced. This divine absence may be the very essence of creation."

Evening had fallen but still Feitelzohn talked. By the time we went outside, it was night. The street lights were on in Bielanska Street, and a thin snow was falling. As usual after speaking at length, Feitelzohn grew silent and cranky, ashamed of his own verbosity. He shook my hand and went off in the direction of Dluga Street. I walked toward Leszno. It felt strange to have a pocketful of money suddenly, an elegant room, even a maid who would make my bed and bring me breakfast. Feitelzohn's words had stirred me. Yes, what was it, actually, that I wanted? I felt drawn to Betty Slonim. Celia's kiss and confession presaged a new affair. I did not want Dora to leave. But was I in love with these women? Well, what else did I want? I had dreamed of writing a perfect book and now I wanted a perfect play, too. The snow grew denser. It made my eyelids blink and caused spearlike beams to radiate from lamp posts and show windows. Feitelzohn's constant insinuations that Celia desired me were puzzling. Was he trying to palm her off on me, or to share her with me? I had heard him say that man was on the verge of trading the instinct of jealousy for the instinct of participation.

I had resolved to work late into the night, but as I climbed the steps to my room, weariness settled over me. Tekla let me in. She wore a short white apron and a cap with lace over her hair, like a maid at a doctor's. She smiled familiarly and showed me the curtains she had hung in my room. She had already made my bed. She asked if I would like some tea. I thanked her and said not now.

I tried to overcome my weariness and sat down to rewrite the first act of *The Ludmir Maiden*, but instead I started to write a play that was completely new. I seemed to have lost control over my pen. It raced faster than my fingers. Although the mistress of the house had installed a desk covered in green felt and a desk lamp with a green shade, things glared before my eyes. Aha, that inner antagonist and saboteur was launching a campaign against me. I knew his tricks by now. I wanted to succeed, but he sought my downfall. I found I was leaving out letters and whole words. I began to consult the books that were supposed to serve as guides for my behavior: Payot's *The Education of the Will* and Charles Baudouin's work on autosuggestion, the notebook in which I had set down rules for living and means of maintaining spiritual hygiene, but fatigue overcame me and I fell on my bed in my clothes.

At once the dreams and nightmares took over. When I opened my eyes, the clock showed a quarter of two. I hardly managed to undress before drifting off again into a deep sleep. In my dreams I was able to analyze what I was going through. Yes, dreams were precisely what Dr. Feitelzohn sought to restore to man— aimlessness, spiritual anarchy, the whims of idolators, the perversions of madmen. In my sleep, Betty and Celia became one, although not altogether. I mated with this plural female, and Haiml stood by and encouraged us. Even this coupling had some connection with the play. *Is Celia the Ludmir Maiden? Is Betty the dybbuk of the adulteress? And am I myself the blind musi-*

cian? But I had never had any special feeling for music.

I had known Betty Slonim less than two days, but here she was participating not only in my daytime fantasies but in my nocturnal visions as well. She was somehow with me and part of me, my deeds and philosophizing. Feitelzohn wanted to return the soul to that primeval chaos from which all things evolved, but how could chaos create anything? Could it be that purpose, not causality was the essence of being? Were the teleologists right after all?

2

I HAD planned to get up at seven, but when I wakened I heard the clock in the living room toll nine times. Someone knocked on my door with the stippled panes and Tekla came in carrying a tray covered with a napkin. She had brought me eggs, rolls, cheese, and coffee. I had slept more than seven hours. I had gone through a dreamy epoch I had forgotten except for one fragment —sliding down a mountain as a band of wild people awaited below with clubs, spears, poles, and axes. They half shouted, half chanted a melody, a remnant of which still lingered in my ears—a dirge of passion and madness.

The girl started to apologize. "I thought you were up."

"Oh, I overslept."

"Shall I take the tray back to the kitchen?"

"No, I'll wash later."

"You have a pitcher of water and a basin right here. A towel, too."

"Thank you, Tekla. Thank you very much."

I was overcome by the feeling that I was being given more than I deserved. Why should this country girl be waiting on me? She had undoubtedly been on her feet since six that morning.

Yesterday, I had seen her washing clothes. I would have liked to give her something, but I couldn't reach the chair where my jacket hung. She smiled, showing a mouthful of teeth without a blemish. She had muscular legs and firm breasts. She placed the tray carefully on the table. She studied me as if trying to fathom my thoughts. "A good appetite!"

"Thank you, Tekla. You're a fine girl."

A dimple showed in her left cheek. "Good health to you." She left the room slowly.

These are the real people, the ones who keep the world going, I thought. They serve as proof that the cabalists are right—not Feitelzohn. An indifferent God, a mad God couldn't have created Tekla. I felt temporarily enamored of this girl. Her cheeks were the color of ripe apples. She gave forth a vigor rooted in the earth, in the sun, in the whole universe. She didn't want to better the world as did Dora; she didn't require roles and reviews as did Betty; she didn't seek thrills as did Celia. She wanted to give, not to take. If the Polish people had produced even one Tekla, they had surely accomplished their mission. I poured a little water from the clay pitcher into the basin on my washstand. I moistened my hands and dried them on the towel. I took a drink of coffee and a bite of the fresh roll. I felt an urge to utter a benediction and thank the powers that made wheat and coffee beans grow, to offer thanks to the chickens that laid these eggs. I had gone to sleep in misery and risen almost happy.

Someone knocked on the door and opened it. It was my landlord's son, Wladek, who, his father had told me, had quit his law studies at Warsaw University and spent all day at home reading trash and listening to the music and chatter on the radio. Wladek was tall, lean, pale, with a high forehead, thin nose. To me, he appeared ill both physically and mentally. The father spoke Polish with a Yiddish accent but Wladek spoke it grammatically and with style. He said, "Excuse me, sir, for disturbing you in the midst of your meal, but you're wanted on the telephone."

I jumped up, nearly spilling my coffee. This was my first call here. I went out into the corridor and snatched up the receiver. It was Celia. "I know that if Mohammed won't come to the mountain, the mountain must come to Mohammed," she said. "The trouble is, I have never considered myself a mountain. I've heard about your successes and I want to congratulate you. I thought we were friends, but if you prefer to remain aloof, of course that's your privilege. Still, I would like you to know I'm delighted for you."

"Not only am I your friend—I love you!" I exclaimed with the light-minded assurance of those who can afford to say whatever comes to their lips.

"Oh, really? Well, that's good to hear. But if that's the case, why haven't I heard from you? When you come to us you're like a friend, a brother. Then you go away—and silence. Is this your nature or is it a system you use?"

"No system. Nothing of any kind. I know how busy you are."

"Busy? With what am I busy? Our Marianna does everything. I sit and read, but how much reading can you do? Morris has been visited lately by hordes of Americans, so I see nothing of him. The second American ambassador to Poland I call him. Besides you two, there's no one in our circle to exchange a few words with. Haiml, God bless him, has gotten himself too involved with the Poale Zion. I believe in Palestine and all that, but England does what she pleases with her mandate. Days go by that I don't speak a word to anyone."

"Madam Chentshiner, whenever you want to meet me, all you need do is call. I miss you too," my mouth said of its own volition.

Again Celia paused. "If you miss me, what's to keep you away? And call me Celia, not Madam Chentshiner. Come over and we'll talk. If you'd rather, we can meet at a confectionery. You're probably busy with the play. Morris told me all about it. But no writer writes ten hours a day. What kind of woman is this Betty Slonim? I expect you're in love with her already."

"No, not in love."

"I sometimes envy women like her. They go straight to the

target. She picked out a rich old man for a lover and he'll do
everything to make her famous. To me, this is prostitution, but
when have women not sold themselves for money? If she gets
two zlotys for it, she's a streetwalker, but when it's many thousands, along with diamonds and furs, she's a lady. I didn't know
you wrote plays. Morris told me the theme. An interesting subject. When will you be over?"

"When shall I come?"

"Come for lunch today. Haiml went to his father's in Lodz.
I'm all alone."

"At what time?"

"Three."

"Fine, I'll see you at three."

"Don't be late!"

I put down the receiver. She was lonely. I had suffered for
years from loneliness; now suddenly my luck had changed. But
for how long? An inner voice, that unconscious which Hartmann
claims is never in error, told me that it wouldn't be for long.
Everything would end in catastrophe. Then why not enjoy the
moment? Sleep had calmed me somewhat, but now tension returned. I wouldn't make the first move with Celia, I decided. I'd
leave all the initiative to her.

I went back to my interrupted breakfast. Yes, I had to find
pleasure before I died and returned to nothing. I reminded myself that I hadn't checked the money I had left overnight in my
jacket pocket. Someone might have robbed me while I was
asleep. Even Tekla could have stuck in her hand and taken
everything. I jumped up and tapped the pocket. No, no one had
robbed me. Tekla was an honest girl. Still, I began to count the
bills even as I felt ashamed of my mistrust.

There was another knock on the door. Tekla had come to see
if I wanted more coffee.

"No, Tekla dear, I've had enough." I gave her a zloty and her
cheeks turned red.

3

EXACTLY at three o'clock I arrived at Haiml's house on Zlota Street. To get there I walked down Iron Street to the juncture of Twarda and Zlota, then turned left. Zlota Street was almost always deserted—a residential street, without stores. Most of the residents were well off, with few or married children. The five-story building where Haiml lived was dark gray, with balconies supported on the shoulders of mythological figures. One had to ring a bell to get in the front entrance. The stairs were of marble but worn, and a spittoon stood on every landing. From the landings one looked out onto a square courtyard, a small enclosed garbage bin with snow on its deck, and a tiny garden where the branches of trees were glazed by the frost and reflected the colors of the rainbow. Celia answered when I rang. Marianna, the maid, had gone to visit her sister, Celia explained. She invited me in. The apartment glistened from cleanliness. In the dining room the table was set. A huge china closet sparkled with crystal and silver. Portraits of men with white beards and of women in wigs and jewelry hung on the walls.

Celia said, "I prepared your favorite dish—potatoes with borscht and meatballs."

She showed me to Haiml's place at the head of the table. From the way she had sounded on the telephone, I expected kisses the moment I came in, an immediate physical intimacy. But her expression told me that she was in no mood for this. She had turned formal. We sat facing each other, far apart. Celia served me. I suspected she had sent the maid away so that we could be alone. The cold walk had given me an appetite and I ate a lot. Celia questioned me about the play, and as I outlined the theme to her, I found myself making unexpected changes. This was a magical theme—like the Torah, it seemed to possess seventy different faces.

Celia said, "Where will you find the actors for such a play? And what about the director? If it doesn't come out absolutely right, it can turn into something terribly vulgar. Our Yiddish actors and actresses in Warsaw are of a low breed. You know this yourself. In all these years I haven't seen anything worthwhile on our stage."

"I'm afraid that I've fallen into a trap."

"Not if you don't hand the play over to them until you're satisfied it's just as you want it. That's my advice."

"Sam Dreiman is about to rent a theater and hire a cast."

"Don't let him do it. From what Morris tells me, he's a common man—a former carpenter. If the thing turns out badly it's *your* reputation that will suffer."

This was not the Celia I had seen on my earlier visit, but I was growing accustomed to abrupt changes both in myself and in others. Modern man may be ashamed of emotion, but he is all affect and temperament. He burns with love and turns cold as ice; he is intimate one moment and aloof the next. I was no longer astonished by these mysterious variations. In fact, I often suspected that I unwillingly hypnotized those with whom I came in contact and inflicted my moods upon them.

After lunch we went into the parlor and Celia offered me cherry liqueur and cookies. The walls were covered with paintings by Jewish artists—Liebermann, Minkowski, Glicenstein, Chagall, Rybak, Rubinlicht, Barlevi. Jewish antiques were displayed in a glass cabinet—spice boxes, a gold-plated wine benediction goblet, Hanukkah candelabra, a Passover bowl, the sheath of a Book of Esther, a Sabbath bread knife with a mother-of-pearl handle, an illuminated marriage contract, a pointer and crown from a Torah scroll. It was difficult for me to accept the fact that this intense Jewishness was merely decoration, its essence long since lost to many of us.

For a while we discussed painting—cubism, futurism, expressionism. Celia had recently attended an exhibition of modern art and been thoroughly disappointed. In what way was a square head and a nose like a trapeze indicative of man and his dilemmas? What could harsh colors that had neither harmony nor basis in reality say to us? As to literature, Celia had read Gottfried Benn, Trackl, Däubler, as well as translations from modern American and French poets. They left her cold. "All they want is surprise and shock," she said. "But we become shock-proof so quickly."

She began to look at me quizzically. It seemed that she was wondering, as I was, why we were behaving so conventionally. She said, "I'm sure that you're infatuated with that Betty Slonim. Tell me about her."

"What is there to tell? She wants the same thing we all do—to grab some pleasure before we vanish forever."

"What do you call pleasure? Sleeping, if you'll forgive me, with a seventy-year-old carpenter?"

"It's payment for other pleasures she's getting."

"What, for instance? I know women who would give up everything to perform on the stage. This seems to me a strange passion. Now, to write a good book, that's something I'd like to do, but I realized early that I hadn't the talent for it. It's the reason I admire writers so."

"What are writers? The same kind of entertainers as magicians. As a matter of fact, I admire someone who can balance a barrel on his feet more than I do a poet."

"Oh, I don't believe you. You play the cynic, but you're really a serious young man. Sometimes it seems to me that I can see right through you."

"What do you see?"

"That you're constantly bored. All people bore you except maybe Morris Feitelzohn. He is exactly like you. He can't find a place for himself anywhere. He wants to be a philosopher, but he's basically an artist. He's a child who breaks all its toys, then cries to have them put together again. Though I'm no artist, I suffer from the same sickness. We might have shared a great love, but he doesn't want this. He tells me how he carries on with servant girls. He continually douses me with cold water, enough to put out the hottest fire. You must give me your solemn word that you won't repeat my words to him. He is deliberately driving me into your arms, and he does this out of insanity. His game consists of igniting the fire in a woman, then leaving her to herself. But he has a heart too, and when he sees those close to him being hurt, it touches his conscience. He is also morbidly curious. He wants to try everything. He's afraid that somewhere there may remain an emotion he hasn't tasted."

"He wants to establish a school of hedonism."

"Foolish fantasies. For years I've been hearing about orgies but I'm sure they provide no satisfaction. They're a lark for fifteen-year-old boys and streetwalkers, not for mature people. You have to be drunk or mad to take part in them. In Paris, for five francs tourists can watch acts of perversion. The few writers who babble about this at the Writers' Club are old and sick people. They can barely stand on their feet."

We were still for a while; then Celia asked, "What about your Communist sweetheart? Has she gone to Stalin's land yet?"

"You know about her, too?"

"Morris speaks of you constantly."

"She's due to go any day now. Everything between us is ended."

"How do you end things? I never could end anything. I hear you finally have a nice room."

"Yes, with Sam Dreiman's money."

"Does it have a balcony?"

"No balcony."

"You once told me that you liked a balcony."

"One can't have everything."

"I sometimes feel that the reason some people get nothing is that they never have the courage to reach out their hands. I am one of those."

"What would happen if I reached out my hands to you now?" I asked.

Celia rocked in her chair. "You can try."

I went over and held out my hands to her.

She looked at me ironically. She stood up. "You may kiss me."

I put my arms around her and we kissed silently for a long time. She moved her lips as if to say something. But no words came out.

Afterward she said, "Don't tell Feitelzohn. He's a jealous little boy."

4

DUSK FELL. The winter day—the like of which would never occur again, unless Nietzsche was right in his theory of perpetual repetition—flickered out like a candle. For a while, a purple pane reflected on the parlor wall, a sign that some part of the sky in the west had cleared preceding sunset. Celia didn't switch on the lights. Her face was in shadow and her eyes shone out of it as if casting their own glow. Then it darkened again. Through the window a star sparkled within a split in the clouds. From where I was sitting I tried to fix it in my memory before it vanished. I toyed with the notion of how it would be if the sky remained constantly overcast and parted for only one second each hundred years, when someone might catch a glimpse of a star. He would tell of his revelation, but no one would believe him. He would be called a liar or accused of having suffered an hallucination. Behind how many clouds does the truth lie concealed now? And what did I know about the star I was looking at? This was a fixed star, not a planet. It might be bigger than the sun. Who could know how many planets rotated around it, how many worlds drew sustenance from it? Who could conceive what kind of creatures lived there, what plants grew, what thoughts were thought there? Well, and there were billions of such fixed stars in our

Milky Way alone. They couldn't be merely physical or chemical accidents. There had to be someone whose commands controlled the infinite universe. His orders traveled faster than light. So omnipotent and omniscient was he that he presided over every atom, every molecule, every mite and microbe. He even knew that Aaron Greidinger had just embarked on an affair with Celia Chentshiner.

The telephone rang and Celia, who had been sitting silently in the easy chair mulling over her own thoughts, lazily stretched out her hand to the small table on which it stood. She drawled in that singsong used in Warsaw exclusively for telephone conversations, "Haiml? Why so late? I thought you'd call earlier . . . What's that? . . . Everything is fine. Haiml, we have a guest— our young friend came for lunch . . . No, *I* called *him*. If he wants to put on airs, I'll be the one to give in. Who am I, a simple housewife, and he a writer, a playwright, and who knows what . . . Yes, we had lunch and I persuaded him to stay to dinner . . . Oh, he has a famous actress now, young and probably pretty, too. What does he need with a woman my age? How is your father? . . . So? Good, let him take his medicine . . . Tomorrow? When tomorrow? On the twelve o'clock train? . . . Good. I'll meet you at the station . . . What else do I have to do with myself. A whole day went by yesterday and no one rang me. So I swallowed my pride and called him . . . Who? To direct? Don't talk nonsense. He knows as much about theater as I do about astronomy . . . You mustn't laugh at me, but a Gentile director would understand the thing better than one of our boors. They at least have studied and seen theater . . . Morris? I haven't heard from him at all. He has forgotten us, too . . . Oy, Haiml, you're one of those types, all right . . . You want to talk to him? I'll give him the phone. Here he is!"

Celia handed me the receiver. The phone had a long cord. Everything in this room was arranged to avoid effort. I heard Haiml's voice, which sounded even more thin and shrill than when we talked directly.

"Tsutsik! How are you? I hear you're working on your play. Good, good. It's high time a young person wrote for our theater. The world goes forward, but we're still stuck with *Chinke Pinke*, and *Dos Pintele Yid*. Each time Celia and I go to the Yiddish theater we vow it's the last. Well, but not to go is no achievement, either. Our conservative Zionists have renounced the diaspora. All good fortune, they say, will come about in Palestine. But let's not forget that Palestine was only our cradle. We should have grown up in those two thousand years. By ignoring the exile they help bring about assimilation. You were kind to come spend time with Celia. Who can she entertain herself with? She has nothing to say to the women in our circle. With them, it's always the same—this dress, that dress, this hat or the other. All gossip. Don't be in any hurry to leave. Don't be bashful . . . Did you say jealous? Nonsense! Who was it said that when people rejoice in one another they exalt the creator, too. When I married Celia and even long before, while we were still engaged, I was terribly jealous. If she so much as spoke or smiled at another man I was ready to trample the two of them to dust. But I once read in a Hasidic volume that when one has a harmful trait and overcomes it, it can completely reverse itself. Today I know that if you really love a woman, her friend can be your friend, her pleasure your pleasure, her ecstasy your ecstasy. Tsutsik, I still want to say something to Celia. Be so good as . . ."

I turned the receiver over to Celia and went off to the room the Chentshiners designated as the library. It was dark there except for the reflection of light from a window across the street. I stood and asked myself, "Are you happy now?" I waited for an answer from that deep source called the inner being, the ego, the superego, the spirit—whatever its name—but no answer came.

Celia opened the door. "What are you doing in the dark like a lost soul? We have no secrets from you."

I could not find words to reply to her, and she said, "How can I begin an affair when I'm seriously thinking about suicide? There are people who at a certain age come to a natural end—all words spoken, all deeds done, and nothing remaining but death. I used to get up each morning with hope. Today I no longer expect anything."

"Why, Celia, why?"

"Oh, I don't fit in anywhere. Haiml is a decent person and I love him, but before he even opens his mouth I know what is going to come out of it. Morris is the very opposite, but you never know where you stand with him. He lives close to desperation. You're too young for me, and unstable. I have the feeling that you won't be staying here in Warsaw long. One day you'll simply pick up and disappear. Morris told me that Sam Dreiman wants to take you to America."

"He's a big talker."

"Such things happen fast. If you have a chance to escape from here, don't wait. We're caught between Hitler and Stalin. Whichever invades the country will bring a cataclysm."

"Why don't *you* leave?"

"Where to? I don't see myself in America."

"What about Palestine?"

"Somehow I don't see myself there, either. It's a place we'll be transported to on a cloud when the Messiah comes."

"You believe this?"

"No, my dear."

· CHAPTER FOUR ·

1

SPRING arrived early this year. By March, the trees were abloom in the Saxony Gardens. My play wasn't ready, but even if it had been, it was too late to present it. By May all the affluent families went off for the summer to Otwock, Świder, Michalin, and Józefow. The play wasn't the only problem. Sam Dreiman had had trouble obtaining a theater. So the première was put off until Succoth, when the Yiddish theaters regularly commenced their season. Sam Dreiman had advanced me another three hundred dollars, which I reckoned would carry me through until fall. He was considering renting a summer home on the Otwock route and I would be assigned a room there to work on the play under Betty's supervision. Sam confided to me that even as he sat in Warsaw doing nothing, he was earning several thousand dollars each and every week.

He said, "Take as much as you need. I won't spend it all in any case."

By now, I was on a first-name basis with Sam and with Betty, and they both called me Tsutsik. Yet I knew that everything depended on the play. Sam Dreiman often used the word "success." He kept warning me that the play must reach audiences both in Warsaw and in New York, where he still planned to take it, along with me, its author.

[65]

He said, "I know the Yiddish theater in America like the back of my hand. What else did we immigrants have except the theater and the Yiddish paper? Each time I came from Detroit to New York, I never failed to enjoy an evening in the theater. I knew them all—the Adlers, Madam Liptzin, Kessler, and Thomashefsky, not to speak of his wife, Bessie. They spoke plain Yiddish—none of that gobbledygook you hear in the art theaters, where they bore the crowds to death with propaganda. People come to the theater to enjoy themselves, not to revolt against Rockefeller's millions."

Betty and I had already kissed, both in front of Sam and behind his back. When we sat over the manuscript, she would take my hand and put it on her knee. Feitelzohn's contention that the instinct of jealousy was becoming vestigial like the appendix, coccyx, and male breasts seemed to hold as true for this couple as for Haiml and Celia. Sam Dreiman smiled and kidded me good-naturedly when Betty kissed me. He often left us alone and went off to play cards with his acquaintance at the consulate.

Feitelzohn went there as well. Recently he had lectured on the subject "Spiritual Vitamins" at the Writers' Club, and he was preparing to launch a series of soul expeditions. A friend of his, the hypnotist Mark Elbinger, had come to Warsaw from Paris. Feitelzohn told me remarkable facts about this man. He could hypnotize his patients over the phone or merely by telepathy. He was also clairvoyant. He had held séances in Berlin, in London, Paris, New York, and South America. He was supposed to take part in the soul expeditions.

Since Sam preferred to play cards rather than to spend his time looking around for a summer place in the still empty resort villages in the Otwock region, he sent Betty and me to find a suitable villa. Sam planned to arrange that the rehearsals of the play take place there. Feitelzohn had promised to hold soul expeditions on "the loin of nature." At the Table of the Impotent there was even talk of an orgy to be organized by that famous master of revelry, Fritz Bander.

One day I met Betty at the Danzig Railroad station. She bought tickets for us, and we waited in line together. It smelled here of beer, sausages, coal smoke, and sweat. Soldiers carrying full field packs waited for a train and passed the time downing huge mugs of beer that a girl drew from a keg. Her cheeks were red and she wore a tight blouse over her bosom. The soldiers joked with her, talked smut, and her pale-blue eyes smiled half in arrogance, half in embarrassment, as if to say, "I'm only one— you can't all have me."

The newspapers talked of how modern the German Army had become, fully mobilized and equipped with the latest weapons, but these Polish soldiers looked just like the Russian soldiers in 1914. They wore heavy greatcoats and the sweat poured from their faces. Their rifles appeared too long and too bulky. All of them were doomed to be massacred, yet they made fun of the Jews in the long gaberdines. One even tugged at a Jew's beard, and they could be heard hissing, "*Żydy, Żydy, Żydy.*"

I hadn't been in a train for years. I never traveled second class, always third or even fourth. But here I sat on an upholstered bench with an American lady, an actress, and looked out at the brick-red buildings of the Citadel, whose roofs were covered with earth and overgrown with grass. This ancient fortress was supposed to defend Warsaw in case of attack. It also contained a prison. The train rode out onto the bridge. The Vistula gleamed, and a strong breeze blew in from it. The sun reflected large and red in the water, and although the hour was long before sunset, a pale moon appeared in the sky. We rode through Wawer, Miedzeszyn, Falenica, Michalin. There were memories connected with each of these stops. In Miedzeszyn I had slept with a girl for the first time—only slept and done nothing else, since she wanted to preserve her virginity for her husband. In Falenica I had delivered a lecture that turned out to be a fiasco.

We got off in Świder, one stop after Jósefow, where Haiml and Celia had their summer house. A real-estate broker was waiting for us at the station. We waded through the sand until we

came to a villa that appeared to me the height of luxury, with
verandas, balconies, flower beds, even hothouses, all surrounded
by woods. Betty seemed so eager to get rid of the broker that
almost immediately she handed him a deposit of two hundred
zlotys. Only then did we learn that the house had no lights, there
was no linen for the beds, and the nearest restaurant or coffee
shop in the neighborhood was kilometers away. The summer
hotels were not open. We had to return to Warsaw and wait for
the contract to be drawn up and sent to Sam Dreiman. The
broker, a little man with a yellow beard and yellow eyes, seemed
suspicious of our intentions. He said to us, "It's too early. The
nights are cold and dark. The summer is not here yet. Everything
has its time."

From a hut a janitor came out with two barking dogs. He
asked the broker to give back the keys to him. We were advised to
go back to the station, because at this time of year the trains did
not run frequently. But Betty insisted that she see the river
Świderek and its waterfall, which the real-estate broker in Warsaw had spoken to her and Sam about. As we walked, a blast of
icy wind brought winter back to us. In a matter of minutes the
sky became overcast, the moon disappeared, and a mixture of
driving rain and hail hit our faces. Betty spoke to me, but I
could not hear her in the clamor of the wind. We had reached
the Świderek River. The beach stretched before us wet and
empty. The low waterfall tumbled with a thundering roar. The
narrow stream shone strange and mysterious and two large winter
birds flew along the surface, all the while screeching warnings,
one to the other, not to get lost in the stormy twilight. Betty's
straw hat lifted itself into the air and landed on the bank across.
Then it started to roll and turn somersaults; it vanished in the
shrubs. Betty clutched with both hands at her disheveled hair as
if it were a wig, and she shrieked, "Let's go! The demons are
after me. It's always like this when a spark of happiness lights
up my life!"

She threw her purse on the sand, put her arms around me, and, pressing me to her, hollered, "Keep away from me! I'm cursed, cursed, cursed!"

2

WINTER returned for a while, and Betty put on her sable coat once more. Then spring moved in for good. Warm breezes blew from the Praga woods through my open window, carrying with them the fragrance of grass, blossoms, and newly turned earth. In Germany, Hitler had solidified his power, but the Warsaw Jews had celebrated the festival of the exodus out of Egypt four thousand years ago. That day I didn't go to Betty at the Hotel Bristol. She came to me instead. Sam Dreiman had gone to Mlawa to attend the funeral of a cousin. Betty refused to go with him. She said to me, "I want to enjoy life, not mourn the death of some strange woman." She was again dressed in a summery outfit—a pale-blue suit and a straw hat. She brought me a bouquet, and Tekla took it and put it in a vase. I had never heard of a woman bringing a man flowers.

The spring wouldn't let us work. Birds flew past the open window with cries and twitters. We left the manuscript on the table and went to the window. The narrow sidewalks swarmed with pedestrians.

Betty said, "Spring in Warsaw makes me crazy. In New York there is no such thing as spring."

After a while we went down into the street. Betty took my arm with her gloved hand and we strolled aimlessly. She said, "You always speak of Krochmalna Street. Why haven't you ever taken me there?"

I didn't answer immediately. "That street is completely bound up with my youth. For you, it won't be anything more than a dirty slum."

"Just the same, I want to see it. We can go by cab."

"No, it's not so far. I can't believe myself that I haven't been back to visit Krochmalna Street since I left there in 1917."

We could have gone by way of Iron Street, but I preferred to walk to Prezejazd and there to turn south. On Bank Place we stopped momentarily before the gate of the old bank with its heavy columns. Just as in my boyhood, carts of money were being trundled in and out, guarded by armed police. Żabia Street was still the millinery center, with rows of windows showing hats that were modern and hats worn only by older women—hats with veils, nets, ostrich plumes, wooden cherries, grapes, and hats with crepe for those in mourning. Behind the iron fence of the Saxony Gardens the chestnut trees were scattering their blossoms.

There were benches on Iron Gate Square and weary passersby were sitting in the sunshine. God in heaven, this walk was wakening in me the enthusiasm of a boy. We stopped before the building called Vienna Hall, where wealthy men had weddings for their daughters catered. Below, among the columns, women still peddled handkerchiefs, needles, pins, buttons, and yard goods of calico, linen—even remnants of velvet and silk. We came out onto Gnoyna Street and my nostrils were assailed by the familiar odor of soap, oil, and horse manure. In this neighborhood were the cheders, studyhouses, and Hasidic prayer houses where I had learned Torah.

We reached Krochmalna Street and the stench I recalled from my childhood struck me first—a blend of burned oil, rotten fruit, and chimney smoke. Everything was the same—the cobblestone pavement, the steep gutter, the balconies hung with wash. We passed a factory with wire-latticed windows and a blind wall with a wooden gate I never saw open in all my youth. Every house here was bound up with memories. No. 5 contained a yeshiva in which I had studied for a term. There was a ritual bath in the courtyard, where matrons came in the evening to immerse themselves. I used to see them emerge clean and flushed. Someone told me that this building had been the home of Rabbi

Itche Meir Alter, the founder of the Gur dynasty generations ago. In my time the yeshiva had been part of the Grodzisk house of prayer. Its beadle was a drunk. When he had a drop too much, he told tales of saints, dybbuks, half-mad squires, and sorcerers. He ate one meal a day and always (except on the Sabbath) stale bread crumbled into borscht.

No. 4 was a huge bazaar, Yanash's Court, which had two gates —one leading into Krochmalna and the other into Mirowska Street. They sold everything here—fruit, vegetables, dairy, geese, fish. There were stores selling secondhand shoes and old clothes of all kinds.

We came to the Place. It always swarmed with prostitutes, pimps, and petty thieves in torn jackets and caps with visors pulled down over their eyes. In my time, the Boss here had been Blind Itche, chief of the pickpockets, proprietor of brothels, a swaggerer and a knife carrier. Somewhere in No. 11 or 13 lived fat Reitzele, a woman who weighed three hundred pounds. Reitzele was supposed to conduct business with white slavers from Buenos Aires. She was also a procurer of servant girls. Many games were played in the Place. You drew numbers from a bag and you could win a police whistle, a chocolate cake, a pen with a view of Cracow, a doll that sat up and cried "Mama."

I stopped with Betty to gape. The same louts, the same flat pronunciation, the same games. I was afraid that all this would disgust her, but she had become infected by my nostalgia. "You should have brought me here the very first day we met!" she said.

"Betty, I'll write a play called *Krochmalna* and you shall play the leading role."

"You're a great promiser."

I didn't know what to show her next—the den in No. 6 where the thieves played cards and dominoes and where the fences came to buy stolen goods; the prayer house in No. 10 where we used to live, or the Radzymin studyhouse in No. 12, to which we later moved; the courtyards where I attended cheder or the stores where my mother used to send me to buy food and kerosene. The

only change I could observe was that the houses had lost most of
their plaster and grown black from smoke. Here and there, a wall
was supported on logs. The gutters seemed even deeper, their
stink even stronger. I stopped before each gate and peered in.
All the garbage bins were heaped high with refuse. Dyers dyed
clothing, tinsmiths patched broken pots, men with sacks on their
shoulders cried, "Ole clo's, ole clo's, I buy rags, ole pants, ole
shoes, ole hats; ole clo's, ole clo's." Here and there, a beggar sang
a song—of the *Titanic,* which had gone down in 1911, of the
striker Baruch Shulman, who had thrown a bomb in 1905 and
been hanged. Magicians were performing the same stunts they
had in my childhood—they swallowed fire, rolled barrels with
their feet, lay down bareback on a bed of nails. I knew it couldn't
be, but I imagined that I recognized the girl who went around
shaking a tambourine hung with bells to collect coins from the
watchers. She wore the same velvet breeches with silver sequins.
Her hair was cut like a boy's. She was tall and slim, flat-chested,
her eyes were shiny black. A parrot with a broken beak perched
on her shoulder.

"If all this could only be transported to America!" Betty said.

I asked her to wait outside and opened the door to the Neustat
prayer house—empty, but the holy ark with the two gilded lions
on the cornice, the pulpit, the reading table and benches gave
witness that Jews still came here to pray. On shelves the holy
books lay and stood in black rows, old and ragged. Since no one
was inside, I called Betty to join me. I shouted and an echo
responded. I pulled apart the curtain before the ark, opened the
door, and glanced at the scrolls in their velvet mantelets and the
gold embroidery tarnished with the years. Betty and I thrust our
heads inside. Her face was hot. We shared a sinful urge to desecrate the sacred and we kissed. At the same time I excused myself
before the scrolls and reminded them that Betty was not a married woman.

We left the prayer house and I looked around the courtyard.
Shmerl the shoemaker once lived and had his workshop here in
a cellar. He had been given the nickname "Shmerl not today."

If you came with shoes or boots to be soled or heeled, he always said, "Not today!" He died while we were still living in Warsaw. A cart drove into the courtyard and took him away to the Hospital for Epidemic Diseases. On Krochmalna Street it was believed that they poisoned patients there. The wags in the courtyard joked that when the Angel of Death with his thousand eyes and sharp sword came for him, Shmerl said, "Not today," but the Angel replied, "Yes, today."

At No. 10 the balcony of what had been our apartment was hung with wash. It had once seemed so high to me, but now I could almost reach it with my fingers. I glanced into the stores. Where were Eli the grocer and his wife, Zeldele? Just as Eli was tall, quick, agile, sharp, and argumentative, Zeldele was small, slow-moving, dull, and good-natured. Zeldele had to be told twice what it was a customer wanted. For her to put out her hand, take a piece of paper, slice off a chunk of cheese, and weigh it could take a quarter of an hour. If you asked her the cost, she began to mull it over and scratch under her wig with a hairpin. If the customer bought on credit and Zeldele marked down the amount, she couldn't make out later what she had written. When the war came and German marks and pfennigs came into use, she grew completely bewildered. Eli abused her in front of the customers and called her "Cow." She became sick during the war and they didn't manage to get her to a hospital. She lay down in bed and went off to sleep like a chick. Eli cried, wailed, and beat his head against the wall. Three months later, he married a plump wench who was just as slow and tranquil as Zeldele.

3

WE ENTERED Yanash's Court and went to the slaughterhouse. The same blood-spattered walls, the hens and roosters going to their deaths shrieking with the same voices: "What have I done to deserve this? Murderers!" Evening had fallen and the harsh light of the lamps reflected off the slaughterers' blades. Women pushed forward, each with her fowl. Porters loaded baskets with dead birds and carried them off to the pluckers. This hell made mockery of all blather about humanism. I had long considered becoming a vegetarian and at that moment I swore never again to touch a piece of meat or fish.

Outside the slaughterhouse, the lamps used to illuminate the courtyard only intensified the darkness. We passed tubs and basins containing live carp, tench, and pike, which the housewives would clean and chop in honor of the Sabbath. We walked on straw, feathers, and slime. The storekeepers scolded and swore the familiar old curses: "A black plague on you!" "A fever in your guts!" "You should lead your daughter to a black wedding canopy!"

We left the bazaar and went into the street again. Before gates and lamp posts stood streetwalkers—some fat with huge bosoms and flowing hips; others slim, draped in shawls. Workers coming from factories and shops on Wola and Iron Streets stopped to talk to the whores and haggle over prices.

Betty said, "Let's get out of here! Besides, I'm hungry."

Suddenly I saw the No. 7 building, where Bashele and her three daughters had moved. Even if the family was still alive, they would have left their apartment years ago. Well, but suppose they hadn't moved out? And Shosha still remembered the tales I used to tell her, our playing house, hide-and-seek, tag? I stopped in front of the gate.

Betty asked, "Why are you standing there? Let's go."

"Betty, I have to find out if by any chance Bashele still lives here."

"Who is this Bashele?"

"Shosha's mother."

"And who is Shosha?"

"Wait, I will explain."

A woman walked into the gate and I asked her if Bashele lived in the courtyard.

"Bashele? Does she have a husband? What's her surname?" the woman asked.

I couldn't recall, or perhaps I had never known the family's last name. "Yes, her husband has a round beard," I answered. "He used to be a clerk at some store. She has a daughter, Shosha. I hope they're alive."

The woman clapped her hands. "I know the one you mean! Basha Schuldiener. They live on the first floor opposite the gate to the left. You're an American, eh?"

I pointed to Betty. "She is an American."

"Family?"

"Just friends. I haven't seen them for almost twenty years."

"Twenty years? Go straight ahead, but be careful. The kids dug a hole in the middle of the yard. You can fall and break a leg. It's dark there. The landlords grab the rent money but they don't believe in lighting a lamp at night."

Betty began to grumble, but I exclaimed, "It's a miracle! A miracle! Many thanks!" I called after the woman. I stood in the courtyard of No. 7 and looked across it into a window with a burning gaslight behind which I might possibly soon meet Bashele and Shosha. As if she finally realized what I was going through, Betty grew silent. I took her arm and led her along. Despite the darkness I spotted the hole and we avoided it. We came to the short flight of unlit stairs that led to the first-floor apartment, I felt about for a doorknob, pushed the door open, and a second miracle unfolded before me. I saw Bashele. She stood at the kitchen table peeling an onion. She had aged little in all this time. Her wig was still blond; her wide fair face had wrinkled slightly, but her eyes looked up with the amiable half smile I remembered from my childhood. Her dress might have come from those days, too. When she saw me, her upper lip lifted —she still had her broad teeth. Her mortar and pestle, the cooking utensils, the closet with the carved molding, the chairs, the table—all were familiar.

"Bashele! You don't recognize me, but I recognize you!" I said.

She put down the onion and knife. "I do recognize you. You're Arele."

In the Pentateuch, when Joseph recognized his brothers, they kissed and embraced, but Bashele wasn't a woman who would kiss a strange man, not even one she had known as a child.

Betty arched her brows. "Is it true that you haven't seen each other for almost twenty years?"

"Wait—yes, almost as long," Bashele said in a common woman's voice, kind, motherly, and yet unique. I would have known it out of a million other voices. "Many years," she added.

"But he was only a child," Betty protested.

"Yes. He and Shosha are the same age," Bashele said.

Betty asked, "How can you recognize someone who left here as a child?"

Bashele shrugged. "As soon as he started speaking, I knew him. I heard you became a writer for the papers. Don't stand there in the doorway. Come in and be welcome. This is probably your wife," she said, nodding toward Betty.

Betty smiled. "No, I'm not his wife. I'm an actress from America and he's writing a play for me."

"I know," Bashele said. "We have a neighbor who reads your things. Every time your name appears in the paper he comes and reads to us. Once it said that a piece by you will be played in the theater."

"Where is Shosha?" I asked.

"Went to the store for sugar. She'll be right back."

As Bashele spoke, Shosha came in. God in heaven—what surprises this day had brought, each greater than the other! Were my eyes deceiving me? Shosha had neither grown nor aged. I gaped at this mystery. After a while, I did observe a slight change in her face and in her height. She had grown perhaps an inch or two. She wore a faded skirt and sleeveless jacket that I could have sworn she wore twenty years ago. She stood holding a paper cone used by grocers to weigh out a quarter pound and looked at us. In her eyes was the same childish fascination I remembered from the times I told her stories.

"Shosha, do you know who this is?" Bashele asked.

Shosha didn't answer.

"It's Arele, the rabbi's son."

"Arele," Shosha repeated, and it was her voice, although not exactly the same.

"Put down the sugar and take off your jacket," Bashele said.

Slowly Shosha put the cone of sugar on the table and took off her jacket. Her figure had remained childlike, although I detected signs of breasts. Her skirt was shorter than those in style and it was hard to tell by the gaslight whether it was blue or black. This was how garments looked that had passed through the disinfection station during the war—shrunken, steamed, faded. Shosha's neck was long, her arms and legs thin. Everyone in Warsaw wore sheer, glossy, colored stockings, but Shosha's appeared to be made of coarse cotton.

Bashele began, "The war, the miserable war destroyed us. Yppe died shortly after you moved to the country. She caught a fever and took to bed. Someone snitched and the hospital wagon came for her. For eight days the fever consumed her. They let none of us into the hospital. On the last day I went to ask about her and the guard at the gate said, '*Bardzo kiepsko,*' and I knew that she was gone. Zelig wasn't in Warsaw. He didn't even go to his daughter's funeral. Four years went by before we could put up a tombstone. Teibele grew up a young lady, God spare her, smart, pretty, educated—everything you could want. She went to the Gymnasium. She is a bookkeeper now in a mattress business. They sell everything wholesale. On Thursdays she figures out what's coming to all the employees and gives the slips to the cashier. If she doesn't sign them, nobody gets paid. The boys run after her but she says, 'I've got plenty of time.' She doesn't live here with us, comes only on Sabbaths and holidays. She has an apartment with a roommate on Grzybowska Street. If you tell people you live on Krochmalna Street it ruins your chances for a good match. Shosha lives at home, as you can see for yourself. Arele, and you, young lady, take off your coats. Shosha, don't stand there like a clod! The lady is from America."

"From America," Shosha repeated.

"Have a seat. I'll make tea. Have you eaten supper?" Bashele asked.

"Thanks, we're not hungry." Betty winked at me.

"Sit down. Arele, your parents still live in the provinces?"

"Father is no longer living."

"He was a dear man, a saint. I used to consult him on questions of religious law. He wouldn't even look at a female. The moment I came in he turned away. He was always at the lectern. Such big books, like in a studyhouse. What did he die of? There are no such Jews any more. Even the Hasidim dress like dandies today—cutaway gaberdines, polished boots. Mother still living?"

"Yes."

"And your brother, Moishele?"

"Moishele is a rabbi."

"Moishele a rabbi? You hear, Shosha? He was such a tiny thing. Didn't even go to cheder then."

"He did go to cheder," Shosha said. "Here in the courtyard at the crazy teacher's."

"Eh? The years go by. Where is Moishele a rabbi?"

"In Galicia."

"In Galicia? Where is that? There are such faraway towns," Bashele said. "When we lived in No. 10, Warsaw was Russia. All the signs had to be in Russian. Then the Germans came, and with them the hunger. Later, the Polacks raised their heads and shouted, '*Nasza Polska!*' Some boys around here went to join Pilsudski's legion and were killed. Pilsudski went with his men to Kiev; then they were pushed back to the Vistula. The people thought the Bolsheviks were coming and the ruffians began to talk about knifing all the rich and taking their money. Then the Bolsheviks were driven back. They were driven here, driven there

—the shortages grew. Zelig is never at home any more. Things happened I will tell you about some other time. People have become selfish. They stopped caring even for their nearest. The zloty is falling, the dollar rises. Here they call dollars 'noodles.' And everything is dearer, dearer. Shosha, set the table."

"With the tablecloth or the oilcloth?"

"Let it be the oilcloth."

Betty signaled that she wanted to tell me something in private. I leaned toward her and she whispered, "I can't eat here. If you want to stay with them, I'll go back to the hotel alone."

I said, "Bashele, Shosha, the fact that I lived to see you again is a great joy to me, but the lady has to leave and I can't let her go alone. I'll come back later. If not tonight, then tomorrow."

"Don't go away," Shosha said. "You went away once and I thought you were never coming back again. One time, our neighbor—Leizer, his name is—said you were in Warsaw and showed us your name in the newspaper, but it didn't say your address. I thought you had forgotten all about us."

"Shosha, a day didn't go by that I didn't think of you."

"Then why didn't you come over? Something you wrote—it had your name on it—was printed in a paper. Not a paper but a book with green covers. Leizer reads everything. He's a watchmaker. He came and read it to us. You described Krochmalna Street accurately."

"Yes, Shosha, I didn't forget anything."

"We moved to No. 7 here and after that you never came over. You got big and you put on phylacteries. I saw you pass by a few times. I wanted to go over to you, but you were walking so fast. You became a Hasid and didn't look at girls. I was shy. Then they said you left the city. Yppe died and there was a funeral. I saw her lying there dead and she was all white."

"Shosha, be quiet!" her mother snapped at her.

"White as chalk. I dreamed about her every night. They made her shroud from my shirt. I got sick and stopped growing. They took me to Dr. Kniaster and he gave me a prescription, but it didn't help. Teibele is tall and pretty."

"You are pretty, too, Shosha," I said.

"I'm like a midget."

"No, Shosha. You have a nice figure."

"I'm grown up and I look like a child. I couldn't go to school. The books were too hard for me. When the Germans took over they began to teach us German. A boy is a *Knabe* to them and how could I remember all that? We were supposed to buy German books and Mama didn't have the money for it. Finally, they sent me home for the second time."

"It's all from not getting enough to eat," Bashele added. "They mixed the bread with turnip or sawdust. It tasted like clay. That winter the potatoes froze and got so sweet you couldn't eat them. I cooked potatoes three times a day. Dr. Kniaster said that Shosha had no blood and he prescribed some brown medicine. She took it three times a day, but when you're hungry, nothing helps. How Teibele—the evil eye spare her—managed to grow up so pretty is God's miracle. When will you be back?"

"Tomorrow."

"Come to lunch tomorrow. You used to be fond of noodles with beans. Come at two. You can bring the lady along. Shosha, this lady is an actress," Bashele said, indicating Betty. "Where do you perform? In the theater?"

"I played in Russia, I played in America, and I hope to appear here in Warsaw," Betty said. "It all depends on Mr. Greidinger."

"He always could write," Shosha said. "He bought a notebook and a pencil and filled three pages. He drew figures, too. One time he drew a house on fire. Flames shot out of every window. He drew the house with a black pencil and the fire with a red pencil. Fire and smoke poured from the chimney. Remember, Arele?"

"I remember. Good night. I'll be here tomorrow at two."

"Don't stay away so long again," Shosha said.

4

I WANTED to walk but Betty hailed a droshky. She told the driver to take us to the restaurant on Leszno Street where we had had our first meal in company with Sam Dreiman and Feitelzohn.

In the droshky, Betty put her hand on my shoulder. "The girl is an idiot. She belongs in an institution. But you're in love with her. The moment you saw her, your eyes lit up in a strange way. I'm beginning to think you aren't in your right mind yourself."

"That may be, Betty."

"Writers are all slightly touched. I'm crazy, too. All talents are. I once read a book about this. I forget the author's name."

"Lombroso."

"Yes, maybe. Or maybe the book was about him. But since each of us is crazy in a different fashion, one can observe the other's madness. Don't start up with that girl. She is sick. If you promise her something and don't keep your word, she'll crack up altogether."

"I know."

"What do you see in her?"

"I see myself."

"Well, you'll fall into a net you'll never be able to untangle yourself from. I don't even believe that such a woman is capable of living with a man. She surely can't have a child."

"I don't need children."

"Instead of your raising her up, she'll drag you down to her level. I know of such a case—a highly intelligent man, an engineer, and he married some unbalanced woman who was older. She bore him a crippled child, a piece of flesh that could neither live nor die. Instead of placing it in an institution, they dragged it to all kinds of clinics, spas, and quacks. It died finally, but the man was ruined."

"I won't have such a freak with Shosha."

"It's typical that the moment something interesting presents itself to me, fate thumbs its nose in my face."

"Betty, you have a lover who is goodness himself, rich as Croesus, and ready to turn the world upside down for you."

"I know what I have. I hope this won't spoil our plans for the play."

"It won't spoil anything."

"If I hadn't seen it with my own eyes, I wouldn't have believed such a thing possible."

I leaned my head against the back of the droshky and looked up above the tin rooftops at the Warsaw sky. It seemed to me that the city had changed. There was something festive and Purim-like in the air. We passed Iron Gate Square again. All the windows of the Vienna Hall were illuminated and I could hear music. Someone must be getting married there this evening. I closed my eyes and put my hand on Betty's lap. The smells of spring came to my nostrils along with the stench of garbage wagons transporting the day's refuse to the fields.

The droshky stopped. Betty wanted to pay but I would not allow it. I helped her out and took her arm. Normally I would have been self-conscious about escorting such an elegant lady to a restaurant, but my encounter with Shosha had dazed me. In the restaurant an orchestra was playing American jazz and hits from Warsaw cabarets. All the tables seemed to be taken. Here they ate the chickens, ducks, geese, and turkeys that had been slaughtered earlier that day. It smelled of roasting, of garlic, horseradish, beer, and cigars. The older men had tucked the huge napkins into their stiff collars. Bellies protruded, necks were thick, and bald pates gleamed like mirrors. The women chattered vivaciously, laughed, and dug their red fingernails into the portions of fowl that couldn't be got at by a fork. Their rouged lips drank from foaming mugs of beer. The headwaiter offered us a table in a niche. They knew Betty here. Sam Dreiman left dollar tips. Skillfully waiters maneuvered among the tables, balancing trays from which steam rose. I sat not facing Betty but alongside her.

The menu didn't feature a single dish that wasn't fish or meat, and I had just vowed to become a vegetarian. After some deliberation I decided the vow would have to wait another day. I ordered broth and meatballs with farfel and carrots, but I had no desire for food. Betty ordered a cocktail and a steak, insisting that it be rare. She took little sips of her drink and looked at me sharply.

She said, "I don't intend to hang around this stinking world too long. Forty years is the maximum. I don't want to live a day longer. What for? If it works out that I can perform a few years the way I want, all the better. If not, I'll put an end to it sooner. Thank God for one gift—the choice to commit suicide."

"You'll live to ninety. You'll be a second Sarah Bernhardt."

"No. Also, I don't choose to be a second anything. It's first or nothing. Sam promises me a huge inheritance, but I'm convinced he'll outlive me, and I hope that he does with all my heart. They don't know how to mix a cocktail here. They try to copy America but imitations are always false. The music's a poor imitation, too. The whole world wants to copy America and America copies the whole world. Why should I be an actress? Actors are all monkeys or parrots. I tried to write once. I still have a bundle of poems lying around—some in Yiddish, some in Russian. Nobody wanted to publish them. I read the magazines and I see that they print the worst rubbish, but from me they demand that I be another Pushkin or Yesenin. Why are you looking at my steak like that? What you said about vegetarianism today is nonsense. If God created the world this way, then that is His will."

"The vegetarians only express a protest."

"How can a bubble protest against the sea? It's arrogant. If a cow lets herself be milked, she must be milked, and if she lets herself be slaughtered, she should be slaughtered. That's what Darwin said."

"Darwin didn't say that."

"No matter, someone said it. Since Sam gives me money, I must take it from him, and since he goes to Mlawa and leaves me alone, I must spend time with someone else."

"Since your father let himself be shot, then—"

"That's vile!"

"Forgive me."

"Basically, you're right. But man must have regard for his fellow man. Even animals don't devour their own species."

"In my uncle's house a tomcat killed his own kittens."

"A tomcat does what nature tells him. Or this could have been a mad tomcat. You're a mad tomcat yourself, and you too will devour somebody. You looked at that stunted girl today with the eyes of a tomcat looking at a canary. You'll give her a few weeks of happiness, then you'll abandon her. I know this as well as I know it's night now."

"All I did was promise her I'd come for lunch tomorrow."

"Go to her tomorrow and tell her you're married. Actually you do have a wife—that Communist you told me about. What's her name? Dora. Since you don't believe in marriage, then the woman you're with *is* your wife."

"In that case, every modern man has dozens of wives."

"Yes, every modern man has dozens of wives and every modern woman has dozens of husbands. If laws no longer have meaning, let the lawlessness apply to everybody."

The music stopped and we grew silent. Betty tasted a piece of her steak and pushed the plate away. The headwaiter noticed and came over to ask if he could bring her something else. She said that she was not hungry. She complained that the cook used too many spices. Our waiter came over and the two men began to discuss the chef. The headwaiter said, "He'll have to go."

"Don't fire him on my account," Betty said.

"It's not a question of only you. He's been told a hundred times not to use so much pepper, but it's like a madness in him. Because he likes pepper he'll end up without a job—isn't that madness?"

"Oh, every chef is half mad," the waiter said.

Both he and the headwaiter lingered around the table while we ate dessert. They were apparently afraid of losing their usual tip, but Betty took out two dollars and gave one to each of them. Both men began to bow and scrape. In Warsaw a family could have eaten for half a week on that sum. A millionaire's mistress apparently had to act like the millionaire himself.

"Come, let's go," Betty said.

"Where?"

"To my place."

5

I GOT home at eight in the morning. On the way to catch my trolley I glanced in a mirror—a pale face, a bristly beard; I had had to leave the hotel early, before the maid brought breakfast. The trolley was full of men and young women going to factories and shops, with lunches under their arms. I yawned and tried to stretch, but there was no room to extend my legs. It had rained during the night and the sky hung overcast and dark as dusk; in the trolley the lights had been turned on. All the faces appeared grim and preoccupied. Everyone seemed to be taking account, wondering at the start of another day, what's the sense of all this effort, and where does it lead to? I imagined that by some common sensitivity they all realized the same mistake and were asking, "How could we have missed something so obvious and why is it too late to correct it?"

At home Tekla let me in. In the corridor her eyes expressed a reproof that seemed to say, "You wild man!" She asked if I wanted breakfast and I told her thanks, but later.

She said to me, "A glass of coffee would be good."

"So be it, dear Tekla." And I handed her a half zloty.

"No, no, no," she protested.

"Take it, Tekla, I like you."

Her cheeks flushed. "You are too good."

I opened the door to my room. My bed stood made and untouched, the shades were lowered—a bit of yesterday lingering and demanding its due. I stretched out on the bed and tried to snatch a few moments' rest. Never had a night seemed as long as this. Once my mother told me the story of a bewitched yeshiva boy who bent down over a water tub to wash his hands before supper and in the second it took him to obtain a pitcher of water lived through a reincarnation of seventy years. Something of this kind had happened to me. During one night I had found my lost love and then succumbed to temptation and betrayed her. I had stolen the concubine of my benefactor, lied to her, aroused her passion by telling her all my lusty adventures, and made her confess sins that filled me with disgust. I had been impotent and then turned into a sexual giant. We got drunk, quarreled, kissed, insulted one another. I had acted like a shameless pervert and an ardent repentant. At dawn, some drunkard tried to break open our door and we were both convinced that Sam Dreiman had come back to surprise us, punish us, perhaps even put us to death. I dozed off and Tekla wakened me with a tray of coffee, fresh rolls, and fried eggs. She no longer paid attention to my wishes but, like a sister or wife, acted on her own initiative. She looked at me knowingly. When she put the tray on the table, I took her around from behind and kissed her nape. She made no move for a moment. Then she turned and murmured, "What are you doing?"

"Give me your mouth."

"Oh, it's forbidden!" She brought her lips to mine.

I kissed her long. She kissed back and her breasts pressed against me. She kept glancing at the door. She risked her reputation, her job. She tore from my arms, panting. She seized my wrists, held them with a peasant's strength, and hissed like a goose, "The mistress could come in!" She shuffled toward the door, dragging her legs with their broad calves. I recalled the phrase from the *Ethics of the Fathers:* "One sin drags another." I sipped the coffee, bit into a roll, tasted the eggs, and took off my shoes. The play lay on my desk, but I couldn't write now. I lay down on the bed and I neither slept nor stayed fully awake. In all the novels I had read, the heroes desired only one woman, but here I was, lusting after the whole female gender.

Finally I dropped off, and in my sleep I wrote the play. The writing became increasingly harder. The pen blotted, ran dry; it scratched the paper and I couldn't make out my own handwriting. I opened my eyes and glanced at my watch—ten past one. I had slept for hours. I was supposed to be at Shosha's at two, and I still must wash and shave. I had decided to take Shosha a box of candy. I no longer needed to steal a groschen or six from my mother to get Shosha chocolate—my pockets were stuffed with Sam Dreiman's banknotes.

I did everything in a hurry. It would take too long to walk to Krochmalna Street, and when I left the confectionary I hailed a droshky. As it pulled up before No. 7, my wristwatch showed five minutes past two. I could feel the mother's and daughter's anxiety. I rushed through the courtyard and nearly fell into the hole I had sidestepped in the dark the evening before. When I opened the door, I walked into a holiday household. The table was set with a tablecloth and china. Shosha wore a Sabbath dress and high-heeled shoes. She no longer looked like a midget, merely a short girl. Her hair was set differently—high, to make her appear taller. Even Bashele had fixed herself up in honor of my visit. I handed Shosha the candy and her blue eyes gazed at me in embarrassed bliss.

Bashele said, "Arele, you are a real gentleman."

"Mama, shall I open it?"

"Why not?"

I helped her. I had asked the confectioner for his best candy. The box was black with little gold stars. The chocolate lay in fluted paper cups, each of a different size and in its own niche.

The color changed on Shosha's face. "Mama, look!"

"You shouldn't have spent so much," Bashele protested.

"Remember, Shosha, how I used to steal money from my mother to buy you chocolate and was lashed for it at home?"

"I remember, Arele."

"Don't eat any chocolate before lunch. It'll spoil your appetite," Bashele said.

"Just one, Mama!" Shosha pleaded. She studied which piece to select, pointing to one and then another, but she couldn't make up her mind. She stopped, bewildered.

I had read in a book on psychiatry that the inability to decide about even small things was a symptom of a spiritual disorder. I picked out three pieces, one for each of us. Shosha held the candy between her thumb and index finger and lifted her pinky with the gesture of the poseurs of Krochmalna Street. She took a bite. "Mama, it melts in your mouth! How delicious!"

"Say thank you, at least."

"Oh, Arele, if you only knew—"

"Give him a kiss," Bashele told her.

"I'd be ashamed."

"What's to be ashamed of? You're a young lady—may the evil eye spare you."

"Not here, then. In the other room." She held out her hand. "Come with me," she said.

I followed her into the other room, which was crowded with bundles, sacks, and old furniture. There was a metal cot, with a straw mattress but no sheet. Shosha stood on tiptoe and I bent down toward her. She took my face in her childlike hands and kissed me on the lips, on both cheeks, on my forehead, and on the nose. Her fingers were hot. I took her in my arms and we stood there clinging to each other.

I asked, "Shosha, you want to be mine?"

"Yes," Shosha replied.

· *CHAPTER FIVE* ·

1

IT WAS early summer, the month of May, and Sam Dreiman had
rented a cottage for himself and Betty in Świder, not far from
Otwock. It wasn't the villa we had seen in March. He had
hired a maid and a cook. Every morning, after breakfast, Sam
went to bathe in the Świderek River. He stood under the low
waterfall with his round shoulders, white-haired chest, swollen
belly, and let the water pour over him. He screamed with pleasure, sneezed, gasped, and barked out his gratitude to the cool
stream. Betty sat on the beach on a folding chair under a parasol
and read a book. Like me, Betty avoided all sports. She could
not swim. In the sun, her skin became sickly-red and developed
blisters. In the attic, a room with a balcony had been set aside
for me, and I used it several weekends. But I stopped going
there. There were constant visitors from Warsaw or America—
guests came even from the American consulate. The majority of
the visitors spoke English, and then when Sam knew I was coming he invited actors and actresses who were scheduled to appear
in our play and demanded that I read scenes to them. They were
all old, but they dressed like young people—the men in narrow
pants, the women in gaudy trousers over their broad hips. They
kept praising me and I couldn't stand the excitement and even

less the undeserved compliments. I had paid another two months' advance on my room on Leszno Street and wasn't about to let it stand empty. Besides, each time I went, Sam complained because I wouldn't bathe in the little river. I was embarrassed about undressing before strangers. I had never freed myself from a notion inherited from generations: the body is a vessel of shame and disgrace, dust in life and worse in death.

But what really kept me in Warsaw was Shosha. I went to see her now daily. I had laid out a program and tried desperately to stick to it. It required me to rise at eight and wash at the stand. The hours from nine to one were to be spent at my desk with the play. But I had also started a novel, which I shouldn't have done. Besides, the few hours of work were full of interruptions. Feitelzohn phoned every day. He had prepared the first soul expedition, which was to take place at Sam Dreiman's summer house. He was planning to read a paper there, to defend his theory that jealousy was about to vanish from human love and sex and be supplemented by a wish to share libidinous enjoyments with others. Celia called me every other day from Jósefow. Each time, she asked the same thing: "Why do you sit in hot Warsaw? Why not enjoy the fresh outdoors?" She and Haiml both described how balmy the air was in Jósefow, how cool the nights, how sweet the song of the birds. They begged me to come to them. Celia argued, "Let's snatch a little peace before another world war breaks out."

I admitted that they were right and promised them, as I promised Sam Dreiman and Betty, that I would come out that very day or the next, but the moment the clock showed one-thirty I headed for Krochmalna Street. I would enter the gate of No. 7 and see Shosha standing at her window watching for me—a blond girl, blue-eyed, with a short nose, thin lips, a slender neck, her hair braided in pigtails. Thank God, she had all her teeth. She spoke the Yiddish of Krochmalna Street. In her own fashion she denied death. Although they had all died, in Shosha's mind Eli and Zeldele still ran the grocery store, David and Mirale still sold butter, raw and boiled milk, as well as sour milk and cottage cheese, Esther still kept the candy store where you could buy chocolate, cheesecake, soda water, and ice cream. Each day Shosha surprised me with something. She got out her old school text-books with the familiar pictures and poems. She had kept the notebooks in which I began my literary career and attempted to paint as well. I noticed that when it came to drawing I hadn't made the slightest progress.

Whenever I was with her, I asked myself, How can this be? How can it be explained? Had Shosha found a magical way to stop the advance of time? Was this the secret of love or the power of retrogression? Oddly, Bashele, like Shosha, showed no surprise at my reappearance. I had come back and I was here. I gave Bashele money to prepare meals for me, and when I arrived at two or a bit later, the house already smelled of new potatoes, mushrooms, tomatoes, cauliflower—whatever she had bought that day. She set the table and the three of us sat down and ate as if we had never been parted.

Bashele's dishes tasted as good as they had when I was a child. No one could give to the borscht such a sweet-and-sour zest as Bashele. She added spices to her dishes. She cooked cabbage with raisins and cream of tartar. She kept jars of cloves, saffron, crushed almonds, cinnamon, and ginger on her kitchen shelves.

Bashele took everything in stride. I told her I had just be-come a vegetarian, and she asked no questions but began to provide meals for me consisting of fruit, eggs, and vegetables. Shosha would go into the alcove to take out her old playthings and lay them out for me as she had done twenty years before. During the meal Bashele and Shosha related all kinds of things. The stone over Yppe's grave had tipped and was leaning on another tombstone. Bashele wanted to set it upright, but the cemetery watchman demanded fifty zlotys. Leizer the watch-maker had a clock with a brass bird that popped out every half hour and sang like a canary. He had a pen that wrote without being dipped in ink and a lens that could light a cigarette when held under the sun. Berl the furrier's daughter had fallen in love with the son of the proprietor of the tough guys' den at No. 6. The mother didn't want to go to the wedding, but the rabbi who came after my father, Joshua the preacher, said this would be a sin. In No. 8, a ditch was dug and they found a dead Russian sapper, with a sword and a revolver. The uniform wasn't yet ruined and medals were still pinned to its lapel. Each time I asked for a person on Krochmalna Street, Bashele knew all about him or her. Most had died. Of those who were still living, many had moved to the provinces or gone to America. One beggar who died in the street was found to be carrying a pouch with golden ducats dating back to the Russian occupation. A whore had been visited by a man from Cracow. He paid her one zloty and went with her to her cellar room. The next day he came again and the day after that, too, and so day after day. He had fallen in love with her. He divorced his wife and married the whore.

Shosha listened in silence. Suddenly she blurted, "She lives in No. 9. She became a decent woman."

It would seem that Shosha understood such things. I glanced at her and she blushed. "Tell me, Shosha," I asked, "did anyone ever propose a match to you?"

Shosha put down her spoon. "They offered me one with a tinsmith from No. 5. His wife died and a matchmaker came to see me."

Bashele shook her head. "Why not tell him about the store manager who wanted you?"

"Who was this manager?" I asked.

"Oh, he worked in a store on Mead Street. A short fellow with a lot of black hair. I didn't like him," Shosha said.

"Why not?"

"He had black teeth. When he laughed, it sounded like 'ech, ech, ech, hee, hee, hee.' "

As Shosha mimicked the man's laughter, she started laughing herself. Then she grew serious and said, "I can't marry without love."

2

NO, SHOSHA hadn't remained completely a child. I kissed her when her mother went shopping and she kissed me back. Her face glowed. I put her on my lap and she kissed my lips and played with my earlobes.

She said, "Arele, I never forgot you. Mama laughed at me. 'He doesn't even know you exist any more,' she told me. 'He probably has a fiancée by now, or a wife and children.' Yppe died, and Teibele went to school. The frosts came, but Teibele always got up early, washed her face, and took her books. She got good grades. Mama was kind to me but she didn't buy me a dress or shoes. When she got angry she said, 'Too bad you didn't die instead of Yppe!' Don't repeat this—she would kill me. During the war Mama began to sell crockery—glasses, ashtrays, saucers, and things like that. She took up a place between the First and the Second Market. She sat there every day and earned next to nothing—a few pfennigs or a mark. I was left alone. They think that I'm a child because I'm small, but I understand everything. Daddy has another woman. He lives with her on Nizka Street. He comes home maybe once every three months. He comes in, counts out some money, and starts right in to yell. He goes to Teibele's—to where she lives. He says, 'She is *my* daughter.' Sometimes he sends the money by her."

"What does your father do? How does he earn money?"

Shosha's face grew solemn. "It's not allowed to say."

"You can tell me."

"I can't tell anybody."

"Shosha, I swear by God I won't tell a soul."

Shosha sat down on a stool next to me and clasped my legs. "With the dead."

"In the burial society?"

"Yes, there. First he worked in a wine and spirits store. When the boss died, the sons pushed him out. On Grzybowska Street there is a society, The True Mercy, and they bury the dead. The boss there went to cheder with Papa."

"Your father drives a hearse?"

"No, a car. This is a kind of car that if someone dies in Mokotów or Szmulewizna, Papa goes and brings him to Warsaw. He has gotten a gray beard but he dyes it and it's black again. The sweetheart—that's what they call her—is with the society, too. Swear that you'll tell nobody."

"Shoshele, whom would I tell? Who of my friends knows you?"

"Mama thinks that no one knows, but they know. There was a lot of trouble about drying the wash in the attic. If you hang it out to dry in the courtyard, it's stolen. Also, a policeman comes and gives a ticket. Whenever it's wash time, a brawl breaks out. The women curse and sometimes hit each other. There isn't enough room for everybody. One woman who sells cracked eggs cut a line with wash hanging on it and all the shirts fell down. The others beat her and she ran to snitch to the cops. Oh, there was such a fuss I had to laugh. The woman got mad at Mama and she yelled, 'Go to the dead, with your husband's sweetheart, and rot with them together!' When Mama came home she got spasms. They had to call the barber-surgeon. If Mama knew that I told you, she'd scream terribly."

"Shosha, I'll tell no one."

"Why did he leave Mama? I saw her once, that sweetheart. She has a voice like a man. It was winter and Mama got sick. We were left without a groschen. You're sure you want to hear?"

"Yes, I do."

"We had to call a doctor, but there was no money for medicine. Or for anything else. Yechiel Nathan, the owner of the grocery store, was still in No. 13 then. You remember him, eh? We used to do all our shopping from them."

"I should say so. He used to pray in the Neustat prayer house."

"Oh, you remember everything! It's good to talk with you—the others know nothing. We were always in debt to them, and when Mama sent me for a loaf of bread, the wife looked into a long ledger and said, 'Enough credit.' I went home, and when I told Mama, she began to cry. She fell asleep and I didn't know what to do. I knew that the society was on Grzybowska Street and I thought maybe Papa would be there. So I went. The windowpanes were white as milk, and a black sign read THE TRUE MERCY. I was afraid to go inside—suppose corpses lay there? I'm a terrible coward. You remember when Yocheved died?"

"Yes, Shoshele."

"They lived on our floor and I was afraid to pass their door at night. During the day too, because it was dark in the hall. At night I dreamed of her."

"Shoshele, I dream about Yocheved till this day."

"You do? She was a little child. What was wrong with her?"

"Scarlet fever."

"You know it all! If you hadn't gone away I wouldn't have gotten sick. I had no one to talk to. Everyone laughed at me. Yes, white panes with black letters. I opened the door and no corpses were lying there. It was a nice room—an office they call it. There was a little window in a wall and people were talking and laughing behind it. An old man carried glasses of tea on a tray. Someone at the little window asked, 'What do you want?' and I told him who I was and that Mama was sick. A woman with yellow hair came in. Her face and hands were covered with freckles. The man said to her, 'This girl is asking about you.' She glared at me and said, 'Who are you?' And I told her. She yelled, 'If you ever come here and bother me again I'll tear out your guts, you little no-good!' She said some filthy words, too. She mentioned that which a girl has—you understand?"

"Yes."

"I wanted to run away, but she opened her purse and dug up some money. When Papa found out about it, he came here and hollered so loud the whole courtyard could hear. He grabbed me by my pigtail and dragged me through the house and spat on me. For three years, maybe, he didn't talk to me when he visited. Mama was angry at me, too. Everyone hollered at me and that's how the years went by. Arele, I could sit with you for a hundred years and not yet finish telling you all of it. Here in our court-yard it's worse than in No. 10. There were bad kids there, too, but they wouldn't beat a girl. They called me names, sometimes they tripped me, but that's all. Remember how we played with nuts on Passover?"

"Yes, Shosha."

"Where was the hole?"

"Inside the gate."

"We played and I won them all. I cleaned you out. I wanted to give you back your nuts, but you wouldn't take them. Velvel the tailor made me a new dress and Mama ordered a pair of shoes from Michael the shoemaker. Suddenly, pious Ytzchokl came out and began to yell at you, 'The rabbi's son plays with a girl! You dreadful boy, I'm going to tell your father this minute and he'll pull out your ears.' Do you remember this?"

"As it happens, this is something I don't remember."

"He chased you and you ran. In those days, Papa still came home all the time. A sheet of matzohs hung in our house. Mama had rendered chicken fat after Hanukkah and we ate so many scraps our bellies nearly burst. They had made you a new gaber-dine. Oh, look how I've been chattering away! In No. 10 it wasn't so bad—here, the thugs throw such big rocks they once made a hole in a girl's head. One fellow dragged a girl down the cellar. She screamed, but if you scream in No. 7, no one bothers to see what's wrong. A lot of the hoodlums carry knives. Mama always says, 'Don't mix in.' Here, if you stick up for someone, you could get stabbed. He did, you know what, to the girl."

"And he wasn't jailed for it?"

"A policeman came and wrote in a book and that was that. The fellow—Paysach is his name—ran away. They run away and the policeman forgets what he has written. Sometimes they send the policeman to another street, or to the higher numbers here. When the Germans came, they threw all the bullies and thieves in jail. Later, they let them all out again. People thought it would get better under the Poles, but they take bribes, too. You slip a zloty into the policeman's hand and he erases what he wrote down."

Shosha stood up. "Arele, you must never go away again. When you are here, I become healthy."

3

WE TOOK a stroll and Shosha clung to my arm. Her fingers stroked my hand, each finger fondling me in a separate fashion. Warmth spread over me and a prickling hair zigzagged across my spine. I barely kept from kissing her in the street. We stopped before every store. Asher the dairyman was still living. His beard had turned gray. This man who rode each day to the train depot to fetch cans of milk was a charitable person, my father's good friend. When we left Warsaw, my father owed him twenty-five rubles. Father went to say goodbye to him and to apologize for his debt, but Asher took fifty German marks from his purse and gave them to Father.

I was supposed to be sitting polishing the play; instead, I was walking with Shosha through the narrow gate of No. 12 to seek out my chum, Berish's son, Mottel. Shosha didn't know him— he belonged to a later period of my life. In the courtyard, I passed by the Radzymin and the Novominsk prayer houses. Afternoon services were already in progress. I wanted to leave Shosha for a minute and look inside to see which of the Hasidim remained alive from among those I had known, but she held on to my arm and wouldn't let go. She was afraid to remain alone in the courtyard. She had not forgotten the old tales of pimps who rode around in carriages snatching girls to sell into white slavery in Buenos Aires. I didn't dare bring a girl into a Hasidic prayer house while the congregation was praying. Only on Simchas Torah were girls allowed inside a house of worship, or when a relative was deathly ill and the family gathered to pray before the holy ark.

A Gentile man carrying a long pipe at the end of which a flame flared went from lamp post to lamp post lighting the street lamps. A pale light fell over the crowds. They shouted, jostled, pushed. Girls laughed noisily. At every other gate stood streetwalkers, beckoning to the men.

I didn't find my friend Mottel. I climbed the dark stairs to where his father lived with his second wife and knocked on the door, but no one answered. Shosha began to shiver. I stopped with her on the landing and kissed her. I pressed her close and thrust my hand inside her blouse and felt her tiny breasts.

She began to tremble. "No, no, no!"

"Shoshele, when you love, such things are permitted."

"Yes, but—"

"I want you to be mine!"

"For real?"

"I love you."

"I'm so small. I can't write."

"I don't need your writing."

"Arele, people will laugh at you."

"I've longed for you all these years."

"Oh, Arele! Is this true?"

"Yes. As soon as I saw you, I knew that I really haven't loved anyone till now."

"Have you had many girls?"

"Not many, but I've slept with some."

Shosha seemed to think it over. "Did you do it with this actress from America?"

"Yes."

"When? Before you came to me?"

I should have answered yes. Instead, I heard myself say, "I slept with her the night after we met." I regretted my words immediately, but confessing and boasting had become a habit with me. Perhaps I learned it from Feitelzohn or in the Writers' Club. I've lost her, I thought. Shosha tried to move away from me, but I held her tight. I had the feeling of a gambler who risks all he possesses in a game, yet makes himself remain quiet. I could hear the pounding of Shosha's heart behind her little left breast.

"Why did you do it? You love her?"

"No, Shoshele. I can do it without love."

"This is what *they* do—you know who I mean."

"The whores and the pimps. That's what we're all becoming, but I'm still able to love you."

"Do you have others, too?" Shosha asked after a pause.

"It happens. I don't want to lie to you."

"No, Arele. You don't need to fool me. I love you as you are. But don't tell Mama. She would raise a fuss and spoil my happiness."

I had expected Shosha to demand details about my affair with Betty. I was ready to give them to her, as well as the fact that I made love to Tekla, though she had a fiancé in the army to whom I wrote letters for her. But Shosha seemed to have forgotten what I told her or to have dismissed it as of no importance. Was she born with the instinct for sharing Feitelzohn talked about? We continued our walk and we came out on Mirowska Street. The fruit stores had closed, but the sidewalk was littered with straw, slats from broken crates, and tissue paper used to wrap oranges. In the First Market, workers were hosing down the tiled floor. The merchants and customers had already dispersed, but the echoes of their shouts hung in the air. In my time, non-kosher sea creatures without scales or fins used to swim here in enormous tubs. The storekeepers sold lobsters and frogs, which Gentiles ate. Huge electric lights lit the market through the night. I led Shosha into a niche and clasped her shoulders. "Shoshele, do you want me?"

"Oh, Arele, do you still have to ask?"

"You'll sleep with me?"

"With you—yes."

"Did anyone ever kiss you?"

"Never. Some lout tried to once, but I ran away. He threw a chunk of wood at me."

Suddenly I had the urge to show off in front of Shosha, to spend money on her. "Shosha, you said just now that you would do whatever I told you."

"Yes, I will."

"I want to take you to the Saxony Gardens. I want to ride with you in a droshky."

"The Saxony Gardens? They don't allow Jews there."

I knew what she meant—under the Russians, Jews in long gaberdines and women in wigs or bonnets had been banned from the park by policemen guarding the gates. But the Poles had since rescinded that order. Besides, I was wearing modern dress. I assured Shosha that we were allowed to go wherever we chose.

Shosha said, "Why take a droshky? We can take 'streetcar No. 11.' Do you know what that means?"

"Yes, go on foot."

"It's a shame to waste money. Mama says, 'Every groschen counts.' You spend a zloty for the droshky and how long is the ride? Maybe half an hour. If you have bundles that's another story."

"Have you ever ridden in a droshky?"

"Never."

"Today you shall ride in a droshky with me. I have a pocketful of zlotys. I told you, I'm writing a play—a theater piece—and they've given me three hundred dollars. I've already spent a hundred and twenty of it, but I've got a hundred and eighty left. A dollar is worth nine zlotys."

"Don't talk so loud. You could be robbed. Once they tried to rob a man from the country, and when he fought, they stabbed him."

We walked down Mirowska Street on the way to Iron Gate
Square. On one side was the First Market, on the other a long
row of flat shacks where Gentile cobblers sold shoes, boots, even
footwear with raised heels and soles for the lame. They were
closing up shop for the night.

Shosha said, "Mama is right. God Himself sent you to me. I've
already told you about Leizer the watchmaker. Mama wanted
to arrange a match between us, but I said, 'I'll stay single.' He's
the best watchmaker in all Warsaw. You give him a broken
watch and he'll fix it so it will run for years. He saw your name
in the paper and he came to us and said, 'Shosha, regards from
your fiancé.' That's what he called you. When he said this, I
knew that you would come to me one day. He says he knew your
daddy."

"Is he in love with you?"

"In love with me? I don't know. He's fifty years old, maybe
more."

A droshky came up and I hailed it.

Shosha trembled. "Arele, what are you doing? Mama—"

"Step up." I helped her and got in beside her. The driver in the
oilcloth cap with the metal number in back turned around suspiciously. "Where to?"

"Ujazdow Boulevard," I said.

"That's a double fare."

We rode out before Iron Gate Square. Each time the droshky
made a turn, Shosha fell against me. "Oh, I'm dizzy."

"I'll bring you home again."

"See how the street looks from a droshky! I feel as if I were an
empress. When Mama hears about this, she'll say you're a spendthrift. Arele, I'm sitting with you in a droshky and it seems like
a dream to me."

"To me, too."

"So many streetcars! And how bright it is here! Like daytime.
Are we going to the elegant streets?"

"You could call them that."

"Arele, since that time I went to The True Mercy I've never been out of Krochmalna Street. Teibele goes everywhere. She goes to Falenica, to Michalin—where doesn't she go? Arele, where are you taking me?"

"To a wild forest where demons cook little children in kettles full of snakes and naked witches with teats on their navels eat them with mustard."

"You're joking, aren't you?"

"Yes, my darling."

"Oh, one never knows what can happen. Mama always teased me, 'Nobody will take *you* except the Angel of Death.' I thought, They'll put me next to Yppe. And then I came home with a cone of sugar and there you were. Arele, what's that?"

"A restaurant."

"Look how many lamps!"

"It's a fancy restaurant."

"Oh, see the dolls in that store window! Like alive! What street is this?"

"The New World."

"So many trees grow here—like a park. And the ladies with the hats, how tall they are! You smell sweetness? What is it?"

"Lilac."

"Arele, I want to ask you something, but don't get mad."

"What do you want to ask?"

"Do you really love me?"

"Yes, Shosha. Very much."

"Why?"

"No whys about it. Just because."

"So long as you weren't there, you weren't there. But if you went away now and didn't come back, I'd die a thousand deaths."

"I'll never leave you again."

"Is that the truth? Leizer the watchmaker once said that all writers are like bums, they walk near the soles of their shoes. Leizer doesn't believe there is a God. He says everything came from itself. How can that be?"

"There is a God."

"Look, the sky is red, just like from a fire. Who lives in these beautiful buildings?"

"Rich people."

"Jews or Gentiles?"

"Mostly Gentiles."

"Arele, take me home. I'm afraid."

"There's no reason to be afraid. If it comes to it that we must die, we'll die together," I said, startled at my own words.

"Is it permitted to put a boy and a girl in the same grave?"

I didn't answer her, and Shosha leaned her head on my shoulder.

4

I RODE back in the droshky to the gate of No. 7, having decided to walk from there to Leszno Street, but Shosha clung to my arm. She was afraid to go through the dark gate, the dark courtyard, and to climb the half flight of stairs alone. The gate was locked and we had to wait some minutes for the janitor to come and open it. In the courtyard, we bumped into a short little man—Leizer the watchmaker. Shosha asked him what he was doing out so late and he told us he was taking a walk.

"This is Arele." Shosha introduced me.

"I know. I understand. Good evening. I read what you write—including the translations you have done."

It was hard to see him clearly, but in the dim light coming from a few windows I could make out a pale face with big black eyes. He wore no jacket or hat. He spoke in a soft voice. He said, "Mr. Greidinger—or should I call you Comrade Greidinger? It's not that I'm a socialist, but it says somewhere that all Jews are comrades. I know your Shosha since they moved into

this building. I used to visit Bashele at a time when her husband
was still a respectable man. I don't want to keep you, but she
began talking about you the day we met and she's never
stopped. Arele this and Arele that. I knew your father, too, may
he rest in peace. I was in your house once. It was during a *din
torah*—I came to give testimony. A few years ago when I saw
your name in a magazine, I wrote you a letter addressed to the
editorial office, but there was no answer. They don't generally
answer in editorial offices, I know. It's the same with publishers.
Once, Shosha and I went to look for you. In any case, you showed
up eventually, and I hear that Romeo and Juliet have found
each other again. There are such loves, yes, there are. In this
world, there is everything. Nature has a pattern for every piece
of goods. If you look for madness, there's no lack of that, either.
What do they say in your circles about the world—I mean Hitler
and Stalin and that scum?"

"What can they say? Man doesn't want peace."

"Why do you say 'man'? I want peace and Shosha wants peace
and so do millions of others. I still maintain that most people in
the world don't want wars, even revolutions. They would choose
to live out their lives the best way they could. With more, with
less, in palaces, in cellar rooms, so long as they had a piece of
bread and a pillow to lay their heads on. Isn't that true, Shosha?"

"Yes, true."

"The trouble is that the quiet, patient people are passive and
those in power, the malefactors, are aggressive. If a decent majority would decide once and for all to take power in their hands,
maybe there would be peace."

"They'll neither decide nor will they ever get power," I said.
"Power and passivity don't mix."

"Is that your view?"

"It's the experience of generations."

"Then things are bitter."

"Yes, Reb Leizer, it isn't good."

"What will become of us Jews? Evil winds are blowing. Well, I won't keep you. I sit all day in the house, and before going to bed I take a little stroll. Right here in the courtyard, from the gate to the garbage bin and back again. What can you do? Maybe there are better worlds somewhere else? Good night. For me it was an honor to meet you. I still have respect for the printed word."

"Good night. I hope we meet again," I said.

Only now did I become aware that Bashele was standing at the window watching us. She was obviously worried. I would have to go in for a moment. She opened the door, and as we walked up the stairs she exclaimed, "Where have you been! Why so late? I thought the worst!"

"Mama, we rode in a droshky."

"In a droshky? Why, of all things? Where to? How do you like that!"

Shosha began to tell her mother of our wanderings—we had ridden down the boulevards, gone into a confectionary, eaten cake and drunk lemonade.

Bashele arched her eyebrows and shook her head reproachfully. "For the life of me I can't see the sense of squandering all those zlotys. If I'd known you were going to *those* streets, I would have ironed your white dress. These days you can't be sure of your life. I stopped at the neighbor's and we heard a speech on the radio by that madman Hitler. He screamed so, you could go deaf. Since you haven't eaten supper, I'll make something."

"Bashele, I'm not hungry. I must go home."

"What? Now? Don't you know it's almost midnight? Where will you go so late? You'll spend the night here. I'll fix the bed in the alcove. But you have to eat, too."

Immediately Bashele began to pour water into a pan of flour. She lit the stove. Shosha led me into the alcove to show me the iron bed where Teibele used to sleep. She lit a small gas lamp. There were clothes and laundry piled here, along with baskets and boxes accumulated from the time Zelig was a traveling salesman.

Shosha said, "Arele, I'd like you to spend every night here. I'd like to be with you always—eat with you, drink with you, walk with you. I won't forget this night, not till the day they put shards over my eyelids—the droshky, the confectionary, all of it. I want to kiss your feet!"

"Shosha, what's the matter with you?"

"Let me!" She fell to her knees and began to kiss my shoes. I struggled with her and tried to pick her up, but she kept crying, "Let me! Let me!"

5

ALTHOUGH I was no longer accustomed to a straw pallet, I fell into a deep sleep in Bashele's alcove that night. I opened my eyes in fright. A white image stood at my bed, bending over me and touching my face with thin fingers. "Who is this?" I asked.

"It's me—Shosha."

It took me a while to remember where I was. Had Shosha come to my bed as Ruth went to Boaz?

"Shosha, what is it?"

"Arele, I'm afraid." Shosha spoke in a wavering voice, like a child about to burst out crying.

I sat up. "What are you afraid of?"

"Arele, don't be angry. I didn't want to wake you, but I have been lying there for three hours and I cannot fall asleep. May I sit on your bed?"

"Yes, yes."

"I was lying in bed and my brain turned like a mill. I wanted to wake up Mother, but she would have yelled at me. She's busy with the house all day long and at night she collapses."

"What were you thinking about?"

"About you. Crazy thoughts came into my head—that it wasn't

you, that you were already dead and had disguised yourself as Arele. A demon screamed in my ear, 'He's dead, dead!' He made such a racket I thought everybody in the courtyard would hear and there would be a riot. I wanted to recite the Shema, but he spat in my ear and spoke queer words."

"What did he say?"

"Oh, I'm ashamed to repeat them."

"Tell me."

"He said that God is a chimney sweep, and that when we marry I will wet the bed. He butted me with his horns. He tore off the cover and whipped me you-know-where."

"Shoshele, it's all your nerves. When we are together, I'll take you to a doctor and he will make you healthy."

"Can I still sit a little?"

"Yes, but if your mother wakes up she will think that—"

"She will not wake up. Dead people come to me the moment I close my eyes. Dead women tear at my hair. I'm old enough to be a mother but I still haven't gotten my period. A few times I began to bleed and my mother gave me cotton and rags, but then it all stopped. Mother talked about it to a woman peddler—she sold shirts, kerchiefs, bloomers—and this woman told everyone that I'm not a virgin any more and that I'm pregnant. Mother began to pull my hair and call me ugly names. Bullies in the courtyard threw stones at me. This was years ago, not now. When my daddy heard what happened, he gave Mother ten zlotys to take me to a women's doctor, who said it was all a big lie. A neighbor came to us and said that I should be taken to a rabbi, to get a paper saying that I am a *mukasetz*. This means a girl who lost her innocence without a man, by accident. Your father had left Warsaw years before and we went to a rabbi on Smocza Street. He ordered me taken to a mikvah and examined there. I didn't want to go, but Mother dragged me. The woman in charge undressed me until I was naked, and I had to show her everything. I almost died from shame. She touched me and fumbled around. Then she said that I was kosher. The rabbi had asked thirty zlotys for the certificate and we could not afford it, so we let it go. Now that you're here, I'm worried that someone may come and tell you bad things about me."

"Shoshele, no one will come, and I will listen to no one. I didn't know there were still such fanatics in Warsaw."

"Arele, strange things come into my head—perhaps this, perhaps that. Until I was three, I used to wet the bed. Even now, sometimes I wake up in the middle of the night. The room is cold, but I'm soaked with sweat. The pillow is wet. I never drink before I go to bed, but when I wake up I need to go so badly that until I reach the chamber pot I make on the floor. In the daytime, I go to the outhouse in the yard and it is as dark as night, and there are rats as big as cats. You can't sit down. Once a rat bit me. The doors don't close—where there's a chain, there's no hook; where there's a hook, there's no chain. I try not to go, and I've gotten so used to it that days and weeks go by and I don't go. Porters come there from Yanash's Bazaar, and hoodlums, too. When they see a girl, they begin to say nasty words. In some apartments there are water closets. You pull a string and the water flushes. There is light also and toilet paper. Here, there is nothing."

"Shoshele, we are not going to live here forever. I don't earn enough now, but I'm writing a book. And then there's my play for the theater. If I don't succeed this time, I will succeed another time. I will take you away from here."

"Where will you take me? Other girls can read and write, but I never learned how. Maybe you remember when they sent me home from school. I was sitting in class, and the teacher read something to us, but it didn't go into my head. I always saw funny faces. When they called me to the blackboard, I knew nothing and began to cry."

"What did you see?" I asked.

"Oh, I'm afraid to tell you. A woman combing her daughter's hair with a fine comb and putting kerosene on it to get out the lice. Suddenly, lice came from all over—bedbugs, too—and the girl began to scream like mad. I don't remember now if she was a Jewish girl or a shiksa. In a minute the lice ate up the mother and the girl, and only their bones were left. When I walked on the street I thought, What will happen if a balcony falls down on my head? When I passed by a policeman I thought, Perhaps he will say that I stole something and take me to prison. Arele, you will think that I'm out of my mind."

"No, Shoshele, it's nothing but nerves."

"What are nerves? Tell me."

"Fear of all the misfortunes that can happen and do happen to human beings."

"Leizer reads the paper to us, and awful things happen every day. A man crossed the street and was run over by a droshky. A girl from No. 9 tried to get into the trolley car before it stopped, and she lost her leg. Only last week, a tinsmith fixing a roof fell down and the gutter was red from blood. With such things in my head, I could not pay attention to my lessons. When Mother sent me to buy something, I held the money tight in my fist—then when I got to the store it was lost. How can this be?"

"Every person has an enemy inside who spites him."

"Then why doesn't Teibele have one? Arele, I want you to know the truth so that you won't think that we are fooling you."

"Shoshele, no one has fooled me. I will help you."

"How? If it's so bad now, what will happen when Hitler comes? Oy, Mother is waking up!" Shosha ran from the alcove. I heard the sound of her shirt tearing as she caught it on a nail in the door.

· CHAPTER SIX ·

1

ACH DAY—no, each hour—brought a new crisis, but I had
become accustomed to the dangers attending my lot. I compared myself to a criminal who knows that he will be punished
but until he is seized he squanders his loot. Sam Dreiman had
given me a new advance and Betty had reconstructed my play to
suit her whims. She had introduced new characters, even edited
my language. I realized with amazement that the passion to
write can strike anyone capable of holding a pen. Betty had
introduced more action into the drama and added "lyrics," but
the play no longer held together. Though Betty mocked and
mimicked the American Yiddish, she anglicized mine. The blind
musician now declaimed like the villain in a melodrama. Fritz
Bander, who had been cast to play a wealthy Hasid in love with
the Ludmir Maiden, demanded that his role be larger, and Betty
gave him permission to extend it with lengthy monologues. He
still retained some Galician Yiddish mixed with German. Fritz
Bander also demanded a part for his German mistress, Gretel,
who knew no Yiddish. He pointed out that Jews often employed
German maids and this was a part she could handle.

Betty had several copies of her version of the play typed up—
one for her, one for Sam Dreiman, one for Fritz Bander, one for

David Lipman, one for me, and for others. Each person made changes, and the text was typed again and the revisions commenced all over. Sam Dreiman had rented a theater on Smocza Street and ordered the sets, though basic decisions about the production were still to be settled. The Actors Union demanded that jobs be introduced for additional actors as well as for extras. I was forced to write in parts for a beadle, a madman, and an anti-Hasid who berated the Hasidim. The cast grew so large that dialogue essential to its content had to be deleted.

At first, I resisted. I rewrote Betty's and Bander's revisions, corrected their grammar and spelling, but I soon saw that the contradictions, the different styles, and grotesqueries grew faster than I could repair them. I couldn't believe it, but Sam Dreiman also took a hand in the writing. It reminded me of a story I had heard as a child from my mother about a band of spirits who seized a village and turned everything upside down—the water-carrier became the rabbi, the rabbi a bathhouse attendant, the horse thief a scribe, the scribe a teamster. A hobgoblin posed as head of a yeshiva and in the studyhouse preached a sermon filled with blasphemies. The leech, a demon, prescribed goat droppings and calf feathers for the sick, along with moon juice and turkey semen. A devil with the legs of a rooster and the horns of a buck became a cantor and turned the rejoicing of Simchas Torah into the lamentations of Tisha Bov. Such a mystic comedy could have been created from my play.

The telephone in the corridor outside my room never stopped ringing. Tekla no longer bothered to pick up the receiver—invariably the call was for me. The actors and actresses were bickering with each other, with Betty, and with David Lipman, who was threatening to quit. The secretary of the union raised new demands almost daily. The actors complained that the American millionaire had deceived them regarding their wages. The theater owner decided he had signed an unfair contract and would have to have more money. Sam Dreiman screamed at me until I had to hold the receiver away from my ear. If Jews were capable of such deceit and intrigue, he said, then Hitler was right.

I tried to calm the spirits of the others, but I feared a nervous breakdown myself.

The days passed in turmoil. I stopped talking to Shosha and Bashele. When I went to them for lunch, I sat at the table in silence. I even forgot to eat and had to be reminded that the soup was getting cold. At night after two or three hours' sleep I awoke with my heart pounding, the pillowcase drenched in sweat. In my sleep, my own complications had mingled with the problems of the world. Hitler, Mussolini, and Stalin wrangled about my play, and then went to war. Shosha attempted to defend me. I sat up and listened to the echoes of cries and mayhem that still lingered in my brain. My hair pierced my skull. I itched and scratched. I had wakened with a thirst, a gnawing in my intestines, a stinging in my bladder. My nose was stuffed and a shudder kept running down my spine.

Day would be breaking, and I would still sit and take reckoning. I had accepted more money from Sam Dreiman than I had intended. I gave Bashele more for my meals and helped her with her rent as well. I had given Dora a loan I knew I would never get back.

That night I fell asleep at three. At ten to nine, the ringing of the telephone woke me. Tekla poked the door ajar. "It's for you."

It was Betty. She asked, "Did I wake you?"

"Yes, no."

"I had a terrible night. I wouldn't wish it on my worst enemies."

"What happened?"

"Oh, Sam is torturing me. He makes ugly scenes. He says such wild things I'm beginning to think he's losing his mind. Yesterday, he drank maybe a half bottle of cognac. He shouldn't touch it—he has a bad heart and an enlarged prostate."

"What does he want?"

"To destroy himself and everything. He doesn't want the play any more. Every second he gets a new notion. He made such a fuss you could hear him through the whole hotel. I want to remind you that we are rehearsing today. I have about as much strength to perform after last night as you have to dance on the roof, but I can't leave things hanging in the air any longer. At times I'd like to pick myself up and run off to the ends of the earth."

"You too?"

"Yes, me too. He's become jealous all of a sudden. He seems to know about us!" Betty said, changing her tone.

"What does he know?"

"He's listening right now. I have to stop."

I stood by the telephone with the premonition that presently it would ring again. And so it did. I lifted the receiver and said, "Yes, Celia?"

No one answered and I assumed I had been wrong, but after a while I heard Celia's voice. "Have you become a prophet, or a gypsy?"

"The Gemara says that when the Temple was destroyed God gave the power of prophecy to madmen."

"Is that what the Gemara says? You are crazy, but you are also committing literary suicide. I lay awake half the night worrying about you. Haiml sleeps like a log. The minute his head hits the pillow he begins to whistle through his nose and goes on until morning. But I keep waking up. At times it seems that you wake me. I hear you calling 'Celia!' It's all my nerves. One time it even seemed that I saw you in the doorway. Was it your astral body? There's something not of the ordinary about you. My dear, Morris has read your play. Sam Dreiman gave him a copy. I don't want to repeat what he said. I hear it's no longer your play, everything's distorted. Really, what's the sense of it all?"

"The sense is that I'm losing my senses."

2

WHEN I entered the theater for the rehearsal, coming in from the bright light I bumped against the seats and nearly tripped, but gradually I grew accustomed to the dark. I took a seat in the front row. Sam Dreiman sat two rows behind me. He coughed and grunted and mumbled to himself in English. Celia and Haiml were present, too. Critics aren't usually invited to rehearsals, but I spotted one of them in the audience. In their articles, the critics often decried the state of the Yiddish theater and denounced young writers for allowing kitsch to dominate the stage and for not writing serious plays; yet I knew that they hoped my play would fail. They had launched a campaign against Betty Slonim. In the leftist publications they dubbed Sam Dreiman an American "all-rightnik" and a "Golden Calf." Some theatrical writers pointed out that a mystic play about a girl who presided over Hasidic banquets with a veil over her face, preached the Torah to Hasidim, and was possessed by the dybbuks of a whore and a musician didn't befit the tragic circumstances of Polish Jewry. What was called for were plays that reflected the dangers of Fascism and Hitlerism and the need of resistance by the Jewish masses, not dramas that brought back the superstitions of the Middle Ages.

Two seats away from me sat David Lipman and his wife, Estusia. She peeled oranges and handed sections to him. Because of a heart condition he required constant nourishment. He wore a velour jacket and a flowing tie. The whole play wasn't being performed, merely individual scenes. Fritz Bander, portraying Reb Ezekiel Prager, the Hasid, declared his love for the Ludmir Maiden—Betty. Although I had told Bander time and again not to shout, he thundered away. In those places where he should have lowered his voice, he roared; and he whispered or skipped over those places where he should have been forceful. He swallowed words and improvised. He didn't remember his lines and the prompter had to keep feeding him his speeches. Bander jumbled and fractured the quotations from the Gemara, the Midrash, and the books of the cabala. I had assumed that David Lipman, who was allegedly versed in these matters, would correct him, but he kept silent. He was in awe of Fritz Bander because he had performed in Berlin. Once in a while David Lipman made observations and indicated directions, but he ignored essentials and confined himself to petty details. Betty also had trouble with her lines. She made errors in her Hebrew and even in the Yiddish words. Some of the words she pronounced in a Polish accent, others in a Lithuanian. Where she was supposed to portray both the whore and the blind musician, she lost her bearings altogether.

I sat slumped over, from time to time closing my eyes to lose sight of my disgrace. Betty might be critical of the trash of the American Yiddish theater, but she had adapted its mannerisms. I recalled my mother's saying "words that walk on stilts." Curiously, when Betty spoke to me in private, her Yiddish was fluent and precise. As I gazed at the stage, I knew I had failed completely. My own mistakes were only too clear to me, but I had no idea how to correct them.

The moment the lights went on, Sam Dreiman came charging at me. "We can't put on this monstrosity!"

"No is no."

"I sat there and didn't understand what on earth they were babbling about, and if I didn't understand it, you can't expect anyone else to. I thought you were going to write in plain Yiddish."

"Dybbuks don't speak a plain Yiddish."

Betty, Fritz Bander, and Gretel came up.

"Betty darling, we'll have to postpone the play!" Sam Dreiman shouted.

"Postpone? Until when?"

"I don't know when. I brought you here to be a success, not to have rotten potatoes heaved at you."

"Sam, don't say that."

"Betty darling, the sooner you act on a mistake, the better. Forty years ago I put up a building in Detroit and in the midst of the construction it turned out that the plumbing and everything else wouldn't work. I'd sunk a fortune into the project, but I ordered everything torn down and the building begun all over again. If I hadn't done this, I would have gone to jail. I had a friend, also a builder, and he put up a factory six flights high. Suddenly, while the building was filled with workers, it collapsed and killed seventeen men. He died in prison."

"Well, I knew it! I knew it all! The evil powers have started their tricks again. I'm through as an actress. My luck—"

"Your luck, sweetheart, is as bright as the sun in the sky!" Sam Dreiman hollered. "You will perform in Warsaw, in Paris, in London, and in New York. The name of Betty Slonim will light up Broadway in huge letters, but in a drama that the world wants to see, not in some crazy farce for insane cabalists. Mr. Greidinger, I don't want to be cruel, but what you've given us is unfit for the public. Betty, we'll get another play. He isn't the only writer in Warsaw."

"You can put on all the plays you want, but without me," Betty said. "This is my final card. With my luck, if you put on a masterpiece it would fail. It's all my fault! Mine! Mine!"

"It's mine, too," Sam Dreiman said. "When he brought us the first two scenes and I read them, I saw at once that this wasn't for us. I thought it might be fixed, but not everything can be fixed. It's like that building—the foundation was poorly laid at the start. I fired the architect and began with another. I'll do the same thing right now."

"You can do it, but without me."

"With you, Betty darling, only with you!"

· CHAPTER SEVEN ·

1

A T THIS time, the logic of my pride was that nothing remained to me but to hide from all those involved with me and my profession. I still had over one hundred dollars from Sam Dreiman's third advance—money that I must pay back if I were not to consider myself a thief. My calculations turned around this sum, which was worth about nine hundred zlotys. According to the agreement with the man from whom I sublet my room on Leszno Street, I had to give a month's notice before I moved out, and I certainly did not intend to break this agreement. I considered suicide, but that would be possible only if I could take with me those who had hung all their hopes on me. Meanwhile, I had to be careful with every penny. I stopped sleeping on Leszno Street, which saved me the expense of paying for a taxi when I went home late in the evening. On the bed in Bashele's alcove I covered whole sheets of paper with figures. The publisher for whom I had translated some German books owed me money, but I was far from sure that he would ever pay it. I was working for the literary magazine, but weeks passed without my getting a penny from them. I reminded myself that about three million Jews lived in Poland and managed to make a living somehow. I did not fool Bashele. She knew my situation. I had promised to marry her daughter but we had never set a date. They would not send out warrants for my arrest if I should disappear. Judging by the way Hitler occupied one territory after another and the Allies sat back and did nothing, there was no hope for the Jews in Poland. But running away and leaving at bay those who were dear to me was not in my nature.

Yiddish newspapers in Warsaw reported that the play Sam Dreiman, the American millionaire, had been planning to produce had been canceled. The Yiddish theater season began on Succoth and there was not time for him to find a new play. They also mentioned that he was negotiating with a playwright in America. Of *The Ludmir Maiden,* a journalist wrote in the humor section that it could not be produced because it was possessed by a dybbuk. Leizer the watchmaker read all these stories of my failure to Shosha and Bashele.

In the month of August, a strong heat spell hit Warsaw. When I was a boy, almost no one on Krochmalna Street took vacations and went to the country in the summer. Only the wealthy and rich did this. But times had changed. Workers were now given vacations and they went to Miedzeszyn, Falenica, and even to Zakopane in the mountains. The workers' unions had summer colonies in Karwia at the Baltic Sea in the "corridor" that divided East Germany from West Germany and that Hitler vowed to take back. I heard that Feitelzohn stayed a few weeks in Jósefow with Celia and Haiml. I had spoken to Tekla on the telephone and she told me that Celia kept calling me. Tekla asked why I hadn't come home for so long. She also asked for my telephone number and the address where I was staying so that she could tell people how to get in touch with me. I said I was busy with work and didn't want to be disturbed. Even Tekla knew that my play had fizzled. She heard it from Wladek, who read about it in the Polish Jewish newspaper *Nasz Przegląd.*

During the day I seldom left the apartment on Krochmalna Street. My old bashfulness had returned to me, with all its complications and neuroses. Some tenants of No. 7 knew me. From

Leizer they had heard about me and my love for Shosha. They had also read of my forthcoming play. The girls used to watch from the windows when I passed with Shosha on the way to the gate. I was ashamed before these girls now and imagined that they laughed at me. I even avoided going to the outhouse during the day. The heels of my shoes were worn down, but I could not pay to have them fixed. My hat was faded and stained. I would put on a fresh shirt and a few hours later it would be soaked with sweat, and dirty. The little hair left on my head began to fall out. When I wiped the perspiration from my skull, I found red hair on my handkerchief. I had begun to have all kinds of mishaps around the house. Bashele would give me a glass of tea and it would slip from my hands. Each time I shaved, I cut myself. I kept losing my fountain pen, my notebook. Money dropped from my pockets. In my mouth a molar began to loosen, but I could not afford to go to a dentist. Anyway, what did I need a dentist for, since my weeks or days were numbered?

I had brought with me a few of the books in which I always sought solace whenever there was a crisis in my life—which was often. This time I couldn't find a trace of comfort in them. Spinoza's "substance" had no will, no compassion, no feeling for justice. He was a prisoner of his own laws. Schopenhauer's "blind will" seemed to be more blind than ever. Of course there was no hope for me in Hegel's *Zeitgeist* or in Nietzsche's Zarathustra. Payot's *Education of the Will* was addressed chiefly to students whose wealthy parents paid for their board and tuition. Coué's and Charles Baudouin's patients had homes, professions, well-to-do families, accounts in the banks. I sat on the edge of the bed all day long and let perspiration run over my hot body. Shosha sat near me on her little stool and talked to me or to herself. Occasionally she spoke to Yppe. For some reason Bashele frequently left the house. Shosha would ask her, "Mommy, where are you going?" And Bashele would say, "Where my eyes carry me."

Now that I had failed for everyone to see, I realized that the failure was my own fault. Instead of working on the play, I had spent hours with Shosha every day. Even though Betty kept warning me that the work on the play was of the highest import- ance, she made me go with her to museums, to cafés, on long walks, and sabotaged all my plans for work. I should have gone with her in the evenings to see serious plays from which I could learn about the construction of a drama. Instead, she took me to see silly Hollywood movies from which there was nothing to be learned. I wasted precious hours discussing Yiddish literature in the Writers' Club, playing chess, and telling jokes. I even squan- dered time with Tekla, listening to her complaints about her mistress and her stories about the village where she came from, her unloving stepmother, and of Bolek, to whom she was be- trothed and who had left her to go to work in the coal mines of France. Our conversations always ended by our falling down on the bed together. I wasn't really awake in those months. My lazi- ness, my passion, and my empty fantasies had kept me in a hypnotic amnesia. Now I could hear my mother saying, "No enemy can do to a man as much evil as he does to himself."

"Arele, what are you thinking about?" Shosha asked me.

"Nothing, Shoshele. As long as I have you, there is still some sense to my life."

"You will not leave me alone?"

"No, Shoshele, I will stay with you as long as I live."

2

AT NIGHT I lay awake for hours. From the heat I continuously ran to the sink to drink water and then I had to urinate. Bashele had put a chamber pot under my bed and it soon became full. I stood without any clothes before the window of my alcove—a little window with four panes—and let the breeze that came into the courtyard once in a while blow over me. I looked at the few stars that could be seen moving slowly from one roof to the other. Though I had nothing to expect on earth when the Nazis arrived except starvation and concentration camps, perhaps there was some spark of hope in the heavenly bodies? However, from the popular books about astronomy which I had read, I knew that the stars consisted of the same elements as the sun and the earth. If other planets were inhabited by living creatures, their conditions could be like those on earth: struggle for a bite of food, for a secure place to lay one's head. I was overcome by a rage against creation, God, nature—whatever this wretchedness was called. I felt that the only way of protesting cosmic violence was to reject life, even if I had to take Shosha with me. The animals and the insects did not possess such a choice.

But how would I accomplish this, actually? If I were to throw myself out the window of my room on Leszno Street, I would risk remaining alive with possibly a broken spine. If I were to fling myself under a trolley or a train, I might end up without feet or arms. Should I get rat poison and slowly burn out my insides? Should I hang myself and burden those who loved me with arranging my burial? After much brooding I decided that the best way to end it all would be to throw myself into deep water, where I would molest no one and would even help the fish with a meal. The Vistula was too shallow in the summer. Every day the newspapers wrote about ships that got stuck in the sand. The only way of doing it right would be go to Danzig or Gdynia and board a ship that sailed the Baltic. A travel agency was advertising a cruise to Denmark for which no foreign passport or visa was necessary. The price was reasonable. It was enough for the passenger to show a Polish inland passport. The trouble was, I didn't possess even this kind of document. In the process of moving from one furnished room to another with my books and confusion of manuscripts, I had lost my draft card, my birth certificate, and all other proof of my citizenship. I would have to travel to the village where I was born and bring to the

City Hall witnesses who could attest to the day of my birth or my circumcision feast. The archives of births and deaths had burned down in the German bombardments in 1915. With all my anxiety I had to laugh. I needed to go through a lot of red tape to be able to commit suicide.

That night I fell asleep at dawn. I opened my eyes. Shosha was shaking my shoulder. I looked at her bewildered. It took me a while to remember where I was and who was waking me. "Arele," she said, "a young lady is waiting for you. The actress from America."

After a while Bashele stuck her head in the room. I asked her and Shosha to please leave and close the door. In a rush I put on my underwear, my pants, my shirt, and my jacket. For a minute I thought I had lost the hundred dollars that I carried in the left pocket of my pants. I needed money to buy a train ticket and ship card to go ahead with my plan. Had someone stolen my money? I touched all my pockets with the turmoil of one who wants to live, not to die. Thank God, the banknotes were in a pocket of my vest. My shirt was crumpled, my collar had a spot, I had lost the cuff link of my right sleeve. I screamed through the closed door, "Betty, wait! I will soon be out." The sun was already scorching me through the open window. From the court-yard I heard the voices: "Bagels, hot bagels! Plums, fresh plums!" A beggar was already scratching out a plaintive melody on a fiddle and his female companion was beating on a little drum with bells, calling for alms. I touched my cheeks. Although I kept on losing the hair on my head, my beard grew with wild impetus. The stubble felt stiff and prickly. Disordered and frowzy, I opened the door and saw Betty freshly made up in a straw hat with a green ribbon, a suit that I had not seen, and white shoes with open toes—a novelty to me. I began to apologize for my appearance.

Betty said, "Everything is all right. You don't have to compete in a beauty contest."

"When I fell asleep day was breaking, and—"

"Stop it. I didn't come to look you over."

"Why don't you sit down?" Bashele said to Betty. "I keep asking the young lady to sit down, but she has been standing all this time. We don't live in luxury but our chairs are clean. I dust them every morning. I wanted to make tea, but the young lady refuses everything."

"I'm sorry. I just had breakfast. Thank you very much. Tsutsik, forgive me for coming so early in the morning. Actually, my watch shows ten minutes to ten. I came, as they say in America, on business. If you like, we can go out somewhere and talk it over."

"Arele, don't go for long," Shosha said. "We have prepared breakfast and later we will have dinner. Mommy bought sorrel and potatoes and sour cream. The lady can eat with us."

"We have enough for both of you," Bashele agreed.

"How can I eat if I've had breakfast already?"

"Shoshele, we will only go out for half an hour," I said. "It's not convenient for us to talk here. Let me find my cuff link and change my collar. One minute, Betty."

I rushed into the alcove and Shosha followed me. She closed the door. "Arele, don't go with her," she said. "She wants to take you away from me. She looks like a witch."

"A witch? Don't talk nonsense."

"She has such sharp eyes. You told me yourself that you lay with her in bed."

"I told you? Well, never mind. Between her and me everything is finished."

"If you want to begin with her again, better kill me first."

"The way things are going, I will kill you anyhow. I will take you on a ship and we will both jump into the sea."

"Is there a sea in Warsaw?"

"Not in Warsaw. We will go to Gdynia or Danzig."

"Yes, Arele, you can do with me whatever you want. Throw me in first or take me to Yppe's grave and bury me there. As long as you do it, it is good. But don't leave me alone. Here is your cuff link."

Shosha bent down and gave it to me. I put my arms around

her and kissed her. I said, "Shoshele, I have sworn by God and
by the soul of my father that I will never abandon you. It's about
time that you trust me."

"Yes, I trust you. But when I saw her, my heart began to
pound. She is dressed as if she were going to a wedding. All new
to please you. She thinks I don't understand, but I understand
everything. When will you be back?"

"As quickly as possible."

"Remember that no one loves you as I do."

"Sweet child, I love you, too."

"Wait, I have a fresh handkerchief for you."

3

BETTY and I passed the courtyard; it looked like a marketplace.
Peddlers were hawking smoked herring, blueberries, watermelons.
A peasant had ridden in with his horse and buggy, and he was
selling chickens, eggs, mushrooms, onions, carrots, parsley. In
other streets, this kind of business was not allowed, but Krochmalna had its own laws. An old woman carrying a sack on her
back stood near the garbage bin and with a stick poked through
for rags to make paper and for bones used in sugar factories. Betty
tried to take my arm, but I gave her a sign not to do it, since I
was sure that Bashele and Shosha were watching us from the
window. We were watched from other windows, too. Girls wearing loose dresses over their bouncing breasts were shaking thread-
bare carpets as well as featherbeds, pillows, and mangy fur coats
that would be worn when winter began. One could hear the
noise of sewing machines, cobbler's hammers, the planing and
sawing of carpenters. From the Hasidic studyhouse came the
voices of young men chanting the Talmud. In the cheder, little
boys recited the Pentateuch. On the other side of the gate Betty

took my arm and said, "I didn't know the number of the house, but after I called and called you on Leszno Street and the maid always replied that you were not there, I decided you must be here on your beloved Krochmalna Street. What kind of a swamp have you fallen into? It absolutely stinks here! Please forgive me, but this Shosha of yours is a perfect imbecile. She asked me to sit down at least ten times. I told her I preferred to stand, but she asked over and over again. I really think you are mad."

"You are right. You are right."

"Don't tell me how right I am. You are one of those men who like to sink. In Russia they call them *brodyagi*. Gorky wrote about them. In New York there is a street called the Bowery, and you see them lying on the sidewalk drunk and half naked. Some of them are intelligent, with higher education. Come, let's get out of this sewage. An urchin has already tried to grab my purse. You haven't had breakfast, and I am hungry myself from walking so long around here trying to find the house. All I remembered from my first visit was that there was a ditch in the courtyard. But it seems that they filled it up. Where can we get a cup of coffee?"

"There is a coffee shop at No. 6, but the underworld goes there."

"I don't want to stay on this street another minute. Hurry, here's a droshky. Hey! Stop!"

Betty jumped in and I after her. She said, "Would you like to have breakfast in the Writers' Club?"

"Absolutely not."

"Did you have a quarrel with someone? They say you've stopped coming there. How about Gertner's Restaurant, where we met the first time. My God, it seems so long ago."

"Madame, where to?" The coachman turned his head.

Betty gave him the address. "Tsutsik, why are you hiding from people? I met your best friend, Dr. Feitelzohn, and he told me you've severed connections with him and everybody else. I can understand in a way that you wouldn't want to have anything to do with me, because I'm responsible for what happened, although I had only good intentions. But what's the sense of a young writer burying himself in such squalor? Why don't you at least stay in your room on Leszno Street—you pay the rent, after all. Sam is deeply upset about the way you run away from us."

"I hear he's negotiating a play with some trashy writer from New York."

"Nothing will come of it. I'm definitely not going to play in that kind of junk. I've told you already it's entirely my bad luck. Everyone who's involved with me shares my miserable fate. But I told you I came on business and I'm not lying. The story is this. Sam's not well and I'm afraid he's sicker than I realized. He's planning to go back to America. We've done a lot of talking in the past few days, much of it about you. Now that there's no longer a deadline I've had time and the peace of mind to read your play again. It's not nearly as bad as that short little critic with the tin-framed glasses made it out to be. The insolence of a writer tearing down a piece before it's been performed! That can happen only among the Yiddishists. Such a malicious worm. Someone introduced me to him and I gave him a piece of my mind. He began to excuse himself and flatter me and twist his tongue like a snake. Actually, I think it's a good literary play. The trouble is, you don't know the stage. In America we have men who are called play doctors. They can't write a line themselves, but somehow they know how to rearrange a piece and make it right for the stage. I'll make it short—we want to buy your play and try it out in America."

"*Buy* it? Mr. Dreiman already gave me seven or eight hundred dollars. It's his if he wants it. I'm terribly sorry that I'm not able to give him back the money, but he certainly can do what he likes with the play."

"Well, I can see you're not much of a businessman. I'll tell you something. He's loaded with money. America is beginning to go through a new period of prosperity, and without lifting a finger, he is making a fortune. If he wants to pay you, take the money.

He promised to leave me a large inheritance, but according to the law he has to leave a part of his fortune to his Xanthippe, and perhaps also to his children, though they hate him and defy him. With my luck, I'll probably get nothing. If he's willing to give some to you, there's no reason you should refuse. You won't be able to write if you remain where you are now. I looked into that alcove of yours. It's a hole, not a room. You could suffocate in there. What's the point of it? Even if you want to commit suicide, such a death is too ugly. Here is Gertner's."

Betty tried to open her purse, but I had the fare ready in my hand and I gave it to the coachman.

Betty threw me an angry look. "What's the matter with you? Do you want to finance Sam Dreiman?"

"I don't want to take any more from him."

"Well, everyone is crazy in his own way. Bevies of schnorrers run after him and you are trying to support him. Come, madman. I haven't been here in God knows how long. I even thought they might not be open so early. In New York there are restaurants where the day begins at lunchtime. Now you may kiss me. We can never really be complete strangers."

4

THE HEADWAITER rushed toward us and gave us the table in the niche that Sam and Betty always got when they ate here. He said he was sorry he hadn't seen her and Sam lately. Even though it was still early, there were people already at the tables, eating fish and meat and drinking beer. Betty ordered coffee with cake for herself and made me take rolls with eggs and coffee. The waiter gave us a look of reproach for ordering a late breakfast instead of an early lunch. Those at the other tables gazed at us questioningly. Betty looked too elegant to be my companion. She was saying, "How long is it since we've seen one another? It seems to me an eternity. Sam wants me to return to America, but in spite of all my disappointments I fell in love with Warsaw. What would I do in America? In New York they know everything that is happening everywhere. In the Actors Union they have surely heard of my defeat, and my stock there will have dropped lower than ever. They sit in the Café Royal and make mountains out of molehills. What's left to them except to gossip? Some of them saved when times were good. Those who have nothing get relief from the government. In the summer they play a few weeks in the hotels in the Catskill Mountains. America has become a country where one is not compelled to work if he doesn't want to. They drink coffee and chatter. They play cards. Without cards and gossip they would expire from boredom. My trouble is that I don't play cards. Sam tried to teach me, but I couldn't learn even the names of the suits. A stubborn instinct in me refuses to learn. Tsutsik, I'm as good as finished. This was my last game. I've nothing left except to commit suicide."

"You too?"

"Who else? Is this why you are going to marry Shosha—to make her a widow?"

"I'll take her with me."

"Well, you are, as they say, healthy, fresh, and meshugga. In my case I tried to play year after year after year, and I always failed. Besides, I'm older than you. But why should you fall into such despair? You are a writer of stories, not a playwright. So far as the theater goes, you're still a greenhorn—I think with talent. Oh, here is my cake and your eggs. I used to wonder why those condemned to the electric chair bother to pick out a special last meal. They ask for a rare steak and a tasty dessert. Why should a person care what he eats if he's going to be dead an hour later? It seems that life and death have nothing in common. You may decide to die tomorrow but today you still want to eat for pleasure and sleep in a warm bed. What are your real plans?"

"Really, to get through with the whole botched-up mess."

"My God, when I was on the ship to Europe I never thought I would drive someone into such a state because of my foolish ambitions."

"Betty, it's not your fault."

"Whose fault is it?"

"Oh, it's everything together. The Jews in Poland are trapped. When I said this in the Writers' Club, they attacked me. They had let themselves fall into a stupid kind of optimism, but I know for sure that we will all be destroyed. The Poles want to get rid of us. They consider us a nation within a nation, a strange and malignant body. They lack the courage to finish us off themselves, but they wouldn't shed tears if Hitler did it for them. Stalin will certainly not defend us. Since the Trotskyite opposition began, the Communists have become our worst enemies. Trotsky is called Judas in Russia. The fact is that the Trotskyites are almost all Jews. If you give a Jew one revolution, he demands another revolution—a permanent one. If you give him one Messiah, he asks for another Messiah. As to Palestine, the world doesn't want us to have a state. The bitter truth is that many Jews today don't want to be Jews any more. But it's too late for total assimilation. Whoever is going to win this coming war will liquidate us."

"Maybe the democracies will win."

"The democracies are committing suicide."

"Well, don't let your coffee get cold. If you hadn't decided to carry that silly Shosha on your shoulders, you could easily get yourself to America. There the Jew can still muddle through. I can go back, but the very thought of it makes me shudder. Sam can't stay at home even one night. He always has to go somewhere—usually to that Café Royal. There he meets the writers he supports and the actresses he used to have affairs with. This is the only place where he is somebody. It's funny, but there is only one little place in the whole world—a third-rate restaurant —where he feels at home. He eats the blintzes the doctors have forbidden him. He fills up his belly with twenty cups of coffee each day. He smokes the cigars he knows are poison for him. He demands that I go with him, but for me this café is a nest of snakes. They always hated me, but now that I am with Sam they would like to swallow me alive. The Yiddish theater where he takes me at least twice a week has reached its lowest point. To sit there with him and listen to their stale jokes and see sixty-year-old yentas play eighteen-year-old girls is a physical pain. The sad truth is that for me there isn't *one* place in the whole world where I feel at home."

"Well, we're a well-matched pair."

"We could have been, but you didn't want it. What do you say to this Shosha all day long?"

"I don't say much."

"What is this with you, an act of masochism?"

"No, Betty, I really love her."

"There are things you must see to believe. You can never foresee them in your imagination: you and Shosha, me and Sam Dreiman. At least he finds some comfort among his cronies. Tsutsik, look who's here!"

I raised my eyes and saw Feitelzohn. He stood a few steps from our table with a cigar in his mouth, his Panama hat pushed back, and a cane hooked over his shoulder. I had not seen him with a cane before. He looked older and changed. He smiled with familiar shrewdness, but I imagined that his cheeks had fallen in, as if he had lost his teeth. He approached our table with small steps. "Is this how things are?" he said with a muffled voice, and then took out the cigar. "Well, really, Tsutsik, I begin to believe in your hidden powers." He leaned the cigar in the ashtray on our table. "I passed by and it occurred to me, 'Perhaps Tsutsik is there.' Good morning, Miss Slonim. I've become so mixed up that I forgot to greet you. How do you do? It's nice to see you again. What was it I wanted to say? Yes, Tsutsik. I said to myself, 'What would he do here so early? He only comes here with Sam Dreiman and not this early in the day.' I was about to continue my walk but somehow my feet brought me in by their own choice. You should be ashamed of yourself, Tsutsik. Why are you keeping away from your friends? We have all been looking for you—Haiml, Celia, I. I called you perhaps twenty times, but the maid had one answer: 'Not home.' What's wrong? You have better friends in Warsaw?"

"Dr. Feitelzohn, sit down with us," Betty said. "Why are you standing?"

"Since you two are huddling in a corner, no doubt you have your secrets. But one can say hello in any case."

"We have no secrets. We were talking business and we have finished. Sit down."

"I really don't know what to say," I began to stammer.

"If you don't know, don't say. I will say it for you. You have been a little boy and you will remain one for the rest of your life. Look at you," Feitelzohn said.

"Where did you get a cane all of a sudden?" I asked, just to change the conversation.

"Oh, I stole it. One of my Americans left it to me. Lately my feet have been making monkey business. I walk on a flat road and suddenly my feet begin to run by themselves as if I were ice skating or going downhill. What kind of a malady is this? I will have to ask our literary physician Dr. Lipkin, who understands as much about medicine as he understands about literature. Meanwhile, I have decided that a cane cannot do any damage. Tsutsik, you look pale. What's the matter? Are you sick?"

"He's perfectly well and crazy," Betty said. "A first-class maniac."

5

FEITELZOHN assured us that he had eaten breakfast, and when Betty ordered rolls, an omelette, and coffee for him, he smiled and said, "If one lives in America a few years, one becomes an American. What would the world do without America? When I lived there I complained of Uncle Sam steadily—talked only about his shortcomings. But now that I'm here, I miss America. I could go back if I chose, on a tourist visa. It might even be that I could get a visa as a professor. But in New York and Boston no university would give me a permanent job. And to teach in those small colleges somewhere in the Midwest means dying of boredom. I cannot sit all day long and read like a bookworm. The students there are more childlike than our cheder boys. All they talk about is football, and the professors are not much cleverer. America is a country of children. The New Yorkers are a little more grown up, but not much. Once some friend of mine put me on a ferry to Coney Island. This, Tsutsik, I wish you could see. It is a city in which everything is for play—shooting at tin ducklings, visiting a museum where they show a girl with two heads, letting an astrologer plot your horoscope and a medium call up the soul of your grandfather in the beyond. No place lacks vulgarity, but the vulgarity of Coney Island is of a special kind, friendly, with a tolerance that says, 'I play my game and you play your game.' As I walked around there and ate a hot dog—this is what they call a sausage—it occurred to me that I was seeing the future of mankind. You can even call it the time of the Messiah. One day all people will realize there is not a single idea that can really be called true—that everything is a game—nationalism, internationalism, religion, atheism, spiritualism, materialism, even suicide. You know, Tsutsik, that I am a great admirer of David Hume. In my eyes he is the only philosopher who has not become obsolete—he is as fresh and clear today as he was in his own time. Coney Island fits David Hume's philosophy. Since we are sure of nothing and there is even no evidence that the sun will rise tomorrow, play is the very essence of human endeavor, perhaps even the thing-in-itself. God is a player, the cosmos a playground. For years I have searched for a basis of ethics and gave up hope. Suddenly it became clear to me.

The basis of ethics is man's right to play the games of his choice. I will not trample on your toys and you will not trample on mine; I won't spit on your idol and you will not spit on mine. There is no reason why hedonism, the cabala, polygamy, asceticism, even our friend Haiml's blend of eroticism and Hasidism could not exist in a play-city or play-world, a sort of a universal Coney Island where everyone would play according to his or her desire. I'm sure, Miss Slonim, that you have visited Coney Island more than once."

"Yes, but I never came to your philosophical conclusions. By the way, who is David Hume? I've never heard of him."

"David Hume was an English philosopher and a friend of Jean Jacques Rousseau before he became a disgusting schnorrer."

"Here is your omelette, Dr. Feitelzohn," Betty said. "I have heard of Jean Jacques Rousseau. I've even read his *Confessions*."

"It is easy to read David Hume, too. A child can understand him. I'm sure, Tsutsik, you know that $7 + 5 = 12$ has been judged an analytic sentence, not a synthetic a priori one. Hume was right, not Kant. But you still haven't explained what happened to you. You vanished like a wishing ring. I began to think you had gone to Jerusalem and were sitting in a cave trying to bring the Redemption."

"Dr. Feitelzohn, his cave is on Krochmalna Street." Betty turned to me. "May I tell him the truth?"

"If you like. I don't care any more."

"Dr. Feitelzohn, your Tsutsik has found himself a bride-to-be on Krochmalna Street."

Feitelzohn put down his fork. "Is that so? According to the way you used to praise that madman Otto Weininger, I thought you would turn into an old bachelor."

I wanted to answer him, but Betty prevented me. "He could have remained a bachelor, but he found such a treasure—her name is Shosha—that he had to break all his principles and convictions."

"She's making fun of me," I managed to say.

"What? You cannot run away from the female species. Sooner or later you fall into their net. Celia was looking for you desperately. Shosha? A modern girl with such an old-fashioned name? What is she, a fighting Yiddishist?"

Again I tried to answer and again Betty interrupted me: "It would be hard to say just what she is, but if such a connoisseur of women as your Tsutsik decides to marry, you know she has to be something extraordinary. If your David Hume had met her, he would have divorced his wife and run away with Shosha to Coney Island."

"I don't think David Hume had a wife," Feitelzohn said after some hesitation. "Well, mazel tov, Tsutsik, mazel tov."

Only now did Betty let me speak. "She makes fun of me," I said. "Shosha is a girl from my childhood. We used to play together before I went to cheder. We were neighbors at No. 10 Krochmalna. Later I went away and for many years . . ."

Feitelzohn picked up his fork. "Whatever the case, you don't run away from your friends. If you get married, you cannot keep it a secret. If you love her, we want to know her and accept her as one of us. May I call up Celia and tell her the good tidings?"

I saw that Betty was about to come out with some new joke and I said to her, "Do me a favor, Betty, and don't speak in my name. And please don't be so sarcastic. Dr. Feitelzohn, it's not such good tidings and I don't want Celia to know about it. Not yet. Shosha is a poor girl without any education. I loved her as a child and I was never able to forget her. I was sure that she was dead but I found her—thanks to Betty, as a matter of fact."

"I wasn't being sarcastic. I meant it all seriously"—Betty tried to defend herself.

"Why isn't Celia allowed to know the truth?" Feitelzohn asked. "Whenever I expect life to remain status quo, something unexpected pops up. World history is made of the same dough as bagels. It must be fresh. This is why democracy and capitalism are going down the drain. They have become stale. This is the reason idolatry was so exciting. You could buy a new god every year. We Jews burdened the nations with an eternal God, and therefore they hate us. Gibbon tried so hard to find the reason for the fall of the Roman Empire. It fell only because it had become old. I hear that there is a passion for newness in the sky also. A star gets tired of being a star and it explodes and becomes a nova. The Milky Way got weary of its sour milk and began to run to the devil knows where. Does she have a job? I mean your fiancée, not the Milky Way."

"She has no job and she cannot have one," I said.

"Is she sick?"

"Yes, sick."

"When the body gets tired of being healthy, it becomes sick. When it gets tired of living, it dies. When it has enough of being dead, it reincarnates into a frog or a windmill. The coffee here is the best in the whole of Warsaw. May I order another glass, Miss Slonim?"

"Ten glasses, but please don't call me Miss Slonim—my name is Betty."

"I drink too much coffee and I smoke too many cigars. How is it possible that one never gets tired of tobacco and coffee? This is really a riddle."

· PART TWO ·

· CHAPTER EIGHT ·

1

TWO DAYS before Yom Kippur eve, Bashele bought two hens with which to perform the sacrificial ceremony, one for herself and the other for Shosha. She wanted to buy a rooster for me, but I refused to let a rooster die for my sins. Certain writers in the Yiddish newspapers had come out against this rite, calling it idolatrous. The Zionist supporters proposed sacrificing money instead, which would go to the Jewish National Fund for Palestine. Still, from all the apartments on Krochmalna Street one could hear the clucking of hens and the crowing of roosters. When Bashele went to Yanash's Court to have the hens slaughtered, she didn't return for two hours. The crowd was so large she couldn't get to the slaughterers. Toward evening, the street emptied even of pickpockets. The den at No. 6 was closed down. Candles were lit in the brothels and no visitors were permitted. Even the Communists were hiding somewhere. Bashele had bought a seat in a synagogue. Toward the evening meal, she lit a large candle stuck in a pot of sand—a "soul candle"—and put on a silk holiday dress that went back to the time we had lived at No. 10. She took out of a chest two prayer books she had received as a wedding present, and went off to services. Before leaving, she blessed Shosha and me. She placed her hands on my head and mumbled the benediction as if I were her son: "God make thee as Ephraim and as Manasseh."

I stayed with Shosha for some time. I tried to kiss her and she admonished me that it was forbidden. She had been busy all day long helping her mother prepare for the after-holiday meal, and she kept yawning and falling asleep. She looked pale. She asked me again and again to read some prayers from her grandmother's prayer book, with its faded pages and spots made by tallow candles and tears, but I refused. After a while I wished her a good holiday and left. Dr. Feitelzohn had invited me to spend the evening with him.

A silence had descended over all the Jewish streets. The trolleys made their way empty, and shops were closed. Overhead, the stars flickered like the flames of memorial candles. Even the prison on Dluga Street, the "Arsenal," appeared veiled in reverent melancholy with its dim glow behind the barred windows. I imagined that the night itself took score of its mission. Feitelzohn's apartment was in a house near Freta Street. He had told me no other Jewish tenants lived there besides him. At times I felt that no Gentiles lived there, either. The front windows were never lit in the evenings, nor were there lights at the gate entrance. I climbed the four flights of stone stairs to his place and not a rustle could be heard from behind a single door. I often played with the idea that this was a house of ghosts.

I knocked, and Feitelzohn opened. The apartment consisted of a huge, almost empty room, with gray walls and a high ceiling with a solitary lamp. A door led to a tiny kitchen. How strange, this erudite man owned hardly a book except for an old German encyclopedia. Nor did he have a desk. He slept not in a bed but on a couch, which was covered with a black blanket. Mark Elbinger sat on the couch now—erect, tense.

I had apparently interrupted a dispute between them, for after a long pause Feitelzohn said, "Mark, of all the errors Jews have made, our greatest was to delude ourselves—and later other peoples—that God is merciful, loves His creatures, hates malefactors, and all the rest of it our saints and prophets preached, from Moses down to Chafetz Chaim. The ancient Greeks never nursed this delusion and that was their greatness. While the Jews accused other nations of idolatry, they themselves served an idol of justice. Christianity is an outcome of this wishful thinking. Hitler, savage that he is, is now trying to dehypnotize the world from these fallacies, but—oh, the telephone again! On Yom Kippur!"

I was not in a mood to take part in any discussions and I went over to the window. On the right side I could see the Vistula. A three-quarter moon cast silver nets upon the dark water. Elbinger materialized at my side. He murmured, "A strange person, our Feitelzohn."

"What is he?"

"I've known him over thirty years and I don't begin to fathom what he is. All his words have one aim—to cover up what he's really thinking."

"What is he really thinking?"

"Gloomy thoughts. He is disappointed in everything, but mostly in himself. His father was an ascetic. He may still be alive somewhere. Morris has a daughter whom he last saw in her diapers. I myself have known two women who committed suicide over him. One a German in Berlin, and the other a missionary's daughter in London . . ."

Feitelzohn grunted and put down the receiver. "It's my opinion that woman's number-one passion isn't sex but talking," he said.

"What does she want?" Elbinger asked.

"You ought to know, you're the mind reader."

The conversation turned to occultism, and Feitelzohn said, "There are unknown forces here, yes, there are, but they're all part of the mystery called nature. What nature is no one knows, and I suspect that she doesn't know herself. I can easily visualize the Almighty sitting on the Throne of Glory in the Seventh Heaven, Metatron on His right, Sandalphon on His left, and God asking them, 'Who am I? How did I come about? Did I create Myself? Who gave Me these powers? After all, it couldn't be that I've existed forever. I remember only the past hundred trillion years. Everything before that is hazy. Well, how long will it go on?' Wait, Mark, I'll get you your cognac. Something to nibble on? I have cookies as old as Methuselah."

Feitelzohn went into the kitchen. He came back after a long time with a plate holding two glasses of cognac and a few biscuits. I had told him I was fasting, not because I believed that this was God's will, but to remain in some way a part of my family and all the other Jews. Feitelzohn clinked his glass with Elbinger's. "*L'chaim!* We Jews keep on wishing ourselves eternal life, or at least immortality of the soul. In fact, eternal life would be a calamity. Imagine some little storekeeper dying and his soul flying around for millions of years still remembering that once it sold chicory, yeast, and beans, and that a customer owes it eighteen groschen. Or the soul of an author ten million years later resenting a bad review he got."

"Souls don't stay the same. They grow," Elbinger said.

"If they forget the past, they are no longer the same. And if they remember all of the pettiness of life, then they cannot grow. I have no doubt that soul and body are two sides of the same coin. In this respect Spinoza had more courage than Kant. Kant's soul is nothing but a false figure in a false system of bookkeeping. *L'chaim!* Let's sit down."

The conversation turned again and again to the secret powers, and Elbinger said, "Yes, they exist, but what they represent I do not know. My own experience with them started when I was still a child. We were living in a village so small I could never find it on any map—Sencymin. Actually, it was a hamlet into which two to three dozen Jewish families had moved. My father, a *melamed,* was a pauper. We occupied two rooms—one used for the cheder; the other for the kitchen, the bedroom, and every-thing else. I had an older sister, Tzipa, and an older brother, Yonkel. I was named Moshe Mottel after a great-grandfather, but

I was called Mottele, which later evolved into Mark. I recall a number of episodes in my life as far back as the age of two. My bed was set up in the cheder room, where the children studied by day. The two windows there had shutters and they must have faced east, because the sun shone through them in the mornings. What I'm speaking of now has no connection with the so-called occult but with a feeling that everything is full of mysteries. I recall that once I woke quite early—my parents, brother, and sister were still asleep. The rising sun shone through the cracks in the shutters, and columns of dust rose from sunbeams. I remember that morning with remarkable clarity. Obviously, I was too young to think in the context of words, but I wondered, 'What is all this? Where does it all come from?' Other children no doubt go through the same thing, but on that morning my feeling was unusually strong, and I knew instinctively that I shouldn't ask about this and that my parents couldn't supply any answers. Our ceiling had beams, and a web of sun and shadow played across it. I realized that I myself and what I was seeing— the walls, the floor, the pillow on which I rested my head—were all one. In later years I read about cosmic consciousness, monism, pantheism, but I never experienced it with such impact. More, it provided me with a rare pleasure. I had merged with eternity and I relished it. At times I think it was like the state of passing over from life to what we call death. We may experience it in the final moments or perhaps immediately after. I say this because no matter how many dead people I have seen in my life, they have had the same expression on their faces: *Aha, so that's what it is! If I had only known! What a shame I can't tell the others about it!* Even a dead bird or mouse presents this expression, although not as distinctly as man.

"My first psychic experiences—if you can call them that—were of a kind that might have come in a dream or while I was awake, although I'm as convinced that they weren't dreams as I am that my sitting here with you now is no dream. I remember one time leaving our house at night. Our house—actually, all the Jewish houses were built around a sandy area called the Market. The shops were there, the prayer house and a ritual bath, as well as the tavern. I couldn't say how late it was, but the Market was deserted, all the stores were shut, and the shutters closed. I managed to slip out of bed and open the door. The night was bright —if not from the moon, perhaps from the stars.

"Across the way from us stood another house. The peasant shacks had roofs of straw, while the Jewish houses had crooked shingle roofs. Needless to say, the houses were low. The moment I stepped outside I saw something sitting on the roof across the way. I imagined it was a man, yet different. For one thing, he had no arms or legs. For another, he didn't stand on the roof, he didn't sit—he hovered there. He didn't speak to me, but I understood that he wanted me to come up to him, and I knew that to go up would be the same as going to where my dead brother and sister had gone. Just the same, I felt a strong urge to go to him. I stood gaping in indecision, frightened and disbelieving my own eyes.

"Suddenly I was aware that the man or monster had begun berating me—still in silence—and he lowered a spade toward me. The spade was not a spade at all but something that emerged from his body. It was a kind of tongue, so long and wide that it couldn't have come from any mouth. It stretched out so close to me that I knew it would catch me at any moment. I was overcome by a dreadful fear and ran back into the house screaming. The household wakened. They blew on me and, it seems, uttered incantations over me. My mother, father, Tzipa, and Yonkel— all of them barefoot and in their nightclothes—asked why I was crying so desperately, but I neither could nor wanted to answer them, knowing that I wouldn't be able to find the right words for it, that they would not believe me, and above all, that it would be better for me if I said nothing. Actually, I'm telling this for the very first time tonight. From then on, I became a kind of secret visionary. I saw things that some sense told me not to reveal. In the daytime I often saw shadows on the walls of our house, shadows not connected to the phenomena of light and shade. These were beings that crawled over the walls and into the walls. At times, two came together from opposite directions and one swallowed the other. Some were tall; their heads touched the ceiling—if you could call them heads. Others were small. At times I saw them on the floor, too, and outside on other houses, and in the air. They were always busy—coming, going, rushing. Rarely did one stop for a moment. I tell myself today that I saw ghosts, but this is merely an appellation. One thing does come to mind—I separated them into males and females. I wasn't afraid of them. It would be more accurate to say that I was curious.

"One night after I had gone to sleep and my mother had put out the light and the moon shone in through the cracks in the shutters, I heard a rustling. How shall I describe it? It was like a dried palm leaf shaking, like beating osier branches, like spraying water, and like something else to which there is no comparison. The walls began to hum and buzz, particularly in the corners, and the shapes that till then I had seen only by day now raced in thick whirls. Today, I would express it as a kind of panic among them. They hurried here and there, merged in the corners from which the noise came, raced over the beams and across the floor. My bed began to vibrate. Everything beneath me shook and tossed, and the straw in my mattress seemed animated. For once I was terrified, but I didn't dare cry out, fearing a blow or some other punishment. When I grew older, I speculated that this vibration might have been the result of an earthquake, but when I casually asked my parents and other townspeople if they had ever been through an earthquake, they all replied in the negative. I don't know if Poland has ever suffered an earthquake. The noise and dashing about lasted a long time. You can tell me my venture outside the house and the experiences that night were dreams or nightmares, but I know this isn't so.

"In later years I almost ceased having these visions, or whatever they may have been, but others evolved. I got an urge for girls—for Gentile girls, too—and I gradually realized that if I thought about a girl long enough or intensely enough, she grew magnetized and came to me. I'm not one to ascribe unusual powers to myself. Essentially, I'm a rationalist. I know coincidences occur that, in terms of probability, couldn't happen. When I play the game of dreidel with myself and the dreidel falls on the same letter five or six times because I will it to do so, I can assume that it happened by chance. However, when I spin the dreidel ten times and it comes out the same, I know that chance has nothing to do with it. I'm sure you'd rather hear about girls than dreidels. It came to the point where I would mentally order a woman to come to this and that street, and this and that number—we were then living in Warsaw—and she would come. I can't prove this to you. I can't even demonstrate with a dreidel each and every time. These powers are strangely inclined to be spiteful. They are mischievous, and they hate to be put to the test with pencils and watches. I would say that they hate science and scientists. Believe me, even to my own ears this sounds like nonsense. Who are these powers? Are they living beings? And why should they hate science and statistics? It sounds like a pretext for lying, and I've been called a liar more than once. I myself considered mediums liars if they couldn't demonstrate their powers when they were being controlled, so to say, scientifically. Well, but aren't our sex organs full of caprices, and aren't they, in a sense, antiscience? Morris, if you were told to sleep with a woman in the presence of ten professors with cameras and meters and all kinds of measuring instruments, you wouldn't be such a Don Juan. Well, and what would have happened to poets like Goethe or Heine, if they had been placed at a table surrounded by professors and instruments and ordered to write a great poem? You can play a violin in a bright hall before hundreds of people, but it's a moot point whether Beethoven or Mozart could have written their symphonies under such circumstances. I tell you that although I've managed many things under strict controls and before huge crowds, I've experienced my most significant events only when I've been alone. No one watched for results, and I didn't have to worry that I would be jeered or whistled at. Shyness is a tremendous force—occasionally a negative one. There are many men who would go to brothels, but they don't because with a prostitute they would become impotent. Why should the occult powers be any less capricious than the genitals? I can hypnotize in front of an audience today. I had to learn to do this. I've conquered my fear of failure, but not altogether. If I bang my fist on the table, the table bangs the fist back in return. This is true in spiritual matters as well. Every hypnosis has its counterhypnosis. If I'm afraid that I won't be able to sleep, I lie awake all night, and if professors from another planet sat around me on a single visit, they might conclude that I never slept at all. Why is it so hard to be a good actor and to speak and behave naturally onstage? At home, every woman is a Sarah Bernhardt. I've seen great scholars face an audience unable to utter a lucid sentence on a subject in which they were world experts.

"Yes, I did things that amazed me and convinced me I could dominate other souls, often those whom I barely knew—perhaps they had glanced at me just once. My success with women was so great that it frightened me. What is hypnotism, anyway? My theory is that it's a language with which one soul communicates directly with another.

"Our conscious hypnotic powers have limits. I don't believe that I hypnotized the dreidel. Perhaps I hypnotized my hand to spin the dreidel in such a way that it fell where I wanted it to. But who says that hypnotism is merely a biological force? Maybe it's physical, too? Maybe gravity is a kind of hypnotism? Maybe magnetism is hypnotism? Maybe God is a hypnotist with such strong hypnotic powers that He can say, 'Let there be light,' and there is light? I heard of a woman who ordered a chair to walk, and the chair walked from wall to wall and even danced. A poltergeist lifts plates and breaks them, throws stones, and opens locked doors. A woman came to me once and swore on all that was holy to her that one time when she entered her kitchen a pot rose, soared toward her, and slowly came to rest at her feet. This was an elderly woman, a lawyer's widow, a mother of grown sons and daughters, a person of education and dignity. She had no possible reason to make up such a story. She came to me hoping I could explain the mystery. It had plagued her for years. She told me that the pot didn't *fall* at her feet but laid itself down carefully. From that day on, she was afraid of the pot. She waited for it to pull another stunt, but no, it remained a pot like all pots. The woman cried as she spoke to me. Could this have been a greeting from her late husband? She spent two hours with me, hoping I could provide her with an explanation, but the only thing I could tell her was that the pot hadn't acted on its own, but that some force—an unseen hand—had lifted it and laid it down at her feet. I recall her saying, 'Maybe the pot wanted to play a joke?' "

"If this story is true, we must reexamine all our values, our concept of the world," Feitelzohn said. "Still, why doesn't it happen that a pot or some other object rises in the presence of a physicist or a chemist or at least a photographer with a camera? How is it that these wonders always occur in quiet widows' kitchens? Why don't they happen in a kitchen where there are several cooks present? Can it be that pots are bashful, too?"

At ten-thirty, Elbinger announced that he must leave. He had an appointment. I wanted to leave with him, but Feitelzohn insisted I stay.

He lit a cigar and said, "That big hero is a hypochondriac. He has hypnotized himself into believing that he suffers from a dozen ailments. He is convinced that he hasn't slept in years. He has ulcers. He is supposedly impotent, too. Women are crazy for him, but he practices celibacy. The history of mankind is the history of hypnotism. It's my firm conviction that all epidemics are mass hypnosis. When the papers announce an outbreak of influenza, people start to die from influenza. I myself talked all kinds of insanities into myself. I can't even read a book any more. At the end of the first sentence, I start to yawn. I'm sick of women. Their talking puts me off. Take our Celia. She would come here for an hour or two, and for an hour or two she would chatter. That Haiml is a homosexual. At times it seems to me I'm another. Don't be afraid, I wouldn't lay a hand on you."

Again the telephone rang. Feitelzohn let it ring. He stood there and looked at me in a new way—there was something fatherly and older-brotherly in his look.

He said, "It's Celia. I see you're tired. Go home if you want. Tsutsik, don't stay in Poland. A holocaust is coming here that will be worse than in Chmielnitsky's time. If you can get a visa—even a tourist visa—escape! A good holiday."

Then he walked over to the telephone, which had kept on ringing.

2

WARSAW was so quiet I could hear the echo of my own footsteps. Candles still burned in the windows. The gate in the house on Leszno Street was closed, and the janitor was slow in coming to open it. He grumbled, as if he knew that I intended to move out soon. Although I had my key to the elevator with me, I walked up the dark stairs.

I knocked at the apartment door and Tekla opened it. She said, "The phone rang for you today maybe a hundred times. Miss Betty."

"Thank you, Tekla."

"You don't go to the synagogue on such a holy day?" she asked with reproof.

I didn't know how to answer her. I went to my room. Without putting on the lights, I took off my clothes and lay down, but even though I was tired I couldn't sleep. What would I do after the few zlotys I had left were gone? I saw no possibility of earning money. I lay there, frightened by my situation. Feitelzohn had at least a semblance of a living from his lectures. He took money from Celia and from other women, too. He had a rent-controlled apartment, for which he paid no more than thirty zlotys a month. I had accepted the responsibility for a sick girl.

I fell asleep and wakened with a start. The phone in the corridor was ringing. On my watch the luminous hands showed a quarter past two. I heard the sound of bare feet—Tekla was running to answer. I heard her whispering. The door to my room opened. "It's for you!" Her voice expressed the indignation of a Jew forced to desecrate the holiest day of the year.

I got out of bed and bumped into her. She was wearing only her nightgown. In the hall I picked up the receiver and heard Betty's voice. It was hoarse and grating, like that of someone in the midst of a quarrel. She said, "You must come over to the hotel at once! If I call you in the middle of Yom Kippur night, it's not because of some trifle."

"What's happened?"

"I've been calling you all day. Where do you wander off to on Yom Kippur eve? I didn't sleep a wink last night and I haven't closed my eyes tonight. Sam is very sick. He has to have an operation. I told him all about us."

"What's the matter with him? Why did you need to tell him?"

"Last night he got up to go to the toilet, but he couldn't pass water. He was in such pain I had to call the First Aid. They relieved him with a catheter, but he requires an operation. He refuses to go to the hospital here and insists on returning to America to his own doctor. The doctor who saw him today told me that he has a weak heart and is not likely to recover from surgery. My dear, I have a feeling he won't make it. He called me to his side and said, 'Betty, I'm cashing in my chips, but I want to provide for you.' He talked in such a way that I couldn't withhold anything from him. I told him the whole truth. He wants to talk to you. Catch a cab and come right over. He's acting like a father to me—closer than a father. I know it's Yom Kippur, but this can't wait. Will you come?"

"Yes, of course, but you shouldn't have told him!"

"I shouldn't have been born! Be quick!" She hung up the receiver.

I tried to put on my clothes in a hurry, and they slipped from my fumbling fingers. The button fell out of my collar and rolled under the bed. I stooped to pick it up and knocked my forehead against the rail. The room was warm, but I felt a chill. I closed the door behind me and began to race down the unlit stairs. For the second time that night I rang the bell and waited for the janitor to open the gate. The pavement outside was wet—it must have been raining. The street lay deserted. I stood at the curb hoping for a taxi to come by but soon realized I could stand all night without one coming. I went in the direction of Bielanska Street and the Cracow suburb. The only streetcar that passed was headed in the opposite direction. I didn't walk but ran. I came to the hotel. The clerk dozed before the honeycomb of key boxes. I knocked on Betty's door. No one answered. I knocked again, this time on Sam Dreiman's door, and Betty let me in. She was wearing pajamas and slippers. Inside, the lights glared with a middle-of-the-night tension. Sam lay with his eyes closed, his head resting on two pillows, seemingly asleep. From under the bedding a little hose ran into a container. Betty's face was sallow and drawn, her hair disordered. "What took you so long?" she asked in a choked voice that hid a scream.

"I couldn't get a cab. I ran all the way."

"Oh. He just now fell asleep. He took a pill."

"Why do you have the room so bright here?"

"I don't know. I'll turn the lights down. I don't know what's happening to me any more. One calamity after another—look at my eyes. Come closer!"

She took me by the arm and pulled me to the other end of the room near the window. She gestured to me to be quiet. She began to talk in a whisper, but from time to time she emitted a shriek as if so many words had collected in her they could no longer be contained.

"I started calling you at ten this morning and on into the night. Where were you—still with that Shosha? Tsutsik, I have no one here but you. I tell you, Sam is a saint. I never knew he had such a noble soul. Oh, if I had known, I would have been nicer to him. I would have been faithful. But I'm afraid it's too late now. He had a hemorrhage in his nose. Tomorrow they're holding a consultation here. I called the American consulate and they arranged everything. They wanted to check him into a private clinic, where he can have the best doctors, but he insisted he would only be operated on in America. In the midst of the commotion he called me to him and said, 'Betty, I know that you love Tsutsik and there's no point in your denying it.' This was such a blow to me that I confessed everything. I began to cry and he kissed me and called me 'daughter.' He has children, but their mother filled them with hate against him. They dragged him to court and tried to grab their inheritance while he was still alive. Wait, he's waking up."

I heard a tossing about and a groan.

"Betty, where are you? Why is the room so dark?"

She ran to the bed. "Sam darling! I thought you would sleep longer. Tsutsik is here!"

"Tsutsik, come over. Betty, turn up the lights. So long as I can draw breath I don't want to be in the dark. Tsutsik, you can see for yourself I'm a sick man. I want to talk to you like a father. I have two sons, both lawyers, but all my life they treated me not like a father but worse than a stranger. I have a son-in-law, and he's no better. Living with him has turned my daughter into a bitch. I haven't felt good for a long time. Old age has suddenly caught me—the head, the stomach, the legs. Twenty times a day I run—if you'll excuse me—to the toilet, but my bladder is blocked up. In New York I have a doctor who watches over me. He gives me a checkup every three months, treats me with massages. He didn't want me to have an operation because my heart is making monkey business. In Warsaw I have no doctor. Besides, we were so busy with the theater I put off everything. My doctor ordered me not to drink—whiskey irritates the prostate and isn't good for the bladder, either—but you don't want to admit you're washed up. Take a chair, sit down. That's it. You, too, Betty darling. What was I saying, eh? Well, I'm afraid God wants me up there with Him. He's probably in the real-estate business and wants Sam Dreiman to advise Him. When the time comes, you got to go. Even if I survive the operation, it won't be for long. I was supposed to lose weight while I was here. Instead, I gained twenty pounds. How can you diet when you're away from home? I love your Warsaw dishes—they have that homey taste. Well . . ."

Sam Dreiman closed his eyes, then shook himself and opened them again. "Tsutsik, today is Yom Kippur. I thought I'd be able to go to the synagogue. I wanted to go to the one on Tlomacka Street as well as to the Hasidim on Nalewki. I bought the tickets. But man proposes and God disposes. I'll be frank with you—if I should pass away, I don't want to leave Betty to the fates. I know about your affair—she confessed everything to me. I knew about it even before. After all, she's a young woman and I'm an old man. I used to be a great lover, I could raise hell with the best of them, but once you pass into your seventies and have high blood pressure you're no longer the big hero you were. She kept on praising you. She accused herself of having brought you bad luck. I hoped the play would be a success, but it wasn't fated. We did a lot of talking. Hear me out, don't interrupt, I beg you, and think over what I'm going to say, because I look at things in a clear-headed way. You're a poor young man. You have talent, but talent is like a diamond—it has to be polished. I've been told you're involved with some sick, undeveloped girl. She is poor, too, and what is the saying? Two corpses go dancing. Things will not end well in Poland. That beast Hitler will soon come with his Nazis. There'll be a great war. Americans will lend a hand and they'll do what they did in the last war, but before that the Nazis will attack the Jews and there'll be nothing but grief for you here. The Yiddish papers are in trouble already, there are no book publishers, and what goes on on the stage is disgusting. How will you make a living? A writer has to eat, too. Even Moses had to eat. That's what the holy books say.

"Tsutsik, Betty loves you and I gather you don't hate her, either. I'm going to leave her a lot of money—exactly how much I'll tell you another time. I want to make a deal with you—a regular business transaction. I don't know yet what's going to happen to me. It's possible I'll leave this world soon, though if God is willing, I may be around for another few years yet. If they remove my prostate I may not be left a whole man in the true sense of the word. Here is my plan: I want you two to marry. I'll establish a trust fund. A lawyer will explain it all to you. You won't be a parasite supported by his wife but just the opposite—you'll support her. I only ask one promise from you—that as long as I live she can remain my friend. I'll be your publisher, your manager, anything you like. If you write a good play, I'll produce it. When you have a book ready, I'll publish it or give it to another publisher. In America, writers have agents to represent them, and I'll be your agent. You'll be my son and I'll be a father to you. I'll hire people who'll see to it that everything is in order."

"Mr. Dreiman—"

"I know, I know what you want to say. You want to know what will happen to the girl—what's her name? Shosha. Don't think I would leave her to God's mercy in Warsaw so she should starve. Sam Dreiman doesn't do such things. We'll bring her over to America. She is sick and should have help—a psychiatrist maybe. The consul is my friend, but he can't issue a permanent visa. There is a quota and not even the President can get around it. But I've figured how we can manage. We'll take her along as our maid. She won't be anyone's maid, but saying she is can get her a visa. If she's cured there, this would be a hundred times better for her than if she becomes your wife and starves to death

here. You have only to agree that Betty can remain my friend and
not leave me alone when I'm old and sick, and she won't take you
to court if you should want to give your Shosha a kiss or whatever. Isn't that so, Betty?"

"Yes, Sam darling, anything you say is all right with me."

"Do you hear? So that's my plan. It's her plan, too. We talked
frankly. Just one thing more—I must leave for America soon, so
everything has to be done fast. If you say yes, you'll have to
marry at once. If not, we'll say goodbye, and may God help you."

Sam Dreiman closed his eyes. After a while, he opened them
and said, "Betty, take him to your room. I have to . . ." He mumbled a few words in English that I didn't understand.

3

IN THE hallway between her room and Sam's, Betty began to kiss
me. Her face was wet from crying, and within a moment my face
was drenched. She whispered, "My husband, that's the way God
intended it!"

She opened the door to her room for me and immediately went
back to Sam's side. She hadn't put on the lights and I stood in
the dark. After a while, I lay down on the sofa, my mind blank.
I assumed that Betty would come right back, but she was away
a long time. The shade was drawn over the window, but it
seemed to me that day had started to break. Gradually, I began
to take account of the situation. After I had given up on everything, a perspective had opened such as I never dared dream of—
a visa to America and the chance to write without worrying
about money! I could take Shosha along, too. Something inside
me both laughed and marveled. From the time I reached man-
hood, I had told myself I would marry a girl just like my mother
—a decent, chaste Jewish daughter. I always felt pity for men

with dissolute wives. They lived with harlots and could never be sure that their children were their own. These women sullied their homes. Now I was considering taking one of this ilk for my own. What Betty had told me about her adventures in Russia and in America stayed in my mind. During the Revolution she had carried on with a Red Army man, with some sailor, with the director of a traveling actors' troupe. She had sold herself to Sam Dreiman for money. Not only did she have an ugly past, but Sam Dreiman had now stipulated that as long as he lived she would remain his friend—which was to say his lover. "Run!" a voice cried within me. "You'll sink into a slime from which you'll never be able to get out. They'll drag you into the abyss!" It was my father's voice. In the light of dawn I saw his high brow and piercing eyes. "Don't shame me, your mother, and your holy ancestors! All your deeds are noted in heaven." Then the voice began to abuse me. "Heathen! Betrayer of Israel! See what happens when you deny the Almighty! 'You shall utterly detest it and you shall utterly abhor it, for it is a cursed thing!'"

I lay there shaken. Since my father had died, I had been unable to conjure up his face. He never appeared in my dreams. His death had brought with it a kind of amnesia. Often, before going to sleep, I implored him to reveal himself to me wherever he might be and to give me a sign, but my pleas had not been answered. Suddenly here he was beside Betty's sofa, and on the Day of Atonement. Glowing and awesome, he shed his own light. I recalled what the Midrash said of Joseph: as he was about to sin with Potiphar's wife, his father, Jacob, appeared before him. These apparitions come only in the height of distress.

I sat up, my eyes wide open. "Father, save me!" As I pleaded, Father's image dissolved.

The door opened. "Are you asleep?" Betty asked.

It took a while before I could answer. "No."

"Shall I turn on the light?"

"No, no!"

"What's the matter with you? Today is more than Yom Kippur

for me. Before you came, I took a nap on the sofa and my father came to me in a dream. He looked just as I knew him in life, only handsomer. His eyes glistened. The murderers shot him in the face and crushed his skull, but he stood before me unmarked. Well, what's your answer?"

I could only say, "Not now."

"If you don't want me, I won't throw myself at you. I've still retained some pride. One has to be a saint to treat us the way Sam Dreiman is offering to do. But if it's a disgrace for you to become my husband, say so and don't leave me dangling. I've done some ugly things in my time, but I didn't have anyone then and I owed nothing to anyone. My blood burned like fire. Those men weren't even real to me. I swear to you that I've forgotten them all. I wouldn't recognize them if I saw them on the street. Why was I fool enough to tell you about them? I've always been my own worst enemy."

"Betty, Shosha would die if I did this to her," I said.

"Eh? The truth is, she'd be cured in America, but here she'll starve to death. Already their house reeks of decay. She looks ready for the grave. How long can she go on like that? I don't have to get married—not to you or to anybody. That was purely Sam's idea. A real father wouldn't be as good to me as he has been. I'd sooner cut off my hand than just leave him. I've already told you he is barely a man now. All he needs is a kiss, a pat, a kind word. If you can't even let him have that, then be on your way. If I am ready to take Shosha into my house—that ninny— then you needn't act so superior toward Sam. He has more insight in his little finger than you have in your whole body, you goddamn idiot!"

She went out and slammed the door behind her. A moment later she was back. "So what shall I tell Sam? Give me a straight answer."

"Well, all right, we'll marry," I said.

Betty paused a moment. "Is this your decision or are you just trying to make a fool out of me? If you're going to go around burning with jealousy and thinking of me as a whore, we'll call the whole thing off right now."

"Betty, if I can look after Shosha, you can be with Sam."

"What do you think—that I'd post a guard by your bed like that sultan in the *Thousand and One Nights?* I realize you feel close to her. I'm prepared to accept it. But I demand the same from you. The times when a man could indulge all his swinish urges while the woman remained a slave are over. So long as Sam lives—and may God grant him the years he deserves—we must all live together. Try to think of him as my father. That's what he has become. I haven't given up on the theater—I still plan to make another try at it. In America we can revise this play. There no one will harass us or rush us. The fact that you'll be diddling around with your Shosha bothers me as much as last year's frost. I doubt if she's even capable of *being* a woman. Have you got her started yet?"

"No, no."

"Well, a lion can't be jealous of a fly. All I can tell you is that in a hundred and twenty years, when Sam is no more, I won't be looking for anyone else. This, I could swear to you before black candles."

"You don't need to swear."

"We must get married at once. Whatever happens, I want Sam to be there."

"Yes."

"I know that you have a mother and a brother, but this can't be put off. If things go well, we'll bring your family over to America, too."

"Thank you, Betty, thank you."

"Tsutsik, I'll be better to you than you can imagine. I've already had enough filth in my life. I want to wipe the slate clean and start fresh. What it is I see in you I'm not sure myself. You have a thousand faults. But there is something about you that draws me. What is it? You tell me."

"I wouldn't know, Betty."

"When I'm with you, things are interesting. Without you, I'm miserable and bored. Come here, wish me mazel tov!"

4

I HAD fallen into a deep sleep on Betty's sofa. When I opened my eyes, I saw her standing beside me. It was day. She looked bedraggled and upset. She said, "Tsutsik, get up!"

I had wakened with a headache. It was a few seconds before I could remember what I was doing here.

Betty bent over me with maternal concern. "They're taking Sam to the hospital. I'm going with him."

"What happened?"

"He has to be operated on immediately! Where shall I look for you? You'd better stay in this room so I can call you."

"I will, Betty."

"You remember our agreement?"

"Yes."

"Pray to God for him! I don't want to lose him. If, God forbid, something should happen, I'd be left in the cold." She leaned down and kissed me on the mouth. She said, "The ambulance is downstairs. If you need to go out, leave the key with the desk clerk. If you want to go to Shosha's, you can, but you have to break off with that Celia once and for all. I won't stand for a fifth wheel on the wagon. I would have liked you to say goodbye to Sam, but I don't want him to know you spent the night here. I told him you went home. Pray to God for us!"

She left and I stayed on the sofa. I glanced at my wristwatch. It had stopped at the hour of four. I closed my eyes again. From what Betty said, I couldn't understand whether Sam had already made a new will or was planning to. Even if he had, his family would destroy it. I was dismayed at the trend my thoughts were taking. Money matters had always been alien to me. In none of my fantasies had it ever occurred to me to marry for money or for any practical reason. *It's the visa, not the money,* I justified myself—*the fear of falling into the hands of the Nazis.*

Suddenly I felt as if something had bitten me. Break off with Celia? Betty had no right to make such a demand on me while she remained Sam's mistress. I'd go straight to Celia's! I rubbed my jowls—a heavy stubble had sprouted. I stood up, but my legs had grown wobbly from sleeping on the sofa. A mirror hung over the washstand. I raised the window shade and gazed at my reflection: withered face, bloodshot eyes, a wrinkled collar. I went to the window and looked out. There was no vehicle of any kind at the hotel entrance. The ambulance had already carried them to the hospital. Betty hadn't even given me its name. From the slant of the sun's rays, I estimated that it was not early.

"What shall I tell Shosha?" I asked myself. "All she would understand was that I married someone else. She wouldn't live through it." I stood looking out at the street, the empty streetcars and droshkies. Even the Gentile neighborhoods seemed deserted in honor of Yom Kippur. I took off my jacket and washed my face, even though it was forbidden on this sacred holiday. I went out. I walked downstairs step by step. There was no reason to hurry. For the first time I felt close to Sam. He wanted the same as I— the impossible.

I passed a barbershop and went in. I was the only patron and the barber treated me with particular politeness. He wrapped me in a white sheet, like a corpse in a shroud. He stroked my beard before he began to lather. He said, "What kind of city is this Warsaw? It's Yom Kippur by the sheenies and the whole city acts dead. And this is supposed to be the capital, the crown of our Polish nation. It's really funny!"

He had mistaken me for a Gentile. I wanted to answer him, but realized that the moment I spoke more than a word or two my accent would give me away. I nodded, grunting a single word that wouldn't compromise me: *"Tak."*

"They've taken over all Poland," he went on. "The cities are lousy with them. Once, they only stank up Nalewki, Grzybowska, and Krochmalna Streets, but lately they swarm like vermin everywhere. They've even crawled as far as Wilanów. There's one consolation—Hitler will smoke them out like bedbugs."

I barely kept from trembling. The man held the edge of the razor at my throat. I looked up, and his greenish eyes briefly held mine. Did he suspect that I was a Jew?

"I'll tell you something, dear sir. The modern Jews, those who shave, who speak a proper Polish, and who try to ape real Poles, are even worse than the old-fashioned Hebes with their long gaberdines, wild beards, and earlocks. They, at least, don't go where they aren't wanted. They sit in their stores in their long capotes and shake over their Talmud like bedouins. They babble away in their jargon, and when a Christian falls into their clutches, they swindle a few groschen out of him. But at least they don't go to the theater, the cafés, the opera. Those that shave and dress modern are the real danger. They sit in our Sejm and make treaties with our worst enemies, the Ruthenians, the White Russians, the Lithuanians. Every one of them is a secret Communist and a Soviet spy. They have one aim—to root out us Christians and hand over the power to the Bolsheviks, the Masons, and the radicals. You might find it hard to believe this, dear sir, but their millionaires have a secret pact with Hitler. The Rothschilds finance him and Roosevelt is the middleman. His real name isn't Roosevelt but Rosenfeld, a converted Jew. They supposedly assume the Christian faith, but with one goal in mind—to bore from within and infect everything and everybody. Funny, don't you think?"

I emitted a half grunt, half sigh.

"They come here for a shave and a haircut all year, but not today. Yom Kippur is a holy day even for those that are rich and modern. More than half the stores are closed here and on Marshalkowska Street. They don't go to the Hasidic prayer houses in fur-edged hats and prayer shawls like the old-fashioned sheenies—oh no, they put on top hats and drive to the synagogue on Tlomacka Street in private cars. But Hitler will clean them out! He promises their millionaires that he'll protect their capital, but once the Nazis are armed he'll fix them all—ha, ha, ha! It's too bad that he'll attack our country, but since we haven't had the guts to sweep away this filth ourselves, we have to let the enemy do it for us. What will happen later, no one can know. The fault for it all lies with those traitors, the Protestants, who sold their souls to the devil. They're the Pope's deadliest enemies. Did you know, dear sir, that Luther was a secret Jew?"

"No."

"It's an established fact."

The barber had gone over my face twice with the razor. He now splashed me with eau-de-cologne and dusted me with powder. He brushed off my suit and with two fingers removed some stray hairs from my shoulders. I paid him and left. By the time I closed the shop door my shirt was soaked. I began to race, not knowing in what direction I was going. *No, I wouldn't stay in Poland! I'd leave at any price!* I crossed the street and a car nearly ran me down. This was the most tragic day of my life. I, too, had sold my soul to the devil. Maybe go to a synagogue? No, I would desecrate the holy place. My stomach churned and I felt an urge to urinate. Sweat ran from me, and pain stabbed my bladder. I knew that if I didn't void immediately I would wet myself. I came to a restaurant and tried to enter, but the glass door wouldn't give. Was it locked? It couldn't be—I could see diners inside and waiters carrying trays.

A man with a dog on a leash came up and said, "Don't pull, push!"

"Oh, many thanks!"

I asked the waiter for the way to the restroom and he pointed to a door. But when I walked in that direction the door vanished as if by magic. People looked up from their breakfasts and stared at me. A woman laughed aloud.

The waiter came up. "Here!" And he opened a door for me.

I ran to the urinal, but just as with Sam Dreiman, the urine had become blocked inside me.

· CHAPTER NINE ·

1

I DIDN'T go to Celia. I spent Yom Kippur with Shosha. Bashele had gone to the synagogue. The big commemorative candle she had lit the day before still burned, casting almost no light. I lay on the bed next to Shosha in my clothes, dulled by the sleep-less night. I dropped off, began dreaming, and awoke. Shosha spoke to me, but even though I heard her voice I didn't follow what she was saying. It had to do with the war, the typhus epi-demics, the hunger, Yppe's death. Shosha placed her childlike hand on my loins. We both had fasted.

From time to time I opened an eye and noticed how the sun-light moved up across the opposite wall. A Yom Kippur quiet lay over the courtyard, and I could hear the twittering of a bird. I had made a decision and knew that I would keep it, but why I had made it was something I couldn't explain to myself or to anyone else. Did it have to do with the vision—or hallucination —of my father? Had the barber influenced me with his poisonous words? I was rejecting a woman of passion, of talent, with the capability of taking me to wealthy America, and condemning myself to poverty and death from a Nazi bullet. Had it been jealousy of Sam Dreiman? Such great love for Shosha? Did I lack the courage to disappoint Bashele? I posed a question to my subconscious or unconscious, but no answer came back. This is precisely the case with those who commit suicide, I said to myself. They find a hook in the ceiling, fashion a noose, place a chair underneath, and until the final second they don't know why they are doing it. Who says that everything nature or human nature does can be expressed in motives and words? I had been aware for a long time that literature could only describe facts or let the characters invent excuses for their acts. All motivations in fiction are either obvious or false.

I fell asleep. It was dusk when I awoke. A final sliver of sunset blazed in the pane of a garret window. Shosha said, "Arele, you slept nicely."

"And you, Shoshele?"

"Oh, I slept."

The room filled with shadows. On the table the memorial candle began to flicker. The flame flared up once and soon grew so small it barely touched the wick. Shosha said, "Last year I went with Mommy to the synagogue on Yom Kippur night. A man with a white beard blew the ram's horn."

"Yes, I know."

"When three stars appear in the sky, we'll be able to eat."

"Are you hungry?"

"When you are with me, it's better than eating."

I said, "Shoshele, we'll soon be husband and wife. After the holidays."

As I spoke, I wanted to caution Shosha to say nothing of this to her mother for now, but just then the door opened, Bashele came in, and Shosha ran to meet her. "Mommy, Arele is going to marry me after Succoth!" She shouted this in a louder voice than I had ever heard from her. She hugged her mother and began to kiss her. Bashele quickly put down her two prayer books and cast a questioning look at me that was full of joyful astonishment.

"Yes, it's true," I said.

Bashele clapped her hands. "God the merciful has heard my prayers. I stood on my feet all day and prayed only for you, daughter, and for you, Arele, my son. Only God in heaven knows how many tears I shed for you two today. Daughter, apple of my eye, mazel tov!"

They kissed, hugged, and swayed, as if unable to break apart. Then Bashele held out her arms to me. There came from her the aroma of the fast, of the naphthalene in which her dress had been lying a whole year, and of something womanly and festive —an aroma familiar from my childhood, when our living room was turned into a women's synagogue during the Days of Awe. Bashele's voice, too, had grown louder and stronger. She began to speak in the style of the Yiddish supplication book: "It's all from heaven, from heaven. God has seen my grief, my broken spirit. Father in heaven, this is the happiest day of my wretched life. Help us, God, for we have suffered enough. Sweet Father, let me live to enjoy the satisfaction of leading my first-born child to the wedding canopy!" She raised her hands high. A motherly bliss shone in her eyes. Shosha burst into tears. Then Bashele exclaimed, "What's wrong with me? He fasted all day, this treasure of mine, my precious heir. You'll soon have food!"

She raced to the credenza and came back with a beaker of cherry brandy. The liqueur must have been standing there from long ago, awaiting some joyous occasion. Shosha received the same offering. We drank a toast and kissed. Shosha's lips did not feel like those of a child but like those of a ripe woman. The door opened and Teibele came in, pretty, in a dress that looked new to me. I had met her for the last time on Rosh Hashanah, when she came to share the holiday feast with her mother and sister. Teibele was tall, erect, and resembled her father with her dark hair and brown eyes. Although she had been only three when the family moved from No. 10 to No. 7, she remembered me and called me Arele. On Rosh Hashanah she had brought a slice of pineapple with which to make the New Year benedictions. As soon as she heard the news, something like a mixture of happiness and laughter appeared in her eyes. "Arele, is this true?"

Before I could answer, she embraced me, held me close, and

began kissing me. "Mazel tov! Mazel tov! It's a fated thing! And
on Yom Kippur! Somehow my heart told me—Arele, I never had
a brother, and from now on you'll be my brother, even closer
than a brother. When Daddy hears this, he will . . ." Teibele
trotted to the door on her high heels.

Bashele asked, "Where are you running in such a hurry?"

"To telephone Daddy," Teibele called back from the hallway.

"Why him? What does this happy event have to do with him?"
Bashele shouted after her. "He abandoned us, sick and lonely,
and went off to live with a slut—may all the fires of hell consume
her. That's no father but a murderer. If it had been left to him,
you'd have all starved to death. I was the one who fed you and
gave my last bit of strength so that you should live. God in
heaven, You know the truth. It was because of that rascal and
his filthy ways that we lost Yppe—may she rest in paradise with
the sainted souls."

Bashele said all this to herself, to Shosha, and to me, since
Teibele had slammed the door behind her.

Shosha asked, "Where will she call from? Is the delicatessen
open?"

"Let her call. Let her suck around him, that old whoremonger.
To me he's as *trayf* as pork. I never want to see his face again.
He was no father when we starved and ailed and spat out our
lungs, and I don't want him as a father now when luck has come
to us, may it only stay with us. Shoshele, why are you standing
there like a ninny? Kiss him, hold him! He is already as good as
your husband and to me he's as dear as my own child. We never
forgot him, never. A day didn't go by that we didn't think of him.
We didn't know where he was or if he lived, so many young
people perished in all the fires. When Leizer brought us the good
news that he was alive and writing for the newspaper, it was like
a holiday in the house. How long ago was this? My head is so
muddled I don't know what or when. *I* will lead you to the wedding canopy, my darling daughter—not your cruel father. Arele,
my child, God should only grant you as much happiness as you

have granted us this night." Bashele began to cry, and Shosha cried with her.

After a while, Bashele put on an apron and started fussing with pots, pans, plates. The two chickens that had been offered in sacrifice on Yom Kippur eve lay already cooked, and Bashele quickly sliced them and served them with challah and horse-radish. Later, she scolded herself that she had forgotten to serve the gefilte fish first.

She hovered over me. "Eat, child of mine. You're probably weak from fasting. For myself, my soul was so burdened I didn't even realize I was fasting. To me fasting is no novelty. More than one night I went to bed without a bite in my stomach so that my little swallows should have bigger portions. Eat, Shoshele, eat, my bride! God hearkened to your longing. Worthy ancestors interceded in your behalf. For you, today is not the end of Yom Kippur but Simchas Torah. What happened to Teibele? Why is she staying away so long? He blotted her out as a daughter and still she keeps herself close to him just because he has a nice apartment and throws her a trinket from time to time. A shame and a disgrace! A sin before God."

Bashele sat down to eat, but every few seconds she turned to face the door. Finally, Teibele came back. "Mommy, I have good news for you, but first swallow your food, because when you get excited, you start to choke."

"What news? I don't want news from him."

"Mommy, listen to me! When Daddy heard of Shosha and Arele he became another person. He fell in love with that red-head, and love makes people mad. Daddy told me two things, and I want you to hear carefully, because he's waiting for an answer. First, he said that he would provide Shosha with a trousseau for the wedding and he would give her one thousand zlotys for a dowry. This isn't much, but it's better to begin with a little money than with none. Second, he said that if you, Mother, will agree to a divorce, he'll give you a thousand zlotys, too. Hush! I know how little this is for all your years of suffering, but since you two can't ever be together again, what's the point of spiting each other? You're not that old, and if you dressed yourself up you could still find a suitor. Those were *his* words, not mine. My advice is, forget the past wrongs and come to a settlement once and for all."

The whole time Teibele was talking, Bashele's face twisted with revulsion and impatience. "*Now* he's going to divorce me—when my blood is congealed and the marrow is dried in my bones? I no longer need a husband and have no desire to please anyone. All my life I lived only for you children, only for you. Now that Shosha has found her destined one, I have but one wish—that you should do the same, Teibele. He doesn't have to be a writer or a scholar. What does a writer earn, anyway? Nothing with nothing. I would be satisfied with a merchant, a clerk, even a tradesman. Does it make any difference what a husband does? The main thing is, he should be decent and have one God and one wife, not—"

"Mommy, decency is *not* everything. You have to feel something for a husband, to love him, to be able to talk to him. To tie up with some tailor or clerk and begin cooking and washing diapers is not for me. But why waste time talking about that? Better think over what I told you. I promised Daddy an answer."

"An answer already? I waited for him longer. Hoo-hah, the great squire! The only reason he's got so much gall is that he has money and we're paupers. He'll get no answer today. Sit down and eat with us. In this house, today is a double holiday. We're poor but we don't come from dirt. We had a preacher in our family—Reb Zekele Preacher, they called him. Your father, that skirt-chaser, will have to wait."

"Mommy, there's an expression—strike while the iron is hot. You know Daddy—all moods. Tomorrow he may change his mind. What will you do then?"

"I'll do what I've done all these years—suffer and place my hope in the Almighty. Arele loves Shosha, not her clothes. You can put a dress on a mannequin, too. An educated person considers the soul. Isn't that true, Arele?"

"Yes, Bashele."

"Oh, please call me Mother. May your mother live to a hundred and twenty, but you haven't a better friend than me in the whole world. If someone told me to lay down my life for your tiniest fingernail, as God is my witness, I wouldn't hesitate." Bashele began to cough.

"Arele, there are no words for how much we all love you," Shosha said.

"Well, you two love, but don't try to sell me to some clerk," Teibele said. "I want to love, too. If only I could meet the right person, my soul would open to him fast enough."

That night, Bashele set the date for the wedding—the week of Hanukkah. She suggested that I write a letter to my mother at once in Old Stykov, where my brother Moishe was now rabbi in my father's place.

Teibele, ever practical, asked, "Where will the newlyweds live? An apartment is like gold these days."

"They'll live here with me," Bashele replied. "And when I cook for two, there'll be enough for three."

2

I HAD committed the worst folly of my life, but I had no regrets. Neither was I elated, as those in love usually are. The day after Yom Kippur I gave notice at Leszno Street that I would be moving out at the end of the month. I might have condemned myself to penury but not yet to death. I still had my room for four weeks. I could pay Bashele for my food until some time after the holidays. I was amazed by my light-mindedness, but not shocked. I had heard that Sam Dreiman had been operated on at the Jewish hospital on Czysta Street and would go off with Betty to recuperate. When Tekla heard that I would be moving out after the Jewish holiday, she came to ask the reason. Was I dissatisfied with the service? Did she, Tekla, neglect to convey an important message to me? Did she insult me in some way? For the first time I saw tears in her pale-blue eyes. I put my arms around her, kissed her, and said, "Tekla dear, it's not your fault. You were good to me. I'll remember you to my last breath."

"Where will you live? Are you going with Miss Betty to America?"

"No, I'm staying right here in Warsaw."

"Bad times are coming for Jews here," she said, after some hesitation.

"Yes, I know."

"If a war should break out, it won't be good for Christians, either."

"Also true. But the history of all peoples is one long chain of wars."

"Why is it so? What do the educated people say—those who write the books?"

"The best thing they find to say is that if there were no wars, no epidemics, and no famines, people would multiply like rabbits and there soon wouldn't be enough for everybody to eat."

"Doesn't enough rye grow in the fields for bread?"

"Not enough for thousands of millions of people."

"Why didn't God make it so there'd be enough for all?"

"I can't answer that."

"Do you know where you will be staying? I'll miss you. I'm off Sundays, but somehow I can't seem to get close to anybody," Tekla said. "The other maids go out with soldiers, with fellows they meet in the street or in Karcelak Place. But I can't make friends with a lout who kisses you one day and doesn't want to know you the next. They drink and fight. They get a girl pregnant and later they don't want to know her. Is that just?"

"No, Tekla."

"Sometimes I think I'd like to become a Jewess. The Jewish boys read newspapers and books. They know what's going on in the world. They treat a girl better than our fellows do."

"Don't do it, Tekla. When the Nazis come, the Jews will be the first victims."

"Where will you move to?"

"No. 7 Krochmalna Street."

"Can I come visit on Sunday?"

"Yes. Wait for me by the gate at noon."

"Will you definitely be there?"

"Yes."

"Is that a holy promise?"

"Yes, my dear."

"You'll be living there with someone, eh?"

"Whoever I live with, I'll miss you."

"I will come!" Tekla dashed from my room. A slipper fell off her foot. She picked it up with one hand and clapped the other over her mouth so that her employer wouldn't hear her crying.

That afternoon I sat down to work on a sketch, and later on a novel based on the life of the false Messiah, Jacob Frank. I had already gathered a substantial amount of material about him. In two days I completed three sketches and took them to the newspaper that had published things from me earlier. All hope was gone, but so was all tension. To my surprise, the editor accepted all three. He even asked me to write other short pieces for him. The power that guides man's lot had postponed my death sentence.

My success with the sketches gave me the courage to phone Celia. I told her everything. Celia heard me out, sighed; from time to time she laughed a short laugh. When I finished she said, "Bring her and let me look her over. Whatever may be, your room still stands ready for you here. You can move in with anyone you like."

"Celia, she's infantile—physically and mentally backward."

"Well, and what are you? What are all writers? Lunatics."

Things began to happen quietly and as if mechanically, I had given up free choice, and causality took over. I let Tekla and her mistress know that I would be staying on another month, and both of them congratulated me and expressed the hope that I would stay even longer. On the last day of Succoth, Teibele called to invite me to her apartment. Zelig wanted to meet me. I put on my good suit, bought candy for Teibele, and took a droshky, so that I wouldn't arrive in a sweat. The girl who shared Teibele's apartment had gone to the opera. Zelig sat at a table in the living room, which was set with liquor and food. With his dyed hair and beard, he looked not much older than he had twenty years ago. He was broad-shouldered, stocky, with a short neck, a pointed belly. His nose was red and had the broken veins of a drinker. He spoke to me with the crudeness of burial-society members. He smelled of alcohol and smoked one cigarette after another. If he were my age, he said, he wouldn't marry a sluggard like Shosha. He complained that Bashele had refused to divorce him and for so many years had kept him from marrying the woman he loved. He compared Bashele to a dog sitting on a pile of hay he couldn't eat himself but wouldn't let another creature have. He told me what I already knew: that he was prepared to come to Shosha's wedding and give her a thousand zlotys' dowry. Like a proper father-in-law to be, he questioned me about my prospects of earning a living at writing. He poured himself half a glass of the vodka Teibele had put out and asked brusquely, "Be honest, what do you see in my Shosha? No front and no behind—a board and a hole is what we'd call her."

"Papa, you shame me!" Teibele cried.

"What's there to be ashamed of? In the burial society we know the truth. A woman can fix herself up for the outside world, cover everything with rouge and powder and corsets, but when we strip her for the shrouds . . ."

"If you don't stop, I'll leave!" Teibele warned.

"Well, daughter, don't be angry. That's how we are. That's why we drink. Without booze, none of us would last. You don't drink, eh?" he said, turning to me.

"Seldom."

"Tell my wife she's waited long enough. It's now or never if she wants to marry again. If she puts it off for a few more years, she can become a virgin again, ha, ha, ha!"

"I'm going, Papa."

"All right, I won't say another word. Wait, Arele, I've got a present for you."

Zelig took a watch and chain from his breast pocket. I blushed and he said, "Whatever I may be and whatever they say about me, I'm still Shosha's father. If she ever has a child—and I can't imagine how, unless they perform a Caesarean—I'll be a grandfather. I knew your father, may he rest in peace. We were neighbors for years. At times when there was a wedding at your house, they called me in to make a quorum. He always sat over his Gemaras. I also remember your mother. Not a bad-looking woman, though too skinny for my taste. You look like her. What will be with this Hitler? People are all terrified, but not me. If things get bad enough, I'll dig myself a grave, take a shot of brandy, and go to sleep. When you see death every day, you stop being afraid of it. What's life, anyway? You give the throat a squeeze and it's all over. Here, take this watch. That's my wedding present to you. It's silver and it has seventeen jewels. Bashele's father gave it to me to sleep with *his* daughter, and now I give it to you to sleep with *my* daughter. If you take care of it, one day you may give it to the fellow who'll do the favor for *your* daughter."

"Oh, Papa, what's to be done with you?"

"Teibele, give up—you can't do anything with me. I have a present ready for you too, when you find the right man. There is no God. I went to synagogue on Rosh Hashanah and Yom Kippur, but I didn't do much praying."

"So where does the world come from?" Teibele asked.

Zelig pinched his beard. "Where does everything come from? It's there and that's all. In Praga, there were two friends and one got sick. Before dying, he made a deal with his friend that if there was another world he'd come back to give him greetings.

He told his friend to light the candles in the Hanukkah lamp on the last day of the mourning period and he would come put them out. The friend did as he was told. On the last day of mourning he lit the Hanukkah lamp. But he was tired from working and he dropped off. Suddenly he woke up. A candle had fallen from the lamp and started a fire. His gaberdine was burning. He ran outside and rolled in the gutter. He had to spend two months in the hospital."

"And what's to be made from this?"

"Nothing. There is no such thing as a soul. I've buried more rabbis and holy Jews than you've got hairs on your head. You stick them in the grave and that's where they rot."

No one spoke for a while; then Zelig asked, "Shosha doesn't sleep so much any more? That time when she got the sleeping sickness she slept nearly a whole year. They woke her, fed her, and she went right back to sleep. How long ago was it—fifteen years already, eh?"

"Papa, what's wrong with you?" Teibele exclaimed.

"I'm drunk. I didn't say anything. She's recovered now."

· CHAPTER TEN ·

1

DORA was supposed to have gone to Russia months earlier, but she was still in Warsaw. Her sister Liza called me at the Writers' Club to tell me Dora had attempted suicide by drinking iodine. It seemed that Wolf Felhendler, a fellow Communist who had gone to Russia a year and a half before, had broken out of Soviet exile and smuggled his way back into Poland. The news he brought was dismaying: Dora's best friend, Irka, had been shot there. A whole group of comrades who had gone to the Soviet Union were either in prison or had been sent to the north to dig for gold. As word of his report spread, the Stalinists in Warsaw accused Wolf Felhendler of being a Fascist traitor and a spy for the Polish Secret Service. However, within Poland trust in Stalin's justice suffered a mighty blow. Even before this, whole cells had become disillusioned and gone over to the Trotskyites, and many Communists had switched to the Jewish Bund or the Polish Socialist Party. Others had become Zionists or turned to religion.

After Dora's stomach had been pumped out, Liza arranged for her to spend a few days in Otwock. Back in her apartment, Dora telephoned me, and I went to visit her in the evening. Behind the door I heard a man's voice—Felhendler's. I hadn't the slightest urge to meet with him. He used to warn the anti-

Communists at the Writers' Club that when the revolution came
he would see them hanged from the nearest lamp post. Still, I
knocked. In a few minutes, Dora opened the door. Even though
it was half dark in the corridor, I could see that she looked pale
and wasted. She clasped my hand and said, "I thought you would
never want to see my face again."

"I hear you have company."

"It's Felhendler. He'll be leaving soon."

"Don't keep him here. I don't have the patience for him."

"He's not the same person. He's gone through hell."

Dora spoke softly and didn't let go of my hand. She led me
into the living room, where Felhendler sat at the head of the
table. If I hadn't known who he was, I wouldn't have recognized
him. He was thinner, aged; his hair had fallen out. His attitude
toward me had always been arrogant—he addressed me as if
the revolution already had come and he had been appointed a
commissar. But now he jumped to his feet. He smiled and I saw
that his front teeth were missing. He held out a clammy hand to
me and said, "I called you at your room, but you weren't home."

Even his voice had grown meek. I couldn't bring myself to take
revenge upon a person so beaten, although I knew that, if it had
been within his power, he would have subjected me to the very
treatment he himself had received. He said, "I've thought of you
more than you know. Did your ears ever burn?"

"Ears burn when you talk about someone, not when you think
of him," Dora observed.

"You're right, of course. Lately, I've begun to forget things.
For a time I even forgot the names of my own family. You've
probably heard what happened to me. Well, I've paid my dues,
as they say. But I didn't only think about you, I actually spoke
of you. I shared a cell with a man by the name of Mendel Leiter-
man, who had once been a reader of *The Literary Magazine*.
Forty of us were jammed in a cell made for eight. We sat on the
floor and talked. The greatest privilege was to be next to the wall
where you could lean your head."

I assumed Felhendler would say goodbye and leave; instead, he settled down again. His suit hung so loosely that it seemed not to be his size. In the past, he had always worn a stiff collar and tie, but now his collar was open, revealing a scrawny neck. He said, "Yes, I recalled your words. You predicted everything in detail—you might have been some kind of prophet who had put a curse on me. I don't mean this in a bad sense—I haven't yet reached such a stage of superstitious nonsense. But words aren't lost. At night when I lay on the bare floor, sick and grimy, my head reeling from the stink of the slop bucket—that is, if they let me lie and didn't drag me off for an interrogation—and I heard the doors being opened to take someone else to be tortured, I thought, what would Aaron Greidinger say if he could see all this? It didn't occur to me for a second that I would live to meet and talk with you again. We were all condemned to death or to work in the gold mines, which is worse than death. No, they don't let you die so fast and easy. One time they questioned me for twenty-six hours straight. This kind of physical torture—I'm not speaking of the spiritual pain—I wouldn't wish on my worst enemies, not even on Stalin's minions. I don't believe they were as cruel during the Inquisition or that it's being done in Mussolini's prisons. A man can take torture from an enemy, but when your friend turns out to be the enemy, then the anguish is beyond endurance. They wanted one thing from me—to confess that I was a spy sent by the Polish Secret Service. They literally begged me to do them the favor and confess, but I swore to myself, anything but this."

"Wolf, stop talking about it. It's making you sick," Dora said.

"Eh? I couldn't be sicker than I am. I said to them, 'How can I be a Polish spy when I did time in every Polish jail for our ideal? How can I be a Fascist when for years I was an editor of a magazine that attacked the Zionists, the Bund, the P.P.S., and that openly preached the dictatorship of the proletariat? My family was from the poorest of the poor, and all my life I've suffered hunger and want. Socialism was my only comfort. Why

would I become a spy for the reactionary and anti-Semitic Polish
regime? What military institutions was I being allowed to get
near? Where has your sense of reason gone? Even in madness
there has to be a trace of logic,' I said. But the fellow who sat
facing me toyed with his revolver the whole time, smoked cigarettes, and drank tea while I was standing on swollen feet and
everything inside me was shriveling from lack of food, water,
and sleep. He glared at me. His eyes were murderous. 'I've heard
all your lousy excuses,' he said. 'You are a Fascist dog, a counter-
revolutionary traitor, and a Hitler spy. Sign the confession before
I tear the tongue out of your pig's snout.' He called me 'thou,'
that Russky. He lit a candle, took out a needle, held it to the
flame, and said, 'If you don't sign, I'll jam this under your filthy
fingernails.' I knew what pain that meant, for the Polish Fascists
had done it to me, but still I couldn't label myself a spy. I looked
at him—someone who should have been the defender of the
working class and of the Revolution—and for all my anguish I
started to laugh. This was bad theater, the worst kind of trash.
Even Nowaczynski in the wildest stretches of his sick imagination
couldn't have dreamed up such an idiotic plot.

"I stuck out my hand and told him, 'Go ahead. If this is what
the Revolution needs, do with me as you will.' He was called out
and a new executioner took his place—a new executioner who
was rested and full. That's how they questioned me for twenty-six
hours by the clock. I pleaded with them, 'Shoot me and put an
end to it.' "

"Wolf, I can't listen to any more!" Dora cried.

"You can't, can't you? You have to! We are responsible for this.
We spread the propaganda to bring it about. In 1926, when the
news began to come out against Trotsky, we called him an agent
for the Pilsudskis, the Mussolinis, the Rockefellers, the MacDon-
alds. We stuffed our ears and refused to hear the truth."

"Felhendler, I don't want to rub salt in your wounds," I said,
"but if Trotsky was in power, he wouldn't act any differently
from Stalin."

A mixture of irony and anger showed in Felhendler's eyes. "How do you know how Trotsky would act? How dare you make assumptions about things that never happened?"

"They've happened in all the revolutions. Whenever blood is spilled in the name of humanity, of religion, or of any other cause, it leads inevitably to this kind of terror."

"So according to you the working class should keep silent over what is happening in Russia, allow Hitler and Mussolini to seize the world and let itself be trampled like ants. Is this what you preach?"

"I don't preach."

"Yes, you do. If you can say that Trotsky would be no better than Stalin, it means that the whole human race is corrupt and there is no hope—that we must surrender to all the murderers, the Fascists, those who instigate pogroms and turn the clock back to the Dark Ages, to the Inquisitions, to the Crusades."

"Felhendler, England, France, and America haven't resorted to inquisitions and crusades."

"Oh, haven't they? America has locked its gates and is letting no one in. England, France, Canada, Australia—all the capitalist countries—are doing the same. In India, thousands of people die of hunger each day. English travelers admit this themselves. When Gandhi, submissive as he is, uttered a word, they threw him in jail. Is this true or not? Gandhi babbles about passive resistance. What a swindle! How can resistance be passive? It's exactly as if you would say hot snow, cold fire."

"Then you're still for revolution?"

"Yes, Aaron Greidinger, yes! If you went to a dentist and instead of pulling a rotten tooth he purposely pulled three healthy teeth, this would surely be a tragedy and a crime. But the rotten tooth would still have to be pulled. Otherwise it could infect the whole mouth—even lead to gangrene."

"Right! One hundred percent correct!" Dora exclaimed.

"I hate to dash your hopes," I said, "but I will make another prediction for you: Trotsky's permanent revolution, or whatever revolution it may be, will duplicate precisely what the Stalinists are doing now. I do not want you to have to say again that I was right. You've suffered enough."

"No," Felhendler said. "If I were to think in your terms, I'd have to hang myself this very night."

"Enough," Dora said. "I'll put up tea."

2

WE DRANK tea, ate bread with herring, and Felhendler recounted his experiences from the time he crossed the border into Russia and was met by a delegate of the Comintern. He was taken to Moscow and assigned a room with another delegate from Poland, a Comrade Wysocki from Upper Silesia. Every other evening, they attended free performances of the theater or the opera or some new Soviet film. Suddenly in the middle of a night there was a knock on his door and he was placed under arrest. Five weeks he sat behind bars without knowing the charges against him. He comforted himself with the idea that his imprisonment was an error—he had obviously been mistaken for some other Felhendler and everything would be cleared up at the interrogation. He shared a cell with both political and criminal prisoners. The thieves, murderers, and rapists beat the politicals and took away their food rations. They played cards among themselves, using slips of paper, and gambled for each other's rations, clothing, and the right to sleep on the hard bench instead of the floor. When one of the players lost all he possessed, he played for blows —the winner could slug the loser. Many of the criminals practiced homosexuality. A new prisoner who didn't want to participate was raped. The Red authorities made no effort to protect the victims.

Felhendler said, "In the Polish prisons, even in such a tough jail as Wronki, where I spent three years, they gave us books. I went through a whole library there. But in the land of socialism, we—the fighters for justice!—sat for weeks on end going mad. We kneaded chess pieces out of the claylike bread that they gave us, but there wasn't enough room on the floor to set up a board to play on. None of the political prisoners had the slightest notion of what crimes they had been picked up for. Yet nearly every one of them remained dedicated to the cause. They put the blame on the lower officials of the G.P.U. without once accusing Stalin or anyone in the Central Committee or the Politburo. But I slowly became aware of the quicksand in which we were caught. Some of the prisoners confided to me that they had been forced to make false accusations against their closest comrades."

It was midnight when Felhendler left. The moment he closed the door, Dora burst into tears. "What can one do? How is one to live?"

She clasped me by my wrists and drew me to her. She leaned her forehead on my shoulder and sobbed. I stood there gawking at the opposite wall. From the day I had left my father's house I had existed in a state of perpetual despair. Occasionally, I considered the notion of repentance, of returning to real Jewishness. But to live like my father, my grandfathers, and great-grandfathers, without their faith—was this possible? Each time I went into a library, I felt a spark of hope that perhaps in one of the books there might be some indication of how a person of my disposition and world outlook could make peace with himself. I didn't find it—not in Tolstoy or in Kropotkin, not in Spinoza or in William James, not in Schopenhauer, not in the Scriptures. Certainly the Prophets preached a high morality, but their promises of plentiful harvests, of fruitful olive trees and vineyards, protection against one's enemies, made no appeal to me. I knew that the world had always been and would always remain as it was now. What the moralists called evil was actually the order of life.

Dora wiped her tears. "Arele, I must move from here at once. The apartment isn't mine, and even if it was, I couldn't pay for it. Also, I'm afraid that my ex-comrades will turn me in to the Secret Service."

"The Secret Service knows about you, anyway."

"They could provide the necessary proof. You know how it is with the Stalinists—whoever isn't for them must be liquidated."

"You yourself used to preach this."

"To my shame, yes."

"The Trotskyites follow the same principles."

"What shall I do? You tell me!"

"I can't tell you anything."

"I could be arrested any day. The last time you slept here I was still full of expectation. I even dreamed you might sooner or later come to me in Russia. Now I don't look forward to anything."

"A half hour ago, you agreed with Felhendler's Trotskyism."

"I'm no longer sure. I should have thrown myself out the window instead of drinking iodine."

That night I lay next to Dora, but that was all. I couldn't sleep. Each time I heard the bell at the house gate I assumed it was the police coming to take us in. I rose at dawn and before I went I gave Dora some of the money I had with me.

Dora said, "I thank you, but if you should hear that I've done away with myself, don't feel too bad. I've been left with nothing."

"Dora, for the time being, don't get involved with the Trotsky-ites. A permanent revolution is about as possible as permanent surgery."

"What will *you* do?"

"Oh, live from day to day—or from hour to hour."

We said goodbye. I was afraid that a secret agent might be waiting by the gate to arrest me, but no one was there. I headed back to my room and my manuscript.

On the way, I glanced at the high tower of the church on Nowolipki Street. In buildings around the enormous courtyard encircled by an iron picket fence lived nuns—Jesus's brides. I often saw them pass in their starched cowls, long black robes, and mannish shoes, their bosoms hung with crucifixes. On Karmelicka Street I passed the "Workers' Home," the club of the left-wing Poale Zion. In there, they espoused both Communism and Zionism, believing that only when the proletariat seized power would the Jews be able to have their own homeland in Palestine and become a socialistic nation. In No. 36 Leszno Street was the Groser Library of the Jewish Bund, as well as a cooperative store for workers and their families. The Bund totally rejected Zionism. Their program was cultural autonomy and common socialist struggle against capitalism. The Bundists themselves had split into two factions, one in favor of democracy and one in favor of immediate dictatorship by the proletariat. In another courtyard was the club of the Revisionists, the followers of Jabotinsky, extreme Zionists. They encouraged Jews to learn to use firearms and contended that only acts of terror against the English, who held the mandate, could restore Palestine to the Jews. The Revisionists in Warsaw had a semi-military unit that from time to time paraded through the streets carrying wooden swords and shouting slogans against those Zionists who, like Weizmann, believed in mediation and compromise with England. Nearly all the Jewish parties had their clubs in this area. Each year added some new splinter group and another office.

I had won a moral victory over Dora, Felhendler, and their comrades, but everything had grown so wildly tangled that I could no longer sneer at anyone else's wrongheadedness.

I went to my room, which I now decided to keep until the wedding, but I was too tired to work. I stretched out on the bed, dozed off, and in my mind heard over and over Felhendler's words and Dora's lament: *What can one do? How is one to live?*

· *CHAPTER ELEVEN* ·

1

A FEW DAYS before the wedding, my mother and Moishe arrived, and I met them at the Danzig depot. The train pulled in at 8 a.m. I barely recognized them. Mother seemed smaller, stooped, and as old as a crone. Her nose had lengthened; it curved down like a bird's beak. Creases cut deep into her forehead and cheeks. Only the gray eyes still showed a youthful sharpness. She no longer wore a wig; a kerchief covered her head. Her skirt reached the floor, and she had on a blouse that I remembered from the time I lived at home. Moishe had grown tall. He had a ragged blond beard and earlocks hanging to his shoulders. His rabbinical hat was flecked and mangy, and his fur coat was ratty. The unbuttoned shirt collar exposed a soft, childish throat.

He gazed at me with amazement in his blue eyes and said, "A real German."

After I had kissed my mother, she asked, "Arele, are you sick, God forbid? You're as pale and drawn as if you just got out of a sickbed, may it never happen."

"I didn't sleep the whole night."

"We've been on the road two days and nights. The wagon that took us to the train in Rawa Ruska turned over in the mud. It's a miracle we weren't hurt. One woman broke her arm. That's

why we missed the train we intended to take and had to wait
twenty hours for another. The Gentiles became unruly. They
wanted to cut off Moishele's earlocks. The Jew is helpless. If it's
this bad now, how will it be when the murderers come? People
shake in their skins."

"Mama, the Almighty will help," Moishe said. "There have
been many Hamans and they all came to a bad end."

"Before they came to their bad end, they killed off plenty of
Jews," Mother replied.

I had rented a room for Mother and Moishe in a kosher boardinghouse on Gnoyna Street. The proprietor was a Hasid. I called
a droshky to take them there, but Moishe said, "I don't ride in
droshkies."

"Why not?"

"The seat may be linsey-woolsey."

After lengthy discussion it was decided that Mother would
spread her shawl over the seat. Moishe had brought along a
basket that closed with a wire and a little lock—the kind once
used by yeshiva students. Mother carried her things wrapped in
a sheet. Passersby stopped to stare at us. The driver went slowly,
since the road was blocked by trolleys, taxis, freight wagons, and
buses. The nag looked skeletal; it limped. Moishe began to sway
and murmur. He was either commencing his morning prayers
or reciting Psalms.

Mother said, "Arele, child, for the fact that I've lived to see
you again, and about to be a bridegroom at that, I must thank
the Almighty, but why didn't your father, too, live to see it? He
studied the Torah almost to the last minute. I didn't realize
myself what a saint he was. Alas, I plagued him for dragging us
off to such a faraway hole, but he accepted it all in good spirits.
I eat my heart out now and don't sleep nights on account of
this. Whatever punishment is visited upon me I deserve. Arele,
I can't stay in Old Stykov any more. I don't want to speak against
Moishele's wife, my daughter-in-law—may she stay healthy and
strong—but I can't live with her. She's a country girl, her father

is a farmer. In Galicia, Jews were always allowed to own land. She does and says things that displease me. I hear well, thank God, but she screams into my ears as if I were deaf. Her mind is always on petty things. It's true that I've sinned, but how much can a person take?"

"Well, ah, well!" Moishe put two fingers to his lips—a sign that Mother's words were slander and that he wasn't permitted to speak now during prayer.

"*Well, ah well* here, and *well, ah well* there! Certainly my words are sinful, but what flesh and blood can suffer has a limit. She hates me because I read books and she barely knows how to pray. But what do I have now besides my books? When I open *The Duty of the Hearts* I forget where I am and what's become of me in my old age. Arele, I don't want to die in Old Stykov. True, your father is buried there, but the few years or months allotted me to creep around in this world I don't want to spend among boors. It's bitter for Moishele, too. They pay him no wages. On Thursdays the beadle goes around with a sack collecting handfuls of wheat, corn, and groats—the way the Russians pay their priests, beg the comparison. The Gentiles there are Ruthenians and some of them boast that Hitler is on their side. They fight among themselves, too. One of them chopped off a girl's head right outside our window, just because she'd been going around with another fellow. Our lives are in danger every minute. I pray for death. Each day I beg the Almighty to take me from here, but just because you want to die, you live."

"Well, ah well!"

"Stop with those *well, ah's*. You won't go to my Gehenna. Arele, I want to say something to you, but I don't want you to get angry at me. I will not go back to Old Stykov. Even if I have to sleep in the streets, I'll stay here in Warsaw."

"Mama, you won't sleep in the streets," I said.

"Have pity on me. I hear there's no longer a rabbi on Krochmalna Street. Maybe Moishele could get some job here? I myself am ready to go into an old-age home or wherever I can find a place to lay my head. What kind of girl is this Shosha? How did you happen to choose her? Well, it all comes from heaven."

The droshky pulled up before a gate on Gnoyna Street. Some of the courtyards here were over a hundred years old. There were alleys where farmers came at dawn with their produce from the nearby villages. Eggs were stored in lime in the cellars. In No. 3 was Krel's studyhouse, where I went to read a page of the Gemara on my own after I had left cheder. In No. 5 was a synagogue and another studyhouse. The ritual bath where my mother went when she was a young woman was still in operation nearby. Even the oil cakes, the chick-peas with beans, and the potato cakes sold here smelled as I remembered them.

Mother said, "Nothing has changed."

Several wagons were parked in front of the building where we had stopped. The horses were eating a mixture of oats and chopped straw from feedbags. Pigeons and sparrows pecked at the seeds dropped from them. Men in short sheepskin coats and caps carried sacks, crates, baskets. Through the partially frosted-over windows could be seen bottles, pots, diapers hanging to dry. From one window came the sound of children reciting a chant from the Pentateuch—a cheder. Muddy stairs led up to the boardinghouse on the third floor.

After each half flight, Mother paused. "I'm not used to climbing stairs any more."

On the third floor I opened a door leading off the dark hallway. The boardinghouse consisted of a sitting room and a few small rooms. In the sitting room one man prayed in his prayer shawl and phylacteries, another packed paper boxes into a sack, and a third ate his breakfast. Two women, one in a wig and the other in a bonnet, sat on a bench mending a fur coat with a huge needle and string. The proprietor, with a pitch-black beard and wearing a skullcap, showed us to a room with two beds, where Mother and Moishe would spend the night.

Moishe said, "It's getting late and I want to pray. Is there a house of worship here?"

"There are two prayer houses in the courtyard—one of the Kozienica Hasidim, the other of the Blendew Hasidim. There is a synagogue, too, but those who pray there are all Litvaks."

"I'll go to the Kozienica prayer house."

"Would you want some breakfast?" the proprietor asked Mother.

"Is it strictly kosher?"

"What a question! Rabbis eat here."

"Maybe a glass of tea for now."

"Something to nibble with it?"

"I've lost my teeth. Would you have some soft bread?"

"There isn't a thing I don't have." He went to fetch the bread and tea.

A washstand stood in one corner of the room, with a basin of water, a dipper, and a dirty towel hanging on a hook. Mother said, "Compared to Old Stykov, this is a mansion. We live in a shack with a straw roof. It leaks. There is a stove, but the flue is broken and the smoke won't go up through the chimney. When will I get to see the bride?"

"I'll bring her here."

2

IT WAS the first night of Hanukkah. The owner of the boarding-house lighted and blessed the first of the eight Hanukkah candles for his guests, but my mother and Moishe refused to accept another person performing so holy a ceremony for them. Besides, he had lighted a candle, not a wick in oil. I went down to the street and bought a tin Hanukkah lamp for them, as well as a bottle of oil, wicks, and a special candle called "the beadle," which is used for lighting the wicks. In their room, Moishe poured the oil into the first little bowl, put a wick in place, lit the beadle, touched the wick with it, and recited the benedictions. Then he began to chant the liturgy: "O Fortress, Rock of my Salvation . . ." These were my father's tunes, even his gestures. At first the wick refused to catch fire, and Moishe had to try to light it again and again. When it did burn finally, it smoked and sputtered. Moishe had placed the little lamp on the window according to the law, so that the miracle of Hanukkah should be shown to the world, even though the courtyard below had three blind walls and no one was there. The window was not tight; wind blew in. Every few seconds the little light fluttered, but it did not go out. Moishe said, "Just like the Jewish people. In each generation our enemies rise up to destroy us, and the Holy One, blessed be He, is saving us from their hands."

"It's high time our enemies should be praying for miracles," I said.

Moishe clutched his beard. "Who are we to tell Him what to do and when to do it? Only yesterday you told Mother that the more the astronomers ponder and measure the stars, the larger they become. You said that many of them are larger than the sun. So how can insignificant creatures like us, with our tiny brains, understand what He is doing?"

Moishe spoke with my father's voice. Only a few years ago my father was arguing with me: "You can spill ink but it won't write a letter by itself. The unbelievers are not only vicious but also fools."

Moishe left for the studyhouse after watching the Hanukkah light for half an hour. He found books there that he could never get in Old Stykov. With the little money he had, he bought *The Roar of a Lion, The Responsa of Rabbi Akiva Eiger,* and *The Face of Joshua.* He promised Mother he would not be late. She sat on her bed, propped up by a pillow, and her large gray eyes stared at the flickering light with curiosity, as if she were seeing such a light for the first time. I remembered her being medium in height, even somewhat taller than Father, but now she appeared shriveled. Her head kept nodding in a constant "yes,

yes, yes." Then she said to me, "Arele, God forbid, I don't intend to nag you, you are already an adult, I hope you outlive my bones, but what was the sense of it?"

"What do you mean?"

"You know very well what I mean."

"Mother, not everything one does has to make sense."

My mother's eyes showed the beginning of a smile. "What is it? Love?"

"You can call it that."

"There is a saying that love is blind, but even love isn't completely without reason. A shoemaker's apprentice would not fall in love with a princess, and he certainly would not marry her."

"Even this can happen."

"What? In novels, not in real life. When we lived in Warsaw, I used to read the novels serialized in the newspaper. Your father —peace be with him—disliked newspapers and their writers. He said that they defiled the holy Jewish letters. Only when the war broke out and he wanted to know the news did he glance into a paper. Even in those trashy novels there was some logic. Now you come and marry Shosha. True, she's a gentle child, unfortunately sick, perhaps a victim of her father, but couldn't you find something better in the whole of Warsaw? I'm sinning, I know I'm sinning. I shouldn't say these things. I'm losing the world to come. Look, the light is out!"

We sat in silence. The air smelled of burned oil and of something sweet and long forgotten. Then Mother went on, "My child, it's all so destined. My father, your grandfather—he should rest in peace—had the name of a genius. He could have become a rabbi in a big city, but he was content to stay in his little corner in a forsaken village, and there he remained until his end. Your paternal grandfather, the one from Tomaszów, hid from people altogether. All his years he wrote commentaries on the cabala. Before his demise, he called one of his grandchildren and told him to burn his manuscripts. Only one page was left accidentally, and those who read it maintained it was full of the mysteries of the Torah. He was so unworldly he did not know the difference between one coin and another. If your grandmother Temerl hadn't skimped and saved, there wouldn't have been a piece of bread in the house. She was a saint in her own right. When she went to visit the rabbi of Belz, he invited her to sit down on a chair even though she was a woman. What am I in comparison to them? I'm steeped in sin. Of course I love you, and I would like you to get a good wife, but if heaven ordains differently, I should have the power to curb my tongue. I say all this to remind you that you should remember your origin. We didn't come to this world to indulge in our passions. Look at me and see what happens to blood and flesh. I was a beautiful girl. When I passed Lublin Street, people stopped to stare. I had the smallest feet in town and I shined my shoes every day with polish, even when it rained. I used to polish them a hundred times with the brush. I had a pleated skirt, and every second day I ironed the pleats. People denounced me to your grandfather for being vain. How old was I altogether? Fifteen years. At fifteen and a half I became engaged to your father. A year later I was led to the wedding canopy. A girl is not allowed to study Torah, but I stood behind the door and listened as your grandfather lectured to the yeshiva boys. If one of them made a mistake, I knew it. I also began to look into morality books in Hebrew. By that time, I realized that I'm hot-blooded and that I had to control my impulses. How did this come to me? I hope to God that the children will take after you, not after Shosha."

"Mother, we won't have any children."

"Why not? Heaven wants there to be a world and Jews."

"No one knows what heaven wants. If God had wanted the Jews to live, He wouldn't have created Hitlers."

"Woe to me that you speak such things!"

"No one has ascended to heaven and spoken to God."

"One doesn't need to ascend to heaven, one can see the truth right here on earth. Three days before Meitel's Esther won the lottery, I saw in a dream the letter carrier handing me a paper full of numbers. I wanted to take it, but suddenly Meitel materialized—she was already dead then. Her face was yellow and she wore a white cowl. She said to me, 'It's not for you, my daughter Esther is going to win a lot of money on this.' And she handed the letter carrier a bunch of straw stalks. I was only a ten-year-old child at the time, I didn't even know that there was such a thing as a lottery. I told the dream to everybody in our house. They shrugged their shoulders. After three days a telegram came saying Esther had won the grand prize. When I had this dream they had not yet drawn the numbers. Two years later, I witnessed a case of a haunted house. For weeks an evil spirit kept on knocking on the window frame in the house of Abraham the ritual slaughterer. Soldiers were sent to search the rooms, the cellar, the attic, but nothing could be found to account for this racket. My child, the world is full of so many mysteries that if the scholars continued to study for a million years, they could not solve even a millionth part of them."

"Mother, all this cannot give comfort to the tortured Jews in Dachau, and in other such hells."

"The comfort is that there is no death. Your own Shosha told me her dead sister was visiting her. She's not shrewd enough to invent such a lie."

3

BASHELE intended to invite my mother and Moishe for either lunch or supper but Mother told me plainly she wouldn't eat in Bashele's house. Neither she nor Moishe had confidence that the food in her kitchen was strictly kosher. However, in order not to shame her, Mother and Moishe agreed to come for tea and fruit. I don't know how they learned that the late rabbi's wife and her two sons would be visiting Bashele's. Around three o'clock in the

afternoon when I brought them from the boardinghouse and
opened Bashele's door, I saw to my amazement a room full of
people: old women in bonnets of beads and ribbons, men with
white beards and sidelocks, also a few young men and girls, who,
it seemed, read the literary journal. There were tea glasses, Sabbath cookies, and saucers with gooseberry jam on the table, which
was covered with a holiday tablecloth. The old women had
brought little gifts wrapped in handkerchiefs—gingerbread, cake,
and cookies, raisins, prunes, almonds. My God, we were not completely forgotten on Krochmalna Street! The war, the epidemics,
and hunger had worked with the Angel of Death, but a few of
those who knew our family remained alive. Bonnets shook,
shrunken mouths mumbled blessings and greetings, reminisced
about former times. Tears rolled down faded cheeks. The men
had all been followers of the late rabbi of Radzymin. He had
passed away without an heir, and his court had disintegrated.
The Hasidim said that if the rabbi had consented to go through
an operation, he might still be living, but to the last day he was
true to his conviction that a knife is for cutting bread, not human
flesh. He gave up his sacred soul after long suffering. Rabbis from
the whole of Poland came to his funeral. He was buried near the
grave of his grandfather Rabbi Yankele, who waged war with
the demons all his life and performed countless miracles. It was
known that corpses came to him at night to confess their mis-
deeds while alive, and that his garret teemed with spirits.

While the Hasidim greeted Moishe and asked him about the
Hasidic courts in Galicia—the courts of Belz, Sieniawa, Ropczyca
—the young men and girls introduced themselves to me. They
praised the sketches and articles I wrote. They spoke to me in a
literary Yiddish with illiterate errors. They had heard about my
play that had failed and complained about the state of the Yiddish theater. Civilization was on the verge of collapse, but they
were still producing the kitsch plays of fifty years ago. Teibele
had come to the reception and she had brought with her her lover
the bookkeeper, a little man with a pointed belly and gold teeth

in the front of his mouth. Some of the girls gathered around Shosha. I heard one of them ask her, "How does it feel to be engaged to a writer?"

Shosha answered, "Nothing, just like a human being."

"How did you two come together?" another girl asked.

"We both lived in No. 10," Shosha said. "Arele lived in the apartment with the balcony. Our windows faced the courtyard just across the horse stable."

The girls looked at one another and smiled. They exchanged side glances that asked, "What does he see in her?"

Bashele had placed Moishe at the head of the table, with the old men on either side of him. Moishe hinted that it was not in the Hasidic tradition for men and women to sit at the same table, and Bashele put chairs for the old women in the middle of the room. The boys and the girls remained standing. The Hasidim continued to discuss Hasidic topics: What is the difference between the court of Belz and the court of Bobow? Why are the Hungarian rabbis against the world organization of Orthodox Jews? What kind of a saint is the rabbi of Rydnik? Is it true that the rabbi of Rozwadow has inherited the sense of humor of his great-grandfather, the rabbi of Ropczyca? They said it was a pity so little was known about the rabbis of Galicia in this part of the country.

"Why is it important to know?" Moishe asked. "Everyone serves God in his own manner."

"What do they say in Galicia about the tribulations of our time?" one of them asked.

Moishe answered the question with a question: "What is there to say? These are the birth pains of the Messiah. The prophet has already foreseen that at the End of Days the Lord will come with fire and with His chariots like a whirlwind to render His anger with fury and His rebuke with flames of fire. The evil ones don't surrender so easily. When Satan realizes that his kingdom is shaky, he creates a furor throughout the universe. There are dark powers even in the higher spheres. What is Nogah? Good and evil mixed together. The roots of evil reach as far as the legs of the Throne of Glory. Since God had to create a vacuum and dim His light in order to create the world, His face has to be hidden. Without diminishing the power of His radiance there would be no free choice. Redemption will not come at once but gradually. God's war with Amalek is going to last long and will bring great distress and many temptations. One of our sages said about the Messiah, 'Let Him come, but I don't wish to live to see Him.' The Mishnah has foreseen that before the Messiah comes human arrogance will reach its height and . . ."

"Woe to us, the water is up to our necks," said an old Hasid, Mendele Wyszkower, with a sigh.

"What? Evil possesses enormous powers," Moishe said. "In quiet times the vicious try to cover up their intentions and disguise themselves as innocent lambs. But in times of decision they reveal their true faces. Ecclesiastes has said, 'I saw under the sun the place of judgment, that wickedness was there.' The men of iniquity aspire to a world of murder, lechery, theft, and robbery. They want the iniquities to be considered virtues. Their aim is to erase the 'Thou shalt not' from the Ten Commandments. They scheme to put honest men in prison and thieves to be their judges. Whole communities degenerate. What was Sodom, with its judges Chillek and Billek? What was the Generation of the Flood? Who were the rebels who built the Tower of Babel? One sheep can make the whole herd leprous. One spark of fire can burn a mansion. Hitler—his name should be blotted out—is not the only villain. There are Hitlers in every city, in every community. If we forget the Lord for a second, we are immediately on the side of defilement."

"Oy, it's difficult, very difficult," said another old man, and he groaned.

"Where is it written that things have to be easy?" Moishe asked.

"Our strength is waning," a third old man moaned.

" 'They that wait upon the Lord shall renew strength,' " Moishe replied.

The old women kept still and cupped their ears to hear better. Even the young men and girls who had come to debate culture, literature, Yiddishism, and progress with me became silent.

Suddenly Shosha asked, "Mommy, is this really Moishe?"

There was laughter. Even the old women laughed with their toothless mouths.

Bashele became embarrassed. "Daughter, what's the matter with you?"

"Oy, Mommy, Moishele is a real rabbi, just like his daddy." Shosha covered her eyes with a handkerchief and cried.

4

TWO DAYS before my wedding it started to snow and went on without letup. When it finally stopped, frost set in. The streets were buried under drifts of snow as dry as salt. Not even sleighs could make their way through them. Huge icicles hung from the eaves and balconies. The wires running above the rooftops had grown thick and were glittering with sparks of frost. Here and there a bird's beak or a cat's head peeped from the snow. On Krochmalna Street the Place was deserted. Little snow eddies swirled—imps trying to catch their own tails. The thieves, whores, and pimps were hiding in their cellar rooms or garrets. The vendors who usually sat before Yanash's Court vanished.

The wedding was to take place at eight that evening at a rabbi's on Panska Street. With Zelig's contribution, Bashele had been able to prepare a modest trousseau for Shosha—a few dresses, shoes, and underwear—but I had made no preparations of any kind. From the short pieces I sold and a little money I got from my publisher for translating, I had scratched together enough for my mother's and Moishe's expenses at the boarding-house, but I had very little left.

On my wedding morning, I rose later than usual. I had stayed awake and could hear the chiming of the grandfather clock and the wailing of the wind until daybreak. It was ten by the time I got out of bed and began to wash and shave.

Tekla pushed open the door. "Shall I bring your breakfast?"

"Yes, Tekla—if you feel like it."

She left and soon came back. "A lady has come with flowers for you."

I had planned to keep everything secret. I started to tell Tekla to let no one in, but at that moment the door opened and I saw Dora. She wore a faded coat, boots, and a hat that looked like an upside-down pot. She held a bouquet wrapped in heavy paper. Tekla grimaced and turned her head.

Dora said, "My dear, there are no secrets. Congratulations!"

My cheeks were covered with soap. I put down the razor and asked, "What kind of nonsense is this?"

"Don't you know you can't keep anything from me? It's true you didn't ask me to the ceremony, but there will always be a kinship between us. No one can erase the years we spent together. Here—may it be with happiness and prosperity."

"Who told you about it, eh?"

"Oh, I have connections. Someone who works with the Secret Service would know everything that goes on in Warsaw."

Dora was referring to the Stalinists who, ever since she had left the Party, had accused her of being an agent for the Polish Secret Police.

I took the flowers from her reluctantly and stuck them into the jug that held my wash water.

Dora said, "Yes, I know everything. I've even had the honor of meeting your bride."

"How did you accomplish that?"

"Oh, I knocked on her door and pretended I was collecting for some charitable cause. I spoke Yiddish to her but she didn't understand what I was talking about, and I thought, She speaks only Polish, but I soon saw that she doesn't know Polish too well either. I don't want to needle you. Since you love her, what difference does it make, anyway? People fall in love with the blind, the deaf, the hunchbacked. May I sit down?"

"Yes, Dora, do sit down. You shouldn't have spent money for flowers."

"I wanted to bring something. I have my reasons. I'm getting married too, and if I give you a wedding present, you'll have to give me one. I have an ulterior motive for everything I do." Dora blinked and sat on the edge of the bed. Rivulets of melted snow ran from her boots onto the floor. She took out a cigarette and lit it.

"Felhendler?" I asked.

"Yes, my dearest. We're both renegades, Fascists, traitors, and provocateurs. Could there be a more perfect match? We'll stand together on the barricades and shoot the workers and peasants. That is, if we don't happen to be in prison at the time. Do the reactionaries know that we're their friends? By the way, what happened to that play you were supposed to have written? You drifted away from me, but I remember each hour we spent together. When something of yours is published, I read it not once but three times. I hear that Dr. Feitelzohn is planning to put out a magazine."

"He's been planning this magazine for years."

Tekla opened the door with her toe and brought in my breakfast tray.

I asked, "Would you join me, Dora?"

"I've had breakfast already, thank you, but I would have a glass of coffee." While Tekla went to bring the coffee, Dora looked around. "Will your wife come to live here with you or will you move in with her?" she asked. "I'm nosy as always."

"I don't know anything yet."

"I don't understand you—but what's the point of upsetting you with questions? You don't know the answer, anyway. As for me, I don't love Wolf. We're too much alike. Lately, he's become exceedingly sarcastic. He keeps making those awful jokes. Our being together is futile, anyway. Either he'll be arrested or I'll be arrested. The police play with us like cats with mice. But so long as we remain on this side of the bars, we don't feel like being alone. As soon as he leaves the house, I start looking up at the ceiling for a hook. When I go downstairs I have to cross the street to avoid my former comrades. If they see me, they spit and shake their fists. You once told me things that I didn't grasp at the time, but since all this has happened, they're starting to come back to me."

"What things?"

"Oh, that you can't help mankind and that those who worry too much about the fate of man must sooner or later become cruel. How did you know this? I hardly dare say it, but I lie in bed next to him and I think of you. He's both ironic and grim. He smiles as if he knows the final truth and I can't stand that smirk, because he smiled the exact same smile when he was a Stalinist. Just the same, I can't be alone any more."

"He moved in?" I asked.

"I can't pay the rent by myself. He got some kind of part-time job in a union."

The door opened again and Tekla came in with a glass of coffee. Her eyes sparkled with laughter. "Miss Betty is here with flowers," she announced.

Before I could answer, Betty appeared on the threshold in a blond fur coat, a fur hat to match, and fur-trimmed boots. She carried a huge bouquet. When she saw Dora she took a step backward. An urge to laugh came over me. "You, too?"

"May I come in?"

"Of course, come in, Betty."

"It's some blizzard outside! Seven witches must have hanged themselves."

"Betty, this is Dora. I've told you about her. Dora, this is Betty Slonim."

"Yes, I know—the actress from America. I recognize you from your picture in the newspaper," Dora said.

"What shall I do with the flowers?"

"Tekla, could you bring a vase?"

"All the vases are full. The mistress keeps kasha in them."

"Bring whatever there is. Take the flowers."

Tekla held out her hand. She seemed to be doing everything in a mocking fashion.

Betty began to hop up and down in her boots. "A terrible frost. You can't cross the street. It's the way it used to be in Moscow. It's like this in Canada, too. In New York they clear away the snow—at least on the main streets. Help me off with my coat. Now that you're about to marry, be a gentleman."

I helped Betty off with her coat. She was wearing a red dress that clashed with her red hair. She looked pale and thin. She said, "You're probably wondering why I came. It's because you bring flowers for a bridegroom and you bring flowers for a corpse, and when the bridegroom is also a corpse, he deserves a double bouquet." She spoke the words as if she had prepared them in advance.

Dora smiled. "Not badly said. I'll be running along. I don't want to disturb you."

"You're not disturbing anybody," Betty said. "What I have to say everyone can hear."

"Shall I bring more coffee?" Tekla asked.

"Not for me," Betty said. "I've had maybe ten glasses today already. May I smoke?"

Betty took out a cigarette, lit it, and after a while offered one to Dora. Both women seemed to fence momentarily with the tips of their cigarettes. It was like the remnant of some heathen rite.

5

DORA still sat on the bed. I had given Betty my chair and I sat on a bench by the washstand. Betty spoke of Eugene O'Neill, one of whose plays had been translated into Yiddish. She would be appearing in it in Warsaw. She said, "I know it's going to be a flop. They don't understand O'Neill even in America, so how will the Warsaw Jews understand him? The translation isn't any good, either. But Sam insisted that I appear in Poland before we go back to America. Oh, how I envy a writer! He doesn't have to deal with people all the time. He sits at his desk with paper and pen and says whatever he wants. But actors are always dependent on others. At times the urge to write comes over me. I've tried to write a play—a novel, too—but I read what I've written and I don't like it, and I tear it up on the spot. Tsutsik—may I still call you Tsutsik?—here in Poland the situation is deteriorating fast. Sometimes I worry about getting stuck here."

"With an American passport, you've got nothing to worry about," Dora said. "Even Hitler wouldn't start up with America."

"What's a passport? A piece of paper. And what's a play? Paper, too. And what are reviews? Again, paper. Well, and traveler's checks and banknotes are also only paper. One time when I couldn't sleep I started thinking—there was once a Stone Age; now we're in the Paper Age. Some tools have remained from the Stone Age, but from the Paper Age nothing will remain. At night the most bizarre thoughts come to mind. Once, I woke up and began musing about my genealogy. I know only a little bit about my grandfathers and nothing at all about my great-grand-fathers and great-grandmothers. Well, and what about the great-great-grandfathers? I figured that when you go back enough generations, everyone stems from thousands of forebears, and from each of them he has inherited some trait. By day, this is nothing more than a passing thought, but at night it becomes terribly relevant and even scary. Tsutsik, you write about dybbuks. The past generations are our dybbuks. They sit within us and usually remain silent. But suddenly one of them cries out. The grandmothers aren't so dreadful, but the grandfathers terrify me. A person is literally a cemetery where multitudes of living corpses are buried. Tsutsik, has this ever occurred to you?"

"All kinds of crazy things occur to me."

"Among the generations there have probably been madmen, and their voices must be heard," Betty went on. "I'm not only a cemetery—in my brain there's an insane asylum, too. I hear the lunatics shriek their wild laughter. They pull at the bars and try to escape. Heredity cells aren't lost. If man is descended from an ape, he carries the genes of an ape in him, and if from a fish, there is something of the fish in him, too. Isn't that funny and frightening at the same time?"

Dora crushed the butt of her cigarette. "Excuse me, Miss Slonim, but did you ever consider that such thoughts have a social undertone? If you have the right pieces of paper, as you've described them—the passport, the checks, the ticket to America —you can indulge in the luxury of probing into all kinds of vagaries. But if you must pay the rent the next day and don't have a groschen and you're apt to be forced out into the cold and they're about to put you in jail for some crime you haven't committed and you're hungry besides—that's when you concentrate on reality. Ninety percent of mankind—ninety-nine percent—is uncertain of its tomorrow, and often of its today. What they have to concern themselves with is the most basic needs. When writers like H. G. Wells or Hans Heinz Evers, or maybe even our own Aaron Greidinger, come out with fantasies about wars between planets or about a girl with two dybbuks who want to get married—excuse me for being so blunt—they're talking to each other. I never read the writer O'Neill, but I have a feeling he's one of those who spin dreams. Miss Slonim, you should appear

in something that touches everybody. Then you will be understood and you will have an audience. Forgive my frankness."

Betty bristled. "What should I play in? A propaganda piece
preaching Communism? First, I'd be arrested and they'd close
down the theater. Second, I come from Russia and I've seen what
Communism really is. Third . . ."

"I'm not proposing you should do a Communist play," Dora
interrupted her. "How could you? No one knows any more where
Stalinism ends and Fascism—or whatever you choose to call it
—begins. Still, it remains a fact that the masses suffer and their
suffering grows steadily worse. If the Nazis attack Poland, it's the
poor who will be the victims. The rich will all flee abroad. If
you can show a bank book with a hundred thousand dollars and
if you travel strictly for pleasure, then the whole world is open to
you. They'll even let you into Palestine if you can show one
thousand pounds sterling. Is that true or not, Aaron?"

"A novel or a play that said all this wouldn't change anything,"
I said. "The masses already know that's how things are. Besides,
you said before the very opposite of what you're saying now."

"I didn't say the opposite. I have my doubts, but the masses
remain dear to me. They should be taught how to resist this ex-
ploitation."

"Dora, you speak of the masses as if they were innocent lambs
and only a few villains are responsible for the human tragedy.
Actually, a large part of the masses themselves want to kill,
plunder, rape, and do what Hitler, Stalin, and tyrants like them
have always done. Chmielnitsky's Cossacks weren't capitalists,
neither were Petlura's murderers. Petlura himself was a pauper
right up to the time Schwartzbard did him in. He starved in
Paris."

"Who sent a hundred thousand soldiers to die at Verdun?
Wilhelm and Foch."

"Wilhelm and Foch couldn't have sent them unless a big
enough percentage had been willing to go. The ugly truth is
that a great number of men—young men in particular—have a

passion to kill. They only need a pretext or a cause. One time, it's for religion; another, it may be for Fascism or to defend democracy. Their urge to kill is so great it surpasses their fear of being killed. This is a truth forbidden to utter, but true nonetheless. Those Nazis ready to kill and die for Hitler would under other circumstances be as ready to do the same for Stalin. There hasn't been a foolish ambition or an insanity for which people weren't ready to die. If the Jews were to become independent, you could start a war between the Litvaks and the Galicianers."

"If that is true, then there is no hope."

"Who says there is?"

"A hypocrite!" Betty said after Dora had gone. "I've seen her ilk in Russia. They put on leather jackets, hung revolvers at their hips, and became Chekaists. Now they're being liquidated. They richly deserve it. Tsutsik, come kiss me. For the last time."

· CHAPTER TWELVE ·

1

I N THE afternoon more snow began to fall. A dusky murkiness showed through the windowpanes. The sky loomed low, gray, neither cloudy nor clear but looking as if, through some change in creation, the world had acquired another climate. Where was it written that the Ice Age couldn't suddenly come back? What was to prevent the earth's tearing loose from the gravitational force of the sun and straying from the Milky Way in the direction of some other galaxy? After Dora and Betty left, it grew quiet in the apartment. The telephone didn't ring, nor did Tekla come to straighten up and take away the tray. I lay down in my clothes on the unmade bed and closed my eyes.

Around seven-thirty I'd have to take a droshky, a sleigh, or a cab and go to the boardinghouse on Gnoyna Street where my mother and Moishe were waiting for me. Mother was undoubtedly sitting on a chair or on the bed, waiting absorbed in *The Duty of the Hearts,* which she had brought with her. My marriage to Shosha had robbed her of the last hope of returning to Warsaw. Moishe was probably in the studyhouse browsing through books there. He hadn't uttered a word against Shosha, but his eyes laughed momentarily when he first heard her name. The boys in the cheder where he went used to mimic Shosha. I was sure he was thinking that those who strayed from the path of righteousness also strayed when it came to worldly matters. Well, and what about Feitelzohn, Celia, and Haiml? Even Teibele had reacted with a hint of contempt when she heard I would be marrying her sister. I had already determined never to take Shosha to the Writers' Club. They would ridicule her—and me.

Evening fell abruptly. My room grew dark. The sky had acquired a violet tinge. I got up from my bed and stood at the window. The passersby were not walking but struggling against the blizzard; occasionally they danced with the whirlwind. Vast piles of snow transformed the street into valleys and hills. What are the sparrows doing now? I wondered. According to Spinoza, the frost, the birds, and I were all modes of the same substance. But one mode whistled, whined, and drove a cold wave from the North Pole; a second hid in a hole in a wall, shivering and starving; a third was getting ready to marry Shosha.

It wasn't yet seven when I went outside to find a droshky. I had put on my good suit and a fresh shirt. Haiml and Celia had reserved a room in a hotel for us in Otwock, where we would spend a week. This was to be their wedding gift and our honeymoon, and I had packed a satchel with manuscripts, some clothing, and a toothbrush. I did it all with the feeling that it was never my decision but that some unknown power had decided for me. The illusion of free choice had vanished from within me. Perhaps this is the way all people marry? Perhaps this is how men steal, murder, go to war, commit suicide? Something in me laughed. The fatalists are right after all. I'll never blame anyone for anything. I waited in front of the gate for fifteen minutes, but all the sleighs and taxis that passed were taken. Nor were any of the trolleys with their frosted-over windows heading in the direction of Gnoyna. I started off on foot, carrying the satchel, and the snow sprayed my face at an angle. My eyelids became swollen. The snow-covered street lights cast trails of fog. I stumbled along in the wintry chaos with the uncertainty of a blind man. Even though I wore rubbers, my feet were soon wet. I passed Solna and

Electoralna Streets, and from Zimna came out on Gnoyna. How would I take Mother and Moishe through such a storm to Panska? She could barely take a step in normal weather. I glanced at my wristwatch, but I couldn't read the numbers on the dial.

I climbed the three flights of wet and slippery stairs that led up to the boardinghouse. Mother sat in the living room in a velvet dress, a silk kerchief over her head, her face pointed and white. I could see in her eyes both a pious acquiescence in God's verdicts and a tinge of worldly irony. Moishe had already put on his rabbinical fur-lined coat with the mangy collar and his broad-brimmed hat. There were other men and women in the place, guests who had spent the night there, possibly stranded in Warsaw by the snowstorm. They apparently knew who was expected and guessed the circumstances, for when I came in a tumult broke out and a clapping of hands.

Someone exclaimed, "Mazel tov, the groom is here!"

A whirl of steam covered my face and for a moment I saw nothing and heard only a mixture of male and female laughter.

A youth—he may have been an employee of the house—volunteered to go downstairs and help us get a sleigh or droshky. Mother wasn't able to climb in, and I had to lift her and place her in her seat. Moishe didn't forget to be suspicious that the seat cover was of forbidden cloth, and he spread his handkerchief over it for a partition. The droshky had already started off when I realized I didn't have my satchel. I began to shout to the driver to stop. At that moment the youth—Mother designated him an angel from heaven—raced up and threw it in beside me. I wanted to reward him, but I had no change. I yelled my thanks and the wind blew my words away. The droshky's canopy was up; it was dark inside. I heard Moishe say, "Well, thank the Almighty you came. It was getting late and we were afraid something had happened. You know how Mother worries."

"I couldn't get a droshky. I had to walk the whole way."

"God forbid you didn't catch a cold," Mother said. "Ask Bashele to give you an aspirin."

"It all comes from heaven, it's all from heaven," Moishe said. "In everything man does there are obstacles so that he can discern the hand of Providence. If everything were to go smoothly, man would say, 'My power and the might of mine hands hath gotten me this wealth.' When evildoers achieve success, they believe it to be due to their own ability, but not always is the path of evil successful. That Hitler—may his name be blotted out—will be dealt his punishment, nor will Stalin, that wicked monster, have his way either."

"Until they receive their deserved punishment, who knows how many innocent people will perish," Mother said.

"Eh? Accounts are kept in heaven. Rabbi Sholom Belzer once said, 'Not a pinch of snuff is ignored in the Celestial Council of Justice!' He who knows the truth relies completely on God."

The droshky dragged along, rocking. From time to time the horse stopped, turned his head, and glanced back, seemingly wondering why people should drive in weather like this. The driver said in Yiddish, "On a night like this, a droshky is no good and a sleigh is worthless, too. On a night like this, it's good to sit by the stove and eat broth with noodles."

"You'll have to give him a few groschen more," Mother whispered.

"Yes, Mama, I will."

When we got to the rabbi's, everyone was waiting: Shosha, Bashele, Zelig, Teibele, Feitelzohn, Haiml, Celia. They greeted me with smiles, winks. Celia's eyes seemed to ask, Are you really so blind? Or do you see something the others can never see? Maybe they had suspected I would change my mind at the last minute. Mother's old-fashioned clothes brought a condescending expression from the rebbitzen, a stout woman in a black curled wig; she had a broad face and a huge bosom. There was not a trace of feminine well-wishing in her stern gaze. Counting the rabbi and his son—a swarthy youth with hardly any earlocks and the stiff collar of a half Hasid, half dandy—there were seven males present, and the rabbi sent his son out to collar three men from the courtyard or the street to complete the quorum.

Shosha had on a new dress. Her hair done in a pompadour and her high-heeled shoes made her look taller. When we came in, she stretched out her arms and made a gesture as if to run up to us, but Bashele indicated to her that she should stand still. Bashele had brought a bottle of wine, a bottle of whiskey, and a bag of cookies. The rabbi, a tall, erect man with a pointed black beard, didn't appear pious like my father or Moishe, but a worldly person, all business. There was a telephone in his apartment. Mother and Moishe looked at each other, surprised. It never occurred to Father to install a gadget like this in his house.

Since Zelig had already deposited a thousand zlotys with a lawyer to be paid to Bashele after the divorce, the former husband and wife avoided each other. Zelig paced to and fro in a black suit, a stiff collar, and a tie with a pearl stickpin. His shoes squeaked. He was smoking a cigar. He was already properly drunk, as befitted a member of the burial society. He called Mother *"mechutayneste"* (in-law), and reminded her of the time when we had been neighbors. Feitelzohn was having a conversation with Moishe, displaying his knowledge of the Gemara and the Midrash. I heard Moishe say to him, "You are a scholar, but erudition demands practice."

"For that you need what I lack—faith," Feitelzohn replied.

"Sometimes the faith comes later."

Feitelzohn had already met Shosha at Celia's. He had praised her childish beauty to me, said that she reminded him of an English girl friend of his of olden times, even spoke of having Shosha take part in some future soul expedition of his, together with me. He added, "Tsutsik, in my eyes she has a million times more charm than that American actress—what is her name? If you would have married her, I would have considered it a degradation."

The rabbi sat down to fill out the marriage contract. He wiped the point of his pen on his skullcap. When he asked if the bride was a virgin, Zelig replied, "Certified."

The rabbi's son came back with three men dressed in padded jackets, heavy boots, fur caps. One wore a rope tied across his

loins. They didn't want to wait for refreshments until after the
ceremony and immediately poured themselves glasses of whiskey.
Their faces, raw from the cold outside, blackened and wrinkled
from age and hard work, expressed disdain for all the hopes of
the young. Their moist eyes behind bushy brows were saying,
Just wait a few years and you will know what we know. From
behind the stove the rabbi's son brought a canopy and four poles.
The rabbi quickly read the ketubbah, the marriage contract
written in Aramaic. He swallowed words. I promised Shosha two
hundred gulden in the event I divorced her, and the same sum
of money from my heirs should she be widowed.

I hadn't bought a wedding ring. Bashele told me that no
jeweler would be able to supply a ring to fit Shosha's index
finger, which was as slender as a child's. Bashele now gave me the
ring that Zelig had given her over thirty years ago. I would use it
just for that occasion. She burst into tears when the rabbi began
to chant the holy words. Teibele wiped a tear from her left eye
with a corner of her handkerchief. Shosha moved her lips several
times, as if about to ask or to say something, but each time
Bashele shook her head in warning.

I noticed that my mother was barely able to stand. From time
to time she wavered and took hold of Moishe's shoulder. Moishe
swayed as if he were mumbling a prayer.

Haiml and Celia had planned a reception for us at a restaurant, but it had to be canceled. Mother and Moishe let it be
known that they didn't trust the big-city restaurants to be strictly
kosher. Besides, the last train to Otwock, where a room stood
ready for Shosha and me, departed too early to leave enough time
for a reception. Bashele had packed a supper for us to eat on the
train. Mother and Moishe intended to go back to Old Stykov the
first thing the next morning. Haiml and Celia would take them
to the station. When Shosha and I returned from Otwock, we
would move in with the Chentshiners.

I knew that all who were present at the ceremony—perhaps
even Bashele and Shosha herself deep down where a vestige of

sane judgment always remains—felt that I was committing a terrible folly, but the general mood was a kind of jubilant solemnity. Feitelzohn, who was wont to make jokes even at funerals to show how consistent he was in his cynicism, conducted himself almost paternally. He squeezed my hand and wished me good luck. He bent down and gallantly kissed Shosha on her little hand. Haiml and Celia both cried.

Zelig said, "Getting married and dying are two things you can't avoid." And he handed me a stack of banknotes wrapped in tissue paper.

Mother wasn't crying. I hugged and kissed her, but she didn't kiss me back. She said, "Since you went ahead and did it, it was obviously ordained."

2

THE TRAIN was scheduled to leave at twenty to twelve, but at midnight it still hadn't moved. The car in which we were seated was empty. The tiny gas lamp blinded more than it illuminated. Bashele and Teibele, who escorted us to the train, had gone home. It was nearly as cold in the car as outside, and I put on the two sweaters I had packed in my satchel. Shosha had brought along a fur collar and a muff that may have come from before the war and had undoubtedly belonged to her mother. The collar had a fox head with two glass eyes. Shosha pressed against me and her body vibrated, like that of some small animal.

Had we made a mistake and boarded an empty train that was scheduled to stand all night in the station? I wanted to take a look in the other cars, but Shosha clung to me and said she wouldn't be left alone. Eventually we heard a whistle and the train began to glide hesitantly over the slippery rails.

Shosha opened the bag Bashele had given us and we ate a

cold meal. Everything she did took a long time: untying the
bag, deciding which portion was meant for her and which for me.
She seemed to waver at every bite. I had promised Haiml and
Celia, those generous benefactors of ours, that when we lived
with them Shosha would help out with the housekeeping chores,
since Celia's Marianna had gone off to be married, but Shosha's
indecision each time she had to make the pettiest choice convinced me that she would be of little use. She picked up a slice
of sour pickle and it fell from her fingers. She took a crumb of a
roll, then put it down again. Her slim fingers had almost no
nails and I could not make out whether she had bitten them off
or whether they had stopped growing. She began to chew and
somehow forgot that she had food in her mouth.

We rode past the Praga cemetery, a city of headstones envel-
oped in snowy shrouds, and Shosha said, "Here lies Yppe."

"Yes, I know."

"Oh, Arele, I'm afraid!"

"Afraid of what?" I asked.

Shosha didn't answer and I assumed she had forgotten what I
had asked. Then she said, "The train may get lost."

"How? A train runs on tracks."

Shosha thought this over.

"Arele, I won't be able to have children. The doctor once
said I'm too narrow. You know where."

"I don't want children. You are my child."

"Arele, are you my husband already?"

"Yes, Shoshele."

"And I'm really your wife?"

"According to the law."

"Arele, I'm afraid."

"What are you afraid of now?"

"Oh, I don't know. Of God. Of Hitler."

"So far, Hitler is in Germany, not here. As to God . . ."

"Arele, I forgot to bring along my little pillow."

"We'll be back in a week and you'll have your pillow again."

"Without my pillow I won't be able to fall asleep."

"You'll sleep. We'll lie in one bed."

"Oh, Arele, I'm going to cry." She burst out in a clamor, like a little girl. I put my arms around her. She trembled and I felt the beating of her heart. I counted her ribs through her dress.

The conductor came in to punch the tickets. He asked, "Why is she crying?"

"Oh, she forgot to bring along her pillow."

"Your daughter, eh?"

"No. Yes."

"Don't cry, little girl. You'll get another pillow." He threw her a kiss and left.

In the midst of crying, Shosha began to laugh. "He thought you're my daddy?"

"That's what I am."

"How is that possible? You're fooling!"

She became still and I put my cheek against hers. She shivered from the cold, but her cheek felt hot. I was cold, too, yet at the same time I was overcome by a desire different from any I had felt before—passion without association, without thought, as if the body, the corporeal stuff, were acting on its own. I listened to my desire and it struck me that if metal could feel, my feeling was that of a needle drawn to a magnet.

Shosha must have read my mind, because she said, "Oh, your beard pricks like needles!"

I started to answer her, but the wheels made a scraping sound, then came to a halt. We were somewhere between Wawer and Miedzeszyn. A white wasteland stretched beyond the other side of the pane. It had stopped snowing and the sky reflected the snow. For all the frost, it seemed to glow of an other-worldly summer.

The conductor came by and announced hastily that the rails were iced over.

"Arele, I'm afraid!"

"Afraid of what?"

"Your mother has grown so old. She looks near death."

"She's not that old."

"Arele, I want to go home."

"Don't you want to be with me?"

"Yes, with you and with my mommy."

"In a week, not before."

"I want it now!"

I didn't answer. She laid her head on my shoulder. A feeling of despair settled over me, together with the comfort brought about by the awareness that I was not responsible for this entanglement. In the half darkness I winked to my other self, my mad dictator, and congratulated him on his droll victory. I closed my eyes and felt the warmth flowing from Shosha's head to my face. What did I have to lose? Nothing more than what everyone loses anyway.

3

WE WERE the only passengers to get off in Otwock. There was no one from whom to ask the way to the hotel, and we wandered into a wooded area. I must have been half asleep. I started to address someone—it turned out to be a tree. Shosha had become strangely silent. All of a sudden a man materialized as if from the ground and conducted us to the hotel. A servant had been sent to meet us at the station but had missed us. He mumbled who he was and remained mute all the way. He walked so quickly that Shosha could barely follow him. Every few minutes he became lost among the trees and then emerged again in a midnight game of hide-and-seek.

The room they gave us was in the attic and was large and cold. It had one big brass bed and a narrow cot, each with huge pillows and heavy blankets. It smelled of pine and lavender. Through a pane that was not frosted over one could see pines laden with snow-covered cones and draped with icicles like the Christmas trees of the Gentiles. Shosha was ashamed to undress before me, and I had to stand facing the window while she got ready for bed. I had assumed that wandering astray through the cold woods would put Shosha in a panic, but the real danger seemed to have left her indifferent. I saw her reflection in the clean part of the windowpane as she took off her camisole and put on her nightgown. After fussing a long time with buttons and hooks, she got into bed. "Arele, it's cold as ice!" she exclaimed.

Shosha demanded that I lie on the cot, but I lay down beside her. Her body was warm, while mine was half frozen. In my cold arms she fluttered like a sacrificial chicken. Except for her little breasts, which were those of a girl just starting to mature, she was skin and bones. We lay together quietly and waited for the bedding to warm up. Cold came in through the window frame, and the panes rattled. From time to time the wind whistled and dropped to a drawn-out moan like that of a woman giving birth. Sometimes a wailing of different voices could be heard, as if packs of wolves were roaming the Otwock forests.

"Arele, it aches."

"What is it?"

"You're sticking me with your knees."

I pulled my knees away.

"My stomach is rumbling."

"It's my stomach, not yours."

"No, it's mine. Do you hear? Like the crying of a baby."

I felt her abdomen. She shook. "Cold fingers!"

"I'll warm myself on you."

"Oh, Arele, you're not allowed to do this to a female."

"Shoshele, you're my wife."

"Arele, I'm ashamed. Oh, you're tickling me!" Shosha began to laugh, but abruptly the laughter turned into a sob.

"Why are you crying, Shoshele?"

"It's all so strange. When Leizer the watchmaker came to read what you wrote in the newspaper, I thought, How can this be?

Is he actually there? I took out the papers you had painted with the colors and they had dried out. We went to look for you at the newspaper and an old man, the one who serves the tea, yelled, 'Not here!' We didn't go back. One evening I played with a shadow on the wall and suddenly it jumped down and slapped me. Oh, you have hair on your chest! I lay sick all year and Dr. Kniasler said I would die."

"When was this?"

She didn't answer. Even as she was talking, she fell asleep. Her breath came quick and soft. I pulled her closer, and in her sleep she cuddled up to me with such force it was as if she were trying to bore inside my guts. How can such a weak creature give off so much heat? I wondered. Is there a physiological reason for it? Or does it have to do with the mind?

I closed my eyes. The tremendous urge for Shosha that had seized me in the train had dissipated. Was I suddenly impotent? I fell asleep and dreamed. Someone shrieked wildly. Animals with long teats dragged me, tore chunks from me with fang and claw. I was wandering through a cellar that was also a slaughter-house and a cemetery strewn with unburied corpses. I awoke excited. I grabbed Shosha, and before she could even wake up, I mounted her. She choked and resisted. A stream of hot blood burned my thigh. I tried to pacify her, but she broke out in a wail. I was sure she had awakened everyone in the hotel. Had I injured her? I got out of bed and searched for the light switch, but I couldn't find it. I tapped around and bumped into the stove. In my distress I prayed to God to protect her.

"Shoshele, don't cry! People will come running! It was all out of love."

"Where are you?"

I found the switch and turned on the light. For a moment I couldn't see. There was a washstand here with a pitcher of water and two towels hanging at the side. Shosha was sitting up in the bed, no longer crying.

"Arele, am I a wife now?"

4

ON OUR third day in Otwock, while I was sitting with Shosha in the hotel dining room eating lunch, I was summoned to the telephone. The call was from Warsaw. I was sure it would be Celia, but it turned out to be Feitelzohn.

"Tsutsik, I have good news for you."

"Good news for me? That's something I hear for the first time."

"Yes, good news. But first tell me how things are going with the honeymoon."

"Fine, thanks."

"No crises?"

"Yes, but—"

"Your Shosha didn't die of fright?"

"Nearly. But now she is happy again."

"I like her. With her at your side, your talent will grow."

"From your mouth to God's ears."

"Tsutsik, I told Shapiro, the editor of the evening paper—what's it called?—that you're writing a novel about Jacob Frank, and he wants you to write Frank's biography for him. He wants to print it in six installments a week and pay you three hundred zlotys a month. I told him that was too little and he may up it a few zlotys."

"Three hundred zlotys is too little? That's a fortune!"

"Some fortune! Tsutsik, you're made! He told me you'll be able to drag the thing through a year, or as long as your imagination holds out."

"That really is a stroke of fortune!"

"Are you still moving in with the Chentshiners."

"Now I won't do it. Shosha will pine away without her mother."

"Don't do it, Tsutsik. You know I'm not jealous of you. Just the opposite. But to live there wouldn't be a good idea. Tsutsik, I'll go bankrupt from this call. We'll celebrate when you come back. Regards to Shosha. Adieu."

I wanted to tell Feitelzohn how grateful I was and that I would pay for the call, but he had already hung up. I went back to the table. "Shoshele, you've brought me luck. I have a job on a newspaper. We won't be moving in with Celia!"

"Oh, Arele, God has answered me. I didn't want to be there. I prayed. She tries to take you away from me. What will you do on the paper?"

"Write the life of a false Messiah who preached that God wants people to sin. The false Messiah himself slept with his own daughter and with the wives of his disciples."

"He had such a wide bed?"

"Not all at the same time—or maybe all together, too. He was rich enough to afford a bed as wide as all Otwock."

"You knew him?"

"He died some hundred and fifty years ago."

"Arele, I pray to God, and everything I ask for He does. When you went to the post office, a blind man came up and I gave him ten groschen, and that's the reason God did all this. Arele, I love you so terribly! I'd like to be with you every minute, every second. When you go to the toilet I start to worry that you may have gotten lost or fallen. I miss Mommy, too. I haven't seen her for so long. I would like to be with you and with her day and night for a myriad of years."

"Shoshele, your mother will be divorced soon and she may remarry. And it will be impossible for me to be with you every minute. In Warsaw I'll have to go to the editorial office, to the library. Sometimes I'll have to meet Feitelzohn. It was he who got me the job."

"He has no wife?"

"He has many women, but not one wife."

"Is he the false Messiah?"

"In a way, Shoshele—that's not a bad comparison."

"Arele, I want to tell you something, but I'm ashamed."

"You have nothing to be ashamed of before me. I've already seen you naked."

"I want more."

"More what?"

"I want to lie in bed. You know what."

"When? Now?"

"Yes."

"Wait, the waitress hasn't brought us our tea yet."

"I'm not thirsty."

The waitress came with two glasses of tea and two slices of sugar cake on a tray. We were the only guests in the hotel. Another couple was expected but not until the next day.

It had stopped snowing and the sun shone. I had been planning to take a walk with Shosha, maybe as far as Świder. I wanted to see if the river was frozen over and how the waterfall looked with its huge icicles gleaming in the sun, but Shosha's words changed everything. The waitress, a short woman with a broad face, high cheekbones, and liquid black eyes, didn't turn back to the kitchen right away. She said, "Mr. Greidinger, you eat everything up, but your wife leaves everything. That's why she's so thin. She barely touched the appetizer, the soup, the meat, the vegetables. It's not good to eat so little. People come here to gain weight, not to lose."

Shosha made a face. "I can't eat so much. I have a small stomach."

"It's not the stomach, Mrs. Greidinger. My grandmother used to say, 'The intestine has no bottom.' It's the appetite. My boss here lost her appetite and she went to a Dr. Schmaltzbaum. He gave her a prescription for iron and she gained back ten pounds."

"Iron?" Shosha asked. "Can you eat iron?"

The waitress laughed, exposing a mouthful of gold teeth. Her eyes contracted to the size of two berries. "Iron is a medicine. No one is told to eat nails." She walked away, scraping her large shoes across the floor. When she reached the kitchen door, she cast an amused glance back toward us.

Shosha said, "I don't like her. I like only you and Mommy. I like Teibele too, but not as much as you two. I would like to be with you a thousand years."

5

THE NIGHT was long. We went to sleep before nine and at twelve we both awoke. Shosha asked, "Arele, you don't sleep any more?"

"No, Shoshele."

"Neither do I. Every time I wake up I think it was all a fairy tale—you, the wedding, everything. But I touch you and I see you are here."

"Once there was a philosopher and he believed that everything was a dream. God is dreaming and the world is His dream."

"Is this written in the books?" Shosha asked.

"Yes, in the books."

"Yesterday—no, the day before yesterday—I dreamed that I was home and you came in. After you closed the door you came in again. There was not one Arele, but two, three, four, five, ten —a whole row of Areles. What is a dream?"

"No one knows."

"What do the books say?"

"The books don't know, either."

"How can this be? Arele, Leizer the watchmaker said that you are an unbeliever—is this true?"

"No, Shoshele, I believe in God, but I don't believe that He revealed Himself and told the rabbis all the little laws that they added through generations."

"Where is God? In heaven?"

"He must be somewhere."

"Why doesn't He punish Hitler?"

"Oh, He doesn't punish anybody. He created the cat and the mouse. The cat cannot eat grass, she must eat flesh. It's not her fault that she kills mice. The mice are certainly not guilty. He created the wolves and the sheep, the slaughterers and the chickens, the feet and the worms on which they step."

"God is no good?"

"Not as we see it."

"He has no pity?"

"Not as we understand it."

"Arele, I'm afraid."

"I'm afraid too, but Hitler won't come tonight. Move over to me. So."

"Arele, I want to have a child with you, a little baby with blue eyes and red hair. The doctor said that if they cut up my belly a living child would come out."

"And you would want that?"

"Yes, Arele. Your child. If it should be a boy, he would read the same books as you."

"It isn't worth cutting up a belly to read books."

"It's worth it. I would suckle him and my breasts would grow bigger."

"They are big enough for me."

"What else is written in the books?"

"Oh, all kinds of things. They found out that the stars run away with us. Myriads of miles every day."

"Where do they run?"

"Into empty space far away."

"They will never come back?"

"They will be extinguished and get cold first, and then they will fall back with such might they will grow hot, and the whole swinish business will begin all over again."

"Where do the books say Yppe is?"

"If there is a soul, she is somewhere. And if there isn't any, then—"

"Arele, she was here. She knows about us. She came to wish me mazel tov."

"When? Where?"

"Here. Yesterday. No, the day before yesterday. How does she know that we are in Otwock? She stood at the door, near the mezuzah, and she smiled. She wore a white dress, not a shroud. When she was alive, two of her front teeth were missing. Now she has a full mouth of teeth."

"There must be good dentists in the hereafter."

"Arele, are you making fun of me?"

"No, I'm not."

"She came to me in Warsaw, too. It was before you visited us for the first time—I sat on my stool and she came in. The door was bolted. Mother was out, and she told me to bolt the door because of the hoodlums. Suddenly Yppe was there. How could she do it? She spoke to me, like one sister to another. I had undone my hair, and she braided it. She played cat's cradle with me, but without string. And then that day before Yom Kippur I saw her in the chicken soup. She had a wreath of flowers on her head, like a Gentile bride, and I knew that something was going to happen. You were there, but I didn't want to say anything. When I mention Yppe, Mother screams. She says that I'm crazy."

"You are not crazy."

"What am I?"

"A sweet soul."

"What do you make of it?"

"You might have dreamed it."

"In the middle of the day?"

"Sometimes one dreams in the daytime."

"Arele, I am afraid."

"What are you afraid of this time?"

"The sky, the stars, the books. Tell me the story about the giant. I forget his name."

"Og, the king of Bashan."

"Yes, about him. Is it true that he could not get a wife because he was so big?"

"That is the story. When the flood came and Noah and his sons and all the animals and fowl went into the Ark, Og could not enter because he was so big, and he sat on the roof. Forty days and forty nights it rained on him, but he didn't drown."

"Was he naked?"

"What tailor could sew a pair of pants big enough for him?"

"Oy, Arele, it is good to be with you. What will we do when the Nazis come?"

"We will die."

"Together?"

"Yes, Shoshele."

"The Messiah isn't coming?"

"Not so quickly."

"Arele, I just remembered a song."

"What song?"

Shosha began to sing in a thin voice.

> *"He was called Beans,*
> *Noodles was her name,*
> *They married on Friday*
> *And nobody came."*

She cuddled up to me and said, "Oy, Arele, it's good to lie with you even if we die."

· *CHAPTER THIRTEEN* ·

1

Iᴺ ᴛʜᴇ afternoon paper where the biography of Jacob Frank—
it was actually a blend of biography and fantasy—had already
been dragging on for months, the news worsened. Hitler and
Mussolini had met at the Brenner Pass and no doubt reached
decisions regarding the destruction of Poland and the Jews, but
a large part of the Polish press kept attacking the Jewish minority
as if it were the nation's greatest danger. Representatives of the
Hitler government came to Poland and were received by the
dictator, General Rydz-Śmigly, and his ministers. In the Soviet
Union the purges, mass arrests, and trials of Trotskyites, old Bolsheviks, right- and left-wing dissidents, Zionists, and Hebrewists
became a permanent terror. In Polish cities, unemployment grew.
In the villages, particularly where Ukrainians and White Russians lived, the peasants starved. Many *Volksdeutschen,* as the
Germans in Poland called themselves, proclaimed themselves
Nazis. The Comintern had dissolved the Polish Communist
Party. The charging of Bukharin, Kamenev, Zinoviev, and Rykov
with sabotage and espionage and the designation of them as
Fascist lackeys and agents of Hitler evoked protests even from
sworn Stalinists. But circulation did not drop in the Yiddish
newspapers in Warsaw, including the afternoon daily for which

I worked. On the contrary, more newspapers were read now than
before. The story of the false Messiah Jacob Frank and his disciples had to end, but I was ready with a list of other false Mes-
siahs—Reuveyni, Shlomo Mulkho, Sabbatai Zevi.

There was a time when I had to make up some pretext whenever
I came home late or didn't come home at all, but gradually Bashele
and Shosha became accustomed to asking no questions. What did
they know about the writing profession? I had told Leizer the
watchmaker that I served as night editor a couple of times a week,
and Leizer had explained the facts to Bashele and Shosha. Leizer
came by each day and read to them the latest installment of my
biography of Jacob Frank. Everyone on Krochmalna Street was
reading it—the thieves, the streetwalkers, the old-line Stalinists,
and the new-fledged Trotskyites. Sometimes when I walked down
the street I heard the market vendors talking about Jacob Frank
—his miracles, orgies, and lunacies. The leftists still complained
that this kind of writing was an opiate for the masses, but after
they finished reading the political news on the front page and
the local news on page 5 the masses needed an opiate.

Before I moved into the alcove at Bashele's she had had the
walls painted and installed an iron stove, and thrown out the
sacks and rags that had been accumulating for twenty-odd years.
Shosha couldn't be by herself even an hour. The moment she
was left alone she was overcome by melancholy. On the other
hand, I couldn't be with her all the time. I had never given up
my room on Leszno Street or told my landlords that I was married. True, I seldom spent nights there, but even Tekla had
learned that writers are impulsive and confused creatures. She
had stopped asking what I did, whom I spent time with, where I
dragged around in the nights. I paid my rent and each week I
gave her a zloty. On Christmas and Easter I brought her a gift.
Every time I gave her something, she flushed, protested that she
didn't need it, that it wasn't necessary. She would seize my hand
and kiss it, as peasants had done for generations.

Because I couldn't be with Shosha all the time, coming home to her was always a wonder to me. She and Bashele had food ready for me to eat before I lay down—rice with milk, tea with a Sabbath cookie, a baked apple. Each night before coming to bed Shosha washed herself and often washed her hair as well. She discussed with me the latest installment of the Jacob Frank story. How could a man have so many women? Was it black magic? Had he sold his soul to the devil? How could a father have doings with his own daughter? Sometimes Shosha provided the answer: those were different times. Didn't King Solomon have a thousand wives? She remembered what I had told her when we lived at No. 10.

Basically, Shosha had stayed the same—the same childish face, the same childish figure. Still, changes had become apparent. In former times, Bashele had been the only one to prepare our meals. She hadn't let Shosha go near the kitchen or entrusted her with the marketing. She only sent her occasionally to the nearby store for a half pound of sugar, a few ounces of butter, a piece of cheese, or a loaf of bread—all bought on credit. I doubted whether Shosha knew the value of coins. Suddenly I observed her bustling about in the kitchen. She accompanied her mother to market in Yanash's Court. I heard her discussing with Bashele the vegetarian dishes that wouldn't upset my digestion. This concern for my diet always baffled me. I wasn't accustomed to anyone's paying attention to my needs. But to Shosha I was a husband, and to Bashele a son-in-law. It had never occurred to me that Shosha could sew or darn, but one day I saw her darning my socks over a tea glass. She began to look after my shirts, handkerchiefs, and collars, and to take my shoes to be heeled at the shoemaker's. I couldn't, or didn't want to be a husband in the accepted sense of the word, but Shosha gradually assumed the duties of a wife.

When I came home in the evenings I still found her seated on her stool, but no longer surrounded by playthings. Nor did she read her schoolbook any more. Surprises constantly awaited me.

Shosha would be wearing shoes with high heels and flesh-colored stockings not only when she went visiting but also at home. Her mother had bought her dresses and nightgowns with lace. Occasionally she changed the way she wore her hair.

Shosha's interest in my writing increased. The novel about Jacob Frank had come to an end. The new novel, about Sabbatai Zevi, described with much detail the Jewish longing for redemption in an epoch that displayed similarities to our own. What Hitler threatened to do to the Jews Bogdan Chmielnitsky had done some three hundred years earlier. From the day they were exiled from their land, Jews had lived in anticipation of death or the coming of the Messiah. In Poland, in the Ukraine, in the lands ruled by the Turks, and most of all in the Holy Land, cabalists sought to bring the End of Days through prayers, fasts, the utterance of holy names. They probed the mysteries of the Book of Daniel. They never forgot the passage in the Gemara which stated that the Messiah would come when the generation was either totally innocent or totally guilty. Every day, Leizer had to read to Shosha the latest installment and explain to her the references to Jewish law and Jewish history. I heard her say to her mother, "Oh, Mommy, it's exactly like today!"

Teibele still hadn't found a husband. She had been choosy so long, Bashele complained, that she had become an old maid. Instead of a husband, she had taken a lover, a married bookkeeper with five children. Any day, he was allegedly going to divorce his wife, who was a common piece, but two years had gone by with no divorce in sight. Instead of satisfaction, Teibele provided her mother only with shame.

Teibele would often visit her mother and sister. She, too, liked to discuss Jacob Frank, Sabbatai Zevi, and their disciples with me. She brought small gifts for Bashele and Shosha, and occasionally for me as well—a book, a magazine, a notebook. Her lover was spending more and more nights at home with his wife. He had turned out to be a hypochondriac, Teibele said. He had convinced himself that he suffered from heart trouble. When

Bashele reminded Teibele that it was getting late and she shouldn't be starting for home at such an hour, Teibele said in jest, "I'll lie down with them," pointing at Shosha and me. Or she would say, "What difference does it make? We're all doomed anyhow."

At night in bed, Shosha no longer talked about dolls, toys, children of neighbors she had known twenty years ago, but quite often she spoke of things I cared about. Was there truly a God up in heaven? Did He know every person's thoughts? Was it true that He loved Jews above all other people? Did He create the Gentiles, too, or only the Jews? Sometimes she questioned me about my novel. How could I be sure of what had occurred several hundred years ago? Had I read it in a book or did I make it up in my head? She asked me to tell her what would occur in the installment tomorrow and in the days after. I began to tell her things I hadn't yet written. I conducted a literary experiment with her—let my tongue wag freely and say whatever came to my lips. I had read and heard from Mark Elbinger about automatic writing. I had also read in a literary magazine about the kind of literature called the "stream of consciousness." I could test all this on Shosha. She listened to everything with the same sense of curiosity—children's stories I had heard from my mother when I was five or six; sexual fantasies no Yiddish writer would have allowed himself to publish; my own hypotheses or dreams about God, world creation, immortality of the soul, the future of mankind, as well as reveries of triumph over Hitler and Stalin. I had constructed an airplane of a material whose atoms were so densely compressed, one square centimeter weighed thousands of tons. It flew at a speed of a million miles a minute. It could pierce mountains, bore through the earth, reach to the farthest planets. It contained a clairvoyant telephone that tuned me in to the thoughts and plans of every human being on earth. I became so mighty I rendered all wars obsolete. When the Bolsheviks, Nazis, anti-Semites, swindlers, thieves, and rapists heard of my powers, they promptly surrendered. I instituted a world order based on Dr. Feitelzohn's philosophy of play. In my airplane I kept a harem of eighteen wives, but the queen and sovereign would be no one other than Shosha herself.

"And where would Mommy be?"

"I would give Mommy twenty million zlotys and she would live in a palace."

"And Teibele?"

"Teibele would become a princess."

"I would miss Mommy."

"We'd come to see her every Sabbath."

For a long time Shosha didn't speak. Then she said, "Arele, I miss Yppe."

"I would bring Yppe back to life."

"How is this possible?"

I elaborated to Shosha the theory that world history was a book man could read only forward. He could never turn the pages of this world book backward. But everything that had ever been still existed. Yppe lived somewhere. The hens, geese, and ducks the butchers in Yanash's Court slaughtered each day still lived, clucked, quacked, and crowed on the other pages of the world book—the right-hand pages, since the world book was written in Yiddish, which reads from right to left.

Shosha caught her breath. "Will we live in No. 10?"

"Yes, Shoshele, on the other pages of the book we still live in No. 10."

"But different people have moved in."

"They live there on the open pages, not the closed ones."

"Mommy once said that before we moved in, a tailor used to live there."

"The tailor lives there, too."

"Everyone together?"

"Each in another time."

I had gradually ceased being ashamed of Shosha. She dressed better, she appeared taller, I took her to Celia's, and both Celia and Haiml were enchanted by her simplicity, her honesty, her naïveté. I had taught her how to handle a knife and fork. She spoke in a childish fashion, but not stupidly.

On one visit Celia had detected a similarity between Shosha and her own deceased daughter. She showed me a yellowed photograph of the child and it struck me, too, that there was a certain resemblance. Haiml, who was growing ever more inclined toward mysticism and occultism, played with the idea that the soul of their little girl might have transmigrated into Shosha and that I was actually his and Celia's son-in-law. Souls weren't lost. They came back and sought bodies through which to reveal themselves to their loved ones. There was no such thing as chance. The forces that guided man and his fate always united those who were destined to meet.

Elbinger happened to be visiting the Chentshiners that evening and he repeated what he had said about Shosha on an earlier occasion—that he thought she possessed the qualities of a medium. All true mediums that he had met displayed the same primitivism, directness, sincerity. Once, he made an attempt to hypnotize Shosha, and as soon as he told her to, she fell into a deep sleep. Elbinger had trouble waking her. Before leaving, he kissed Shosha's forehead.

After Elbinger had gone, Shosha said, "He is not a person."

"What is he?" Haiml and Celia asked in unison.

"I don't know."

"An angel? A demon?" Celia asked.

"Perhaps from the sky," Shosha replied.

Haiml clapped his brow. "Tsutsik, this is a memorable evening for me. I won't forget this evening as long as I live!"

2

THIS Friday night, as always, I came home to Shosha. I did not keep the Jewish laws, Shosha did not go to the ritual bath, but I yielded to Bashele and pronounced the benediction over the wine on Friday night and on Saturday morning. Bashele prepared vegetarian Sabbath meals for me. She even baked a vegetarian Sabbath stew with kasha and beans and a kugel made of rice and cinnamon. Shosha blessed the candles every Friday before dusk. She put them in silver candlesticks that Haiml and Celia had given us. Two challahs were covered with a cloth that Bashele had embroidered thirty years ago for Zelig. The family also owned a knife with a handle made of mother-of-pearl on which the words "Holy Sabbath" were engraved. That Friday evening Bashele and Shosha ate gefilte fish with chicken, and for me they made noodles with cottage cheese and carrot stew. They put on their Sabbath clothes and dressy shoes. Through the open window I saw the Sabbath candles in other apartments and heard table chants. The simple Jews sang, "Peace and light to the Jews on the day of rest and the day of joy." The Hasidim sang a cabalist poem by the Holy Isaac Luria, written in Aramaic, about a heavenly apple orchard, a heavenly bridegroom and bride, heavenly bridesmaids and best men—all in highly erotic verses that would shock readers and critics even today. Bashele and Shosha conversed about the facts that food was getting more expensive and that it was increasingly difficult to find a place to hang the wash in the attic. Bashele mentioned with nostalgia the custom of past years to spread yellow sand on the floors before the Sabbath. Peasants from nearby villages used to bring carts of the sand in wooden kegs. They called out their merchandise in the streets. Now this was out of fashion. Today women liked to shellac their floors. Another thing, pious matrons used to go from house to house on Friday and collect challah, fish, and tripe—even cubes of sugar—for the poor. The new generation did not believe in this kind of charity. The Communists came in and asked for money for the Jews in Birobidjan, a region deep in Russia, somewhere at the edge of the world. They said that there was a Jewish land there. Only God knows if they were telling the truth.

"Mommy, what comes after the edge of the world? Is it dark there?"

Bashele shook her head. "You tell her, Arele."

"There is no edge of the world. The earth is round like an apple."

"Where do the black people live?" Shosha asked.

"In Africa."

"And where is Hitler?"

"In Germany."

"Oh, they used to teach us all this in school but I could never remember," Shosha said. "Is it true that in America there is a big Jewish man who must sign every dollar or the money isn't worth anything? Leizer the watchmaker said so."

"Yes, Shoshele. But he doesn't sign by hand. They print his signature."

"On the Sabbath one shouldn't talk about money," Bashele said. "There was a pious little rabbi, Reb Fivke, and on the Sabbath he spoke only in the Holy Tongue. He lived on Smocza Street, but on Friday he used to go around with a sack in Yanash's Court and collect food for the poor. After twelve o'clock on Friday he stopped talking, because Friday afternoon is almost as sacred as the Sabbath. When they gave him alms he just nodded or he mumbled some words in the Holy Tongue. One Friday he didn't come with his sack and someone said that he was sick in the poorhouse. After a few weeks he came again with his sack, but he had stopped talking altogether. He just went from store to store like a mute man. Someone said that he had had an operation on his throat and they cut out his windpipe. One Friday he entered a butcher shop and the butcher gave him some chicken feet or a gizzard. A man from the burial society—a gravedigger—happened to be in the store, and when he saw Reb Fivke, he let out a terrible scream and fainted. Reb Fivke immediately disappeared. They revived the gravedigger with cold water and by rubbing his temples with vinegar, and when he came to himself he swore a holy oath that Reb Fivke had died, that he had buried him himself. People couldn't believe it and said that the man was mistaken, but Reb Fivke never came again. Some curious men investigated the matter and they found his widow. He had been dead for months when this happened. I know, because Zelig still used to come home once in a while and the gravedigger was his best chum."

"As far as I know, your former husband does not believe in such things," I said.

"Now he believes in nothing. Then he was still a decent person," Bashele said.

"Oh, I will be afraid to go to sleep," Shosha said.

"Nothing to be afraid of," Bashele said. "Good people don't become spiteful after death. Just the opposite. Sometimes a corpse doesn't realize that he is dead and he leaves his grave and walks among the living. I heard of a man who came home when his family was sitting shiva for him. He opened the door and when he saw his wife and daughters sitting on low stools in their stocking feet, the mirror covered with a black sheet, and his sons with rended lapels, he asked, 'What's going on here? Who died?' And his wife, who was a mean shrew, answered, 'You!' At that moment he vanished."

"Oh, I'm going to have bad dreams."

"Just say, 'In Thy hands I commend my soul,' and you will sleep peacefully," Bashele advised.

After the dessert, Bashele served tea with Sabbath cookies she baked herself. Then I went out with Shosha on a walk from No. 7 to No. 25; one could walk that far safely even at night. Farther there was danger of being attacked by some hooligan or drunk. On some streets there were Jewish stores that were kept open on the Sabbath, but not on Krochmalna Street. Only one tea shop had its door half open on the Sabbath, and the customers drank tea on credit. Even the Communists were not allowed to pay in cash. Bashele remembered times when gangsters used to attack young couples or newlywed pairs and make them pay a few groschen a week in order not to be molested. But this took place in past years, she told me. At the time of the revolution in 1905 the socialists waged war with the toughs of the underworld, and many thieves, pimps, and racketeers were beaten up. A number of brothels were destroyed and the whores dispersed. The brothels and the thieves came back, but the racketeers disappeared forever.

Shosha and I walked. We passed the almost empty Place. When we reached No. 13, across the street from No. 10, Shosha stopped. "Here we lived once."

"Yes, you say it every time we pass."

"You stood on the balcony and caught flies."

"Don't remind me of that," I said.

"Why not?"

"Because we do to God's creatures what the Nazis do to us."

"Flies bite."

"They must bite. This is the way God created them."

"Why did God create them this way?" Shosha asked.

"Shoshele, there is no answer to this."

"Arele, I want to look inside the gate of No. 10."

"You've done it a thousand times already."

"Let me."

We crossed the street and looked into the dark courtyard. Everything remained as it had been twenty years before, except that most of the tenants had died. Shosha said, "Is there still a horse in the stable? When we lived here the horse was brown and it had a white patch on its nose. How long can a horse live?"

"About twenty years."

"Why not longer? A horse is so strong."

"Sometimes a horse lives until thirty."

"Why not until a hundred?"

"I don't know."

"When we lived there a demon entered the stable at night and plaited little braids in the horse's tail, and in its mane," Shosha said. "The demon mounted the horse and rode it from wall to wall all night long. In the morning the horse was wet from perspiration. It had foam on its mouth. It almost died. Why do demons do such things?"

"I'm not sure it's true."

"I saw the horse that morning. It was all wet. Arele, I want to look into the stable. I want to see if the horse is still the same."

"It's dark in the stable."

"I see a light there."

"You see nothing. Let's go."

We continued to walk until we reached No. 16. Then Shosha stopped. This was always a sign that she wanted to say something. Shosha could not walk and talk.

"What is it, Shoshele?"

"Arele, I want to have a child with you."

"Why suddenly?"

"I want to be a mother. Let's go home. I want you to do to me you know what."

"Shoshele, I told you, I don't want any children."

"I want to be a mother."

We turned back and Shosha said, "You go away to the newspaper and I am lonesome. I sit there and queer thoughts come to my mind. I see funny faces."

"What faces?"

"I don't know. They grimace and say things I don't understand. They are not people. Sometimes they laugh. Then they all begin to wail like at a funeral. Who are they?"

"I don't know. You tell me."

"They are many. Some of them look like soldiers. They ride horses, too. They sing a sad song, a silent song. I am frightened."

"Shoshele, you're imagining things. Perhaps you're dreaming."

"No, Arele. I want a child to say kaddish for me when I die."

"You'll live."

"No, they call me to go with them."

We passed No. 10 again, and Shosha said, "Let's look inside the gate."

"Again?"

"Let me!"

· CHAPTER FOURTEEN ·

1

HAIML's father died and left Haiml buildings and real estate worth several million zlotys. Friends and relatives advised Haiml to move to Lodz, where he could keep a closer eye on his main properties, but Haiml said to me, "Tsutsik, a person is like a tree. You can't chop it from its roots and plant it in other ground. Here, I have Morris, you, my friends from the Poale Zion. Somewhere in the cemetery here lie the bones of my little daughter. In Lodz I'd have to look at my stepmother's face each day. The main thing is, Celia would feel unhappy there. Who would she have to talk to? Let there only be peace in the world and we'll get through the years somehow where we are."

At one time Feitelzohn planned to go back to America, but he had long since given up this plan. From Palestine a number of his friends wrote that if he were to come there, there was a good possibility of a position at the Hebrew University in Jerusalem, but Feitelzohn refused. "The German Jews run things there," he told me. "Many of them are more Prussian than the Prussians. I would fit in about as well as you would fit in among Eskimos. I'll have to sneak through my years somehow without universities."

We all lived for the present—the whole Jewish community.

Feitelzohn compared this epoch to the year 1000, when the Christians in all Europe awaited the Second Coming and the destruction of the world. So long as Hitler didn't attack, so long as no revolution or pogrom erupted, each day was a gift from God. Feitelzohn often recalled his beloved philosopher, Veihinger, and his philosophy of "as if." The day will come when all truth will be recognized as arbitrary definitions, all values as rules of a game. Feitelzohn toyed with the plan of building a play-temple for ideas, for samples of cultural diversions, for systems of behavior, for religions without revelations—a kind of theater where people would come to act out their thoughts and emotions. The audience would be the performers. Those who hadn't yet decided what kind of games they preferred would participate in soul expeditions with him or with someone of his caliber to discover what would amuse or inspire them most.

I heard Feitelzohn say, "Tsutsik, I know very well that it's all sheer nonsense. Hitler wouldn't accept any other game but his own. Neither would Stalin, nor even some of our own fanatics. But I lie in bed at night and imagine a world of all play—play-gods, play-nations, play-marriages, play-sciences. What happened to mathematics after Lobachevsky and Riemann? What is Kantor's ℵ or the "set of all sets" or Einstein's theory of relativity? Nothing but wordplay. And what are all these parts of the atom that grow like mushrooms after a rain? And what is the receding universe? Tsutsik, the world goes in your direction—everything is becoming fiction. Why are you grimacing, Haiml? You're more of a hedonist than I am."

"Hedonist shmedonist," Haiml answered. "If we're fated to die, let us die together. I have an idea! In the Sochaczów study-house the greatest joy came on the second evening of a holiday. Let us establish in our house that *every day* should be the second evening of a holiday. Who can forbid us to create our own calendar, our own holidays? If all life is nothing but make-believe, let us make believe that every night is the second night of a holiday. Celia will prepare a festive meal for us, and we'll make

kiddush, sing table chants, and talk about Hasidism. To me,
Morris, you are my rebbe. Your every word is filled with wisdom
and love of God as well. There is such a thing as heretical fear
of God. You can sin and still be God-fearing. Sabbatai Zevi wasn't
the liar he was made out to be. The true Hasid isn't so afraid of
sin. You can frighten a non-Hasid with Gehenna and the bed
of nails, but not us. Since everything is supposed to be a part of
the godhead, why is Gehenna inferior to paradise? I'm looking
for pleasure, but to be joyous today people need noisy music,
vulgar chansonettes, women in chinchilla furs, and who knows
what else, and even then gloom prevails. I go to Lurse's, to the
Ziemianska. They sit there gazing into magazines with pictures
of whores and dictators. There's not even a trace of the bliss we
used to have in the Sochaczów studyhouse, with its torn books, a
kerosene ceiling lamp, and a bunch of bearded Jews with untidy
earlocks and ragged satin gaberdines. Morris, you know it, and
Tsutsik, you know it, too. If God needs a Hitler and a Stalin and
icy winds and mad dogs, let Him have them. I need you, Morris,
and you, Tsutsik, and if there is no merciful truth, I take the lie
that gives me warmth and moments of joy."

"One day we will move in with you," Feitelzohn said.

"When? When Hitler stands at the gates of Warsaw?"

Haiml proposed to Feitelzohn that he publish the magazine he
had been planning for years and write a book about the revival
and modernization of the play called *Hasidis*. Haiml would
finance both and have them translated into a number of languages. All great and revolutionary experiments had originated
and been conducted in precarious circumstances, Haiml contended. He suggested that the first temple of play be built in
Jerusalem, or at least in Tel Aviv. The Jews, Haiml said, unlike
the Gentiles, hadn't spilled blood in two thousand years. Jews
were perhaps the only group that played with words and ideas
instead of with swords and guns. According to Jewish legend,
when the Messiah came, Jews would go to the Land of Israel not
on a metal bridge but on one made of paper. Well, and could

it be mere chance that the Jews dominated Hollywood, the world press, the publishing houses? The Jew would bring the world deliverance of play and Morris Feitelzohn would be the Messiah.

"Before I become the Messiah," Feitelzohn said to me, "maybe you could lend me five zlotys?"

2

I STAYED the night with Haiml and Celia. For some time, my relations with Celia had become platonic. There were times when I ridiculed this word and what it meant, but neither Celia nor I had had much interest lately in sexual experiments. Both she and Haiml still tried to persuade Feitelzohn and me, with Shosha, to move into their apartment and live like one family. Lately, Celia had turned gray. Haiml had mentioned that she was under a doctor's care and that in normal circumstances she would have gone to Carlsbad or Franzenbad or some other spa, but he never said what was wrong with her.

That night, as so often before, the conversation ended with the question why were we not leaving Warsaw, and each of us gave more or less the same answer. I couldn't leave Shosha. Haiml wouldn't go without Celia. Besides, what was the sense of running away when three million Jews remained? Some rich industrialists in Lodz had run away to Russia in 1914 and three years later were murdered by the Bolsheviks. I could see that Haiml feared more the bother of travel than the persecution of the Nazis. I heard Celia say, "If I felt that I still had the strength to begin over, I wouldn't remain here another day. My mother and grandmother as well as my father all died at my age—in fact, younger. I keep myself going only with the force of inertia, or call it what you will. I don't want to go to a foreign land and lie sick in some hotel room or hospital. I want to die in my own home. I don't want to rest in a strange cemetery. What more can Hitler do to me? I don't recall who said it, that a corpse is all-powerful, afraid of no one. All the living want and ever hope to achieve the dead already have—complete peace, total independence. There were times when I was terrified of death. You couldn't mention the word in my presence. When I bought a newspaper, I quickly skipped over the obituaries. The notion that I would one day stop eating, breathing, thinking, reading, seemed so horrible that nothing in life agreed with me any more. Then gradually I began to make peace with the concept of death, and more than that—death became the solution to all problems, actually my ideal. Today when I'm brought the newspapers I quickly turn to the obituaries. When I read that someone has died, I envy him. The reasons I don't commit suicide are first, Haiml—I want to go together with him—and second, death is too important to absorb all at once. It is like a precious wine to be savored slowly. Those who commit suicide want to escape death once and for all. But those who aren't such cowards learn to enjoy its taste."

We went to sleep late. Haiml began to snore immediately and I could hear Celia turning in her bed, sighing, murmuring. She put on the night lamp and put it out. She went to the kitchen to make herself tea, perhaps to take a pill. If everything was nothing but a game as Feitelzohn maintained, our love game was over, or at least postponed indefinitely. It was actually more his game than ours. I always felt his presence when I was with her. Often when Celia talked to me she repeated almost literally things he told me. She had acquired his sex jargon, caprices, mannerisms. She called me Morris and by some of his pet names. Whenever our love play failed, Feitelzohn was lying between us. I even imagined that I could smell the aroma of his cigar. It was dawn when I fell asleep. The morning came up cloudy and a bit damp —it had rained in the middle of the night—but there were signs that it would be clearing later. After breakfast I went to Shosha's and stayed there for lunch. Then I left for my room on Leszno Street. Although it would have been quicker to go down Iron

Street, I walked on Gnoyna, Zimna, and Orla. On Iron Street
you were vulnerable to a blow from a Polish Fascist. I had laid
out my own ghetto. Certain streets were always dangerous. Other
streets you could walk boldly by day but not at night. Still others
had remained more or less safe for the present. The corner of
Leszno and Iron Streets always posed a measure of danger.
Although I had turned away from the Jewish path, I carried the
diaspora upon me.

As I came closer to the gate, I started to run. Safe inside, I
caught my breath. I climbed the three flights of stairs slowly. I
had lots of work to do this day and in the days to come. I was
behind with my novel for the newspaper. I had promised a story
for a literary anthology. I had started another novel about the
Sabbatai Zevi movement in Poland. This was intended to be a
serious work, not for serialization in an afternoon daily. I rang
the bell and Tekla opened the door. She was polishing the corridor floor and had her dress tucked up over her bare legs.

She smiled and said, "Guess who called three times last evening?"

"Who?"

"Guess!"

I mentioned several names, but she shook her head. "You give
up?"

"I give up."

"Miss Betty."

"Betty from America?"

"She is here in Warsaw."

I was silent a moment. Feitelzohn had learned from one of the
American tourists that Sam Dreiman had died and left Betty a
large share of his inheritance, and that Sam's widow and children
had contested the will. Now Betty had come to Warsaw. And
when? At a time when every Jew in Poland was dreaming of
escape. Even as I stood there marveling, the telephone rang and
Tekla said, "It's her. She said she'd call in the morning."

3

ALTHOUGH it didn't seem to me so long ago since Betty had returned with Sam Dreiman to America, I barely recognized the woman I faced that day at the Hotel Bristol. She looked years older, middle-aged. Her hair had become thin and was no longer naturally red but an ugly mixture of yellow and red. Her face beneath the rouge and powder appeared somehow broader and flatter; there were wrinkles, and traces of hair on her upper lip and chin. Had she been ailing all this time? Had she grieved so over Sam's death? Something had happened to her teeth, and I noticed a spot on her neck she had not had before. She wore a kimono and slippers. She measured me from head to toe and back again, then said, "Already completely bald? Who wore you out so? I thought you were taller. Is it possible at your age to start shrinking? Well, don't take it seriously, I live entirely by my impressions. I lack all sense for what they call objective truth. I hardly recognized Warsaw. Even the hotel didn't seem the same. Before we left Poland I collected a whole stack of photographs of you and the others, but they got lost along with many of my papers. Sit down, we must talk. What can I offer you? Tea? Coffee? . . . Nothing? What's the sense of nothing? I'll order coffee."

Betty ordered coffee by phone. She spoke in a mixture of Polish and English.

She sat down in an easy chair facing me and said, "You're probably wondering why I came, particularly at such a time. I wonder myself or, to put it more accurately, I've stopped wondering not only about what others do but about my own actions as well. You probably know that Sam is dead. He went back to America and I believed he was well. He threw himself into his business as energetically as ever. Suddenly he dropped dead. One second he was alive, the next he was dead. For all my grief, I envied him. To people like me, death is a long process. We begin dying just as we're starting to mature."

Her voice had also changed—it was hoarser, somewhat shrill. The waiter rang and rolled in a silver service on a cart. It had coffee, cream, and hot milk. Betty handed him a dollar.

We drank our coffee and Betty said, "Everyone aboard ship kept asking the same thing: 'Why are you going to Poland?' They were all going to Paris. I told them the truth, that I have an old aunt in Slonim—the very city whose name I bear—and I wanted to see her before she died. They all believe that today or tomorrow Hitler will start the war, but I'm not so sure. What good would a war do him, since whatever he wants they bring him on a silver platter? The Americans and the whole democratic world have lost the most valuable possession—character. There's a form of tolerance that's worse than syphilis, worse than murder, worse than madness. Don't look at me that way. I'm the same person. It's just that in the time we were apart I lived whole ages. I suffered a complete nervous breakdown. I often heard the term used but didn't know what it meant. In my case, it showed itself in total apathy. One night I went to bed ostensibly normal, and when I woke up I was alive physically but I was neither hungry nor thirsty, nor did I have the slightest urge to get up. You should forgive me, but I didn't even want to go to the bathroom. I lay all day and my mind was blank. After Sam's death I had started smoking heavily. I drank too much, too, although alcohol had never been a passion with me. Sam's Xanthippe and his greedy children took me to court over his will and their lawyer was something it would take the devil himself to invent. Just looking at his face made me sick. I gave up everything and fled for my life. When the actors found out that Sam had left me part of his fortune, they became as tender with me as they would be with a boil. They even offered me membership in the Hebrew Actors Union. I was promised leading roles and whatnot. But my ambition for the stage was gone. What is theater, anyway? False mimicry. Literature is the same. Sam—may he rest in peace—never read anything, and we often argued about this, since I was a voracious reader from childhood. Now I'm beginning to understand him. Why didn't you answer my letters?"

"What letters? I got just one letter from you and you didn't even include a return address."

"How is that possible? I wrote several times. I cabled you, too."

"When? I swear on everything that's holy to me that I received nothing but one letter."

"What's holy to you? First I wrote to the address on Leszno, and when you didn't answer I wrote you in care of the Writers' Club."

"I no longer go to the Writers' Club."

"But that was your second home."

"I decided to stop going."

"And you're capable of sticking to a decision? Maybe my letters are still lying there?"

"What was the cable about?"

"Oh, it's no longer important. Life is full of surprises. If a person thinks no more surprises await him, it's only because he has shut his eyes and doesn't want to know. What about you? Did you break up with that freak Shosha?"

"Break up? Where do you get such notions?"

"How is it you've kept your old room? I didn't call there believing I'd find you—I only hoped they might know your new address."

"I work there. It's my study."

"You have an apartment with her?"

"We live with her mother."

A trace of laughter showed in Betty's eyes. "On that foul street among the thieves and brothels?"

"Yes, there."

"What kind of life do you lead with her, if I may ask?"

"A kind of life."

"Do the two of your ever go anywhere?"

"Rarely."

"You never go out of the house?"

"Sometimes. We take a turn around the garbage bin at night. To get a little air."

"Well, you've remained the same. At least you're crazy in your own fashion. In New York I was stopped in the street by an actor who made guest appearances here and he told me that you've become a big success and have published a novel everyone is reading. Is this true?"

"I'm having a novel printed in a newspaper and I barely earn enough to feed us."

"You're probably running around with ten others."

"That's not true, either."

"What is true?"

"How about you?" I asked. "Surely, you've had affairs."

"Are you jealous? I could have had. Men still chase after me. But when you're deathly ill and each day isn't one crisis but a thousand, you don't want affairs. Is that hocus-pocus Elbinger still in Warsaw?"

"Yes. He fell in love with a Gentile woman who was the mistress of the famous medium Kluski."

"I think I heard of him once. What did he do?"

"The dead came to him and left impressions of their hands in a pail of paraffin."

"You're scoffing, eh? I really believe that the dead are all around us somewhere. What has happened to that short, rich fellow—I've already forgotten his name. His wife was your sweetheart."

"Haiml and Celia. They are here."

"Yes, them. How is it they've stayed in Warsaw? I hear many rich Jews have escaped abroad."

"They want to die."

"Well, you're in one of *those* moods today. I've missed you. That's the truth."

4

I COULDN'T believe my ears, but after all those angry words about theater in general and Yiddish theater in particular, Betty Slonim had come to Warsaw with a play and was seeking a producer. I shouldn't have been surprised. Many of my colleagues, the writers, behaved precisely this way. They announced that they were laying aside (or breaking) their pens, and soon afterward they launched a novel or a long poem—even announced plans for a trilogy. They heaped invective upon a critic, maintained that he had no conception of literature, and the next day they begged him to write a few kind words about them. The play Betty brought was her own. I stayed the night, and we read it. It was the drama of a young woman, an artist (Betty had made her a painter) unable to fit into any environment. She couldn't find the right husband or lover, or even any interesting girlfriend. The play featured a psychoanalyst who tried to convince the heroine that she hated her father and was jealous of her mother, while in fact the woman worshipped her parents. There was a scene in which the heroine searches for an end to her loneliness by trying to become a lesbian and fails. The play contained possibilities for humor, but Betty handled everything in tragic fashion. The long monologues were packed with clichés. It ran some three hundred pages and was full of observations about painting by someone who knew nothing about it.

Dawn had begun to break by the time I got through with the fourth act. I said to Betty, "The play is good in essence, but it's not for Warsaw, just as mine wasn't for any place."

"What is for Warsaw?" she asked.

"I'm afraid nothing is for Warsaw any more."

"It seems to me this play is just right for the Polish Jews. They are like my heroine—they cannot fit in anywhere, neither among the Communists nor among the capitalists. Certainly not among the Fascists. At times I think nothing is left them except suicide."

"Whether that's true or not, the Warsaw Jews don't want to hear it. Certainly not in the theater."

I was so tired from reading that I lay down on the bed and fell asleep in my clothes. I wanted to tell Betty that she herself was proof that no person or collective has the strength fully to resign, but I was too exhausted to bring out the words. In my sleep I reread the play, gave Betty advice, even wrote new scenes. Betty had left the lights on and from time to time I opened an eye. She was busy in the bathroom. She had put on a magnificent nightgown. She came over to the bed and took off my shoes and pulled off my shirt. In my sleep I laughed at her and her urge to seize all the pleasures at once. That's what suicides are, I thought—hedonists who attempt to enjoy more excitement than they are capable of. This possibly was the answer to my own riddle.

I opened my eyes and saw that it was day. Betty sat at the desk in her nightgown and slippers, cigarette in mouth, writing something on a sheet of paper. My wristwatch showed a few minutes before eight. I sat up. "What are you doing? Rewriting the play?"

She turned her head toward me. Her face was ashen, her eyes had become strangely stern and determined. "You slept but I couldn't shut an eye. No, not the play. For me the play is dead. But I could save you."

"What do you mean?"

"The Jews here are all going to perish. You'll sit with that Shosha until Hitler marches in. I've been reading the paper half the night. What sense does it make, eh? Does it pay to die on account of such a moron?"

"What do you suggest I do?"

"Tsutsik, after I see my aunt I have no reason to stay here, but I want to help you nevertheless. Aboard ship I met an official of the American consulate and we spoke of various things. He even began flirting with me, but he wasn't my type. A military man, a drinker. They drown everything with whiskey—it's their answer to all problems. I asked him about bringing someone to America and he told me that outside the quota this is impossible. But it's easy to obtain a tourist visa if you apply with some goal in mind and can prove that you won't become a public charge. In America, when a tourist marries a citizen, he immediately gets a visa outside the quota and is allowed to remain. I want to tell you something. I see in advance that all my plans and hopes will come to nothing. But if I can help someone who is close to me before I die, I want to do it, and even though you told me coldbloodedly last night that I have nothing to hope for from you, I consider you somebody close. As a matter of fact, you are the closest person I have outside Sam—may he rest in peace—and my sisters and brothers lost somewhere in the Red hell—I don't even know if any of them are still alive. Tsutsik, since you assure me the play is worth a kick in the ground, as the Litvaks say, I have nothing more to do here, and I can't go back to America all by myself. Between a yes and a no I could arrange a tourist visa for you and you could go with me. Do you have official papers with Shosha? Were you married in court?"

"Only by a rabbi."

"Is it written on your passport that you're married?"

"Nothing is written on the passport."

"You can get a tourist visa immediately if I give you an affidavit. I'll say you've written a play and we want to put it on in America. I'll say I will be appearing in it. There is even a chance that this might really happen. I can show them a bank book and whatever they require. I don't consider death a tragedy. It's actually a release from all trouble. But to live day in, day out with death is too much even for a masochist like you."

"But what could I do with Shosha?"

"They wouldn't give Shosha a tourist visa. If they took one look at her, they wouldn't give one to you."

"Betty, I can't leave her here."

"You can't, eh? That means you're ready to give up your life for her."

"If I have to die, I'll die."

"I didn't know you were so madly in love with her."

"It's not only love."

"What is it?"

"I can't kill a child. I cannot break my promise either."

"If you go to America, there might be a chance you could send for her. You'd at least be able to send her money. As it is, you will both perish."

"Betty, I can't do it."

"If you can't, you can't. According to what you've told me, you never had such consideration for women. When you got tired of one, you found another."

"Those were adults. They had families, friends. Shosha—"

"Well, you don't have to justify yourself. When a person stands ready to offer his life for another, he obviously knows what he's doing. I wouldn't have believed you capable of such a sacrifice, but you never know what a human being is capable of. Not that those who make the sacrifices are always saints. People sacrificed themselves for Stalin, for Petlura, for Machno, for every pogromist. Millions of fools will give their empty heads for Hitler. At times I think men go around with a candle looking for an opportunity to sacrifice themselves."

Neither of us spoke for a while. Then Betty said, "I'm leaving now to visit my aunt and we may never meet again. Tell me, why did you do it? Even if you lie to me, I want to hear what you'll say."

"You mean marrying Shosha?"

"Yes."

"I really don't know, but I'll tell you, anyway. She is the only woman I can trust," I said, shocked at my own words.

Betty's eyes lit up with laughter. For an instant she became young again. "My God, this is the truth. As simple as that!"

"Perhaps."

"You're both a godless lecher and a fanatical Jew—as bigoted as my great-grandfather! How is it possible?"

"We are running away and Mount Sinai runs after us. This chase has made us sick and mad."

"Don't include me. I am sick and mad, but Mount Sinai has nothing to do with it. As a matter of fact, you're lying. You are no more afraid of Mount Sinai than I am. It's your miserable pride, your silly fear of losing your filthy male honor. You once told me what one of your cronies said about the impossibility of always betraying and never being betrayed. Who was it—Feitelzohn?"

"I don't remember. Either Feitelzohn or Haiml."

"Haiml couldn't have said it. Well, it doesn't matter. You're crazy, but a good many other idiots of your kind went to their deaths to save the reputation of some whore. No, Shosha won't betray you—unless she is raped by a Nazi."

"Goodbye, Betty."

"Goodbye forever."

5

I HAD left the hotel without breakfast—I couldn't have stayed because the room-service waitress would have seen me. For the second time I had given up the chance to save myself. I walked without a definite direction. My legs led me by themselves from Trebacka Street to Theater Place. I didn't have the slightest doubt that to remain in Warsaw this time meant falling into the hands of the Nazis, but somehow I didn't feel any fear. I was tired from so little sleep, from reading Betty's play, and from her talk. I had given her the opportunity to scold me and so made our parting less solemn. Only now did it occur to me that she had never before mentioned her aunt in Poland and that she

never had gone to see her. She certainly would not have come to
Poland especially to see her now. Like me, Betty was ready to
perish. A passage of the Pentateuch came to my mind: "I am at
the point of dying and what profit shall this birthright be to me?"

I had thrown away four thousand years of Jewishness and exchanged it for meaningless literature, Yiddishism, Feitelzohnism.
All I was left with was a membership booklet from the Writers'
Club and some worthless manuscripts. I stopped at store windows
and stared. Any day the destruction might begin, but in the
meantime, here they displayed pianos, cars, jewelry, fancy nightgowns, new books in Polish, as well as translations from German,
English, Russian, French. One book had the title *The Twilight
of Israel*. Well, but the sky was summery blue, the trees on both
sides of the street were lusciously green, the ladies wore the latest
styles of dresses, hats, shoes, purses. The men looked them over
with expert appraisal. Their legs in nylon stockings still promised the never-realized delights. Although I was doomed, I too
glanced at hips, calves, breasts, throats. The generations that will
come after us, I said to myself, will think that we all went to our
death in repentance. They will consider all of us holy martyrs.
They will recite kaddish after us and "God Full of Mercy."
Actually, every one of us will die with the same passions he lived
with.

They still played the familiar operas in the opera house:
Carmen, Aida, Faust, The Barber of Seville. They were just un-
loading from a truck the faded sets that in the evening would
create the deception of mountains, rivers, gardens, palaces. I went
to a café. The smell of coffee and fresh rolls whetted my appetite.
With my coffee a waiter brought me two newspapers. Marshal
Rydz-Śmigly again assured the nation that the Polish armed
forces had the means to repulse all attacks from the right and the
left. Foreign Minister Beck had received new guarantees from
England and France. The old anti-Semite Nawaczynski attacked
the Jews, who, together with the Masons, the Communists, the
Nazis, and the American bankers conspired to destroy the Cath-

olic faith and to replace it with pagan materialism. He still quoted the Protocols of the Elders of Zion. Somewhere I had had a trace of faith in free will, but this morning I felt sure that man possessed as much choice as the clockwork of my wristwatch or the fly that stopped on the edge of my saucer. The same powers were driving Hitler, Stalin, the Pope, the Rabbi of Gur, a molecule in the center of the earth, and a galaxy billions of light-years distant from the Milky Way. Blind powers? Seeing powers? It did not matter any more. We were fated to play our little games and to be crushed.

6

USUALLY when I didn't spend the night at Shosha's I came home the day after for lunch, but this morning I decided to go back to her early. I was too tired to try to work at my desk on Leszno Street. I paid for my breakfast and went by way of Senator Street to Bank Place and from there to Gnoyna and Krochmalna. In the Jewish streets they bustled and rushed as every day. In the brokerage houses on Przcehodnia they figured the value of the zloty against the dollar. Those on the black market paid a few pennies more for the dollar. In the yeshivas they studied the Talmud. In the Hasidic studyhouses they conversed on Hasidic topics. That morning I had the feeling I was seeing all this for the last time. I tried to engrave in my memory each alley, each building, each store, each face. I thought that this was how a condemned man would be looking at the world on his way to the gallows. I was taking leave of every peddler, porter, market woman—even of the horses of the droshkies. I saw in each of them expressions I had never noticed before. Even the horses seemed to know that this was their last journey. There was knowledge and consent in their large eyes, dark with pupil.

On Gnoyna Street I stopped for a moment at the large study-house in No. 5. The walls were blackened, the books stained and torn, but young men with long sidelocks still swayed over these ancient volumes and chanted the sacred words with the same mournful chant. At the lectern by the Ark the cantor was praising God for his promise to resurrect the dead. A little man with a yellow face and a yellow beard sold boiled chick-peas and beans that he doled out in a wooden cup. Is he the eternal Jew? One of the thirty-six saints that are the pillars of the world? A disguised Elder of Zion in secret pact with Roosevelt, Goebbels, and Léon Blum to bring about the kingdom of Satan?

I entered Krochmalna and the gate of No. 7. The baker's daughter stood there with large baskets of warm bagels. She must have been one of my readers, because she smiled and winked at me. I imagined that she was saying to me: "Like you I must play my game to the last minute." I passed through the yard, opened the door to Bashele's apartment, and what I saw was so bewildering that I stood in the doorway staring. Tekla was sitting at the table drinking tea or coffee with chicory from a large cup. Shosha sat beside her. Something has happened to my mother, I thought. A telegram must have come announcing that she died! Tekla saw me now and jumped to her feet. Shosha rose, too. She clapped her hands. "Arele, God Himself sent you!"

"What's going on here? Am I already in the World of Delusion?"

"What? Come in. Arele, this Gentile girl came and said she was looking for you. She called you by name. She brought a basket with her belongings. There it is. She said something about a fiancé—I don't know what she's talking about. It's a good thing Mommy went shopping or she might have thought who knows what. I told her you wouldn't be home till lunchtime, but she said she'd wait."

Tekla stood there obviously eager to speak, but she waited respectfully until Shosha had finished. Tekla looked pale and disheveled, as if she hadn't slept. She said, "Forgive me, sir, but something bad has happened to me. Last evening someone knocked on the kitchen door. I thought it might be a neighbor returning a glass of salt she had borrowed, or one of the maids from the courtyard. I opened the door and in came a lout—one of our kind, a Christian. He was dressed in city style. He said, 'Tekla, don't you recognize me?' It was Bolek, my ex-fiancé. He's come back from France from the coal mines and he says he wants to marry me. I was scared to death. I said, 'Why didn't you write all these years? You went away and it was as if the earth swallowed you.' And he said, 'I can't write, and neither could any of the other miners.' Well, between this and that, he sat down on my bed and started talking as if nothing had passed since we last saw each other. He brought me a present, too—some trinket. It's God's miracle I didn't die on the spot. I said, 'Bolek, since you didn't write so long, we are no longer engaged and everything between us is finished.' But he started yelling, 'What's the matter? Got somebody else? Or are you in love with that Jew who wrote those letters to me for you?' He was drunk and grabbed a knife. My mistress heard the commotion and she came running, and he started cursing the Jews and threatened to kill us all. The mistress said, 'So far, Hitler isn't here yet. So get out of my house.' Wladek called the police, but a policeman didn't show up till three hours later, after Bolek had gone. He swore he would come back again today, and he warned me that if I didn't go with him to a priest straight off and marry him, he'd kill me. After he left, the mistress came in and said, 'Tekla, you've served me faithfully, but I'm old and weak and I don't have the strength for such goings-on. Take your luggage and leave.' I persuaded her to let me spend the night. This morning she paid me what was coming to me, added five zlotys, and sent me on my way. You once gave me your address on Krochmalna Street, so I came here. The young lady said she's your wife and that you'd be back for lunch, but where could I go? I know no one in Warsaw. I was sure you wouldn't throw me out."

"Throw you out? Tekla, I'm your friend for life!"

"Oh, thank you. What shall I do? I can't go home to our village, because Bolek said if I did he'd come after me. He has a
whole gang of thugs who served in the army and came back with
revolvers and bayonets. He said he'd saved up a thousand zlotys
and some French money besides, but my heart is no longer his.
He can get plenty of other girls. He stank of vodka and he talked
like a roughneck. I've grown unused to that kind of coarseness."

"Arele, when Mommy comes back and hears this, she'll get
nervous," Shosha said. "If the man is threatening with a knife,
you mustn't go to that place. But what will she do here? We
hardly have space to lay our own heads. Mommy says each time
she goes out to let no one in. She used to say the same when we
lived at No. 10—remember?"

"Yes, Shoshele, I remember. Tekla is a decent girl and she
won't give anyone any trouble. I'll take her away in a minute."
In Yiddish I said, "Shoshele, I'm going with her for a while.
When your mother comes back, tell her nothing."

"Oh, she'll know it, anyway. Everyone in the courtyard looks
out the window, and when someone who doesn't belong here
goes in or out they know it and start to gossip: 'What's she doing
here? What does she want?' The younger women are busy with
their children, but the old ones want to know everything."

"Well, I'll be back around lunchtime. Tekla, come with me."

"Shall I bring my basket?"

"Yes, bring it."

"Arele, don't be late. When you're late, Mommy starts to
worry that maybe you no longer want us, and things like that. I
start thinking all kinds of things myself. Last night I could barely
sleep a wink. If she's hungry, I can give her bread and herring to
take along."

"She'll eat. Come, Tekla."

We walked out under the watchful gaze of eyes that seemed to
ask, "Where is he off to so early with this peasant girl? And what
is she carrying in the basket?" I answered them in my mind,
"You may try to solve the puzzles in the newspaper, but never

the mysteries of life. For seven days and seven nights you could rub your brows like the Sages of Chelm and you'd still never figure out the answer."

In front of the gate, I stood for a long time thinking what to do next. Should I try to find a room for her? Should I go with her to some coffee shop and look up advertisements for maids' agencies? I would have let her stay with Shosha for a while, but I had never told either her or Bashele of my room on Leszno Street. They believed that I slept at the newspaper, and Bashele would begin a long interrogation. Suddenly I knew what to do. The solution was so simple I wondered that it hadn't occurred to me immediately. I walked with Tekla to the delicatessen in No. 12, told her to wait for me by the door, and went inside to phone Celia. Only a few days earlier, she had bewailed the fact that ever since Marianna had left her, she hadn't been able to find a decent maid. I heard Celia's dull voice—one that seemed to say without putting it in words, Whoever it may be, I can expect nothing.

I said, "Celia, this is Tsutsik."

"Tsutsik? What's happened? Has the Messiah come?"

"The Messiah hasn't come, but I have a maid for you."

"A maid? You? For me?"

"Yes, Celia, and a part-time boarder in the bargain."

"Bless me if I know what you mean. What boarder?"

"I am the boarder."

"Are you making fun of me?"

I told Celia what had happened. "I can't stay in my room on Leszno Street any longer. A rowdy peasant is threatening Tekla and me." Celia did not interrupt me, apparently stunned by the turn of events. I could hear her breathing on the other side of the line. From time to time I glanced through the glass door to where Tekla waited. She stood with humble patience. She did not put down the heavy basket but held it in both her hands, pressed to her belly. At home on Leszno Street she showed big-city shrewdness, but overnight she seemed to have lost it all and become a peasant again.

"Will you bring Shosha with you?"

"Whenever she is able to stay apart from her mother."

Celia seemed to ponder the implication of my words. Then she said, "Bring her as often as you want to. This is going to be your second home. Where you go she should go."

"Celia, you are saving my life!" I exclaimed.

Again Celia paused. "Tsutsik, take a taxi and come at once. If I live a little longer, something good may happen even to me. If only it isn't too late."

· EPILOGUE ·

1

THIRTEEN years had gone by. In New York, I had saved two thousand dollars out of my salary from the Yiddish newspaper. I had also received a five-hundred-dollar advance for a novel that would be translated into English, and I took a trip to London, Paris, and Israel. London still had craters and ruins left over from the German bombs. In Paris, I ate in a restaurant that obtained its food from the black market. In Marseilles I boarded a ship bound for Haifa with a stopover in Genoa. The singing of the young passengers rang through the nights—the old familiar songs, as well as new songs that had come out of the war with the Arabs between 1948 and 1951. After six days, we arrived in Haifa. It was an experience to see Hebrew signs over the stores and streets bearing the names of writers, rabbis, and leaders, to hear Hebrew spoken in the Sephardic style, to see Jewish soldiers of both sexes. In Tel Aviv I stopped at a hotel on Yarkon Street. Although Tel Aviv was a new city, the houses looked old and dingy. The telephone didn't work properly, the bathtub seldom had hot water, and the electricity often went off at night. The food was bad.

There was a notice in a newspaper announcing my arrival, and

I began to receive visits from writers, journalists, old friends from Warsaw, distant relatives. Some of them had numbers tattooed on their arms from Auschwitz, others had already lost sons in the battles for Jerusalem or Safad. I heard the same horror stories about Nazi brutalities and the savagery of the N.K.V.D. that I had heard in New York, in London, in Paris, and aboard ship.

One morning as I ate breakfast in the hotel dining room, a tiny person with a milk-white beard that extended like a fan came into the room. He wore an unbuttoned shirt with an open collar, a straw hat, shabby trousers, and sandals on his bare feet. I was sure that I had known him once, but I couldn't identify him. How can such a little man have such a large beard? I wondered. He approached my table with hasty steps. He had young black eyes that resembled the olives on my plate. He pointed a finger and said in a familiar Warsaw Yiddish, "There he is! Peace to you, Tsutsik!"

It was Haiml Chentshiner. I got up and we kissed and held each other for a moment. My face filled with beard. I asked him to have breakfast with me but he told me that he had eaten, and I ordered coffee for him. I had heard that he and Celia perished in the Warsaw Ghetto, but encounters with those supposedly dead had ceased to surprise me. Feitelzohn I knew was no longer alive, for I had read of his death in the paper years ago.

We drank the coffee and Haiml said, "Forgive me for calling you Tsutsik—it remains a term of affection for me."

"Yes, but I'm an old dog now."

"To me you will always remain Tsutsik. If Celia were alive, she'd call you the same thing. How old are you?"

"Forty-three."

"Not so very old. I'm in my late fifties. It seems to me I'm as old as Methuselah. The things we went through during those years! Not one life but a hundred."

"Where were you, Haiml?"

"Where *was* I? Where wasn't I! In Vilna, in Kovno, in Kiev, in Moscow, in Kazakhstan, among the Kalmucks, the Chunchuz, or whatever they're called. A hundred times I virtually looked the Angel of Death in the eye, but when you're fated to stay alive miracles occur. So long as a breath of life remains in the body, it crawls like a worm, and I crawled and avoided the feet that squash worms till I came to the Jewish land. Here again, we suffered war, hunger, steady danger. Bullets flew over my head. Bombs exploded a few steps away. But here no one went like a sheep to the slaughter. Our lads from Warsaw, Lodz, Rawa Ruska, and Minsk suddenly turned into heroes like the fighters in the time of Masada. Piff-poff! The greatest optimist wouldn't have believed it possible. You probably know what happened to Celia."

"Not a thing."

"How could you, after all? How about going out on the terrace? I like to look at the sea."

We went to the terrace and took a table in the shade. A waiter came over and I ordered more coffee and cookies. For a long time we both stared out to sea, which changed color from green to blue. On the horizon a sailboat rocked. The beach swarmed with men and women. Some exercised, others played ball, sunbathed, or lay under umbrellas. Some splashed at the edge of the water, others swam far out. A man urged a dog to go into the water, but the animal was unwilling to bathe.

Haiml said, "Well, a Jewish land, a Jewish sea. Who would have believed this ten years ago? Such a thought was beyond daring. All our dreams centered around a crust of bread, a plate of groats, a clean shirt. Feitelzohn once said something I often repeat: "A man has no imagination either in his pessimism or his optimism." Who could have figured that the Gentiles would vote for a Jewish nation? Nu, but the birth throes are far from over. The Arabs haven't made peace with the situation. It's hard here. Thousands of refugees live in tin shacks. I lived in one of them myself. The sun roasts you all day like fire, and at night you freeze. The women are at each other's throats. Refugees have come from Africa who've never seen a handkerchief—literally people from Abraham's time. Who knows what they are—maybe descendants of Keturah. I hear you've become famous in America."

"Far from it."

"Well, you're known. They used to read your books in the camps in Germany. Things were reprinted in the papers there. Each time I saw your name, I cried, 'Tsutsik!' They thought I was crazy. Today when I saw the notice in *Hayom* that you were here, I began to jump in the air. My wife asked, 'What happened—have you gone mad?' I got married again."

"Here?"

"No, in Landsberg. She had lost her husband and the children were taken away from her to the gas chamber. I was wandering around alone. I didn't have anyone to so much as make me a glass of tea. I remember your words: 'The world is a slaughterhouse and a brothel.' At the time it seemed to me an exaggeration, but it's the bitter truth. They consider you a mystic, while the fact is, you're an out-and-out realist. Still, everything is forced upon us, even hope. The dictator on high, the celestial Stalin, says, 'You must hope!' And if he says you must, you hope. But what can I hope for any more? Only for death. Where is the sugar?"

"Right here."

"This coffee tastes like dishwater. How long is it since I've seen you—thirteen years? Yes, in September it will be exactly thirteen years. Shosha is no longer alive, eh?"

"Shosha died on the second day we left Warsaw."

"Died? On the way?"

"Yes, like Mother Rachel."

"We knew nothing, nothing. News came from others. There were Jews in Bialystok and Vilna who became mail carriers, messengers. They brought letters to wives across the borders. But you vanished like a stone in water. What happened to you? I first found out you were alive in 1946. I came to Munich with a large group of refugees and someone gave me a newspaper published there. I opened it and saw your name. It said that you were in New York. How did you manage to get to New York?"

"Through Shanghai."

"Who sent you the affidavit?"

"Remember Betty?"

"What a question! I remember everybody."

"Betty married a Gentile, a colonel in the American Army, and he sent me the affidavit."

"You knew her address?"

"I learned it by chance."

"Well, I'm not religious, I don't pray, I don't observe the Sabbath, I don't believe in God, but I acknowledge that some hand guides our world—this, no one can deny. A vicious hand, a bloody hand, occasionally merciful. Where does Betty live—in New York?"

"Betty committed suicide a year ago."

"Why?"

"No one knows."

"What happened to Shosha? If it's painful for you to talk about it, you don't have to tell me."

"I'll tell you anyway. She died exactly as I saw it in a dream a few years before. We were walking along a road that led to Bialystok. It was toward evening. The others walked fast and Shosha couldn't keep up. She began to stop every few minutes. Suddenly she sat down, and a minute later she was dead. I had told this dream to Celia. Maybe to you, too."

"Not to me. I would remember it. What a sweet child she was. In her own fashion, a saint. What was it, a heart attack?"

"I don't know. I think she simply didn't want to live any more."

"What happened to her sister—what was her name, Teibele?" Haiml asked. "And how about her mother?"

"Bashele perished for sure. About Teibele, I don't know what happened. She might have run away to Russia. She had a friend —a bookkeeper. Perhaps she's here, although it doesn't seem probable, since I have heard nothing from her in all these years."

"I'm afraid to ask, but what happened to your mother and your brother?"

"After 1941, the Russians saved them by taking them in a cattle train to Kazakhstan. The trip took two weeks. I met a man who was with them in the same train, and he told me the details. They are both dead. How my mother could last several months after the experience of this trip, I still don't grasp. They were taken to a forest in the middle of the Russian winter and told to build themselves log cabins. My brother died almost immediately after he arrived."

"What happened to your Communist girl friend, what was her name?"

"Dora? I don't know. Got crushed somewhere, either by the do-gooders or by the do-badders."

"Tsutsik, I'll be right back—don't go away."

"What a thing to say!"

"Anything can happen."

Haiml left and I turned toward the sea again. Two women splashed each other and lost their balance from the force of their laughter. A father and son played with a balloon. A Sephardic Jew in a white cloak, barefoot, and with a scraggly white beard and earlocks dangling to his shoulders, went around begging from the people on the beach. No one gave him anything. Who would go begging on a beach? I wondered. He was probably not in his right mind. At that moment I heard my name called on the public-address system. I was wanted on the telephone.

2

I CAME back from the phone. Haiml sat at the table, facing the door with a childish eagerness. When I came out, he made a move as if to stand, but kept his seat. I sat down and he asked, "Where did you go?"

"I was called to the phone."

"When you come here, they don't leave you alone for a minute. Well, there were notices about you in the newspapers, but how did they know it when *I* came? People called whom I thought were long buried. Every such meeting was like the resurrection of the dead. Who knows? If we could live to see the miracle that the Jews have a country again, maybe we shall see the Messiah come, after all? Maybe the dead *will* be resurrected? Tsutsik, you know I'm a freethinker. But somewhere inside me I have the feeling that Celia is here, that Morris is here, that my father— may he rest in peace—is here. Your Shosha is here, too. How is it possible, after all, that someone should simply vanish? How can someone who lived, loved, hoped, and wrangled with God and with himself just disappear? I don't know how and in what sense but they're here. Since time is an illusion, why shouldn't everything remain? I once heard you say—or quote someone— that time is a book whose pages you can turn forward, not back. Maybe *we* can't, but some forces can. How is it possible that Celia should stop being Celia? For Morris to stop being Morris? I live with them, speak with them. At times I hear Celia talking to me. You won't believe this, but Celia told me to marry my present wife. I lay in that camp near Landsberg, sick, hungry, lonely, dejected. Suddenly I heard Celia's voice: 'Haiml, marry Genia!' That's my wife's name, Genia. Sure, you can explain this psychologically. I know, I know. Nevertheless, I heard her voice. What do you say to that, eh?"

"I don't know."

"You still don't know? How long can you go on not knowing? Tsutsik, I seem to be able to make peace with everything but death. How can it be that all the generations are dead and only we shlemiels are allegedly living? You turn the page and can't turn it back again, but on page so-and-so they're all right there in an archive of spirits."

"What do they do there?" I asked.

"That answer I don't have. Perhaps we are there already, dreaming the same dream. Either everything is dead or every-

thing is alive. I want you to know that it was only after you left
that Morris became great—he never had been as great as he was
in those months. He lived with us on Zlota Street until the Jews
were herded into the ghetto in October of 1940, which was more
than a year after the Germans came in. As you know, before the
war he could have gone to England as well as to America. The
American consul urged him to leave. The war with America
didn't start until 1941. He could have traveled through Rumania,
through Hungary, even through Germany. With an American
visa they let you pass. But he stayed with us. One time I said to
Celia, 'I'm ready to die but I want one favor from you and the
Almighty if He exists—that I never see a Nazi.' Celia said to me,
'Haiml, I promise you that you won't see their faces.' How could
she have promised such a thing? She herself had grown in stature.
She wasn't the same Celia any more. Our situation and Morris's
moving in with us uplifted her to a degree that can't be put
into words. She became beautiful!"

"Were you jealous of him?"

"Don't talk nonsense. I too grew a bit. The Angel of Death
waved his sword but I stuck out my tongue at him. Outside, it
was the destruction of the Temple, but inside our house it was
Simchas Torah and Yom Kippur rolled into one. Next to them I,
too, became cheerful. I'm not telling these things in proper
order—how can you speak of such things in order? My only uncle
died in the month of October. It wasn't possible to go to Lodz—
a Jew couldn't show his face anywhere. Still, I dared the dangers.
I walked the whole distance on foot. The trip there and back
was a real odyssey.

"As you know, Celia had prepared a room we called the Cave
of Machpelah. She started to prepare it while you were still in
Warsaw, but the day they announced on the radio that all men
were to cross the Praga Bridge and you decided to leave together
with Shosha, that day the room became Feitelzohn's and my only
place. We ate there, we slept there. Morris did his writing there.
I had brought money from Lodz—not paper money, but golden
ducats my father left with my uncle for me. They were saved

from the time of the Russians. Just the fact that I had returned with such a treasure to Warsaw and wasn't searched or killed on the way is beyond belief. But I did come back. Then Celia had her jewelry. At that time you could get everything for money. A black market developed almost at once.

"After my odyssey, I was so depleted that my last drop of courage drained away. Like Morris, I wouldn't go into the street, and Celia became our contact with the outside world. Each time she went, we weren't sure we'd see her again. Your Tekla, too, ran errands for us. She risked her life. She had to go back to her village because her father died.

"The days were days of sorrow. Our life started at night. There wasn't much to eat, but we drank hot tea and Morris talked. He talked those nights as I never heard him talk before. The heritage of generations had wakened within him, and he hurled sulphur and brimstone against the Almighty; at the same time the words themselves blazed with a religious fire. He castigated Him for all His sins since the Creation. He still maintained that the whole universe was a game, but he elevated this game until it became divine. That was probably how the Seer of Lublin, Rabbi Bunim, and the Kotzker spoke. The essence of his words was that since God is eternally silent, we owe Him nothing. It seems I once heard similar words from you—or maybe you were quoting Morris. True religion, Morris argued, was not to serve God but to spite Him. If He wanted evil, we had to aspire to the opposite. If He wanted wars, inquisitions, crucifixions, Hitlers, we must want righteousness, Hasidism, our own version of grace. The Ten Commandments weren't His but ours. God wanted Jews to seize the Land of Israel from the Canaanites and to wage wars against the Philistines, but the real Jew, who began to be what he is in exile, wanted the Gemara with its commentaries, the Zohar, *The Tree of Life, The Beginning of Wisdom.* The Gentiles didn't drive us into the ghetto, Morris said, the Jew went on his own, because he grew weary of waging war and bringing up warriors and heroes of the battlefield. Each night Morris erected a new structure.

"We could have escaped up to the time they locked the Jews
in the ghetto; people went back and forth to Russia. In Bialystok
there was a Jew from Warsaw, a half writer, half madman, and
a whole martyr. His name was Yonkel Pentzak. He kept going
from Bialystok to Warsaw and back again—a kind of holy
messenger or a divine smuggler. He smuggled letters from wives
to husbands and from husbands to wives. You can imagine the
risk connected with such journeys! The Nazis finally got him,
but until they did, he served as a sacred mail carrier. He brought
me a few letters. Some friends of mine had gone there and they
begged us to join them, but Celia didn't want to and Morris
didn't want to, and after all, I couldn't leave them behind. What
was there for me in that alien world? The whole crew of writers
and leaders that sent us greetings had overnight turned about
and become ardent Communists. Denouncing one's fellow was
now the order of the day. Their writing consisted of praising
Stalin, and the reward for this was at first a plate of groats and
a bed, and later jail and exile and liquidation. I came to the
conclusion that what people call life is death and what people
call death is life. Don't ask any questions. Where is it written
that a bedbug lives and the sun is dead? Maybe it's the other way
around? Love? It wasn't simply love. Tsutsik, do you have a
match, maybe? I've gotten into the habit of smoking, actually
right here in the Jewish land."

I went to get Haiml matches, and at the same time I bought
him two packs of American cigarettes.

He shook his head. "Are those for me? So help me, you're a
spendthrift."

"I took more from you than two packs of cigarettes."

"Eh? We didn't forget you. Celia kept asking about you—
maybe someone had heard something, maybe something of yours
had been printed. After you left Warsaw, where did you go—not
to Bialystok?"

"To Druskenik."

"You were able to get there?"

"I smuggled myself over."

"What did you do in Druskenik?"

"Worked in a hotel."

"Well, you did the right thing to stay away from the writers. You couldn't become a Communist, and the anti-Communists were soon sent to Siberia. Later they did the same to most zealous Stalinists. What did you do in 1941?"

"Kept on going."

"Where to?"

"I dragged along till I came to Kovno, and from there I went to Shanghai."

"Got a visa, eh? And what did you do in Shanghai?"

"Became a typesetter."

"What did you set?

"The *Shitah Mekubbetzet*."

"Well, a crazy race, the Jews. I heard there was a yeshiva there that published books. You didn't write?"

"I did that, too."

"When did you go to America?"

"At the beginning of 1948."

"I left Warsaw in May of 1941. Morris died in March."

"Why didn't you take Celia along?"

"There was no one to take along."

"Was she sick?"

"She died exactly a month after Morris, in what they call a natural death."

3

HAIML and I squeezed our way into a bus going to Hadar Joseph, a suburb of Tel Aviv with housing for new immigrants. The passengers cursed each other in Yiddish, Polish, German, and in broken Hebrew. The women fought over seats and the men took sides. One woman had brought along a live chicken. The bird tore loose from the basket and began to fly over the heads of the passengers. The driver shouted that he would throw out anyone who caused a disturbance. After a while things quieted down and I heard Haiml say, "Well, a Jewish nation. The new-comers are all out of their minds—victims of Hitler, bundles of nerves. They always suspect they're being persecuted. First they cursed Hitler, now they curse Ben-Gurion. Their children or perhaps their grandchildren will be normal if the Almighty doesn't send a new catastrophe down upon us. What can you know of what we went through! You haven't said anything, but you're probably wondering why I had to marry again after Celia. Before, Genia and I were two worms crawling separately; then we began to crawl together. Until recently we lived in a tin shack. Later, we got the apartment we have now. How much can a body tolerate? She isn't Celia, but she's a good person. Her husband was a teacher in a Yiddish school in Pietrkow. A Bund-ist. Genia believed in Stalin for a while, until she got a taste of him. Funny, she knew Feitelzohn. She once went to a lecture of his about Spengler and he autographed a book for her. She's an orderly in a hospital where they bring the wounded in ambu-lances. The Red Mogen David. It just so happens she's off today. She knows all about you. I gave her your books to read."

We came to Hadar Joseph. Lines of wash stretched from one flat roof to the other. Half-naked children played in the sand. Cement steps led directly into Haiml's kitchen. Outside, it stank of garbage, asphalt, and something else sticky and sweet-ish that was hard to identify. The kitchen smelled of sorrel and garlic. Next to the gas range stood a short woman with short-trimmed hair—black, mixed with gray. She wore a calico dress and over her bare feet cracked slippers. She had apparently undergone surgery, since the left side of her face was compressed, full of scars under the chin, and her mouth was crooked. When we came in she was watering a flower in a pot.

Haiml called out, "Genia, guess who this is!"

"Tsutsik."

Haiml seemed embarrassed. "He has a name."

"It doesn't matter. Just the opposite," I said.

"Excuse me, that's how we refer to you," Genia said. "Four years I've been hearing it day and night—'Tsutsik,' 'Tsutsik.' When my husband thinks well of someone, he speaks of him without stopping. I had the honor of meeting Dr. Feitelzohn, but I only know you from a picture that appeared in the Yiddish paper. Finally I see you in person. Why didn't you tell me you were bringing someone to the house?" she said, turning to Haiml. "I would have put the place in order. We battle here constantly with flies, beetles, even mice. Years ago I didn't consider that insects or mice were God's creatures, too; but since I've been treated as if I were a beetle myself, I've come to accept things one doesn't want to accept. Please, go into the other room. Such an unexpected guest. What an honor!"

"You see her cheek?" Haiml pointed. "That's where a Nazi hit her with a piece of pipe."

"Well, why talk about it?" Genia said. "Go in the other room. Excuse me for the state it's in."

We went into the other room. A big sofa stood there, one of those that serve as a sofa by day and a bed at night. The apartment had no bathtub, only a toilet and a sink. This room seemed to serve both as a bedroom and a dining room. There was a bookcase, where I spotted Feitelzohn's *Spiritual Hormones* and several of my books.

Haiml said, "This is our land, this is our home. Here, maybe we'll have the privilege of dying if we're not driven into the sea."

After a while, Genia came in and began to straighten up. Even as we sat there, she swept the floor and spread a cloth over the table. She excused herself again and again for the mess. Evening was beginning to fall by the time she served dinner—some meat for herself and Haiml, vegetables for me. It struck me that the couple mixed meat dishes with dairy. I had assumed that despite

the fact Haiml talked like a heretic he would be observing Jewishness in the Land of Israel.

I asked, "Since you aren't religious, why did you grow a
beard?"

Genia put down her spoon. "That's what I want to know."

"Oh, a Jew should have a beard," Haiml replied. "You have
to be different from Gentiles in some way."

"The way you have lived, you're a Gentile, too," Genia said.

"As long as I have never beaten or killed anybody, I can call
myself a Jew."

"It's written somewhere that whoever breaks one of the Ten
Commandments must break them all," Genia said.

"Genia, the Ten Commandments were written by a man, not
by God," Haiml said. "As long as you don't harm anyone, you
can live any way you want. I loved Feitelzohn. If they told me to
give up my life so that he could live again, I wouldn't hesitate.
If there is a God, let Him be witness to what I say. I love Tsutsik,
too. The time of property will soon pass and there will evolve a
man with new instincts—those of sharing: Morris's very words."

"Then why were you such an anti-Communist in Russia?"
Genia asked.

"They don't want to share—they want to grab."

It grew silent and I heard a cricket—the same sound that came
from the cricket that chirped in our kitchen when I was a boy.
The room filled with shadows.

Haiml said, "I am religious—in my own fashion. I am religious! I believe in the immortality of the soul. If a rock can
exist for millions of years, why should the human soul, or whatever you choose to call it, be extinguished? I'm with those who
died. I live with them. The moment I close my eyes they are all
with me. If a ray of light can travel and radiate for billions of
years, why can't a spirit? A new science founded on this premise
will emerge."

"When does the bus go back to Tel Aviv?" I asked.

"Tsutsik, you can sleep here," Haiml said.

"Thanks, Haiml, but someone is coming to see me early in the morning."

Genia cleared the dishes and went to the kitchen. I heard her close the front door, but Haiml didn't switch on the lights. A pale glow shone in through the windows.

Haiml began speaking to me, to himself, and to no one in particular: "Where did all the years go to? Who will remember them after we're gone? The writers will write, but they'll get everything topsy-turvy. There must be a place somewhere where everything is preserved, inscribed down to the smallest detail. Let us say that a fly has fallen into a spiderweb and the spider has sucked her dry. This is a fact of the universe and such a fact cannot be forgotten. If such a fact should be forgotten, it would create a blemish in the universe. Do you understand me or not?"

"Yes, Haiml."

"Tsutsik, those are your words!"

"I don't remember saying them."

"You don't remember, but I do. I remember everything that Morris said, that you said, and that Celia said. At times you uttered ridiculous foolishness, and I remember that, too. If God is wisdom, how can there be foolishness? And if God is life, how can there be death? I lie at night, a little man, a half-squashed fly, and I talk with the dead, with the living, with God—if He exists—and with Satan, who certainly does exist. I ask them, 'What need was there for all this?' and I wait for an answer. What do you think, Tsutsik, is there an answer somewhere or not?"

"No, no answer."

"Why not?"

"There can't be any answer for suffering—not for the sufferer."

"In that case, what am I waiting for?"

Genia opened the door. "Why are you two sitting in the dark, eh?"

Haiml laughed. "We're waiting for an answer."